VAINGLORY

VAINGLORY

Geraldine McCaughrean

ARROW BOOKS

Arrow Books Limited
20 Vauxhall Bridge Road, London SW1V 2SA

An imprint of the Random Century Group

London Melbourne Sydney Auckland
Johannesburg and agencies throughout
the world

First published in Great Britain in 1991
by Jonathan Cape

Arrow edition 1992

1 3 5 7 9 10 8 6 4 2

Printed and bound in Great Britain by
Cox & Wyman Ltd., Reading, Berkshire

ISBN 0 09 993290 3

for Ailsa

'From the Devil they came,
and to the Devil they shall go'

Saint Bernard
on the family of Henry Plantagenet

Contents

PART III

PART IV

THE HOUSE OF GLORIOLE

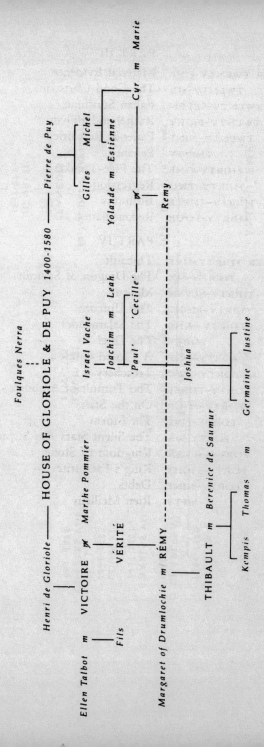

THE ROYAL HOUSES OF FRANCE

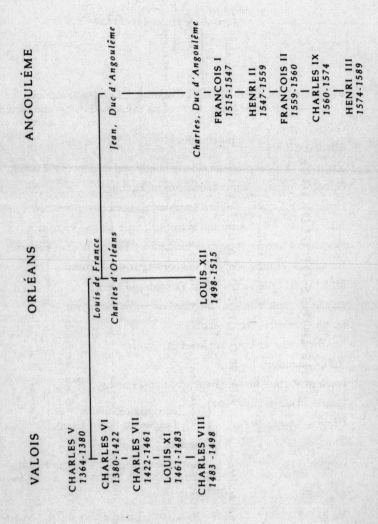

VALOIS **ORLÉANS** **ANGOULÊME**

CHARLES V
1364-1380

CHARLES VI
1380-1422

CHARLES VII
1422-1461

LOUIS XI
1461-1483

CHARLES VIII
1483-1498

Louis de France

Charles d'Orléans

LOUIS XII
1498-1515

Jean, Duc d'Angoulême

Charles, Duc d'Angoulême

FRANCOIS I
1515-1547

HENRI II
1547-1559

FRANCOIS II
1559-1560

CHARLES IX
1560-1574

HENRI III
1574-1589

List of Characters

VICTOIRE DE GLORIOLE – Comte de Gloriole-sur-Sablois, dispossessed before birth of his castle by the wars and the English.

Gilles de Puy
Michel de Puy
} – his cousins.

Viscomte de Bruberac – an elderly knight and student of the occult.

Gilbert Lespines – comrade-in-arms of Victoire.

Humphrey Talbot – English occupier of Gloriole-sur-Sablois.

Ellen Talbot – his cousin and betrothed, later wife of Victoire.

Flockhart – Master-at-arms to Humphrey Talbot, later to Victoire.

Barnabas – a priest; chaplain and corn-factor to Victoire.

FILS DE GLORIOLE – son of Victoire and Ellen.

Angèle de Belles-Boises – intended to be Fils' betrothed.

Jeanne – sexual companion of Fils.

Marthe Pommier – peasant lover of Victoire.

Vache – a money-lender.

Joachim Vache – his son; merchant to the nobility.

Charles, Duc de Charolais
Charles, Duc de Berry
} – conspirators in the League for Public Good.

The Gonpliers – a family of painters.

Charles, Duc d'Orléans – cousin of King Charles VII, captured at Agincourt and held prisoner by the English for twenty-five years.

Bastard Dunois – his half-brother.

VÉRITÉ DE GLORIOLE – bastard daughter of Victoire and Marthe.

The Little Sisters of Pity – a holy order of nuns run on Franciscan tenets, for the orphans of cabinet-makers.

Jehan Bourré – builder and occupier of Plessis-Bourré Chateau.

Geoffroi de Puy – son of Michel.

Estienne de Puy – his elder son.

Cyr de Puy – his younger son, later CYR DE GLORIOLE.

Yolande de Puy – wife of Estienne.

Marie de Puy – wife of Cyr.

de Dénezé – a sculptor.

Mère Catherine – *mère ancille* and oldest of the Little Sisters of Pity.

Malatesti – an Italian nobleman and patron of the arts.

Giulio Gigliamo – an Italian painter.

'Cecille' – the Christian name adopted by the daughter of Joachim Vache, admitted to the Little Sisters of Pity.

Queen Jeanne – divorced wife of Louise XII.

Il Diavolo – an Italian architect.

RÉMY DE GLORIOLE – son of Cyr and Cecille.

Margaret of Drumlochie – his deaf wife.

Balon and Batonne – married dwarfs.

Queen Anne, Duchess of Britanny – wife of both Charles VIII and Louis XII.

Joshua Vache – grandson of Joachim the merchant.

THIBAULT DE GLORIOLE – son of Rémy and Margaret.

Rose Tolon-Peque – his betrothed.

Berenice de Saumur – his wife.

Sebastian de Puy – grandson of Estienne, cousin and companion of Thibault.

Thomas |
Kempis | – twin sons of Thibault and Berenice.

Madame Dideron – Thibault's mistress.

Baron Dideron – her husband.

Dickie Dideron – her son.

Prince of Condé – a conspirator against Francis II.

Cardinal de Guise – all-powerful mentor and minister of Francis II.

Urania – an astrologer.

xii

PART I

The whole course of the interminable medieval wars between France and England was radically changed by the appearance on the scene of a young mystic called Jeanne Darc. Her talk of victory put heart into the uncrowned French Dauphin and into his troops. In 1429, Jeanne's avowal to lift the siege of Orléans brought the French Army – its whores and its heroes – to the valley of the River Loire.

ONE

1429

'The best or nothing,' he told the page. He could hardly help it: a nervous reflex, a family cliché, a failed attempt to behave with panache. 'The best or nothing,' he said, but he did not mean it. He hoped the boy would not take him at his word and bring no one up from the yard below. He needed a woman. He needed something soft to touch before putting on the unrelenting hardness of armour. He needed something pretty before the ugliness of war. He needed an outlet for the surfeit of life that seemed to be bursting his heart and brain and bloodstream.

That day, Life flourished inside him – so sweet that his body felt powerless to contain it. The prospect of the coming campaign made him clench tight his eyes, his mouth, his hands to trap Life inside. And yet Victoire de Gloriole could almost see the face and figure of Death approaching – an oystermonger with a knife ready to prise his soul from its shell.

His armour lay waiting along the floor, but suddenly looked too small for a body so engorged with the ambition to stay alive. It looked like the carapace sloughed off a crab leaving it soft-backed and vulnerable to the gulls. Truthfully, the whole seedy magnificence of Blois Castle, which now wrapped him round in its curtains of stone, was not big enough to encompass his lust for life. 'The best or nothing,' he had told the lewd, grinning face so eager to please. But he had no expectation of the best. The whole castle and its grounds were lousy with wriggling desperation, shrill with the need to laugh, debauched by the urgent need of three thousand men for one last creature comfort, one last comforting creature before the expedition to Orléans. The best of the whores would be already occupied. Let the page bring anyone, so long as he came soon. The good Dauphin Charles had God's 'Holy Maid' to put heart in him. Lesser men must make do with something earthier.

Victoire slumped down in his chair with his boots resting on

3

the end of the bed, legs crossed at the ankle. It was the way men sat while they were waiting for a woman: he had seen them do it. But he was no sooner settled than nervous energy twitched him to his feet again to look out of the window and chew the inner flesh of his cheek.

It looked more like market-day or mardi gras than the eve of battle. The whole castle courtyard was teeming with men and horses, priests and whores. Crucifixes had been rammed home into the brackets which usually held torches. Even a wooden madonna had ventured out of the Church of Saint-Sauveur across the way, to stand on a trestle table, and half a dozen prayer-stools stood drunkenly in front of her, their feet in dung. Near by, a woman sat on a soldier's knee to suckle her baby.

The courtyard was furry with dung. It gave off a sweet, wholesome savour and steamed a little, so that a fool might have mistaken it for a chamber of Hell and the crowds to be picking their feet up trippingly over the infernal peat fires. The sergeants with their long forks-of-office made do for demons.

'The best or nothing,' he said, and the page brought him Lucette. He hustled her into the room, gripping her elbows from behind, steering her towards Victoire as though she might not find him otherwise in the dim, cavernous anteroom. She saw him. She rested her eyes on his face, but they were shineless, vacant eyes. The sockets were the shape of empty oystershells.

Still, none of her teeth were missing and her face was clean – even pretty. Lucette had come from beside the bonfire and smelt a little of woodsmoke: a charred smell. She also carried a silver spoon and a purse, on a leather cord under her skirt: cold against warm, hard against soft. She might not be the best, but on the morning of the ride towards Orléans, Lucette was a great deal better than nothing.

'What are you, then?' she said, afterwards, unwilling to go back down to the draughty courtyard. 'Proper gentry?'

When he told her, 'The Comte de Gloriole,' her eyes widened, but no spark animated them. 'You've a chateau, then? Lands?'

'I have an inheritance. A seat,' he said, and coloured slightly. 'Not far from here, in fact. On the Sablois. Gloriole-sur-Sablois. But I was raised in Poictou. I'm of the House of Anjou. Somewhat.' She thought him a liar. She thought him a sparrow putting on eagle plumes. He thought he could see it written in her face.

But all that was actually written in her face was self-interest. 'A gentleman wouldn't take twice what he's only once paid for.'

He had not thought to have her twice. But his body had taken on an independent impetus, and he paid her a second time and somehow the cord got broken that dangled her purse and silver spoon – as if an unruly dog had escaped its leash.

Men bury their treasure before the enemy arrive. Victoire de Gloriole had precious little else to bury but his seed, and no better land to bury it in.

'I've never seen my estates,' he said, although he had not meant to admit it. 'My grandfather lost them to the English. The dog Talbot has given it to some runt in his litter.'

'So you hate the English, do you?'

He looked back in that instant on a childhood peculiarly dislocated, like a limb from its socket. His whole life had been overshadowed by the English. They had grown over his House like convolvulus and strangled all his father's hopes. What remained but to pull them down, chance by chance? The will to slaughter Englishmen had been bequeathed him along with his pale brown eyes and coat-of-arms and overburdening passion for Life. What else did he have to occupy him, in any case, whose fields were under an enemy's scythe. What an absurd question.

'Of course I hate them.'

Lucette only shrugged her indifference. 'They're all right. You men are all the same in bed anyway, aren't you? Some of the women say Burgundies are worse, but what I say is you're all the same in bed.'

She laid the blasphemy there, on the pillow. He was too slow turning his head, and he breathed in the sin of it. '*You've slept with the English?*'

''Course. Burgundies, too, though they like to keep to their own kind. English are easy, no matter who. Anything in an apron for them. Had a couple of Scotsmen, too, but they're so wild they're not Christian hardly. Don't think I could do it with a heathen. Or a blackamoor.'

He wanted to run, but he was lying against the wall, and to escape he would have to climb over her, lay hands on her. His gorge heaved: he was infected with her sin: it cleaved to him, sticky as tar. He was full of superstitious dread that he should inadvertently have coupled with this traitress. It was as inauspicious as if a magpie had flown in and roosted on his shoulder.

5

Lucette did not even notice his panic. 'What's that beast on your shield? Wolf, is it?'

'No.'

She got up and began to pick over the pieces of his armour. She picked up his sword: her touch would make the blade brittle, the bindings fray. He fled the bed, snatching the things out of her hands, and began to accoutre, but without due regard for superstition. There was an order to be followed: mail-collar, greaves, poleyns, back and front . . . she made him neglect it, this woman of ill-omen.

'I ought to have you drawn for an English spy,' he mumbled. The smell of smoke on her hair was not from the bonfires at all, but from the stews of Hell. Her cheeks were red with subterranean scorching.

'Why, then? Are the English worse than you Dauphin's men? What gentleman'd fight for a bastard, eh? Bastard of Bourges, isn't that what they call him? Ragamuffin bully . . . And you can give me back my spoon.' Her bottom lip jutted like a child on the verge of tears. But the leather cord was wrapped tight round his arm and was as hard to free as a snake. She had to help him disentangle it.

Closeness once more implicated him in her sin, and he knew he would not have her flogged or branded for giving succour to the enemy. She was no older than he, and though sixteen had seemed the prime of manhood that morning, it seemed only a neighbour to childhood now. Like a child he sought reassurance that she would never again entertain Englishman or Burgundian. She was quicker than he could have hoped with her reassurances.

'Oh no. Best keep with the winners now,' she said. 'Even rats know when to leave a ship that's done for.'

It brought him up short. He did not want to exchange another word with her – and yet he longed to share that absolute certainty of hers. 'You do acknowledge, then, that God will give the victory to the French,' he jeered aggressively.

'Oh, no question. Now they've got the Maid's witchery to tell 'em what and where and when.'

'*Witchery?*' He put his helmet on. He lowered his bevor. He shut out the sight of her. Worse and worse! Nothing would have been better than this! No one. 'Jeanne Darc is God's instrument on Earth. Witchery? You foul-mouth.'

'Magic, then. Whatever you choose to call it. Now the Dauphin's got himself a white witch, you won't find me going with the English. They're done for.' She was in a hurry to be gone now. The trumpets were blowing to muster the army to Holy Sacrament. Unless she was quick, there would be no time to earn another handful of coins. Victoire was left shouting the Maid's holy virtues down a draughty passageway, after the retreating shape of a beggarly whore.

The Maid's voice was shrill and penetrating. It ricocheted off the round towers of Blois, like shot from a culverin, and made horses shy and flick their ears. But when Jeanne Darc spoke, the wooden madonna was forgotten.

Here was a Whitsun of renewed hope. The troops of Dauphin Charles did not fully understand just what had caught their imagination, only that the same magic had caught everyone they knew. They could beat the English: the Maid had told them so.

Now the fleur-de-lys blossomed in the windcrack of a thousand royal-blue banners. The skyward slant of every pike and bill and bow and banner and tentpole represented a scaling ladder up against the walls of Heaven.

Jeanne Darc knew where to cast her bread. She broke it with the Dauphin, then fed it to his troops. The politicking nobility she ignored. They had seen too many lost battles and too many convenient little miracle-workers arriving with messages from God. But the common soldiers believed; they wanted to believe, and she rewarded their belief by bringing them here, to the grandeur of this courtyard, and by sending servile priests flapping to and fro with bread and wine to wait on them like so many innkeepers' daughters.

The soldiers swaggered under their shredded canopy of banners. Their sins drained away down the culverts like piss. They were washed clean with words, and if they felt spent, well then it was thanks to the Maid and nothing to do with the whores they had just left panting beyond the wall. She told her troops that they were the soldiers of God.

Victoire de Gloriole came down to the spectacle feeling as empty as an unworn suit of armour; hollow, so that the sanctified wine made his head spin. But as the Maid spoke, all the evil presentiments which had pressed against his heart melted away. Though his legs trembled a little, it was not with fear. The Maid filled him with her rhetoric, filled him like a grail with hot blood. It was the wooing of three thousand bachelors. She was God's artillery. She picked them off, rank by regiment. She told them they would triumph in this world and the next.

So when she told them, too, that they had no need of whores, they believed her. When she told them that the camp-following harlots would sap their virtue, weaken their resolve and dull their radiance in the eye of God, they were overtaken by quite miraculous chastity. They were as eager to be rid of their sins as a drowning man is to kick off his boots. In their zeal, they ran from the courtyard, grabbing up pebbles and clods of dung. It was God's work.

Like hounds leaping between the feet of hunters, the women bayed and yelped, snapped and tumbled – a rout colourful with red undershifts and stringy liripipe hoods. Their shawls made footclothes for the horses. It must have seemed like an ambush – these soft-hooved horses, these hard-handed men, all out of nowhere. This treachery.

No one could credit how slow the harlots were to understand. They wanted reasons. They wanted pity. They wanted to shout reminiscences at the men they recognized. They fouled this act of purification with calling on God and Mary and 'Holy Jeanne' for protection. Single infantrymen were cornered and beset by obstinate, agile girls plucking at them with questions and pleas or clinging to them bodily, on their knees, in the mud. The men's hard resolve was dented by women's foreheads banging into their groins, women's fingers dragging on their hose. Shiny sallet helmets rolled in the mud as men ran for cover. Decisive action was needed, and yet it was the women who took the initiative and ran for the Church of Saint-Sauveur to seek sanctuary. They must be headed off.

'Go to it,' said a knight, riding his horse into Victoire's back as he stood, still unmounted, watching the farce from beside the castle gate. 'Do you mean to wait out the war, boy?' The knight drew his sword.

'Lay blade to a woman?' said Victoire, incredulous.

'. . . not women . . . whores.' The words were shot through with the screams of women trying to reach the castle and appeal to Holy Jeanne. The knight threw Victoire a weapon from his own saddle – a massively long wood truncheon, brass-bound at the tip and with a spike that all but took out his eye. '. . . if you won't use a sword . . . some discipline, for Jesu's . . .' The sentence was torn apart by the mob of women.

The plançon was too long to swing on foot. Victoire mounted up and weighed it in his fist. His horse danced with terror at the unaccustomed shadow, and plunged off through the gate.

He wheeled between the church steps and the stampeded women,

8

wielding his staff like a flail to separate the Devil's tares from God's wheat. Single-handedly he saved the church from desecration. So delicate a piece of riding was it that, for a time, he overlooked the absence of a war to justify it. Then the thought came, and marred all the pleasure.

This was not a chevauchée. Where was the pageantry? Where was the chivalry? There were only bleating women, terrified, or too stupid to be terrified.

And yet, like the shark who, at any touch on its jaw cannot help but chew and shake and rend, the chevaliers of the Royal Army routinely brought to bear all their noble arts. They started with shouts and brandishing. But soon trials of skill came into play: to cut laces with a sword-tip at full gallop, to lift skirts with a billhook, or clip rosaries from a belt with the tip of a lance. And when their aim was not so true (as can't be helped with crude battle weapons), there was the show of blood, the scream of pain and that primordial pang of pleasure that overrides all.

The plançon turned easily on its leather wrist-strap. The brass binding left its bright orbit on the eye: the spike whistled. Like a chivalric hero making show-of-arms in the lists, so Victoire de Gloriole passed in among the whores of Blois, herding them along the river quays, spilling their belongings out of their arms.

'No call for bloodshed,' he told himself, disgusted by the sight of a woman with one breast cut away. 'No call for cruelty,' he told a foot-soldier who was rolling and punching a woman on the ground, demanding the money she had 'cheated' him of an hour before. Victoire prided himself on the closeness with which he could swing the mace without doing injury. And had she not stopped running and turned, the plançon would never have fouled that one short woollen skirt. In its upward arc, the whirling truncheon lifted both smock and over-dresses so that the spike came to rest in the top of the thigh.

Even sword blows are not felt at the time. When Victoire first recognised Lucette, her expression was one of affronted surprise. Her eyes ran up the great length of the plançon and she took its weight in both hands. 'Most brave,' she said, and it was the horse that shied away from her and withdrew the spike out of the wound.

The tide of persecution was ebbing. The women who had not jumped into the Loire were milling across the bridge with a biblical weeping and wailing. Trumpet fanfares were calling the soldiers back to the fortress. The Purge was done. The spiritual grace of Charles's army was assured. The first battle of the campaign had been won with a decisive victory.

Victoire de Gloriole bore down in his stirrups and his horse staggered clumsily backwards away from the red-skirted whore, away from the first intimations of pain, away from the loose-blowing hair that smelled of smoke. Her own would take care of her. Let her go back to the English or the Burgundians and sap their vigour and tarnish their souls. And the aching regret that griped at Victoire? – well, as philosophy told him, all animals are sad after coition.

He allowed the river's unaltering flow to pacify him. He let it carry his eyes and thoughts downstream. That huge, sinuous artery threading the heart of France. The slow pulse of it overrode his own. It was blue with the Touraine sky; it was grey with the reflection of the castle. Somewhere, not far from here, on a calmer tributary still, where the water looped round a circle of rocky ground, his own castle turned the Touraine blue to grey. The fish swimming by him even now might pause to feed, within a day or two, at the foot of his walls. The birds in the riverside trees could fly there more directly. He had never seen it. It lay in the hands of the English. And yet its sheer existence held him on course like a lighthouse at sea: Gloriole-sur-Sablois. The selfsame sap that ran through the trunk of this river branched out into the Sablois and brought spring life to his chateau. The sap in his own body rose at the thought of it. It was not the first time that he had stood by rivers and let them water his dreams. But now they stood to bear fruit, watered by the special magic of this Loire. Near by, a whore who had thrown herself into the river to escape the rout pulled herself ashore. When she saw him, she froze with terror, as though her muddy brownness might camouflage her against the mud. She looked him in the eye, preparing to throw herself backwards into the water again. Victoire looked away, turned the eyes of his horse away, too, as though from an unpleasantness, and started back along the quay.

In the courtyard of Blois, Renaud de Chartres, Archbishop of Reims, presented Jeanne Darc with her own banner of white silk scattered with fleur-de-lys. On a field of white, God gripped the Earth like a boules player with all the planets in hand yet to be played. Two angels, armed with lilies, danced to an unheard music in the wind.

And when they saw the Dauphin present her with a sword, even those who had, in their hearts, thought him a knock-kneed, anxious, underfed, graceless little gentleman, disowned by his mother and despaired of by his tailor, could see how the Divinity of Kings had newly lighted on Charles and wrought a miracle. There was certainly some kind of magic at work.

Whatever else, it was sound military strategy. In instructing Jeanne Darc to rout the whores, God might just as well have phrased Himself in terms of tactics as of chastity. Camp-followers are an impediment in time of siege and pitched battle. Their contribution to morale no longer compensates for their sheer nuisance value. There was good precedent for the purge at Blois. A short way downriver, eight thousand whores had once been drowned before a battle, and the commander had never even invoked moral purity. Expediency solely.

The corporate tragedy of the women was soon dissipated. Some went this way, some went that. Some sought out the outlaws of the Sologne and the poachers of the forests of Blois. Some carried their goodwill to the English troops in Troyes and Le Lude and Gloriole-sur-Sablois. And some simply went home to the villages and farms from where war had turfed them up like truffles in the snouts of pigs.

Some, with more politics than Lucette, prayed earnestly every day for the Maid to raise the siege of Orléans and drive out the English. Somehow they did not associate their sufferings with the little white-armoured saint. They had suffered at the hands of men, as they were well accustomed to doing.

And when their prayers came true, it gave them joy to think what a glorious blow Jeanne had made on behalf of all Womankind.

TWO

White and Black

Magic. It preyed on Victoire's mind, that word. Even after the rout was forgotten, the wounded whore blotted out by later, more vivid experiences, those words of Lucette's still besieged Victoire's mind. Magic. Witchery.

The English said that Jeanne Darc's magic was the stuff of the Devil. The English goddams ran away at the sight of her. They deserted at the very mention of her. They declared themselves dazzled by hosts of golden butterflies. The English said Jeanne Darc was a witch.

The Royal Army continued to carry her at the head of their column, a silvered icon capable of miracles. But there were times – when Jeanne charged English fortifications all alone and bright with ecstasy and swore that there were four thousand at her back – that Frenchmen drew away, and crossed themselves, and lay with their faces to the campfire and fell asleep asking, *'Four thousand what?'*

Did the Maid's magic pour down out of Heaven or did it well up like magma out of . . . another place?

His friends discussed it openly over the campfire. They laughed. They revelled in jokes about necrophiles and goat-licking and virgins. But they were older: Gilbert Lespines, the Viscomte de Bruberac, and Victoire's cousin, Gilles de Puy. To them, the words were worn coins they had carried in their pockets for year upon year. But Victoire was young, and the words still held their full value, their full terror. Once, just once, on the eve of a battle, he took his cousin aside in the hope of some seasoned advice that might settle his mind.

'Is there such a thing as white magic?' he asked. *'Could* the Maid use witchery and still be God's instrument?'

He had a strongly vested interest in knowing. After all, he had been sheltering under the selfsame protection as Jeanne Darc, like two riders sharing the same canopy. He had come through unscathed.

He had acquitted himself well – as well as most – without knowing where his swordskills came from or how he succeeded each time in overcoming his craven fright on the eve of a battle. He had always rendered up thanks to God for his survival. But what if the Maid's magic were not God-given at all? It was a fearful possibility.

Gilles de Puy, a man with crisp, brittle hair and angry, brittle skin that blurred the outline of his dry lips, looked at Victoire, scanning his face as if it were a page of writing. His eyes travelled critically over each separate feature. He appeared to be about to answer, but then allowed his stare to slip away over Victoire's shoulder, and said, 'The blacksmith's free and my horse needs a shoe. Can we save philosophy for another time, cousin?'

Gilles de Puy was as landless as Victoire, dispossessed of his home by the same English incursion. Indeed, his home was a few unprepossessing acres among the vast hills, woods and fields of Gloriole. Even if it were recovered, he would share the farm with his brother Michel and an ancient, insidious father. But exile from his land had given Gilles more than it had taken away. It had made him a *collector*, a gatherer together of facts and fancies. Nothing was passed over without due consideration of its usefulness: not a battle-field corpse, not an unlocked outhouse, not a word or a weakness in his colleagues. He took Victoire's question like a magpie seizing on a bright thing, and flew away with it to the smithy. Turning it over and over in his mind, he applied himself to wondering what profit could be made of it – a young man's superstition. That night, he seated himself opposite Victoire, on the far side of the fire from him, and through the baffle of smutty smoke, permitted himself to study his cousin, unobserved.

How long, he wondered, before Victoire pulled down death on himself? He was only a boy, and yet he went into battle as though he had only yesterdays to lose. Comforting to discover that there was, after all, *something* which frightened him. And in that there must be some advantage, some profit, some clue as to how he could rid himself of his young and chivalric cousin.

Not that de Puy felt any strong personal animosity towards the boy. It was impossible; nobody managed it. That doe-eyed, ingenuous face was still too rounded and smooth for dislike to get a foothold. But there was a question of property at stake. And if Talbot's English troops were truly to be driven out of the Loire Valley, Victoire stood to regain thirty-three thousand acres.

And Gilles de Puy stood next in line. No. Victoire must not

be allowed to survive the next day's battle. When the conversation lulled, Gilles sat up and said, 'My cousin wants to know if the Maid's in league with the Devil.'

Victoire blushed vividly. He was appalled to see his private fears paraded in public; angry and embarrassed in equal parts. Bruberac and Lespines were staring at him. 'I simply wondered if there were truly two kinds of magic – white and black,' he mumbled defensively. Then the full horror of his doubt overtook him and he rose up on his knees, holding his hands out towards each man in turn. 'Well? Are there? I want nothing to do with witchery!'

But the others had lapsed back into complacency: nothing more than an etymological quibble. Gilbert Lespines returned to opening and closing the visor of his helmet, working pig grease into the hinge. 'All the difference in the world between white and black. White's natural. Nothing wrong with love philtres and horse plasters.'

'And the Maid's miracles? Miracles must be a kind of white magic? Yes? The Maid does miracles, not magic.'

'Miracles' did not tally exactly with what Lespines had been talking about, but he let that pass. 'Nothing wrong with miracles, no. Goes without saying.'

Bruberac kept silent, his great top lip bulging over the lower like snow overhanging a roof. He dissected the lark on his platter with extreme delicacy: a man of science, a man of analytical methodology.

Gilles de Puy poked the fire with a forked stick, trying to dislodge a piece of bubbling cheese. When he spoke, the casual, facetious tone barely concealed the deliberateness with which he picked his way from word to word. 'Well I'm sorry to shock you virgins, but I know better. I know for a fact the Maid owes her luck to the Black Arts.'

All at once he was the centre of attention. It gave him a pang of pleasure. It made him stretch and recurl his body like a contented cat beside the fire. He allowed time for their imaginations to gorge on the words, like tapeworms inside them: 'the Maid owes her luck to the Black Arts'.

The canopy of God's grace blew away from over Victoire's head. His Divine Protection was gone. And yet no. It was unthinkable that he should have been sheltering all this time under the raven-wing of Satanism. He would sooner have ridden naked into battle. Gilles de Puy watched and saw his words strike home as sharp as the arrow piercing Achilles' heel.

Lespines was the first to break the silence. He gave a snort of derisive laughter. 'Pay no heed, Victoire. I think it's de Puy's notion of a jest. What's this, Gilles? A story for All Soul's Night?'

De Puy continued to grin – still joking, still in earnest. 'Oh, I can show you proof of it. You want proof? I can give you proof.'

'Give it, then!' Victoire came at him over the fire, scattering hot ashes, breaking up the circle of friends. But de Puy only rolled out of the way, roaring with laughter. 'Green boy! What's the matter? What's so very *dire*, eh? So long as the magic holds and we keep skinning the English – what's it to you where the power comes from?'

'Have a care, you men,' Lespines protested peaceably, grabbing the back of Victoire's wadding jacket and trying to pull him away. It was all the assistance de Puy needed to unbalance his cousin and roll him on his face in the ashes. Kneeling astride him, he twisted an arm until the boy was holding his own plait of hair.

Victoire writhed with impotent outrage. 'What's it to me? I'm closer attached to my immortal soul, that's plain! Fight with Satan at my back? Not for all the crowns in Christendom! – Nor would you, I dare swear! *What's your "proof"?*'

Bruberac, who had seemed mesmerized by the violence of the quarrel, did at last lumber to his feet like an ox at the water's edge, his head travelling from side to side and his breath pushed from his lungs in groans. 'Yes, de Puy, hold your tongue. Keep your "proofs" to yourself. No one wants 'em.' Bruberac too was afraid.

Lespines grew more and more irritated, obliged now to pity the old man as well as the boy. He loosed a kick at de Puy and told him to stop baiting his betters. De Puy broke away, as if he were suddenly tired of the joke. 'Tomorrow. After the day's business. Why don't I tell you my proofs tomorrow?'

Victoire rose to his knees, spitting out grass and spleen. 'Tomorrow then! As God grants us grace to live through it.' But the formula tasted sour in his mouth, as though he were no longer entitled to bless himself with it.

'If the Black Arts keep us alive, you mean,' said de Puy, laughing quite unjustifiably loud and long, before ducking beneath the flap of his tent. From inside came a clearly audible, 'Green boy.'

Lespines threw his rind of pork fat against the canvas and flopped down again beside the fire. 'Take no notice, Victoire. That's what passes for comedy when there's famine of wit.'

15

The Comte had barely moved, his eyes still resting where his cousin had stood, wondering whether to go after him, wondering whether he should challenge the man to mortal combat. 'He meant it, Gilbert. I ought to know my own cousin.'

'You ought to, that's true,' said Lespines, but more to himself than to Victoire. He had glimpsed the ambition in de Puy, the envy, the resentment at being born one remove from Victoire's noble title. Lespines knew the man a thousand times better than his naive young cousin did. Equally he knew it would be futile to voice his suspicions: that jealousy or subtlety were at work here. Victoire would never listen: a nobleman's first loyalty is to his kin. And anyway, Lespines was hard put to see how that carefully engineered argument had furthered de Puy's interests. All he could do was persuade Victoire that the whole thing had been a joke in poor taste. He turned to Bruberac to help him do it.

But the Viscomte Bruberac had gone – lumbered away into the darkness like a cow swallowed up by a bog.

He squeezed under the canvas at the back of the tent, staining his knees and the crown of his belly a dark brown. De Puy was waiting for him, reclining along his bed, holding in the crook of one arm the morocco-bound book he had taken from among Bruberac's belongings. 'I was expecting you, my dear Viscomte,' said de Puy without looking round.

The old man was sweating, despite the cold of the evening. He wallowed across the ground towards de Puy like a drowning man towards a raft. His mouth was awash with words. 'What are you about? What did you mean? Tell him? Tell him what? You won't tell him! What I said to you was secret! Deepest, closest secret. One friend to another!' He saw the volume lying open on de Puy's forearm. '*You took my book, Hell blast you! What're you doing with my book?*' He grasped at it like a mother wanting her child from a stranger. De Puy let him have it, allowed him to snatch it, and Bruberac cradled it to his breast where it jerked with the sobbings of his breath. It seemed as if the demons and goblins sketched inside it were anxious to be loose.

The Viscomte kept on repeating, 'Why did I tell you? Why did I show you my studies? Why would I show you but as one friend to another?'

De Puy let him blubber his way to silence. When Gilles at last spoke, his voice was full of patronizing condescension. 'It was an honour indeed that you should tell me your little secret. And I was *wonderfully* enlightened to hear where your studies have taken you – all those merry rites and rituals . . .'

'Experiments! I'm a scientist merely!' Bruberac's desperate spittle glistened on de Puy's jacket; the old man saw it, went to wipe it off and overbalanced against de Puy, his big jowl pressing intimately against the other's cheek. Gilles did not recoil and Bruberac took encouragement from it – as though bodily contact must arouse some pity, restore de Puy to his former congenial nature. After all, he had seemed so agreeable once – had shown such a very sympathetic interest in every treasured secret he was allowed to share . . . Otherwise Bruberac would never have introduced him to his lovely coterie of spirits and ghouls and beasts-of-darkness. 'You don't mean to tell the boy about me, do you? I know you better, Gilles. You're a gentleman by nature. Say you'd never tell the boy about my studies. He's white as milk. He takes Mass every day! He'd run to the priests and have me burned. He's too young to understand how it is for us scholars – us students of the ancient mysteries . . .'

De Puy could feel the old man's tears creep down his own cheek like lice but still did not push him away. He simply whispered to him tenderly, like a lover. 'Tell cousin Victoire? My dear old friend, of course I don't mean to tell him.'

Bruberac's sobs stopped panting in his ear: the old man was holding his breath, listening for his reprieve. 'You won't tell him I practise?'

'I shan't have to. Tomorrow, I said. Didn't you hear me say I'd furnish my proof "tomorrow"? . . . And Victoire won't be alive tomorrow night, will he?'

'Not alive?' Bruberac laughed unconvincingly. 'Who can say? Who can read the future?'

'I take it you mean to see your Friends tonight?'

'What? No! No, no. No!' and his long jowls rattled with the lie which he almost instantly abandoned. 'They won't always come. They don't always come when I bid them. Why?'

'Well, and if you should see them – if you should, I say – Beelzeboal and Bual and Asteroth and . . . who was that other charming fellow?' He tapped at the book in Bruberac's arms, re-calling its sketches of pot-bellied elephants, snake-haired harpies, mandrakes astride worms, their nostrils oozing brimstone. 'Ah yes, Asmodeus the Pander. I say, if you *should* conjure the spirits tonight, you'll have a pleasant present for them, won't you?'

'Present? No! A goat! A kid! No, nothing.'

'Nothing, Viscomte? Do you call the soul of my esteemed cousin Victoire de Gloriole nothing?'

'De Gloriole? Never. He's a pure man. It couldn't be done,' said Bruberac categorically. The subject was closed: he sat back on his fat haunches.

'Oh but you underestimate yourself, Viscomte!' De Puy spoke still more softly, raising the flaky weals of his eyebrows and widening his eyes ingenuously. 'You've studied the Occult Arts so very assiduously – made such sacrifices! I don't doubt but that your excellent Masters will grant the prayers of their faithful servant. Didn't you tell me once that they'd grant you anything, so long as it was damnable? A day's sport? They'd thank you for it. And sure, they'd want to preserve your life, wouldn't they? Your spirits from the Underworld?'

'My life?'

'But of course, Viscomte. Your life. Naturally, if Victoire lives, I'm bound by my word to show him proof – that there's black magic abroad in the Royal Army. Aren't I? And regrettably that would mean the pincers and the fire for you, my dear old comrade. You can see that, surely?' He paused. 'You *can* see that, can't you?'

'You mean to be Comte de Gloriole,' said Bruberac with a sudden dispassionate despair. 'You want me to conjure spirits to steal the boy's life away, just so that you can steal away his castle. You don't even want to dirty your hands with murdering him. You son of a whore.'

The old man loosed a punch, but de Puy only caught the fist in both hands and pushed it away, laughing. 'I commend you to God, old friend. And if He won't have you, then I commend you to your comrades down below. In the Grate, so to speak.' He addressed this to Bruberac's rump, for the man was squeezing his way out under the tent flap, his stomach scraping the earth, his fists rounded in the dirt.

De Puy lay back and crossed himself in routine preparation for sleep. His stomach was lined with adrenalin as warm as wine at the prospect of next day's battle. Even if Bruberac's blasphemous pastimes were nothing but the delusions of mad old age, it did not matter. Victoire would probably die anyway. His shield of righteous self-confidence was dented: he no longer knew whether he was fighting under God's banner or the Devil's pitchfork.

18

But by and large, de Puy was inclined to believe in the grotesques and gargoyles sketched in Bruberac's red *Book of Sin*. There were plenty of others in the King's Army who let slip indiscretions when they were drunk – of things they had seen, of beings they had conjured, favours enjoyed in return for kissing a goat's rump. Not Gilles. He was too cautious and clever a man to risk damnation. He congratulated himself. Without becoming implicated, without trading his soul for their services, he had succeeded in recruiting half the demons in Hell to ambush Victoire on the Field of Patay, to pike him off his horse with their toasting forks, to hurry him hence to Hell, leaving the castle on the Sablois to be reclaimed some day soon by his only surviving relations. Let Bruberac grovel on his knees to the angels of Satan and pay them libations of blood and lights; de Puy had put them to work in his own service, and that made him more powerful than Lucifer himself.

The English did not fare well on the field of Patay. They blamed it on malign magic, but it may have been more to do with Sir John Talbot and Sir John Falstoffe bickering their way through the day. They were too preoccupied to keep at bay the daring young French chevaliers who leapt on their archers like deer crashing through an osier break.

By noon, the goddams had begun to see omens of destruction written in the sky, then obstinately to fulfil them by dying in bloody swathes. The horses of the French whirled them into a wheeling vortex of flight made ever smaller until, like rats in a scythed field, the few survivors broke and fled for open countryside. No truce trumpet blew. Such parlour niceties of war had long since fallen into disuse. Afterwards, the wounded goddams too hurt to move and with no ransom to offer, threw their surcoats over their faces so as not to see the plançons come thudding down.

The adrenalin of battle, the congratulations of the King himself, the smile of his Holy Maid raised Victoire's heart to a height from which the events of the previous day looked small and distant. He set about finding his cousin. He would confront these 'proofs' of his – give the lie to them. Without the prospect of imminent battle fraying at his nerves, Victoire was even inclined to forgive Gilles for making a joke at his expense, baiting him, teasing him – making mischief simply to pass the time. The Royal Army was free of demon-worshippers, the fleur-de-lys too glistening white to smear with filth. His soul magnified the Lord. His senses magnified the glories of being alive. And clutching these truths to him, Victoire sought out his cousin, Gilles de Puy, childishly eager to be reconciled with his kin.

But Gilles had not outlived the day. A peculiar death. His horse had died of heart failure at full gallop and had pitched its rider forwards, sword outstretched. The tip embedded in the ground, the blade broke, and the jagged metal found the narrow gap between bevor and breastplate.

The Viscomte de Bruberac asked to see the body, and even drew a sketch of it into a great red scholarly ledger. He gave a copy to Victoire, along with his condolences on the loss of a comrade and relation. Victoire kept the sketch for many years afterwards and often wept when he found it among his possessions.

Bruberac had always liked the young Comte. He would have hated to see him die. So while the French Army was singing its *Te Deums* in gratitude for victory, Bruberac stood in a chalk circle in the depth of a wood near by, and paid his own debt of gratitude. Pouring another vial of lamb's blood on to a stone still glistening from the night before, he thanked the Father of Demons for answering his prayers: for snatching away with hooks and grapples the life and soul of Gilles de Puy; for preserving the life of the boy. He even knelt and asked, in all humility, Hell's continued protection over the head of Victoire, Comte de Gloriole.

THREE

Vigil

When the French Army disbanded for the winter of 1429, the Viscomte de Bruberac went home to his estates and retired from campaigning. No one criticized him for it: he was old and had done good service to the King before and since the coronation: advice, gifts, flattery, loans.

Victoire de Gloriole kept him informed with long, observant letters, as the Royal Army tacked back and forth across France and drove the English north, surrounding and swamping the remaining little islands of Empire like a tide climbing an uneven beach. Bruberac was gratified. He made a note of each victory in his large red book. Some old soldiers cannot bear to be out of the fray, but the Viscomte showed no such foolishness. 'I did my part,' he would say. And sometimes, when a second-rate wine infected him with melancholy, or Victoire wrote of the death of a comrade of long standing, Bruberac would stare into his pewter jug and mumble that some gave their lives while others gave . . . more.

Bruberac's occult 'studies' widened after the battle of Patay, though he did not write to de Gloriole about them. Victoire remained in total ignorance. In fact no one knew about those studies but a hand-picked team of apprentice scientists – handsome young Spanish brothers charitably adopted during a pilgrimage to Santiago di Campostello.

There were other acts of charity. Bruberac built a monastery in the grounds of his chateau near Ormes, and invited a small community to occupy it. It was carping of them to complain that the chapel, in the eyes of tradition, faced the wrong way. After all, God is omnidirectional. It was carping, too, for the townspeople to ignore his kind adoption of vagrants and orphans, saying that he would feed them, clothe them and see to the welfare of their souls. It was probably envy at work, for Bruberac invariably made these offers to outsiders – destitute refugees or outcasts straggling through the estate lands in flight from war or famine. The Abbot said at first that it was Christlike. The people of the town said worse. When the vagrants disappeared, the Spanish boys and the peasants said nothing at all.

After the birth of her son, Lucette walked sixty miles to Gloriole – that heap of ruined masonry on the Sablois river. She had taken it into her head that the father of her baby, restored to his estates once more, might take a sentimental interest in the fruits of his youth. The Bastard Dunois, the Bastard of Orléans – these were the military heroes of the hour. So why not a Bastard Gloriole, a Bastard of Sablois? There was no doubting that the baby sprang from Gloriole's loins: its mother had not been able to ply her trade after the ousting of the whores by Jeanne Darc, owing to the wound in her thigh. Besides, it had his looks, his coppery eyes, his black hair.

But when she at last found the place he had told her was his, the castle was still occupied by the English – a sorry pocket of ill-founded optimism, cut off from succour, living in hopes of a major reverse in the war or of a negotiated peace. The knight with the eyes of dark copper and the wolfish device on his shield was not yet restored to his title. Indeed, he was probably dead on some mire of a battlefield such as Patay or Paris. She saw his failure to be there as yet one more betrayal in a life of betrayals, and grew vindictive in her disappointment.

Had he not hated the English worse than death, that sweet-faced boy in the chamber at Blois, that barbarian with the plançon? And would he not make good the extravagant hopes she had harboured as she trudged those sixty miles? Then she would give his son to the English and let them breed a warrior to kill Frenchmen. A fitting revenge for her strange diagonal gait, for the worn side to her moccasin, for the dusty groove her dragging leg left behind her on the roads.

So she set the baby down – soft against hard – at the foot of the gate bastion, just inside the sentry's alcove, while the child was sleeping. He did not wake.

She turned and recrossed the drawbridge, listening for him to stir and cry, but he did not. She was once more free to ply her trade: she would have twitched her skirts at the sentries, but that would have been reckless: they could hang a woman for abandoning her child. The wind leaned into her face and the thistles snagged her skirts. An inclement March wept over her. But she had left starvation there on the stone ledge; she looked back at the castle and congratulated herself on it.

The boy would not starve, either, though she perceived his future only dimly. But like a mirage it was bright and glistening. His looks alone – that perfect, small face was burned on her eye like the sun's scorch-mark – would guarantee that he was loved and cared for. He invited affection, tenderness. Treasures would be heaped upon his youth, and glory on his adulthood. After all, his looks would not disgrace a Queen's cradle, a King's throne. Was he not, after all, the bastard of a nobleman with a wolfish thing for his device and armour bright as alchemy? It was a thing well done. Azay had not even cried.

Suddenly, unaccountably, she found herself sitting in the wet grass, howling like a wolfish thing, bending her head forward in great arcs of sorrow until there was mud on her forehead like the mark of Cain.

For a year she had been walking towards that infinite point at which the lines of necessity crossed. There had never been another option. She had not armed herself, therefore, against the pain. Necessity caught her like wire under the chin and made her gulp and choke. A post-natal agony convulsed her, took the wind out of her lungs and convulsed the womb where she had carried him. It was not physically possible to go any further from the castle: like a dog tethered to its kennel, she only pulled the leash tighter round her throat the further she tried to go.

She would go back before the sentry woke, before Azay woke and alerted the sentry. She would say she had lain him down, out of the draught, only while she relieved herself on the river bank, or while she entertained a lover. They would not care why she had done it, so they were rid of the trouble of a squalling brat. That's all a child is to anyone but its mother, after all.

But as she reached the drawbridge again, she could hear the unmistakable voice of her son, wailing on a rising crescendo. There was a babble of voices, too – of swearing militia and squawking women. A bleary crowd had gathered round the sentry-house door. She saw the rag of cloth passed from hand to hand on which she had sewn his name, 'Azay'.

They were shrill with indignation. They were righteous with outrage. It was a villainous thing, they said. The work of an unnatural woman. A damnable sin. A hanging sin. Then they looked up and saw her on the far side of the moat.

So she shrugged, as though she were a passer-by with her mind fixed on a far-distant destination and no time to be curious about strangers. And she hunched her shawl about her head and walked leisurely on, with her halt, diagonal gait and no backward glance. And a cock crew three times in the castle yard.

To my most dear and honoured Viscomte Bruberac,

I pray God my letter finds you in health and happiness and with the ear of God inclined towards your prayers. I have a very special need of your prayers, sir, for the King has placed under me a detachment of five hundred men and we lie three leagues from the banks of the Sablois. Tomorrow we either take or lay siege to the towers of Gloriole.

My hopes are high. After they took the Holy Maid and martyred her,

(The paper was gouged, and the words drowned in their own ink.)

I feared that our heads were no longer covered by her blessed grace. I even doubted (God forgive me) that God would allow such a death to come to her if she were truly His elected servant. But it would seem that her prayers intercede for us still in Heaven. For the English fall back from us on every side and begin to talk of truces.

Today I rode to the top of a bluff and saw, for the first time in my life, the halls of my inheritance. I have only seen them before built of words by my father. Everything was as he described, and yet the wholeness was beyond my imaginings. Not the towers only, but the water at their feet, the hills at their back, the great vastness of woodland and heath, the beasts hidden in the forest, the souls moving upon the fields and the souls planted beneath the earth, the fruits and the grain and the birds where they build their nests – they are all mine by right of sword and of blood. These are the joys I have languished so far from. These are the treasures the English stole from my House.

Tonight I shall keep vigil in the Chapel Saint-Cloud – on my own estates. That devil Shrewsbury has razed the little place to ruination. (What cause can a man find for doing such things, unless he is in debt to the Devil?) I shall pray God to grant me the restoration of my lands, or else a grave in my own ground. To this end I write to you, being now my closest friend indeed,

24

since only a few leagues separate us! Knowing you to be a man greater than I in honour and virtue and therefore more likely to catch the ear of God, I crave your prayers and blessing on my sword. Though my own poor deserts may not warrant them, I trust to the merits of my father who had the honour, I know, to title himself

Your friend and fellow Christian,

VICTOIRE DE GLORIOLE.

The Viscomte smiled indulgently over the letter and rewarded the messenger who brought it. 'Tell your master that we shall give him better than prayers,' he said, though he did not explain himself.

Solid night: it climbs in at a man's mouth, bangs at his eardrums, stuffs up his nostrils, leans against his eyeballs until they ache at the pressure. In keeping vigil, Victoire de Gloriole was pitting his courage against the whole dark universe. Just as the physician bleeds a man to drain off an evil humour, so Victoire was hoping the great black leech of night would drain off all his remaining fear. But it seemed there was a reservoir in him that never quite ran dry.

He spread his horse blanket on the floor of the ruined chapel and sat down on it cross-legged. His lantern, wedged into a crevice which had once held holy water, guttered and animated every piece of rubble, every broken column, the misericord and the lectern and the font. The chapel danced around him, capering, conjuring, making unintelligible magic.

'Oh God, give us victory tomorrow and I will make this chapel an honour to thy name and an imitation of thy Kingdom!' He said it aloud, but his voice was no sooner out of his mouth than it was ambushed and smothered by the bandit dark. He said his other prayers in silence, only his lips moving, and his throat cramping with the exertion.

In this black, treacly night minutes swelled to twice, three times their size. Outside, his horse champing on her bit sounded as if she was crunching bones. Sleep searched for chinks in his armour and posted dreams between his eyelids. Only the fear of demons stealing his soul stopped him from surrendering his cheek to the soft wool of the blanket.

His kneecaps ached from sitting in the one position; the pain was an ally in the struggle to keep awake. He lost count of the Aves,

Misereres and Paternosters he said, and was annoyed because a tally would have made a ready reckoner for the passage of time. Dewfall came at midnight and laid beaded drops on his cuirass and poleyns, so that he thought for a moment he had sweated cold fear all the way through his armour.

'Oh God, give me back my lands that I may worship thee with all the dignity and means of a nobleman. Oh God forgive the death of thy saint, Jeanne, whom we did nothing, nothing, *nothing* to save!' (And his fist beat on his knee and his throat ached like a man about to weep.) 'Let the sin of it not hang on my sword tomorrow!'

'Jeanne Darc! Duchess of Hell! Thou fiend incomparable! Thou angel of Dis! Thou mistress of Satan! Thou womb of magic! Thou drinker of my blood: *Come up!*'

The heat of the yew-wood fire sent a thaw of sweat rolling down Bruberac's snow-white body. He loosened the collar of his green velvet coat and the blood vessels in his thick neck leapt with relief.

'Oh Jeanne, Queen of witches, burned like the Phoenix, come now to torment your enemies with the fires of Hell!'

Over the months since Bruberac's retirement, the vaulted cellar of his fortress had been transformed into a scene of unseamed illusion. The five false walls, reshaping the room to a pentagon, were painted black and eyed with mirrors which glanced the light of candleflames, one to another, without ever shaming the dark. A crucifix hung upside down from the tie-beam, and a Bible lay face down under the feet of a tripod and wide dish of flame. Caballistic signs in silver studded the wooden vaulting, and horned skulls held little reservoirs of burning oil in their brain-pans and cast monstrous faces on to the ceiling.

Bruberac threw more fuller's earth on to the shallow dish and thrilled to his own illusions, slavishly obeying his own ritual, inventing his own damnation. His Spanish boys stood about with sleepless eyes hollower than the skulls above them.

'I offer this Mass in the name of Victoire de Gloriole, that I may one day bind him in love to you as I myself am bound! Rise and revenge yourself on the men of Albion! Rise and take the fortress of Gloriole! Break its walls like an egg. Sow confusion and despair. Sharpen the sword of this said Victoire, its rightful tenant. Open the gates of Hell to his enemies.'

One of the boys gave a snicker of helpless, nervous giggles and, to conceal it, declared himself possessed by a demon and threw himself on the floor. The others, fearing he was canvassing special favours, quickly followed suit, and only the boy holding the sacrifice was handicapped from joining in. The sacrifice wriggled. The pentagonal room, full of smoke, incenses and noxious fumes, took on the dense, choking climate of a house being fumigated against plague with priests in attendance to intone the apothecary's incantations:

'*Te abjuro! Te abjuro! Veni me! Veni me! Amata mea!*'

'Oh God, if it be thy will, give me this place and I will be a faithful guardian of your laws. Give these lands into my charge – these fields, these vines, these woods, these rides, these orchards and lakes, and this river! Give me the fief and I will be just in feu.' Victoire's mind wandered on, ahead of his prayers, down the paths and drives of his hopes, up stairways and along passages to a great hammer-beamed room with a tall carved chair at the head of a table spread with white pewter. A roll of white bread in every trencher, a huge fire in a huger grate, charring the settle. The stables below were full of horses and the eaves full of doves. A woman in a gown of white wool looked up from the far end of the table and smiled and unlaced her bodice to feed a child.

'Oh God!' he roared, having exhausted the scope of words. 'Oh God, *please!*'

'And now I give unto thee blood and flesh and soul, according to the laws of Solomon who summoned the demons and named their names! Blood for blood spilled, flesh burned for flesh burned, the soul of an innocent that Hell may triumph! Look! Are you here? Can you see? Oh show yourself to me! Come to me as you come in my dreams! Come now! Oh Beelzeboal, free her to me! *Behold what I give thee!*'

Before sunrise, the Spanish boys, seven sons of the same father, carried their master, catatonic with ecstasy and exhaustion, out of the chamber and up to his bed. They undressed him and put him to rest.

Theirs was such a vacant, stunted life that their own terror came and went as their hunger came and went. They had not the mental faculty to reflect on it, and so it stayed behind, in that five-sided room. Oh they knew that the Viscomte was a devil, a beast, a damned thing. But with the emphatic loyalty dogs feel for the man who feeds them, they also knew an inarticulate pity for the lonely old man. He had no visitors but demons. With their imperfect understanding of the language, they rather thought that his Masses conjured up the spirit of a dead wife, and that touched a sentimental Spanish chord in their pigeon-breasts. They would never inform on him, because then not only would the Devil break out of the black room to tear out their hearts, but the old man would be arrested and burned, and that would mean an end to the white-bread sops and the vegetable potage. Besides, they were certain that the holy fathers across the yard knew and did nothing; such things must therefore be acceptable in the eyes of God.

Bruberac crawled from under the narcoleptic influence of the incense at dawn. He was stiff in one arm and had difficulty in writing his formal best wishes to Victoire. There was a certain twist to his mouth, as well, which his boys did not recall – up at one corner and down at the other. Superstitiously, they said he must have been pulling faces when the wind changed direction.

Victoire woke with his chin on his breastplate and a stiffness in his legs which quite prevented him getting up at first. He had to sit rubbing the backs of his calves, and listen to the unmistakable clanking of pack animals approaching the church. Gathering up various pieces of armour discarded during the night, he rolled off the apse floor and into hiding behind the rood screen. But his burned-out lamp still stood on the stoop, and his sword lay on the high altar. The noise came closer and veered away, closer and veered away, following the zig-zag path over the hill. It was impossible that a traveller should pass a chapel and not step inside to say a Paternoster. And who could such travellers be but English-men, goddam Talbots? He was a Frenchman alone on thirty-three thousand acres of English territory.

It was a whole donkey-train. He could tell by the quick, scrabbling hooves. He cursed himself that he had not thought of it before; that the hill gave an important strategic advantage in any battle to take the fortress. It reared up higher than the donjon tower, so that a man in daylight could peer down it like a chimney. And it dominated the approach road. Any well-mounted defence would make sure to secure the chapel before attackers arrived.

Archers. Though he could not see them, he was sure they must be archers, with panniers of arrows bristling their donkeys into porcupines. Victoire knelt up, his loose apron of chain-mail hissing treacherously to give him away. He looked over the broken wall of the chantry. Thirty pink, flame-shaped ears wagged above the last fold in the hillside, and goads slashed the air. A dozen men, heads down, were driving the animals up the precipitous path. Victoire curled himself into an angle of the wall, as full of self-hatred as if he had metamorphosed into a woodlouse in that mouldy grey crevice. He remembered his horse, tethered at the rear of the chapel. They must surely see it and come looking for its rider to kill him. Fear possessed him like a demon, and he prayed for God to cast it out and leave him free use of his faculties. For his folded legs were not his to command and his hands were full of sweat. The magic madness of battle eluded him; it lay with his sword on the desecrated altar.

The scrabbling hooves were all around him now – to front and back of the chapel. The flame-shaped ears flickered around him like the burning fiery furnace. He wanted to retract his prayer for a grave in his own earth – to distract God's attention from it with a clamour of other pleas – for the clouds to descend, for the earth to move, for a detachment of angels to intervene with flaming, two-edged swords. A donkey poked a curious nose in at the door, reminded perhaps of its byre. But the blow of a goad lifted a gust of white dust out of its twitching hide; it backed away, leaving the chapel full of honking. This was more than Victoire's dignity could stand.

He rose to his feet. He walked to the altar and picked up his sword. He weighed the hilt between his hands. Dust lapped over the walls in waves, full of the warm, comfortable smell of donkeys.

But then the flood rejoined – a confluence of donkeys spilling on down the far side of the hill. He cleared the dust out of his throat; he spoke an Our Father under his breath, and still no snort of surprise greeted the sight of his horse, no cry pounced at him over the wall, no arrow-fletch rattled against its knocking.

'The godless Picts!' he remarked to himself. 'To pass a chapel and not so much as stoop to say an Ave! No wonder they're losing the war!'

He jumped up on to the font. It rocked unsteadily under him but from it he could glimpse, over the broken wall, the massed rumps of a dozen donkeys all swinging their bellrope tails; the heads of their drovers confused amid the clutter of pans and panniers. There was not an arrow in sight. They had not come to man a defensive position. They went hurrying on down, with all the concentrated determination of Lot's family leaving behind them Sodom and Gomorrah. He felt like calling after them: a schoolboy jeer. He felt like pitching stones after them, pursuing them on foot with sword and dagger. The greatest day of his life was begun hugger-mugger and inglorious. His old-fashioned folly of a vigil had been turned into farce, his prayers nullified by his cowardice. He needed to recoup the day. But the pieces of his armour still lay squandered on the chapel floor, and he should long since have rejoined his men.

Not until the dust settled could he see the strayed horse himself, nicely camouflaged by the dapple of an ash tree, a shout away down the hill. The sound of the donkey-train was gradually erased by the noise of a large army detachment on the move: his troops were arriving to lay siege to Gloriole-sur-Sablois.

But even so, he took time, at the crest of the hill, to buckle on the various pieces of his armour. For the clear morning light brought interesting revelations. It was a perfect vantage point. He could see the great loop of the river embracing the crumbling heap of white and brown rock, its broken walls as irregular as coral. He could see almost all of the inner courtyard, the bailey motte, the house at the foot of the keep, disproportionately small in comparison with the massive weight of the curtain walls and their round corner towers. It was a cairn of rocks that generations had kicked at with only limited success. A section of the curtain wall was all but down. A king progressing from chateau to palace along the lovely Loire would not have turned his head to glance at it. But to Victoire de Gloriole it was a plot in Eden, his ancestral seat, a gift extended to him by the ghostly hands of ancestors long dead. His spirits soared, with theirs, towards God.

FOUR

Taking Gloriole

'I thought the English must've found you trespassing,' said Lespines. 'I had to give orders to march in your place.'

All Victoire said was, 'Send thirty archers to hold that hill yonder. It gives mastery of the road. Is the bridge secured?'

Lespines noted the change in Victoire. He noted it with the kind of chagrin a father feels at his son's first show of beard. Overnight their relative status had changed: Gloriole had become a comte, like Elijah lifted up high in a chariot of fire. 'The air of your estates suits you my lord Comte.'

'Holding them will suit me better, Gilbert. But lend me a rag, will you? I can't take possession with all the shine off my armour. Where are the peasants? I should speak to my peasants.'

'Boarded up in the village church, as I take it. Do you want them fetched out?'

'No! And a pox on the man who goes harassing them. I don't want them more frightened than they are. I count on you, Gilbert. I need my church and I need my peasants. Unburned. If I've the leisure later, I'll go down to the church and introduce myself to them – put their minds at rest.' His eyes drifted yet again towards the massive crag of masonry: brown stone for the most part, brown as dung deposited by the blinding bright streak of the river. He said with affected contempt, 'It's a sorry pile, Gilbert. It should be easy enough to take, though. The moat's silted and there's a length of curtain wall fallen outwards on the west side.'

'I saw it,' said Lespines.

'The breach is low enough. We can cross it with scaling ladders. I shall go in that way with a small advance party.'

'You don't lay much store by the parley, then?' said Lespines affectionately, amused by Victoire's everlasting heroics.

'I'll tell you why that is,' said Victoire, removing a strand of hair from his mouth with a feminine delicacy, despite mail gloves. 'You may sound parley if you please, but I doubt you'll get an answer, since there's no one inside. No soldiers, I mean. None on guard, at least. From up there, there's a clear view of the inner yards and battlements. There's life in the donjon – there's smoke rising – but the place is ungarrisoned. So. As I say. I shall go in at the breach.' He looked to Lespines for encouragement, but saw that he had just forfeited the right of inexperienced youth to lean on the older man. 'Will you come with me, Gilbert, or wait here for me to raise the cullis from inside?'

Lespines examined the brass horn in his lap. Then he slung it across his back. 'We'll sound parley inside – at the foot of the donjon. God grant you a few hostages at least to brighten your economy, my lord.'

'Amen.' And they turned their horses and spurred them in the direction of the engineers and ordnance men and their clutter of unwieldy engines and ladders.

It was a treacherous scramble across the improvised bridge of ladders and felled saplings. The masonry shifted under the grapples like stones rolled by a tide, and the advance party scurried across on all fours, knowing their backs to be vulnerable to any sudden flurry of arrows from the slits in the high, inscrutable keep.

But it was a lamentable set of defences, for all its ugly grandeur. And beyond the breach in the wall there was no detachment of archers, no phalanx of English goddams waiting to fall on them, no one to stop them seizing the inner yard and opening the portcullis. With the drawbridge down, the cavalry came over, and then the foot-soldiers, eyeing the rotten planks dubiously and breaking stride with little grace steps so as not to set it bowing. All that greeted them was a storm of flies from the midden and a smell of – what? – Englishmen. Each nation's spoor smells insanitary to another. It was an old smell, a dead trail.

The blare of the parley trumpet ricocheted from wall to wall. Victoire's horse, infected with the emotions of her rider, pitched and stamped, and swivelled her ears. He creamed sweat off her neck in handfuls. The mercenaries began to root about in the lean-to sheds between the buttresses, and to break open the doors of the yard buildings. Victoire turned paler with each crunch of breaking timber, as if the fibres breaking were his own flesh. He turned his horse and turned it and turned it again, telling himself he was impatient, insulted, irritated – anything so as to quell the childish excitement that kept capering through him.

Every man in the yard suddenly looked up. A clatter of mailed heels was descending the spiral staircase of the keep. Though the owner of the heels was invisible, the men's eyes traced his progress down, round, down, round from the high chamber to the wooden door at the tower's base. The rain-swelled door scuffed and graunched open in answer to a kick from within, and a cavalier in a Plantagenet surcoat came stumping out, his scabbard-tip dragging on the ground.

Squinting against the light, the man took his bearing from the clutch of banners and pennants mustered in the yard and immediately addressed himself to Lespines. 'You, I take it, are the so-called Comte de Gloriole.' He had a face like a wall, grey-lichened with patches of beard and in need of repointing: angular scars that had healed without aid of a surgeon.

Victoire laughed, 'Why didn't you answer parley? We might have taken you for a sortie and shot you.'

The broken water-spout of a nose turned in his direction and sniffed. 'The House of Talbot disdains to waste its wind on the likes of vagabonds and bandits.'

'Oh splendid!' snorted Victoire, and his horse wagged her head appreciatively, too.

'Are you de Gloriole?' The possibility seemed to shake the warrior to the depth of his rocky foundations. 'My trade is with you then, boy. Sir Humphrey Talbot sends me, his Champion, to demand single combat with your lordship. To decide the matter of ransom.'

There was an outburst of raucous laughter, unsettling doves from their cote in an end gable. Lespines nudged his horse closer to the man on foot, who made no move to get out of the way. 'Don't talk horse-shit, man. Tell Talbot he's a taken prisoner already. He can offer ransom or have his throat cut. As he chooses. And so can you.'

Victoire said, 'He could at least have offered to fight me himself.'

'My master is of tender years, sir,' said the Champion, 'but blessed with a strong sense of honour – which I find wanting in the French if you will refuse my . . .'

'How tender?' said Victoire.

'Fourteen years.'

'Fourteen? My castle given to a child? Pshah! Tell him to pack his toys and nightshirt and I'll put him to a wet-nurse till his ransom's

33

paid.' In her agitation, Victoire's horse turned round twice in pursuit of her own tail.

The Wall remained unmoved, however. 'Sir Humphrey will never surrender up the castle to you, sir, unless God gives you victory in a trial of arms with me.'

'I *have* the castle, man!'

'While he holds the donjon, he holds the castle.'

It was an undeniable truth. The keep was the spine in the body, the centrepost in the tent, the maypole in the dance. Victoire, for all his five hundred men, was still a cat scratching on the outside of a locked door.

'Fetch straw from the stables!' he shouted, standing up in his stirrups. 'Pile it round the door and stand by with a torch! . . . The parley is over, sir. Tell your master, if he won't surrender himself instantly, let him roast. The terms of his ransom are ten thousand livres!'

'Sir! There are others . . . the household . . .' said the Champion. And the features of his face reorganized themselves, as the stones of the wall had stirred under the grapples.

'I assumed it. His ransom secures their lives too.'

'Women! Children!'

'The more reason for Sir Humphrey to yield to common sense. Are you going to deliver terms, sir, or am I to light the straw?'

Suddenly the English Champion made a snatch at the bridle of Victoire's horse, seized both her cheek straps and pulled down her head for a clearer confrontation with the rider. A dozen swords rasped out of the scabbard to offer him death. 'A pass or two, sir! For honour's sake! The lad won't budge, sir! He's never met with a setback in all his life! He's never met with the word "no"! A pass or two, for God's sake!'

The man was a monument to the wars. Each scar attested another man's death; his mortal clay had been chipped away and yet he had survived better than his adversaries. He did not for a moment turn his eyes away from Victoire despite Lespines' swordpoint wavering alongside his throat.

'Give him your horse, Gilbert. And find us two lances apiece,' said Victoire. 'I'll fight Talbot's proxy.'

'The devil you will! We'll smoke 'em out. You! Climb up and say so!'

But Victoire knocked Lespines' blade away from the Champion with his own. 'I had enough smoked herring in Poictou, Gilbert!

More than I could eat. Live hostages are more of a novelty to me. So give the man your horse.'

'Where's his own horse?' muttered Lespines as he stood by and watched the two mares being caparisoned in front armour for the joust.

'Stolen by the grooms, sir, overnight,' replied the Champion curtly in his peculiar roughcast French. (As the currier observed, 'They speak without their noses, these Englishmen.') 'Our parley-horn, likewise,' he added. 'That's why we couldn't answer yours.' Victoire recollected the donkey-train, and suddenly realized that his fortress had been stripped bare, within hours of his coming, by opportunist English deserters.

A single thought occupied him as the two horses turned tail on one another and swayed to opposite ends of the yard. He should have taken time to see inside the manor-house with its beamed upper room and long table and fireplace: to have seen it in more than his dreams.

'The fellow's mad,' said Lespines, walking alongside as Victoire's parrain, carrying his second lance. 'He knows full well if he kills you we'll cut him down and burn the rest alive.'

'Sounds less than honourable to me. You must do as you see fit, Gilbert, but I say let them go. Bide by the passage-of-arms . . . If I go down . . . Michel de Puy's my heir, you know. The castle's his if I go down. I dare say he wishes me all the ill-luck in the world, now I look at it that way.' He peered among the ranks of assembled men, but could not glimpse his young cousin in the crowd.

'God be in your lance, my lord,' said Lespines with all the nonchalance he could muster, and Victoire replied:

'Oh no doubt of it. Besides, I used up my store of cowardice this morning – on my fine, brave vigil.'

So to expiate the fear he had felt kneeling in the Chapel Saint-Cloud that morning, Victoire de Gloriole couched his lance and rode against Humphrey Talbot's proxy. He could imagine, as he rode, the wide, childish eyes that must be watching through the donjon slits, willing him dead.

They were not the long, flexing tourney lances, but short, rigid battle weapons, undecorated, ungilded, unribboned. On the first pass, the horses, without benefit of a list fence to lean their shoulders to, arced wide of each other. The beasts were acquainted, after all. On the second pass, both men dug in their spurs and the

35

leap of their horses drove cries out of the riders – out of the pits of their stomachs – unconnected with speech.

At the last moment, the Champion dropped the tip of his lance and let his shield fall aside. Victoire's lance hit him square in the breast, rent the surcoat and buckled the armour underneath into a sunburst of creases. As he saw the man hurled out of the saddle by the impact and somersaulted over the tail of his horse, it occurred to Victoire that his feet must already have been out of the stirrups: he had not wanted to suffer that indignity, peculiarly dreadful to cavalrymen, of being dragged and trampled by his own horse.

Victoire had dismounted even before the hollow rattle of the two dropped lances came to an end. He raised the Englishman's head on to his knees and unfastened the stoven breastplate, heaving up the ribcage with both hands. The wind rushed back into the lungs, like the breath of God reanimating Adam, and made the limbs twitch.

'You let go the lance, boy. If you hadn't, I'd be dead.'

'Only because I saw you drop your shield, man!' said Victoire. 'Don't you know suicide's a sin?'

The head rolled like a boulder in his lap. 'My wife and children are in the keep. It was the only way. Now honour's satisfied, maybe the lad will swallow his defeat. It's new to him you understand.'

'New to Talbots everywhere.'

'Oho! You don't suppose you're fighting another John Talbot, do you? Two of him and we'd never have lost the Loire. This branch is a rotten branch. Grafted on. Grafted on. I . . . My wife and daughters are in your protection, sir! As you love honour, keep your men off them!' He deflated then like a leaky wine skin, and the hollows of his cheeks subsided, his stocky body seeming to diminish in size.

'Tend to him the best you know how,' he told his surgeon. 'I'd have him for one of mine if he weren't an Englishman.' The capering exuberance returned three-fold to Victoire. He and Lespines ran back on foot to the monumental tourney prize, to the captured donjon . . .

The door was locked, bolted and barred against them. Sir Humphrey Talbot, who had never been gainsaid, never met with a setback, leave alone defeat, had no intention of honouring the passage-of-arms.

'You are my prisoner, Sir Humphrey! Come down and sur-render arms!' It made Victoire dizzy to crane his neck and bellow.

The shrill, disjointed retaliation showered over the rim of a stone sill, like bird droppings. 'Not! Not! Shan't!'

Victoire gave orders for the wounded Champion to be carried off the yard.

'He has shamed me. My curse on the little bastard,' said the old knight, and he put one arm over his face, so as not to see the straw lit round the base of the castle keep.

The horror of that animated, leaping fire cleaving to those inanimate stones came back to Victoire in nightmares. Soft against hard. It haunted him with images of the burning of Jeanne Darc – a small white figure raised up high above the faggots, enveloped by the smoke, corrugated by the heat, dying even out of reach of the flames, in Hell before being in Heaven.

Victoire all but kicked the straw away from the door himself. He armed twenty men with forks and spears and rakes, keeping them so close in readiness that they reddened and sweated in the heat. A banshee screaming broke from the arrow slits – women, children, a baby – as the smoke belched under the door and gushed up the great flue of a building. Unimaginably soon, it was filtering out of the topmost slits, like light between shutters. Bags of saltpetre against the door blew it to splinters, and the smoke redoubled its efforts to clamber up the spiral stair.

'Surrender, Talbot! Surrender, you turd! You dishonoured brat!'

'I surrender! I surrender!' came the shrill, retching squawk. Victoire snatched a pike from a nearby soldier and dragged away the first stook of blazing straw; it scattered about their feet.

Lespines was the first on to the stair, with Victoire close on his heels. Slits of light fell across the steps, marking their ascent, round and up, round and up. The smoke was still thick in the air, but de Gloriole was euphoric. 'It's mine, Gilbert! I've taken it!' He was panting and his eyes streamed with the smoke, but here was the Tree of Knowledge in the centre of his Eden, here was Paradise regained. 'And you'll be my Master-at-Arms if you're willing! Will you, Gilbert? Will you stay on with me? You my right-hand . . .' A broad funnel of light poured on to them from above. The staircase was accomplished.

Suddenly the legs ahead of him fetched up short – the tendons shortened and the heels slid backwards off the uneven stone. Lespines fell forward into the room, twisting as he fell, landing on his back.

37

The crossbow bolt had passed clean through mail and leather to pierce his stomach.

When Victoire jumped over and astride his friend, he found the noble Lord Talbot crouched on buckled legs against the far wall of the room. There was a pool of urine at his feet. At the sight of a second adversary, Humphrey threw the empty crossbow inaccurately at Victoire's head and snatched to him instead a woman and a baby. The woman he held round the neck, with his dagger against her cheek, the baby by its clouts, dangling alongside his sword.

The room was full of smuts – floating black fragments of smoke like blood clots from a lethal wound. It seemed to Victoire that the vessels in his eyes were bursting, spotting his vision with apoplexy.

'I'll kill them! I will! I'll kill them!' screamed the Talbot, his acned face gibbering and his teeth clattering round his tongue. 'Don't come any closer or I'll kill them!'

'What's that to me?' said Victoire. But though he raised his sword, he did not step forward. He did not want to unstopper the stairs and let more troops pour into the upper room. He kept them behind him on the steps.

The baby was screaming, red-faced, golden-eyed. The noise filled the room with horror and, almost as if to be rid of the sound, Humphrey thrust the child out through the slit, scraping it against the stone, soft against hard. There was a gasp from all the women present. But Victoire, his sword outstretched like Solomon, found himself wondering why he could not tell which among them was the baby's mother.

'Think on your soul, Talbot. Bring the child in. Let the woman go. And I'll shrive you before I quarter you.' He did not recognize his own voice so distorted was it by violence. Straddling the body of his friend, he felt it slacken into death at his feet.

The boy hesitated. He tried to pull in the baby: it had turned in his grip and would not come back through the slit. He tugged and tugged. He turned his head to see what he was doing.

And the woman under his arm pulled the dagger away from her cheek and drove it sideways into the acned neck. The falling baby's crying diminished, then abruptly ceased with a noise like a dropped bag of flour bursting, soft against hard.

Victoire's swordblow gave the Talbot a swifter death than he deserved. The members of his household spat on the young Sir

Humphrey one by one and delivered themselves into the protection of his killer, as the large, round chamber gradually filled up with French soldiers from below.

FIVE

The Chicheface

'Whose was the child?' asked Victoire, but no one could tell him. A foundling, they said. A thing of no account. They said it by way of sycophancy, not wishing him to see any trace of blame in their eyes. It was not that they were indifferent; their priests had taught them better than to scorn little children. They had found it on the drawbridge, hadn't they? But now it was dead there was no one to grieve and certainly no one who wished their captor to feel an unnecessary burden of guilt. They wanted him as sweet-natured as his face promised, as chivalric as the passage-of-arms had implied. They required his pity to be directed towards the living and not wasted on the dead. He even heard some of his own men say that it was a lucky thing, a blood sacrifice – though he called them pagan devils for saying it.

He put all his remaining prisoners under guard in the dungeon below the keep, all but the woman who had been held hostage by Humphrey. He could not tell why he chose her to question – why her more than another.

'Why would he not surrender and be ransomed?' he asked, squatting beside the body.

'He was told there'd be none. His relations in England – they told him to fight or fly, but not to be taken – not to expect ransoming, in any case. He and his father, they were tubers from the rose. Sapping the bush. There were strange stories about the father. Great excesses. Debts. The Great John – that's to say, Sir John Talbot – took this castle and a tenant was needed to hold it against the . . . to hold it. So the father was ordered here. It pleased everyone – to have him gone from England. Him and his son. His wife fled him long since. He was sick already when he sailed. He died last month.'

'Not greatly mourned, I take it.'

'I couldn't say.' But she could and did say a multitude more –

as though, like Orpheus, the music of her voice was all that was keeping the wild beasts at bay.

She was as tall as Victoire and as thin as a hazel twig. Like hazel, too, in answer to some unseen current of water, she trembled violently, her hands clasped awkwardly in front of her, her straight arms braced and her diaphragm quaking behind the blue wool of her dress. He could recognize it for fright, but had no notion that he was the cause. Well, no more than he had a notion, somewhere at the back of his mind, that she was the most beautiful woman he had ever stood alone with in a room.

'When he knew he was dying, the father sent post-haste to England to make a match for his son. He lacked money, he said, to make good the fortifications.' She swung her clasped hands towards the slit, towards the yard. 'The money didn't come, as you see: the Loire was lost already. Then he sent to Sir John Talbot to say he would cede the fortress if a wife wasn't found for his boy. And I was sent, and came here ten days ago. And I'd be married by now but for . . .' She hesitated. She seemed to have forgotten the reason. '. . . But for the span of mourning.'

'Who to? Married to whom?' said Victoire foolishly. 'To that?' He pointed the blade of his sword at the body on the floor, its half-cloak thrown over its face and its legs twisted in opposite directions so that the codpiece gaped.

'Wife and widow in a week,' she said, as though she should see the comedy but somehow could not. All the while, she was turning paler and paler, like a sheet of paper held up to the light – an intriguing, translucent white that held the eye, though his stare threw her into a greater and greater panic. 'I was sent by way of an insult.'

'Mademoiselle! Would that my relations would pay me so handsome an insult. In what way are you an insult? Do you have no dowry?'

'Oh yes!' She said it before she thought. 'There had to be a dowry. That was the point of the match.' Her voice was drying up like a stream in summer. As if to divert his train of thought, she blurted out, 'The locusts have stripped your fields bare, monsieur. When it was known that the French . . . that you were coming, the household thought Humphrey would fly – him – all of us – fly. But he had nowhere to go. And he dared not surrender without hope of a ransom. And if he had got to England, what then? He'd be penniless, landless, unthought of, not wanted. He relished his title greatly. He

41

said it was God-given – like the Divinity of Kings . . . No small opinion of his worth, you see.' Her agitation took her between the two bodies: she stood and looked down at them absently, the hem of her dress drinking up the spilled blood, thread by purpling thread. 'Humphrey persuaded himself you would offer a *turnois* – a bribe of some sort, to buy him out . . .'

'Would that I had the means, mademoiselle.'

'So when the rest saw he'd not surrender or fly, the hired soldiers and the grooms and the servants, they stripped the house bare. They carried off all that could be carried. My trousseau all unpacked. My . . . ah . . . dowry. The horses, too. They took the horses. You wonder at the loyalty of my master's household? To stand by him and let themselves fall into . . . let themselves be taken. The poor souls had no horses, you see? No horses, no boats. You would have fewer prisoners to triumph over but for the thieving of our own servants. God have mercy on us. Now . . .' Her hand suddenly flew to her mouth and her dark eyes strained wide over the gag of her own fingers as she looked this way and that for somewhere to be sick.

'Pray lie down,' he said, alarmed. The donjon was furnished as a dormitory and whatever else the castle now lacked in furnishings, it had mattresses in plenty. 'Pray do lie down, mademoiselle!' But he only elicited a banshee wail, and she fell on her knees, her hands covering her head, dragging forward the coif. Then the whole concealed mass of her dark hair escaped in a cascade into her lap. (What hair! What a quantity of hair!)

'I would take my life! I would, but you do such things to suicides in this country, such foul things! Why do you do such terrible things?'

'Jesu, woman! Because it's damnable! Kill yourself? Jesu! Why should you want to . . . ?'

'It's not damnable! There've been saints . . . But to be fed to the dogs! *You* could kill me, though, couldn't you?' Her eyes were riveted to his sword.

He threw it on to the farthest bed and tried to lift her to her feet to reason with her. But he felt, like Jacob wrestling with the angel, that this could go on all night. 'mademoiselle! Were you so very fond of that – that *person* yonder? I'm sorry – listen to me! – I'm sorry to maim your marriage plans, but he shot my friend! After surrender! Look there! He shot my comrade! And it seems to me that a wretch who'd fight by proxy, defame a truce, shelter behind a woman and kill a baby lacks something of chivalry!' He groaned: his words were not reaching their mark. At last he protested, 'Forgive me, mademoiselle. I know I'm green, but I don't understand such an excess of grief for such a . . .' (Her hair smelt of herbs – savonnerie and lavender.)

'Chivalry. Chivalry? What do the French know of chivalry?' she demanded, and reared up, beating at him with her fists. He took a restraining hold of her forearms.

'Forgive me, but I believe we invented it.'

'And is it chivalry your men are showing now to our women and children down below?'

'I hope and trust so!' He cocked an apprehensive ear, for fear her hearing was more acute than his. 'They are under orders . . . I need *ransoms*, mademoiselle! Look around you. I *need* ransoms!' But she was oblivious to argument.

'We know what you are. We know what you do!'

'And, pray, what's that, mademoiselle? What wonderful reputation have we earned in England?' He was panting with the exertion of restraining her, and as she began to kick at his shins and lift her knees sharply into him, he was obliged to pin her against the wall with his body in self-defence. The hilt of his sword hooked up a swag of her dress. She opened her mouth and screamed full in his face, so that he felt as if his brain was glass and had shattered. 'Holy saints and angels,' he whispered and shook his head to empty it of the fragments.

Into the silence which followed fell, drop by drop, elucidation. He could feel the stiffening in her bodice flex and hollow, flex and hollow against his arm. He wished he had taken off his mail gloves and could feel her hair breaking now over his hands.

Here was the precious property of his enemy, fragile, breakable, unenjoyed; a Talbot's bride snatched intacta from under his very thigh, a doe of the Talbot herd, run off, cornered, unstagged.

And he would be no more than fulfilling her expectations. It was the single most inciting thought he had ever entertained. He leaned his full weight against her and bent his face forwards into the angle of her throat. It seemed the most natural thing in the world to do. 'What's your name?'

'Ellen Talbot.'

'How old are you, Ellen?'

'Twenty.'

'A poor match for fourteen.'

43

'Common enough.'

'Was that the insult?'

'No. I don't know. I don't know the insult intended.' She was breathing so shallowly that the words barely stirred in her throat. 'You're not long from a boy yourself.' He could feel her jugular pulsing against his cheek.

'Eighteen. I'm eighteen,' he said. 'But the war, you know. The war makes men out of . . .' He broke away from her suddenly into the centre of the room. When he spoke again, it was in a haste to be gone. 'The war makes barbarians out of Christian men. I'm sorry, you must excuse me. The pillagers are not long gone. If I dispatch a troop of horse, I can maybe redeem some portion of my worldly goods – and your dowry. Also, I must see to the obsequies for my friend . . . Do I take it there will be no ransom paid for anyone here?'

'None. John Talbot forbade it.' Still pressed against the wall, she held both hands over her throat as if to hide a strawberry stain or a blemish.

'I can't afford to feed any of them. You can tell those in the cellar – they may have their throats cut or leave here and chance their fortunes downriver. I'll put all that want to go in a boat and send them down to the sea under a warrant of passage. All but the man who fought me. I'll make him my Master-at-Arms if he'll turn his coat. He and his wife and daughter may stay.'

'And may I go too?' She whispered, as if speaking aloud might wake some dragon sleeping in the room with them.

He only half looked at her, his hand raised as if to shield his eyes from an irritating glare. He pressed the cold back of his glove to his cheeks. 'No. Not yet. I don't know. I think not. But I'll confine you in the manorhouse. You'll be more comfortable there than here. Later, perhaps you'll grant me the honour of your company.'

He summoned soldiers to remove the bodies: Lespines first, to be washed then coffined in the castle chapel, then Humphrey Talbot.

'What's to do with this one?' asked the soldiers, carrying the body between them with as little reverence as possible. They winked confidences at one another, because of the screaming they had heard, because of the way the woman stood, because of the way their young commander was looking at her.

'Can I hear dogs?' asked Victoire.

'Yes sir! A fine kennel! Best thing in the place. Twenty-five hounds or more.'

'Then have the chaplain say a prayer for his soul and feed Sir Humphrey to the dogs. I won't have him buried in my land . . . You may keep such clothes as fit you . . . Oh, and lady' – he spoke with his back to her – 'if Satan should tempt you to suicide again while I'm gone, you may rest assured I'll do the same with your body, though without the prayers. Your servant, mademoiselle.'

There was a great deal to be accomplished before sunset. The estate peasants, persuaded to open the doors of the village church at last, greeted Victoire with a look he recognized from a stray dog he had once fed and been bitten by after. They swore they had paid *aides* and *taille* and *feu* to the Talbot only a week or so before, that they had been bled white by his bailiff and robbed of their last sou by the deserting English. The English bailiff (who was among the prisoners in the cellar) produced account books, however, showing countless taxes unpaid. They had blamed the French, then, saying that disbanded French militia had stripped the villages bare. It was probably truer than their excuses now: the peasants were simply tempering their excuses to suit the listener. But it made little difference to the parlous state of his economy. The shorn sheep can't be quickly shorn again.

'I shall need builders to restore the west wall. And builders and carpenters and joiners to begin a great-barn, too.'

'A great-barn?'

'And a new miller. The last was English, so I hear.' They hung back inside the church door, kneeling on the hard stone floor. 'Let it be known generally – for fifty miles around at least – that I'm selling the franchise on the mill to the highest bidder – so long as he's honest. I'll be the judge of that myself, after one year.'

They stared at him as if they had grown too accustomed to the English dialect to make sense of his aristocratic French. 'Selling the franchise?'

'I mean to restore the Chapel Saint-Cloud, too, and glorify it. Was the relic stolen by the English or put into hiding?'

'Stolen? Safe-keeping?'

'And the King in his grace has granted me toll rights on the river. I must construct a boom tower on the far bank. The blacksmith can start forging a chain as heavy as ever he thought of, and make it a shade longer than the length of the bridge.'

'Boom tower.'

'Oh, and if there is anyone here who was in service at the castle yesterday and took my furniture and ornaments into safe-keeping, I thank you and charge you to present yourself for employment again at tomorrow dawn. With your treasure. But anyone who thinks to gain at my expense will be hunted and hanged for a thief . . . Informants will be well rewarded. As for my troops, it may ease your minds to know that they are not mine and must be sent back to the King post-haste. I'll not disband them here.'

'Not disband them?'

'Not disband them to loot your homes and rape your women, no. They're still under orders to the King. Oh, and I won't be raising a levy of men for the wars until this place of mine is put to rights.'

'God save the King,' ventured a small, dubious voice.

'Amen. And God put you in mind of my father — those of you who remember him. That you may rejoice in the restoration of his name. I'm sure he was a just and kind fief and I mean to imitate him.'

'Always just and kind,' they said, kneeling side-on to him, wringing their hoods, rolling the heels of their boots. They were like Moors being catechized into the true faith. They rubbed their necks where the sword-edge might still fall if they spoke the wrong words. They reserved judgment on this new liege of theirs. They were far too preoccupied trying to foresee the next blight in store for them.

'I need a boat. There are none left at the castle,' said Victoire. 'Now. I need a boat now. Where are the apple barges?'

They flinched at the sudden call for thought. 'Apple barges. Further upriver. By the orchards.'

'Fetch me one down, and a man who can take it as far as the sea.'

'The sea.'

Most had not seen the sea. They took its existence on faith. People said it was full of monsters. None of the monsters were more implausible than this peculiar youth talking of barges and barns and boom towers.

He would not have talked so fast nor attempted so much except that he was lonely; lonely past daring to think how much. For years he had lived in tents and billets, in the company of men, and then he had struggled to separate his thoughts from the common pool and bend them towards a future time, laid up in store for him like Heaven. Now, with Lespines dead, he felt he had outlived a war

46

in which the rest of the world had died. All his life he had lived in anticipation of coming home. But now he came to inspect his prize, he did not know behind which door to look for Happiness.

In the long hall of the manor-house, the tapestry rails hung askew and empty where the looters had torn down the hangings. The logs had been tipped out for the sake of their wicker basket. The hanging lamps were gone. The arms of the chair at the head of the table were carved with dog-heads – talbots – and John Talbot's portrait hung over the chimney breast.

The woman prisoner, he knew, sat perfectly still in the adjacent room, hoping that if she did not make a sound, he would forget her existence. It was a vain hope. 'Be so good as to come and sit with me!' he called out. He heard the rattle of a rosary as she dropped it out of her hands, but she did not come. 'Lady Ellen. Be so good as to lend me your company,' he called again, and she came, bent at the shoulder-blades and hips. She had exchanged her clothing with another of the women, so as to be dressed in black. It made her look like a birchtree after a brushfire.

He thought: '*She is the door,*' and was immediately at a loss to know what the phrase meant. It made no sense whatever. All at once, though, his mood was put to rights. The anticlimax was dispelled. The day's significance was restored. He sat back in the carved chair and his spirit expanded to fill it. His hands muzzled the dog-heads on the arm-ends. 'I swore to my father I would retake this place. It's a fine estate, don't you think? A little dilapidated, but that's soon mended. I have plans. I have such plans!'

She did not reply, and he did not press her to make conversation, but turned to calculating, with chalk on slate, his potential income and the projects on which to spend it. The chalk squealed with horror at the silence in the room.

'I had not understood,' she said. 'This is your ancestral home. You are Sablois.'

'No, I'm Gloriole. Sablois is the river,' he said, smiling down at the slate.

'I'm sorry. The letters that summoned me called it Talbot-Sablois. I imagined . . .'

'The gall of the man! Talbot-Sablois? Pshah! I wonder the post-messengers ever found their way here. It's been the fortress of Gloriole-sur-Sablois since it was built. An ancestor of mine built it. Foulques Nerra. Along with nearly every fortress on the Loire. Between crusading and fighting his neighbours. A tower here, a fortress there. This one was to hold the Sablois and the land between Sablois and the Loire. At least, he built the donjon and the curtain wall. The fiefdom was a gift to my great-great grandfather by Saint Louis himself. This manor-house was my grandfather's work. It is pleasant, don't you think?'

'I have heard of Nerra. Is it true he had his wife burned alive?' she asked.

But his excitement refused to be doused. He simply withdrew to his calculations, saying, 'It was a very long time ago.' Her body arced like a longbow over the breviary in her lap. He knew he must lay his arrow to the bow. He stood up.

Just then a scuffling on the stairs announced the arrival of his cousin, Michel de Puy.

The young chevalier had made an excuse of bringing the Comte's food, but as soon as he set it down and bowed, he pulled up a chair close to Victoire's. 'So! You are restored to happiness, my lord cousin!' said Michel, plunging his clasped hands between his knees and leaning forward precipitately. 'A glorious day for our families! My father and I rejoice in your good fortune!'

'I wish your brother Gilles were alive to share my good fortune,' said Victoire. But he saw that it was unkind to interrupt: the young knight was endeavouring to remember a rehearsed speech. He knitted his brows and fixed his eyes somewhere over Victoire's head so as not to be distracted.

'On this auspicious day, my father bids me urge you to a greater happiness.'

'How very rhetorical of him,' said Victoire, setting about his sardine sop while it was hot. 'Do you think he can direct me to a good master of hounds? And a stable of hunters? It might be my making with the King.'

'He begs you to take moves to ensure that the achievements of today are assured for all time, and the honour of your name preserved to all generations!'

'By Saint John! Let him write it in a letter, Michel. You eat your dinner. Eloquence at mealtimes? It makes for colic.'

'Consider. As a hero of many campaigns, you more than most men must have seen mortality in your own reflection!'

It promptly occurred to Victoire that mirrors too must have been stolen from the room. 'I see mortality in the body of Gilbert Lespines, sir, who lies in the chapel in place of me. I hardly need to look further for proof of mortality.'

'Exactly!' agreed Michel with tactless delight. 'So let our two families redouble the triumph of today with the incomparable joy . . . of a *marriage*.'

Victoire, his head low over the bowl, fixed de Puy with a gaze so glittering and odd that Michel sat back abruptly in his chair and began to chew his nails. He saw the Englishwoman looking at him, too, and wagged his tongue at her suggestively. Knowing how his esteemed cousin detested the English, he assumed he was beholden to do something of the kind. Presumably she was there to be humiliated.

Once again, loneliness clambered up the walls of the manor-house, as tangible as belladonna.

'Yes. I must marry,' said Victoire suddenly. 'Who is your father suggesting?'

'You agree! Praise God!'

'Who?'

'God. Praise God.'

'No, Michel. I meant who may I hope to marry?'

'Oh! My sister, of course. Victorine. Victoire and Victorine! A match commended by the very names! It must signify . . .'

'Forgive me. I didn't know you had a sister, Michel.'

'Oh yes! A great beauty! And strong. And healthy. And . . .'

'Have you her portrait?' Victoire asked. Michel giggled away the unlikelihood of having his sister's portrait. 'And when could the marriage take place?'

Victoire's eyes left his cousin in peace, and strayed towards the woman in black. Black like a blackthorn; she pricked him and made his blood flow.

'The betrothal at once. Within the week.'

'And the marriage?'

(Her coiled hair pushed against the coif like a live thing inside a poacher's bag.)

'Perhaps when she's twelve? A little later, a little earlier, according to when Nature breaches her.'

Victoire saw his own dismay mirrored in the woman's face. 'And, very roughly speaking, how far is Nature off breaching your sister, Michel?'

'I . . . ah . . . well. She's, let me think. She will very soon be four, sir, with God's grace.'

Victoire shot out of his chair as if to conceal the upward flight of his eyebrows. 'Oh then let God be gracious indeed, cousin! He's going to have to fend off my mortality for another ten years at least!'

Michel de Puy leapt to his feet in an ecstasy of relief. 'No fears there! No fears in the world. It's agreed, then! I'll write to my father instantly.' He had reached the door before Victoire called him back.

'I must crave your indulgence, Michel. For a day or two, at least. The estate makes calls on me that I should, in all fairness, answer before I allow myself the selfish luxury of love. I shall write to your father myself with my considered answer.'

'Oh.' Crestfallen, Michel de Puy went to sit down again, but could not do so until the Comte seated himself. He soon perceived that he was being invited to go and, after a bow as rehearsed as the speech had been, he left the room, pausing only to pluck the coif off the head of the woman in black. It was intended as a tribute to his nephew's rape of the English in general.

After the door had shut, Victoire went to stand behind Ellen, picking up her hair in both hands, as if he would replace it in the cap. 'My cousin has an infernal impudence – beyond his manners, I mean. My relations must hold me extraordinary green if they think I'll leap into a match with my little relation, be she ever so *healthy*.'

'It would call for a great *restraint*, my lord,' she said with undisguised contempt and leaned further and further forward, away from him.

'It would call for an even greater want of worldliness, lady. I'm a landed Comte now, dwelling in the light of the countenance of the King, and unless I deceive myself, brides of four and brides of four-and-forty will very shortly come tripping it with tracts of land and noble alliances and golden dowries and foreign favours stuffed under their skirts. Why should I hold my mortality in check for ten years just to *join farms* with my next-door kin? Still, I suppose Michel's not to blame. He's only the conveyor of his father's message. And you must forgive his manners, lady. He is very young.'

'That was not reason enough for you to forgive Sir Humphrey Talbot.'

'No. There was too much to forgive. I'm not a saint. And besides . . .' He twisted the hair through his hand and it coiled round his wrist, cold and shiny, then fell again like water from a pump. The skin of her neck and hairlines had a bloom of fine, dark hair, like a newborn baby. 'Besides . . . he had what I wanted.'

'You mean your estates, my lord. He had your estates.'

'My estates? Yes. But I find he had something he merited even less and that I want even more. Something altogether free from dilapidation.'

The hair went taut in his hand. 'You mistake, my lord, if you mean me. My spirit is quite in ruins. I am all despair.'

He went and crouched down in front of her chair. 'Mademoiselle, where is your dowry?'

White rims showed above and below her dark irises. 'I told you. It was stolen, along with everything else.'

He took hold of her fists and forced them open inside his grip. They were lovely hands, long and thin, springing from forearms as delicate as the fetlocks of a deer and flecked with dark freckles. 'Did I tell you? I've secured an excellent vessel for your friends. For their journey downriver. The apple barge I got down was none too sound. But while I was at the river today, trying to make repairs, what should the merciful God supply but a far better boat newly come upriver. So newly come, in fact, that its master was still ignorant of the . . . altered situation hereabouts. He sailed into us, you see. Like a fly into a web.' His thumbs stroking the palms of her hands expressed small drops of sweat, as certain leaves, in bruising, release their liquor. 'Shall I tell you what he had aboard, lady? It was a truly wonderful cargo – worth the listing.'

'What had he aboard?' The tip of her long, straight nose was pulled in by the stiffening of her cheeks and top lip.

'One thousand livres in gold, in two chests of white ash. And bed linen and three rolls of cloth – wool, damask and Italian velvet. Two books, a chalice and a silver chain. Oh and a great quantity of sardines – by way of camouflage, I take it – unless of course sardines were in the terms of your dowry?'

'My dowry?'

'Sure, the boatmaster was very heartfelt on the subject. He was at pains to tell me the merits of the lady whose dowry he was delivering. Any woman would be proud to match such a description.'

'Then you have certainly robbed some worthy lady of her future hopes, monsieur, but as for me . . .'

'Robbed? Well, I admit the sardines were uncommon useful for feeding the men. But as to the rest – if I knew the lady in question, I might return her goods to her.'

'Oh yes? Very likely.' Her eyes took on a vacant, stony malevolence, though not, this time, towards him. 'He would not marry till

51

it came. Humphrey, I mean. He feared a deception. He thought the family would cheat him and not send a penny. He was waiting for the ship to arrive. That's why I was not a wife when the French . . . when you came. Did you kill the boatmaster?'

'No! Hearing his refined French, I took him for a man fallen on hard times, reduced to the sardine trade. But then I thought, Who could be entrusted with a thousand livres in gold unless he'd a vested interest in delivering them? Your brother Stephen doesn't greatly resemble you, does he? Ah, but then he tells me you two are born of different mothers, isn't that right? . . . I've put him with the rest in the donjon cellar.'

She got to her feet, but he did not move, so that her abdomen was brought close to his face, eliciting a kind of groan from him. She abruptly sat down again.

'Mademoiselle, I mean to lie with you,' he said.

'Sir, I know it.'

'So.' He smiled a smile of dazzling ambiguity. 'So you'll be my mistress and profit by that beauty which makes you so *indispensable* to me. And sweep it through the court in satins and velvets, and catch the eye of King Charles himself, and share with me in the glories of Gloriole!'

Her face was like an icon – exaggeratedly huge at the eyes, the rest lifeless and two-dimensional. Even the sunburn on her cheeks was flaked, like old gilding. 'No, sir. I shall not. You can't so easily unburden your sins on to my conscience. You will take what you want, but I'll never give it voluntarily.'

'Not even for your brother's life?'

She had long since anticipated him. 'Of course. For my brother's life. For any man's or woman's life. I'm not so wicked as to price my maidenhead above the meanest of lives. But extortion will only buy you a quiet bedfellow, not a willing one. You only double your sin by threatening innocent lives in such a vile cause.'

'Yes. I know.'

He got up and fetched his shield from its peg on the wall. 'I have misled you, Ellen. I do mean to seize your dowry.'

'I never doubted it.'

'Do you know what animal this is?'

It was some time before she could be persuaded even to glance in the direction of the shield with its battered and scratched device. 'A mangy wolf? It befits you.'

He held the shield out at arm's length, as if looking at it himself for the first time. 'All my life I've wished ill on the man who gave our family this for an achievement. Until now. And no, it's not a wolf, nor a badly painted fox, neither. Its name is Chicheface. A legendary beast. Mythical. Rare to the point of extinction. Noah would be hard pressed to find a pair. It's the diet, you see. Once it was fat and sleek, and the ribs didn't gape. Now it's a starved, forlorn thing like this. Do you know what it eats, lady?'

Her eyes scudded back to her lap. 'Honourable Frenchmen?' and he laughed, and bowed.

'No. The poor beast eats only the flesh of pure women and faithful wives, you see. And that's a wondrous rare commodity these days.'

'It suits you all the better,' she said between her teeth.

'Yes, but a *pure woman*! A thing to be hunted down by every means, don't you agree? A thing to be seized on, tooth and paw, and never let go? A thing to be wolfed down?' He placed his hand over his crop. Or possibly his heart. 'If you believed in my honour, I'd base my claim on it. If you believed in my chivalry, I'd trust my cause to it. But since you think nothing good of me . . .'

To his dismay, the tripling towers of his rhetoric suddenly crumbled to dust inside his head. He laid down the shield and took himself off to the far end of the room, and sat down with his head in his hands.

'I am the Chicheface,' he said, aghast. 'It's the family curse. We crave . . . more than our fellow men. *Rien meilleur*. Nothing's better. Nothing but the best . . . Haven't you seen it carved on the lintels? That's why . . . That's why I must possess you. It's a question of appetite, you see? I'll starve else. And it goes against Nature to starve within sight of food.' He spread his big hands towards her in a futile appeal to reason, and let them drop again. 'So. I shall marry you, by whatever *extortion* you see fit to name. Because my soul's hungry for a perfect woman, and to forswear you would be to forswear women. As I said, I'm not that ambitious to be a saint. What do you say? Well, what can you say? You will do it. I'll give you no alternative.' He rubbed his hands to and fro through his hair until, with the muscles of his cheeks pulled tight and his mouth set hard and half open, he did somewhat resemble the forlorn creature on the shield. Then he simply stared at her, blinking his golden eyes overfast, as if against a flickering light, and growing visibly younger the longer it took her to speak.

'*Marry* you?'

'Marry me.'

'What about the brides tripping it from hither and yon, all stuffed with benefits?'

'The King would press me to marry one of them quite soon. That's why I must make haste and marry you. They'll think I was greedy for your dowry, or overcome by the thought of cuckolding a Talbot. That's believable.'

'But neither one's your motive.'

'No. Desire's my motive. It's all the Chicheface knows. Though I'll be right glad of the thousand livres, believe me!'

'You might have had that in any case,' she said, struggling to grasp his logic. 'What if I had agreed to be your . . . your . . . whore? Of my own free will.'

'I should have sent you home in your shift with the rest. And kept your maidenhead. Like a foxbrush for my wall – not much prized, you know, but proof of vermin ridded.'

She studied his face like a tangle of multi-coloured threads too hard to unravel. 'And what about the insult?'

'Insult? Oh, the insult!' He ventured an uncertain smile which she felt strangely compelled to return. 'You swear you don't know the nature of the insult?'

'No. I don't know it.'

'Well, what then? Sure! Any insult paid to one Talbot by another must be a boon to me, mustn't it?'

She said, like one trying to fathom a legal paragraph, 'So. I must marry you, must I? A foreigner and a sworn enemy of my kin.'

'Who sent you for an insult.'

'Who sent me for an insult. To marry a vile boy and fortify a lost cause. I don't much care about their motives. But yours . . . You're right. The Chicheface is a rare beast. And mad too, I think.'

'It's the fire in its blood, mademoiselle. It burns like sulphur. Enough to drive a poor beast mad.'

And then she sat and looked at him for a long time, and all the while he turned paler and paler, like a sheet of paper held up to the light. If she had not been taught from birth her utter subjection to the male sex, she would have sworn he went in fear and trembling of her.

SIX

Winning Approval

There were wild lamentations at the landing stage, and a fish-wharf kind of row. Women clung to each other and children wailed. The men squinted dubiously at the keelless, shallow-draughted boat, and shook their heads and scraped the dung off their boots on to the bulwarks and looked up at the big, balmy sky as though it promised hail. They were all flushed and slightly dishevelled from several hours of dancing, and most of them were drunk.

De Gloriole's household had been sent for from Poictou and, arriving on the eve of the wedding, had been unclear as to which were guests and which were English prisoners. Alliances had formed which were not quite appropriate to wartime, but the example of their betters had confused the poor creatures and it was only to be expected. A French ecurie was kissing an English seamstress behind a fold of sail.

It was Ellen's brother who had insisted they set sail immediately after the wedding. He suspected treachery on the part of the Comte de Gloriole. Nobody lets valuable hostages go in exchange for a bride, however excellent the woman – not when he can have woman and dowry and still keep his hostages. Victoire said they should stay till morning and spend one less night under the gabardine shrouds of the sardine boat. But Stephen Talbot was adamant.

His suspicions, though, had not kept him from participating in the wedding – giving his sister to the enemy with a mixture of sullen surliness, breast-broaching agony and hasty efficiency. Now he was lacrimose with emotion and claret and knelt on the dipping landing stage at her feet and pressed her hands to his lips. 'I shall give Father not a moment's peace till he sends ransom to deliver you, as you have delivered me!'

'But I'm married now, Stephen,' she said (who had not been drinking). 'You saw it duly done, according to religion.'

'It's no true marriage. Not made under duress! May God never pardon me till I bring you safe home again out of this foul Sodom!'

Ellen looked behind her to where her bridegroom sat on a grassy knoll, aloof, his knees drawn up and his hands round his thighs. She said a little briskly, 'If this is Sodom, Stephen, I've nothing to fear from the occupants, have I?'

'Worse! Worse!' Talbot had no wish to diminish the horrors in store for her in the Frenchman's bed. To have done so would have diminished his grounds for bitter self-reproach and he was relishing it far too much.

'Haven't you enjoyed our wedding, Stephen?' she said, taking the coronet of flowers from her head and resting it affectionately on his. 'It seemed to me that you were every whit as merry as the Comte's men.'

Her brother's knees cracked loudly and he got to his feet. 'You have great fortitude, Ellen,' he sniffed, rather than reply to the question.

She stood on tiptoe to whisper in his ear. 'If you'll not betray a secret, Stephen, I'll tell you: I'm rather too curious to trouble with "fortitude". This is a wondrous strange rape. The man has honoured my virginity, dressed me in white silk, showered me with presents and entertained my entire household, as well as freeing them. I'm secretly curious to know when the suffering begins.'

'Tonight! Tonight!' hooted the Talbot balefully, and more tears (or claret) escaped him at the eye and nose.

'I suppose I must believe you,' she said with an expression which did not in the least support the remark. 'So won't you stay to comfort me in the morning? Sail tomorrow. Stay tonight.'

The reminder of his own peril galvanized Stephen wonderfully. 'He would slit our throats while we slept!'

And he sprang aboard the boat, manhandled the ecurie ashore and began fumbling with the ropes. As the boat put out, the women had to lift their skirts and leap aboard or be left behind. A bundle fell into the river and was pulled out again. The fishy smell of the sardine boat receded downstream. Stephen Talbot stood on the stern wagging the flower wreath in farewell, so that white petals fell like tears on to the face of the river.

Ellen went and sat down beside her husband. He took the coronet of flowers from his own head and replaced hers without comment. They watched the boat pick up speed.

Then, a short way downriver, a noisy commotion arose. The blacksmith's new chain – forty fathoms long – had been wound up between the castle and a temporary wooden tower on the opposite bank to form a barricade across the river. The boat glided into it and the impact almost dislodged Stephen Talbot from his gunwale. The craft rocked excitedly, held prisoner in a manacle of chain.

Victoire felt a shudder go through the woman beside him.

'He was right,' she said under her breath. 'You never meant to let them go. You mean to keep them – or kill them. That's it! You mean to drown them in front of my eyes, you . . .!' She jumped up and started to run along the towpath. And judging that she meant to throw herself in to spite him, he ran after her. His household, thinking they were witnessing some playful nuptial dalliance, laughed and applauded dutifully, and cheered as he closed the gap.

The boat had turned side-on to the current, its rubbing strake catching against the chain. The occupants sat stock-still, their eyes caught by the movement on the bank – the billowing milk-white skirts, the cloud of trailing black hair, the pursuing scarlet doublet on the bank. They sat rigid and tried to guess the meaning of the chase and the meaning of the chain.

Victoire could have brought her down, but he was loath to muddy the glistening, spotless silk or to roll them both in the deep nettles that haunched the narrow towpath. So he let her reach the bridge, reach the centre of the bridge, before drawing level and catching hold of her arm. 'Pray don't dirty yourself, madam!' She pulled free. 'Or tear yourself on the roughcast.' She launched a blow at him. 'Or put me to the trouble of swimming. I can do it if you make me.'

'You liar! You French devil! You never meant to keep your word!'

He stepped in close and pinned her arms to her sides with his own, clasping his hands in the small of her back, as if to snap her spine with a jerk. He pressed her backwards against the parapet of the bridge. 'I did intend it, Ellen. I did *mean* to keep my word. But I found it ran against my conscience.' She tried savagely to bite his ear or cheek. 'Against my conscience, you hear! To marry a woman under durance. To make her buy her brother's life with her maidenhead.' He loosened his grip. 'Today you honoured our agreement. Every syllable. So. You choose. I've held back the boat for you to go aboard. If you want. If you choose.' He let go of her altogether, showing her his open hands like a conjuror or a surrendering prisoner.

She turned away from him and leaned over the parapet of the

57

bridge, still breathless. The boat lay almost below, resting in the bow of the chain. The bridge's arch gulped the river down as if to quench the dryness in her own throat. He leaned across the parapet beside her.

'Why? Has the Chicheface lost its appetite?' she said.

'No. But that's no matter. From a distance you won't even hear it howl. Much as that might gratify you.'

She was looking down into the upturned dish of her brother's white, uncomprehending face. He called something. She could not make it out. In his exasperation he pitched the flower circlet out of his fist into the water.

'I'd be breaking my wedding vows,' she said.

'There's no legal marriage without the bed,' said Victoire to the river.

'And you would truly let us go? Stephen and me and the rest?'

'The toll-keeper has orders to obey your word as if it were mine.'

She took the flower garland off her head and this time gave it to the river to wear. The bridge swallowed the two floating coronets, and she crossed to see them emerge on the other side. She and Victoire watched for a long time as the two circlets spun downstream until hers disintegrated and his washed into the lee of a stone buttress and was held there by slack water. When she glanced sideways at Victoire, she felt as if she were watching a swimmer trapped under ice.

She went back to the upriver parapet and signalled to the toll-keeper to drop the chain, to let the sardine boat continue on its way. The hull pecked awkwardly over the massive tripwire and grazed through the centre arch of the bridge with a great deal of shouting and fending off.

'I'm not dressed for a sea voyage,' she told him, kicking the nettles out of her hems. 'Let's go back to the house. There are still some important people to be entertained. To listen to you, anyone would think a wedding was to do with taking a wife. Everyone knows it's a matter of greasing the axletree, making the wheels turn.' She chose to ignore the short, hard breathing beside her – as of a man who has narrowly escaped drowning. It gave her a peculiarly immodest burning sensation in her bowels which she did not in the least understand.

The wheel of the year turned so fast that the peasants of the Gloriole estate felt they were aboard a runaway wagon. They turned reproachful, bewildered eyes on their new owner as they hurtled by. Or was it he who went hurtling by them? Either way, it was a strain on the eyes to keep sight of him. One moment he was out at the mill climbing the paddles to demonstrate where they were out of true; the next he was up at the barn explaining how transverse oak caps on the stone bases would keep damp from rising into the posts. He had seen such-and-such in Poictou; he had seen so-and-so on campaign in Brittany. He had read this and that in an Italian thesis. They allowed him a good eye for horses and dogs – the sort of thing a nobleman ought to concern himself with. But this Comte had met a horticulturalist while he was billeted in a monastery. This Comte had seen counter-planting to keep off pests. This Comte knew how to use saltpetre to shift a tree stump in an hour rather than a day. The peasants put their hands over their ears, shut their eyes tight, and ducked their heads against the explosion into their lives of Victoire de Gloriole. And when a new curate – one Barnabas – was assigned to them by the absentee incumbent of the parish, they rushed to him with their unhappiness:

'He works us to death! He watches us to find fault! He wants to change the old ways – the ways God ordained!'

Victoire came face-to-face with Barnabas for the first time across the pulpit rail of the Gloriole chapel. Obliged to visit his old comrade Bruberac, who was poorly, he had therefore entrusted to his wife the task of welcoming the young man to the parish. She reported a certain air of hostility, but said that it might have been her fault: her Englishness brought out rudeness in a great many Frenchmen. So Victoire cheerfully extended an invitation to Barnabas to hold Mass at the chateau. On the morning in question the Comte stood with his personal chaplain to his left and Ellen to his right, as the young Barnabas tripped up the pulpit steps with a thud. The shuffling, chattering household craned their necks to see if he would finally emerge.

Then he addressed himself to the parable of the rich man and his barn.

His knuckles were white where he gripped the balustrade, and the congregation could hear his fingernails scratching the stone. His lips were bone white, furled firmly over his teeth. This resemblance to a tortoise was exaggerated by the hooked beak of his nose, and he had the diction of a man with his mouth full of stones. His elbows juddered under his surplice. His washed-out grey eyes darted towards Victoire and skirted away again, like small dogs attacking a tethered bear.

'The fellow's a damned Leveller,' whispered the chaplain at one point. 'You'll have to turn him off!' But the Comte did not seem to understand what he meant, or else was too preoccupied to be listening to the sermon. It was certainly none too articulate a homily, made up of dark allusions to *barns* torn down and *bigger* ones put up; to the hoarding of *false earthly treasures*; to *fools* not rich in godliness; to *oppressors of the poor*.

Barnabas bumped down the pulpit stairs. At the end of Mass, he stood round-shouldered in the yard and was cut dead by such members of the household as had been paying attention. Victoire himself must have fallen asleep and missed all the impertinent remarks, however, for he put a cordial arm round the priest's shoulders and invited him to visit the restoration work in hand on the Chapel Saint-Cloud.

'Does the priest's house suit you?' he asked as they walked up the zig-zag path towards the hilltop chapel.

Barnabas snorted. 'I? Live in the priest's house? It was built for the Bishop.'

'But the Bishop doesn't live here. The man has seventy livings. He can't live in all of them.'

'But he can keep a place for when he does come.'

'Of course. So where do you sleep, sir?'

'I have a cell. In the grounds,' said Barnabas irritably. It confirmed his conviction that the Comte was obsessed with buildings.

The chapel had hardly progressed at all in comparison with the mill and barn. The broken walls had simply been dismantled and the ground levelled in preparation for fresh building. 'I mean to use bright white tufa from over the river, in place of the schist. I've sent for quarrymen from Troo. They know the stuff. There's enough yonder to build a city. I can't think why my ancestor contented himself with the schist on this side. Look. See there? You can see the rides I'm cutting through the forest. I shall put up a hunting pavilion in due course – in case the King descends on me, you know, and finds me wanting. And yonder's the mill. I may put up post-mills, too: my father told me the water drops as low as useless in a long summer. And over yonder, of course, are the beginnings of the great-barn. Though it won't be finished this season. Not till next harvest-time, I don't suppose. A hundred cubits long, thirty cubits wide and thirty-two cubits high. A veritable ark of a barn, wouldn't you say?'

Barnabas shot him a glance which implied he fully understood his situation. The Tempter had brought him, Barnabas, to this high place to put him to the test. His lips curled inwards again. He steeled himself to speak the truth, come what may. 'And then you'll buy in at low prices and hoard till famine raises the price of bread so that you can sell at huge profit. That's the new way, so I understand it.' The tortoise shrank back into its shell.

But the Comte gave a cheer, spun round on his heel, grinning, and stabbed Barnabas in the chest with his forefinger. 'So *that's* the reason! *That's* why I'm harangued from the pulpit. *That's* why they watch the barn go up as if it were the Tower of Babel. My dear Barnabas, you have done me a great service. You've no idea how I've racked my brains for why the peasants won't work. I tell you, man, the mind of a peasant is harder to fathom than the will of God, sometimes. And yet along you come and within days you understand everything. Well! Now you've revealed the mystery of the problem, you can damn well reveal the solution. How do I ease their misgivings? How do I convince them I'm not sweating their hides off so that I can starve them to beggary?'

The tortoise called darkly, timidly high-pitched, from inside his shell, 'Time will prove you. Good or ill.'

'Yes, yes. But in the meantime! Some days I feel like I'm dragging a cart without the wheels on. I know! I have it! You can be my corn-factor.'

'I . . .?'

'Break even. A profit's not important so long as you pay for your own hire and the upkeep of the barn. My only concern is to *even out* our prospects.'

'*Our* . . .'

His gestures became huge and graphic. 'Offset the years of famine against the years of plenty. Like Joseph in Egypt, yes? Joseph in Egypt. Seven years of plenty, seven years of want. I'd like to hear you preach on the subject of Joseph and his stockpiling, brother. Indeed I would . . . Yes! You shall be my corn-factor. You can have the tallat loft over the west door of the barn for your cell – when it's built, I mean. In the interim, till it's finished, you would oblige me by occupying the priest's house. I'd as soon maintain a house over a head that's present as one that isn't. Absenteeism irks me. Is it agreed?'

It was not fair. Christ Himself had not been bombarded with such a motley assortment of temptations, or at such high speed. The Tempter in the Bible seemed lethargic in comparison with this . . . this . . .

'In the meantime, on my knees I implore you, be my intelligencer among the peasants!'

(Ah! The snare and hooks of hell. Here was the price too high, the treachery too fell. To deliver up dissenters for flogging, sure.)

'Let me know their gripes and fears before they grow into discontent. There's so much to be accomplished. I need their goodwill. I need universal contentment. Thrive one, thrive all. Would you commend the concept to them? I'd be endlessly grateful. Oh, and would you read the Bible in French in future? Or would the Bishop forbid it?'

'*The Bible in French?* I've never *seen* a Bible in French!' He added hastily (for fear of being thought ignorant), 'I've heard they exist, of course.'

'Oh, I have one in my library. Please make free to read it whenever you have the leisure.'

'Your *library*? You have a library?'

'Sure, what kind of a barbarian do you take me for, man? Music and books are the food of civilization. The mulch on the vine. Use my library whenever you care to – so long as you'll dispute with me from time to time. I pine somewhat for the well-read men I knew in the army. Come and eat, won't you?'

He need not have bothered justifying his aims or revealing his virtuous intents towards the peasants. For the sight of a Bible in French, for a glimpse of *The Four Sons of Aymon*, to open the covers of *The Shepherd's Calendar*, Barnabas would have bound his soul in service to Victoire de Gloriole, and blessed him from one harvest to the next. A peasant boy educated from books but never able so much as to clasp one in his arms, he would have pawned his redemption for the friendship of a man with a library. On the way down the zig-zag path, he was a beast transformed. He skipped and skidded, letting his arms fly loose and the smiles restructure his bony face. He was as excited as a child at the sight of a horseman galloping down the north road.

'God's blessed me with poor eyesight, my lord. Who's that raising dust?'

Victoire overtook him at a run, tempering his oaths only a

little to the company. At such a distance it was just possible to be mistaken about the box pannier behind the rider's thigh; it might not be a fleur-de-lys it bore, and the man's surcoat might not be of the royal household. 'Now, God forgive my sins, Barnabas, and spare me the honour of a royal visit as soon as this.'

'The *King*?' shrieked the priest. 'Coming to Sablois?'

Without looking back, de Gloriole beckoned him on. 'You'll lend me your assistance, man, even if I keep you waiting a day and a half for your dinner!'

Charles Valois, most gracious and happy King of France, saluted his dearly beloved subject, Victoire, Comte de Gloriole, and craved the honour to call on him in company with certain of his household. In the mouth of the chevaucheur, it sounded an exceeding honour. When it took on form and shape, the honour was . . . overwhelming.

Beasts queued to be slaughtered in the kitchen yard. Hay wagons full of fresh straw grated wheelhubs with those fetching utensils and pans in from Ormes. The stables were cleaned with Herculean energy and speed, the old tedding raked out and scattered around the feet of ladders erected for the hanging of banners and pennants. The skins of roasting sheep were rapidly cured and dressed to replace the soot-black fleeces at certain of the windows. Without the hasty improvements wrought for the wedding, Victoire might have sent word forestalling the King – pleaded plague or siege or sudden death. Even now, in comparison with any of the chateaux in the Valley, he knew that Gloriole-sur-Sablois was a dilapidated cow-byre, that his household was ragged and small, that the luxuries he could offer were Spartan hardships compared with those the King had acquired recently. From a throneless ragamuffin, Charles had become more splendid than any of his forebears and did not like to lay such splendours aside, even on his royal progresses. In fact he had no need to, for the gentlemen of Court vied hotly to outdo each other in royal hospitality. It meant they must live on vegetables and beans for the rest of the year, but the benefits bestowed by a successful royal visit made the expense well worthwhile.

De Gloriole was not immune to ambition, but he had less fat to fall back on. His revenues were all tied up in restoration and improvement. He had to pillage his peasants (which vexed him) and go into debt with the merchants to mount anything resembling a royal reception. And he had no idea how long the honour of Charles's presence might persist. His wife told him the castle looked fit to receive God and Saint Michael both, to which he replied that God was wont to make do with stables whereas the King was not.

His fears were confirmed by the King's face, as he rode across the bowing drawbridge and under the mildewed arch, sniffing the air with a slight curl of the lip. From behind him, fanning out like an assault corps and scattering the assembled party of welcome, burst his bodyguard of Scottish archers. Behind them came esquires of the stable and table, breadbearers and cupbearers, chamberlains, baggage and chamber varlets, chevaucheurs, a surgeon and apothecary and astrologer, and a pack of German crossbowmen. The red liveries, like a trick of mirrors, seemed to stretch to infinity down the north road.

'My dear Comte!' The smile confirmed Victoire happy. 'What a change you've wrought on this . . . *castle* of yours. I heard you have some exceptional dogs, and have taken the liberty of coming to see for myself!'

Victoire wondered at the intelligence system which had carried news of his dogs to the King's own Court. It crossed his mind to be glad he had no more unworthy secret. 'My Lord, they can't compare with the King's own kennel,' he said, his knee pressed to the fallen instep of the outstretched kingly foot. 'But they have given me cause to share His Majesty's own admiration for things Scottish.'

'They're Scotch?'

'Like your archers, sir. With as true an aim and as great a courage.' And the dogs, as if sentient of their diplomatic importance, pitched themselves against the palings of their run and cheered themselves hoarse at the scent of royalty. King Charles reminded a chamberlain or two of the services done by the Comte at Patay and Orléans and Paris, and the tight knot of apprehension relaxed in Victoire's stomach. Inadvertently he took his wife's hand and squeezed it. He wished Charles would find a kind word to say to her that would remove the anxious flex in her eyebrows. In his heart of hearts he thought her rather worthier of a king's admiration than his hunting dogs.

But not until dinner was the matter of their wedding even touched upon.

The King had exchanged his green riding tunic for an equally short green doublet of velvet and sat halfway down the long table. His host and hostess (in their wedding clothes for lack of anything else adequate to the occasion) sat opposite. Now and again the huge plain of wood shifted at the sheer pressure of guests around it. It gave somewhat the impression of a raft clutched at by far too many drowning sailors. Two-deep they surrounded the food, the varlets and bearers standing as far back as the heat of the fire or the size of the room would allow, the rest jostling elbows and reaching across one another for the Gargantuan assortment of fillers and crude quantities of meat. It was as if they wished to conceal the banquet from the King before he noticed the lengths to which de Gloriole had gone to afford hospitality. The musicians were crushed into a corner, drowned out by the din. On the stairs outside sat a dozen more courtiers, eating from linen squares and passing a jug of wine between them.

Charles, ironically, laid very little store by food and barely noticed what he ate. He was abstemious too with his wine. It had no opportunity to dull his perceptions of the house. Looking round at the walls draped (for lack of tapestries) with swags of cloth from Ellen's dowry, he said, 'You must see my argentier, Gloriole. He has a wonderful stock of goods just now – clothes, hangings, jewellery. And what he doesn't have he can get. He loans cash, too.'

'I admit, I have neglected the chateau in favour of the estates, my lord. They were sorely run down.'

'Ah yes! First things first. A man must see to his forests. Horses and hunting before houses, I always say.'

Ellen smiled at how poorly this described her husband's idea of estate management. The smile caught the King's eye, though up until then, nothing she had said had caught his interest sufficiently for him to speak to her.

'So. You are married, de Gloriole. A thousand regrets that I was not present. Alas, horses could barely travel fast enough to fetch me the news before the deed was done. A veritable *coup d'amour*, was it not? You can imagine the amazement it caused among those you fought with at Patay: de Gloriole – the great slayer of the English – contracted to England. A secret compact made with the Talbots.'

The food turned to stone in Victoire's gullet. He felt the eyes converge on him from up and down the table. So this was the true purpose of the King's visit. It was written in every supercilious face. Someone had whispered in Charles's ear that the Comte de Gloriole had married the enemy. Already the treachery of it was common gossip at Court. Protestations of innocence would have been foolish and counter-productive.

65

Instead, Victoire sat back in his chair, tore off a morsel of bread and looked sideways at his wife, as if amused that so small a thing should have given rise to so great a stir. 'My lord! It was hardly a contract with the English! You might say that, having sunk one of Talbot's ships, I salvaged such cargo as took my fancy. The dogs and a wife.'

'And a master-at-arms.'

'Ah yes. And a master-at-arms. Your Majesty is so very well informed. Though I hardly think of Flockhart as an Englishman. He's so thoroughly disaffected from his former masters.'

'And you have withdrawn from the wars.'

'To consolidate a strategic position, yes, my lord. But I shall muster again next spring and every spring that proves necessary to get the English out of France. Why, is there a campaign presently where I could do you service? I thought there was a lull. But if there's cause, of course, no estate business in the world would keep me from mustering a levy, such as I'm able. It's still my chiefest ambition to see John Talbot on his face in the grass.'

The King chewed his food between his front teeth, and the tip of his long Valois nose flexed to and fro. 'The picture seems rather different from the one I was painted.'

'Then would that I knew the name of your painter, my lord, so as to avoid the mistake of commissioning him.'

Charles looked malevolently up and down the room, but clearly the man who had informed against Victoire was not present. 'What became of the English garrison?'

'It fled before I arrived.'

'And the suzerain?'

Victoire nodded curtly at his wife who flinched a little and ducked her head. 'My husband fed him to the dogs, Your Highness.'

'Oh excellent!' The King gave a noisy cheer and clapped his palms together and glared around him with a look which seemed to imply, 'I told you all as much.' 'It was indeed hard to believe that de Gloriole the goddam-slayer had been so quick to make his peace with the English.' Relief sapped Victoire's resilience to a new angle of attack. The King had not finished with him yet. 'But marriage, my dear Victoire! That was . . . impetuous, was it not? Extraordinary impetuous.' All eyes in the room came to rest on Ellen, all knowing better what should have been done with her. 'I see your English wife scorns to follow French fashion. Is it that she is contemptuous of our ladies' tastes, or does she lack their . . . advantages?'

66

'Sure, it's the fault of my ignorance, my lord, and no lack of willingness,' said Ellen.

Still he would not address her, though his eyes had trailed over her continuously throughout the meal. 'Then why doesn't she show her breasts, Gloriole? The ladies of the Court all wear their dresses open to the waist these days. You must surely have heard. An excellent fashion – proof of an open and cheerful disposition.'

Victoire felt the sweat spring out at his hairline and cursed his readiness to blush. 'Remarkable. I had no idea, my lord. Forgive my ignorance. I am become a provincial entirely. Had my wife attempted to dress like that this evening, I'm afraid I'd've mistaken her modesty and forbidden it. I'm only a crude soldier. I thought only whores and nursing mothers unlaced in company.'

He was seething with indignation. He was awash with the animal instinct of possessiveness. He was filled with antagonism towards the rows of staring eyes fixed on his wife's high, modest lacings.

A red-haired chamberlain leaned across the table to dig his fingers into the carcase of a chicken. 'But now you know better, surely she'll bend her English ways to your French will, I warrant she will. I warrant she must.' And his companions all nodded and wiped their lips with finger and thumb.

It was a test. It was a threat. Victoire looked sideways at his wife and indicated she should leave the room. When she had gone, he wanted to go after her and apologize for what had happened – apologize for his King, apologize for the French. He tipped his chair back on to two legs and adopted that barrack-room delivery that had always tasted like tar in his mouth. 'I was loath to say it while she was present, my lord. It lacks chivalry. But if you'll believe me, unlacing would do nothing to enhance my lady's charms. She has a good face and a fair manner and came with a useful dowry, but sure under the covers there's not a lot to take a hold of, if you understand me.'

'She has an arse like a boy, too,' conceded the King, but was plainly unconvinced. With a snicker of amused recollection he asked, 'Did you really feed her lover to the dogs?'

'I thought it would teach her to come to heel,' he said, and the lie tasted worse than pitch.

There was a noisy murmur on the stairs outside, and the door opened. His wife re-entered, her hair let down and her dress unfastened to the waist. One side of the bodice hung forward like the petal of a rose revealing the rosehip. Ellen went and presented herself to the King and curtseyed again to him as low as the floor.

'Now that my marriage has raised me to the status of a French-woman, I want as earnestly to be thought French as to see my husband appreciated. He is the King's most loyal and faithful gentleman. I know I'd fain be as obedient to my husband as he is obedient to Your Majesty.'

The King raised her to her feet then stood himself. 'Gloriole, you're a liar,' he said, and the whole assembly gave a small frisson of delighted horror. Victoire too stood up.

'A liar, my lord?'

'A liar and a self-serving deceiver! They're as fine as any I've seen at Court. And you wanted to make a secret of them!' And plunging his fingers through the corsage, he widened the gap and lifted each breast further into view. 'There, my dear. So that the nipples show fully. That's the fashion.' He leaned back and admired his handiwork. 'Madam! I thought the chateau bare when I arrived, but I find it is furnished with comforts and attractions on a par with any palace. I shall visit often, so you will offer me such hospital-ity. Now! To see these famous dogs. Scottish hounds fed on an Englishman. I can think of no pack I'd sooner hunt with. Victoire! A hunt tomorrow! And a bed now, so that we can all rise early!'

'You should not have done it,' he said as they lay rolled together in the narrow gully of his army truckle bed. They had given up their own to the King, and every other bed of quality to members of the upper royal household.

'It seemed necessary. I'm sorry it offended you.'

He pulled her forehead against his mouth and kissed it. 'I'd rather be thought a traitor than a pander to my own wife.'

'I hear it *is* the fashion at Court,' she said, as if to extenuate the King's behaviour.

'Then for God's sake let's shun the Court and live quietly. I never thought to harbour the thoughts I did tonight. If I made you a Frenchwoman when I married you, he all but made me an Englishman tonight. When he touched you I understood the English vice – the murder of kings, I mean.'

'Abraham lent his wife to the Kings of Egypt. I read it in the Bible.'

'My God, if it should come to that!' They clasped each other close like children in the darkness. Beyond the arras dividing their alcove from the rest of the room his own household slept in various forms of discomfort.

'What? If it should come that, what?' she whispered. 'You must have a pension. You must have a royal office to help pay for the barn and the lodges and the mills and the chapel and the boom tower.'

'What do you take me for?' His whispers became less and less circumspect. 'An Egyptian pox on Abraham, if he pimped Sarah for the sake of a poxy Egyptian pension!'

'Shshsh! He did it to preserve his safety. To keep from being killed! You see what powerful enemies you have? They were quick to make much of the marriage.'

'I didn't know before today that I had any enemies.'

'But the marriage was – what did he call it? – remarkably impetuous. And I'd hate to see you suffer for it. Not if it's in my power . . .'

His hands felt for the contours of her face. Through his fingers she could see only the shine of his eyes. 'Not for the world, do you hear? Not for a king. Not for the world.'

'Not for the world, Victoire. No. Not just for that, but for you . . .'

He put his hand over her mouth. 'It would split me, Ellen! The simple thought of it goes through me like a knife. God knows I'm a loyal subject. Charles Valois is appointed master over me by God. So he can have my blood. He can send me to the front like David sent Uriah, but I shan't leave Bathsheba behind for him to toy with. He can have my chateau, for all the good it could do him, and he can have my feu. But if ever he oversteps his due, I'll away to Italy or Germany and be a mercenary. So long as I have you to myself. My love, my own love.'

He had not known he would say it. It shocked him to hear himself: not the discounting of his chateau, for war had taught him not to lay much store by possession; but to hear him begrudging the King anything. It was like a little ship breaking adrift from a great continent and, from its decks, seeing the land diminish to the size of an island on the horizon. The King was, after all, only a man, and men are, after all, part good, part bad, part friend, part enemy. This sad, cynical discovery made Victoire cling tighter to his woman in the dark and mourn his lost innocence like Adam. The only difference between him and Adam was that his Eve seemed a better recompense than anything he might have lost.

Ellen's father did not send a ransom or make any attempt to redeem his daughter. He told her, in eloquent terms, that her bed was made and that she must lie on it.

My dear Father,

Your letter did not startle me nor cause me the consternation you anticipated. I did not suppose that Stephen would persuade you to send a ransom when the Great Sir John expressly forbade it.

When I left England, obedient to your will, I did not cherish hopes of return, nor of enjoying great happiness in this world. Sir Humphrey, my bridegroom, in no way changed my outlook, and although our nuptials were never joined, he left me in no doubt as to the subjection a wife should expect in marriage. I also found the claim to be true – that the accursed French in no way resemble our own pure-bred English stock. For I fell from the grip of Humphrey into the jaws of the Comte de Gloriole and there was a very different breed of man.

In short I found that whereas the husband to whom you sent me was foul in habit, language, deportment and intent, the one to whom I fell prey is ever gentle, honourable, mindful, loving, quite wonderfully industrious and fair. The burden on me is great indeed, since I must bear so many kindnesses at his hands, so much unlooked-for joy and pleasure in my marriage bed.

If I say that I have found the best husband in all France, you will say that is no great commendation, so I shall say rather that I have found the best husband in all the world, nay, in all the history of the world. His enemies are therefore my sworn adversaries, and his friends and country I cleave to as water cleaves to salt.

Knowing full well how you cherish my welfare, Father, I know just how much you will rejoice at my happiness and that of my dear Victoire, your son-in-law. If any doubt still remains, let me wipe it quite out of mind by writing that the seed of de Gloriole newly planted in my English womb confirms me happiest among all the daughters of men.

Your affectionate daughter,

ELLEN, COMTESSE DE GLORIOLE

Gloriole-sur-Sablois, September 1430.

SEVEN

A Made Man

The woods were scorched to a papery extravagance of gold leaf –
a gilt frieze between the ancient oaks and elms which held up the
canopy of sky. The crisp litter of the forest's floor hissed like surf
under the horses' hooves, and the dogs moved through it chest-
deep, snapping at the flurries of twigs and leaves thrown up by the
dog in front.

In his anxious agitation, Victoire imagined his hounds, unaccustomed to so huge a contingent of riders, running amok and
scattering, or turning on the huntsmen, hamstringing the horses,
unseating the King and chewing him to pieces. But their ambition
was only to be free and running, out from under the Master's whip,
out from under the horses' hooves and away in an undulating breaker
of fur, washing aside the small things, the dross, and engulfing the
larger prey.

Carpenters in the crosstrees and eaves of the half-built hunting
lodge drew up their knees as the dogs flooded by below. They
glimpsed a green tunic and fifty red ones besides, and ran home
to tell their children they had seen the King of France.

The birds rose like dust from a shaken carpet. The hollow green
light of dense forest, as with the approach of a storm, first twitched
with the panic of wildlife, then the sobbing, panting pack of hounds,
then the thunder of hooves, then the lightning flash of the oblique
sun on sword, on javelin, on bright harness. And at the shock, the
trees let fall their leaves in torrential cascades. Now and then a man
struck by the forked bolt of a branch cried out or went down, red
livery sprawled like blood under a tree. The woods were scoured,
the woods were scarified, raked clean by the stampede, and settled
behind it into silence, then into renewed birdsong.

Better than battle, which is confused and often ignobly sordid,
here was pure adventure. For each man and horse was pitted against
his own barrier of fear, and overleapt it almost despite himself. Man

encouraged horse, horse encouraged man, and the unified beast, the man-horse, was as strange and wondrous a hybrid as any centaur. The Scottish bowmen were out of their element – thorny crayfish snagged in a tumble of kelp. The field was to the smooth men, lying forward across their horses' sweating necks, threading their thinness between jagged trunks, slipping through the breaks on lower trajectories than the high-springing deer. Their clothes were sleek and close-fitting, their wits were swept by the slipstream into the tail-ends of their hair, their eyes adapted to the rapid alteration of sunlight and shade.

The hounds brought down a muntjac deer and could not be whipped off till the guts had been spilled and fought over. Then they wanted water to slake their salt-blood thirsts, and the headlong career of the hunt faltered and bunched and came trotting to a halt beside a stream, in among its dogs. It was breathless with delight, panting and thirsty and raucous with excitement. There was little to put between hunter and hound.

'Is it true you use a sword, de Gloriole?' shouted the King, his voice high and breathless. 'A *sword* for boar?' The fact was obvious. The weapon hung down beside Victoire's saddle in an elaborate, broad scabbard. The question implied pretensions of courage on Victoire's part: courage above his fellow men.

'Specially made for the sport, my lord. Not a battle sword. I'm not in such haste to kill myself! A present from my wife. A taste of the English hunt. Would your Majesty care to use it?' He drew out the sword – five feet long – a solid poker for half its length and hammered flat below the bolt-hole into a flame-shaped, scalloped tip. Men crouching by the water eyed the weapon with professional curiosity and feigned scorn.

'Didn't she find your own long enough, Victoire?' called a chamberlain, making an obscene gesture. They were envious, chiefly of his having something new, something novel to offer the King.

But the thought crossed the King's mind – it showed in his face – that de Gloriole was one of the few knights who had carried a broadsword in battle and been capable of using it. The boar-sword was massively heavy. 'A spear's the thing,' he said. 'Where's the finesse without a spear?' And he weighed the light haft of his own in his hand, so that Victoire knew he had no need to part with the sword Ellen had given him.

In the middle of their drinking, the dogs picked up the scent of a boar and were away again. The King had been brought drink in the saddle, and de Gloriole had stayed mounted, the better to oversee his guests. The rest were on foot by the water. Charles took a childlike glee in finding himself at an advantage over them, and leapt the stream in pursuit of the hounds, scattering his courtiers underfoot, claiming the kill for himself. Instantly the look on the faces of his entourage was one of panic: nursemaids whose charge had plunged wayward into a busy thoroughfare. They threw the water out of their hands; they scrabbled for their reins; they snatched for their stirrups; they set their horses dancing with alarm, because of their own. Victoire took off after the King, his hunter dragging its heels through the stream and pitching uncomfortably up a steep slope before drawing level with Charles who had halted on the bare crest of a hillock. The pack was momentarily lost from sight among deep bracken. Victoire, too, reined in.

Sablois Forest lay all around him – a kingdom of trees lifting their branches in fealty. Out of respect for Victoire, the sap rose in a million trunks. He had left his secret back at the chateau, in the tiny hiding place of his wife's womb, and yet it sprang up to greet him here, now, in a great roaring of green, cheering trees: hosts of well-wishers, legions of singing subjects who had stood patiently waiting since Unrecorded Time solely to see the joy of this morning, this moment, this man.

'My wife is with child!' he shouted breathlessly to the King. 'She told me this morning! By way of telling me to take care!'

The King craned this way and that in search of the dogs. The news did not excite him. 'Women hate the hunt. They like to think they're the sole thing we go in chase of.'

'Indeed, I never thought to take a woman's interference so kindly, my lord, and I like the reason well enough!'

After a moment's thought, Charles conceded congratulations. 'I shall pray God send you a son, de Gloriole. A son's the thing. I have a son, you know? Fine boy.' It was a strange way to speak of the Dauphin of France. 'Yes, a son's the thing. You may call yours Charles if you wish, or Louis, like mine.'

'You do me great honour,' said Victoire and he meant it, for as the flies spiralled out of the sun he could see, with perfect acuity, how the glory of kingship had descended, father to son, from Saint Louis to this most honoured visitor of his. Heredity suddenly seemed as powerful a force as any in the universe. And the prayers of God's Anointed could not fail to guarantee him a son.

'*There!*' cried the King as a pale shape, amorphous as a globule of mercury, slipped across a clearing below them. The dogs were working their prey, pursuing it, turning it, braying on a different, more triumphant note. The two riders could hear the boar racketing up and down, fraying its evil temper to breaking point against the tree trunks. Charles went down the slope brandishing his boar-spear with its metal cross-piece for all the world like a crusader's crucifix brandished over the heathen. Past Victoire came a Scotsman of the bodyguard, cursing under his breath in Gaelic and contorted in the saddle with anxiety. He barked reproach at the Comte – 'Could you no keep up with him, man?' – then plunged his horse over the edge of an embankment in a manoeuvre which made the horse scream with fear. Victoire thought it patronizing that they should so wet-nurse the King, scurrying after him like a merchant after his carts, trying to protect their assets. Why should Charles be picketed about like a prize bull and protected from enjoying himself, shielded from venturing his life on a halloo?

The forest cloaked a terrain which ran, wave-form, down to the river. It was possible to sense the presence of the water without actually glimpsing its hidden straits, for the trees yearned somehow towards its brightness and the ground was puddled with myriad different flowers and fungi. Patches of spongy bog grew emerald-green grass. A banneret in a treetop marked the spot where half a dozen fresh horses awaited use by the huntsmen. Victoire knew that Charles's horse was tiring and that the man would opt for a change of mount before going after the boar. So he sidled his own horse downhill towards the banneret, by the shortest route – if only to prove to the Scotsman that he could keep up with the King if he chose but was not so ill-mannered as to compete for the spoil.

Then the boar, trapped between the river and the dogs, swerved clear across his path. It seemed to come from nowhere, erupting out of a bush with the speed of a landslip, as black as Satan and half the size of an ox. It was gone again – submerged in bracken – so fast that he might have thought it imaginary if his horse had not turned rigid under him, stiff-legged and trembling, the bit held fast between its teeth. Its haunches sank down, then recovered with a stagger.

Below the tree flying the banneret, Charles had dismounted and a groom was transferring his saddle to a bay mare. The Scotsman had caught up, and he too dismounted, glaring about him for someone to share the responsibility of the King's safety. Away to the right the dogs encountered the boar in a hellish confusion of violent noise that made the tethered horses squeal and buck. The beast had turned. Its flight was done. Its rage was on it. The boar was primed to kill whatsoever lay in its path.

Then Victoire sympathized with the courtiers at the loss of their precious charge. Then he envisaged the King's death: on his hands, under his protection. The throne emptied. The war lost. The country fallen in pieces like cracked plate. The blame attributed. The shame incurred. The everlasting remorse. The irretrievable grace. All in a split second his responsibility for the King came home to him. It contorted and buckled him in the saddle as his horse edged gingerly down the tree-cluttered incline towards the men on foot. The King was transferring his weapons from one horse to the next. With a prosaic thud the cross-bolt fell out of its socket in the spear and bruised the majestical foot.

When the boar came out of the trees, Charles just had time to put the spear into the hands of his bodyguard and let the man step in front of him to receive the charge. From close-to Victoire saw the look on the Scotsman's face as the monstrous avalanche of black flesh and bristle bore down on him. The groom fled. The King stepped a little to one side, as if to let a lady pass, his shoulders hunched, his fists clenched by his side and his eyes fast shut.

The spear went in at the mouth, but because there was no cross-bolt the boar came on and came on and came on, swallowing the six feet of iron into the maze of its guts until the Scotsman's hands were between its lips. The sheer impetus of the charge buried the boar's forehead in the man's chest and carried him backwards into a tree where tusks ripped him and split him, like a gaff used overmuch to land a dying fish. The boar hesitated, leaned back on its short, foolish legs, fixed the King with its small, black eye and turned awkwardly towards him. It seemed barely to notice the encumbrance of a spear through its gullet and entrails.

The sudden jibbing of his horse helped to propel Victoire out of the saddle. The sword was in his left hand, its cross-bolt in his right. Thus, one-handed he could no more than clip the beast across the rump with the blade-tip to catch its attention. It did not turn. Perhaps it could not turn, transfixed as it was from stem to stern. But it paused long enough for Victoire to place himself in front of the King and push home the metal bolt halfway down the blade of his sword and level it, both hands on the hilt.

The spear-end protruded from the animal's mouth and its tongue flapped. The bristles stood up stiff and separate, as black as crow quills, across the grotesque mound of the shoulders. The tusks still carried scraps of the Scotsman's clothing. The dilated nostrils drizzled rheum. Like a siege engine it came on, implacable, impervious to pain, an involuntary grin nailed to its mouth and no intimation of death in its small black eyes. Double-handed, the sword down by his hips and his feet wide apart, Victoire did not so much lunge as catch the second charge on his blade.

As heedlessly, as stupidly, as indestructibly as before, it swallowed down the sword: a fairground trick, a feat of no consequence. Only when the cross-bolt jammed in the corners of its mouth was it checked and did its hooves scrabble in the dirt. He pitched the sum of his weight into the sword-hilt. The beast in return pitched its weight into him. He had only to let go of the hilt for the tusks to shred him: their bony yellow implied a skeleton bursting through the superfluous meat, impervious to blades. At a distance, Victoire could hear his own voice screaming at the boar to die and be damned.

At last some vital organ burst; the legs splayed. With a monumental wrench of the sword, he turned it on its back and it lay perfectly still with the four hooves curled demurely on to its belly. The King ran it through once, twice, a dozen times with a spear from the pile of reserve weapons. Some at least of the riders descending the slope must have seen what happened.

The blood was singing so loud in Victoire's ears that the others appeared to ride out of silence and array themselves about the clearing in tableau. He found himself on his knees, and deduced that his head was thrown back, for he could see the banneret drooping from the treetop like a parched tongue. Nobody spoke. Two grooms removed from sight the offensive remains of the Scots bodyguard.

At last the King bent and withdrew the boar-sword from between the grinning jaws and wiped the blade across the bristly back. There was a patter of applause, exclamations of wonder at the size of the carcase, words of admiration for the tusks.

'De Gloriole finished it off, of course,' said the King.

'It was dead already, my lord,' said Victoire, 'I did nothing.' His voice broke: his throat was sore from yelling.

'It is a fine sword,' said the King, weighing it in both hands, the tip resting on the dead brute.

'Keep it, my lord. In commemoration of a remarkable kill.'

'Damned good of you, de Gloriole. I'll have my armourer cast one from it, with more flourish to the guard. I favour a cord-bound hilt, you know, but you broadsworders never have much use for fine detail.' An ecurie cut off the ears of the boar and gave them to Charles who put them in the pouch at his belt. The adulation gathered momentum. Courtiers crowded round, stepping over de Gloriole, pulling the carcase this way and that, voicing shrill and florid phrases hoping that the King had met with no harm. Once or twice a hand furtively, fleetingly gripped Victoire's shoulder or perhaps it was simply someone steadying himself as he congratulated Charles. Then a chamberlain helped the Comte to his feet and to his horse, and something was said in his ear which might or might not have been '. . . a made man . . .' and a festive cavalcade of triumph unlaced itself from the confused tangle of over-excitement. The King declared his need to return to Angers before nightfall. The boar was not even spit-roasted for its insolence, just flayed and salted and hung in obscure anonymity in a cellar of Gloriole-sur-Sablois.

Suddenly they were gone, helping themselves to this and that, purloining removable objects like sentimental lovers pillaging an innocent field of its flowers. The royal cavalcade withdrew from the fortress as twisted and red as the sword drawn out of the boar and fetched out, like the viscera, all the thankful excitable household staff and local peasantry to wave and cheer.

Victoire could not wave. He found by afternoon that the muscles of his chest and shoulders had so seized up that he could not lift the weight of his own arms and had to go without supper to avoid drawing his wife's attention to the fact. Unfortunately, the concealment cost him such effort that he quite omitted to hide the uncharacteristic mood that had settled on him: he was preoccupied and irritable. As often as she dared, Ellen made tentative attempts to appease him and to guess at the cause.

'Well, so the King's gone. And never a shred more lewdness talked of,' she said. 'What fools we were to lose sleep casting such dire suspicions on His Majesty . . . Unless he said something more to you during the hunt?'

'What? Oh. No. Fools, yes we were. I told him you were pregnant. He said he would pray for a son.'

Later she said, 'I see he took your boar-sword. I shall have to have you another made. Was it a satisfactory hunt? Did the King admire your forests?'

'What? Oh. Yes. The hunt was a great success. The King made

77

a fine kill. The horses were greatly admired. and the dogs . . . I had a great many offers for the dogs.'

'And did someone offer you an offence, too, Victoire?'

'What? What are you talking about? Must you prattle?' And he declared his intention of going to bed, now that his bed was his own again. He did not invite her to follow. An hour later she found him sitting on the edge of the bed and, though she did not realize it, equally unable to get out of his clothes as out of the small obsession to which his thoughts had confined him.

'Did you hope for mention of a Court position today, Victoire?' she asked, pulling off his boots. 'Was nothing said?' All she got by way of a reply was a scowl which said such thoughts should be beneath her as they were beneath him. 'Well, and what did happen today to make such foul weather?' she asked, losing patience. Slipping off her dress, she climbed into bed behind him. 'You were all sunshine when you left here this morning.' Still he continued to sit in his unfastened doublet and breeches.

'Something–nothing. An incident.' Something about the way he said it made the blood huddle under her heart for warmth. She knelt up behind him and gathered his hair into the nape of his neck: it made him shiver. 'Something came at me. Just a pig thing. A piglet almost. But ugly, yes? Ugly as death, to tell the truth. Nothing to speak of. Just a matter of putting out my sword, you know?'

'Perhaps not quite so small.'

'Perhaps not. A little bigger than small.'

'And?'

'And I cursed God.'

'*Victoire!*'

'The Devil must have put it into my head. But it seemed to me that God was envious – had to ensure His . . . *supremacy of bliss.*' His hands were locked together in his lap as if he were still holding the hilt of a broadsword. 'I would not be parted from you. I *could* not be parted from you. I looked round me and there wasn't a door left in the world that I was ready to pass through to be out of this one.' He looked at her sharply over his shoulder. It was a reprimand. 'That's not what I was raised to, Ellen. "A vale of tears." "Man rises up and is cast down." That's what I was bred on. A year ago it was all well and good. All I had to do was to kill the English until they killed me. But now! Damn you, woman. I've got so much! I feel so poxy vulnerable. You in one hand, the baby

78

in the other, the estates held between my teeth – I'm prey to the first bandit who . . . Too much to lose, damn it. Too high not to be pulled down, do you see? Too happy not to be turned out of Paradise for it.'

'Yes, Victoire. I see.' Her arms were gone from round his neck. 'I was raised on the same black bread. I've thought the same thoughts. But if we do our best . . . ! If we don't do wrong –'

'And the King says you're narrow,' he interrupted. '"Deuced narrow for whelping", as he put it. I'd forgotten there could be a danger.'

'As you forgot your promise to take care in the hunt. Every time you go to the forest, must I wait for them to fetch you back across your horse?'

Their mutual terror of losing one another lay like a cold sword down the centre of the bed and brought them to the very verge of hatred. God is as clever as Satan, thought Victoire.

At three o'clock, she woke to find him hard to his own side of the mattress, on the outside of the covers. 'Why are you still in your clothes, you unsanitary Frenchman?' she whispered.

'Damn it, because I strained myself skewering a boar and I can't get out of 'em!' he said in peevish disgust, and submitted to the tenderness of her assistance and sorrow and remonstrance and sympathy.

EIGHT

Just Rewards

The rewards began to arrive within days. First there was notification of a post as Grand Echanson, and then a donat of ten thousand écus 'for the equipping and fortification of a castle of the King's domaine'. Three cartloads of furniture, 'rendered surplus to the King's needs by improvements to the royal seat of Angers', no sooner stood empty in the yard than the King's argentier arrived with a small bazaar of sample merchandise: everything to accommodate the nobleman of taste and his retinue. The argentier's account books afforded him the delightful (if startling) information that Victoire stood stronger in credit than almost any other gentleman of his clientèle.

The bareness of Gloriole-sur-Sablois plainly caused the man physical pain. He urged Victoire to buy tapestries, fire-irons, lamps and statuary with the urgency of a doctor prescribing medicines. Victoire was very conscious of his castle's shortcomings and could understand the merchant's insistence. He was less clear why the man should be so insistent on selling him embroidered nightshirts. '*Nightshirts?* You mean I should put on a different shirt to go to bed?'

'Not *here*, perhaps not *here*,' giggled the little argentier. He concealed, beneath a stuffed black fustian gown, a trading fortune which put him on a par with dukes and marquises but could not free him of his striking resemblance to a vole. 'But in the King's bedchamber?'

'What the devil would I be doing in the King's bedchamber?' said Victoire, bewildered. 'I'm Grand Echanson, not Valet of the Bedchamber!'

The argentier gaped a little, ducked his head once into the collar of his robe and sprang directly to the subject of saddlery and harness. He never again raised the subject of nightshirts. 'And is there any other service I can do the honoured Comte?' he enquired, folding away a list of commissions that reached almost to the ground.

'Yes. If you'd be so kind, you can direct me to a talented painter.' He added, without thinking, 'The best or nothing.'

The man was offended. 'Naturally the best or nothing, sir. I am argentier to the King!' He applied himself to a notebook. 'But you must give me some intimation: Ascension, Nativity, Old Testament, patron saint, landscape . . .?'

'A portrait.'

'Ah. A portrait. Most à la mode.'

'Of my wife.'

'Ah yes, indeed. A fitting subject for any artist. Here is the man for your needs. Armand Gonplier. He's painted the King himself in the character of Saint John. Do you wish me to commission the man? Then the subject of . . . remuneration need not pass between you.'

But for all the argentier's fiscal discretion, he was heard to ask of several clients (as he broke his journey back to Court at various chateaux along the Loire) what *particular* favour had elevated Victoire de Gloriole to such heights of royal esteem. He got no satisfactory answer. Nobody understood it any better than he.

In the meantime, at Sablois, the Bishop came scurrying, full of grief that the rigours of work had kept him so many, many months from his duty and the pleasure of the Comte's company. He arrived, he and his entourage, stately as the Three Magi, and was rather disorientated to find that the dilapidated Nazarene stable he dimly remembered as smelling of horses and dogs was undergoing a transformation.

In fact the old stables had been demolished and a new block built, on-the-square, where the western wall had once stood. The new wall was to embrace a far larger plot. Everywhere he looked, there were charcoal diagrams drawn on the wall, made by either Victoire or his architect to demonstrate an intention, to explore a possibility. Indeed, scaffolding cross-hatched so much of the structure already that from a distance the castle appeared to have been scratched out by an impatient draughtsman in favour of a new design. The Bishop gazed about him, leaving his mouth a little ajar. He did not expect the Comte de Gloriole to descend, like Elijah, from the clouds.

'Barnabas is here, I think, if you've been looking for him,' said Victoire, dulling the shine of the Bishop's ring with his breath after the exertion of climbing down a scaffold to greet him. 'We'll take refreshment in the library. My wife manages to keep it as free of dust as anywhere. I have cider, too! I'm building a new apple press and the brewer sent down a tun. Experimental but it tastes well enough to me.'

'I only partake of wine. Because of my *donations*,' said the Bishop obscurely, but allowed himself to be hurried unceremoniously towards the manor-house. A stonemason working over the door showered his pate with dust as he stood admiring the interior alterations. There was a smell like Saint Lawrence roasting on his gridiron.

'It's the glazier. Leading,' said Victoire, when he saw the Bishop sniff. 'Every window is being glazed. Every window, think of it! My wife has a pretty eye for detail, too. All octagons and pentagons, and our initials interlaced.'

'I trust your wife's no alchemist, sir!' exclaimed the Bishop, ruffled by finding himself so soon on the notorious topic of de Gloriole's wife. 'Octagons . . . pentagons?'

'What? Oh yes! Excellent witty, my lord Bishop!' And if Victoire realized his guest was not joking, it did not for one moment show. 'Sure, now I think of it, she is an alchemist, if you'll believe me. She can make the leadenest day pure gold just by walking into a room.' But the Bishop stared at him as if he were speaking a foreign language. Victoire coughed nervously and opened the new, quarter-panelled door into the library.

Each of the fourteen books Gloriole owned was now housed in its own sideboard. These dark, ornately carved pieces of furniture stood about the room, ceiling high, like household altars to a pantheon of gods. Candleholders jutted out above each small central cupboard where, locked away like the sacramental Host, lay a single well-thumbed volume. Barnabas appeared to be at his devotions when they entered, for he was kneeling on a chair in front of one of the sideboards, the candle lit, and his elbows resting on a scrolled wooden shelf.

'I've told you, Barnabas! Why don't you lift it down and read at the table?'

'I don't like to . . . The bindings, you know,' said Barnabas scrambling awkwardly down from the chair and rubbing his shins. It amused Victoire to see the wood carvings on this particular sideboard; they depicted a deer-hunt rather than any biblical scene. But he would never have drawn the Bishop's attention to the fact that they had caught Barnabas reading *The Very Parfit Art of Venerye* instead of a holy book.

The Bishop needed no extra grounds for punishing his parish proxy: he was no sooner introduced to Barnabas than he declared him banished to Scotland. 'Do you realize, sir, that this villain has been living in *my house*, indulging himself in *sins of luxury*, profaning my *own bed!*'

'How "profaning"?' Victoire was at once amazed and breathless with curiosity.

'God knows, sir! God knows!' breathed the Bishop darkly.

'Ah. Aha. Might I say, my lord Bishop, before you lay too much to Barnabas' charge, that I *instructed* him to live in the presbytery. A house keeps better with someone living in it, and I admit I do hate and abhor dilapidation. The arrangement's only temporary. Barnabas is an excellent man. I'd be sorry to have the Scots benefit at my expense.'

There was nothing the Bishop could do but extricate himself laboriously, like a ram out of a thicket, and to feign delight in the praises both Comte and Comtesse heaped on Barnabas. As they did so, they plied the visitor with wine from the Gloriole vines. It was excellent wine. He took a deal of comfort from it. The more cardinal-red he became, the more cardinal-grand he grew until, when Victoire assembled the staff for a blessing, the solemn gravity of the churchman's voice and the expansive sweep of his benediction dissolved several of the women into tears of devout gratitude.

There, before the whole assembled household, the Bishop turned on Victoire a full orational broadside. '*The King has sent you cannon, I believe!*'

'Yes. A pair of bronze culverin. Never saw prettier. Do you want to see them?'

'*I too have a donation to make to the armoury of so excellent a servant to the King!*' He clapped his hands over his head, so that the whole room flinched, and his servants fled in search of the Bishop's gift.

'Your benediction itself is present enough, my lord,' said Victoire, feeling intuitively that he should avoid catching his wife's eye.

'*You are a young man. A modern man. You have undoubtedly discovered the merits of corned gunpowder. You corn your gunpowder, do you not?*'

'Yes. Er . . . yes. Naturally we corned our gunpowder on campaign . . .' But the lower Victoire dropped his voice the louder the Bishop intoned.

'*And with what do you corn your gunpowder?*'

Faces began to push forward in rapt fascination. Wives turned to their husbands and clearly did not believe the whispered answers they got, for they jabbed their menfolk in the ribs with impatient elbows.

'In the field?' said Victoire.

'*In the field!*' bellowed the Bishop.

'Master-at-Arms!' snapped Victoire at the old English Champion. 'Sir!'

'Tell the Bishop how we corn gunpowder in the field.'

There was a pause.

'*Piss on it, your lordship,*' announced the Master-at-Arms with military briskness and volume. Faces turned unanimously towards the Bishop, mouths dropping open.

'*And you cannot fail to know, therefore, the proven fact that the urine of a wine drinker is surpassed only by the urine of a bishop who has partaken only of wine.*'

Victoire found he could not speak. He nodded towards Flockhart again who delivered his clipped response to the hall: '*I have heard as much, your lordship!*'

At that moment, the Bishop's servants returned bearing (as indeed the Queen of Sheba's had before them) gifts of rare worth. These were two large stoneware urns, lugged like Greek amphora and discreetly worked with depictions of the angels fetching wine to Elijah in the desert.

Ellen gave a kind of yelp and ran from the room. The Bishop's eyes trailed after her, and Victoire felt the need to explain: 'My wife is with child, my lord. She is easily overcome by emotion.' The Bishop was reassured.

'It is my intention to make donations at all the great armouries in the land. But when I heard of His Majesty honouring you with the gift of cannon, I felt called to make my best efforts to aid the excellent Comte de Gloriole and those men of my parish who muster under him at the clarion call to war.' He raised his eyebrows; he looked around him, hands crossed on his stomach, and he waited for Victoire's formal thanks.

'Indeed. I cannot express the depth of my . . . amazement that you should entrust me with a gift of such immeasurable . . . imagination or one that has cost you such personal . . . exertions,' said Victoire. 'I pray you will not overtax yourself, my lord, in the war effort.'

And so the Bishop departed happy, not pausing long enough to celebrate Mass or deliver a sermon. Most of his flock never knew he had even visited his see.

Ellen insisted they fire a parting salute from one of the culverin on the roof. But the Master-at-Arms would not waste the precious donation – 'in case there was some truth in the matter' – and undertook (given a pint of wine) to corn gunpowder 'enough for a salute the Pope himself will hear in Rome!'

After the Bishop, came the artist – a young man of infinite enthusiasms who esteemed de Gloriole not because of any monetary riches but because he had 'limed the most beautiful finch in all Europe'. Armand Gonplier was not in the least disenchanted that the woman kept vomiting while he sketched her, and when she excused herself on grounds of pregnancy, he at once declared that he would paint her as the Madonna, her breasts bared for the Christ child. She laughed out loud – a high, singing, immodest laugh. But the husband said, in rather strained and icy tones, 'Let us not tread worn grass, Monsieur Gonplier. *Not* the Madonna suckling.'

'Perhaps Ruth at the feet of Boaz would be less presumptuous and more fitting,' suggested Ellen diplomatically. 'I am a foreigner, after all. And in the background we shall have Victoire's great-barn . . . and the chateau, of course.'

The portrait did not resemble Ellen: Victoire did not expect it to. It resembled perfect womanhood, as was its duty. The forehead was high and hairless, not overhung with viny tendrils of escaping black. The Madonna's eyes were small and vacant, full of the Other World; Ellen's were gazelle dark and full of reflections: of candles as she oversaw dinner; of flowers as she planted out a kitchen garden; of doves as she perfumed the dovecote; of saints as she watched the mural-painter at work in the chapel; of stars as the decorators gilded the roof of the Great Hall; of words as she sat opposite Victoire in the library and read. The portrait was buxom and fleshy, not thin, fragile, singing like a cricket. Its hands were prim and empty, not rough from tacking the espaliers to the garden wall, not quick and saucy, not always at his fingertips like the nose of a favourite dog. The portrait did not satisfy Victoire. Its skin was not sunburned from riding out to the furthest limits of the estate to lend her opinion on a new hawk or to fetch him some piece of news. The portrait's skin was pale as death.

The dress was accurate. Only one other thing about the portrait was faithful to life. Its subject was in the foreground, almost filling the canvas, and behind her, tiny and insubstantial, were the estates and buildings of Gloriole. They were grand. They were grander than anything that had stood in that silver loop of river since Time began. And yet, for all its importance, even the river itself was reduced to a silver ribbon that had floated to the ground, unnoticed, from out of Ruth's hair.

One night Ellen found him, during the hours of great darkness, sitting in front of the easel with a candle, staring at the picture.

'What's the matter?' she wanted to know. 'Has he made a mistake with the great-barn?'

'He should have painted you as Jael,' was all he would say, and she did not understand him. How could she? Jael drove her tentpeg through a man's skull while he was asleep – brought him butter in a lordly dish then squandered his brains.

For Victoire there was no regaining mastery of his spilt wits: they were squandered at his wife's feet like the ungleaned corn around Ruth's skirt in the portrait. It was all for her: his every thought, ambition, passion.

'Who do you favour, madam?' he heard Gonplier ask as he laid aside his brushes for the last time. 'Who, beyond God, favoured you with such a wealth of beauty?'

'I shan't be sorry to be out of the way of your flattery, Armand,' she said. 'My mother's side I suppose. Not my father, certainly. But I have no memory of my mother. She died when I was born, you see. Like my grandmother. She died when my mother was . . . Ai Jesu! Enough.'

Gonplier rammed his brushes into their wallet with uncareful haste and rolled it with one hand while he collapsed his easel with the other. 'Indeed, I swear you don't resemble anyone at all. You're a journeyman's sample. Unique. Unprecedented.' But he did not kiss her hand as he had done every day previously. He left with a curlicue of flourishes, initialling the air with his cap. He was embarrassed, as people are with the terminally sick.

As he passed Victoire in the door he cast on him a look so close to pity as to breach all etiquette. 'You seem such a good man, de Gloriole. What did you do for God to reward you so vilely?'

And Victoire, searching his conscience like a man brought unwarned to the gallows, said, 'Nothing. Nothing. Nothing. Nothing. Nothing.'

NINE

The Possession of Loss

He did not recognize Lucette and she did not try to wake a recollection. It would not have been safe. She let him think she was fooled by the disguise – the shabby cloak inadequately hiding his expensive black buckram doublet. She did not chase contact with the golden eyes which refused to meet hers. They examined the sagging ceiling festooned with cobwebs; they analysed the bedding blanket by rag; they swept the floor where no broom had swept before them; they clambered out of the ragged hole punched in the wall to let in light and flies. The eyes came to rest on the table where a lacemaker's hook lay among the caked deposits of oatmeal porridge and coins from his own pouch. She picked up the hook and put it in her pocket: there was no lace in the room but the cobwebs. He could not bring Ellen here. It would have to be elsewhere.

'I hear you're a midwife.'

'You hear more'n that, sir, or you'd not come sprinkling money.'

He went to pick up the coins again, but she was too quick for him. 'What's the girl?' she asked.

'What's that to you?'

'Hush–tush! Shan't a midwife ask about her patient?'

'You wouldn't know her.'

'Well that's no great matter. I meant what's her state?'

'Above yours.'

Lucette sighed patiently, savouring her power over this unhappy, guilt-stricken man.

She had no clear knowledge of what had become of her son, her little Azay. His presence within the castle had held her in the neighbourhood like a ship with its sea anchor snagged among rocks. Even now it held her: even now that he was gone. She knew he was no longer there, but knew nothing of the circumstances. She knew that he had been there among the English, and

gone after the French came. Disappeared. Never seen or heard of
again.

By then a career had accidentally settled upon her. She said
she was a midwife. She had brought a baby into the world,
hadn't she? Mothers do as much, but they have a baby to show for
it afterwards. Lucette must therefore be a midwife. That was how
she came to think of herself. And after she realized Azay was dead,
it seemed a natural progression to graduate to the more lucrative end
of the profession. She had built up, too, a profitable sideline in 'waste
products'. They were bought avidly by the mad old Viscomte de
Bruberac over by Ormes. It was dangerous, but somehow fear of
the hangman remained a less real emotion in Lucette than the thrill
of such encounters as this, the gratification of money clinking in the
purse under her skirts, the satisfaction of knowing another mother
was without her son. 'How far gone is your . . .'

'Halfway.'

'So late? You shouldn't have wasted so long in thinking. She
won't pass for a virgin after.'

'That's no matter.'

'Ah! I see it's your sister, then. Or some lady in holy orders,
perhaps.'

'You filthy . . . It's my wife. My wife, woman. My wife.'

'Lay astray, did she, while you were at the war? Common
enough.'

He would have hit her but was too demoralized and too much in
need of her help. The situation was unreal. He moved through it as
if in a dream. 'I've consulted surgeons. They say it's impossible she
should have an easy time.' But it was not the surgeons' words he
carried in his pocket. It was a letter from his father-in-law, scrawled
across the paper like a demonic incantation. He had carried it with
him for a week now – kept it from his wife, mentioned it to no
one. It seemed to weigh heavier than the forty écus he had just
unburdened on to the table.

*A curse on you, Frenchman, and on all your nation. May the
race die out. May the name of France fall from maps as the wick
of Gloriole is set to burn down to extinction. The same curse light
on you as blighted me in my first wife – a mare sold me unsound
– five generations of female out of female and each one killing
her dam and never a son in recompense. Thus I was betrayed and
thus I betray you!*

Did you never learn how the Devil gives his worst snares the best outsides? Beautiful is she not? And hot in lechery herself, so I judge from her letters. But such women are sent to tempt a man to lust and punish him for it. My daughter is like her mother — the Devil's eel-trap, monsieur. You may put your fist inside, but nothing will ever escape it by the same door. Nothing but girls, and then to be cut from the pod. I see God's hand at work. I sent a Spanish fig to my cousin but God saw fit to deliver it to you. So, Frenchman! You looked to rape the English and find your seed sewn up in a shroud. I am glad of it! May all your hopes end thus — in worthless and wretched wombs.

Every Englishman ever to die on his sword's point or dangling from his lance was one too few for Victoire by the time he had read and digested this answer to his own letter. It had been hard enough to write to the enemy in civil terms, but he had done so. He had written begging for reassurance. He had been stiltedly polite, painfully conciliatory. Only for Ellen would he have sunk so low. Now the remainder of his life would not be long enough to pay back the English for this humiliation.

But for all his oaths and spleen, Victoire could not help but understand the man's hatred of women — a hatred which encompassed even his own daughter. Victoire knew that he too would never trust women again if Ellen betrayed him and died.

'It's not safe for her to bear children,' he said simply and succinctly, and the abortionist was startled out of her squalid speculations.

'What's that to you? A man? A man must breed. Especially . . .' She broke off dangerously close to saying that a comte must have an heir.

'I won't justify myself to you, witch. Can you deliver her or not?'

'Maybe. There's a danger. There's always a danger. You've left it wonderful late. You must give me your word as a . . . gentleman that you'll not hold me to blame if the lady dies, though I did my best work.'

'Hold you to blame, woman? I'd hold you to iron and fire. I'd draw and quarter you. She must not die.'

The words terrified her. Everything about the young man in the hooded cloak, holding his hands in check with the swordbelt round his hips, frightened her till her head spun with fear. But she would have done the work for nothing: for forty pieces or for nothing.

To rip his heir to pieces in the womb; to dismember his very own son. He had let her Azay die. To empty this wife of his, whom he loved with such tenderness as she had never believed existed in the world. Let the woman die. As soon as the job was done, Lucette would leave the district. The anchor-rope binding her to the neighbourhood would be quite cut through with that little lace-making hook of hers, and she could go where she wished, take her art to one of the thousand-and-one towns where it was wanted.

'Bring her to me tonight.'

'Not here. I'll not bring her here.'

'Where, then? At the . . . at your house? I must have peace and privacy. And no one at hand to hear.'

'In the forest. I'll send a horse and man to fetch you there at dusk. I have a lodge there. I'm a . . . forester.'

'As I'm a midwife,' she said under her breath, and she lifted her skirts and scooped the dirty money into her purse. Something about the action triggered a recollection in Victoire – of someone he had known, if he could but remember where or when.

'Come and see! I've bought you an owl! Come and see! Come and see!' his wife greeted him, taking him by the hand.

The hunting owl stood in the aviary among the other hawks and falcons, its head-feathers horned like the Devil and its yellow, baleful eyes utterly filling its face. Those eyes. They devoured him, those eyes.

'It should have a hood. Where's its hood?'

'It's being made. See, it's there on the last. It'll be finished in a few days. Isn't he fine, though? Isn't he?'

'Can't its eyes be covered up? Can't you cover up its eyes?' He found he had to turn his back on the watching, blinking, dilating, membranous eyes. Only then could he say, 'It's a fine bird, Ellen. Thank you. I have a present for you, too. But you must come to the hunting lodge to get it.'

'Now? Tonight? What's the matter, Chicheface? Tell me quick. Why so melancholy? And why are you wearing that dreadful cloak?' She had long since stopped allowing him the luxury of brooding: it was as if she resented any waste of time in coming to the point.

'Fetch some shifts and your breviary. I'll tell you as we ride.'

'Ah, it's the nunnery for me then, is it? You've found another lover with less of a belly to thwart you . . . It's only yesterday you forbade me to ride, Victoire! Because of the baby. And don't rub your hair like that: you'll wear it thin.'

He could not bear to look at her. Her eyes seemed as big as the owl's. He simply took the letter from his pouch and rammed it into her hands, to fend them off touching him. And while she read it, he saddled her a horse and explained the arrangement he had been making with the 'midwife' in Rocheblanche. He was businesslike and methodical. But the horse grunted at the force with which he fastened the cinch.

She handed him back the letter and unconsciously wiped her hands on her skirt as if they were dirty. 'But the King's praying for a boy. It will be a boy,' she said.

He rent the letter in pieces. 'It'll be nothing. It won't *be*. I have the woman's word. Let the King keep to curing scrofula, I'll not rely on his prayers.'

'No heir for Gloriole?'

He went on bridling the horse. 'Let Michel de Puy have it after us. The de Puys crave the place. You saw at the wedding how they crave the place. What's the matter? What's a name? It's in the stone, anyway. Our initials. Our devices. We're carved in the lintels now. The rain won't scuff us out for a thousand years. We'll leave our mark another way, you and I. We don't need heirs.'

'A thousand years.'

The horse was ready. There was nothing left to occupy his hands. He led the animals outside to the mounting block. Her peaceable voice came after him, but she came only as far as the doorway herself.

'A thousand years. That's how long I'd burn.'

'What?'

'And another thousand after. And then another. I'd be damned, Victoire. For ever.' It was hard to bring him to a halt – like thrusting a spoke into a racing wheel. 'Have you lost all your religion, man? What you're talking about is damnable. I'd no sooner go to meet your midwife than I'd go to a Black Sabbath and sign my soul away in blood. The King's praying for a boy and I shall have a boy. An heir for Sablois. A Comte de Gloriole. When you were born your father was "eating the bread of affliction", as they say, wasn't he? He might have thought you better unborn. But he must have been pleased enough to have you, in all conscience. I know I am. No. We shall have a son, and if I die in the doing –'

'*Yes? And what then?*' he said, malevolent with passion.

'Then I shall escape seeing my husband bettered by my son in the tilt yard – or sending him off to war to fight my relations – or suffering him to fetch home unsuitable foreign brides . . . Victoire, I am afraid. Just like you. More than you, maybe. I've been afraid since the first. Since before I told you. I'm not ready to die. I'm not courageous enough to go anywhere without you. But even if it's true – even if God is envious of us, I don't believe you'd send me into everlasting fires just to spite Him. And I don't believe you'd separate us two for all Eternity just for the sake of not parting from me now . . . Besides, it's not *now*.' She came and led the horse back inside the stable. The aviary fluttered at the disturbance. The owl gaped its yellow eyes. 'It's a wealth of weeks away . . . And my father's a lonely, vindictive old man. Take no notice. Pay him no heed.'

He called after her: 'I might be content with a girl! As long as I had you to help me bring her up!'

But she dismissed the idea. 'Pshah! You, a daughter? If she weren't Joan of Arc you'd send her out to do washing.'

So Lucette waited in vain all night at the hunting lodge for her customer. Indeed, with no horse, she was marooned, there where the escort had brought her. She had to walk home. For all she had pocketed a vast sum without incurring risk or exerting her skills, she was peevish in the extreme and muttered and cursed like some ancient hag as she dragged her maimed leg through the leaf-mould, scraping to death fleshy white mushrooms on the forest floor. She would not have parted with the night's work for all the safety of idleness.

Besides, safety and peace are not the long-term lot of the likes of Lucette. Within the week, a sudden inexplicable upsurge in moral fervour brought a mob to her door. They dismantled her hovel, clod by wattle. They hanged her from a chestnut tree. The guard from the castle, arriving too late to prevent the incident or to make any arrests, comforted themselves that the lynching was natural justice and had saved the cost of a trial. They did not waste much time burying the body deep at the crossroads: she would not have received a Christian burial in any event. Everyone knew abortionists were in league with the Devil.

While her neighbours were struggling to dislodge the ladder from against the gallows tree, and to prise the woman's fingers and feet off the rungs, Lucette was heard to curse aloud the Comte de Gloriole. 'He set you on to this! Devil rack him! Devil tear him! Do it to him, not me! Do it to him! Murderer!'

But it was not Victoire who had roused the mob.

The Viscomte de Bruberac, now prey to irrational outbursts of rage at the smallest of setbacks, had been stirred by her mention of a certain 'very special' piece of merchandise. When she failed to deliver it, his temper burst like a plague rat. A night's ritual in the subterranean cellar of his fortress had had to be abandoned. His vengeance may have been disproportionately violent, but he orchestrated the lynching with the pedantic efficiency only a madman can muster.

During her pregnancy, Ellen laid out the gardens at Gloriole – an eminently practical array of cabbages, onions, beans, berries, salad, and fruit trees but arranged with such pretty geometry that the vine-covered perimeter walk seemed to enclose a mosaic floor of variegated green, red and white. She inadvertently instilled in the gardener such a passion for his work that it became a very real problem to wrest away a cabbage for supper. It would ruin his symmetry, he complained. His plaintive cry echoed through the garden like a hoopoe, bemoaning the rape of his shallots, the rack of his lettuces, the pillaging of his beetroot and artichokes.

The herbs, Ellen tended herself: rosemary, hyssop, chervil and the like for the kitchen and verbena, mauve, menthol and a dozen more for their medicinal worth. It was as though she had been born with a knowledge of herbal remedies, for she could not recall at whose knee she had learned them. There was not an injury, an ailment, an evil humour or a nervous affliction that she could not ease with some infusion or compound, cataplasm or balm of herbs from her garden domain. There was oregano for the boatswain's bronchitis and vulneraire for a baby's gastritis in Rocheblanche; vermifuge for the horse's colic and camomile to soothe an old lady's fright when the demobbed soldiers passed through. With consummate ingratitude, the peasants suspected her at first of witchcraft and English sorcery. But, like weeds in the garden of Gloriole, such suspicions could not thrive long.

The rumour of love potions and amorous philtres prospered longest. No one could otherwise quite explain how the Goddam-Slayer came to worship an Englishwoman. But popular spite did not survive acquaintance with the new Comte and Comtesse. The men who saw Ellen appreciated that such a woman did not need the help of magic; and their wives, on meeting Victoire, did not want to credit him with either folly or bad taste.

The peasants sensed, like cattle sniffing the wind, a certain unrepeatable good fortune in the air. They prayed for nothing to change, for Time to stop still, for an end to seasonal variation, for the Year's wheel to bog down in the autumn and winter rains: as the gardener would have liked to keep his garden unpicked, in a perfect state of perpetual fruition.

No one laughed at the quaint ardour of the love-match. The planets hung in a happy conjunction in their heaven, and simple minds governed by portents saw a kind of pattern at work. Everything was growing and coming to fruition: the Comtesse Ellen, the grain-barn, the chateau, the hunting lodge, the cider press, the hilltop chapel, the Comte's unconcealable happiness.

Only the midwife ventured a laugh when she heard how Ellen had sent for red menthol that morning to ease stomach cramps and backache. 'It'll take more than red menthol, madam, to ease a baby into the world!' she said, and laughed herself ruddy as she helped Ellen back into the great bed.

Next morning it was the midwife who fetched Barnabas. It was she who reminded the kitchen that food must be set by for the priest. She was a practical, down-to-earth woman. She knew how often the common decencies are overlooked at such a time. 'Be sure and set by a meal for the priest,' she told the cook.

But Barnabas did not emerge from the bedchamber for lunch or supper. He could not. He would not. He refused to leave Victoire alone with the body of his dead wife.

Victoire would not allow the lady's body to be removed to the chapel for the customary lying-in and vigil. He insisted it stay on the marriage bed. He said, 'The fiends will go first to the chapel. It'll take longer for them to find her here.'

'No fiends will trouble to make the journey,' said Barnabas with trite and routine reassurance. He had sat through many such nights, when the demons, getting wind of death, come searching for an easy soul to steal. He had never seen them come.

'They will,' said Victoire. 'They're coming already. Don't you smell them? Go if you like.'

The smells were real enough: sweet corruption and the sweaty struggle with death. It was the first time Barnabas had seen Caesar's cut made. Usually, when peasant women struggled to give birth and failed the child was allowed to die with its mother, inside her. Barnabas had no ambition to see Caesar's cut made again. Nor was it a thing Victoire should have watched, whatever sights he had seen in the wars. 'Let her be washed and taken to the chapel, my lord.'

'No. But you go or stay. As you choose,' said Victoire. Such a small degree of irritability.

'I'll stay, my lord.'

But he, who had been trained to sit, kneel and stand through endless hours of devotions, had to marvel at the stillness de Gloriole could maintain – sitting on his heels near the wall, well back from the bed, his eyes fixed on his wife's face. Except for a slight rocking, forward and back, there was nothing to suggest more than mild apprehension in the man. He did not blink. He did not utter a sound.

And yet this silence was not devotional. There was something about the quality of it which petrified the kneeling priest and held him pinned in place, as if there were a forked stick across his throat. He must push it aside. He must speak.

'What will you call the boy, my lord? Let me christen him before I leave. It's best, even if you have a baptism in the grand style at a time more fitting. Sure, you must have a name chosen already.'

Victoire turned very slowly towards him. After a long silence he said, 'Why? Is it easier cursed with a name?'

'My lord?'

'Why should I give it a name? I've got no wish to speak to it or wish it other than damned? God grant it torments more than hers.'

'My lord Comte! For God's sake! What kind of a . . .' He collected himself, laughed, cajoled. 'Your own son? No name for your own heir? The fruit of your marriage? Come now . . .'

'Call it what you like. It's a son, isn't it? Call it by its function, then. Call it "son". But don't disturb me. I have demons to fend off and my soul's not well armed to do it.'

Barnabas snatched at the opportunity to keep the silence at bay. 'Do you want to make Confession, then? It will pass the time till morning?'

'Why should I want to pass the time till morning? I'll be in Hell by morning . . . But yes, I'll make Confession to you.' The eyes glanced sidelong at him only briefly this time. They were dry, dark and glittering. 'I'll confess a present wish to kill a great many people. Not least you.'

'Me, my lord?'

'For offering her the joys of bliss. What inducements could I offer to compete with that? To keep her here on Earth.'

'Oh. I see. But who else?'

'Henry Talbot for letting me see her. Humphrey Talbot for letting me have her. Her mother for giving her birth. My own for the same favour. The midwife for her blade-whetting. *Myself for putting in the dagger.*'

'You didn't, Victoire. You did no such thing.' But for the life of him Barnabas could not remember what had become of the midwife's blade. He wished he could.

'Myself for putting in the dagger . . .' Victoire repeated, and broke off, spreading one hand across his chest. His face displayed a sudden, abject, death's-head horror – a terror absolute. 'Barnabas . . . Can you exorcize demons? Do you know how?'

'There are no demons here,' said the priest.

'But there are! They came for her, but they'll take possession of me instead. She'll see to it! They've come. They're here. I feel them – rending and tearing!' He plucked at the fastenings of his doublet as if, like Hercules' shirt, it were molten fire cleaving to his skin. 'Claws and hooks tearing!'

Barnabas slid himself closer across the cold, pottery tiles of the floor, closer and closer. 'There *are no demons*, Victoire.'

'I should have worn a breastplate! I should have put on armour!' The fur collar of his doublet glistened with fallen sweat. He was like a bear rolled in the dew.

Barnabas reached out one hand. He was still out of reach and slid closer yet. 'You can't arm against grief, Victoire. You're possessed by grief. I can't scare that back to Hell.'

'A demon . . . Here. Fetch the midwife to cut it out of me!'

Barnabas grabbed the fur collar in his fist. '*Grieve, you fool! Weep! Cry, why don't you?* You're not keeping vigil before a battle, man! You're keeping watch over your wife – over Ellen! Your sweet good wife, man! Mourn, you stupid –!'

Victoire propelled himself off his heels and launched himself at Barnabas only to land short of him, on hands and knees. 'For what? For a *woman*? They die all the time! Everyone knows that! It's commonplace, damn you! The graveyards are full of them! How could there be this kind of pain? In the Natural Order of things? At God's ordaining? It's not possible! She was a witch, Barnabas! She had me in thrall and now she's dead her familiar is clawing my guts to pieces. I feel it! I feel it! She needs to cut out my soul to get her a place in Paradise!' Outstripping his breath, he panted and choked on what he was saying. 'Did you never read the story of Aristotle? You must have! I never go into my library but you're there! Sure, you've read it! Did you never read how when he was old the great philosopher fell in love? He fell in love with a young whore – a young trollop? And she made him go on hands and knees while she rode on his back for all the world to see what fools love makes of wise men! Look at me! Look at me now! Aristotle on all fours!'

Barnabas put his elbows to the floor. It was the only way he could bring his mouth close enough to the other man's ear and shout, 'At least he would have had the wisdom to weep when she died!'

'What do you know, you gelding? You eunuch! She's a succubus! She drank my blood while I slept!'

'*Mourn, man! Mourn!* Hate won't serve now! Courage won't serve now! Do you think you can bear it like a battle-wound?'

The first drop of a hailstorm hit the new glazing in the window with a whip-sharp crack. Startled by the noise, Victoire sprang clear through the priest's arms to the bed and spreadeagled himself across his dead wife. '*You shan't have her! You shan't take her! In the name of Christ, take me instead!*'

But no demons burst through the glass, shark-jawed, gagging on the netting of lead. And when he looked once more at the rainy window it seemed to Victoire, in his mind's eye, that the whole chateau had been wrapped in the web of a voracious spider, every window latticed with strands of black, and he cocooned inside for ever.

'How shall I live without her, Barnabas?' he asked, resting his forearms against the priest's chest as both men got to their feet.

'In her son, my lord. In the plans you both made for Gloriole. And in her son.'

But in the morning they put his son into his arms. And Victoire, who had ridden hock-deep through bloody war and seen the sun eclipsed by carrion flocks of birds – who had seen the bough bend on the local gibbet-tree – who had seen the smoke rise up over Bruberac's hall – believed this the first murder he had ever been party to, and his son the first murderer.

PART II

Some said it was impossible the war should ever end. It stretched back beyond the recollections of a lifetime, beyond generations of memories – Englishmen slaughtering Frenchmen, Frenchmen slaughtering Englishmen – since before men thought of themselves as either French or English.

But in 1435, King Charles made peace with the Burgundians. The following year the English, robbed of their allies, evacuated Paris. By 1444 a standing army of twelve thousand French professionals stirred at the King's command, with artillery at their back and powder corned by a multitude of bishops.

Then King Charles gave his niece Margaret to the English King Henry, in exchange for Anjou and Maine. And within the year two nations who had sworn to hate one another till the end of the world were locked in a loving embrace.

Unfortunately, it takes more than a royal marriage to end such a tradition of war. Hatred, like a boulder, gathers momentum as it careers down a century of battlefields. A few loving words won't stop a broadsword in its downward arc.

TEN

Out of the Pit

For the construction of great buildings, chestnut trees a century old are felled in winter and their bark removed. Rough-hewn into square beams, still bleeding their sap, they are lowered into a river and left for many years before they can be used to satisfy the ambitions of architects. Under the surface of the Sablois river, chestnuts from the forests of Gloriole-sur-Sablois lay inert while the running years made of their fibres as dense a fabric as stone.

No political treaty-mongering could root out Victoire de Gloriole's inbred and ingrained loathing for the English, any more than John Talbot could be kennelled up in Shrewsbury with his battle scars and reminiscences, to keep bees and cultivate his wardrobe. By the age of forty, de Gloriole had campaigned so long and hard that he had the look of a grizzled bear newly escaped from the pit – a look exaggerated by his habit of wearing a bearskin round the shoulders of his armour. Even between campaigns he kept to his black under-wadding or a dark hardicote. He scorned the long, voluminous houppelande which impedes a man's movement and occupies his hands on the stairs. Nothing was allowed to impede his movements nor the quick cycle of his busy years. When the famines of '31 and '35 stretched their jaws to consume the countryside, they could not swallow down Sablois: they gagged on the husbanded plenty of the great-barn, the lesser barns, the pannage, the sheer concerted refusal of the community to be panicked into starvation. The peasants of Gloriole had no respect for famine – only for their Comte – that quick, black, fur-shouldered shape always in the corner of their eye like a bear newly escaped.

And yet everyone knew he had escaped the pit twenty years before. Everyone knew that the hatred he had vowed to feel for his son had lasted no more than a matter of months, a season of madness.

They had hidden the child away from him at first, as if it were some monstrous aberration, some guilty miscreant. They named it, as they had been instructed, 'Fils', and housed the wet-nurse at the furthermost end of the enlarged house. But in those days, while the chestnut beams lay maturing on the riverbed and the quarrymen were still hewing white masonry from the cliffs, the chateau remained too small to keep a baby's crying out of any of the rooms. Victoire lay awake at night and listened, in the narrow bed to which he had confined himself. The great bed he had burned, hangings and all, in the stable yard. He began to think of those cries as his own disembodied grief haunting the furthest recesses of the house, held in by the sorcery of initials written in stone on the lintels, written in lead in the white-glass casements.

Then one night the nurse woke with a cry of fright to find the dark, stocky shadow of the Comte bending over the crib holding a candle. His knuckles and the coverlet were leprous with dripping wax and the unsteady light distorted the features of his face.

'Don't harm him, my lord!' said the nurse, consumed with fear. 'There's no hurt in him, little scrap!'

He did not seem to register what she said, only that he was no longer alone with his thoughts and was required to speak. 'He has black hair,' he said

'Yes sir. Black like your own.'

'Black like hers.'

'He has his mother's features altogether,' admitted the nurse, although she had been loath to say so before.

His eyes glared at her through the dark. 'Will that wash? Her features in a lad? She was so . . . *female*.'

She crawled down the bed on hands and knees. 'Well he's never been taken for a girl yet, my lord,' and ventured closer to the crib. 'Proper little man. Long and thin.'

'And narrow at the hips.'

'What? Not where it matters, sir, no sir, why? Would you like to hold him, sir? Though he's fractious first off and blarts a bit.'

He blew out the candle. 'No! No, why should I want to hold him? Leave me be! Get back to bed, woman!'

The wet-nurse hurried to tell the priest next day – chiefly in case anyone had seen de Gloriole enter her room and carried the wrong word back to her husband in the village. But Barnabas had immediately asked for the boy out of her arms and carried him to the retraite where Victoire tackled his correspondence.

'Isn't he a fine boy?' said Barnabas dumping the baby down naked in the centre of the desk and leaping backwards as if to admire a pot of plants.

'I don't have the leisure for a sermon . . .' protested Victoire.

'No, but isn't he a fine boy?'

'You overstep your mark, Barnabas.'

'I know, but isn't he a fine boy?'

'He's pissing on the register of muster!'

But Barnabas only repeated, as bright and ingenuous as the first time, 'Yes, but isn't he a fine boy?'

Victoire was obliged to pick up the child himself: he held it between both hands, at arm's length, as he would an unhooded hawk whose beak might take out his eyes.

'Isn't he a fine boy?' said Barnabas remorselessly.

'Damn you, priest. He'll catch cold.' Only then did Barnabas restore the child to its nurse.

When the weather cleared, she took Fils into the garden to 'air' him among the mauve and the peppermint, and was aware of being watched from the window of the armoury. She carried the boy conspicuously high, on one shoulder. One day the Comte rapped on the windowpane with his knuckles and the baby looked up and smiled. Shortly afterwards, the nurse found that she was not required to take the boy for a daily airing. The Comte himself said he would do that.

Victoire thought he had staunched the wound, but with the bandage off, the blood kept flowing. He thought he had dammed up the river with dry boulders and sharp rocks, but he found the river had simply gone underground to re-emerge further on. All the love he had felt for Ellen revived and devolved on to her son, transmuted into a mixture of pride, protective tenderness and vaulting ambition. He could be seen walking – even riding – with Fils in the angle of his arm like a tall, black-eyed falcon – to see the hunting lodges thatched, the hay ricked, the apple barges launched downriver, the herons culled and the rams put to the ewes.

When Fils was three, as well as a whipping top, his father gave him a round-tower turret newly crowned with a conical roof of black-Angers slate that gleamed like silver in the sun. When Fils was seven, in place of a toy flag Victoire struck the heir's device on shield and banner and hung them in the armoury. He overpainted the heraldry on the great fireplace of the main hall with the inverted tessellations of the first-born son.

'. . . as if the place were the boy's already,' said the King dyspeptically, eyeing the device as he sat relaxing with his feet on Victoire's table after a day spent killing Victoire's deer. But then the King was jaundiced against sons that particular summer. His own was in league with the rebellious Duke Alençon.

'Of course Louis is just Alençon's pawn, you know,' he said, lightly dismissing a revolt that was pulling the country in two. 'He thinks he lacks advancement because I was installed Dauphin at fourteen and he's seventeen and still waiting. I've told him – all in good time, "when he shall come back in humility". But I want a few heads on poles first.'

Charles was not a man sensitive to atmosphere. He had a long but selective memory and, recalling that de Gloriole had once been married to an Englishwoman, had persuaded himself that Victoire was, like himself, in favour of peace with the English. De Gloriole did not enlighten him. He did not mention that Alençon and the Bastard Dunois had come to Gloriole, had sought to enlist his aid, had urged him to muster in the cause of Louis and oust the King.

'First peace with Burgundy, and now the English!' they had said, beating their mailed fists on the selfsame table. 'Will you sit by while he sells the honour of France for the sake of a full exchequer? You? The Goddam-Slayer? You? The flower of French chivalry?'

They called him comrade-at-arms and clapped him on the back and embraced him as if to pass on their fury to him as dogs pass on their fleas. They had no need to infest him with their rage: he had enough of his own already.

Scorchers – disbanded professional soldiers suddenly cheated of their war – were burning up the countryside, pillaging the French for want of English victims. They had destroyed two post-mills, sacked the lovely Chapel Saint-Cloud and killed twelve of his peasants: a new breed of land pirate, well trained and well equipped – by King Charles-the-Veryvictorious. Peace at all costs was the King's gospel now. The small matter of Jeanne Darc's burning was glossed over – a grass fire started accidentally by a few careless prelates; an unfortunate incident and probably for the best. Prisoners who had languished in England since Agincourt and earlier went unredeemed, their ransoms unpaid, while their gaolers were wooed with soft words.

'He doesn't want my brother released!' cried Dunois in anguish. 'The Duke of Orléans! His own cousin! Means him to rot in England!'

'I heard as much,' said de Gloriole. 'I am very sorry for it.'

'He's afraid of the comparisons people would draw once they saw a truly great man! That's the reason! Well? Are you for us or against us, Victoire?'

He sympathized with their grievances. He shared their frustration, their indignation. And yet this was the same Charles they were maligning who had elevated him from trooper to lord, had made him rich, had eaten at his table. This was the Charles to whom God had sent the little Maid Jeanne, to raise him up to the Divinity of Kings. This was the King who had prayed for Ellen to have a son.

'If anger were virtue,' he said at last, 'I should be your equal in merit, gentlemen. But as it is, I am a mere galley slave at my oar, chained by fealty. I vowed lifelong loyalty to my lord King and I see no course I could steer to bring me over to your side. Not without my soul foundering. I'm sorry. I can't join your rebellion.'

And they had accepted his answer; not cursed him, not unsaid their praise of his manhood, not unravelled their comradeship. He loved Dunois and Alençon. They were truly good men.

Now the King sat and criticized the labelled coat-of-arms on Victoire's chimney breast, because 'a man should trust only to himself, Gloriole! Sons aren't to be trusted. No more'n scurvy courtiers'.

Fils looked up at his father over the brim of his milk, blinking his black eyes in confused alarm. Victoire winked at him: the most fleeting of signals between two collaborators.

'Take your cousin, de Gloriole!'

'De Puy?' said Victoire, startled out of his silence. 'De Puy sided with Alençon? No! Sure! I'd've heard of it.'

'No, no. I was talking treachery, that's all. It was that son of his that came tattling to me that you were plotting secret alliances with the English. You know? Years ago . . . When you tupped that Talbot beauty with the small rump? Should've heard the way he phrased it. Good as made you out a turncoat. Not nice. Not civil. You can't trust kin. They're not to be trusted.'

'A misreading of the situation on Michel's part,' said Victoire mildly. 'An honest mistake, I dare say.'

But he made a mental note of de Puy's treachery, just as he noted the King's opinion of sons.

Cures can be concocted and medicines devised, but the endemic disease of war still recurs. Despite the Truce of Tours and the marriage of Henry VI to Margaret of Anjou, by the time Fils was fifteen the King had declared war once more on the English and sworn to drive them out of even Normandy. Those who fell from grace at Court now were those tainted by dealings with the goddams. And Victoire was once more wielding his sword in the King's service, this time with his son beside him.

They became a familiar and renowned sight on the field, for Fils was left-handed and Victoire right, so that they made on horseback an unassailable twin barb, one double-bladed creature like the angel at the gates of Eden, expelling the English from Paradise.

At night, by the campfires, other knights and squires would stand about just to watch father and son play *la morra*. For it defied belief to see how they could play it. Others could strike lucky once or twice; by fluke they sometimes guessed right three times in a row. But Victoire and Fils could play a whole minute together, one throwing wide his palm, the other simultaneously guessing the number of fingers held up. Sceptics said that the two worked a system between them to impress – but they did not say so to Victoire. The Comte de Gloriole was no longer a youth to be teased or baited.

On 17 July he woke to his fortieth birthday camped amid the obscure beauty of the Dordogne. All around him villages perched on hilltops like mast-broken ships on the crests of a pitching sea. And on one, the fortification of Castillon flew flags of smoke. It was under bombardment by English artillery.

Some people, faced with death, invent epitaphs: 'If I should die, write over me . . .' But Victoire and Fils communicated in a different way, perfunctory and businesslike:

'Don't neglect to clad the east wing.'

'Well then, make something more of the moat, the way I described.' They carried their chateau to war with them and their schemes scrolled up inside their wadding.

'And remember to fill the portlogs after the scaffolding's down!'

'And plant elms across the river to break up the northerlies!' Their embrace was casual, only a moment longer than those they exchanged, as gestures of good luck, with their fellow chevaliers.

Culverin-fire broke up the earth like the ice of a frozen lake, the smoke engulfed riders as though they had fallen through the ragged holes into oblivion. Spouts of flame erupted from the salamander cannon, and the air was coarse-grained as sacking with dust and ash. It smothered a man and blinded him, made of his foes indiscernible and shapeless shadows wading through the mire. The heraldry on surcoats was effaced, a blur of blood and whorls of dirt and tattered holes. By their helmets they knew each other; by the shape of sallets: two incompatible breeds of snail crawling across the glistening ground.

The English and their Gascon allies had overreached themselves. Castillon was securely held and heavily manned. Talbot's siege of the town was impractical, even before French reinforcements arrived. The goddam siegers found de Gloriole and his Sablois levy at their backs, cutting off their retreat. Once they were joined in hand-to-hand fighting, however, the cannonfire from the castle rained down indiscriminately on English and French alike.

Square, ordered ranks of riders were gradually broken up, as a river in flood disintegrates a raft of debris and scatters it whirling downstream. Now and then a trumpeter would rein in to sound a command – lip-service to stratagems devised at smooth tables on quiet nights by rational men. Then the buglers would be engulfed like bellowing livestock in an unpremeditated stampede. Craters opened in the ground as though Hell were a rabbit warren to be entered by a thousand different burrows.

In the suffocating noise, Victoire and Fils were separated, parted knee from knee by a French cannon ball that rived their horses apart. Through a vent in the smoke Victoire saw, with perfect clarity, the corner turret of Castillon blasted away, the collapsed floor suspended inside and a slow haemorrhage of furniture through the gaping hole: a press, a bed, a post, a man, a log, a chair – jostling together down a slope of planks then somersaulting in a silent fall into the dry moat. The choked culvert in the sagging roof broke and spilled cold rain-water down into the room. He could feel it trickling. He could feel the cold draught of air sucked into the void by the explosion, could feel the mortar blasted from between the bricks of the buttress. And he thought he felt it because Fils was gone from his side, because a meteorite had separated the constellations of Castor and Pollux.

It was only when his horse went down, knelt down, flopped down lazily under him for no apparent reason that he realized the cannon ball had burst and the fragments of stone shattered like a pot in the firing. His pauldron was blown clean away; the vambrace housing his left arm was open at every hinge and coiled down his arm in a jagged spiral. To the blue cords fastening the bent coudière around his elbow were added knotty strings of dark red. He could not open his hand.

Victoire disentangled himself from the horse and walked away. Impatiently he parried the hysterical onslaught of a Gascon who, in his zeal, overbalanced and was readily hamstrung from behind. Irritated to find his way barred by a brace of Englishmen, Victoire took one below the ear and the other low down, through the mail stomacher, before tramping on into the shade of a tree and sitting down with his back to the trunk. He took off his helmet and thought peevishly, If any bastard hampers Fils . . . A cannon ball flew through the branches of the tree and showered him with twigs and leaves. Affronted, he brushed them off with his right hand.

The pleat of steel curving over his crop was stoven in and constricted his diaphragm's rise and fall. Besides, he was loath to fall asleep until he had seen that Fils was not inconvenienced, before he had satisfied himself that the boy was not in need of a loan of armour, a new horse . . .

This wet grass would make for rust; he should not sit in it. He certainly should not lie down in it. But there were toadstools growing from the trunk of the tree – huge, flat-domed toadstools like bare, bony kneecaps. They captured his interest and held his eye. A spider lowered itself out of the grass on to his hand. He had an irrational hatred of spiders and their geometric webs. That was the beauty of chestnut for building, he told himself: it repelled spiders. He must remind Fils of that. One day every roof- and tie-beam in Gloriole would be carved from the chestnut matured beneath the surface of the Sablois.

A cold place; a place where breathing is difficult, where the sap freezes in the fibres of the timber like sweat in the pores of a man's skin . . .

Next he knew, the air was washing past him on all sides like water. There were hands spread flat beneath his shoulders, his back, his hips, his legs, raising him up into the cold, blue, steep-raked sky. He thought he must be carried to the graveyard at a run, for a panted Latin chant flew up from a half-dozen mouths below him and the hands jarred in his back.

'Sanguis Christi maneat in te sicut Christus fecit in se.'
'Sanguis Christi maneat in te sicut Christus fecit in se.'

'Sanguis Christi maneat . . .'

It was the invocation to stop the flow of blood. He recollected it now. He had recited it over a hundred wounded men in his time. For whom, he wondered, should he be saying it now?

'God blast all Gascons! God split all Englishmen!' he said, and the voices beneath him panted an 'Amen'. Not a prisoner, then. His right gauntlet was off and two hands were holding his. But he found he dared not turn his head, dared not look down from this dizzy, careering roost, for fear it was not . . . as he hoped. For fear it was not . . .

They carried him to Limbourn Priory. They cut off ventail, brassard and coudière with pliers. They poured hot oil into the gashes the armour had made. They hauled on the arm until its overlapping fragments of bone fell back into alignment, and splinted it between slats of wood. But the first time that Victoire's composure deserted him was when, emerging from the fire-rimmed darkness, Fils leaned over him and kissed him on the cheek.

The tears rose irresistibly and filled Victoire's eyes. He was impatient of them; they marred his vision, stopped him seeing his son clearly. His free hand travelled clumsily over the boy's chest and face, plucking and pulling at him, searching him for signs of injury. The pouches of his jaw laboured with speech. 'Son! Son! Son! Whatever was I thinking of? Are you hurt? Let me see you! Not hurt? You're sure you're not hurt? Why the devil did I bring you here? What the devil right did I have? That nag of yours isn't fast enough in the turn! I should've changed her long since! Godforsaken place! Turn around! Let me see you're not hurt! God forgive me for risking you –'

'Father! I'm not wounded! It's *you* who's wounded.'

'Not hurt? No credit to me, then. Why did I put you to it? What was I doing, setting you on to fight Talbots? Christ, you're a Talbot yourself! Your mother would never have let me . . . Jesus! Is that blood on you?'

'It's yours if it is, Father. Or English. Will you lie back, man?'

'Oh God quit me, but you're half English yourself! You shouldn't be here! What was I doing, making you a target to your own kin! I don't know how the thing could've escaped me all these years! You've got no quarrel with these scum! You've got no call to fight! I've got no right to lay you open to danger! What would your mother have done to me?'

Fils silenced him with a kiss on the lips. 'Father. Listen. I came here to bring you a present. A piece of news. A birthday present for you. Are you listening?'

'God quit me . . . What? Yes, yes.'

'Castillon's secured in the King's name. The English are driven off.'

'Oh good, good.'

'And do you know who they'll find among their dead? Do you know who the English lost today? To my sword? Do you?'

Victoire raised himself up on one elbow, incredulous. 'To your sword?'

'John Talbot, Earl of Shrewsbury.'

'We blasted him with culverin – he wouldn't die! We had him in '49 – in Rouen – and let him go!'

'And now I've let go his soul. I thought you'd prize his sword for a present. But these monks here wouldn't let me bring it in to you. So we shall put off fêting your birthday till we can do it at Gloriole. What do you say?'

Victoire said nothing. He rested his forearm across his eyes. He plucked the blanket over his face. The cavity of his body was filling up with pride: only a constriction in his throat stopped it from overflowing; it throbbed and seared in his arm and grew so big that it pressed up against his heart. Like a bereavement.

On the brink of sleep it occurred to him that Sir John Talbot must have been even older than him, that Sir John Talbot had been the cause of his marriage. And he began to count how many years it was since he had stopped thinking of Talbot as the Devil Incarnate.

Victoire returned to Gloriole after the Battle of Castillon, but Fils was obliged to stay on with the King's Army until Bordeaux fell in October. By then, any such charitable thoughts towards the memory of John Talbot had long since evaporated. Other considerations had been occupying the Comte's mind: so much so that Barnabas and Flockhart found him irascible and short-tempered, and could not fathom why.

He discontinued all work on the chateau. Three new blocks, planned and half-built, remained a single-storey annexe – truncated – unlinked by the lacy arcading Fils had sketched. There was not so much as a covered-way to save guests arriving on a rainy day from having their boots all mired with loose clay off the yard. The cloisters stood open to the sky – no more than a mask held up in front of the building.

Nevertheless, there was no concealing that the chateau had been all set to become the finest north of the Loire. Everyone said so: all of the two hundred guests invited to celebrate Fils' homecoming. Pyramids of white tufa blocks lined the river bank. Ziggurats of stacked and seasoned timber lay wherever there was a patch of land flat enough not to warp them. A campanile stood on the hilltop alongside the Chapel Saint-Cloud, its bells huddled together at the foot like unhatched eggs at the feet of a white swan.

'Twenty livres a bell,' said Victoire, when they asked him why the bells had not been hung. 'Who can afford a tax like that?' But few took him at his word. The Comte de Gloriole was simply not poor.

Certainly no expense had been spared to fête Fils on his return. So many guests! Such a deal of food! Such a wealth of music! From a carved wooden gallery suspended, so it seemed, from the very vaulting of the great-hall a coopful of musicians showered down notes from lute, hautbois, cornet and flute, while the great-serpent hung over the gallery's side and set the air vibrating with its deep, droning bellow. Shallow bronze dishes larger than cymbals rested here and there on wooden tripods, inviting guests to wash their hands between courses. And bellicose tapestries of conquering heroes – Julius Caesar, Alexander the Great and Charlemagne – rippled their golden fringing in the draught from the fire.

In the hearth, twin andirons depicting a man and a woman supported one huge, blazing log while the iron back-plate had been forged into the shape of a phoenix, so that it seemed to fly up out of the flames towards the heraldic blazon on the chimney breast. And over the mantel hung the newest tapestry in Victoire's collection. It was out of keeping with the other warlike ones and depicted the return of the Prodigal Son. It hid the coat-of-arms on the fireplace. An exceedingly *dangerous* place to hang a tapestry, said some of the ladies, noting how soot from the fire was already blackening the braid.

Twice the size of the original room, the great-hall now sported twin barrel vaults coffered with gilded carvings, each square a deep dark blue spangled with stars. The vaulting had been extended at the time when the end wall was knocked away to incorporate the stairs and two landings at lower levels – terraces set with additional tables for the squires and ecuries. There were presents for both wives and mistresses, and swags of golden autumnal flowers hung dying in tawny nets beneath every window and portrait.

It was almost as if Victoire had something to prove to the remote and tenuous acquaintances who found themselves – rather to their surprise – sharing in Fils' homecoming. There had never before been such an assembly of miscellaneous noblemen and country squires. Those chroniclers of the times, the Court gossips, could be seen counting the candles and reckoning up the goblets so as to give an accurate account whenever they next held centre-stage. They boggled around them, envious of the signs of evident royal esteem, and pondered afresh what favours Gloriole could possibly have done the King. As courtiers went, Victoire was not a notoriously gregarious man. He was normally too absorbed in his peculiar obsession with estate management. So here was a novel opportunity, for those who spent all their time revelling, to revel in this austerely elegant setting of the Sablois chateau, and to wolf down the Comte's food.

The Comte himself was dressed in lavish imitation of his usual clothes: no grand houppelande but a black velvet doublet and loose black wool breeches and a new bearskin of so glossy a black sheen that it added a quite inappropriate and animate menace to his every gesture. Only his own household found it strange that he should have chosen to place his own great-chair on the dais against the end wall – lonely, unaccompanied – where he sat to dispense justice over the comté and not where he sat to eat dinner with Fils.

The ancient Flockhart fretted to and fro, like a canary on its perch, his gnarled claws knocking up against one another in agitation as everyone awaited the arrival of Fils and his troupe. Over the years, the young man had unobtrusively fulfilled Flockhart's function as Master-at-Arms and had thus allowed the Englishman to grow old in his post. Old and anxious and fond, somewhere along the way Flockhart had become so adjunct to the father that he had acquired a fatherly devotion to the son: on some days he even confused their names.

But if Flockhart was confused on that damp October evening, waiting for Fils to come home, it was not because of his great old age. Canary-like he fluttered up against Father Barnabas and plucked at his robe with one claw. 'Why does he scowl so? Why does he sit there like that? Does he think the boy won't come? Why doesn't he go up on the roof to watch for him? Eh? Eh? I would! I would, if it weren't for the rungs . . .'

Barnabas soothed the old man. 'I've been up on the roof, Flockhart, and even I could make out Fils and that horse of his. Up by the alder trees. He must be on the bridge by now.'

The sound of a trumpet confirmed Flockhart happy, and he teetered away to the window, to watch Fils' arrival. He wobbled to the sill, as precarious on his unsound legs as the bricks of an unpointed chimney. Barnabas did not follow: he was busy watching the Comte draw back into his great-chair, nurse his left wrist in his right hand, gripping it so hard that the veins swelled purple and the knuckles whitened.

With an innate sense of ceremony, the visitors fell back from the centre of the room and left a pathway clear for the guest of honour. The ladies smoothed the cornflour more deeply into their temples and throats and eased the bodices lower on their immodest dresses. Fils de Gloriole was spoken of throughout the Loire for the face God had graced him with.

The gossips hoped for a travel-stained, horse-smelling battle garb and two days of beard, but were disappointed. Fils' short felt tunic with its high, stiff collar was stitch-pleated to the shape of his body so that his belt served no purpose and hung low round his narrow hips. The bellow sleeves were slashed, freeing his forearms through the red-lined slits and showing the tight maroon velvet sleeves of the doublet below. He carried his roundlet cap in his hand and its leafy dagging sweeping the floor.

That was all Victoire saw. From the far end of the room he saw only that Fils' long curly black hair was uncovered and that he dragged the dagging of his cap along the floor in a token of humility and respect. He did not get up from the chair.

Fils looked around the room, taken aback by the huge number of people – even more so by the daunting walk and untoward formality that separated him from his father. But he was only momentarily dismayed. As he and his squires advanced towards the dais, he saw his father's eyes assimilate first the sword of Talbot wrapped in a fold of canvas, then the shaggy white chaos of puppies that came spilling into the room behind Fils. Their paws skidding on the slippery tiles, they barged and wrestled and jumped over each other, until their leads were tangled and plaited. They swept the floor with their dangling white ears, and slavered at the smell of so much food and human sweat. They were as woolly and grubby as sheep and, among a crowd of France's finest decked out in finery, far more disreputable. The puppies brought half Touraine into the hall on the underside of their long-furred tails.

'Talbot-hounds, my lord father,' said Fils simply, signalling that his squire should tie them up to the leg of the table. 'And Talbot's sword as I promised you.' The second squire laid the sword on the table, and a flurry of guests pressed forward for a closer look. 'Tokens of love borne you by a grateful and dutiful son.'

The delight was unconcealable. Sure, there could be no mistaking it. Though his father, as a swordsman, never gave much warning of his moves, his laughs, his smiles, still Fils could not have mistaken the insupportable delight that stood momentarily in his father's face. Consequently, though Fils was a swordsman too, and quick to parry as a rule, he mistook entirely his father's sudden move out of his chair.

Fils smiled broadly and spread his arms to receive the embrace. He did not even draw back from the blow Victoire delivered, open-handed, to the side of his head.

ELEVEN

My God Is a Jealous God

The room was in consternation. The guests examining the sword had not seen what had happened and looked for an explanation of the general gasp. Others did not believe what they had seen. Still more laughed it off nervously: a stock joke perhaps between father and son – a domestic comedy.

'Father, are you quite well?' said Fils, with only half a voice. He was answered with a blow back-handed to the other side of his face. He fell back from the force of it and afterwards put tentative fingers to the corners of his mouth as if, like the disciple Thomas, he needed proof of the wound.

'Faction-monger! Self-seeking puppy! Underhanded upstart! Did you suppose I was struck deaf by that cannon ball? Fancied yourself closer to your inheritance, did you? Well, see here! I've the use of both my arms: I can still cuff a sly sneaking son as well with either!'

This was not strictly true. The arm had not mended as flexible or as strong as before. Fils caught the left hand short of his face but allowed it to continue on its way, and held it in place against his cheek like a benison, so that Victoire snatched it away with a snort of disgust. 'What have I done, Father?'

Beside Barnabas, Flockhart sobbed in a whisper, 'Liars! Dissemblers! There's been lies told! He's been maligned. The boy's been . . .' Barnabas took a firm grip on the old man to preserve him from structural collapse, and silenced him with a shake.

Michel de Puy's wife tried to exchange a meaningful and knowing look with her husband, but he was watching too intently to trouble with her 'pssts' and 'hissts' and nudges. He watched with the concentration of a gambler whose last penny is riding on a game of *la morra*. Victoire had turned his son's back to the wall and his fists, knotted in the low, loose belt, jerked him up against the fresh paintwork.

'Will you shame me before all your guests, Father?'

'Before all France if you dishonour my fealty and play fast-and-loose with the King's enemies!'

A different, a comprehending murmur went through the room. Fils said nothing.

'Word reaches me that you went to the Dauphin's wedding. Did you think to keep it hid from me? A wedding expressly forbidden by the King? Did you think word of it wouldn't reach me at last?'

'So long since!' said Fils, unresisting. 'I all but forgot.'

'Ay! Ay, son! I know what you forgot! I know the weakness of your memory! In the matter of fealty your memory's as sound as rotten wood! But I can change that. Before God, and these my friends and kin, I mean to!'

A dangerous, feverish flush came to Fils' face as he hovered between astonishment and outrage. 'What then? "Before God and these our friends and kin." Will you flog me?'

Victoire picked up the Talbot sword. Some of the women screamed. The musicians stared like monkeys through the bars of their wooden cage. Flockhart broke away from Barnabas and went to push his way forward through the press, mumbling, 'I must stop this. I must speak out for the lad. There's some mistake!' But somehow he tripped over the priest's outstretched foot and tumbled down and slowed his fall by clutching at the clothing of those nearest: impatiently they shook off the interruption.

'That's my prerogative. But first I'll have your apology. 'Fore God and these my friends and kin, I'll have your oath and I'll have your penitence. See here?' Victoire had crossed to the chimney breast and, with the point of the sword, lifted the tapestry of the Prodigal Son to show the labelled heraldic device underneath. 'See how your heir's label's blotted out? Well so it stays! Till you show me the penitence of the other Prodigal who wasted his portion on whores! And till I hear your oath made afresh to the King *from whom you draw life*!' He made a sudden sabre-cut which passed so close to Fils that the point might have deepened the pleating in the maroon felt. Fils' blush darkened ten-fold and he ran a hand round his neck like a man washing. The puppies set up a cacophonous barking which obliged him to shout, 'My oath, then! Before God and these . . . others.'

'To serve the King in feu and fealty all the days of his life!'

'God knows, I never did anything less,' said Fils, but with the blade wavering a hair's breadth from his face, and his heir's blazon shrouded out of sight, he knelt and he swore. And after that he swore never more to consort with the Dauphin Louis, and added to his oaths the words of the Prodigal Son: '*Father I have sinned before heaven and in thy sight and am no more worthy to be called thy son.*'

Women burst into uncontrollable tears. Men turned to speak to one another and found their mouths still full of unchewed food, overlooked in the excitement. There was a great drinking down of wine.

'Await my chastisement in the garden,' said Victoire. And Fils – a man of twenty-two, who had killed the Earl of Shrewsbury in the field – bowed with stiff formality to his father and left the room, signalling his army companions to remain where they were. Victoire stayed only to deliver a peremptory apology to his white-faced guests and to beg them make free with his hospitality, before he too made for the door. Mothers swept their children out of his path: he was still carrying the Talbot sword. As soon as both men were gone, plates rattled on to the table, feet clattered across the floor and a gaping, gawping flock as single-minded as sheep pushed and pressed for a view from the several windows. Barnabas offered to help Flockhart to his feet, but the old soldier shook him off and cursed him for a boneless eel.

'Follow me,' said Victoire, overtaking his son and striding fast across the kitchen garden. A vine-covered trellis canopied the gradual incline down towards the walled garden. He lunged ahead into the dappled tunnel, and Fils fell in behind him, at a distance, like a kicked whelp. It would not have been hard to fall behind: the Comte was moving at such a pace.

The year's grapes were gone and the leaves were already ragged so that their view of the house was barely marred as they descended the slope, scuffing pebbles in among the roots of the vines and skidding on the wet clay.

'Well?' called Fils, endeavouring to keep up without breaking into a run.

'Well,' returned his father.

'Was it quite wise to call the Dauphin a whore?'

'Is that what I did? Perhaps I did. You could've contradicted me.'

'God forbid!' panted Fils. 'I'm not so foolhardy.'

They passed between the statues of Flora and Dionysus and into the warmer, still air of the high-walled quadrangle. Out of the sight of the house. Once there, Victoire raised the Talbot sword over his head like a javelin and threw it, point-first, into the trunk of the ancient apple tree. Then he turned on his heel and caught up his son in his arms, like a heathen embracing salvation.

Round and round he whirled him, in a venting of emotion unrestrained to the point of hysteria. He said, 'Let me look at you! Let me look at you!' but could only hold Fils to his chest, his eyes shut so tightly that though he thought he saw the fan-trained trees of his garden it was only the espaliered veins of his eyelids.

At length Fils held him at arm's length and said, with all the feeling in the world, 'For God's sake! For God's sake! I thought you'd kill me!' The words had a sobering effect at last.

'Kill you? I'd as soon kill myself,' Victoire said fondly, holding the narrow, fawn-shaped face between his hands as though to reacquaint himself with every feature. 'By Saint Joseph, son, I've missed you these three months!'

They sat down together on the circular bench at the centre of the garden.

'Was there a letter, Father? Did you write to me and the letter went astray? I walked into that unwarned, you know?'

'I didn't dare trust to letters. I didn't dare risk you showing anything but surprise.'

'Well! I must've shown that in plenty! That and blind fright. It's as well you can still judge your distances with a sword! I thought you'd maim me with that lunge . . . Well? Is there an explanation? Are you going to tell me why you as good as called me a traitor in front of all Touraine's finest and fairest? Is the Dauphin really so dangerous a pond to dabble in?'

'Don't you know?'

'Forgive me, but how would I know, Father? I'm barely acquainted with the man. Not well enough to go to his wedding, anyway!'

Victoire was picking dog-hairs off his breeches and did not look up for some time. 'Show me the man who can recall who came to his wedding, and I'll show you a liar. The Dauphin will never deny you were there. I tell you, the whole substance of the crime won't outlive the week. All that'll be remembered a year from now is that you're the Dauphin's man and I'm the King's. They've seen it split us apart. With their own eyes, they've seen it. I invited the whole world round about. All Tours and Anjou will believe it from today onwards.'

'As they believe their Creed,' Fils agreed. 'And just why exactly have they seen it? Are you ready to tell me?'

Victoire narrowed his eyes, the better to study, branch by twig by bract, each twist and gesture of the plum tree, the lemon tree, the orange. His hands clasped his thighs – as if to stop them shaking. 'Have you heard the news of Jacques Coeur?'

'Yes, but I hardly see . .'

'He's banished. Exiled. His house and goods are forfeit to the Crown.'

'So? You expect clemency for the man who poisoned the lovely Agnès and filched a million from the King's coffers?'

'No. Precisely. You have it. I don't. I expect such a man in quarters and his guts in the fire and his soul in Hell. And where's Jacques Coeur today? On Chios, under a warm sun. The man who poisoned the King's mistress . . . or carried the blame for someone else who did. Someone beyond scope of the King's justice.'

Fils drew in breath so sharply that he choked on his own saliva. 'The Dauphin? Dauphin Louis poisoned Agnès Sorel?'

'God knows. I only say it's what the King believes. Whether whisperers put it into his head or solid proofs, I couldn't say. But because of it I do know there's a time coming when the King will split from Louis for evermore – worse than when Alençon split them. Worse than Louis' marriage split them.' Victoire was silent for a long while.

For three months he had mustered and organized his thoughts towards this end, but it was tiring to search out enough words to express them now. He wished Fils would simply read his mind, as he had when they played la morra. But young men of twenty-two have rarely seen enough of the world to grasp its subtleties or the sophisticated sins of the politician. Out of the corner of his eye, he could see Fils struggle to think with the cynicism of middle age.

'They're not father and son like you and I, Fils. There's no natural affection there. And the rancour goes deep. One day soon Louis will pass into eclipse – and all those seen to favour him will be eclipsed too. Then the King will die and Louis will come from behind his cloud – and shine on those his father put in shadow. I'm not going to let Gloriole drop between the two of 'em. If you value your inheritance, you'll be for Louis and I'll be for Charles. And the whole world will think they knew it all along.'

Fils digested this as best he could. 'And what will become of you when King Charles dies, Father? If Louis thinks you're his sworn enemy?'

'Then I'll have the consolation of knowing you shine as bright in the new King's eyes as I shone in his father's.'

'Yes, but what will become of you?' Victoire brushed the question aside as an irrelevance. 'And is he a man worth shining for anyway?'

'He'll be the King. What more is there to say? God chose him before he was born. He'll be the King.'

Fils was not convinced. 'Are you sure? God choose a poisoner? It doesn't speak well of the Almighty's discretion. I mean, did God truly choose someone who'd clap his son's crimes on an innocent man? Poor Coeur! Jesus, the man mended the whole economy of France!'

'Ah! You remember the man's merits all of a sudden, do you, now you doubt his guilt? Yes, poor Coeur. Now the King has an excuse to seize on a house and fortunes he's always coveted. He's even now melting down the spoons and candlesticks. Coeur's bedhangings are already up around the King's bed. That's why I've stopped the building work here – for fear Gloriole takes the King's fancy in the same way. "My God is a jealous God", you see.'

'And you still think he's a fit man to rule France? A man who'd scapegoat Coeur to get his spoons? If I believed it, I really might up and side with Louis!'

'Oh believe it, Fils.'

'They say he takes young girls three and four at a time. And men too. Is it true?'

'Behind the curtains he filched from Jacques Coeur, I don't doubt it. Though you should never trouble with gossip. I thought I taught you better.'

'And this is the man . . . ?'

'*Yes!* And this is the man God made King. This is the man to whom we owe our fortune and our house. This is the man that made me. This is the man who, on my seventeenth birthday, I saw crowned at Reims and kneeled down and swore perpetual devotion to, with sentimental tears streaming down my face! *And this is the man you swore allegiance to not a half-hour since.* On pain of disinheritance. Because if there's a purpose to the Universe, there's a purpose to the Descent of Kings . . . You're too young to remember. I never told you this before. But once, when you were small, I came close to rebellion. As close as you to me. And I searched my conscience and I found this one obstacle, big as Ossa. If there's an order to the Universe, then there's an order to the estates of man, and you and

I are fixed in fealty to King Charles as others are in fealty to us. There's no sense without it. Nor safety. And where God doesn't bind me to him in fealty, gratitude binds me to Charles. He made me a rich man – and you a rich one after me – if you play the game as I say . . . Oh son, son, why trouble your head with it? I don't understand it either. Maybe greater men need greater sins, I don't know.' He laid his hand on the back of Fils' neck. 'Just consider how they lack the consolation you and I have. We have each other. We have a common purpose, you and I. We have Gloriole – *to be unto countless generations*. And I'd sooner have that than all France and the ruling of it . . . And I'd sooner lose that than have my son hate and resent me as Louis hates and resents his father.'

Victoire stood up, recovered the Talbot sword from the tree, and trudged slowly back to the vine-covered walk, nursing the present between his hands with a tenderness akin to passion, wondering at the sheer arithmetical laws that allowed such volumes of pride to be invested in such a slight young man. He would not put the puppies in with the hunting pack. They would be house-dogs, always with him. Like Fils.

To Fils, watching from the walled garden, it seemed that his father had aged a little in the course of the last hour and that the bearskin stooped a little more under the weight of the future Victoire had irrevocably sealed for himself that afternoon.

He got up and followed, walking a few feet behind as before. 'Father!' he called blithely. 'It *does* console me to be your son and heir and to see what pains you've gone to for my future happiness. But if you ever show me the point of a sword so close as today – so help me but I'll teach you your shortcomings as a swordsman! You frightened the bowels out of me with that thrust!'

The crowds watching from the windows of the great-hall witnessed an embrace then which put them in mind of the tapestry flapping in the heat from the log fire. They assumed that the Prodigal Son had been chastised and was now magnanimously forgiven. They could not possibly know – how could they? – that it was the father who was asking forgiveness of the son.

Next day, Victoire was put to the inconvenience of making Confession. He pondered how to tackle the problem. There was an unusual and awkward silence in the ante-chamber to his bedroom where he and Barnabas knelt face-to-face on the hard floor. He had consolidated the posts of priest and chaplain ten years before. In the end, Victoire decided to test out the ground before venturing into Confession at all.

'And what did you make of yesterday's proceedings, Father?'

'Oh, a splendid party. Excellent music,' said Barnabas ingenuously.

'And the rest . . . ?'

'Ah. That,' said Barnabas sitting back on his heels and directing his eyes a little above the Comte's head. 'Well it seems to me there was a great deal of *theatre* staged hereabouts yesterday, and I was always partial to theatre.'

Victoire too sat back. They looked like two men about to play nine-men's-morris on the flags. 'So transparent, Barnabas? If I am, it'll all have been for nothing.'

'Ah, only transparent to me, sir. You forget, I've been cleaning the glass these ten years. I'd be a wondrous failure if I hadn't made you transparent by now – to myself, I mean.'

'To yourself. And what about the rest?'

'As opaque as lead, sir, if your Master-at-Arms is anyone to judge by. If you've a shred of pity in you, you'll let me put Flockhart's mind at rest at least. It seems like the sun and the moon at war to Flockhart, to think of a rift between you and Fils.'

'That can't be helped. You'd better shrive me for my unkindness, but while Fils and Gloriole depend on it, I'll swear on Holy Writ that we're at daggers-drawn, my boy and I.'

'Then I'd better shrive you for perjury, too, sir,' said Barnabas with smug prudery.

'And you'll swear to it, too.'

'Ah. Well. Swear to it? Well, I don't know. I could maybe *intimate* it. Now and then. If you feel there's a need.'

When wind of the homecoming and the quarrel reached the King, he could not make up his mind whether to be gratified or offended. He cherished a notion of himself as an affectionate and forgiving father, and liked to cite letters and gifts from Louis as proofs of his son's obedient devotion. But given the renown of Victoire and Fils as the Roland-and-Oliver of the battlefields, he could not fail to be flattered. His sound advice regarding sons had after all been taken to heart by the Comte de Gloriole. It was confirmation, too, that that peculiar joy of theirs had indeed been baseless self-deception: paternal love had melted away in the heat of Victoire's more natural love for his royal master. So after some deliberation Charles found a solution with three-fold benefits. He would reward de Gloriole for his loyalty, curb any genuine threat from Fils as an ally of the Dauphin, and deliver a slap to the young man more lasting than the one delivered by his father.

He would marry Fils to Angèle de Belles-Boises. Dauphin Louis had a declared detestation of the family, despite their eminent and unimpeachable breeding, and possibly because of their perfect loyalty to the Crown. And the child herself was so detestable and so far off marriageable age that Fils would be confined to a purgatorial ante-chamber of marriage, hard put to judge which was worse: enforced bachelorhood or the prospect of it ending in Angèle.

King Charles sent the eleven-year-old with a covering letter, urging Victoire to effect the betrothal at once and afford her 'a period of society with Fils, that they might become thoroughly acquainted'. Because she came without prior warning, she arrived when her hosts were engaged, up to their waists, in mending a sluice-gate on the ornamental lake.

Angèle was a trophy from the battleground of her parents' bed. Her mother and father, finding each other too unpleasant to bear, had turned all their attentions on their daughter and lavished upon her every expense and effort to make her resemble them. She was as bellicose as her father and as vain as her mother and, in keeping with her status as a trophy, came wrapped in the hides of dead animals. The coat she arrived in was of otter fur, sleek and flat, her shoes of snakeskin, and her hat resembled the horns of an ox. The dress she had brought for the betrothal had cost the eyes of an entire peacock tail, had the gilded claws of osprey for its clasps, and had ermines crawling up its pelvis from all points of the compass like furry leeches. Even at eleven in the morning she was all flourishes and paint, too, like the plain, wood-carved madonnas that foolish peasants made gaudy and grotesque with gathers of cloth, lurid paint and jewels. Her little fists were arthritic with gemstones. She clenched them in insupportable rage as her sensibilities were subjected to the scene on the South Prospect.

Village women from the estates were sitting along the edge of the lake with their feet and skirts in the water and buckets in their laps, laughing inordinately at the efforts of their dozen menfolk to trap and evacuate fat carp into the buckets. Two white dogs continually jumping in and out of the water shook themselves over the women making them shriek and laugh all the more. Victoire and Fils were up to their chests in water, wrestling with a broken sluice-gate.

At first Angèle de Belles-Boises refused to believe that the two men labouring in the lake were indeed the Grand Echanson of the Court Royal and the heir to his estates. She preferred to believe that Flockhart was the Comte, which thoroughly embarrassed him. 'My lord! My lord Comte!' he called plaintively across the water – a cry to be rescued. Victoire, thinking the Master-at-Arms' failing eyes could not locate him among the rest, waved an acknowledging hand over his head and shielded his eyes against the glare off the water. Angèle swore obscenely.

'Why wasn't I met? I am Angèle de Belles-Boises! Why wasn't I met?' she demanded, standing imperiously on the flight of crescent steps that headed the new lake. 'The King won't like it when I tell him!' As Victoire waded towards her, his shirt-tail floating out behind him, she held out the King's rolled letter as though it, like Cleopatra's carpet, contained the very person of Majesty. She looked him up and down and the same scowl that obliterated her blonde-lashed, tiny eyes drew up her top lip to reveal small, forward-pointing dog-teeth. They put him in mind of the blades on Roman chariot-wheels. As he dried his hands on his shirt-front, she observed, 'I don't *like* men who *do* things,' and was most taken aback when he laughed.

'My humble apologies, mademoiselle, for such an indecorous welcome. The sluices keep jamming open, you see. We were in danger of losing all the fish into the river. But if you want me to read that letter, you'd best come down where I can reach it. I don't have on my breeches.'

With all the distaste of Persephone descending into Hell, she took two steps down. 'I don't *like* fish,' she said.

His face betrayed very little of his emotions as he read. Begging her to make herself comfortable in the house, he bowed with all the civility possible while waist-deep in water, and waded back to the sluice-gate. Her voice came trailing over the water after him: 'Those dogs! My dogs won't *like* those dogs!'

The parchment trembled, and the King's words ran like tears between Fils' wet hands, as he in turn read the letter. Between their thighs, hopeful little fish escaped through the broken sluice – away to the Sablois and the Loire, where hungry pike and perch would cut them off in a matter of days. 'My God, Father. What have you brought me to?' asked Fils under his breath.

And over the lake came the shrill, incisive statement, 'I don't think noblemen *ought* to take their breeches off!'

TWELVE

Solace

'There has to be a simple remedy to this, Fils,' said his father.
'Do let's maintain a level of *sang froid.*'

'Very well for you to say it! She's afraid of you: I don't have
your advantages. Father, please! Appeal to the King for clemency!
Appeal to the parents to take her away!'

'We'll see. We'll see,' said Victoire. But inwardly he felt cornered and resourceless, his powers of ingenuity worn down by the
constant bleat that waited in ambush for him round every corner:
'I don't *like* . . . !'

For two weeks he had been civil, attentive, chivalric, compli-
mentary to the child, and fastidious in his dress. But he was not
accustomed to being criticized for his greyness and shortage of hair,
to being told to shave his beard, commanded to put down his dogs
or asked incessantly when he meant to die and make Fils a comte.
Angèle was like a needle left accidentally by a tailor in the seam of
a garment.

Quite involuntarily one morning he put a thumb to Angèle's
reddened cheek and wiped off the rouge, strangely fascinated to
see the natural colour underneath.

'I don't *like* men who touch!' she said, punching him in the
stomach.

'Then you'd best take Holy Orders, my dear, and disappoint my
unfortunate son,' he said. 'Touching's the way of men.' After that
he adopted his usual suit of black wadding, and grew if anything
more bearlike and rustic.

Angèle did not *like* his looks. She did not *like* his chateau. She
did not *like* his gardens. She did not *like* the idea of marrying anyone
less than a duc. She did not *like* soldiers. She did not *like* the device
of the chicheface and would change it as soon as . . . she was able.
But never again did she ask Victoire when he might see fit to die.
And she avoided him at all but mealtimes. Instead, she dogged Fils'

steps and plagued him with questions about his war, writing down his answers in a little book so as to pass them on to her cousins. It vexed her terribly that he would not put a figure to the number of men he had killed or describe in detail their dying.

'And have you raped many women?' she asked.

He replied incredulously, 'Would you become betrothed to me if I had?'

After some consideration she decided, 'So long as they were English women. Or peasants.'

'Father, she has no moral sense!' protested Fils, rubbing his temples with the heels of his hands. 'You must speak to the King for me!'

'I'll do what I can,' conceded Victoire dubiously.

Fils dropped his voice. 'To tell the truth, I'm burning to marry. But I'd sooner enter the priesthood than marry that . . . that . . . *doll*.'

'It would be best if you waited, and married to please Louis,' said Victoire. But he knew that already he had kept his son unfairly from marriage for five years too long. It was time to cease his search for another Ellen and to settle for a compromise between Heaven and Hell, between angel and Angèle: a woman from the middle-ground of acceptability. In his disappointment for his son he snapped impatiently, 'Have patience, can't you? I'll think of something! No good comes of haste. You *wench*, don't you?'

'As much as you do,' said Fils with crushing dignity. 'I did on campaign, yes. But having found it was . . . not the local custom hereabouts, I've followed your example. So if you could either arrange a good marriage or a war or change the custom – I'd be indebted to you.' Victoire's guilt redoubled. He had assumed his son was at least taking solace with the local women.

A fortuitous summons to attend the King at Tours saved him inventing an excuse to visit Court. And before he left, he took discreet measures to ensure Fils' happiness. He let it be known that young, personable widows who might find pleasure in the company of the Oldest Son would be welcome to dine at the chateau following church on the sabbath. 'Just so long as they don't actually earn their living on their backs,' Victoire added.

It was a luncheon which lived a long time in the communal memory of the estates. The food was manna to be wondered at – though portions were small owing to the unexpectedly large number of women who climbed aboard the wagon sent to wait outside the church. Victoire had supposed there to be some ten or fifteen young war widows on his estates, and in the event three times that number took up his invitation and arrived in the finest clothes their mothers, sisters and friends could lend them. If they were all widows, then some had carelessly forgotten the battles at which their husbands died. And if some did not earn their living on their backs, well, they received a great many male visitors at unsocial hours. The Steward installed himself in the musicians' gallery and drew a diagram of those seated at table, crossing through certain guests with puritanical fervour. He knew the local population more thoroughly than Victoire ever could.

Only one woman was debarred at Victoire's command – a sweet-faced, still-handed girl to whom the Steward had no objection at all. Fils was ready to protest that she was quite the best there, until he saw the depth of distress in his father's face and noted the way his eyes travelled from this thin, dark-haired fawn to the portrait of his wife on the wall. Catching his son's eyes on him, Victoire shrugged and gave a wry grin. 'Some things would be too much to bear,' he said sheepishly.

Fils sat at the head of the table, being agreeable to all indiscriminately and trying not to leave his eyes on any one face for long enough to raise false hopes.

'What are all these *dirty* people doing here?' demanded Angèle de Belles-Boises, scuffing her heelless shoes through the great-hall.

'Eating. It's a traditional feast of the agricultural year,' replied Victoire, hunching his bearskin round his ears. 'It precedes the sowing of oats.'

'I don't like the way those women speak to Fils!' she yowled above the cacophonous bawdy of women enjoying themselves. 'You should put out their eyes for *looking* like that!'

'They're hoping to be touched,' he responded, deadpan. 'It ensures prosperity in the coming year.'

'I don't *like* to be . . .' said the child. But seeing the way the Comte looked at her, she swallowed down the end of the sentence and scuffed her way out again.

Fils opted for a large, handsome woman his own age, named Jeanne (after the Maid of Orléans). Victoire took her aside and rather peremptorily (because of his need to leave for Tours immediately) awarded her a pension of twenty blancs a year 'while Fils' use was exclusive', and a guarantee that any children born to her would have a paid entrée to the Church.

She welcomed her good fortune with clapped hands, a little dancing jig and the cry, 'Oh and we do so *like* your good son, lordship!
We'd have done it for nought if he'd asked us!' He thanked the other
ladies for accepting his invitation and presented them with parcels of
woollen cloth, enough for a dress apiece. Then he put on red livery,
called for his horse, and rode with all speed to attend the King.

After the other candidates had gone, the rolling cart spilling
their laughter and singing like grain from a haywain, Fils and Jeanne
retired to the silence of the second state chamber. A sense of the
sheer unmerited generosity of Life quite enveloped Fils, along with
Jeanne's arms and thighs and hair and enthusiastic peasant brawn.
It was not until she interrupted his labours with a polite cough in
the ear that he was aware of anything else in the world, let alone
of Angèle de Belles-Boises standing beside the door watching, the
little notebook open in her hand.

'I don't think I *like* oats,' said Angèle puzzlingly.

'Desiccated,' said the King lying back among the pillows as though
the weight of his vast nose had finally become too much for his
thin neck to bear. A wicker cage under Jacques Coeur's one-time
bedcover hinted at some injury to leg or foot.

To Victoire's dismay, he found that his invitation to Court
was not part of a general summons, but that he was the King's
sole visitor. And yet there appeared to be no firm reason for the
summons. A name picked at random. A whim. A fancy.

This was the age when Charles ruled by arbitrary punishment
and reward, trusting to a mixture of nervousness and greed to keep
his courtiers to heel. A fortune would topple one day, a mignon be
elected to high office the next, and it had not a thing to do with
justice or desert. It simply kept men jumping, like loggers riding
felled timber down the Loire.

'Did your Majesty have a fall on the hunt?' enquired Victoire.

'What? No! Desiccated. I'll swear to it. Did you hear the rumour?
Alençon has a powder. He brags about it. Put it in a man's laundry
and he's desiccated. He said it! He boasted of it! That's the cause,
I dare swear.' He did not say it with any great conviction, and it
seemed to Victoire that Charles could think of other causes for the
blatant agonies in his leg. Not desiccation so much as dissipation.
From time to time Charles writhed with pain, and all the colour
drained from his face, leaving the nose floating like an iceberg
among the oceanic pillows.

'How does that son of yours care for Mademoiselle de Belles-Boises?'

'Ah,' said Victoire, and gave every impression of a man unwilling to say more.

'Tell me! Tell me!'

Victoire recruited and disposed his words carefully, with military strategy. 'I just wonder . . . no, no. That would be unfatherly of me.'

'Say it! Say it!'

'Well, I simply wonder . . . I can't help wondering whether my son really merited such a great kindness. But maybe that's the jealousy of a disenchanted father speaking.'

'What?! Kindness? What d'you mean, "kindness"?'

'Oh, but the match was an instant success. The child is so very . . . precocious. Fils is quite besotted. He's keen to marry her even before she's breached – as soon as the Church will allow, anyway.'

'She's a saddle sore! She's an enema!'

Victoire rocked his head from side to side. 'I own, she's not to my taste: I never like them young and pert. But my son and I grow more unlike in our tastes every day that passes. Some days I feel it must be pure spite toward me that makes him fawn on her so. But I can barely keep 'em apart. She's hot as pepper for the taste of a man.'

The King gave a cry of pain or rage or disbelief. 'Keep him close-quartered, Gloriole! Keep him under lock and key! Keep him dry as August, Gloriole! Make'm burn!'

'I do what I can,' said Victoire doubtfully.

'See them betrothed, then send the girl home.'

'And she has such strange political views,' Gloriole persisted, so seemingly wrapped in thought as to be deaf to the King. 'It's as though to defy her parents – or to please my son, I don't know which – she's all *Louis*. The child never saw your son the Dauphin, I take it? No? It's just that she seems so *devoted* to the thought of him. We hear nothing else from dawn till dusk but of the *eye* of the Dauphin, the *calf* of the Dauphin, the *wit* of the Dauphin, the *thigh* of . . . If Fils weren't so much of an admirer himself, I'd look for him to break out in jealousy at her overpraising of the Dauphin. La! how I detest children disobedient to their parents' politics . . . But I tire Your Majesty with my tedious opinions. The world belongs to the young, you'll tell me. Men like me should dwell on Heaven and what's past and leave the young to make the future, no matter how it rankles.'

'Devil take their calves and their thighs!' mumbled the King, his cartilaginous face so contorted with pain and spleen that it seemed to have no bones at all. For want of a better target for his spiteful disappointment, he launched out at the only person within reach. *'Why don't you sing, damn you?'*

'Sing, Your Majesty?'

'It's what you're kept for, isn't it? Grand Echanson? These titles. These posts. D'you think they're given for nothing? Can you sing or not?'

Victoire had heard tell of favourites ruined overnight – of purges, of archaic posts abolished, of economies among the red liveries. He weighed up the easiest route to the King's displeasure: to sing or not to sing. 'Forgive me. Your Majesty must show forbearance . . .'

'No I mustn't! Why should I?' demanded the King, turning this way and that in an effort to find some furrow in the bed that was not sown with pain.

'I mean, my lord, that I would have brought a lutenist with me if I'd had the wit to anticipate Your Majesty's wishes. What should I sing?' (Panic suggested to Victoire that the only songs he had ever sung were psalms and marching songs. And it was not the right time for ballads of young love.)

'Sing what you like. Sing what you like, damn your eyes.'

So, for the first time since Fils had ridden in the angle of his arm and gone to sleep to the sound of his father's voice, Victoire sang a Touraine lullaby. In fact, he had a clear, sweet voice, higher than his build implied.

Not for thee the twig and briar;
Not for thee the bed of bark,
Winter's cold nor summer's fire,
For thou art no little lark.

Not for thee the rocky byre;
Not for thee the woolly dam,
Summer's drought nor winter's mire,
For thou art no little lamb.

Not for thee the stony cavern;
Not for thee the icy lair,
Summer's slaughter, winter's raven,
For thou art no little bear.

Warmer than in palace tower,
Safer than in castle wall
Shall my arms fold for thy bower,
For thou art my best of all.

Sullen depression clung to the King's face these days, even when he was asleep. Hated by his mother, disowned by his father, betrayed by his friends and disappointed by his son, there was no possibility that the song held such associations for Charles as it held for Victoire. But vexation or pain or a stray eyelash had gouged a tear from the corner of the King's eye. It ran down into the corner of his open mouth. De Gloriole checked himself dangerously short of pitying the Veryvictorious King.

Somewhere on the road the King's chevauchée must have overtaken Victoire. For as he arrived back on his estates, he was astonished to see his own carriage approach and pass him on the Sablois–Loire turnpike. The child in the rear had spotted him and was shouting up at the coachman, 'Don't stop! Don't slow down! Don't stop! Don't speak to him!' At the sight of his master, the coachman naturally made as if to rein in, but Victoire waved him on, as if to say he would not dream of delaying them on their journey. The lashless small eyes that glared out at him were red with weeping, and the short nose drizzled. Angèle de Belles-Boises had received the royal command to return home. Her piercing cry of 'I don't *like* you!' Victoire took, not personally, but as a generic damnation of the whole human race.

Fils was cock-a-hoop. He was free of Angèle, and he saw marriage – true marriage – no more than a word away. He could barely believe his ears when his father still forbade it. 'To hell with the King! To hell with the Dauphin! I want a wife. I want a son. I want an heir!' he protested.

'And what's so fine about sons and heirs?' his father retorted sourly. 'They're wilful and obstinate and they neglect your estates once they've discovered *free-will*.' He forbade Fils to mention marriage again: 'Not till you can marry to please Louis without inviting Charles's wrath. In the meantime you can vent yourself on your wench and be content.'

'And how long will that be? Till I'm old and dry like you?' Fils retaliated with childish pique. In his agitation he quite forgot

132

to connect Angèle's departure with his father's trip to see the King, and so expressed no gratitude at all.

When he woke in the night, he found Victoire sitting by his bed. Having failed to wake Fils with small, uncertain 'hums' and 'ahems', he had settled into a contemplation of the candleflame and was quite absorbed in his own thoughts. There was candle wax accumulating on the backs of his hands.

'I'm sorry, Father,' said Fils, making him start. 'To sink to abuse.'

'Don't mention it. Don't mention it. Perhaps I have more in common with the King than I cared to think. Some jealousies are . . . perennial between father and son.'

Fils was encouraged. He reverted tirelessly to his favourite subject. 'So you'll let me marry! Consider, Father! You did it! You risked ruin to marry! Why shouldn't I?' he said sitting up in bed.

Victoire frowned. 'Because you have more to lose and less to gain. If there were a woman in prospect the match of your mother, I'd do anything to clear your way. But there isn't. And until there is, you can rest content.' He closed the subject by peremptorily blowing out the candle. Out of the darkness a different breed of voice said, 'I came to tell you. If you'd just listen. I don't think you'll have to wait long. Something in the King's face. I've seen it often enough, God knows. In the field, off it. The King's carrying his death in him. He's dying. Trust me.'

'*The King? Dying?*' The news held such personal promise for Fils and such novelty that his head filled excitably with amazement and wild possibilities. He was fuddled with sleep, slow to remember the implication for his father. They came back to him suddenly like a pain in the gut. But by the time he could muster some inarticulate expression of concern, of anxiety, the more solid blackness had gone from out of the thin, unshifting dark and there was no one else in the room.

Death was patient with King Charles. As months turned to years, Fils felt cheated, hoodwinked. But if Victoire seemed mistaken in his prediction, he was proved wise in his caution. The Dauphin Louis fled France for Burgundy and began to hatch hostile alliances. Charles took charge once more of the tenatory of the Dauphiné, and friends of his son's disappeared like mirages from the King's highway. He sent dispatches, too.

133

Honoured Gloriole,

As the King cherishes your loyalty and well-being, confine under lock-and-key any knight among your household who may think well of Our enemies. These are treacherous times. Trust not to kinship, nor hope for kindness to be rewarded with honesty. Bind fast any who have ever spoken out in favour of traitors. The times admit no bonds of love but those deep-sworn in fealty. I pray you, Gloriole, do not trust to filial obedience or a father's soft words but to locked doors and barred windows . . .

So for a time, Fils lived as a prisoner at Gloriole-sur-Sablois. Flockhart was his baleful, lamenting gaoler. Every evening, to his wife and daughters, he wailed and bemoaned the terrible injustice. It was unnatural, he said, that any father should confine his son on the command of a worthless, knock-kneed French Pretender.

But Flockhart was deaf and his eyesight was failing. His wife and daughters smiled and nodded and got on with their sewing. They could not fail to notice with what ease the woman Jeanne came and went through the 'prisoner's' locked doors, or how many hours Victoire spent playing chess with his 'detainee'. It was even rumoured that ward and warder were seen hunting heron when the weather was good, and were building an ornamental barge in the cellars of the chateau.

Then, in 1461, King Charles VII, called The Veryvictorious, died at Mehun-sur-Yèvre. He starved to death, too afraid of poisoners to let food pass between his pursed and embittered lips.

THIRTEEN

The Kingdom of Caves

'It's insupportable! It's not to be borne!'

'Ah nonsense, son. We've slept in places far worse on campaign. It'll do.'

From the tall golden bluffs of Sablois had come twenty years of tufa. The slabs of pale rock had been hacked and blasted out of the valley's bones, and shipped like pagan monoliths across the water and downriver to Gloriole. There a new castle, emerging like a lovely winged thing from an ugly chrysalid of grey boulders, had split the confines of its dour beginnings and spread itself over motte and river bank and beyond the bridge to the foot of the Saint Cloud hill. Thwarted and incomplete, still Gloriole had clad itself in white tufa like a knight returning battle-soiled from the war and putting on soft doeskin and linen. Only the massive keep, ugly but potent and central, thrust out like an old, stained codpiece left to prove the knight no less a man than before.

In mining the tufa, the quarrymen had made a honeycomb of the yellow rock, pitting the bluff with caves of all shapes and dimensions. No sooner were they cut than the green profusion of the encroaching forest spilled fresh vegetation over the brim. It fell like hair over a pock-marked face, smothered the ragged aftermath of quarrying and obliterated the rock face, so that the caves were no more than dark eyes peering out, or a deeper variegation of green.

Already some of the peasant families made homeless by the delinquent Scorchers had found that by creeping into a cave neither rain nor the worst of the wind's cold could find them. Here they huddled together until destruction and violence faded to a memory and a cave seemed almost a home.

When Louis at last came into his own, he came like a bailiff, grasping possessions, griping up old debts, dispossessing, evicting, ousting, forcing himself on France, as though she would never have submitted out of love. Up were his friends. Down were his enemies. And those who fell under the shadow of his dislike snatched up their lives, like cloaks from beside the door, and fled.

'You see what provision I took for my comfort,' said Victoire, drawing aside the creeper and ducking his head inside the cave. 'I had it in mind all along: stone for the house and a country retreat for my old age. Don't make such heavy weather, Fils. You're unnerving the horses.'

'Father, I can speak for you to the Dauphin – the King, I mean! I've been declared Grand Echanson! God knows, that should give me the King's ear! What could he charge you with? What law would let him do you any mischief?'

'A few furs and fleeces and carpets, and I'll be snug as Moses in the bulrushes . . . King's Pleasure, Fils: that's what law.' Victoire began off-loading the few packages and kegs they had managed to load aboard their saddle horses and two pack animals – the bare essentials of survival. Fils was irritably impatient with his father, then, for numbering among the necessities of life the portrait of his wife, the tapestry of the Prodigal Son, the *Roman de la Rose* and a flute.

'Aesthetics, Fils,' his father had said implacably. 'A man's life's more than bread and carving knives. I've always wanted to learn the flute. And the hanging will serve to keep out a draught or two.'

'Father! This is sheer folly! I can't allow it!'

'Fils, when?' snapped his father. 'Enough. It's time-wasting and profitless. You'd do better helping me unpack. York! Suffolk! Where are those damn dogs? They'll go astray if they wander too far.' But the two white talbots came back between forays, to take bearings, reassure themselves with familiar smells, then range away again, nose-down, like ploughshares furrowing the undergrowth.

Willow and rose-bay willow, ivy and dock, blue convolvulus and white dog-roses, sloe and purple-fruiting brambles cascaded down the escarpment. Random excavations of the rain had left tree roots scrabbling to keep hold of the crumbling tufa. Sloping strata of red and brown rock made bold chevrons of colour beneath the tatting of plants. Only the river at the base of the bluff held back the rampant lusty forest like a restraining arm.

There was no view, however distant, of the chateau downriver. Two bends in the river and a barricade of forest blotted it out so completely that it might never have existed.

Fils propped the portrait of his mother against a side wall of the cave. Having grown up over-looked by the painting, he had in turn overlooked it. He only now paid attention to its detail, to its allegory, to its subject. He knew the dress. It still lay in a press in the first state chamber. Fils looked round the cave. Sunlight had never touched the rear wall: it was a mere impenetrable blackness. He must bring his father a gross more of candles. And yet it was insupportable. It was not to be borne. The man's dreadful cheeriness and acceptance were of no help to Fils. He could not let his father go on with the foolishness.

'Best go now, Fils,' said Victoire's voice from outside the cave. 'Before the horses are seen. Leave me in peace to settle myself.'

Fils ducked out of the cave entrance and in doing so ran his face against a clump of elderberries, so that the purple stain ran vivid down his cheek. Turning from talking to his horse (whom he would perhaps never ride again, perhaps never see again) Victoire was unnerved to see red trickling down his son's face. The ground lurched beneath his feet. The cave shouted foul presentiments through its open mouth.

He covered the space that separated them in two strides and took the face between his hands and then the shoulders and then the entire man within his arms. 'Come often, son! Come often and tell me how the world stands. And who's out and who's in and how the crops harvest and how the works go on . . .' He collected himself a little. 'Not so often as to make for rumours, of course. No one must suspect you.'

'It's futile! Give it up!' pleaded Fils. 'The whole estate will know where you are by tomorrow! And if the King offers a price on your head . . .'

'. . . And you must slander me night and morning, Fils. Think on!' Victoire shook him furiously, as if he could shake a right understanding into him. 'All my efforts were aimed at this. To see Sablois still in Gloriole hands. To see you well placed with the new King. All my comfort's in knowing you have the estates still, and can thrive in them. It's all the comfort I need, but I need it above bread or books or carving knives. Don't undo me now with your buts and bluster.' He felt his son physically submit. Now it was Fils' turn laboriously to put on an imitation of cheerfulness and confidence as his eyes rooted about his father's face.

'Well, and you're sure you'll be warm enough? And you'll

manage with cooking? And not set the forest ablaze? Or sing too loud, so your neighbours hear.'

'There's not a soul for a league, upriver or down. But no, I'll not sing loud – or freeze in my cot, you old woman. I swear it.'

He watched Fils tackle the awkward descent from the cave to the river bank, too encumbered by the horses to turn and wave or lift his eyes from the steep, treacherous track. 'No, Fils, I won't be singing,' he said, and walked slowly back to begin his solitary exile, to go to earth like a hunted fox, to hibernate in a cave until the long winter of King Louis' dislike – or his life – came to an end.

The roof was coffered and corniced with spiders' webs. The hill was a barrow, the caves its burial chambers. He had cut open the mountain to build his chateau and now he was to live like a bacterium in the wound until the hole healed over him, the vegetation scabbed over the injury and he was trapped inside.

Night came sooner than he wanted, sucking the daylight away into the river. He lit a candle and tried to read, but an illiterate draught or spiteful demon blew it out and plunged him into a full understanding of his loneliness. Hellequin's damned souls or a family of wolves howled at a distance, and the trees of the forest, their roots clutching and clawing downwards towards his cave, tossed and whispered, Medusa-haired in the night sky.

'Fils is safe. Fils is assured. Fils will come to visit me,' he told himself. 'I am in Fils. My blood lives in Fils. Even now, I'm laying down my head in Gloriole, I'm drawing the covers over me . . . God quit me, haven't I the imagination to picture it? Can't a man live in his mind? Can't a man give up his place to his own son and be glad?'

'On his deathbed, perhaps,' said the Darkness curled up in the rear of the cave like a troll. 'Your purpose is served. Victoire is dead, long live Fils. Why go on living, Enemy of the State? What's your function? To live like a wild animal? To be a wolf's-head on your own estates? Waiting to be betrayed for a half-dozen sous? Waiting to exchange one cell for another of the King's choosing?'

Fear and cold and hard stone circled him round. Victoire heaped contempt on his self-pity, but he could not help wondering whether, in dividing his substance with his son, he had left himself too small a portion to live on for very long.

He dreamed he had fallen into a well, its sides too sheer and slimy to offer the smallest purchase, the water so cold that it made the blood clog in his veins and opened all the scars in his left arm. He was treading water, tiring, drowning. He called out for Fils, but the water came in at his mouth, full of beetles and spiders. When he woke up, his cry was still echoing round the cave.

The following morning he was unaware of being awake, of listening to the cacophonous rabble of birds outside, until a disturbance to their singing made him crouch up suddenly and reach for the sword beside his bed. There was something moving about near the entrance to the cave.

'Here?'

'Here. Look where the horses were.' Peasants. Futile, he thought, to have tried to keep anything a secret from his peasants. This was their habitat, not his. He had been lying on his sword arm, and it raged with cramp. He cursed the great age of forty-eight, that it left a man no better fitted to fight than a callow youngster on his first vigil.

The creepers twitched. Someone cut down a swathe of nettles with the blow of a stick. He looked at the picture of his wife – and to his great discomposure, seemed to smell a scent reminiscent of his Ellen, all mixed up with the savour of fresh bread.

After a time, there was no more movement outside the cave. He rolled off the bed and ventured through the elderberry archway, tenting the way ahead with small cuts of his swordpoint. But for all his vigilance, he nearly stepped in the bowl of blackberries. He had not expected to be waylaid by picked fruit, but there it was, along with a loaf of bread, a pail of water, a bunch of savonnerie, a faggot of firewood and a large wicker basket. There was no sign of anyone. The birds whistled and chuckled and sang, but there was not a soul about. Even so Victoire, his sword tucked between his knees, eased down his shirt and brushed his hair into some semblance of order, knowing that there might be eyes watching which expected some decorum from the Comte de Gloriole.

First the cave-dwellers and finally every carl and varlet learned where the Comte was hiding from the new King's displeasure. But they did not betray him. On the contrary, they murmured outrage and disaffection from the Crown that it should have driven their protector to lay down his head in a bear-den.

When the notices of reward were posted for assistance in the arrest of the Comte, unseasonably high winds tore them down overnight. When a King's chevalier cried the same announcement aloud in Croix-Rouge, he had night-water tipped over his head. A mistake, the woman said.

The community discovered a God-given opportunity to get to Heaven. They would protect the persecuted; succour the helpless. Their priest, Father Barnabas, appeared to agree with their theology, for he never once urged them from the pulpit to surrender up the missing Comte. And when their feus and taxes for the year – O annus mirabilis! – happened to drop, they knew that God was fully on their side, and smiling on their loyalty.

They cherished the secret of their fugitive, as they cherished the contents of the great-barn, the pannage in the woods, the apples in the press-loft. Any blight or dilapidation would be their corporate loss. Besides, it was the best excitement anyone had invented since the wars, and a great deal more entertaining.

So every morning, Victoire would find outside his cave little votive offerings of food, comfort or decoration: a carved crucifix, a slab of cheese, a fish still twitching from the river, a thumb-stick, a cabbage, a pair of dice. After a time his benefactors did not take such pains to disappear from sight, but would acknowledge him with a departing nod over one shoulder, or stand about talking to each other half a league off, until they had looked him over. They were like children, who play in parallel before they dare play together. They would be there when he went out to cut wood; not close enough for conversation, but showing a friendly interest, a companionable curiosity in his ability to manage. The woman in the nearest cave showed him one day how to milk her goat, beckoning him closer, but never speaking so much as a word. It was somehow understood between them that he should feel free to milk her goat whenever he was passing that way.

But they never paid visits. A moat of deferential awe, a gulf of rank excluded them.

So Victoire thought he must be dreaming when the tread of feet halted outside the cave one afternoon. He could see a woman plainly intent on entering. Still, it was raining torrentially that day; he had got soaked to the skin himself fetching in his firewood out of the downpour. While his clothes dried, he had slept, partly to escape boredom, partly to keep warm under the pelts that now smothered his bed. Outdoors, the sky between the trees was not blue but simply a different, more bilious shade of green, and the run-off had turned the tracks and paths into little yellow cataracts, rolling their pebbles together into new shoals and furrows. The Medusa trees had swallowed up every last bird, and the hiss of their leaves and the hiss of the rain and the hiss of the rolling pebbles merged into a sound so loud as to mesmerize like silence.

The woman puzzled for a moment with the warp and weft of creepers draping the cave mouth, then slipped through. He supposed she must be sheltering from the weather. He was loath to speak, in case she thought the cave uninhabited and took fright. Even when she took off her cloak, she was simply a dark outline for him, a shape against the poor light source. She, it seemed, could see him better and had certainly been expecting to find him there. 'Are you ill?' she said as he emerged from the skins, still drowsy.

'I was cold,' he said.

She came closer. And then he held still, for fear of waking. For this was a dream, no question of it. There was the taupe-coloured skirt, the flocked bodice, stiff as a castle wall, the gathers under the breast. (It was, after all, a maternity gown.) There were the bunched sleeves, the undershift spilling up like spume between the lacings and over the corsage. And the black hair, clinging wetly to the contours of her breasts. And the face – neither aged nor much altered from the one he remembered, given the poor likeness of the portrait and the dim light of the cave.

'Ellen?' he said, and was too late to stop his heart dropping its drawbridge with a painful, jarring thud.

Only slowly, stupidly, hampered by sleep and an adrenal cramping of his stomach, did he realize that she was afraid. She had muddied the dress.

'The beautiful dress!' She held it awkwardly, hitched up in both hands to the height where peasant clothes more usually hung, up round her knees. Her feet were bare. 'The rain! It came over me, good master. I never meant . . . It's only the hem that's dirtied!' She began to take off the dress, clumsy with haste and the unfamiliarity of the fastenings, trying still to keep it up off the stone. 'I'm not insolent! Truly! I'll kneel down presently! When I'm out of it.' He did nothing to ease her predicament. He lay silent in the bed and watched her, his hand on his swordhilt where it had been since he first heard steps on the path – where it rested habitually as he woke. He would not even have realized he was holding it, had her eyes not darted there a third and fourth time. At last she said, struggling free of the toils of the dress and kneeling with it cradled in outstretched arms, 'Please, lord! Don't kill me for soiling it! It was the rain's doing!'

He remembered where he had seen her now: at the selection of a comforter for Fils. He had sent her away for resembling his wife. Now she knelt in his wife's smock, holding out his wife's dress to him, as much in terror of her life as his wife had once been, but for dirtying a frock.

'Oh Fils, Fils. What an idea!' he said aloud in helpless reproof. 'Tell me your name, woman.'

'Marthe was give me, good master – by your ciderman, my pa. But so it please you I'll answer to anything if you'd rather!'

'Marthe will serve perfectly well. Put down the dress, Marthe.'

She looked around her anxiously. The only stool was already draped with his wet clothes. But he had managed to suspend from the ceiling, by two ropes, out of the way of rats, the portrait of Ellen. 'Hang it over the picture,' he said. 'But you must wear it in future and not mind the dirt. It was made to be worn.'

'Faith! It's much too good to be worn!' she exclaimed, hanging up the precious fabric with all the reverence of a priest covering the sanctuary for Lent. The wet tails of her hair were making the shoulders and bodice of the smock progressively more transparent.

He turned back the pelts that covered him.

'Oh!' she exclaimed with unfeigned astonishment, and stared, as her father was wont to stare at a prime consignment of apples. 'You're lovely!'

He took it for flattery. 'I'm old, Marthe.'

But she continued to stare and asked with equal surprise and a genuine interest to know, 'Where, lordship? Nowhere that shows.' Hers was not the social order for flattery. 'They told me rich men don't wane early as poor ones. But maybe it's you being a soldier and a rider and not one as sits about and rots.'

She had asked a whole platoon of saints to help make her acceptable to him. Now her prayers were answered, she continued to recite devout thanksgivings as she lay down against him and flapped close the glossy hides.

It was built like a charcoal-burner's fire that bed – layer upon layer heaped up into a dark, compacted mound. And once a fire was lit at its heart, it engendered such a deal of heat as to temper the softest wood, to maintain combustion for days untended.

The incessant, the ceaseless sensual hiss of rain on the trees, on the river, on the stones lost all its serpentine menace, and softened to the sibilant shushing of a mother soothing her son to sleep. The watching peasants judged it unnecessary and unwise to deliver more presents to the cave, for a day or two at least.

Fils was embarrassed by his father's privation. It shook him to the core that a comte of the *noblesse d'épée* should be forced to live like a pigman. At first he visited often – too often for safety, truthfully – bringing furnishings and luxuries for the cave. But their altered circumstances, their sudden inversion of dependence, stood between them like a prison grille. He could not bring himself to look Victoire in the face. He could not find adequate words of regret and, in the end, failed to find any words at all.

Most men's eyes diminish with age, withdraw into their face, like heads drawn back inside the windows of a house, more indifferent, more insular. But his father's eyes remained full of animated interest in all aspects of Fils' welfare, living vicariously as he was in his son's fortunes. He was forever pressing to know that Fils was happy, and Fils did not find it legitimate to be happy when his father was living like a prehistoric man in a quarryhole under the Forest of Sablois.

He could not bring himself to believe that the gradual change which overtook Victoire was anything more than polished acting, an actor finding more and more tricks by which to lend conviction to his role. Even though it had been his idea to send Marthe to the cave dressed in Ellen's gown, he could not believe that such a small service would render any lasting comfort. Nor that the life of a peasant could ever be tolerated with better than suppressed despair.

Arriving at the cave one day, he was advised by Marthe that his father was down by the river. He recognized the dogs before he recognized Victoire. The talbot-hounds were lying drying on the bank after a swim, like great ravelling pieces of laundry still in need of scrubbing. The fisherman beside them was wearing only knee-breeches and a straw hat, and sat with his feet in the water, camouflaged by the dapple of a willow tree.

For fear his disguise was inadequate, Fils thought to skirt silently round the angler and proceed cautiously until he found his father. But the fisherman turned round, alerted by the sound of grassblades trodden underfoot, and greeted him with the broadest of smiles. As though in continuation of a conversation that had been going on between them for hours, his father said, 'You must plant roses – red and white on either side of the colonnade. White for the Yorkists, red for the Lancastrians. And tend them so they grow up equal. They can wrestle themselves to a standstill over our broadwalk, why not? In commemoration of York thrashing the Queen at Towton, eh? They're mad, these English! They've torn themselves to pieces from the inside out with their civil war. Done better than we could've done with quartering irons. Do you want to swim, son?'

'What? Thank you. No. I don't think so.'

'Well? Don't just stand there sweating. Give me a kiss, boy, and tell me how the world goes with you. Did you see the den? Marthe's wondrous proud of it. She fetches women round to view the hangings and carpets. It's acclaimed the finest cave from here to Troo and back.'

Fils winced at the thought. He caught sight of his father's shirt hanging demurely on a branch. Its lace was torn away at the collar. Victoire intercepted the look. 'An experiment. I was trying to build a bait-trap. In at one end, net the other, no escape. Hey ho. No profit to science there. Are you sure you won't swim? I could show you the eel-traps I've put down. *They* work. One of God's small miracles, the osier and the ingenious eel-trap. Wait! You must stay and eat with us. Marthe can make eels taste like the Bread of Life.' He eased himself off the bank and swam leisurely through the water, breaking its rime of sunlight into black diamonds and dazzle. One of the dogs lifted its head, slowly succumbed to the suggestion, and flopped inelegantly into the river to meet him halfway back from the eelbeds. It snapped at the eels trapped inside the osier basket. Victoire pulled both dog and basket ashore and found Fils sitting nursing the straw hat on his lap. 'Like it? I made that, too. A sworn initiate to the guild of reed- and osiermen, me. Have it! I'll make myself another.'

'I wouldn't rob you,' said Fils handing back the hat.

'Good. I have to admit, I'm fond of it – being my first effort, you know. I'll make you one before you come again . . . God's sake, son, what's the matter? The sun's in Heaven, the honey's in the hive – has someone died or what?'

Fils picked burrs off his hose and shook his head. In a voice as low as Jericho, he admitted at last that he was betrothed to be married. The lady in question came with the King's commendation and a marriage portion of twenty thousand écus. She owned land in Maine and Oise, and her stock was as old as the Loire.

There was a short pause only. 'That's good, Fils. Every man should have the company of a wife. I did wrong to keep you mewed up so long as a bachelor. And the King's choice! You're a made man, Grand Echanson. Is she a beauty? When's the wedding? Where?'

'Two months. At Gloriole. All the county and half the Court will be there.'

'Excellent.'

'But not you, Papa. You won't be there. You'll be here, wearing raffia and eating eel-pie.' He kicked at the basket and one of the eels inside fell out on to the ground. It slithered back towards the river. It repelled him: it had the look of the Serpent escaping back into Eden.

'You can have my blessing now, if you want it, child.' Victoire reached out his hand, but Fils snatched his head away.

'Your name won't be spoken. It won't be mentioned that you exist. You'll be a space in the air of your own home for strangers to walk through! What's it to you if she's a beauty? *You* won't be setting eyes on her!'

Cold after his swim, Victoire plucked his shirt from the branch and put it on. It adhered to his wet body. 'You want me to see her? Bring her out hunting partridge and I'll view her from a treetop – like Zacheas up his sycamore tree spying on the Saviour.'

'*Oh Christ!*'

'That's the man. That's your benefactor. He and the excellent King Louis, whom God defend.'

'Papa, how can you say it!'

'*Because he's the King, man!* Haven't I taught you anything?'

The river ran by, its warp and weft perfectly even but for a few broken reeds like pulled threads where its selvedge snagged against the banks: the industry of a tireless loom. But it was satin to one man and sacking to the other.

'I can't stay, Father. I'm holding court of assize this afternoon.'

'I know it. You're trying my little neighbour Monsieur Poulet for debt, aren't you? Want some advice from a reliable witness? Poulet does owe Vache what the bastard claims. But it's the interest on a loan. And what rates! That man Vache makes the Pharisees look like philanthropists. Tell him *Pecunia pecuniam non parit*, then ask him if he still wants to proceed against Poulet. That should frighten him off. There's more than Poulet have been fleeced bare, poor creatures. Lord, I hate usurers worse than ever, now I see them from the underside! . . .' He broke off, seeing that his advice was going unheard. 'Ah, Fils! A bridegroom always has doubts on the eve of his wedding! It's a thing to be rejoiced in! I rejoice in it.

145

I'll rejoice as well here as yonder. So pray don't look for grievances where there's none to be found. And as you love me, don't question God's disposition of His assets.'

They embraced, and Fils emptied his pockets of the brignole cherries and dragées he had brought. 'I'll give them to Marthe,' said Victoire delightedly. 'She'll think she's in Paradise.'

'As you shall surely be before me,' said Fils self-pityingly.

'As I am already on days like this, when my son comes to see me,' returned Victoire. 'Think on, now. Red and white roses along the colonnade. Oh, and bring some cork another time, if you can remember – for the luxury of a fishing float that works. I've caught nothing but a roach all morning, but what couldn't I do with a piece of cork to my name?'

Fils toiled away up the river embankment, sweating under the weight of his costly clothes and the cloak concealing them. He did not yet dare trust the peasants' loyalty. There was a lot Fils did not dare believe, thought Victoire, as he returned beneath his canopy of willow, and the ermine-shaped shadows rested cool on his sunburnt shoulders. Fils saw his father as exiled from all the things that mattered most in life. And yet here were Court pomp and ceremonial enough for any man: it simply took hours, days, weeks of sitting and settling to see them: the bloody escutcheons of the poppies, the silver shields of the lakes emblazoned with water lilies, the cardinal purple of the thistles. Each reed in the river was crowned with its own heraldic device of seeds, and the banneret reflection of bulrushes fluttered in the water. The Court gossip of natterjack toads started up near by, and bright-liveried birds flashed to and fro on missions of critical importance to the welfare of the State. Come King, go King, live man or die, this complacent tyranny of beauty would reign everlastingly, and grant asylum to any exile fleeing through its gates.

FOURTEEN

The Nativity

Next winter the liquid river turned to rock – at least to thin, pale slates, then to paving stones, then to great slabs of frozen water that tumbled against each other into a moraine of boulder-ice. Overglutted with cold, the Loire, Cher and Sablois choked on ice and voided a dirty, jagged rubble of it on to their banks. Gloriole barges were crushed between frozen jaws, and the toll-chain, wrenched by deep sinews of cold in the river, was torn out of the boom-tower wall like the umbilical cord from a badly delivered child.

On Christmas Eve, Fils de Gloriole took delivery of a nativity commissioned from Court painter Jean Fouquet. He hung it at one end of the great-hall, in the space vacated by the portrait of his mother. Without giving it careful thought, Fils felt it faintly appropriate that a madonna should hang in place of Ellen's portrait. She had, after all, been cherished with all the reverence of holiness by his father.

The painting invited the praise of every Christmas house-guest. The household, summoned together to view it, gazed with such speechless wonder that the only sound was of Flockhart's wife describing the piece to her purblind husband.

A smiling madonna, her heart-shaped face surmounted by a horned headdress of silver decked with gauzy streamers, sat amid the pillows of a great bed, the covers concealing one breast but not the other, from which issued a small constellation of stars. Her hands were pressed together in devout prayer around a jewelled rosary which lay glittering on the figured brocade of the coverlet. The crisp white sheets were tight tucked, and cherubs full of awe drew back the tapestry hangings to let in shafts of heavenly light. Doves rose on updraughts of song hymned by a trio of angels, one with a lute, one with a cornet and one with a portable organ, its ribbons fluttering multi-coloured. The walls of Mary's chamber were hung with tapestries depicting scenes of Old Testament prophecy, and a little fire glimmered in the grate at which a lady-in-waiting had just filled a copper warming pan with comforting coals.

There stood Joseph, his lukha robe trimmed with bright fox-fur and his eyes turned towards Heaven – a patriarch with fulsome white beard and cheery cheeks. But even Joseph was dwarfed by the patron-figures who stood round about him – the men who had paid for the painting. Incense wreathed upwards from a prelate's censor.

Smoke from the snow-sodden wood choked the small confines of the cave. Those inside blundered through it, coughing and hawking, wiping their running noses on the backs of their arms. A woman pushed Victoire aside because his bigness, bundled up in layer upon layer of wrappings, blocked the heat from the fire. He was still cold, for all his cloak and bearskin. The very earth of the embankment seemed frozen to the marrow, and now and then the wind pushed brazenly in at the door and sent the smoke cowering back into the rear of the cave. Bats, like hanged goblins, were illuminated by a flaring of the fire, and any heat was swept away by the wind.

But Marthe, naked on top of the straw-strewn bed, did not seem to feel the cold. Sweat rolled down the red apoplexy of her face and over the purple-veined grossness of her distended belly. Her fists pulled tufts of wool from the fleece under her and colostrum dribbled like pus from her bloated breasts, much as the obscenities and prayers spilled from her mouth. Between pangs – those spasms of violence in which her body convulsed and the women surrounding her bellowed out their bullying commands – she addressed her prayers to the mildewed tapestry of Tamburlaine the Great that hung opposite her: she had always mistaken it for God's triumphant Second Coming. The mad cacophony of screams, orders, yelping dogs and his own unanswered questions hammered down on Victoire out of the spidery void overhead.

They did not want him there; they had done everything they could to oust him. But outside was nothing but a world of cold gnashing at him, and even when he did go out into it the pain of the cold did nothing to ease the frantic, impotent guilt, the vicarious agony. He kept coming back to the cave. He was, after all, responsible for this suffering.

Between her legs the bloody mouth of Hell gaped and steamed. What had possessed him to do this twice – to inflict this torment on the two women that had given him most – the two women he cared for most? There were not pains enough in Hell to requite him, a mere man, for this, for causing this.

The Three Magi knelt demurely on the hearthrug and offered up gold, frankincense and myrrh on silver salvers. Of the three, Melchior physically outscaled his companions. His face was that of Fils de Gloriole. Within the curve of his arm he sheltered the patrons – one his father-in-law, one the Bishop – both of whom, by offering to share the cost of the commission, had made plain their desire to be included. The midwife (who bore an enhanced resemblance to Fils' wife) smiled in a preoccupied way over their heads and held up a tiny throne from which a serenely beatific baby, haloed in gold, blessed the onlookers with two fat fingers. Beyond the window, bearing (inaccurately) the etched initials of Fils and Francine, the fields and towers of Gloriole stood piled, without perspective, in a Jerusalem mountain of splendour and status.

The householders looked for some sign, some disguised symbol of the Comte, but Fils knew well enough when to sacrifice sentiment to common sense. It was as if Gloriole were already in the hands of its heir, as the heraldic blazon over the fireplace indeed implied it was.

The household returned to its task of preparing for the Christmas festivities and contending with the fearsome cold which laid siege to the chateau. Fils, though his time was his own to stand and admire Fouquet's excellent work, found he could spare it no more time than the servants. Instead he stood by the long windows looking out at the leprous canker of snow and hoar and ice, at the transfixed and tortured river, at the buckled ornamental lake which had smashed its sluice-gates like matchwood.

Upriver, out of sight, cut off by drifts horse-deep and by a new geography of ice, his father fasted in frost. Over his head, the great black troll of the forest scrabbled at the earth with rooty claws, searching for sustenance. Wild beasts, less merciful than any bailiff, were evicting peasants for the sake of their lairs, and the sky rested so heavy on the bristle-shoulders of the trees that they would crack and concertina all of a sudden, with a noise that carried miles.

Fils wanted, like Wenceslas, to carry meat and fire to the forest fence. But he had the vigilance of a wife to contend with these days. She was a patriot, she said. She cherished the image of the old Comte as a foul demon, a nameless wolf's-head to be found and destroyed. 'As soon as that treacherous old dog is put down . . .' she would say.

Fils looked again at the picture and resented the factual inaccuracy of his wife holding aloft a baby. There was no baby. He believed the woman Marthe must be near her time. But without a child of his own within the chateau and unable to be Wenceslas and go bearing gifts, Fils was dull to the spirit of Christmas.

Christmas, it seemed, was unable to attend the festivities at Gloriole-sur-Sablois that year, owing to the weather's inclemency.

'You have a daughter, good master,' said the midwife, dirty-handed and violent as she dragged the filthy object from its repulsive lair – like a gamekeeper culling badger cubs at the mouth of a set.

'Christ, Christ, Christ,' said Victoire. 'We have a daughter, Marthe, we have a daughter.'

'So if the King's men ever come . . . they may let her live?' She panted. She burrowed into his clothing; she could feel the cold now, though the wind had changed direction and the fire began to win out against it. He had not realized before that such thoughts troubled her; she had never mentioned them.

'No, love. No slaughter of the innocents, I swear it.'

'And you'll let her be a Daughter of Joy and go to Heaven?'

'All in good time. All in good time. Pshah, Marthe, she's only just arrived! Let's not hurry her away.' And she smiled and looked his face over as if it were a wonder made everlastingly new.

The baby they gave into his arms in no way resembled the purple vernixed rat evicted from his woman's belly. Though the midwife lacked courtesy, grace and a good wash, she had a certain innate sense of ceremony and gave him the package as though it contained a gift of immeasurable worth. Indeed, not the most precious of kingly gifts could have seemed as beautiful as that miracle-in-adversity, that whiffling, blarting, curled container for a mortal soul presented to him wrapped in his wife's shift.

Gradually the crowd of dark-clad women withdrew, bidding him good fête. The firelight gained a better hold on the cavern and the dogs stopped their howling and barking, and settled to a glimmer of eyes and pale fur in the corner. Marthe went to sleep in his arms.

And it seemed to Victoire that Christmas was more real and more to be celebrated than ever it had been when he was a child in Poictou or the Comte de Gloriole.

He was wrong in thinking there would be no slaughter of the innocents.

By New Year Marthe was feverish: some infection attributable to dirt but attributed to the Devil. It was not grave: she fed the child, she got up, she waited on Victoire. But she never complained of the cold, because of the false summer in her blood, and the false summer betrayed her lowered defences to the persistent siege of winter.

Fils said: 'Father, I'm sorry to be so long in coming. It's Francine, you know. She watches me all the while . . . Papa?'

Victoire said: 'She was well. She got up. She waited on me. I'd never have left her otherwise.'

'Francine would've suspected something if I'd said I was going riding in the freeze. It wasn't likely I'd risk the horses. I thought for a while she did suspect . . . Look I'm sorry your woman died.'

But Victoire only said: 'It's the wood. It's so scarce, you know. It takes so long to gather, and it burns so fast. But I wasn't gone beyond the daylight hours. And when I came back, I found her. Beside the baby's crib.' He sat on a log beside the river. The water was running again, crazing the ice then melting each fragment into a round, circular wafer which the next wave swallowed down in communion with spring. The bank was in mourning – scorched black around his feet, crushed too hard to be resilient as the woods were resilient, as the fields were proving with their patches of swampy green. Trees uprooted by the thaw hung above them at outlandish angles, the mats of their root-systems dangling threads of earth. They intimidated Fils: he wanted to move away, but his father did not seem sensible to the threat of landslips or falling timber. 'Have you seen the girl? She's quite fetching – for a baby. We call her Vérité.'

'Vérité?'

'Yes, man, Vérité. As the greatest of the virtues. Marthe asked me, "Which of the virtues do you love best?" "We'll call her Vérité, then," she said.' The recollection swallowed him up. He seemed to forget his listener altogether, staring at the palms of his hands as though they contained the past in sandy grains which must not be suffered to drain away.

'In all honesty then, Papa, I must tell you . . .' Fils began. 'There are men – of a like mind with me . . . We've talked often – a great deal. But now the time's past for talking . . . There's Charles, Duc de Charolais . . .'

'He's Burgundian,' murmured Victoire, thus giving the misleading impression of a man paying attention.

'Yes, but a sound man with sound notions. And Charles, Duc de Berry . . . The King's own brother, man!'

'Well, and what of him?'

'He's of a mind with me. Things can't go on as they are. I should never have allowed all this!' The copious sweep of his arm took in river, bank, and quarried embankment. It was intended to encompass the plight of his father, the injustice of a good and loyal man forced to hide away in a rocky, cliff-top hole. He had neglected to notice how his father, over the years, had not just lived like a peasant but had become a peasant – developed a corporate identity with the other peasants on his estates. Victoire assumed that Fils was talking about the peasants.

'You're right. Their lives are too hard to bear. "Like men wading across a lake, chin-deep" . . . who said that? The smallest dip in the slime and down they go. Always looking for the next meal. Always taxing their brains and bodies just to stay alive . . .'

'The League for Public Good we've called ourselves, and we mean to –'

'I'm glad. I'm glad. The name won't matter, so long as you do something. I never want to see another winter like the last. And I so helpless to help. And Marthe . . . And I so helpless to help . . .' He wandered away again into the snowy tracts of a remembered Christmas. Thus he entirely misconstrued what Fils meant when he spoke of the League for Public Good. And his son entirely misconstrued how his father responded, and took it for encouragement to commit treason.

Perhaps in his heart of hearts Fils misconstrued nothing. Perhaps he sensed the danger – like a man walking out on to the melting ice of the Loire. Perhaps he did not really want to reveal to Victoire that he was involved in a plan to overthrow the King. He had come intending to lay the plan before his wronged father like a New Year present. And yet he took the secret home again virtually intact. His father had, after all, taught him perfect loyalty to kings and to fealty, and though it was his father's plight which had undermined those precepts, Victoire was not a man to smile on treachery. Ha! To grace a bastard peasant child with the name 'Vérité' signified as much.

It had not been hard, following that desperate winter, to find a wet-nurse to keep the child alive. Newborn babies had died in plenty. A natural culling of wildstock, as some noblemen saw it, drawing up their annual inventory of goods and chattels, game and

152

serfs. A slaughter of the innocents, as a free-thinking atheist might have blasphemously looked on it. A personal responsibility, as the Comte de Gloriole saw it. But then he was haunted by one particular death, by the death of one insignificant peasant woman in the cave where, despite being feverish, she had waited in tenderest solicitude on a greying, elderly bear.

He no longer slept with his sword by his head. Three years on, after all, it was not possible to sustain the nervous adrenal reflexes of a man in imminent danger. Besides, he trusted his neighbours, was dimly aware of their love for him though he was quite unable to understand it. The daily routine of bargaining with Nature for his fill of food, safety, survival and beauty left him so legitimately weary that he slept soundly, trusting to the birds to wake him.

Nevertheless, he dreamt that night of the taking of Gloriole. Even as he slept, he wondered why he should be put to the trouble of once more capturing its keep.

The donjon seemed far higher now – extended into a Babel Tower reaching towards Heaven. The spiral staircase wound interminably upwards, draining his heart of its stamina, filling his legs with molten lead. Still he had no choice but to continue climbing at a run, for his son's voice was calling him from the top of the lightless shaft, and the whole issue of his heredity hung on successfully securing the keep.

In the small chamber at the top, he emerged into a light so bright that he had to shield his face with his arm. But it was simply a matter, wasn't it, of running-through the rat-shanked English boy and taking possession?

His lunge was too thorough to be halted, and the light too bright for precise identification. So the blade had passed clear through his son's throat before he could recognize the black eyes, the doe-like narrow features, the shining black locks of hair escaping their plait. Fils tried to explain that his hands had been held, his weapon confiscated, but only the smallest sound came to his lips, for his windpipe was cut through and he could not find words . . .

Victoire woke with his arm already raised to fend off the light of the torch thrust into his face. His hair was wet with sweat. His own swordpoint was pressed to his naked chest, just above the covers, just over the windpipe, and the cave was full of men. He recognized Barnabas among them, flustered and flushed with womanish anxiety. 'Good morrow Judas,' he said, and Barnabas blushed peony-red.

'Victoire, Comte de Gloriole?' asked the soldier standing over him. Clearly the man, confronted with this, this *caveman*, was far from sure.

'All's well, Victoire. Nothing to fret about,' said Barnabas, undermining the words by the way he chewed on the side of his hand.

'Long live the King!' exclaimed the soldier, and his swordhand was trembling slightly.

'Amen to that,' said Victoire.

It was a childish, ludicrous way to decide whether to kill a man or spare him, but then the troopers in the cave were bewildered and unhappy. For three years they had thought of Victoire de Gloriole as a treacherous fugitive. Now they had been told a different story.

'We hear you were accused wrongly.'

Victoire did not feel the need to say anything: let them fumble their way without his help. He wiped the sweat out of his hair, but the dream clung, residual.

'We hear you were slandered by your son.'

Victoire looked to Barnabas for a translation. 'Slandered?'

'Slandered, my lord. By your son. The traitor,' said the priest. 'The traitor, yes.'

'But we have held him fast at Loches now, your lordship,' said the sergeant, reversing the sword so that the hilt drooped over Victoire's face. 'He has confessed to being in league with de Berry and Charolais. I suppose he seeks salvation by righting the wrong he's done to you all these months . . . Though why you lay down under it – let him do it – never swore your innocence – well, it baffles the likes of me, sir. A simple man like me.'

Victoire barely noted him. 'What's Loches? That's the chateau of the Sorel woman, isn't it?'

'No more, sir! It's State Prison now, sir. Didn't you know that?' He laughed that Victoire should be so much out of touch with events.

Victoire looked to Barnabas for contradiction. His question, his whole carriage as he rose from the bed was a plea for contradiction. 'Where is Fils?' he asked. The priest's face filled up with apologetic regret.

'As the gentleman said. At Loches, my lord. Arrested for conspiring against the King with the Ducs de Berry and . . .' It was more than the priest could bear. To be shot through with questions by those bronze eyes like Sebastian shot full of arrows. His heart

154

had been breaking all morning. Unable to explain in front of the soldiers, he writhed in his bonds of secrecy.

'And you say all's well, do you?' said Victoire raising his eyebrows in an expression of mildest surprise. But as he quit his cave, without prospect of returning, he said under his breath to Barnabas, 'Never look to me more, priest.'

FIFTEEN

The Room of the Question

'He's between the Ordinary and the Extraordinary Question,' said the sergeant cheerfully. Dressed and mounted, the Comte de Gloriole presented a more plausible figure of nobility and the officer was gradually adjusting to the idea of his innocence. The troop of horse come to bring Victoire news of his exoneration adopted the role of an escort now, falling in behind the two lead horses.

'You'll have to be more plain, my friend,' said Victoire. 'I don't understand the expressions.'

Here the soldier was on familiar ground, and warmed to the subject. 'Well, the Ordinary Question, that's more of an enquiring kind of a question. When they need answers, so to speak. Your son, now, your son for instance, let it out that he'd defamed your lordship, under the Ordinary. And admitted to his treason, of course, though he didn't have many names to give, so I gather. That's no great matter. The rest of the gang'll be taken soon.'

'He's admitted to treason?' said Victoire. The sergeant was not to know that the strange lack of bass register and the even, mechanical intonation to the voice were anything out of the ordinary. 'What's left to say, then? No call for another "Question" as you call it.'

The man pulled a quizzical face. 'You're right: it's an odd use for the word, but it's just how the label grew up. Ordinary. Extraordinary.'

'We are talking tribunals here? Court hearings and depositions?' conjectured the Comte, but a hysteria of terror persisted in gushing upwards inside him – a geyser of adrenalin continually recycled by aching guts and a staggering heart.

'Tribunals, sir?' said the soldier, puzzled. 'No, sir. Just the torture.'

He was disappointed then. The conversation lurched to a halt just when he had been gaining confidence. Gloriole-sur-Sablois was in sight now. When they reached the gates, the sergeant would have no more excuse to ride shoulder to shoulder with a comte: a thing to tell his wife and friends that would impress them. He tried to slow the pace, but Gloriole seemed eager to get home. Understandable after three years in a cave.

'You were going to tell me the difference between the Ordinary and the Extraordinary Question,' said the Comte casually just as they were on the point of parting. The sergeant had not been invited in: it consolidated his poor opinion of the senior ranks: ingrates to a man.

'Oh well, sir. The Ordinary Question's a questioning sort of a torture, as I said – when there's information to be got from a man. Extraordinary, that's for its own sake. Only for special misdemeanours. For those as give particular offence to the King, so to say. They'd maybe let you watch it, if you'd a mind. You've quite a score to settle after all . . . Though Loches is a long way off, and you must have plenty other things to occupy you. God-by-you, sir.' He added dubiously, 'Plenty will rejoice in your restoration, I'm sure.'

They came out to meet him clutching little wisps of straw. As if he were King. But he spoke not a word more to them than secured him a fresh shirt and a horse. Barnabas buzzed round him like a fly, but he swatted him away. The air was hot, like a cheek, with embarrassment. Within the household, circumstances were too dire to acknowledge. Panic had been postponed – plastered over with a terrible congealed normality in which everyone kept to his work station but did nothing. Soldiers had come and taken Fils away: where and why did not bear discussing. No matter. The Comte himself was restored to his chateau. He could come home and tell them all was well – that the Old Order was re-established, even if it meant erasing Fils from their thoughts. All they wanted was comfort and direction.

But then, when he came – fetched back from oblivion – they did not recognize him. They said his mind had probably been turned by living in the caves. They resented the lack of reassurance. They said: *he isn't the man he was. Now God help us.* All he did was change his clothes and quit the chateau again, leaving them to their fears and uncertainties.

Twice he missed the road to Loches. It was three years since he had sat astride a horse and his own was dead. This beast did not know him, made no allowances for his ineptitude, cared nothing for his haste. The muscles of his inner thighs cramped and bruised.

Bare-headed now, in the restoration of his grandeur, his scalp burned under the late summer sun and his head swam with unbidden and unbearable thoughts.

He could not get it out of his mind. Last he knew, Loches had been known as the Chateau de Beauté, 'Beauty's Fortress', for housing little Agnès Sorel at the King's pleasure. Now Sorel was dead of poisoning. And Beauté was poisoned too, as surely as if the water of the Cher had stagnated and ringed it round with pestilential doom. When he reached Loches he barely dared go in.

Louis' State Prison stood well away from Sorel's hall – a building on a different scale, of a different substance and character: as different as male from female. Its vast square keep was pockmarked with the portlogs left by the scaffolding. Its slabs of nerveless rock were pierced through with tiny windows as an ox's skin is pierced with pores. It was a well-shaft driven upwards to tap the sky of foul water.

Afterwards, he could not forget the noise of wings beating inside the tower – pigeons and rooks roosting in the cratered vastness of walls, doomed like Dante's Damned to a perpetual vortex, flapping in everlasting discontent from sill to sill, ledge to ledge, up and down the staircase. Those staircases wound both upwards towards the watchtower and down into the ground. For the King's most prized prisoners were not entrusted to the frail wrappers of twelve-foot walls but were planted deep in the rocky ground. Like the dead.

'I am the Comte de Gloriole. You have my son here. If not him, his body.' It cost him no effort to conceal his emotions: they were imprisoned fast and deep inside him, walled round with the conviction that this was all a mistake, none of it was happening: his son was not here at all. But the Chief Warden of the gaol did not contradict him. He simply led the way to a great wooden door studded with iron, set in the Martelet. He spent an infinity of time lighting a torch, then started confidently down to Hell. 'Does he live still? Or is he dead?' The place, after all, smelt like a charnel house.

'Oh, he lives, sir. He lives. We're not such heathens that we work on the sabbath. He's down for the Extraordinary, but we don't begin on the sabbath. You wouldn't expect us to begin on the sabbath, would you sir? But maybe you only came for a body, sir?' He stopped on the stairs, blocking the way, fearing he would disappoint the Comte by showing him a live prisoner.

'I have no use for a body once the soul's out of it.'

The gaoler laughed nervously. 'The prisoner has no use for it now, sir, believe me. He'd sooner be out than in.'

Orphean strains of lute music floated preposterously up on the stench. And laughter, too.

'Oh, that's the Infante, sir. Prisoner of war. Too valuable to part with, but a very *respectable* gentleman. He's on privileges naturally. His jester's a wonderful rogue, sir. A dwarf from Milan or some such. And he has a minstrel, and a tutor visits to teach him French and music. And he has a little stove, sir, and paints. And books.' A banshee wail pierced the ear like an awl – a scream from the Pit below. 'And a monkey,' said the gaoler laughing good-naturedly. 'We make 'em as comfortable as things allow when they're on privileges.'

There was a way then. Money, as infallible as ever, could serve to cushion Fils against the worst rigours of imprisonment, protect him from brutality. His warders were open to bribes. It was a comfort.

'We've kept your son in the Room of the Question between Ordinary and Extraordinary. It holds their mind to the thing in hand. The Stirrup does especially. Besides, to be honest with you we mislaid the key to the Stirrup. I hear the turd had you banished to a cave these two years.'

'Three. Three years.'

'You must be vexed to have spawned him. Never fret though, sir. We'll put it home to him with a will tomorrow. Sorry: I'll have to make bold to examine your person now, sir, and relieve you of your blades, sir.' He took Victoire's sword and dagger, while the monkey and the dwarf laughed somewhere over his head.

The door of the Room of the Question was a square lattice of timbers thicker than a man's arm – a portcullis side-hinge-hung, with a trench beyond. A rope and pulley outside the door let down a plank bridge across the trench and, when the cell was not in working use, drew it back up against the door. A shaft which might, on some summer noon, have delivered one ray of sunlight from above, dropped a single patch of grey no bigger than a cat on to the straw-covered ground inside. Sun's warmth had never penetrated the clammy cold. Victoire could see nothing and no one at all.

But at the noise of the door opening, something scrabbled in the straw and cried out the *Nunc Dimittis* in French: '*Now lettest thou thy servant depart in peace . . . Now lettest thou thy servant – now lettest thou thy servant . . . Ai Jesu! It's not time yet!*' It was not possible to fix the source of the sound, for it echoed off all sides of the round cellar. If it had not been for the gaoler's torch thrust past his head with a belch of smoke and a reek of pitch, Victoire would have trodden on his son.

The torch was rammed into a bracket on the wall: its light suffocated a few spans from the flame. The door closed again, drawing up its bridge like a contemptuous lower lip. 'Call when you're done with him, your lordship!'

Fils was spreadeagled naked on his back, his feet held off the ground and wide apart by the rings set into an iron bar padlocked between two brick plinths. He was gibbering with cold. Victoire could see the outline of his mouth, white with over-licking, but not his eyes which were shut tight. His hands being free, he had made shift to sweep together a low wreath of straw round him, and the whiteness of his arm tended it as the neck of a brooding swan instinctively bends and sweeps to tend her nest. But at the disturbance of air as Victoire crouched down beside him, he clasped both hands over his genitals, and his teeth showed white and clenched in a grimace of purest fear.

'*Son! Son! Son!*' It was a noise to chill the monkey's blood and set the dwarf's mind to jokes of Hell.

'Put out the light, Father,' said Fils after a great length of time. 'Don't see me like this.'

'See you? Blood and tears! Would to God I could see you! God curse my eyes that they won't let in the sight of you!' And he tried with the touch of his fingers to see the plight of his son. There were pools and patches that might have been sweat or urine or blood – all icy cold.

'Don't touch me!' yelled his son, and the iron bar scraped in its sockets. 'For the love of God, don't touch me.'

'I'll fetch the light close,' said Victoire. But as he rose, Fils snatched hold of his shirt-front, pulling the lace adrift. He drew his father's face down, kissed it and said in a low, quick whisper, 'Let it alone! Speak soft and keep distant. They'll be watching,' then pushed him sharply away.

It might be true. Victoire could see the shape of two figures beyond the door, their heads leaning close in to the grille. When he looked in their direction, they moved quickly aside and out of sight. Fils continued in whispers. 'Best lay on the reproach and curses, Papa. They won't trust to my word that you're a sound man.' His father said nothing. The whisper grew more insistent still. 'If you love me, Father, don't waste what I've done! I've drawn you back into the light of the King's countenance with my "confession". Don't you understand? I told them I denounced you to get possession of the chateau. They don't recall how it really went. The country was in chaos around the coronation; there's no one can contradict me for sure. And why should I say it if it wasn't true? But you must help it along, my story!'

Victoire sat back on his heels and breathed shallowly through an open mouth. The stench had closed up his nostrils. To play-act hatred against this young man? Against this most dear extension of his soul? Like Peter betraying Christ? He could not do it. He would not trouble to do it. But the gaolers could listen and mistake him if they chose. '*Why, Fils? Why did you do it?*'

'For you. For the injustice of it all. Because kings are nothing but random spite and vice. How else could we two come to play such a ludicrous game? Why? For you. Made to live like a bear in a den for the crime of being loyal. For me, made to countenance it. Pandering to their vanity.'

It was Victoire's own doing, then. He had never supposed the guilt to rest anywhere else. Fils had rebelled out of love for his father. Victoire might as well have bound and tied him himself and delivered him up to this stinking midden of rock.

'Were you tried?'

'I was put to trial. It comes to the same thing.'

'What was your sentence?'

'What? I don't understand you. You know the sentence, sure. The Extraordinary Question, of course.'

'That's the trial, not the sentence.'

Fils felt about for his father's hand, as though breaking bad news to a woman. 'That's the sentence, Papa. To the death. Pain till the end of pain. I thought you knew. I thought just now they'd come to begin. I'm ashamed you saw the terror it put in me. You must think me craven cowardly. Well. So I am. I'm glad it was you instead. I'm glad to see you before I die, God knows it.'

Victoire withdrew his hand. He said with austere precision, 'No. You have till tomorrow. It's the sabbath. "Do you expect them to work on the sabbath?" . . . I shall go to Louis. I shall plead compassion. I'll come back tomorrow.'

'*No, Papa!*' It was shouted out with such force of anguish that the watching guards pressed closer, and their knuckles came round the lattice of the door as they tried to see what revenge the Comte was wreaking on his Judas-son. Victoire flinched backwards from the sound and ran his hands over his face and hair several times, trying to collect himself. 'What then?'

Fils' voice dropped back to the softest of whispers. 'You'll leave here rejoicing in royal justice. You'll defame me for a traitor to kith and King. You'll go on pontificating – about the Divinity of Kings and the Absolute Duty of subjects, you know? You'll go back to Gloriole and keep estate. You'll not be seen to grieve or regret – except over the three years I robbed you of. And you'll keep Gloriole. Keep Gloriole! Come King, go King, you'll keep it! Or the whole game's been for nothing!' The whisper was dry and rasping, and outstripped Fils' resources of breath.

'Not grieve,' said Victoire with flat sarcasm.

'Not be seen to grieve, no.'

'Not grieve while my own son . . . Not grieve while my own flesh . . . while the best part of me . . . Not grieve while my own beloved son's torn to pieces by demons? I'd have to be a different man from the one I was born, Fils. I'll join with Charolais and Berry. I'll cut Louis' throat. Let me never rest else.'

'*No!*' (The guards at the door were impressed, and frustrated that they could not see and hear better.) 'No, Papa! I have no posterity! God knows you kept it from me long enough, and now where is there to shed my seed? Eh? Look around you! Fine consummation for a childless man! They'll rip it out of me with hooks and pliers and red-hot – oh Christ have mercy, I'm so afraid, Papa!' He covered his face with both hands and wept out loud.

Victoire slid forward and took hold of the sticky, tangible darkness that was his son's hair. He soothed him as he had as a child, with shushing. He would have sung, had he had a voice: *Richer than in palace tower, Safer than in castle wall* . . . Their faces were close together now. They had barely to lend any breath at all to give shape to their words.

'They keep me from the Sacraments – to frighten me with damnation. Make them shrive me, Papa! At least tomorrow make them shrive me! Now I've tasted Hell, I'm more afraid of it than I was. Make them. Make them.'

'I swear it.'

'And say Masses for my soul!'

'I'll invest a chantry. I swear it, Fils.'

'And make Gloriole my immortality!'

'I –'

'It's all that matters, Papa. Lying here, it's come to be all that matters. Forget Charolais. Forget Berry. You can't keep sight of Grand Causes in this dark. All I can see is Gloriole. I think of the Heavenly City, but all I see is Gloriole. It's all that's left to me. You had a son. I only had Gloriole!'

'And now we both have only Gloriole,' said Victoire.

'All my life, since I've been grown, I've done as you told me, Papa. Why? To keep Gloriole. Come King, go King, that's what you said. God quit you now if you lose it for want of a few deceptions. If you love me, you'll keep up –' Victoire's hand covered his mouth.

'If I love you, Fils? Enough.' His eyes were growing more accustomed to the dark. He could see that the cell had a large fireplace – deep-hearthed and domestic, with an array of tools hanging along the mantel, like orderly cooking utensils in a great man's kitchen. 'You're famished with cold, lad. I'll have a fire lit in here.'

Fils actually laughed. 'God save you, Papa. That fire's not lit for comfort. The hour it's lit is the hour you can lend me your best prayers . . . Look now, there's a favour you might do me in that respect.'

'Name it. You have it. Anything.'

'No. No matter.'

'Fils! What could you ask me that I wouldn't do? My life for yours and welcome. That would be easiest. Small beer. If you'd had a son you'd know it. Tell me what I can do for you.'

Again Fils gave a kind of a laugh and shifted himself on the hard flags like a man trying to get comfortable in bed. 'For shame. You and I, who could play *la morra* for five minutes together, and you need me to tell you?'

They looked each other in the face then, and either the torch flared, or his eyes had adjusted to the dark, or the bonds of amity reforged so strong between father and son that Victoire had not the smallest difficulty in reading that face and the thought behind it. He recoiled physically. 'No, Fils! Never!'

Fils propped himself up on one elbow. 'Please, Papa! You've the strength in your hands to do it easily. No one easier. I'd split my skull on the floor, but that's a mortal sin . . . And you've killed enough men in your time to do it fast and sure!'

'No! No!'

163

'And put it down to righteous anger after!'

'*No!*'

'I'd do as much for you. If you knew what they do to a man in this room, you'd have pity . . .' Fils remembered something and settled back on to his shoulder-blades, and stared at the ceiling. 'But I'm not shriven.'

'No. You're not shriven.' His father seized on the excuse gratefully and jumped to his feet. 'You said yourself – you're in need of a priest. I'll go now and make certain of a priest. Then I'll come back and bear you company. You shan't be alone, I –'

'You'll go now and not come back,' said Fils, still looking at the ceiling. 'Go and keep my dear wife company. Make much of what you saw here. Every detail. And revel in it. Make tomorrow a holiday in honour of what's done to me. You'll find Francine quite merry at the thought. Do you know yet who informed on me to the King? No, I don't know either, but I've got my suspicions. Francine's a right cheerful and "open" lady. If you've a mind to, you can have her. King Louis did. Before he passed her down to me like a used codpiece. She won't trouble you long. There'll be others rushing to marry her just to taste the King's spittle in her mouth and the King's –' The warder's steps came spiralling down the stairs again. 'Keep Gloriole for me, Father! Swear it! It's all I have to think of tomorrow!'

'Fils! I swear it! I'll make a New Jerusalem of it, my Fils.'

'And I'll see you in Heaven, Father?' The voice was rising again towards its childish treble. 'I wish I'd seen that bastard sister of mine. I wish I'd stayed to fish and swim and wear a straw hat rather than seek out Charolais and Berry!'

'Fils –'

'I see you've brought him to remorse, my lord,' said the gaoler, his face pushed close to the grille beside Victoire's head. 'More than we could do, by God it is!'

The plank bridge fell with a crash, and the opening of the door fed the torch more air. So there was no time left to crouch down again, to touch face or hair or to snap his son's neck with a pair of tender hands.

He turned to the warder and said stiltedly, formally, straightening the torn jabot of his shirt-front, 'My religion teaches forgiveness. I shall send to the King for clemency. In the meantime see to it that the man receives Communion. I'll not have a limb of my family tree burn in the Devil's grate. Not even this one. Look to it,' and he pressed two gold coins into the warder's pouch, because the man's hands were full of firewood.

'Too late to send to the King, your lordship. The King's in Guyenne, and the Office of Justice won't stand for any delay once the day's set for a Question.' He had two faggots of wood in either hand which he threw into the grate before pulling the torch out of its bracket. 'Does your lordship want to stay and see the thing carried through? For your own satisfaction?'

'For Christ's . . . ! No. I have better things to do than watch Hector dragged around the walls of Troy. When I was at war it was considered poor chivalry to triumph over one's enemies. Even the likes of this. Well, Fils. Adieu. We had better hope Heaven is wide enough to suffer us both to dwell there, or we'll surely fall to brawling, you and I. I'll go home now and scrape your heir's label off the hearth, and see if I can't build the walls of Gloriole high enough to blot out the sorrow you've brought on my house. God bide by you, Fils de Gloriole.' He ducked his head to clear the door, and the blood was roaring so loud in his ears that he thought he could hear the Tormented in Hell just below his feet and see the hooks snatch for his soul, out of the corner of his eye . . .

He found himself, a moment later, being raised from his knees by the two surveillance officers, and thought for a second that he was under arrest.

'Did he hit his head? I think you hit your head, sir. On the door, sir. I didn't see. I'm sorry, sir. These low doors . . . I think he hit his head . . .'

'Infernal rat-hole,' said the Comte, wrenching himself free. He kept his hand to his head all the way up the stairs: it furnished an excuse for his slowness in climbing, for his legs' unwillingness to climb – up out of Hell like empty-handed Orpheus. Beyond a door, the monkey shrieked with laughter and a jester made tasteless jokes.

Peremptory, graceless and with mechanical efficiency he told the warder, 'I will have the body, now I think of it. To know he's dead and that I'm really free of him.'

The man seemed to hesitate, but it was only that he was uncertain of time factors. 'The prisoner's in fair health. Strong. Fit. Don't send before Tuesday, will you, sir?' He returned the Comte's sword, and clasped his hands for de Gloriole to use in remounting his horse: he weighed surprisingly heavy. The gaoler watched the horse stumbling clumsily over the cobbles of the yard and, a discreet while later, the King's surveillance men following after – though why they should trouble themselves further he could not understand. De Gloriole was patently as sound a king's man as any king could wish.

On a personal level, the gaoler could not find it in him to like the Comte de Gloriole. But then the warder was a family man with two sons of his own. Although he had always known the nobility to be a very different breed from lesser men, he could not help thinking that it took an unnatural father to part from his only son for ever with such cold-blooded equanimity.

SIXTEEN

Potence

It was said to be a way of 'punishing the bricks' for the crime of giving shelter to the King's enemy. No matter that Gloriole-sur-Sablois was no longer the possession of the traitor, nor that his father's rights in it were reinstated. Still the bricks must be punished. It was part and parcel of the sentence, of the dissolution of Fils. The keep – call it what you will – the donjon, the potence – symbol of first-rank nobility – must be demolished.

The Minister of Works himself arrived early on Monday morning to oversee the demolition. All rooms, halls and outbuildings were to be evacuated. Dislodged from their work, the household sat about outside the curtain wall. It lent a falsely festive, holiday air to the proceedings. It was almost as if Fils' injunction was being carried out – that Sablois should holiday in celebration of the Extraordinary Question in progress at Loches.

For a few hours it seemed as though Victoire would be allowed to suffer his purgatory in private. For Francine, his daughter-in-law, had packed and left the chateau for Court – to petition the King for possession of Gloriole-sur-Sablois. She would not find the King: the King was in Guyenne. But she would undoubtedly bring persuasive 'arguments' to bear as soon as Louis returned. If it was true that she had betrayed her husband to the authorities, Louis might well think she deserved just such a reward.

Still, Victoire was grateful to her for her absence, whatever the reason. He could go and beat his head against the spikes that surrounded his wife's little sepulchre and claw up his skin and howl like a wolfish thing, and slaughter the lilies in the brickwork which denoted the King's esteem. He could lie on his face in the chapel and pray to God for mercy. While his son died.

But here now was the Minister of Works. And here were others, too – petty Court peacocks and valets and hangers-on – come to see the spectacle. They watched Victoire, hailed him, circled him closer and closer like Aesop's animals watching the old lion die – donkeys timidly waiting to rush in and kick out his brains. They whispered about him behind their hands. They wrote down each others' witty observations to use for gossip when their friends back at Court asked, 'How did he seem after all this time?'

The Minister of Works, too, showed a close interest in Victoire's state of mind. It was probably among his duties to observe and report on how the suspect responded to the loss of his keep, to the imminent death of his treacherous son. Victoire was on trial himself. The smallest show of sorrow would of course call into question his perfect devotion to the Crown: one tear would damn him for a covert member of the Public League. The reasoning of intelligencers is very simplistic.

But they saw no show of sorrow. They saw no tears. For Victoire had been commissioned to play out his part by one far more influential than King Louis. He had been tutored by Fils in the need for perfect self-containment. No paid intelligencer could possibly match the obligations that bound Victoire to his role in this grotesque charade.

'You understand, of course, the regrettable necessity of this,' said the Minister of Works. 'Your son forced on the King a chastisement which gives him no pleasure in the world. Indeed it grieves him sorely to rob Sablois and your lordship of such a noble donjon.'

'My assets are the assets of the King. His Majesty must of course do as he sees fit. Moreover, I understand the regrettable need for you to refer to Fils de Gloriole as my son, Minister. But pray don't use the word more often than you must. If it weren't that I loved my wife dearly, I'd declare publicly that she laid astray when she got that particular child.'

The sappers, like rats at the base of a sack of grain, were boring holes in the footings of the keep. Others were laying an incendiary trail of faggots throughout the watch-platform which crowned the tower, where the wooden walkway and its thatched roof provided fuel enough to burn. A fire at the summit would weaken the structure prior to demolition: a simpler task than the laying of explosives, it was quickly accomplished. Very probably, its lighting coincided with the lighting of the fire in the Room of the Question.

'Of course it's today that your son's put to death, is it not?' suggested the Minister peering unsubtly into Victoire's face. The coppery eyes rebuffed his stare, hard and metallic.

'I believe so. I've put the matter out of mind – inasmuch as one can dismiss the disappointment of one's hopes.'

'Your hopes lie with the King now, sure.'

'Then I'm fortunate indeed.'

'And yet you were right close to your son once, so I recall. In the war.'

'I've been close to whores in the war, sir. Would you have me maintain the acquaintance when the pox was on them? . . . I'm intrigued to know – how will you persuade the donjon to fall thus, into the yard, rather than backward on to the hall. Not that I doubt the competence of your saltpetremen.'

'Oh never worry, sir! They've had practice in plenty of late. The keeps have been falling hither and yon. Your estate's not alone in its disgrace.'

'I'll trust implicitly to their expertise. I was simply interested, from a professional point of view. Will they use fuses?'

The Minister began to be flustered. He was not accustomed to this kind of reaction from those he visited with his sappers. 'Artillery, Comte. We use artillery. A slow fire under the yard side, for an hour or so, then a blast of cannonfire. You could perhaps go for a ride in the forest till it's over . . .'

'Perhaps I might lend you my culverin. I have a fine pair in bronze on the roof. Most simple to calibrate and wholly accurate.'

'Oh come come, chevalier!' cried the Minister with a sudden outburst of emotion. 'Show a little . . . Such fine buildings! I've had men hang on my robes . . . I've seen men swear and curse and offer me a farm in Normandy if I'd spare their keeps! And yet you . . .' He stalled in the face of the stony regard, the raised eyebrows.

'And did it do them any good, this cursing and bribery?' asked Victoire witheringly. 'It's just a potence, man. Rocks and mortar. As you rightly point out, it won't be the first time a man succumbed to "im-potence". One does not die of it. One is simply dishonoured. After the dishonour my son has done the house, you can barely do worse with a few saltpetremen.'

From a great height of contempt Victoire looked down on the little Minister of Works whose duties of office had degenerated from the beautification of royal chateaux to the punitive demolition of keeps. Perhaps, with his knowledge and love of buildings, he did realize after all how much a fortress meant to the knight who lived there. Or perhaps he simply sought to undermine Victoire's *sang froid* with his pity.

'We have our own cannon, thank you, Comte,' said the Minister, recovering himself. 'We had better retire to a safe distance now, if you please.'

Victoire led the way uphill to the Chapel Saint-Cloud, and as they climbed he heard the hiss and thud of burning arrows fired into the wooden balcony of the keep. A train of chattering courtiers and hangers-on fell in behind, drawing Victoire's attention to how quickly the fire caught, how the smoke made monsters in the sky, how the masonry cracked as the timbers fell blazing into the yard below. They giggled, nervous of their own teasing. He spread his cloak on the ground and sat down where once he had stood and overlooked his family seat for the first time.

His chateau lay spread out beneath him. The square central residence with its four round-tower turrets, dwarfed at present by the keep, spread butterfly wings in the shape of white single-storey extensions. All roofed with steep black-Angers slate, the butterfly glistened, newly hatched, pupating behind the hot smoke from the burning watch-platform. Both wings of the butterfly were brilliantly patterned with parterre all infilled with bright garden beds and pools of shining water. On the South Prospect the lake lay completed, its central island a circle within a circle, and a preposterously pretty barge out-hauled in mid-water. Caught as it was within the river's loop, like a game of cup and ball, it was plain Fils had been right to suggest that spot for the lake.

Through a flurry of aristocratic curses and cuffs, a peasant widow pushed a path to Victoire and dropped down on her hands and knees in front of him. He was hard put to recognize her. She seemed to have no such problems, though of the two he must have been the more changed. 'Is it true? I just heard. Nobody wanted me to know! My ma didn't want nobody to tell it me. Is it true, good master? Is he took prisoner? Where is he, good master? Where is he, for Christ's sake? It's me! It's Jeanne, his comforter!' A gang of oafs gathered round, arms linked over each other's shoulders, making a half ring round the Comte and this hysterical peasant woman, gawping and sniggering.

'He's in Loches Prison, where all traitors should be,' said Victoire looking past her, over her shoulder to where the sappers were poking with pikes at a livid red patch of fire under the base of the keep.

'Well and what's to be done with him? Will they kill him? Will they put him to the torture?'

(So much better informed than he had been, thought Victoire. But then peasants always knew more of life's routine torments than their chatelains and suzerains and masters.) 'Both, woman. Both torture and death.'

'Ai! Mary! Joseph! Jesus! What will they do to him, master?'

'No more than he deserves.'

'But what will they do to my Fils, master?'

'No worse than they've done to his kind before.'

'But what? What will they do? Do you know, gentlemen?' Seeing she would get no reply from Victoire, she foolishly turned her appeal on the gang of loutish courtiers, who grinned and circled her about, their faces pressed close to hers and their fingers jabbing.

'First they'll pour water down him till he's fit to burst.'

'Then they'll put out his eyes . . .'

'. . . Slice off his ears and slit his nose . . .'

'. . . Then they'll break his legs . . .'

'. . . and smash his fingers one by one . . .'

'Then they'll take fire to him here –'

'– and here –'

'– and here, of course –'

'And then a knife.'

'Knife's last, 'cos that lets blood and blood's the start of the end.'

'Between every rib. Through to every bone.'

'And his breasts. Here. Here. Snick-snack.'

'His tongue! We forgot his tongue!'

The woman's screams came to Victoire not as hers at all but as another's, heard over a great distance – from the buildings that lay below him in the loop of the river, white-limbed and unable to crawl away from the remorseless torments of the sappers with their ramrods, burning arrows, carefully placed pikes of fire . . .

'A cut here. A tear there. A rending open so.' They lifted Jeanne's skirts, and fear for herself suspended all fear for Fils.

'I know the part you'd be sorriest to part with. They save that till last. They can make such agonies for a man . . .'

'. . . She'd know about that, wouldn't you, dame?'

'But in the end there's no keeping anything from the torturer's . . .'

Victoire drew his dagger. It would be simple. From where he sat, a single stroke would cut through two sets of hamstrings. He would silence them. He would teach them about pain . . . Then the blast of a cannon stole the air out of every mouth and rammed home its recoil into every ear.

It shattered some of the glass windows in the great-hall – took out its eyes. It burst clear through both walls of the keep and smashed a bony white balustrade beyond. The sappers were streaming out of the gates to get clear of the yard, their brown uniforms like a haemorrhage of arterial blood. Contusions of smoke bruised the air.

Oversized as the charge had been, great as the gash was in the base of the potence, it seemed for a long while to have defied their brutalities. It was strongly built, after all.

But gradually the splits which the fire had opened up at the brim reached down towards the newer fissures at the base, the bricks slid one over another, as though there had never been mortar between them. The great phallus snaked once, threw up a column of white dusty ejaculate, then softened to a thing of no substance at all and dissolved downwards, filling the yard with high-bouncing boulders and the smoke of shattered masonry.

Jeanne broke away from her tormentors and fled down the hill, her hands in her hair.

'Your keep's down, my lord Comte,' said the Minister of Works, gripping his shoulder staunchly. 'I don't doubt the good King will let you raise another shortly.'

'But I shall not,' said Victoire implacably.

'The charge was too great. Incompetents. There'll be some peripheral damage, I fear.'

'It's no matter,' said Victoire.

They dispersed from round him. The householders sitting outside the curtain wall began to trickle back into the yard to pick their way over the rubble and wonder at the sheer quantity of brickwork. The courtiers returned to their horses, laughing and joking about the accidental demolition of the balustered terrace, looking back at Victoire and shrugging their shoulders at his lack of emotion. Living in a cave, they said, had made him as dull-witted and insensitive as a bear.

Through his lashes Victoire watched them observe him. What did they expect to see but stillness? He lay back against the slope of the hill, his hands under his hair and his feet wide apart. Overhead the birds disturbed from their dovecote by the explosion circled in confusion and terror, the content of their guts showering the hill. Thirty-three thousand doves and pigeons – one for every acre of his lands. Not one more, in strict accordance with the Law. They rained their droppings on the dispersing courtiers who squealed and yelped and groaned and swore. He did not laugh at the sight, though it gratified him. He did not weep that his son was dead, that his potence was down. After all, they had put out his eyes and he was unable to weep; cut off his ears and he was deaf to screaming; crushed his limbs and let his blood drain away into this sun-scorched, thirsty hill. They had castrated him with fire and blade. What response did they expect from him who was, after all, a dead man?

A brown habit brushed against his face, and Barnabas, crouching above him on the hill, entered his field of vision. 'I've said Mass for Fils since dawn, my lord. Won't you come and take God's comfort yourself now?'

'What God's that, priest?' asked Victoire matter-of-factly. 'Take yourself and your God and get off my estates before dark. I mean never to waste words on either of you again. If I find you on Sablois land tomorrow, I'll cut your throat so you can carry the message thence in person. Do I make myself plain?'

SEVENTEEN

The Collector

Having expelled God, he set about expelling the vixen from among his vines – the woman Francine. He asked himself what commodity the King prized above a woman's placket and, ironically, it was the frightened pigeons which gave him his answer.

He let it be known that his son, deeper entrenched in villainy than anyone supposed, had begun to establish a system of intelligence-gathering during his years of usurpation. Victoire commissioned his fowler to acquire homing pigeons in twos and threes, discreetly and from wide-spread sources. He was to tag them as carriers and begin to orientate them to Sablois. While this was in hand, the Comte wrote to the King, allowing the letter to intercept him on his return journey from Guyenne:

> *Fils de Gloriole, that traitor lately brought low by Your Majesty's justice, divulged to his inquisitors, I hope, his use of post-fowl to further his confederacy against the Crown.*
>
> *In recompense of the damage done to both State and Throne, I naturally undertake either to dismantle this pigeon loft or to turn its use to the needs and interest of Your Majesty and Your Majesty's officers. I desire only to know your wishes with regard to this – as I might say – hub from which radiate the spokes of an intelligence network stretching, as I believe, as far as Jerusalem and York. Though my knowledge of the science is small, I believe I could, in short time, lay hold on the threads of this most intricate web, to the advantage of State and the comfort of Your Majesty's peace of mind.*
>
> *Otherwise pray send an independent witness to oversee the destruction of these fowl, that no trace of them might remain to the shame of my house.*

Louis was ravished with delight. Once, during the reign of his father, the disgraced banker Jacques Coeur had controlled a pigeon loft which brought economic intelligence from the five corners of Europe. It was not beyond the King's powers, therefore, to imagine a network of communication which would bring him news of friends, enemies and events the world over. He wanted to believe in it and so he did.

Louis did not send to Gloriole demanding that the loft be dismantled. Nor did he grant Francine widow's ownership of the estate (though he kept her a long while at Court deliberating what compensation to make her). Meanwhile, his secretary wrote to Victoire of a grudging willingness to receive '*whatever information touching closely His Majesty which the Comte might see fit to send in plain French, easily digested*'.

Victoire obliged.

From the dovecote at Gloriole-sur-Sablois sprang up a fluted supra-turret. Its conical roof echoed the conical dovecote below and radiated a hundred tiny gablets – roostholes to which the pigeons would return to feed in troughs of the yellowest corn. When the fowler had acquired a hundred or so pigeons and made Sablois the lodestone of their world, Victoire bought the man a farm in Spain and paid him a pension to return every other month for a basket of birds, 'to test how their training holds'. In Spain the man was to acquire fifty more, training them to home on his Spanish farm. On his two-monthly visits to Sablois, he delivered these into Victoire's keeping. These were Gloriole's winged spies. All that remained was to find secrets for the birds to carry to and fro.

So, by night Victoire wrote cryptograms, formulating a cipher of fifty symbols – classical as Greek, flourished with touches of Romanes and leavened with musical notation. And using this he wrote on ribbons of thinnest paper which he rolled round the quill of a feather and sleeved in tin.

He was good at handling birds, but his hawks stood neglected now, his falcons forlornly sidling along their perches. The only birds he handled were pigeons. Whenever a barge left the Sablois wharfs laden with apples or wine, there was aboard it an osier basket crooning full of pigeons. The boatswains, when they reached the sea, would lift the lid to be buffeted like Pandora by the escaping birds. They did not question why this had become part of their duties: the Comte had asked it and so they did it.

Whenever the quarrymen were sent for and given such a basket to take with them as far as Troo or Vendôme, they did not query what purpose it served. The Comte had asked it and so they did it.

Whenever a recruit to the King's Army left Rocheblanche for Paris or Chartres with his sword paid for by Victoire, he carried with him an osier basket fluttering with livestock. The Comte asked him to and so he did it.

Consequently, every few days, ringed pigeons were seen to circle the twin-coned turret in the stable-yard, to fuss and fret their way into the lofts, to rattle their message-cans against the dowelling perches. From west, north, south and east information flocked to the Comte's slated loft – and lo! it was couched in the selfsame secret cipher the Comte had used to communicate with his 'secret foreign sources'. Anyone who had doubted the rumours that de Gloriole was co-ordinating a worldwide intelligence network quickly thought again.

In his retraite once a week, as attentive to his schedule as a priest preparing his Sunday homily, de Gloriole compiled a report for the King's Office of Information, with the help of his secretary. He asked his cousin Michel de Puy to recommend someone reliable and discreet. This guaranteed that the man would be both prying and tell-tale, and tell the de Puys in copious detail everything that Victoire did. 'Well, each day I fetch him the tin sleeves off the legs of any birds that come in; he unfurls the papers – copies the ciphered messages into a leather-bound volume, then scores through half a dozen – the ones of no consequence, as I guess. He reads them through for half an hour or so, then he dictates a report for the King.' The Secretary was convinced. The de Puys were therefore convinced. Victoire de Gloriole spun out his existence at the heart of a spider's web of international secrets.

There were sexual scandals neatly suppressed, incipient alliances between powerful Italian nobles, instances of simony and embezzlement in Rome.

Insurgence was stirring among the Illyrians. A new flintlock had been developed by a German, but was proving unreliable. The banks in Florence were setting aside gold reserves against a possible slump on the commodity market.

The Emperor was minting more coin. Assassination plots were hatching like flying ants. A Portuguese naval commander, believed to have pinpointed the true location of Atlantis, had died on the return voyage without mapping his find.

What though Victoire invented every last word? Somewhere in Germany a prototype flintlock had inevitably blinded its inventor and blown off his hands. The Illyrians had been seething with discontent for a thousand years! Why not today? Undoubtedly the Florentine banks were hoarding gold: that is the nature of banks. No question but there were alliances thought of that never came to fruition, dalliances undertaken that never came to light. Preposterous claims and disappointed hopes. Victoire's 'information' would never be disputed while he wrote as he did.

For he told the King what the King wanted to hear – that men did foul and imaginative things between the sheets; that friends quarrelled and factions plotted; that those wealthier than he would be poorer in the next world for their sins; that the world was full of treasures and monsters; that his enemies were mortal; that the other Kings of Europe were mad or sick or afraid. What merit is there in the truth when lies are just as plausible and more likely to please?

It gratified Victoire to pervert the truth. It confirmed him in the cynical wisdom he had learned – that all the truths he had ever held dear were the Devil's exercises in disinformation. There was no honour among kings. They deserved no sacrificial fealty. They were cattle like the rest and it eased their straining udders to be well milked each morning. So when the Sablois estate began to flow with milk and honey from the King's gratitude, Victoire lapped it up without modesty or argument. He had a need for it.

As the birds migrated to and from his pigeon loft, carrying his ciphered gibberish and fetching it home to him again like ravens to the Ark, his growing reputation fetched in all manner of other information. An intelligencer with the King's ear quickly invites the confidence of amateur spies and tell-tales. News of quite genuine indiscretions were whispered by furtive men with dubious motives. He weighed up the usefulness of what they told him, then decided whether or not it was 'true', whether or not he would pass it on to the King.

Had he attended Court more often, stood closer to more arrases, drunk with more men, slept with more of the gossiping demoiselles, he could certainly have made himself privy to every secret in the country. But he found fiction more interesting than truth and preferred to keep aloof from Court as he always had done, even before it had inspired his contempt. After all, he would never run short of intelligence, not while he coined it, like a forger coining silver, out of tin.

Among the gems of genuine knowledge that came his way was that Francine, his daughter-in-law, was pregnant by a builder of real-tennis courts. This he *did* choose to convey to the King, along with the generous offer that the woman could have the Gloriole estates in Poictou as well as her own in Maine and Oise, so long as it pleased her to live a life of retirement. She clung to the title of Comtesse all her life, doggedly and with *grand hauteur*, though she married a bourgeois Dutchman by the name of Plunk and gave birth to several mongrels.

So Victoire lived on alone at Gloriole, squatting like a fat black spider at the centre of its web. Though he was referred to at Court as the Intelligencer, no such official title was ever awarded him. Those close to the King said it amused him that the archaic title of Grand Echanson should have grown so apt, and that he referred to Victoire affectionately as his 'songbird always singing'. A couple of those courtiers who had slighted the Comte during the years of his disappearance found their careers blighted and the doors of the King's bedchamber closed to their knocking. Louis criticized his Minister of Works for over-hasty demolition of the potence at Gloriole and urged Victoire in the most brotherly terms to rebuild as soon as he chose. In short, Victoire de Gloriole had become a Court favourite.

All the courtiers who had derived such entertainment from that day of the demolition found their names mentioned in dispatches from the pigeon lofts of Gloriole. One by one they fell from grace. But it would not be true to say that Victoire was exacting justice, nor did he ever dignify his work with the name of 'revenge'. For he knew there was only one person to blame for the death of Fils.

Inside his head, there was a trial held at which he was both magistrate and defendant, and judgment was enforced with a fierce rigour. He confiscated from himself the comfort of women, the consolation of music, the use of sheets on his bed. He ate no meat and took no sabbath rest. The priest Barnabas had defied him, and went on living in the tallat loft over the great-barn. Victoire did not send to have him killed or evicted, but he held good to his divorce from God and took no Communion. Whatever he could achieve without outward show of abstinence, he denied himself.

And yet it was nothing. When ascetic living has been a necessity, it is hard to make a virtue of it. He could not fail to be more comfortable than in the cave, and his benevolence towards his peasants was only another kind of guilt, because he had escaped their miserable lifestyle.

It was easy to afflict himself with torments in private. It took more of an effort to keep up the outward show. Still he did it, in accordance with Fils' wishes. He observed scrupulously a measured ascent to opulence. His finances could not fail to thrive while he kept the King entertained with titillating gossip. And King Louis was free with money in a way that his father had never been. Not that it showed in his dress: Louis had been known to make Royal Entry to a town and not be noticed. He was shabby and unremarkable in every respect but for the knobbly deformity of a nose and short upper lip. But he knew how to live frugally, and saved money for the things that really mattered by having other people pay his expenses. He worked his shabby and unremarkable way from one chateau to the next, saddling his friends and noblemen with the housekeeping. He also encouraged them to be generous to his royal songbird.

No one could accuse the Intelligencer of being either shabby or unremarkable. He would not have passed unnoticed, thanks partly to the ferocious forward carriage of his shoulders, the grizzled splendour of his beard, and partly because he cultivated a wardrobe (as his tailor put it) 'of the damnedest good stuff that was ever wore'. It was necessary to abjure black, for fear it be thought he was in mourning for his son. He adopted instead a dark maroon red – 'the very colour (a surgeon once remarked) of blood from a gut wound'. But he had it made up for summer in crash or felt or dowlas linen from Britanny, and for winter in worsted and fustian. His cloaks were frieze or duffel, lined with shalloon, and his shirts were percale cambric. He owned (though they were seldom seen) Court robes of slubbered maroon samite and raw silk – one more compliment to the King that did not pass unnoticed. For Louis had only newly recommended silk-farming to the Loire, and Gloriole had adopted the mulberry trees as others adopted the fleur de lys – as a sign of royal approval. In fact the manufacture was extremely lucrative, and bolts of silk were soon slithering from the looms of Sablois like water's thaw after winter. But Louis believed the enterprise to be entirely in his honour and not for sordid commercial ends. It was not as if de Gloriole needed the money . . .

In truth Victoire needed every franc d'or and écu, every silver blanc and sou. For not only was he extending Gloriole, he was furnishing it with a collection of art the like of which Touraine had never seen. When the King heard this, he was glad. He trusted men who valued material wealth, who coveted *things*.

The butterfly chateau pupated, within a crysalid of scaffolding, into a dragonfly, its body doubling in length, its wings quadrupling.

The central residence was soon only the thorax of a vastly extended body. The four corner turrets with their conical roofs were
duplicated in four more to the west, but this time with steep
corner pavillons in the same black-Angers and with lacy coppered
cresting on the roof-ridges. The machicolations were false: this was
not a time for fortresses so much as palaces. And the gargoyle faces
that emerged from beneath the gutters, though they appeared to be
shouting perpetual curses, were only really a functional means of
directing rainwater down from the steep roofs.

The head of the dragonfly was a ninth domed tower – not a
keep, no, by no means – but an adornment intended to house a
new panelled staircase of nine straight flights, and three galleries of
paintings and tapestries.

They were all of them commissioned – from artists in Paris,
Reims, Angers and Tours and from the tapestry factory at Arras.
The very first was a companion-piece to the Prodigal Son – an
exact duplicate, except that the embrace was the kiss of betrayal
between Judas and Christ. 'These Philistines,' said the designer in
residence at Arras. 'Where's the religious message there? Some of
these sword-wavers will order anything for the sake of symmetry.'
The two tapestries hung on opposite sides of the great-hall whose
walls were now panelled in Cordoba leather red as wine and tooled
with a repeated device: overlapping discs, black over gold. The sun
eclipsed.

Victoire commissioned the second tapestry more locally, for
its design was to depict the Touraine countryside, a great tract of
the Loire mirroring a domestic sky. Between the clouds Daedalus
hung helplessly from a pair of drooping wings while Icarus plunged
flightless into the river. For the myth told how Daedalus had made
his son wings which failed in the heat of the sun.

'A man of catholic tastes, that one,' said the tapissière after
delivering the third wall-hanging. For it was neither biblical nor
classical, but a scene from Roman history. It depicted the bringing
to Brutus of the body of his dead sons after his defeat at Philippi.

From the Scottish artisans at Aubigny-les-Cardeux Victoire commissioned a stained-glass window for the head of the stair. It was of
Absalom caught by his long hair in the branches of a tree and shot
through with arrows by his pursuers.

Though the Comte would not allow Christ to pass his lips at
Communion, he was content that the man should hang at every

turn and angle of his house. Perhaps it appealed to some morbid streak in the Comte, his neighbours argued, for he commissioned no scenes from the Gospels *other* than the Questioning of Christ and the Crucifixion. Nor was he content with coy, prudish conventions, but seemed in pursuit of the painting which would capture fully the agony of a man tortured to death.

It was a phenomenon the painters were familiar with: a kind of pornography of sadism that they despised rather more than the usual requests for nude nymphs, naked boys and Bacchanalian orgies. Why else should a man commission a diptych – poignant as it undoubtedly was – of Medea's elopement? On one side the sorceress Medea sat cutting a little boy into messes; on the other sailed Aeetes, searching the sea for morsels of his only son. But artists are artists and they always greeted the news that Victoire de Gloriole was commissioning yet another painting with excited anticipation. There was a terrible mundane predictability with most commissions: the same themes appeared over and over again. Not so with de Gloriole. Only he, with his bizarre tastes, offered an artist the chance to paint Thyestes (who inadvertently ate his children cooked in a pie) and Caligula (who ripped his unborn son from the womb and ate him to consolidate his power).

In the garden of Gloriole, from a block of marble the size of a tiring house, a sculptor was chipping his slow deliberate way through to the figure imprisoned inside. Hercules.

'And shall he be wrestling with the Nemean lion or capturing the hind of Artemis?' asked the sculptor de Dénezé. 'Or would you like a Hydra?'

'Oh, let's have something jolly,' said de Gloriole clapping him stoutly on the back. 'Give me Hercules in his cups. Roaring drunk and singing.'

'Very well. Why Hercules, then? Why not Bacchus, or I could do you a Saturn?' said the sculptor. He was a little disappointed: he carved an excellent hind. 'Did Hercules drink? I forget.'

'For shame!' exclaimed the Comte, feigning the greatest good humour. 'Don't you recall how he strangled all his children while the drink was on him?'

'Oh,' said de Dénezé somewhat taken aback. 'Something jolly, then. Hercules in his cups.'

When de Dénezé paused for refreshment, he would stroll over to the lake, to where a great cast bronze fountain was being installed midway between bank and island. He had to admit he found the

choice of subject an odd one for a fountain, though the workman-
ship was exquisite. Poseidon might have been more appropriate,
mermaids and dolphins more conventional. Still, the bronze aroused
de Dénezé's professional envy: he had long coveted the opportunity
to carve an Abraham-and-Isaac. It would have given him a chance
to carve a ram caught by its horns in a thicket, and he did a good
ram.

There was no ram on the fountain – only old Abraham and
the son he bound and laid on an altar of faggots ready to offer
him up for obedient sacrifice to God. De Dénezé contemplated
how he would have tackled it: the knife poised at the very moment
in which God called out to the prophet to stay his hand and spare
his son . . .

'Wait! Hold! Move away!'

The plumbers shivering in the water as they worked to connect
pipes to the base of the monumental bronze grumbled back at the
sculptor. 'Whassa matter?'

'The fool! The imbecile! The heathen! What half-brain cast this?'
The plumbers shrugged their indifference, so de Dénezé climbed into
a rowing boat and pulled out for a closer look. No, he had not been
mistaken. The sculptor of the fountain had made the most crass of
errors in his carving of the original plaster mould. There was the
boy Isaac, his head hung back off the faggots, long hair spreading
on to the water itself, his mouth open and screaming. But Abraham's
knife was not halted in mid-air; there was no look of divine revelation
in his old, bearded face – only a terrible brutal determination. And his
big swordsman's fist was pressed hard up under the boy's ribcage,
sinking the blade deep into the body cavity. 'Has the Comte seen
this . . . this *travesty*?'

'Yep. Seemed pleased enough,' said the plumbers, ducking their
shoulders back beneath the water to grope for the faucets.

Last of all, for the drum frieze below the very cupola of the ninth
turret, Victoire commissioned a 'Day of Judgment'. He applied for
it, in fact, to the son of Gonplier who had once painted Ellen. It
employed Gonplier's whole studio of mural painters, and the stairs
cascaded a perpetual stink of tempera down into the base of the
house. A boy was employed full-time in grinding colours.

At the head of the staircase flew Saint Michael with a great coiled
golden horn and wings which engulfed two windows within their
spread. He it was who marshalled the souls of the Dead, sorting the
Saved from the Damned. The Comte had notions of how the angel

should look: fetched along an old oil painting by Gonplier's father, though it was somewhat damaged by mould and damp and it was of a woman. Angels are always a touch androgynous, so Gonplier the Younger did not demur. 'A man, you understand, but featured like this,' said the Comte. 'And with black hair.'

That irked the painter. 'Angels don't have black hair – or black eyes!' he thought of saying, but noticing that the Comte's hair was grey decided to err on the side of caution, and painted black hair.

The fee was handsome (more handsome than the Angel Michael really) so Gonplier exerted his very best efforts to please. From under the archangel's right hand, the Unredeemed Damned were herded by angels with whips and flails, clockwise through pools of fire, running the gauntlet of demon pikemen and chewed on by hideous goblins, towards the yawning jaws of Hell.

A theatrical young man, Gonplier took up a position exactly in front of the angel and, as Victoire came up the stairs for the daily inspection of works, flung his arms wide. 'And here,' he said, flourishing his scale-rod in the direction of the Happy Blessèd, 'here is the figure of the noble Comte. I executed it myself, and I dare swear the likeness is as fair as any that's ever been painted of your lordship in oils.' Conventions had changed since the time of his father. The likeness to de Gloriole was very good.

'You fool! You presumptuous jackanape! You sycophant! Why didn't you ask before you began? Paint it out! Paint it out, you hear!'

Gonplier was too astonished to speak. His assistants were thrown into terrified confusion. Only the dye-boy was left with the presence of mind to say, 'But sir! You must want yourself in the scene! You must! It's the way of Judgments!'

'Yes, yes, yes!' bellowed de Gloriole, and his voice carried down the flighted staircase as far as the cellars. 'But *here*, boy! *Here!* Paint me here!' And he pointed to the column of the Damned picking their way through Purgatory to the unportrayable torments of everlasting Hell.

EIGHTEEN

Now God Stand Up for Bastards

There was one patron of the arts alongside whom de Gloriole paled into insignificance. Charles, Duc d'Orléans, cousin of King Charles VII, had at long last returned from imprisonment in England to the chateau of Blois, and had established a centre of culture there that made Louis look like a pig in mud.

Fils had been to the Duc's wedding while Victoire was fishing and weaving osier, and had been greatly taken with the man, though Victoire thought it somewhat obscene that anyone should marry a thirteen-year-old having reached the age of seventy. Knowing the extreme old age of the Duc, the last thing Victoire expected was for Charles d'Orléans to arrive at his door with this selfsame child-wife and crave 'whatsoever hospitality the excellent Comte might spare out of his busy day'. Charles was carrying a small wicker basket which he presented to Victoire. 'One of your post-men, I believe. It quarrelled with a peregrine falcon of mine, but The Wife has nursed it with all tenderness and I think it'll live. You would if she nursed you the same way. I do. I do.' The frail old man swayed into the entrance hall and perched on the edge of a carved wooden chest.

'I'm greatly obliged to you,' said Victoire, simultaneously dispatching servants to prepare fires, meals, beds. 'How did you know the bird was mine?'

'I brought The Wife and Baby with me. I hope it's not an imposition, but having found her so late in life, I have little enough chance to enjoy 'em, you know?' Since he would not answer a direct question, Victoire naturally assumed he was deaf. But it was plain Charles lacked in no other way. His son was a bonny three-year-old with a strong resemblance to his father, even though six of the Ages of Man separated them. The Duc conducted his movements as though he were directing an orchestra, and after three upward sweeps of the palms, he raised himself painfully off the chest. Victoire quickly came to recognize the gestures and offer help in time to be of use. 'An excuse, the pigeon. An excuse, I admit it. I heard you were gathering up a fine collection of art, and I'd a mind to see it.'

'Such an arduous journey for you, my lord Duc. If you'd sent word, I'd have conveyed the paintings to Blois.'

'Ah, but there are more than paintings.'

'The tapestries too.'

'But there are windows – statues.'

'You are very well informed, my lord.'

'And besides, a work of art is best seen in the place for which it was intended, don't you agree? Yes, an arduous journey. A bed wouldn't come amiss if it won't greatly trouble your household. Anything big enough for two, and a box for The Baby. You have a beautiful chateau, Victoire. It bears you good witness for a man of taste. I may call you Victoire, may I? Thank you.'

The Duc's driver, having quietly familiarized himself with the lie of the house, unceremoniously picked up his master and carried him up the stairs to the great-hall and to the most comfortable chair. On his own initiative, he had already moved it closer to the fire. (It said much of the driver's strength that he made so light of it: the Duc was a lean man but tall and well built.) There he rested, like a drummer during a quiet passage of music, counting the bars. Then he was ready to see the house, and would not be dissuaded from it by either Victoire or The Wife.

His driver carried him as far as the Last Judgment, and from there he made his slow, deliberate way on foot round every gallery of the three-tiered tower. The eyes, blue-milked with age, wandered over the works with a nonchalance that suggested failing sight or limited interest, and he passed no comment. And yet he would not suffer Victoire to hurry him away from a painting. And when the tower was seen, he ambled through the gardens asking which of the statues had been commissioned and which simply bought through an argentier. Victoire saw no harm in answering truthfully. Other house-guests had wandered admiringly among his things; a lady or two had even called them 'pretty' and 'wished she could have one just the same'. They were not titled and he never proffered an explanation. It would have taken a scholarly eye to see all the myths, legends and historical incidents referred to within them. Following Orléans about, watching to catch him if he fell, Victoire's thoughts were entirely taken up with that stray pigeon.

'Ah, the pigeon loft, yes,' said Orléans, beating out ten bars of rest with his index finger as he stopped to admire the architecture of the twin-coned tower.

'Yes, my lord.'

'Yes. Yes, yes. An interesting cipher-code. You must explain it to me. Some time.' A trapdoor opened in Victoire's diaphragm and dropped his heart directly through into his lights, hot and heavy. 'I'm marvellously hungry. Would it be too much to hope that your cooks have had time to muster a bite of bread?'

The meal mustered was of mutton, udder pâté, aspic jelly, teal, bustard, dried medlars, aniseed and cheese. The Wife (whose name was Marie) had as little to say for herself as most seventeen-year-olds, while Orléans spent most of his time trying to persuade The Baby to try new tastes: the child was a true conservative. Victoire was left to wonder whether he was being dangled on a hook or had slipped from an old man's thoughts. But the more asides Orléans made to his wife, the more Victoire doubted any such mental infirmity.

For Charles itemized each and every painting and tapestry he had seen, describing it in copious detail, and never once mistaking the subject matter. 'The Comte is a man overly fond of symbolism, my dear,' he concluded, without looking in Victoire's direction.

The table was cleared and wafers were served with white hippocras. Flockhart's wife brought the little boy a slab of castrelin which Orléans tasted – 'to see it would not take out The Boy's milk teeth'. For the remainder of the evening, he tolerated the child climbing up and down his legs and stomach and chest and sitting in his lap making his clothes and beard sticky with the nougat.

'Some astrologer said this one'll be King of France one day,' he said, ruminatively winding the child's hair around his fingers. 'But I trust the fool was talking nonsense . . . I heard tell of you long since, you know, Victoire?'

'Of me, sir?'

'When I was in England. You had a reputation there, you surely did.'

'Hardly the match of yours, my lord.'

'My dear Victoire, you're not old enough to recall the days of my repute as a knight. I was taken prisoner before you drew your first sword.'

'Your merits were not forgotten. It's to our perpetual shame that you were not ransomed sooner.'

'Oh it was . . . instructive,' said Orléans mildly. 'Twenty-five years in the Tower of London: I met interesting folk. I adopted a new motto, did you know?'

'Yes.'

'Can you recall it?'

'Naturally, my lord.'

'And can you speak it? Or does it go too much against the grain?' Victoire could feel himself shrinking by the moment to the status and incompetence of a schoolboy. '*Nonchaloire*, my lord.'

'Indeed. *Nonchaloire*. "Take life easy", or something to that effect. My chaplain would have preferred "*Let not your heart be troubled*", but it takes up too much wall-space. And yours is what?' He got up and crossed to the hearth, and lifted the Judas tapestry to reveal the heraldry hidden beneath. 'Ah yes. *Rien meilleur*. "The best or nothing". "Nothing but the best". An outlook recommended by your dinner . . . Although I've always thought it rather open to being misconstrued: "Nothing would've been better than this", ha ha! *Rien meilleur*. Yes indeed. I believe your son shared your veneration of the principle.' Victoire did not respond. He was too preoccupied with how Orléans knew the secret of his chimney breast, knew that the tapestry hid a heraldic device. 'I can recommend it to you for a tag. *Nonchaloire*, I mean. Once you've forgiven yourself.'

Marie brushed up a handful of food scraps from the table and, rising, threw them into the fire. 'Pray don't invite violence on yourself, husband. I'll wait for you above. Shall I take Louis?'

'No, no. Leave him. The excellent Comte can carry him for me if there's a need.'

By the time Marie closed the doors behind her, Victoire had retreated within himself to a depth beyond sounding. Or so he thought. To deflect the conversation from himself, he asked Orléans to tell him more of his years in England, and the old man, assessing Victoire's face like a castle wall for scaling, abruptly agreed.

'I was taken at Agincourt, you know. Two score of us were hemmed round by the English cavalry. Shameful fiasco, Agincourt. If it were spoken of oftener here, our youngsters would learn more by it. A rout. We had them outnumbered five-to-one and still they routed us. Over-confidence. It never serves to be cocksure. Anyway. They had us like beans in a pestle, my men and I. Beat out our brains. Good friends. Dear friends. I can remember the sound of them panting. Grunting. Swinging away fit to fight their way out of Hell. Gradually taking fright. Swearing. Praying. Trying not to tread on the ones already down. I fell backwards over a corpse. The rest came down on top of me. One by one. I recall the weight: thought I'd be pressed to death like a heretic. Breastplates, boots, faces. I remember their blood trickling down on to me, all hot. Jesu, the time it took for some of them to die! Good friends. Dear friends. The English found me when they were scavenging. Twenty dead on top of me. It's not the way I'd choose to be buried. Friends close as brothers some of them. So you see I know the guilt-of-the-survivor when I see it. It passes. It passes. If you let it.'

'I never knew the like of that,' said Victoire hastily. 'My war . . .'

'Hoi-toi, who's talking about the war? It must be worse when it's a son whose blood's running down on to you. And a son loved so much. The Little One – this chap – he opened my eyes to it, if I didn't know it already. I'd be something the same if I lost him.'

Victoire's eyes were so narrowed as to show only the colour of oil seething behind an arrow slit, prepared to repel besiegers. 'I own, my son was a great disappointment to me.'

'Oh, was he so!'

Orléans gestured his intention to stand up, and obliged Victoire to carry the little Louis, as he led the way. By the door he paused to finger the leather wall-covering. 'The sun eclipsed. Your wife was English, wasn't she? Quite an influence on your thinking. You even pun in English. The son eclipsed.' Once they reached the head of the stairs, he stood writing a requiem in the air with his forefinger, at the foot of the stained-glass casement. The warrior in the window hung snagged in his thorn-tree by his long, dark hair, pierced through by arrows and by the low evening light. '*O my son Absalom, my son, my son Absalom, would God I had died for thee.* Do I have the words correct? I think so . . . Oh Victoire, Victoire. You can't raise the dead by grieving after them! You should marry again like me! Get more sons!'

Victoire wiped his free hand up over his face and hair – almost as if he were taking off a mask. He was found out. 'And disinherit Fils?' he said undramatically. 'I'm building Fils his immortality. The only kind there is. When it's done – if you suffer it to be done . . .' He broke off, frowning and disorientated. 'Everything I've done dishonourable – the birds – the lies – it was only to that end. To build an immortality for Fils. I hope you believe me. I am a one-time man of honour, after all.'

Orléans beckoned his need of an arm to lean on, but it seemed to Victoire that the hand laid on his sleeve was anything but frail. 'You're wrong. This isn't an immortality, Victoire. It's a mausoleum. A shrine to lost sons. A celebration of desolation. "In my Father's Hell there are many mansions." Eh? Eh? Very beautiful, I grant you, but it'll never be much of a credit to you or to Fils. It faces the wrong way, you know. It faces the wrong way.'

'I heard tell you were an architect,' said Victoire with defensive sarcasm.

'It faces into the Past, man. It'll never catch the sun, you know, while it faces backwards. Learn by me, Victoire. I spent twenty-five years a prisoner and it didn't ease the guilt one shred. Now I have Marie and Louis and Blois, and my music and poetry and books and pictures and tapestries-of-a-million-flowers . . . I'm the happiest of men. I'm *obligated to happiness*, you see. I've twenty-five years to make up for and twenty good men's lives to live for them, since they're not able.' His fist crescendoed into Victoire's upper arm. 'Marry, man! Marry!'

'*For Christ's sake!* I've married twice too many women for their own good! I beg your leave to spare a third!'

Orléans was undeterred from his bright, remorseless chatter. 'Ah yes! The other guilt! You kill your wives with loving, don't you? You know that Marie is my third wife, I suppose? You and I have a great deal in common, don't we, young man?'

'*Young man!*' said Victoire with the weariness of disgust. 'I'm fifty-two.'

The Duc plumped himself down on the top stair, pulling Victoire down with him. (The child was hot and sticky and insisted on putting his hands into Victoire's mouth and laughing him out of countenance.) 'Just so. I do my best, but what wouldn't my wife give, d'you suppose, to be laid down by a fifty-two-year-old rather than by a man of seventy-four? It's all relative, you see. All relative. I've lived most of my life since I was your age. Fitted it in. Perforce. And a fine time it's been . . . Where's that daughter of yours?'

It caught Victoire entirely off guard. He could not for a moment recollect that he had a daughter. Now he was forced to track her down, in the depths of his memory. 'You've set your spies on to me good and true, haven't you, Orléans?'

'Ah well. Since I found your pigeon and its strange little letter, I've made some fair enquiries about you, yes. As I say – you were a name I knew already from the English. Plainly a man worth the enquiry. I never waste my time, you understand. It's much too short.'

'I have no daughter. Only a bastard. *Ow!*' The child had made a deep exploratory bite in his ear.

'Excellent child! Do thus when you're grown and I may let you be King after all . . . Take care, monsieur. You're talking to a man with a great partiality for bastards. You know my brother, sure?'

'The great Dunois. Of course. He came here once. To this house. It did the house more honour than I was able to do him at the time.' Victoire was sheepish. Alongside the name of Dunois, 'Bastard' had always been a title of esteem – carried no reproach whatsoever. Neither had he intended any towards Vérité. None in the world.

'My father 'got Dunois on a city woman. Brought him home proud as Caesar. God knows what my mother thought. But there you are. She was an easy-going woman. I was well pleased. A brother ready-made. And he proved as good a brother as a man could wish for.'

'Yes, yes. I meant no . . .'

'After Agincourt he took it on himself to redeem me from the English. Never rested. Never flagged. Held my name up in front of the King's face when it was the last sight the Veryvictorious wanted to see. Tended my estates. Travelled from Châteaudun to Blois, to and fro like a tennis ball. By Florian, but he was God's best blessing to me! After The Boy, you understand. And if I ever hear you disparage bastards again, I'll fetch out your pigeon-spies and let 'em sing to the King what you've been up to. You hear?'

'I never intended –'

'Did you love the mother?'

'Vérité's mother?' Victoire stared at him. Most noblemen would have kicked him down the stairs for such an admission. Love Marthe? Even Fils would not have stomached such a word in association with a peasant woman. 'Yes, I loved the mother. That's why she's dead. I have a certain happy facility for dispatching the things I'd soonest keep by me. That's why I put the child at the Madeleine. And that's why I've taken a vow to live celibate – which rather prevents me complying with your advice. By your leave.'

'Oh Victoire, no! That I didn't know! Celibate? One of God's best inventions and you've set it aside? What a waste. I'd as soon live without music! What a waste of God's bounty!'

'I don't doubt but that God tired of toying with Man a thousand years since; nor takes the smallest interest in our pain and pleasures.

Let one fuck, let another abstain. Let one die in the Stirrup: the everlasting breeding of the rest will fill up the gap.'

The outburst silenced Orléans in such a way as a shovelful of earth buries a worm: for just so long as it takes to reach the surface and the sunshine again. 'Then pardon my curiosity, but to just whom did you make this vow of yours? Not to God, sure, if you hold Him so indifferent.'

'To myself.'

'And yet you're relying on Judgment Day to complete your punishment. I saw your portrait on that mural – in among the Damned. You're inconsistent, monsieur.'

'By your leave, not at all. I believe devoutly in the Devil. I've seen his works close-to. There's a one whose interest in the Race of Man never falters; *he* pays the perfectest attention to detail, nor never rests from his work on the sabbath.'

'Don't turn to Devil worship, Victoire!' exclaimed Orléans suddenly, abandoning all pretence of levity.

'I won't. We're too much alike, Satan and I, for the fellow to earn such respect.'

'By Saint Jude! Give me The Child before his soul picks up the taint of you!'

The old man's heels were resting on the hem of his robe. As he stood up, he was jerked off balance and pitched forwards. It was only Victoire's quickness of mind and hand that prevented the Duc from plunging face-first down the stairs.

'More! More!' cheered the child, tossed high in the air as Victoire jumped to his feet.

The Duc clung to Victoire's aching left arm, trembling from the fright. His voice was subdued. 'Well. Well. Well. And how's that,' he panted, his voice made frail by fright. 'Well, look now. I have the power to tell the King a thing that would send you to the Stirrup yourself. And yet you stop me falling downstairs. At the risk of incurring your annoyance, I venture to say, sir, that you're a charlatan. As demons go.'

'I'm a swordsman, simply. I'm driven by reflexes,' said Victoire icily. 'Do you mean to send me to the Stirrup, then?'

'Oho! You want things made so easy for you, don't you! No, friend. I won't do you any such favour . . . Bring me my breakfast tomorrow morning early. I'll have decided by then what fate you deserve for your forged intelligences. What punishment to exact. Or blackmail, if you prefer.'

Walking behind Orléans, Victoire carried The Boy as far as the door of the second state chamber. His arm remembered the shape, the weight, the pleasure from another time, long before. So the child's fascination with his face increased as it was able to trace, with a small finger, the interesting course of waterdrops down the creases of cheek and nose into the grey beard – taste them and find them salt.

Next morning, as commanded, Victoire himself took the breakfast tray into his visitors' chamber and, having placed it on the Duc's lap, turned his back out of respect for the Duchesse Marie. He awaited sentence, hands behind his back, wishing he had slept so that the leading of the window would not dance in and out of focus.

But Orléans had nothing at all to say on the subject of the cipher-code or the pigeons, or any aspect of the Comte's role as Intelligencer. In fact, all he mumbled, as he dropped chicken jelly on to the sheets of the great bed, was:

'Vérité? Did you say your daughter's name was Vérité? You realize you can't bring a girl by that name into this house? Either the house or the girl's name will have to change. And it's a very pleasant name. Don't you think so, wife? If we have a girl next, we'll name her Vérité – if you think I can match up to a daughter with such a name. D'you think I can? I think I could. I dare swear de Gloriole matched up to it once.'

A matter of weeks later, Charles, Duc d'Orléans was dead, killed by nothing so malicious as his incomparably happy old age. So there was no constraint on Victoire to do as he was told: no threat of being unmasked, no benign blackmail. He did not fetch his bastard daughter from the Madeleine Convent, refuge for the Daughters of Joy. Such committals are irrevocable, and besides, it had been Marthe's wish that she go there, and thus to Heaven.

Still, he found his own travels often took him close by its forbidding walls. In fact he frequently rested his horse on the patch of grass outside the high, wrought gates. He began to think of those gates as very similar to certain doors in the prison fortress of Loches.

NINETEEN

Daughter of Joy

'Go away! Go away! There's nothing for you here! Jackal! Blue-bottle! Shoo!' The nun flapped her sleeve-ends at him through the grille. Victoire looked over his shoulder. 'It's you I'm talking to! Yes, you! We know you! Go away!'

'I've come to see the Prioress. I want to see the Prioress,' said Victoire feeling even more confused and ill-at-ease than he had the day before, on his journey.

'This isn't a brothel! There's nothing for you here!' declared the nun, and disappeared from sight. He shook the gate agitatedly and swung the rope of a big brass bell suspended over the gate arch. A cluster of inmates gathered to look at him and whisper and giggle, as though he were the exhibit behind bars and not they. A nun with a besom swept them apart, but they regrouped, like mushrooms in a picked patch of shade. Their eyes made Victoire blush. Daughters of Joy – repentant whores and the offspring of illicit unions, irrevocably given to a life behind the veil.

'I am Victoire, Comte de Gloriole,' he said quickly to the next nun who passed near the gate, and so gained admission and an audience with the Prioress.

She was a woman about his own age, with a tissuey skin rumpled around the mouth by a lifetime's constriction of the wimple. She showed none of the fright of the sister at the gate, but all of the suspicion, wrapped up in a kind of charitable contempt. 'So after all these years you make yourself known to us, sir. I take it you have formed an intent. Why do you look so uneasy, Comte? Don't you know there are plenty of your kind? You are no novelty to us.'

'I simply had it in mind to offer you – that's to say offer the convent an endowment.'

'Of course you had. Of course. I never doubted it.'

'Is there any particular lack I can fill?' he persevered, feeling more and more disconcerted. He realized that alms-giving was the duty of every Christian; he had not been hoping for fawning gratitude or amazement. But gifts normally met with a little more enthusiasm and a little less venom.

'You might donate a half-dozen bolts of burrel, for the making of dresses,' said the Prioress curtly.

'Yes! Very good. Excellent. I'll do that!' although he had been thinking more in terms of a building or a chantry.

'And now?'

'Now?'

'You have a request to make in return.'

'I do, yes, but how did you . . . ?'

The Prioress let the air escape between her decayed lower teeth in an expression of extreme impatience. 'Oh you lechers. You debauched centaurs. You come buzzing like wasps round honey and want to be thought of as one of the Magi bearing priceless gifts. You're all alike. All unclean.'

'I –'

'For years my nuns have seen you. Watching. Watching. Others are commonly more direct; they come straight to the gate and think to choose once they're inside. But perhaps you're a man of *discernment*. Perhaps it took you six, seven years to see what you wanted. Do you suppose you went unnoticed, sir? Watching the girls go down to the river for their promenade. Watching them in their time of free converse. Giving ungodly castrelin to the smallest girls.'

'And what's ungodly about castrelin, pray?' said Victoire, gradually understanding. It eased his anxiety wonderfully. So much so that he put his boots up on a second chair.

'The girls are here to be purged of their sins or of the sins of their parents. We arm their souls against mere demons, but we are put to the expense of a high stone wall to keep out the likes of you and your kindred spirits.'

'I never realized the wolves ran in such large packs in this part of the world,' said Victoire. 'You do well to be so vigilant. You have a girl here . . .' (Again the Prioress hissed through her lower teeth like a kettle coming to the boil.) 'You have a girl here I want kept safe from predators.'

'And she will be, sir. Whosoever comes sniffing after her with a mouth full of bribes and a heart full of filth!'

'I mean my daughter.'

If he was expecting the Prioress to blench, gasp with embarrassment, to fall backwards into apology, he was disappointed. It seemed she had almost as great a contempt for fathers as for libertines. 'A fondness for the spoils admits to a fondness for the crime,' she said, clearly not for the first time in her life. 'Don't you repent of your sin?'

He could hardly believe she was serious. 'Naturally I'm sorry that my daughter's mother died. Before I could marry her.'

'But not before you could know her carnally, it would appear.'

'By Frideswide! Know her carnally?' What an expression! He could find no association between it and the memories that came back to him (more and more often these days) of Marthe and of his time in the cave.

'Why do you come here, sir? To what purpose?'

Victoire shrugged. He had thought it too obvious to need explanation. 'To see she's well. To comfort myself she's in good hands. You had scarlet fever here last year. It put a kind of fear into me.'

'You've come more often since. It hasn't gone unnoticed.'

'I want to see my daughter.' He took his boots off the chair. He had not known he was going to say it. It came as more of a surprise to him than to the Prioress.

'I can't allow that. It would unsettle the girl. It would part her mind from the things of Heaven.'

'You're right, I suppose.'

'That was why you placed her here, was it not? To live a life of repentance?'

Repentance. It sounded as if he had packaged up his sins and bound them to the child's back when he sent her with the wet-nurse to be delivered anonymously to the Convent of la Madeleine. Repentance for what? The child had nothing to repent. He found himself thinking that he shared Charles d'Orléans' theology more closely than this bleak, angry woman's. And yet he was on her ground, within her estates, bound by her rules. He began to withdraw. 'If I thought she was happy . . .' But the Prioress did not see the theological function of happiness. It was not a necessary constituent of the religious life.

He had come for nothing. He would not come again. In a couple of years his daughter would enter the novitiate, then take the Veil, drawing it between his life and hers where, in truth, it had always hung. Without believing in Heaven, he had done everything necessary to ensure her a place there.

The Prioress did not ask, 'Who is your daughter? Which is yours?'

195

She had no interest. She was in charge of women and girls to whom men were an irrelevance, an obsolete factor. All men. Everyman. 'You may tour the building. To satisfy yourself that our facilities are adequate. You may supply any you see wanting. Pray do not anticipate thanks or recompense.' And she summoned a child from the garden outside her window to show him about the convent. He noticed she did not know the child's name.

He was about to refuse the invitation. Now that his vague hopes had been so thoroughly quashed, all he wanted was to get away, out from under the repressive gloom of these walls. Perhaps it was true. Perhaps these children and women had each brought with them a burden of sin and guilt. Perhaps it was that which poisoned the atmosphere to the point of suffocation. Then the child arrived from the garden to escort him.

It was Vérité.

He looked between the girl and the Prioress, thinking it was a deliberate act of kindness. But it was not. He thought, then, that the nun must see the likeness and realize her mistake. But the Prioress did not look at faces: her focus was fixed at a distance better suited for scanning souls. He allowed Vérité to lead him silently out of the solar and into the cloisters.

He had never spoken to her on any of his visits. Once, he had given her almonds, but she had been summoned away from him by a nun and slapped and the almonds spilled on the ground. He had never been able to confirm for a certainty that this thin, dark-haired child was, in truth, Vérité. But the older she grew the more she resembled her mother and father until it seemed to him that the whole world must realize, but be too discreet to comment, that this was the daughter of Gloriole.

Nonsense, of course. The face was an amalgamation of mother's and father's, and Marthe's was a face known only to her neighbouring cave-dwellers. Even the child saw nothing of herself in the grand visitor she escorted, walking at a pace which made it plain that she thought him a frail old man. 'What's your name, child?' he asked, for fear it was he who was indulging in self-deception.

'My name is Vérité,' she said. 'Though one day I'll be Sister Stephen.'

'But underneath you'll still be Vérité.'

'Oh!' she said and looked astonishment at him out of eyes that were his – in all truth they were his. It was as if he had guessed a secret she thought she had kept hidden.

'And do you like it here, Vérité?'

'Where?' she said. A stupid question of his. Where else had she ever seen or known?

'This is a very beautiful building.' Certainly, on the inside, the Madeleine had all the unfractured peace of a glass bubble touched only by dry female hands that left no fingermarks to dull the purity.

'I'm not a whore, you know?' said Vérité abruptly. 'Some of the ladies here are. I'm a Daughter of Joy. That's different.'

'I know.'

'It means I haven't gone to bed with a man,' she said. It sounded precocious, but it was nothing more than grasping at definitions, at overheard remarks and crass explanations. 'I'm very wicked, but I'm not so wicked as the whores.'

'I'm sure you're none of you very wicked at all. Tell me, do the . . . older ladies talk to you ever? About the world outside?'

'It's forbidden,' she said in reflex accordance with some well-inculcated rule. It seemed to remind her that she was meant to be showing him the facilities of the Madeleine, and she began to introduce him to rooms, prospects and inanimate objects in a dutiful panic that jarred on all his nerves. The place was, after all, only small. He was reminded of the island to which Caesar Augustus banished his daughter – walked from end to end in a matter of minutes.

'Do you want to . . . Do you girls look forward to being holy sisters?' She did not answer. 'Some do and some don't, I dare say.'

'Ah well, I suppose I wouldn't mind it,' she said. 'But I may not be able to stay here.' She looked furtively around her and stood on tiptoe to whisper. 'My father's a king, you see.'

'Is he so?!' Victoire rather startled her by sitting down abruptly on a monumental urn. 'Which one?'

'Good King René of Sicily and Jerusalem,' she said without a moment's hesitation. 'And one day he'll send for me to live with him in a palace in the Holy City – right beside the Garden of Gethsemane.'

'Fortunate René!'

'*Do you know him? Do you know my father?*'

'Ah – I've met him once or twice. No, no. I don't know René. Not at all, really.'

Still, it was said too late not to excite her. 'What manner of man is he? Tell me about him – everything about him! Please!

Her hands lifted, but she did not touch him. It was as though she were behind the grille already and the only masculine forms with any real substance were Saint Peter and the crucified Christ. Perhaps Victoire was only as real to her as one of the people in her imagination, and that was why she confided in him at all.

Her hair was cut short and unbecomingly, imprisoned under a miserable square of gabardine. Its uneven spikes bobbed against the corners of her mouth. Her face had an unnatural pallor crayoned in with crude greenish shadows under the eyes and cheekbones. The way she had been taught to speak – in a soft, low mumble – showed only her lower teeth so that her broad top lip barely moved. It would have been impossible to smile with such a mouth.

Victoire searched unwillingly for something that might interest a ten-year-old. 'René used to keep a menagerie of animals in his moat. Also poets and artists and writers, though not in the moat, I think.'

'I know. When he jousted at Lannay, two lions on silver chains paraded ahead of him – and a band of drums and trumpets.'

'Good L . . . Good gracious, I didn't know that. But from what I hear, I believe he's as his name says: a good man – a truly good man.'

'I know. He gave money to the Madeleine. We pray for him. That's how I know he's my father. And he gave his other daughter to the King of England. So he must be lonely, mustn't he?'

'I see you know as much about him as I do. Would you pray for me, Vérité? Sometimes? In your private prayers?'

'Why? Are you lonely, too? If you like. If your name's not too hard.'

'I am the Comte de . . . My name's Victoire. Can you remember that?'

She had brought him to the gate. The bellrope was resting through a loop of iron like the Serpent craving re-entry to Eden. As she put him out, he bowed, and she, having learned no social niceties at all, attempted the same herself, awkwardly, gauchely, before turning and walking away. He watched her go: Princess of Sicily and Jerusalem. The titles rested as plausibly on her, he thought, as ever they had on René, the mad old coot. No, not mad. An innocent, the Good 'King' René: readily manipulated by subtle politicians; naive to the point of gullibility; childlike. Levered out of his chateau by the 'real' King's sleight-of-hand, he strolled like a gypsy between a half-dozen country houses with his poets and minstrels. And people loved him. Even this child loved him, to whom he was a name in an orison, a crest on a cornice. She had chosen rightly in her imagination: one innocent's intuitive attraction for another. Better that she should weave her martin's nest of daydreams around the blazon of the King of Jerusalem, then marry a cold-blooded, impotent God sleeping a universe away. Better than disillusioning her with the truth.

Even so, on the ride home, he found himself feeling as malevolent towards Good King René of Jerusalem and Sicily as if they were rivals in love.

During the day, de Gloriole ruled with absolute tyranny over his senses, maintained them on the meanest rations. But to his dismay, they had a way of breaking out at night and overrunning his dreams with bright riots of colour, the anarchical rebellions of happy memories and all the joys of which he had deprived himself. A month or so after visiting La Madeleine, he dreamed music.

It was a braule – a ring-dance – and danced by women and girls in bright dresses, their hair swinging out loose like the tails of a cavalry charge, the unsubtle rhythms beaten out on a tabor. He could see in his dream where the drummer's stick had bruised the drumskin in the same place, over and over, so that it resembled a round white face with deep-sunk cheeks and hollow eyes. When he woke, the rhythm was only the pulsing of blood behind his ears, but the tune was in his mouth like a persistent taste, in his head like a nagging. He could not be rid of it all morning.

His musicians were gone. He had sent them away. But some of their instruments remained where they had left them, like sailors abandoning ship. He fetched them down from the gallery overhanging the great-hall. These days, without friends or a spiritual adviser to question his behaviour, he did not tend to spend long asking himself his motives. Besides, he thought he knew full well why he parcelled up the instruments and sent them, with six bales of Sablois samite, by cart to the Madeleine Convent '. . . having seen no means of music-making among the elsewise charming facilities of your excellent hospice'.

The carter returned after the two-day round journey still mumbling imprecations against 'nuns and whores' for the short shrift he had been given. 'Unload, load it up again. And never a sup of drink or a pob of bread.' The musical instruments and the silk had been returned intact, with a terse note of disparagement from the Prioress:

Sir –

Much as I believe it offered out of well-intentioned charity, I must decline to accept your ill-considered gift of musical objects and lewd stuff. An hour's reflection on the sins of the flesh and upon Our Lord's sorrow will instruct you that a house of Penitential Devotion is not a place for the profane pleasures of secular music. We make adequate music with our voices and have no need of instruments. Only the vanity of the body is served by the sensualities of silk.

Following your regrettable visit to my House, I had cause to chastise novitiate Stephen for wanton secularity of mind . . .

'What's "wanton secularity"?' de Gloriole asked his secretary as he read.

'God knows, sir,' said his secretary inappropriately.

. . . and must make plain that your care for the work of this hospice would be best served by curbing all interference. I cannot entertain the possibility of another interview and must request no donations other than such monies as may be recommended by your prayerful meditations.

'*No music?*' said de Gloriole, throwing aside the letter in disgust.

'*No music?*' said de Gloriole to his steward-of-accounting, as the man endeavoured to explain the merits of bonds over hard currency. The steward was nonplussed.

'*No music?*' said de Gloriole to the argentier trying to interest him in fifty arbalètes for the armoury. 'What became of making a glad noise unto the Lord?' The argentier decided to call another day with a dozen lutes instead.

'*No music?*' said de Gloriole to the woman who brought him his midday meal. 'What's a woman without music?' The woman tried to hum as she left the room.

'*No music?*' said the man who had inflicted silence on himself with deliberate, premeditated masochism. '*No silk?*' said the man who had left off using sheets on his bed for fear his body should ever again enjoy comfort. ' "*Wanton secularity!*" *By Mary, where's the Magnificat in the woman?*' He misremembered the Duc of Orléans once saying he'd as soon give up sex as music. And he nursed his outrage for two whole days, fanning it with exclamations of anger, and slamming doors.

During twenty-five years of campaigning, he had watched young, frightened knights on the eve of a battle pick quarrels with each other and work themselves into a state of hysterical indignation, just so as to throw themselves into battle white-hot and thoughtless. But he did not recognize the same process at work in himself until, from the height of his saddle, he was lashing on the bellrope outside the Convent of the Madeleine and demanding to be let in. The Prioress came to the gate to be rid of him. He dismounted.

'I'm come to take my daughter away.'

'That's quite impossible.'

'I'm come to take away Vérité de Gloriole!'

'There's no one of that name here.'

'As you wish it. Vérité Pommier, daughter of Marthe Pommier.'

'There is no one of that –'

The fingers of his black gauntlets poked through the grille and he pushed his face close to the bars. 'Give her up or I'll write to my excellent friend the King of France and tell him you're running a bawdy-house here. Let me in, woman, and we'll discuss your recompense.'

It was wholly unjust. A part of him knew he was behaving despicably. But another part knew that if he failed to gain access, his pigeons would indeed carry information against the Madeleine that would cause the greatest ecclesiastical scandal of the reign. The Prioress adopted a face which invited martyrdom with its obstinacy. Behind her the early morning courtyard was filling up with women and girls agog with excitement and delicious shock. He could not see Vérité among them. He called to them to fetch her out.

'You're not of sound mind!' said the Prioress.

'No? So? Was it ever a prerequisite of parenthood? Give me up my daughter! What right have you to keep her?'

'What right have you to take her? I wouldn't entrust a mad dog to you, sir! Leave or I'll summon men to drive you off.'

'And I to bring down your walls!'

'Go home and put your soul into frame!'

'So I shall, if you give me my daughter!'

'What do you want with her? Of a sudden? In this desperate, hasty passion?'

'Perhaps I repent me of my unfatherly ways.'

'Perhaps you need her for an advantageous match! Entry here is irrevocable. She's promised to God.'

'Then God must bear up to the disappointment, tell Him. My claim's prior. He may have her hereafter. I need her now.'

'Why? What for? For no good purpose in the world, I know!' She was too slow in her backward leap. A snatch of his glove grasped the corner of her veil and she left her headgear dangling from his fist, her close-cropped hair uncovered like something hidden too long from the sun.

'To make her Chatelaine of my estates! To make her Suzeraine of Gloriole! To make her my heir!'

She glared at him, too afraid to retrieve her headclothes out of his clenched fist, angry that she had not anticipated such a bizarre remark. It set the whores chattering behind her, crediting him with status, dazzled by his folly. 'Vainglorious man!' she declared damningly. And then partly to summon help, but more to escape the shame of being seen bare-headed, she hurried into the solar, commanding everyone else to follow. Her nuns of course obeyed at once, but most of the Daughters of Joy lingered.

Almost in the same moment, one came back to the yard from another direction, pulling Vérité after her. Devilry had made her fetch out the child. But daring failed her and she set Vérité adrift in the open centre of the yard and hid again among the crowd of spectators.

The girl was in penitential sackcloth and, thanks to him, her head had been close-shaved. Someone had made of her a human sacrifice to ugliness.

'*Vérité!*' He called to her, powerless, from beyond the grille. When she recognized him, she recoiled instinctively from the cause of her troubles, but the women behind pushed her forward again as a bearpit crowd shoo the dogs in again to the bear, for the sport of it. 'It's your *father*,' they said with sing-song, playground insolence. 'Your *father* wants you.'

She stared around her for an escape, but the crowd spread out to bar all the doorways off the yard.

'Vérité, I've come to fetch you!' called Victoire, but he could only shake the grille with his two hands and increase her fright.

'Are you the Devil?' It must have seemed like it: this blood-red man come on horseback, waiting at the gate.

'No, I'm not the Devil. Nor a king either! But I am your father! Come with me! I want you with me!' But he was on the outside and she on the in, and it was only like taunting a chained beast. He shook the gates until the mortar trickled at the hinges like blood.

The Prioress, realizing what had happened, called from indoors:

sharp, incisive commands that brooked no discussion: dispatching nuns to fetch the child away, sending others to summon men from the nearby fields. He beat his forehead on the gate. 'Vérité, I'll come back for you! Don't take a vow! Don't be afraid!'

The nuns were trying to force a path through the crowd, but their penitents' mischief had taken on the momentum of a riot; the situation had not been milked for its maximum sport. The whores stood firm, obstructing the nuns. The outlook for Vérité grew worse with every horrifying new twist to the game.

'*Vérité!*' called the stranger beyond the gate – a cry of helpless apology – he looked at her out of eyes that were her own: in all truth they were hers. As the labourers came running round the building to tackle him, he turned away in despair.

'*Wait!*'

Lifting her sackcloth, she took off at full tilt, on her bare feet, along the entrance passageway leading to the gate. She came pelting towards him like a guard dog, and he thought she would hurl herself against the gate. But from a few feet away she leapt up half its height and clambered up the tendrils of iron, while the nuns came flapping after her like great black vultures.

The women in the yard set up a chant, urging her on. Victoire remounted his horse to be higher off the ground and of more help. She thought he was going to ride away and shrieked for him to stop.

At the top of the gates, the spikes curved outward – made to deter intruders rather than escapees. Her little feet fitted exactly between the spikes; her anklebones grazed on the sharp red rust. He saw that her knees were hard-calloused from praying. Beneath her, the nuns began to jump up and to snatch at her robe, and to shake the gate to dislodge her. The Prioress threatened her with the pains of Hell if she persisted. She threatened using the name 'Stephen, novitiate Stephen', over and over again.

'Jump, Vérité!' he said, reaching up his black gauntlets, spurring his horse violently in against the wall to counter its fear of the flapping nuns and the noise.

'Jump! Jump!' yelled the whores.

'This will cost you such a penance!' promised the Prioress, and tipped the balance between one fear and the next.

Vérité hurled herself down with her eyes shut, trusting to Victoire to catch her. His left arm raged with pain at the jolt, and she did not attempt to ease the weight, but dangled rigid from his grasp. He had to slot her legs, like a clothes-peg, across the horse's rump and hang on to the front of her robe with one hand while he gathered up the reins with the other. Unlocked at last, the convent gate swung open and smashed into his horse, so that it sprang sideways and into an immediate gallop. The whores let out a cheer that faltered into silence.

The Prioress, her world healing intact around her in the very moment of her defeat, declined the indignity of running after the sinner. She simply raised her voice to call after him the worst term of abuse she knew: '*Vainglorious man!*'

'You're not really my father, are you? Who are you?' said Vérité. The grip of her arms round his waist had only just relented enough to let him breathe. It was the first time she had ever ridden a horse.

'You'll think me unchivalric if I say it,' he said, glancing quickly over his shoulder at this plucked boiler-chicken of a child, 'but why the devil else would I want you?'

'But you're so *old*,' she said, returning the compliment. 'How old are you?'

'The Good King René's no younger. I'm sixty.'

'No! No one's that old! Not even the Prioress!'

'Methuselah was nine hundred and sixty-nine when he died, oh ignorant one. But I dare say he led a blameless life and wasn't kept too busy abducting girls from convents.'

'What do you want me for?' She had so completely damned herself, was so completely at his mercy, that she seemed to have passed beyond fear.

'I can't remember. It'll come back to me, perhaps, when I'm rested. The memory fails at my age, you know.'

At some level, she seemed to realize that René of Sicily and Jerusalem had been a figment of her imagination. In fact, she proved a peculiar amalgam of fantasy, innocence and borrowed worldly wisdom. 'Must I be your whore?'

'Sancta Maria! Say that again and I'll beat you! As God's my judge, I will!'

'Well, you must be very wicked. You swear terrible oaths.'

'Do I?' It startled him. It reminded him how long he had been out of civilizing influences. Not that he could call this scrawny hen-bustard civilized company: he was hard put to know what he would actually *do* with her to keep her out of sight once they reached Gloriole.

By the time they did so, she had grown so accustomed to the

horse that she would stand up on its rump with one hand on his collar, to look about her. He could not dissuade her from thinking they had crossed three countries and had reached at least as far as the Holy Land or Constantinople. They rode through a biblical geography between the Nile of the Cher and the Euphrates of the Loire.

'What place is that?'

'Where do you think it is?'

'Babylon,' she said at once, thumping down again into his back. 'I can see the gardens.'

'My wife and son laid out the gardens. My first wife, I mean. Not your mother. That's Gloriole-sur-Sablois. That's where I'm taking you.'

'I thought you said you weren't a king. Why did you say you weren't a king?'

'I'm not. I'm a comte simple. Not so much as a duc.' She swung outwards from the saddle and leaned forward, as she did every time she wanted to judge if he was joking or serious. Clearly she decided he was lying between his teeth. Her hands slid from round his waist and she eased herself over the back of the saddle so as not to sit pressed up against a king.

The beauty of Sablois and the Gloriole chateau quite subdued her. It was evening when they arrived, and lights were already lit in each of the nine turrets. The black roofs made a mountain-scape against the red clouds – conical peaks and knife-edge ridges, and the Chapel Saint-Cloud snow-peaking the nearby hill. Pigeons and white doves were circling, after a day spent pillaging the fields, and a skein of geese came in to land on the lake. The dogs in the run were baying an early moon, and the river had picked up the colour of sunset in a rosy phosphorescence.

'What must I do here?' she asked.

'What you can. What you will. So long as you grace and not disgrace my house,' he said as they passed under the portcullis. He pulled a blanket down from the wash-line as they entered the stable-yard: he could wrap her in it and smuggle her into the house – decide what to do with her after that. Looking back on the events of the early morning, he wondered if he were not slipping into the eccentric madness of old age that he could behave so.

'Will your son pretend to be my brother?' she whispered into the nape of his neck. 'Will he want to when he sees me?'

Victoire paused before dismounting and leaned forward on his pommel to test the flexibility of his hips. He found he was too exhausted to stir body or mind. 'My son's been dead these eight years,' he said.

A small, stick-insect hand came over his shoulder momentarily and touched his cheek. 'I am sorry, Your Majesty,' she said.

Loneliness was one of the few abstract concepts Vérité understood – although she had been raised to think of it as a sin – a poverty of spirit, self-inflicted. At the Madeleine she had been lonely because friendships and, for a large part of the day, conversation were forbidden.

It was fortunate that she thought of loneliness as her lot. For at Gloriole there was plenty to be had. Though its buildings straggled over two acres of land, most of its rooms were empty for most of the day. She slept alone, she washed alone, she went walking alone, all the time expecting to overstep her scope, always listening for the voice of correction which never came. It was insecure. It was like walking on a roof without balustrades, in a dense fog.

Foolishly, Victoire put off introducing her to the household until her hair had grown down and he had been able to come by a suitable wardrobe of clothes for her. They avoided her, therefore, as they would any house-guest. They supposed there was a purpose to her being there – an act of charity, they surmised – but would not have dreamed of talking to her.

Flockhart's daughters had married yeomen and lived in Roche-blanche now with daughters of their own. Victoire borrowed clothes from them. Also he gave them Sablois silk and asked t em to make up dresses for their girls and one other for unspecified use. They deduced that he had rescued some needy creature from the leper house or the roadside. The rest of the staff only went as far as to wonder how long she was staying. So, for that matter, did Vérité. So, for that matter, did Victoire. He had promised Marthe that Vérité should be a Daughter of Joy and perhaps, after all, that was what she was best suited for. Though not at the joyless Madeleine, of that much he was resolved. He told her to call him 'monsieur'.

There was no bottom to her ignorance, for she had been taught nothing at all. There was no end to her clumsiness, for she had never been allowed to handle things or own possessions. A spoon, a book and Latin were the full extent of her accomplishments. Victoire watched her over the rim of his tumbler at mealtimes as she struggled to believe in the food set out for her – 'Do I *eat* this or is it for prettiness?' she said of the fruit jelly.

He was not so foolish as to try to educate her. Dogs brought into a pack, rather than whelped there, need time to acclimatize before they can be put to use on the hunt. It seemed a sound principle to follow with this mongrel waif.

Then all of a sudden one morning she was no longer a waif. Her hair, if not luxuriant, no longer looked like mange, and she had ceased to wake up in those ungodly watches of the night fixed by holy orders for prayers: she was well slept. She had been out in the stable-yard watching the horses shoed and her skin was sunny. She had also put on a roundness that evicted the shadows from under her cheekbones and above her collar. He caught sight of her watching him to see how she should eat a pancake and honey. And behold, she had stopped looking like the chicheface on the shield behind her head, and grown to look like the woman in the cherished, battered portrait retrieved from the cave. Better somewhat. If there was an art to eating a pancake and honey correctly, he had never learned it. Showing her his hands and beard smothered in stickiness, he shrugged as if to say, 'You can't do worse, however you try it,' and laughed. She smiled tentatively, as though she were copying that too, then was overtaken by spontaneous giggles and laughed till she got hiccups.

Having mastered the smile, she would barely be parted from it. On the same day that the two raw-silk dresses arrived from Rocheblanche, the draper arrived from Tours with his twin brother the tailor. The dresses were the first presents Victoire gave her. (Malnourished dogs cannot stomach a rich diet all at once.) But somehow once begun, the game of giving took on an irresistible charm.

'Would you be so kind, gentlemen, as to show your wares to the mademoiselle? I shall trust to her judgment. Vérité, please tell the gentlemen which you like best.'

Vérité, dressed in one of the home-made dresses, had been trying to see her reflection in the polished shine of an armoire and tore her eyes away unwillingly; her hands went on patting and stroking the bodice and skirts of silk, savouring the texture of the 'lewd stuff'. The draper humped one bolt of cloth after another on to the table and unfurled it with dextrous skill, showing her how it draped, how it pleated, how it would swag and how the nap or the patterning ran.

'Think about winter as well as summer. Everyday and feast-days,' said Victoire, but omitted to point out just what the cloth was to be used for.

First there was deep green velveteen and she called it moleskin soft and wonderful. Then there was hodden-grey worsted which she said would keep out the worst winter in France. Next there was cornflower-blue velvet which she thought too beautiful for words; and swansdown cotton whose long soft nap she held to her cheek and said was the softest thing in the world.

Then there was samite which she said put her in mind of the river; then satin which she said must be made with metal because it shone so and was so cold to the touch. The flame-coloured foulard she thought the most beautiful cloth eyes had ever seen. Victoire, who had never taken an intrinsic interest in cloth or clothes, found himself reading the draper's tariff and anticipating the pleasure successive bales would bring her. But to his surprise, she gave only half an eye to the pink damask woven with deep red roses, the brocade wrought with a device of seashells, the niñon voile, the white and silver damassin. In fact she could not look at them face-on and turned half away from the table.

'Are they too gaudy for your taste, Vérité?' She did not like to give offence to the draper. 'Would you whisper your objection, lady?'

Giving the table a wide berth, she came round the room to him and whispered in his ear. 'Sure, monsieur cannot wear such things. They're for queens, not kings.'

He digested this solemnly, then whispered back, 'Absolutely. I would have stopped short at the worsted for myself. But we are talking of dresses for you. And having troubled the messieurs to carry their wares all the way from Tours, I think you should do them the courtesy of a fleeting look at least. Personally, I would ask the damassin to dance if I met it at Court.'

'Dresses? For me? But I have a dress! I have two dresses!'

He turned her about, to face the table and its galleon cargo of treasure. 'Pray don't disappoint the gentlemen entirely, my dear.'

She moved along the row of fabrics, each carefully overlaying the one before and cascading off the table to pool and puddle on the floor at her feet. The tailor and draper, as like as two clucks from the same chicken, urged her to feel the weight, examine the reverse, observe the craftsmanship. Her fingers hovered over the plush; she could not bring herself to touch it, then she could not bring herself to lift her fingers away. She reeled visibly from the intoxicating desire to own it; she grew pale at the thought of choosing between one or another.

'If you would be so good as to take measurements, Messieurs Beaujeu, she shall have a gown of each, with two shifts of the swansdown and two of the cambric. Your tariff lists sarcenet. Do you have none with you?'

One of the tailors ran out-of-doors in an ecstasy of apologies and returned with the slight squares of folded tissue in either hand, gold in one, white in the other. With all the theatricality of a fairground magician, he caused the sarcenets to billow out in insubstantial clouds then allowed them to hang from his hands, blowing in the draught from the window. Vérité ran back to Victoire and clung to his arm and hissed in his ear. 'I couldn't wear *that*! You can see right through!'

Victoire took one of the squares and let it fall over her short hair. 'You wear it over your head, lady. Thus. By way of a veil.'

Enveloped in the gauzy cloud, no longer able to distance herself from it all, Vérité closed her eyes against the intolerable bombardment of beauty. The glistening sarcenet was sucked in and billowed out from against her nose and mouth as she breathed shallowly and overfast. He saw her lower lip start to tremble.

'The mademoiselle will take both sarcenets, Beaujeu, but requires some moments' leisure before she is troubled with measuring.'

TWENTY

Clipping Wings

Like angels looking down from the parapets of Heaven, the Little
Sisters of Pity knelt along the gallery carpet and peeped out of the
gablet windows, their eyes as round as wafers and their mouths agape
as if they were singing. But the music was not theirs. It drifted up
from the gardens along with the confused noise of three hundred
guests and entertainments. A visitor using the opportunity of the
party to explore the Comte's art collection strayed up the stairs,
and the nuns rose in a single flock and ran flapping and squealing
along the gallery to the far end. The guest was so disconcerted that
he turned back down the stairs. The nuns remustered one by one:
seagulls disturbed from a rock by an unexpected wave.

'Are you paying heed to me, Vérité?' asked the Comte de Gloriole
sharply.
'Yes, monsieur.'
'And you know what I mean to do? Here? Today?'
'Yes, monsieur. I believe so.' Out-of-doors, a roasting ox slumped
round on a spit turned by dogs in a treadmill. A man was producing
silver blancs from an orange and from behind children's ears. A band
was playing braules and people were dancing, their hair flying out
like the tails of a cavalry charge . . . 'You mean to tell all these
people that I'm your daughter.'
She was dressed in the gown of white and silver damassin which,
though made big for her at nine, fitted her at ten to perfection. Her
peculiarly sturdy black hair, brushed into a cloud of separate strands
around her shoulders, adhered to the sarcenet and moved with it as
it blew in the breeze from the open window.
'That much I shall do, come what may – Vérité, I've told you
before not to bite your lip. And shut the window so you can hear
what I have to say to you.'
With the stiff, inhibited movements of a child feeling alarmingly

beautiful, Vérité crossed to the window. She could not help looking down again to the source of the music. There was a minstrel with a hurdy-gurdy and flame-orange hose.

'I mean to announce more than that, if you'll grant me your leave – Pay attention, Vérité!'

'I am! By my faith, monsieur!'

'And you'll call me "Father" henceforth?'

'If it please you, mon – Father.'

Outside, mountebanks on the tail of a flat wagon were acting out the story of Noah, with animal heads for all the beasts in Creation and a unicorn too. And there was a tilt yard set up, with quintains and keels.

'Come here and put your hands on the Bible. I want you to take an oath. If you're willing.'

'Of course I'm willing. What must I swear?' She hastened to touch the sweat-blackened Bible he held against his chest, but he pulled it away.

'No. It must be thought through. It must be deep-sworn from the seat of your heart.'

'What? What must I swear?'

Outside, a bear was dancing to the music of a bagpipe – there was a dog that could walk on its hind legs, too, and as many skittles lined up as there are soldiers in the King's Army, just waiting to be scattered.

'Would you like to own Gloriole one day?'

'I don't understand.'

'Would you like to be Chatelaine of Gloriole-sur-Sablois? After I'm dead.'

'No. Not if you have to be dead. Of course not.' She picked her way as hastily as possible through what she took for the correct script.

'Everyone must die, child. And everyone must have an heir. Every comte, at least.'

'But I can't be your heir. I'm a girl.'

'What so? Have I a son? It's common. Widows. Daughters. Better you than my cousin's son, eh? Better someone I love, don't you agree?'

'But what would I *do*?' Outside, a man knew how to make a dove disappear from sight and fetch it back again out of his codpiece.

'Whatever it pleases you to do. Fêtes every day, if you choose.

Dresses as you like. There's a wealth of time: I can teach you the way of it, provided that you do want to own Gloriole.'

Fêtes every day? She did not believe him. But to own Gloriole – as she owned the toy house he had given her! To own its peasants as she owned the doll he had given her! To own? To own! Ownership was still a fathomless, mysterious wonder unfolding day by day before a child who had owned nothing before the age of nine. Though she could not entirely grasp the concept, she knew that all happiness stemmed from owning. Before, she had owned nothing – and been nothing to anyone. She could date the day she began to feel loved from the day she first knew ownership. 'Own Gloriole?'

'In exchange you must promise never to marry. I promised your mother you'd be a Daughter of Joy. It's as close as you can keep to her wishes and still be Chatelaine.'

'Not marry? Ever?' Outside there were jugglers walking on stilts as high as a house – and tumblers! – and a man who swallowed down fire and could hold a burning brand to his chest and not even flinch. She had never thought to marry. It was not the lot of Daughters of Joy. 'That's nothing.'

'Swear, then. On the Bible. Swear.' The speed with which he pushed the great grease-mottled volume towards her along the table made her start. She spread her hands on the cover, enjoying the feel of the soft kid leather tooled with golden curlicues. He covered her hands with his.

'I swear never to marry,' she said with a slight shrug of her shoulders.

'And to stay a virgin.'

'What do you mean?'

'Never to take a man into your bed or your body all the days of your life.'

Outside there was a magician with pigeons in his codpiece and a fire-eater who could hold fire to him and did not burn . . .

'Oh. Yes. Of course. I swear. To stay a virgin.'

'And never to bear children.'

'And never to bear –'

'No matter. It's superfluous. It's already sworn.' He freed her hands as abruptly as he had covered them and rubbed at his temples. 'And I shall draw you up a contract of *affrairementum*, and you shall name the heir of your choice when the time's fitting. As today is fitting. Now we'll go outside and I'll tell all our neighbours and kin that you're my daughter and my chosen heir.' The thing seemed to have cost him more than her, for he looked breathless and ashen and his eyes were unnaturally bright. Vérité could see herself in them, all shimmering and gauzy.

She had long since abandoned the effort to find words big enough to house her everyday thank-yous. And here was a thank-you called for bigger than all the rest. However, she had also learned, unconsciously, that it gave the Comte pleasure to be touched. So she put a pair of encouraging arms around his waist and lifted her sarcanet and planted her thank-you as kisses above the grey beard, before disappearing once more inside her cocoon of silver.

'Go outside, child. I'll come and find you shortly.' So she glided towards the door, her wrists arched stiffly outwards, her arms away from her body, like a grand and stately lady dancing a pavane. 'Vérité –'

'Yes . . . Father?' she said, laughing at the idiotic novelty and the difficulty of remembering.

'You look lovely, child,' he said aggressively. 'You grace the house by being in it.' She blushed, and fled away down the corridor with a rustle of silk and hair and a slightly unladylike thud of feet.

Victoire picked up the Bible, meaning to return it to its lectern-shelf, but was overtaken by thought and sat with it clasped to his chest. It was done. He had preserved her against the fate of her mother, against the fate of Ellen, against the curse and blight of his love.

Once again Love had revived within him, taken him unawares. Ever since his first intimation that this child would awake in him what seemed dead, he had fretted how to contain the damage, how to restrict it to the minimum. Love, he could see now, was a malarial infection in his blood. Just when he thought he had shaken it off, the fever flared up in him again, undermining his strength, overtaxing his heart. It would dog him to his deathbed and he was growing too old to suppose he could fight off this last bout.

He had once thought to render his love for Ellen permanent with a son and had killed her in doing so. He had once allowed that son to give him the comfort of a second woman and had killed the woman for her tenderness towards him. He had once thought to ensure the safety and prosperity of his son and had killed him by doing so. But this last time he would let neither ambition nor selfishness on his part condemn this child as he had condemned the others.

Bad enough that he had, out of pure loneliness, prised her from the safe shell of the Madeleine where her soul had been bound for Heaven. Give her Gloriole and he would ensure that a locust swarm of suitors settled on her to strip her bare, to thrust her full of their ambitions, to sweep together her estates between their knees and pin them fast under their hips.

But his women died in childbirth: his children died for the sin of being his offspring. These two observable truths had taught Victoire the only course of action possible. He would give Vérité Gloriole and grant her long life to enjoy it. It was vaunting ambition to want more – to lay claim to immortality with dynasties and descendants. Seal up Vérité's womb and there was an end for him of caring who owned Gloriole. The unborn have no faces: how could it matter to him that he disinherited them?

He had always invested all his love in one person at a time, and now it rested in Vérité. She was the residue of death: the flotsam left floating after the sinking of a fleet. He would not suffer anything to pull her under the icy, all-enveloping ocean.

Time enough to explain these things to her when she was older – when she hankered after marriage or was curious for the taste of a man. God would never set her free of her vow. (In that much He would surely be relied on to recompense Victoire.) After all, the vow was not robbing her of very much. Only of the mindless cruelty of men such as himself, who killed women in pursuit of their lust.

Thus Victoire reasoned, acting on the only wisdom possible; acting on his own experience. He rested his chin on the Bible. The pity of parties was that the organizing of them left a man tired before they even began.

His plan to preserve Vérité had begun to take shape weeks before. He had even made peace with Barnabas in order to enlist his help. Vérité must not want for friends or companionship: his aim was not to preserve a beautiful but miserable fly in amber. So the very first time he spoke to Barnabas after a silence of almost ten years, he bellowed up from the base of the tallat-loft ladder, 'Surely to God there's an order of sisters that finds life a merry thing!'

Barnabas came to the hatch on hands and knees. (It was a terrible place for a man past sixty to live. Victoire suddenly wondered why the priest had not died long ago.) 'You!' was all Barnabas said on looking down.

'Find me an order of sisters. I want to install a convent in the East-turret loft. But they must know how to laugh!' and he had turned and walked out again. The nuns' chastity would make Vérité's own seem natural – the norm. They could not fire her with stories of pleasures unknown to her. (Neither would they give Gloriole the reputation of a bawdy-house, or invite rumours about his own behaviour, something he did not at all relish.)

In those times, it was not hard to find an order, or the sect of an order, or the house of a sect of an order to represent every colour and complexion of Christianity. Barnabas came to the chateau a week later. He said he had found candidates for the East-turret loft in the destitute Little Sisters of Pity, but that he would not let them come.

'Why? What do you mean, you won't let them come?'

'Never.'

'Don't they need a roof over their heads and all found?'

'Yes, but how can I place them at the service of a piece of Devil's meat like you?' said Barnabas, his voice shrill with daring.

'What are you, covetous of martyrdom?' said Victoire, bristling like a boar.

'Don't come near me! You haven't taken the Sacraments for nigh on ten years. You must be thicker in sins than the fleas on a cat! And you expect me to commit a convent of virgins to your care? Pah! That's what I say to you. Pah!'

Inadvertent spittle hit Victoire in the face and he wiped it away. 'A man of strong language, are you, these days? I'd best keep you a distance from my daughter, then, or you'll corrupt her.'

'Your *daughter*?'

'My daughter. The maid in the third state chamber. You've surely caught wind of her. I might as well hide a pig in a press as try to keep a secret from the estate.'

'It's thought she's a wife in training. Or worse. A pastime.' Barnabas considered the true explanation grudgingly. 'Your daughter, you say? I'll let it be known generally. Not for your sake, mind! Only to stop up the lewd influence on the young people. Not for your benefit!'

'I'll spread the news myself in good time. Say nothing for now,' said Victoire.

'Ah yes! I dare say you like to be thought the lusty lover. Just as much as you like to be thought the spy and informer. Well, may God forgive you when all's known!'

'And if He does? If I take Communion and gain forgiveness? Will you forgive me, too?' asked Victoire mildly.

'I'll go and fetch it now,' said Barnabas, setting his lips in the same old smug grin and hurrying for the door.

'I'm not quite bedridden yet. I think I might stumble as far as the chapel to say Confession.'

'But you might fall down the steps on the way and thwart me!' said the priest, and collided with the doorframe in his haste to be gone.

So Victoire was reconciled to God, after ten years treading the scalding rime of Hell, while his priest and observant household held their breath, waiting for the magma to well up and engulf him. Sablois breathed a sigh of relief and there was an outbreak of pilgrimages to Béhuard and Cléry. If a comte went to Hell, there was a tendency to believe he would take his chattels with him for company.

And the Little Sisters of Pity moved in to the East-turret loft, under the knife-edge pavillon of black-Angers. They were to serve as lady's maids, laundresses, seamstresses, nurses and companions, with the understanding that their hours of religious observance would be honoured and their own chapel built on, in due course, at the base of the turret. They were an order made up of the orphans of Touraine cabinet-makers – a class so very specific that, after the original endowment had been used up, no new patron could be found to take an interest in their welfare. They were overjoyed, therefore, to receive Victoire's invitation and, given their background, took a practical hand in establishing their convent. They lined the roof with beech planks, then sawed through the sprung wood floor of the gallery landing and constructed a block and pulley drawbridge that could be raised at night or 'whensoever there were men in the house'. Consequently, when a hunt gathered at Gloriole and guests the worse for drink went in search of the Comte's 'Little Sisters', the nuns fluttered like so many carrier pigeons into their loft and drew up the bridge, leaving only the sound of their laughter on the landing and a tripwire with a bell to warn the unwary of the missing stretch of floor.

The Little Sisters were overjoyed by a great many things. They took their inspiration from the *joculatores Domine* – the Franciscans – whose founding father once said, 'It belongs to the Devil to be sad.' They devoured the Bible in search of passages commending praise, thanksgiving and rejoicing. They held the firm conviction that Heaven would teem with good things housed in beautiful wood cabinets, but they did not let that deter them from enjoying the imperfect world, too.

Consequently, on the day of the party thrown in Vérité's honour, they gathered on the landing to watch, and finally sent word to their benefactor asking whether he thought it would be appropriate for them 'to take a short promenade in the gardens, if we all stay close together'. The Comte replied that he looked forward to them gracing his festivities throughout the afternoon, and they hopped out of the house like a dozen smart-feathered magpies, and danced ring dances with all the little children too small to be welcome in the bigger braules.

Tourney towers had been built for smashing, from split wood and gunny roughly daubed with English heraldries. Heralds in chequered surcoats, posted at the top of each tower, blew ribald trumps every now and then to welcome any latecomers seen straggling in across the river. Funnels of silk filled with wind and sawed to and fro, tethered to poles. A game of *couille de bélier* grew gradually bigger and bloodier as more and more guests permitted their pages and lackeys to join in the aimless battle for possession of a bladder. When it seemed that too many liveries would be destroyed, a more sedate game of soulle was instigated, but the spirit of couille persisted in the fouls.

It was a children's party. The conjurors, the jugglers, the puppet shows: they were all geared to the entertainment of a child. Barnabas saw that, as plain as if it were painted in giant letters on the walls of Gloriole: THIS IS THE INVESTITURE OF VÉRITÉ. And yet the guests seemed not to notice at all. It was a fair, yes, and some had worn shoes which anticipated indoor dancing and a meal at table. But most were a breed of child themselves. For them life consisted of games and sports; they welcomed the chance to play and eat wherever it presented itself, and if these kind of festivities were out of character for de Gloriole, all the more reason to make the most of the opportunity.

There were some, however, who would not be at ease until Victoire's motives were made public. He was an Intelligencer and not to be trusted. He did nothing for fun. He was a rich and cunning man who had still to lay his cards on the political table. Furthermore, he was an old man without heirs. Michel de Puy waited an hour by the steps of the hall, and when Victoire came out, battened on to him close as a leech, towing his grandson along by the sleeve.

'I want to play at quoits, Granpapa!' whined the boy. 'I want to see the tilting!'

'Be quiet, Estienne. And fasten your jerkin aright. You're a button adrift, slut . . . Cousin! Oh cousin, a word! A meeting's such a rare pleasure!'

'Forgive me, Michel. Later. I've business afoot. My mind would not be with you.'

'A rare pleasure! To see you looking so lusty!'

Victoire pressed on at speed, looking this way and that for his daughter. 'We both of us survive, don't we, cousin? The Sablois air must be wholesome.'

'You've not met my boy's boy Estienne – not since the christening! He's grown right promising, wouldn't you say?'

'Don't sell him for less than a fair price, then.' Victoire ducked beneath the guy ropes of the tourney pavilions, but he could not shake off his pursuing cousin.

'If he had his wish, he'd be a page to you, Victoire, and a secretary after perhaps! He plagues his father night and morning. To wear your livery!'

'When he's old enough to ride here and tell me so himself, I'll maybe consider it.'

'By the way, how do you manage, these days? Without the help of a secretary?'

'As well as I did when I had one. I have another helper now, if I could but find her.' He began to be irritated by his failure to find Vérité among the crowds. He did not want her finery dishevelled.

'Yes, and do you hope to breed on her?' shrilled Michel.

Michel burned with pique. It was too unfair. After so many years spent one fence away from inheritance, the prospect of being thwarted a third time was too unjust for words. Had Michel not worked hard enough to earn the inheritance?

Had he not conveyed news of Victoire's 'unpatriotic' marriage, to King Charles? Had he not informed against Fils to the Minister of Information? Only to see Victoire restored to grace! Had he not planted his paid man in the post of Victoire's secretary, to spot how precisely Victoire plundered the King and abused his privileged position? And found nothing.

And was he to be thwarted again by this old man's pitiful lust? For some mystery of a child? Michel de Puy writhed with frustration that his source of information had run dry. But he no longer had a spy among Victoire's household. So what was she? And how could Victoire be stopped from filling her up with his last season of seed? His spy had sworn that the Intelligencer lived celibate. Why could he not have died thus? It was insupportable selfishness.

'Yes, and do you hope to breed on her?'

'How graciously put, Michel,' was all de Gloriole said.

'Well, since you've still such fire in your blood, I trust we'll see you ride to tilt this afternoon, cousin? With your lady's favour at your lance-tip? As you did in the old days? With Fils? I wager you won't risk it at your age!' (There was perhaps still time for the old fool to break his celibate neck.)

Victoire found who he was looking for, and in doing so felt able to grant Michel the full attention of his eyes: witty, scathing eyes. 'If you'll pick up a lance, I'll ride to tilt against you, Michel, whenever you say the word. I had no idea you were so eager to risk life and limb. But first . . . Permit me to introduce you this young lady. You have the honour to meet my daughter, Vérité.'

'Your . . .'

Vérité dropped the quoit she was about to throw and curtseyed, as she had been practising to do. Victoire offered her his arm, and she took it, regally, like an oriental princess.

'This is the vessel in which all my hopes sail, Michel. I was about to make the announcement general – before God and these my neighbours and kin. But seeing as you take such a keen interest in all matters touching Gloriole, you shall be the first to know. This is my bastard daughter. And the heiress to Gloriole-sur-Sablois.'

They climbed to the white balustered terrace which had been reconstructed on a far greater scale after its accidental demolition along with the keep. That destruction of the donjon had cleared a vast open space – enough to contain all of the guests when trumpets summoned them there. They meandered in – from the gardens, from the river bank, from the dry moat, expecting some new entertainment in an afternoon of entertainments. They were entertained instead to an announcement that set them clucking with wonder.

A girl-child made heiress to Gloriole? A girl-child whose very existence came as an amazement to those who had watched the Comte's lonely existence with curious, self-interested eyes. Some had nursed hopes of marrying their daughters or sisters to the wid-owed Comte, but had long since despaired of him, saying he had turned catamite, sure. Some had looked forward to purchasing land from his executors after he died childless, to dividing up the estates among those surrounding it, like a man quartered by horses, leaving only the chateau for the King. And now there was this child!

Who was the mother? They guessed at Vérité's age; they counted the years backwards. Ah! The era of Fils' usurpation! So who had sheltered Victoire during his three-year banishment? The story went that he had lived in the caves, but that was plainly nonsense, for some nobleman's daughter had clearly hidden him under the covers of her bed, and he had begot on her this pretty, elegant thing muffled up in damassin and gauze. The features of the face were so delicate, after all. She carried clothes as the peacock carries its tail – without any encumbrance, clearly accustomed to silken stuffs since a swaddling in lawn. How could they have been so slow to notice the uncommon resemblance between father and daughter? Who did they know in the whole Loire Valley who could have concealed such a daughter, incognito, while she grew? Whose wife? Whose daughter? Which prioress? What cloistered concubine?

There was no consternation, no shocked, prudish gasp of horror: only a deal of envious speculation swiftly followed by one universal topic of conversation. Who would *marry* the girl?

Vérité heard the word. It crept towards her like the tide up a beach, those pebble faces all staring, all turning, all whispering, '*Who will she marry?*' Mothers looked sidelong and thoughtful at their sons and subdued their hair with licked fingertips. Fathers looked around them at the turrets and fascias of Gloriole, and the sun catching the windows glinted in their eyes. Little girls of ten or so looked with unveiled envy at her, easily imagining all the benefits Vérité would enjoy. It drenched her with a fine, cold unease, that tide of faces. It dampened her, that tidal whispering of the one word '. . . *marry?*'

Victoire saw it, too. He thanked God that he had prevailed on Vérité to swear her oath. He breathed the profoundest sigh of relief at the barricade he had built round her to defend her from these covetous, predatory outsiders. He drew off the silver veil as he might have unveiled a new portrait of the Madonna. Virgin intacta. Conceived in immaculate, motiveless love. Small wonder they stared. Small wonder the whispers rose off these congregated faces like half-voiced prayers. Now all that remained was for him to construct a Heaven worthy of this perfect incarnation.

The fête regained momentum after the interruption, and tumbled up against the terrace its gaudy costumes and bawdy comics; blatant pickpockets, busker bands and buskin hams; bamboozling conjurors and grotesque maskers. The chalk-white curved elevation had been rebuilt too high for them to jostle Vérité, and from its stone-wrought balcony she could safely look down and enjoy it all without being engulfed. The Little Sisters of Pity came and gathered round her, all talking at once. They enveloped her in their more ethereal happiness.

At the foot of the stairs, Michel de Puy stood aside as the Comte came down at the run. He noted the quickness of step, the spryness of the legs, but it no longer worried him.

'Well, de Puy? Shall we cross lances once or twice?' said Victoire cheerfully.

'What a notion!' protested Michel simperingly. 'We're both far too old for such follies.'

For, as a burglar moves round from one window to the next in search of a weakness, Michel de Puy had moved on from that particular ploy already, to a less hazardous one. Let Victoire live another few years; it would be all to the de Puy advantage. Quite simply, the twelve-year-old Estienne (now gambling away his substance playing *cherchez-la-femme* with a card-sharper) could marry the bastard heiress. The poor relations would lay hands on the Sablois once and for all. All it needed was a little patience.

Escaping, as he thought, to the peace of the library, Victoire found it already occupied by a guest. Jehan Bourré was examining the device of overlapping circles stamped in the plasterwork, black over gold. 'Coins, are they?' asked the Treasurer of France.

'If you like,' said Victoire.

Bourré was one of the new breed of aristocrat, one of the rich businessmen with whom King Louis had surrounded himself. They bought up tracts of the Valley and built on them with all the industry of termites. Bourré himself was a source of admiration to Victoire, for he had built, in the space of just four years, a chateau of reputed marvels at Plessis-Bourré. But he also invited suspicion, for he was as fast and true a 'Louis-man' as anyone in France; the association dated back to the days of the Dauphinage.

'I didn't expect you to come,' said Victoire rather unguardedly.

'I'm sorry. If I'd known, I wouldn't have accepted your invitation.' Bourré sat down at the table with a copy of *Oger le Danois*.

'I mean, I understand that the King was staying with you presently.'

'Why do you think I'm here?' Bourré said under his breath and began to browse through the book. 'You'll forgive me if I grant myself the luxury of a little relaxation in your excellent house.'

Victoire fetched down *The Golden Legend*, but found the company of a stranger less restful than the peace of an empty room. It annoyed him that he had, of late, to sit so far away from a book to focus on its words, and his concentration seemed to have deserted him for the day. So, by tonight, the King would have heard from Bourré the news of Vérité's investiture. What then? He had not meant to keep it a secret. 'And how is His Majesty?'

'Bored to distraction,' said the Treasurer. 'Bedridden and bored to distraction.'

Oh that the King should be dying! It would solve everything! Victoire appalled himself by thinking it.

'I can understand his choice of sickbed. Your chateau must be a great deal more cheering than Plessis-les-Tours.'

The remark seemed to undermine Bourré's self-control: 'Oh don't think it! An outer chamber of Hell, I assure you! The King assures me so daily. Forgive me, Victoire: I've no right to push my feet under your table, like this, but I'm seeking sanctuary. If the King can't hunt, I tell you, the Royal Presence is no place to be!'

'Is he very sick?'

'No, no. A quinsy. A nothing. But his physician forbids him to leave his bed for a week. What did I ever do to that doctor to deserve it? I tell you, Victoire, praise God and be thankful His Majesty wasn't enjoying your hospitality when he succumbed . . . Ah, I wouldn't talk thus if the illness were grave, you understand!' He added it hastily, realizing all of a sudden that he was talking to the Intelligencer, the King's 'songbird'. In fact he turned quite pale at the thought, and studied the page in front of him with agitated, unfocused eyes.

'Please feel free to stay as long as you like,' said Victoire pacifyingly. 'A man passionate for the hunt, the King. I had heard it didn't do to keep him from it.'

Bourré was hugely relieved. 'I love the King dearly, but he can't brook inactivity. There's been some strange ruins meted out this last week. Three men condemned to prison: one under threat of death. I may run short of servants if the King's quinsy lasts. I beg you to lend me your prayers for his early recovery.'

'Naturally. Clearly I should offer a few thanks for my own deliverance, too.' It was said to put the Treasurer at ease and worked admirably. Bourré settled into his book like a man into a bath of hot water, and gradually nodded off to sleep. Sleep was clearly in short supply at Plessis-Bourré with the King in residence.

But Victoire was not at ease. He had been screwing up his courage for some weeks to call on the King and announce to him the dire illness that had struck down his carrier pigeons. One by one (he had been going to say) they were succumbing to a fearful distemporate disease, their beaks crossing, their feathers dropping. Soon every last one would be found in its feed trough, claws uppermost, eyes glazed over and soul flown. But it was clearly not the time to tell the King with his vile temper plucked ragged by boredom and his spite in full flight.

And yet having carried out one half of Charles d'Orléans' injunction, Victoire was bound to complete the rest. Having now installed Vérité at Gloriole, he must restore to the house the virtue for which he had named her.

He had never expected to operate his 'intelligence network' for so many years without discovery. Indeed, there had been a time, at the beginning, when it had almost been his object to be unmasked – found out – and treated to the King's justice for furnishing such a feast of lies. But now there was Vérité to be considered: her safety; her innocence. So the pigeons must die – one by one or of a sudden, overnight, in an avian Armageddon.

At last *The Golden Legend* drew him in to its golden toils and he read with the same rapt concentration, the same deep breathing and closed eyes as Jehan Bourré. Meanwhile, Gloriole was besieged by the raucous noise and colours of the fête, and the smoke of cooking fires drifted past the windows like burnt cordite. A rowdy moat of delights ringed round the house now, the adults dancing the lawns bald, the children smashing the hedges of the parterre with jumping in them. After they had gone, the barge on the lake was holed and listing, the tourney towers had been smashed down. The funnels of silk blew about in the yard like the sleeves of women after an orgy, and a cutpurse caught in the act of robbery was floating face-down in the river.

It was only the noise of the Little Sisters of Pity that disturbed

Victoire and Jehan, shrieking their way upstairs in flight from a drunken rat-catcher brandishing fistfuls of dead rats.

'A wonderful book,' said Bourré as he woke, politely ignoring the noise overhead.

'Perhaps I could seek the sanctuary of your own library some time in the near future. After the King has gone.' Victoire was embarrassed by the screaming: he spoke louder to mask it, but did not succeed.

'I'd welcome that, de Gloriole. I've very much enjoyed – ai, don't you think you ought to . . .' For it was hard to ignore the protracted scream and loud crash followed by the frenzied barking of dogs. Victoire maintained a dignified pace as he opened the door for the Treasurer and followed him out on to the landing.

The rat-catcher lay with his leg twisted up behind his back, directly beneath the raised drawbridge of the convent-in-the-loft. His pole with its drum-shaped cage at the top had been under him as he fell. Its decoration of dead rats still dangled by their tails, but the one live specimen carried in the cage to denote the man's profession had escaped through the smashed dowelling and was being chased by three talbot puppies in and out of the furniture.

'Holy God, I'm dead,' said the rat-catcher. He had been chasing the Little Sisters, threatening to drop dead rats down their necks. He had not thought to have Christian girls steal the floor from under him. He was mortified with indignation. The tripwire and its warning bell were still tangled round his thigh, and he jingled as the house-varlets extricated his broken leg from under him. The puppies cornered the rat, then took fright at its size and it chased them down the stairs and into the great-hall from where it was plain to hear the copper washbowls on their tripods being turned over one by one.

'Put him in the stables,' said Victoire to the varlets and, to the man on the floor, 'If I put a physician to you, you can unpest the place after. Agreed?'

'I'm dead. Dead!' was all the reply he got.

'You will be, if you trouble my Little Sisters again.' Then he returned to his guest once more as if nothing had happened. 'Perhaps you would be so good as to convey a small gift of Sablois wines to His Majesty, Minister? They can be quite restoring after an illness, I find.'

The rat went to ground in the armoury with a clatter of falling spears.

TWENTY-ONE

The Moat

The Little Sisters, though they imbued the house with a spirit of innocent delight and Christian enthusiasm, were educationally speaking good for nothing much beyond gros-point and joinery. So de Gloriole wrote to his bishop (a new, Louis-loving bishop) and requested the services of a replacement for Barnabas. The estates were more populous than they had ever been; the silk industry alone brought hundreds flocking to the Sablois. A dozen priests now tended the Bishop's see in his inevitable absence. Barnabas could be spared to educate the heir to Gloriole. But until his replacement arrived, and had been counselled in both Divinity and corn-factoring, Barnabas refused to take up the post of tutor. He would have done all three jobs if Victoire had let him.

The offer of the post was partly a way of ensuring that Barnabas would leave the barn and accept lodgings within the chateau. But it also assured Victoire that his daughter would receive an all-round education. For Barnabas was such a voracious reader that there were very few subjects he would not attempt to teach, even where he had the scantest understanding of them himself: heraldry, herbalism and hunting, geometry and geography as well as architecture, the classics, agriculture, viticulture, botany and theology. The steward of accounting was told he must teach Vérité double-entry, the gardeners beekeeping and husbandry. And Victoire himself would supply any essentials he thought lacking: fishing, for instance; Italian, which he had taught himself on campaign, and the selective breeding of dogs. Because she had no preconceived notions of her duties or station, and because she came from such a bleak desert of a childhood, she devoured knowledge, half expecting the opportunity to be snatched away, half expecting a curfew to toll over her days of enlightenment.

It happened only twice that knowledge was withheld from her. The library had grown beyond the luxury of separate sideboards to house each volume. Most were supported now on a sloping shelf that circled the room like a continuous lectern, and much of the big dark furniture had been removed. One sideboard remained – locked as she discovered. 'What's in here?' she asked.

'Oh nothing. An Italian book. You don't have enough of the language,' said her father.

'What's it called? What's it about?'

'I forget. *The Decameron*. A dull thing. The man wrote in Latin later. You may read those easier.' But although her Italian improved, the sideboard remained locked, and bawdy Boccaccio remained a closed book.

But only a week after the party, Vérité, in exploring the pigeon loft, found a carrier at the corn trough still carrying its message-can. Its return had gone unnoticed, so Victoire had omitted to remove its tin sleeve and wring its neck, as he had with most of the others. She produced the cipher-code at dinner and asked what it meant and how anyone was supposed to read it. Her father snatched it out of her hand and threw it into the fire. 'No consequence,' he said, as he had a habit of saying if she asked the meaning of the biblical word 'adultery', say, or what became of Fils. Next day he found her formulating an alphabet for her own amusement, inventing letters and hieroglyphs. And he slapped her a blow that left the imprint of his hand on her cheek, and told her never to draw signs and symbols unless she wanted to be burned as a witch.

It left her with the impression that some sorceress had sent, by pigeon, an airborne curse on the house and that the evil magic had already set to work on her father. As a result, she suffered a string of appalling nightmares – of burning, burning, so the nuns confided in Victoire. They were startled that the news brought such a violent reaction, for he sprang up from his desk in a passionate rage, and went and put on royal livery. 'I'm going to Plessis,' he said accusingly. 'To be away from women's noise.'

In the stable, the rat-catcher was installed on a bed of two straw-bales where, now and then, people remembered to feed him and where he could almost but not quite reach the horses' water. He had adjusted quickly to his recuperation, and had come to think of such unwonted comfort as his right, his compensation for being so rudely dropped through a hole in the floor by malevolent nuns. One eye was cataract-milky, but it was the other he closed in order to fix his victims with a marbly glare and demand 'A sup of something to dull the pain! Your master ordered it!'

Unfortunately, he had been too hurt or too drunk at the time of his fall to recognize Victoire when the Comte came now to fetch his horse out of the stalls, and the sunlight in the doorway was too bright for him to recognize the King's livery. He banged his mended rat-pole on the stone flags and brandished his tin beaker in the direction of the water trough. 'A sup and quick about it!' As he banged, the rats in the top cage were bounced up and down on their claws and wrapped prehensile tails around the dowelling bars. The dead danglers were set jumping too.

'You've caught yourself a fresh menagerie, I see,' said Victoire, crossing for a closer look. 'How did you manage that?'

'I can catch rats in my sleep, I can. They just come to me. Magic like.'

'Because you smell like old cheese, maybe,' said Victoire and snatched the pole out of his hand. 'I have a need for this. I'll return it presently.'

'Give that back, you swyving wolf's-head! Thieving bastard!' The man worked his way up through a soaring trajectory of abuse which suddenly lost height when he caught hold of Victoire by the cloak and discovered it was lambswool.

The Comte drew out his sword. 'I saw amputation a-plenty in the wars. I could maybe call the science of it to mind if you want a speedy cure for that leg of yours.'

The rat-catcher stroked down the pile appeasingly, reverentially, and pushed the sword-tip away with his fingers. 'I could make you a better cage than that, your lordship, if your lordship fancied the profession. I could teach you my arts.'

'Bare-faced gall, that's all you could usefully teach me,' he replied, and mounted up and ducked out under the stable lintel and rode round to the kennels, carrying the rat-pole over his shoulder like a chancellor's mace.

The King's physician must indeed have held a grudge against Jehan Bourré, for he continued to confine Louis to bed at Plessis-Bourré and would not suffer him to make the short journey back to his own chateau at Plessis-les-Tours. Louis, being a thrifty man (as his friends put it), and seeing the saving in housekeeping, did not quibble. At least he did not quibble with the doctor. There was too rich an array of other targets to aim at, from Bourré's cook through to Bourré's wife. His own travelling household were not exempt. Everyone up to and including his own trusty panetier, guardian of the royal dogs, was at risk.

He reigned from his pillows in a frenzy of boredom that smashed most of the wooden rings from their curtain poles and left the bed hangings drooping. The quinsy that had originally afflicted him had been enflamed, by ennui and frustration, into a much more alarming condition, and apothecaries intoned all day long over their pestles and mortars in the kitchens, grinding him concoctions which he threw in their faces. He dispatched ecuries endlessly to les-Tours to fetch more servants, another dog, or yet more personal belongings, damning Bourré's lovely chateau for 'a well', 'a prison', 'a cave', a wasteland of want. He outraged the maidservants, he told the clergy to excommunicate themselves, and he pissed in the grate and deliberately put out the fire when it was newly lit. He had quite decided that Bourré must relocate his villages so as to alter the view, which bored him.

Only the royal dogs escaped calumny. Louis gathered more and more about him: the number rose as his spirits fell. Stag hounds, otter hounds, greyhounds and spaniels attended on his levée and were permitted audience all day, including mealtimes, when he fed them Bourré's 'contemptible' delicacies – quail and lark and fillet of carp. In fact, the servant under condemnation of death was a *valet de chien* who had allowed a spaniel to choke on the ribcage of a quail Louis had fed to the beast.

When de Gloriole arrived, he met the royal surgeon at the door of the bedchamber, carrying a bowl of something red, clotted and steaming. 'You've bled him thus much?' said Victoire in a low voice, suddenly doubting Bourré's mild prognosis of the King's illness.

The surgeon replied by setting the bowl to his lips and drinking off a mouthful or two. 'Hot wine,' he said. 'The dogs've been out for their exercise. He had me wash their feet when they came in. He always has their feet washed in hot wine.'

'Why hot?' asked Victoire.

'Why wine?' asked the surgeon and drank some more, quite past caring what the royal dogs might have trodden in on their walk. Seeing the rats carried over Victoire's shoulder and the large dogs he was leading, he said, 'Are you Court jester?'

'I'm Royal Echanson. I've come to sing the King a song.'

'That should guarantee having your tongue nailed to the door.' The surgeon was halfway down the stairs before he deduced that he had been talking to the Intelligencer, and broke into a sweat at the thought of what he had said.

Louis only granted audience to his 'songbird' in the hope of hearing intelligences at which he could rant and rail and proclaim dooms and dispossessions. He was presented instead with a man carrying a cageful of rats on a pole and leading three huge dogs on choke-chains while talking fast and furious:

'Souillards, Your Majesty! Half as big as a horse and they can bring down a deer and not leave a mark on the hide! And not stags only! Biddable as Belgians and braver than Scotsmen. Thought I'd breed 'em, but I'm loath to breed the best dogs in the country without leave of the King and without knowing that Your Majesty will deign to accept the best of the litters. Of course, I know you have them already, but the breed can be improved, and fewer throwbacks to the English strain . . .'

The King, who was engaged in picking the gold wire off the bullion fringing of the curtain-ties on the bed, looked de Gloriole up and down like a lancer looking for a weakness in armour. 'Your beasts will wake Mistodin.' He indicated the large crib beside his bed, where his favourite dog slept in Court dress of purple drawers and white silk shirt, with a collar of gold studs. The dog raised its hind leg and scratched behind its ear, dislodging its purple bonnet without waking. 'Why haven't you sent me any news of late, Gloriole? Are your pigeons all grown as old and fat as you?'

'Never shall now,' said de Gloriole sadly, sitting down in the window seat. 'They're dead.'

'Dead? How "dead"? What d'you mean, they're dead?'

'Poisoned is my guess. Not difficult, God knows. A blight delivered home to the roost. It only takes one to poison the rest. Like a sailor taking the pox back to a ship.'

'Poisoned? Who poisoned 'em? Send and have him killed! You must get more birds! You must mend the damage! How could you let them be poisoned?' In its apoplectic rage, Louis' face made his father's seem charming in the modesty of its features. With a nose as big as a yule log and a top lip as short as winter solstice, his tongue emerged like a lick of flame to burn up the words as he delivered them. 'I'm not well pleased, Gloriole! You had no call to let them die!'

'I'm bereft,' said Victoire, as if the King had just commiserated with him over the death of a relative. 'I can get more birds – as Your Majesty says – but the training, the reopening of routes . . . So much time. That's why I want to divert myself cross-breeding souillards. Perfecting the breed.'

The King's struggle with indifference was painful to watch, but when he finally overcame his interest in de Gloriole's plans it was with a burst of venomous self-pity. 'What's it to me what you breed? Do I look like a huntsman? Lying here! Closeted up in this piss-hole? Lakey bog! Never a horse under me for a month! Never the promise of a hunt this side of Judgment Day! Pox on your souillards! Take them out of here! And your rats! What d'you bring rats to me for? Will you breed rats, too? Will you furnish me with the plague?'

Victoire shrugged his disappointment. 'The rats were merely to prove the worth of my dogs against yours.' He got up and bowed his way backwards towards the door, encumbered by nigh every dog in the room, for they had gradually become aware of the rats in the cage. They all began to bark.

'Look what you've done, Gloriole!' screamed Louis, shuffling up the bed to watch his own spaniels leap up, snapping at the cage. Mistodin woke up and jumped out of his crib.

'Faith, there's no harm while I keep the cage shut, Your Majesty . . . Not like there'd be if it was open.' And he smiled to himself – a fleeting, reflective smile of the kind a man does not mean to be seen. He reached the door and made a great clumsiness of extricating himself from the room.

'*Open the cage!*' bellowed the King.

De Gloriole made no such hard work of coming back. He unchoked the souillards, then up-ended the rat-pole, tipping out its occupants. After a moment's paralysis, the rats bolted in three different directions, one under the bed, one under a press and one into the folds of the window curtain. Dogs collided in a mountain of multi-coloured fur and scrabbling paws. The floor's surface was slippery and as they pursued the rats they crashed into furniture, into walls, into the King's bodyguard, knocking his legs from under him. At the sound of breakages, others came running, fearing an assassination.

Louis screamed at Victoire, 'Bolt the door! Keep 'em out! Make fast the door or the rats'll get out! My spaniel against your brutes any day! See how slow they are! There!'

The spaniel emerged, scrabbling backwards from under the bed with the tail of a rat clenched in its teeth. But its paws mishandled it and Mistodin bounded over the bed and almost intercepted the prey as it escaped. The biggest mottled rat was climbing up the curtains with remarkable agility until a souillard brought down both curtain and pole in a demolition that left a ewer and basin in shards on the floor. A painted wooden statue toppled and crashed against the window, decapitating the saint so that the haloed head tumbled through the lead-light mesh and into the lake below. The spaniel's jaws closed round the stunned, fallen rat and crushed it with a jet of blood that burst against the wall. The King screamed with pleasure. 'What did I say? What did I say? A spaniel before your souillards!' A second rat committed suicide in the hearth, hoping perhaps for the sanctuary of the chimney but falling back into the fire while six dogs pawed the grate. The smell and the squealing were stomach-turning, but the King revelled in them.

The third rat managed somehow to get in among the bed-clothes, and Louis had to scramble out and stand in his nightshirt and bare feet while the bed was submerged under dogs and viscera spread across the pillows and tapestries. He took the sword out of his bodyguard's hand and used it to prise the burned rat out of the hearth as a reward for Mistodin – ragged now, with purple trousers tangled round his front legs. 'More rats! More rats!' demanded the King, and the bodyguard, still not sure that an assassination was not in progress, stared at Victoire who put his hand to the bolt of the door.

'By your leave, sire, I'll go to the stables and look for some . . .'

'No! Stop! Wait!' Louis had stood up over fast and was feeling the lack of his *disner*, which he had peevishly emptied that morning into the press. Victoire righted a chair knocked over by the dogs, and Louis sat down gingerly on its edge. His spaniel jumped into his lap, red as a belly wound. 'Excellent! Oh excellent sport!' he panted. 'De Gloriole, you're a genius!' Then recollecting himself he added, 'A fool, though. Souillards are all very well for stag, but for rats you need a spaniel. Better still, a terrier. Must get a terrier! Breed me some terriers, why don't you, Songbird!'

'So I will, sire,' said Victoire in a low, soft voice – as one might use in speaking to the sleeping, to insinuate a notion into the unconscious mind. 'I should've thought of it before. I've been so preoccupied with the souillards and the aditz. Did I mention the aditz? I have a contact in Spain. I was thinking in terms of a dozen for the Sablois. For the sake of the hunting, you understand . . .' He slid the bolt. The whole King's Guard burst into the room. They saw the bed; they saw the King, his knees tight together, his lap full of blood as if he were holding his guts. And they fell on Victoire as the dogs had fallen on the rats.

Only slowly did they take in the bright vigour of the King's eye. The spaniel spilled to the floor as he got up. 'Aditz? Import aditz, did you say?' He came and peered over and between the soldiers in an attempt to continue the conversation. He sternly rapped the arm that was impeding Victoire most from speaking. 'Aditz?'

'The climate may not suit, of course.'

'I'll pray to Saint Hubert. My priests say Masses daily to Saint Hubert. For the dogs, you know.'

'Then they cannot fail to thrive,' gasped Victoire buckling under the sheer weight of men.

'Let him go! Imbeciles! What do you think you're doing? Let him go! Desist! Go swim the moat, you scum. You! Fetch more wine to wash the dogs. They're in an infernal mess.'

Bourré came to the door of the bedroom, fetched in from the garden by hysterical servants jabbering that the King was murdered. 'Jesu,' he said involuntarily, at the sight of the desolation of his beautiful room. The scrim wall-covering hung in rags. The prayer-stool was smashed to matchwood. A tapestry arras had been sprayed with blood, and two over-excited dogs were easing themselves against the foot of the bed. A souillard growled menacingly at him. As the Comte de Gloriole came past him, he touched Bourré's shoulder briefly in a gesture of comfort or apology.

'Should've come before!' the King called after him. 'Should've come earlier! Excellent fool!' Bourré thought Louis would pursue the man along the corridor, but he stopped in the doorway and turned congratulations into reproach of his host. 'You should've sent for him before! Why didn't you? Excellent villain! Love'm like a brother!'

The arthritis in Victoire's left arm hurt as if it were broken anew, and he was grazed about the neck and jaw by the blades of the bodyguard. So he found himself a seat on the berm – the narrow promenade between the chateau's walls and moat – and rested there till the Minister of Finance came and found him, leading the three souillards on their choke-chains.

'Victoire, the King says he loves you like a brother. And if he doesn't, I do,' he said, thumping himself down beside the Comte. 'He's a new man. Says he'll hunt tomorrow and go home the day after. Back to Plessis-les-Tours. He swears the impostume's sweated out of him with cheering the dogs. I never saw him so high-spirited.'

'I'm sorry about the furnishings.'

'Furnishings? Tush! I could've spared you a tower or two for a trick like that . . . But can I ask one more favour? Can I prevail on you to tell me – what exactly are aditz? My chaplain has been instructed to intercede with Saint Hubert for their safe delivery. He's not unwilling, but he'd like to know what they are – says it would help the earnestness of his prayers.'

'Lions, man. Little Spanish lions. That size.' He pointed at one of the dogs. 'Smaller, maybe.'

'And you mean to import lions to the Sablois? They'll eat your peasants!'

Victoire rocked his head from side to side. 'But the notion came to me all of a sudden in there. Like divine inspiration. I thought I'd better not fly in the face of divine inspiration. Maybe I'll keep 'em penned up. Maybe I'll keep my peasants penned up. Maybe they only eat Spanish peasants. What do you want, Jehan, miracles? There are limits to my genius.' He looked about him appreciatively. 'There might not be, mind, if I lived with such an outlook. Lord, but this moat of yours is a thing to behold!'

Stranded with sunlight the colour of spun sugar, the lake-moat of Plessis-Bourré mantled its austere elegance with a transparent cloak of water a hundred and thirty feet wide on every side, trapping beneath its meniscus layer not only the sky's colour and spectral dragons of white cloud, but a perfect, unbroken silence.

'I could recommend you my builder,' said Bourré. 'We completed from start to finish in four years. The chateau, the moat. Sure, you have the beginnings already at Gloriole, don't you, with the river half wrapped round you? If you're sure of your soil . . .'

Victoire needed no more encouragement to fetch from under his doublet the sketch he had been engaged upon when Bourré found him. 'Simply a matter of digging out canals here . . . and here . . . and widening the dry-moat to the same width . . .'

Then he would loose the river into the crater like molten metal into a casting, and nothing but a narrow, arched causeway would cross over the water to north and south. He would surround Gloriole with a lake-moat not thirty but eighty yards wide. Half flowing, half artificial, it would double the beauty of his chateau by setting it upon a mirror of gleaming water.

De Gloriole and Bourré sat for some time exchanging ideas on the subject of moats, until they were disturbed by the oaths and arguments of the King's bodyguard shambling in confusion out of the building. Items of clothing already dangled from their hands, and they took off the rest and laid them along the berm in mounds.

'Oh a fine treat for my wife!' said Bourré disconsolately, looking back up at the windows. Louis, redeemed from illness, stood at the broken casement, still spiteful-faced, watching to see his errant bodyguard chastise themselves with swimming the moat, for the crime of trying to arrest his assassin. They eased themselves into the water – men whose bodies had not seen water, some of them, for a year past. Many could not swim.

'They'll drown,' suggested Victoire.

'It's shallowish. I doubt it,' said Bourré. 'They might.'

'How pleasant a thing it is to rest in the King's good favour.'

'Indeed,' said Bourré with feeling.

Bourré quite thought that the conversation concerning the moat had been a polite compliment to his newly completed chateau, or a momentary whim (like the Spanish lions) that would prove too problematic ever to reach fruition. But the aditz did arrive eventually and shivered in the forests of Sablois, in a state of semi-hibernation, until Louis' huntsmen came to put them out of their misery. A second consignment were kept warm in pens and became extremely tame – almost friendly – before being set loose and cut to pieces with sabres and spear and crossbow-fire. Aditz suffered a rapid extinction in the landscapes of the Sablois.

Somehow the intelligence network dependent on Gloriole pigeons never quite re-established itself, however. When she was old enough to understand, Victoire told Vérité that she would be asked, upon his death, to supply all ledgers, all lists of addresses and names that might exist in the house. She was to say that her father kept all such knowledge in his head, for fear of spies, and that it died with him. He taught her, in place of the arts of the intelligencer, how to breed improved strains of souillards and terriers and talbots and otter-hounds.

Deception would die with Victoire. The past would die with Victoire. All but innocence would die with him, and leave Vérité safe from the vicissitudes of politics: come King, go King, safe. Safe within her moated grange.

For the moat came, too, like the aditz. Like the aditz, it was a thing of preposterous prettiness inconsistent with everyday life. At first it was only a dirty gouge in the earth, like a forester's unsuccessful attempts to dig under the roots of a tree to transplant, and it displayed an irritating propensity for subsiding overnight. The chateau's foundations were laid bare, like the receding gums of

234

an old man, but landslips buried three labourers alive before the grassless escarpments could be shored up securely with boulders of schist.

But when, with the last blast of gunpowder, the Sablois river flowed in, it filled a lake-moat five furlongs wide. The drop in the river was such that barges within the reach were stranded briefly on sandbanks. Yellow mud was churned up from the excavations and made of the water a gangrenous mire. The mortar was washed by the impact from between old brickwork in the drawbridge, and hasty repairs were needed. But then the water sealed itself against the white walls; the silt settled, and the fallen shorings, the dead workmen, the staggering cost were all lost beneath the moat, like the Egyptians beneath the closing Red Sea.

He thought he did it for Fils. He told himself that it was the last great debt of beauty payable to the body of the son he had tried to resurrect in stone and glass and chestnut and brick, in oils, in silks and in marble. But it was not true. Like the cabbalist about to perform an act of dangerous magic, Victoire was drawing a magic circle around his house to keep out devils and demons: to keep his daughter safe; to keep the outside world from so much as touching Vérité de Gloriole.

TWENTY-TWO

The Lantern of the Dead

Her sheer unattainability, islanded like Circe in the midst of a silver sea, would have brought suitors to Vérité. Add to that her accomplishments and a remarkable, robust beauty in an age of inbred, litter-runt ladies, and she could have chosen to marry into any of the great trade fortunes. Add to that a dowry of thirty-three thousand acres and the Gloriole chateau, and the savour of her spread far beyond Touraine into Britanny, Anjou and Maine. The King himself gave consideration to her situation. But a girl who vowed never to marry flummoxed him, and he set the problem aside. He assumed it was a ploy to make her more appealing, and considered it laudably successful, for personally he found it quite pricked him on to think of this virgin set like a gem in a ring of silver. De Gloriole was a cunning fellow, no doubt about it.

De Gloriole was cunning, it's true. The regime he created at the chateau was not a dour, oppressive one that invited escape at the first opportunity. It was nursery-cheerful, nursery-innocent, nursery-safe. With regard to the outside world, he simply pointed out that marriage would effectively rob Vérité of everything – deliver her into the hands of a predatory male – and that without it Gloriole was hers to do with as she liked. She might even give it away if the burden proved too great – but not to a husband.

The picture he drew of marriage was of a kind of market stocks in which a woman was pinned helpless and subjected to the abuse and derision of a lesser breed. The lesser breed he depicted not entirely as villains, but as hapless creatures driven by brute passions to wanton temper, cruelty and sin. She had only to read the lives of the saints to see that this was true. The outer world was a place of infinitely terrible possibilities, whereas the world of her inheritance was serene and reliable, rich with variety, dependably the same.

When her character began to reveal itself, she was called in Touraine the finest masterpiece in de Gloriole's collection: his ultimate work of art. The very old and the very young said that she had inherited her father's 'ineffably sweet nature'. The old said it because they were reminded of the handsome flower of chivalry on the fields of Patay and Orléans; the young said it because they had known Victoire only in his old age: a man always half a breath away from smiling; wry and funny and tolerant and slightly eccentric. They likened him to Good King René and to the Duc of Orléans.

His chateau swarmed with jongleurs and storytellers and play-actors, stranded travellers and political dissidents from outside France. Rabbits were suffered to eat his cabbages and deer to break into his parterre and nibble it, since they gave more pleasure to Vérité than caldo verde or boxtrees. Out of the hillside slope leading up to the Chapel Saint-Cloud he fashioned a semi-circular amphitheatre with wooden stage and painted wooden columns, where the priests of the Sablois self-consciously acted mystery plays on feast-days and where Barnabas cajoled them haltingly through Greek tragedies.

And all the while Vérité sat amidst her flock of Little Sisters, so adored by them that they imitated the geese which spontaneously adopt a vulnerable cygnet. They were never apart, except when she and her father went sculling on the moat, and then they clucked and crowed along the banks, cheering on the rowers, racked with impartiality, wanting both to win.

One day Victoire summoned Barnabas to his retraite to confront him with a theological problem. The look on his face was that of a knight who cannot fasten his back-plate armour without assistance. He sat square-on to the priest, his legs splayed, his feet flat on the floor, and his hands on his knees. His beard piled on to his chest in a bright, white cumulus as he rubbed his temples with his good right hand. 'You know the story of the woman married seven times?'

Barnabas felt, as usual, like a passenger trying to jump aboard a cart already moving, and that he was growing a little too old for the running. 'Where are we, pray? Greece? Rome? Bible?'

'The Bible, of course.'

'Old, New or Apocryphal?'

'The Gospels, naturally. Pay attention, will you? Christ and His disciples. One wife, they said. Widowed seven times. Seven successive brothers take her. Which will have her in Heaven? Christ said, "*They neither marry, nor are given in marriage.*" That or some such.' (There was no 'some such' about it: the Bible lay on the table in front of him.)

'Yes. Right. I have you. What about her?'

'A casuistical answer, don't you think? No help to man or beast really. "*Neither marry, nor are given in marriage.*" No help to the seven brothers.'

'They were hypothetical,' said Barnabas, to win time.

'I'm not, though. Must I choose, or what? Or does it mean I must be without either?'

'Ah!' said Barnabas. He could have wept. He could have danced. He could have opened the window and shouted out to the ducks on the moat: Finally! At last! He believes he's going to Heaven! Hallelujah! But Victoire was feeling fierce and bluff. Barnabas' hands climbed up and down the knotted rope of his belt as he held his delight in check.

'Or shall I not see Marthe, because I only knew her carnally? That's the other problem.'

' "Knew her carnally" ? Bless me! What a fearful phrase,' said the priest. 'Do you want the authority of the Church or personal opinion? Personally, I say if there's no marrying in Heaven, then Marthe Pommier can scarce give way to Ellen de Gloriole on those grounds. I take the "casuistical answer", as you put it, to mean that there won't be the same rivalry between the two there might have been if they'd coincided on Earth.'

'Might have been! So. And you think I'll find them both again? Among God's Millions, I mean. Seems to me it could be like looking for your own hat at the Tours hat-market after you've laid it down and forgot where.'

'In my opinion, they'll have the wits to wait at the Gate.'

Victoire was momentarily placated and settled back in his chair before another thought came to him. 'And shall I know them apart? They're damned alike. And now they're both raised to perfection, you know . . .'

'Not in speech, surely? Different accents.'

'Right! If I have a problem, I'll not risk using a name till I've heard 'em speak. Excellent! I'm greatly obliged to –'

'And Fils?' Barnabas saw the diaphragm quake, the hazel eyes narrow at the corners. 'And Fils?' he said again.

'What of him?'

'How will you greet him?'

'Cap in hand.' (And the dagging of that cap dragging along the celestial floor, and the revellers in Heaven parting to make a path between father and son.)

'He'll be blasé already at the good things of Heaven, I suppose,' said Barnabas ruminatively. 'I dare say he'll be glad of the company. Bliss must pall once in a while, I've always thought.'

'Not with Hell to remember,' said Victoire broodingly.

'Oh, do you think so? Myself I can never remember warm in the winter nor cold in the summer. So I never thought of the saints remembering their pain. And I'm sure they never carry their gridirons and cauldrons and bowsaws about with them, however the artists paint them. But as I say, it's only a personal opinion. If the Church has deliberated, I don't know the outcome. I'm sorry.' Victoire cradled his left arm in his right, a daily reminder to him of an old pain that did not lessen with time. Seeing this, Barnabas added, 'Of course you have to remember that there's no pain in Heaven. That's a universally acknowledged fact.'

Victoire assimilated this and nodded. He seemed to be trying not to smile, and his eyes drifted to the window and his thoughts strayed. They returned in an instant, having strayed only as far as the chapel. 'It's time he had a tomb! Have de Dénezé carve a vault. A tomb. Up at the Saint-Cloud. Overlooking the place. It's time enough.' He rummaged within his clothing and brought out a sketch so dog-eared that he must have been carrying it about for years. He pushed it sharply across the desk at Barnabas. 'Like this. Reclining – not on his back, d'you mark? Reclining.'

'Me? Don't tell me. I'm not artistic. I don't rightly comprehend these artistic people. Pray commission it yourself, sir, and spare me.'

Victoire nodded curtly. He did not return the picture to his clothing but, after looking at it for a moment or two, slid it between the pages of the Bible (where Barnabas found it later) saying to himself, and not to the priest, 'Sod what kings make of it. It's time Fils had a fit tomb.'

When he woke next day, the marjoram cataplasm his daughter had prepared for his arm in the evening had worked miracles. He felt no pain at all. He burst into the sewing room: Vérité was reciting a poem by Charles d'Orléans aloud to Barnabas who woke with a start. The tableful of industrious nuns, he could have sworn, rose into the air before fluttering back down to their needles. 'Have you seen what manner of day it is?' Victoire said. 'A row, for Jesu's sake! One circuit of the moat!'

There was a Pythagorean migration of souls out-of-doors. Vérité's particular friend ran behind her, winding the wild black hair into a businesslike plait; others ran ahead to unship the esquifs from their canvas shrouds on the berm. As each runner came out of the dark shade of the rose arcade, the sunlight burst up off the moat to greet them, like the host of golden butterflies the English swore had dazzled them at Orléans. A million million butterflies beating over their heads and fluttering up against the white tufa, dancing in the white windows.

'You may have twenty strokes lead, Papa!' cried Vérité, gathering her profusion of skirts into the white-lined esquif. 'I'm getting very good.'

'Insulting woman. I'll thrash you to a humility!' he replied, pushing off with one foot and unshipping the oars.

The river was running high, swollen with heavy rain over Vendôme, its glassy sinuous currents quite distinct from the calm slack of the artificial ox-bow lake. They eased the boats by hand under the narrow arches of the causeway and aligned themselves with the distinctive stained-glass window overhead. Victoire eased the two hulls further apart, to beyond a clash of oars. Vérité took off her sleeves and threw them to a nun perched on the causeway's parapet. And he thought, as he saw the brown velvet curve through the air, of Ellen throwing her bridal coronet of flowers down from the Gloriole bridge. He said to himself, 'I am happy. Happy past measure. Happy past Man's fit capacity for happiness.' It was perhaps why, on some recent mornings, he felt that he was splitting at the seams, at the sternum weld in that suit of armour the soul puts on to do battle with Life.

'Go!' cried Vérité.

She was a cliff – a sea cliff. However much love he hurled against her, it rebounded on him doubling its volume into a lovely white spray iridescent with rainbows. It quite exhausted him lately, to love her so much and still find her meriting more. His delight in the morning took him fast ahead of her. It was an uneven match: a broadsworder against a girl, but pulling ahead meant that she remained within sight, her boat between the up-pull of his oars. Her black plait was unwinding like the three rivers of the Loire down the flexing spine of France.

She was the soul of Gloriole. Build the body as he might, it had taken Vérité to reanimate the dead stuffs of stone, wood and symbolism. He had spent his life striving for permanence, trying to perpetuate what was beautiful, only to discover that the essence of beauty was in such snatches of ephemera. A row on sunlit water. A dark plait untwisting. A wreath of flower falling through the air.

That was what a man remembered of his life. That was what burst his heart with surfeit of grief and gratification.

Where slack water flanked the moving river in a turbulent cordelière of twisting currents, Vérité overtook her father. It was an uneven match, after all: a seventeen-year-old against an old man. Her oar struck his and (though she did not realize it until his boat dropped behind) knocked it out of his hand. It slid from the rowlock and dipped away through the water, out into the swollen river. He made no attempt to recover it. Gradually, the course of the trailing esquif decayed, and it drifted out of the centre stream and in towards the buttress of the chateau. Vérité stopped rowing, but the natural flow of the river carried her onwards further and further from the diminishing shape of the other boat. She drove in her oars as a brake. 'Father?' But the curve of the river as it rounded its natural bend still threatened to place Gloriole between her and her father – a great white implacable headland, like a quarried escarpment, obstructing the view. She just had time to see the boat hit the buttress full on and unseat its rower. He fell backwards off his cross-bench, and the second oar slipped free of its rowlock and escaped the buttress's eddy. '*Father!*'

They found him lying on his back along the keel, like Christ asleep during the storm on Galilee. His legs were still resting high and wide apart, on the cross-bench. In death, he waited patiently for them till they came; the natural currents of the river always had been drawn irresistibly into that swirl at the angle of buttress and wall. The concave erosion of stone and mortar was proof of it.

The *lanterne des morts* stood at the entrance to the churchyard in Rocheblanche. And though Victoire was to be buried with his wife and son in the Chapel Saint-Cloud – in accordance with plans Barnabas witnessed to – his body was taken to the lantern for the lying-in. It afforded the people of the estates maximum opportunity to pay their respects and, if they wished, to defend the body against the coming-of-demons. So many defenders came that at sunset the lantern was surrounded by a moat of watchers twelve deep, their faces all turned upwards to see the lights lit.

For most corpses the lantern of the dead was a dark-lantern – a feeble array of candles spilling a single trickle of light out across the gloomy graveyard till dawn drowned it out. But on the night Victoire de Gloriole lay there, every narrow window burned as though the sheer energy of light within were splitting open the

241

building at its seams. Moths as many as the pigeons and doves that flocked home off his acres at nightfall spiralled and danced, dazed by this dazzling refutation of night. Now and then, across the yellow apertures of brightness, moved women and priests and close mourners, casting giant shadows over the watchers outside.

Father Barnabas moved through the ritual of death like a man feeling his way through dense cobwebs. He could have wept. He could have railed against God. He could have run to the window and shouted out to the silent, accepting crowd, 'Go away! Go home! You're wrong! Tomorrow he'll wake up and laugh you all to shame!' And yet he was obliged to move sedately on from wick to wick, censor to aspersion, collect to tedious *Te Deum*, as though it were all an acceptable thing. As though a life were a thing to be folded away like purple at the end of Lent.

Vérité undermined him. She would keep asking him to sit down beside the body, on one of the stools set out for visiting mourners, as though his station were equal to that of the Comte's aristocratic neighbours or relations or friends. The Little Sisters undermined him, too: they wept too rarely to do it with any aplomb or religious restraint. And seeing that they agitated the girl, he persuaded them finally to go back to the chateau and say their novenas in the chapel there.

'Go with them, Father,' said Vérité. 'See that they come to no harm on the road. And you must sleep before the service tomorrow.' He was not in a position to argue. In the moment that the Comte's heart stopped beating, his absolute authority had devolved on to the shoulders of the Chatelaine, however slight by comparison, however young.

Vérité, who had thought her father ancient on first meeting and perceived him as younger the better she came to know him, had naturally supposed him to have mastery over Time as he had mastery over the rest of her world. This disillusionment was bitter. Though they said her power had suddenly increased, she knew it to be untrue, for all her power had been in smiling, and now if she smiled she could not persuade her father to smile back. Her power had been in touching, but now if she took hold of Victoire's hand, it did not reward the pressure of hers. Her momentum had been that of a little butty boat towed in the wake of a grand galleon, and now she was cast adrift on empty sea lanes. It was terrible past belief. She owned Gloriole, they said, but all she wished for was to be once again owned herself, to belong to someone, to be held in possession.

'May I trespass on your grief long enough to express my own?'

She thought him a dwarf at first, but he was standing on the stairs, still awaiting her permission to step up into the lantern chamber. 'You must forgive me, sir. I know that we've met, but in these strange surroundings, in this context . . .'

'Geoffroi de Puy, mademoiselle. Son of Michel, beloved cousin of your beloved father.'

'Of course, of course . . .'

'Touched as near by his death as yourself, almost. He was our closest kin.'

She signalled that he should take a seat by the body, and he drew the stool up between his legs as he sat down, so that his knees encompassed hers. She watched his eyes, to see how long passed before they rested on Victoire's body. She had observed how some would look and some would not: it probably indicated the relative fear of death. Geoffroi de Puy must be a man very afraid of death, for he seemed to look only at her. It was hard to say for certain. He had a pronounced squint.

Geoffroi produced from inside his velvet turban a sprig of yellow broom. 'From my son, Estienne. He is feelingly conscious of your grief.'

'How kind. Is he not with you?'

'No. No. He didn't feel it would be . . . appropriate.'

He meant her to ask why, but she was tired and did not care why Estienne de Puy was absent, so long as he remained so and as long as his father would be quickly gone, too. Alone, she would not be so lonely. It was strange to be without her nuns. She wished she could have asked them to stay all night. But not this squinting stranger.

'So I must speak for him.'

'For whom, sir?'

'For Estienne.'

'Please. Don't trouble. Consider his condolences made, as I do.'

'Well, yes, thank you, but no. That's not the burden of my song exactly.'

'Oh?'

'You see, coz – forgive me, Chatelaine – I forget myself. You see, the truth of it is . . .' (He eased his chair a little further from the body and lowered his voice.) 'The truth of it is, the poor lad's in thrall.'

'To what, sir?'

243

'To whom, ma'am.'

'To whom, sir?'

'To you, Chatelaine. To you.'

'I don't rightly understand –' She pressed the back of one hand to her cheeks, vexed with herself for the clammy panic that beset her. There could hardly be a danger. She could hardly be at risk with a hundred peasants a matter of steps away. Not in this holy place. 'These candles give off a deal of heat, don't they? Forgive me – I tax my brain, but I can't think that I've met your esteemed son, monsieur. Have I?'

'I trust not, Chatelaine. Not for a great many years, at least. Not since you were both children. But he's left his sighs hung so thick in the air of your fields and forests, I'm certain you've felt them against your brow often enough. But no, I'd be most displeased to think he had made his presence known to you. It would not have been proper. Until the death of your valiant father, you had no need of a champion. That much I've made very plain to him.'

'I must stop you, honoured –'

'Geoffroi. Pray call me Geoffroi.'

'Please, Geoffroi. I fear I must tell you – I thought it was commonly known – I mean never to marry.'

De Puy put his hands to his back and eased his haunches on the uncomfortable stool. He waited for her eyes to lift out of her lap, then re-engaged them with the earnestness of his crooked gaze. 'Faith, I know *that*, lady! Everyone knows *that!*'

Again she cooled her cheeks, more embarrassed than ever to have made such a dreadful faux pas. 'I'm sorry, mon – Geoffroi. I thought by "sighs" you meant –'

'Love, lady. Love, pure and simple. Estienne wishes only to be your champion and attend on you hourly to the easing of his panting heart. And I can only commend him to you as a right elegant and accomplished lover.'

'Holy Mary! He can't!' she whispered back at him, aghast.

'Can't what, lady?' said Geoffroi condescendingly and patted her hand.

'Can't attend on me. I couldn't possibly entertain a bachelor youth at Gloriole. My father said . . . In the light of my vow . . .'

He sat back, a picture of mortification. 'Well, of course not! It goes without saying! What do you mistake me for? How could we arrive at such a misunderstanding? Vérité! Chatelaine! Did I say my son was a bachelor? Indeed, I did not. He's a Christianly married man!'

She laughed out of sheer relief, out of sheer awkward guilt that she could cause her relation such offence. It was not easy to be a chatelaine. She wanted to pluck Victoire by his white funeral robe and tell him: it was not going to be easy being a chatelaine. He should not have put her to it so young.

De Puy mopped his forehead with a sleeve end. The candles did indeed give off a great deal of heat. 'My poor boy wishes simply to pay court to you as a lover. A knight seeking to carry the favours of his lady. As I say, his love was superfluous while your father lived. But now it's equally inconceivable that you should live all alone at Gloriole without the succour and friendship of a lover. It's simply not *comme il faut* in this age of barbarians and marauders. A woman must have a shield and defender against the world. And if your good father were alive, no one would tell you sooner how apt is Estienne de Puy for such a role.'

She looked round at her father's face. Yes, it was insupportable that she should not be loved any more, having been loved so well by such a father. 'As my father loved me, you mean?'

'Just so. Though without authority over you, of course. Obedient to your every wish. Your servant to command.'

'And you say Victoire – my father would wish it?'

'Devoutly. As he held hopes of Heaven, he would have hoped for such as Estienne to attend on you.'

'Good. Good. Very good. I am greatly obliged to your son for his . . .'

'Love, lady. Say it. Adoration. Words such as one hears in church, are they not? Adoration. Love.' He took a further sprig of broom and placed it on the body, on Victoire's chest, over his heart.

'I shall ask my chaplain, Barnabas. If he says it would be right for me to receive a . . . lover, I shall be glad of Estienne calling at any time. You will sleep at Gloriole tonight, of course? To be rested for the morning? I confess I dread the morning. I've never seen an interment.'

'Then I shall have my son lend you his arm and comfort at the graveside.'

'I thought you said –'

'He waits a way off. Unwilling to derive happiness from a sight of your face in a place where sorrow should rightly reign supreme. Goodnight, sweet coz. God shield you, and may no demons stir from Hell tonight on a fool's errand.'

When he was gone, Vérité twisted the sprig of broom between her fingers and smiled indulgently at the thought of the watcher in the woods, her champion in the lists, the devout hopes of her father fulfilled. It rather alarmed her that she could not put a face to Estienne de Puy, as though he were standing behind her or in ambush around a corner, out of sight. At least her heart quaked, as though in alarm. She hoped he did not have his father's squint. She placed her sprig of broom with the one already between her father's crossed hands, and thanked God that He had provided so well for her with such a family.

Wiping the sticky yellow pollen off his hands, Geoffroi de Puy pushed his way through the uncanny silence of the peasant vigil to where his son stood waiting with the horses.

'Well? Do I have her?' said Estienne.

'That's for you to settle. I can't do everything for you. I can't do more. Short of mounting her. I've lifted her skirts high enough, God knows. All you've got to do is up 'em.'

'I hope she stirs me to it.' Estienne's breeches were tight: it took him a time to climb up on to his horse.

'Christ in Hell, slut, if she doesn't, thirty thousand acres will, or I'll do it myself!'

'Grandfa always meant I should *marry* her,' Estienne said, easing the seams in his crotch before settling into the saddle.

'Marry a bastard? What for? Bastards are easier had than blood-lines. I never meant you should. Just get a child on her and get Gloriole from under her. Never mind how long it takes. Patience is everything . . . There's only one impediment. A priest . . .' (Even as he said it, they passed the wagon laden with Little Sisters of Pity and driven by Barnabas.)

'I knew it. I knew it. I said it couldn't be done,' said Estienne with a whine gathering like a cold in his nasal passages.

'If you're a man, the way'll be cleared by morning,' said his father, feeling the burden of his son like the clog of wood chained to a convict's ankle. 'And if you're not, I suppose I'll have to make shift for you. As usual.'

When they reached Gloriole, the household stewards showed them the way to a bedchamber where ten others were already sleeping, in anticipation of the next day's funeral. Father and son had not long been installed when the Little Sisters could be heard sobbing their way up to the East-turret loft, and Barnabas could be tracked, by an observant watcher, to his own rooms in the West turret.

'May I speak with you, Father?' said Geoffroi, stepping in through the door the moment it was opened. 'May I make Confession to you?'

'I'm very tired. In the morning, I beg you.' Being so full of thoughts of Victoire, Barnabas could not help but feel the same inimical mistrust of the de Puy family, and wanted a night's sleep to restore him to feelings of charity. He thought Geoffroi probably wanted to stake a claim to the household spoons.

'But I owe a debt of guilt towards my father's cousin! I must be free of it tonight. You understand that, sure!'

Barnabas' curiosity was whetted as well as his pity. He sat down on his cot and indicated Geoffroi should kneel in front of him. But Geoffroi too sat down on the bed and pulled the priest's pillow into his lap, the awkward gesture of a man with a great deal weighing heavy on his conscience. His fingers pulled little tufts of flock through the ticking . . .

It was said next day that de Gloriole's spirit had lacked companionship for its journey and had called on Barnabas in the smallest hours of the night. For in the morning the old priest was found dead on his bed, the flock from his tattered pillow resting bright in the strands of his age-discoloured hair. Some even said they had dreamed of a dark figure at the head of the stairs, a bearskin round his shoulders and his beard piled on his chest like cumulus. Surely, he had come for Barnabas his friend, even though it meant leaving the lantern of the dead and fighting his way, perhaps, through battalions of demons. Was it likely that the Goddam-Slayer should have gone peaceably to his glory?

They therefore resolved to bury Barnabas too in the floor of the Chapel Saint-Cloud, close to where the projected family tomb would stand with its two reclining figures (just as the priest had described). They resolved, too, to keep the news from Vérité until after the service. But it quickly came to her in the whisperings of the peasant vigil. 'The priest is dead . . .'

'. . . Barnabas dead . . .'

'. . . fetched him away in the night.'

The two carts passed each other on the road between Gloriole and Rocheblanche, the priest travelling into town to occupy the vacant slab in the *lanterne des morts*, the Comte on his open bier drawn by three horses, back to his estates. Led by pages in black, their black horsecloths trailed the ground, and only their eyes, muzzles and hooves showed. An awning bearing a white velvet cross covered the body but was rolled up on all sides to display the body borne on the lid of its chestnut coffin. A hussier carrying the coat-of-arms walked ahead, and the priests of Sablois behind, carrying the crosses from each church on the estate. And behind them weepers with unlit candles, and a crier: 'Say your Paternosters for the very excellent Comte de Gloriole, named Victoire, and attend on him at the Chapel Saint-Cloud!' As the bier skirted the moat of Gloriole, the overnight guests crossed the causeway and fell into line behind it, forming a cortège, all on foot. Geoffroi, Estienne and some other de Puy, as closest male relations, held out three corners of the funeral pall and were obliged to thrust their hands into the armpits and crotch of the corpse to steady it on the steep, bumpy incline up to the door of the chapel.

The open grave gaped in the floor, the white railing crudely prised up and twisted out of the way by the mechanisms of burial. The chapel had been hung with black cloths and the altar blotted out with black. Thirty shields of Touraine houses hung from the roofbeams, the chicheface suspended over Vérité's waiting chair. She occupied it like a ewe at the slaughter market, every new and noisy ceremony of mourning jarring her closer and closer to the desperation of panic. And had it not been for the estimable Estienne de Puy lending her his arm, the chroniclers said that her grief would have prostrated her entirely.

The requiem reeled round her like a bombardment of cannon. Her Little Sisters seemed to her suddenly like black carrion birds on a battlefield. The Bishop of Sablois browbeat her with biblical allusions to war and sacrifice. They nailed the coffin shut with a noise that stirred the starlings out of the campanile, and they lowered it into the earth while the bells dropped down their noise like the besieged in a keep hurling down rocks. Then the Master-at-Arms – a military man she scarcely knew – threw his sword into the tomb with a deafening clatter, and the Bishop threw heavy clods of earth and boomed out the injunction, 'Pray for the soul of the very excellent Comte de Gloriole, named Victoire!' He should have followed on, after a space for a Paternoster, with 'Pray for the very excellent Chatelaine de Gloriole, named Vérité'. The omission did not go unnoticed by any but Vérité herself.

There was an awkward pause. All eyes were turned on Vérité

and it was necessary for Estienne to whisper in her ear – close to her ear – 'Alms, lady,' before she remembered the forty livres of coin at her belt. She scattered them on the chapel floor with the din of Danaë's falling shower of gold. The cortège remustered, already gossiping about the excellence of the requiem, the generosity of outlay. Their feet scuffed over the coin and left it lying there for the poor to gather up at sunset. Like gleaners in the stubble.

And they left de Gloriole there, too, separated from his wife by sturdy planks of long-enduring chestnut, two sprigs of broom on his breast. Those old enough to attach significance to such things were astounded to see the broom – the *planta genista*. They assumed it must be a reference to his English wife. For why else would a knight who had used up his youth fighting the Plantagenet English be buried with the symbol of his enemies over his heart?

TWENTY-THREE

The Chatelaine

The keys of Gloriole hung from the centre of her belt, so that when she sat on the great raised chair at the head of the hall, to receive visitors and plaintiffs, the keys lay in her lap.

They were symbolic keys only. There were other people charged with the responsibility of keeping the chateau safe from intruders. But the keys symbolized her absolute right to grant or refuse entry to any part of Gloriole-sur-Sablois – from its forest borders to the innermost small cabinet of her bedchamber. To Estienne de Puy she had granted audience in the great-hall. He knelt at her feet and pressed the keys to his lips. He did not let go of them afterwards.

'The philosopher Plato tells us that from birth we carry in our souls the template of a face and form. If ever once we meet a creature whose form and face match that template, then key unfastens lock and lets loose the music of the soul. In seeing you, dear coz, I own I am quite undone.'

Vérité did not know what to do with such a speech – whether to treat it as a joke or not. It encumbered her, like the gift of flowers with which he had filled her arms, leaving her no hands free.

The youth had a large face with a cleft chin and slightly snub nose. His round, domed cheeks suggested he was holding his breath, but then his body too was puffed up a little, with rounded crop and round thighs and kneecaps domed like the cushions of his palms and his spatulate fingertips. The lids of his eyelids closed slowly, but for all their thickness and curling lashes, they left the real fulsome sensuality of his face to the lips. His curly light brown hair was his finest feature, and he plucked it continually over the round lobe of one ear, but never so much as to conceal the pearl that dangled there.

'You didn't bring your wife, sir. I was hoping to make my apologies to her: I barely spoke a word to her at the funeral.'

'Selfishness, I confess it. But of course, if you wish it I shall bring Yolande the very next time I call. A pleasant woman. She's given me only a daughter so far, but I try not to reproach her with it. A small sin among several virtues. I'm sure she tries the best she can.'

Robbed of her childhood's idyll, Vérité was left bluffing her way through the game of real life, grasping for clues to its rules, to its objects. Barnabas was no longer there to help her. But there was Estienne de Puy whose arm had steadied her at the funeral. Surely, if she listened closely enough to him she could deduce how the world worked, without betraying too great an ignorance. It was almost as if he understood her plight and fed her little hints, subtly, genteelly. He was not patronizing like his father; he did not make her feel ignorance was her lasting burden: he would lighten the load.

'I would have welcomed your succour these past days, Estienne,' she said when they were settled by the fire, her nuns strewn about them both on footstools, sewing. 'I've had three proposals of marriage and all couched in such fine language.'

'Jackals,' said Estienne and spat demurely into the fire. 'Hyenas. Closing in on the fatherless foal. Permit me to word you a response you may send to any such unmannerly presumption. We'll leave them in no doubt as to how the land lies.'

'I wouldn't like to give offence! They're all very eminent men.'

'They shall think they came within an inch of success and that nothing but the intervention of angels kept them from griping up your estates.' And he wrote the letters, and signed himself her 'friend', so that the world would suppose they were already lovers.

He made certain of it. Firstly, he came and went at times of day that made it certain she must invite him to stay overnight. He sent her presents by way of the tradesmen – intimate items of clothing and night attire so that rumours spread, with the argentiers, all along the valleys of Sablois, Cher and Loire. He told his mistresses he was too weary from the demands of his 'little nun' to do them justice. And he enlisted the aid of his wife, Yolande, too.

It was the last day of the grape harvest, and the pickers had just called at the chateau with a crucifix made of flowers and vine leaves which they leaned against the carved white terrace and had her splash with bloody wine in the name of tradition. Meanwhile they danced a peculiarly sombre tribute and chanted a paean of feudal praise sprinkled with plentiful alleluiahs. Then the workers, who were many of them itinerant and would not meet again until the following harvest, took leave of each other with embraces and formulaic farewells, slurred a little by the traditional skin of wine.

For many it would be the only wine they tasted in the year.

To preserve her lips from touching the communal wineskin, a pristine cup was filled to the brim for the Chatelaine and her guests. That day Estienne and Yolande were there, as well as de Dénezé the sculptor. He had just completed the de Gloriole tomb in the Chapel Saint-Cloud: two men reclining companionably to read. On the bas-relief frieze a woman knelt without the comfort of a book, in readiness for Vérité's own death. The unveiling had left her a little tearful and perplexed – willing enough to accept the warming cup of wine Estienne continually returned to her hands. Her Little Sisters were locked in their convent loft because of so many rude peasants near the house.

As the pickers hugged each other, Estienne, rising to the traditions of the occasion, embraced de Dénezé thus confirming that the sculptor was well on his way to being drunk. He embraced his wife, then, and passed her into the arms of the sculptor before inviting Vérité similarly to get to her feet. The pickers were gratified to see it. They nodded their approval. But afterwards a great deal of comment was passed on the way de Puy embraced the Chatelaine of Gloriole.

He kissed open-mouthed, pushing his tongue between her teeth while one hand chafed her breasts and the other pushed her black dress between her legs and almost lifted her off her feet. De Dénezé stared at the crudity of it, his eyes bleary, his brain slow to comment. He discovered that he was rather shocked, rather disappointed in the Chatelaine. He checked the wife's reaction, but Yolande was smiling beatifically on the pair. The situation was known then, and condoned. Only he had been slow to learn of it.

Abruptly, de Puy let go and turned his smiles and attentions to the others, taking no measure of the look on Vérité's face. 'Don't forget your tools, Dénezé. They're still in the chapel, remember. An invitation to these thieves here, if they pass it on their way home . . .'

Vérité caught her wind in little inadequate breaths. She smoothed her skirts. The keys tinkled between her shaking knees. Nothing like it had ever happened to her before. She felt like Eve in the Garden, except that she had collided unwittingly with the tree and the apple had forced itself between her teeth. Still . . . what made her think in such terms? What made her associate a kiss with sin? Nothing she had ever been taught. Perhaps it was the latest fashion in kissing. She checked with Yolande de Puy. A fashion, yes, for the woman was smiling at her with an indulgent affection, and no offence in the world. The wine had made Vérité's cheeks burn. She wished she had not drunk so much. She gratefully accepted another full cup from Yolande.

'Did you know that before a sculptor can join his guild he has to work a masterpiece?' Estienne was saying, as he watched de Dénezé move away at a slow, weaving pace towards the chapel to fetch his tools.

When Vérité did not answer, Yolande said, 'Sure, that's only to be supposed, husband. What else?'

'Seemingly there's a cave near here where they do it – carve their masterpieces, I mean. Every new sculptor. To join the guild. Or is it the compagne? Strange place. Wondrous to see, so I've heard. It's their initiation rite, seemingly. I'd like to see it. I'd like to see what de Dénezé did as a youngster. Wouldn't you, Chatelaine?'

She regained her stride. 'Yes! Yes! I'd like that very much! I mean to commission a statue of my father. Perhaps I could choose a bronze-worker from the styles there. I'd like that. Let's go there soon. Yes, yes, I'd like that.' She found the words bubbled out of her like wine from a bottle fallen on its side in the grass.

Estienne, too, excused himself – the wine, he said, though he had not drunk so very much – and she was left alone briefly with Yolande, a small barrel of a woman hooped round with mourning bands. 'Your husband is a great comfort to me,' Vérité said, feeling gauche and, for some reason, apologetic.

'I wish you'd allow him to be,' said Yolande, looking her over with sparrow eyes and a sparrow cocking of the head. 'I can see you like him.'

'I fear I trespass too much on his time already. He fills a great emptiness in my life. I trust the debt I owe him is not too onerous?'

'Well, of course he *does* suffer,' said Yolande cheerfully and, once asked her opinion, lent it with an energy and gusto that cornered Vérité against the terrace wall. 'It's not natural for a man to love unrequited without suffering. But that was his choosing. I'm always telling him so. I worry for his health, of course I do. But it's *you* I fret for more than Estienne. He has me, after all. And what do you have? Eh? Tell me that. That's what keeps me awake and worrying at night. What do you have?' The question was rhetorical. Vérité listened attentively to find out what it was that she lacked. 'I *wish* you'd let him pleasure you as a lover. However do you manage without it? Eh?' Vérité's mouth fell open but she did not have an answer for Yolande. '. . . Of course, I mustn't thrust Estienne at you as if he were the only fellow apt. Another would serve just as well. But he does so *pant* after you. And he's as fair a practitioner as any, I'll vouch for that . . . Yes, yes, I know! You'll say I'm biased, ha-ha! But he does know how to give a woman joy . . . I mean you are a *natural* woman, aren't you, Vérité? Right-minded? You have natural longings? As God intended? Don't you? Ah! I can see you think I'm biased. You do, don't you? Ha-ha!'

'No! No. I'm sure I believe you. I'm sure.'

She was filled with the panic of a refugee among foreign languages – nearing the familiar rise and fall of speech but unable to make sense of it. She was ashamed: ashamed not to understand: too ashamed to admit to this affectionate, well-intentioned woman that she did not know what kindness Estienne possibly could do her that he did not already do. Perhaps she was *not* a natural woman after all. Perhaps there had been some cruel excision made during her babyhood at the Madeleine: some gelding of the brain that had left her incapable of understanding. Perhaps her father had preserved her from knowing she was, in truth, a simpleton such as rocked on the village green sucking his fingers. Worst of all, perhaps her father had simply preserved her from knowing how men and women behave, kept her darkling, for reasons of his own. Resentment stirred small as mustard-seed.

Or perhaps she was wickeder than this good-hearted woman could ever imagine. For to tell the truth longings had stirred in Vérité – pictures on the verge of sleep, dreams on the verge of waking. But they could not be what Yolande was speaking of! They were dark, primordial things which drove the angels from round her bed and left her thinking of Satan. They were bestial things of the kind animals did in her fields and runs and pens!

Strung up thus between ignorance and guilt, Vérité swung like a gallows corpse, and every way the wind turned her, there was someone waiting with a smile. She drank off the last of the wine before Estienne and de Dénezé returned.

Estienne was saying, 'The Chatelaine wishes to visit the Cave of Initiation, man. She'd like to see the journeymen's pieces.'

'Yes, yes I would!' said Vérité or the wine.

'That's quite impossible,' said the sculptor in aside to Estienne, and then to Vérité, 'The place is secret. It's not possible. I regret

'. . . Only the initiates . . . How did madam hear of it? No, no, it's out of the question.'

'Madam is considering the commissioning of a statue,' said de Puy, tipping his head forward to look at de Dénezé through his long top lashes.

'That's right. I am!' she agreed eagerly, failing to notice that the artist took it for a threat of loss of patronage, as Estienne had meant he should. He felt an even greater disappointment in the girl.

'And why not now, Dénezé? As good a time as any,' urged de Puy.

'And be back by nightfall? Impossible.'

'Nonsense, man! It can't be more than five leagues,' said Estienne, proving that he had been there before. But the sculptor was too fuddled by drink to pounce on the mistake.

He found himself on a horse, leading the way up-valley ahead of de Puy and his lover. The noisily obliging Yolande said that since the path defied carriages, and her shape – ha-ha! – defied horseback riding, she would stay behind, but on no account were the others to miss their outing because of her.

Vérité relished the ride, thinking it would clear her head. But Estienne had brought more wine to refresh them on the journey. There was seemingly no end to the harvest cup or to the gallant enquiries after her thirst, her comfort, her well-being. She began to find it just a little oppressive, as her mare found Estienne's stallion oppressive and would nip at it impatiently each time it rubbed its sweaty shoulder into her flank.

De Dénezé was far less gracious than de Puy. He showed the way to the cave with infinite bad grace, all the time looking around for any who could report on his treachery to the compagne.

'If you're so uneasy, take the horses and stand well off with 'em. We can make shift without you,' said de Puy sharply. And feeling that he was in some way Pandarus to a disreputable Troilus and Cressida, the sculptor did as he was told. He had no thought for the Chatelaine's virtue, thinking it a thing spent already.

There was an acrid smell of guano, and they arrived in time to see the bats leave their roosts in the deeper caverns of the natural grottoes and fill the sky. A black Charybdis, they spiralled out of the rock engulfing starlings, moths and the bright evening light and seeming to suck Vérité irresistibly closer on a dangerous undertow.

'There won't be light enough to see,' she said, hanging back from the entrance. But Estienne was even then brandishing a pitchy, unlit flare. He held it over her, like a slightly flabby Hercules brandishing his club in triumph over a slender Stamphylian crane. 'I had imagined a workshop,' she said.

'No, no! This is a place of initiation – like the masons, you know? A tribute to the powers of magic.' And only from this close range was it possible to make out the cabbalistic shapes and symbols carved along the lichen-covered lintel. Vérité suddenly put her hand to her cheek. It felt warm, as if from a slap. 'What's the matter, coz?'

'My father once . . .'

'Ay? What did he?'

'Hit me . . .' She stopped and did not want to go on. She did not want to bring the memory of her father any further into this cave, even though it seemed she must go deeper herself. For had she not been the one who suggested coming here? And how could she reward the estimable Estienne with foolish second thoughts?

'If I'd known that, I'd've thrashed him till he begged your forgiveness,' said Estienne, and she looked him up and down and thought, Don't be ridiculous, but did not say so, because it would have been impolite. She lowered her head, penitent at the ungracious thought . . . and saw a white dismembered hand lying on the floor. It was stone. She realized it was stone. After a second.

The flare proved unnecessary. The low evening sun followed them into the cave which was shallow for most of its area and whose floor barely shelved. The sculptors had, after all, needed light by which to carve their initiates' masterpieces.

The figures stood drunkenly about – some leaning against the wall, some left knee-deep in the stone block from which they had been carved. The very earliest had been chiselled from the very stalactites and stalagmites of the cave. Already these were grotesquely goitred by new deposits of petrifaction, dewdropping from noses, tumorous on breasts and grossly engorging the lust of priapic gargoyles.

For the cave was a shrine to eroticism – crude as all craft initiations are crude; the work of adolescents, glorifying adolescent obsessions and egged on by older men to greater and greater excesses of bad taste.

The wine curdled in her bloodstream. The lees settled heavy through her trunk, and the vapour made her light-headed. Estienne was saying, 'I don't wonder you wanted to come here, lady. It is very . . . rousing. They do say barren wives come here and kiss the statues, and the blight's off'em within a twelvemonth. See where they kiss? See? See, where the parts get wore away?'

To see it all was to stand by and witness what Lot's wife saw, looking back at Sodom, before she turned to salt: white, naked salt beaded with sweat in the heat of falling brimstone and fire.

'Will you kiss, lady?'

'What? No!'

'Not the statues, lady. Not the statues.' And he backed her in among the satyrs and fawns, the succubae and nymphs, leaning against her as one does against a cow to persuade it into the slaughter-pen. He kissed as he had kissed her before, in front of the grape-pickers, and she suffered herself to be kissed. The narrow passages of his small snub-nose obliged him to stop and draw breath. He began to unfasten her dress. She watched him do it. Her spirit seemed to hover above their heads, watching with dispassionate curiosity.

'Is that what people mean when they speak of . . . ?' She pointed behind him at a statue depicting a man and woman, though it more nearly resembled Romulus suckled by the wolf, the one animal overarching the other. 'Is that what lovers do?' But she already knew. The mysterious geography of the sexes gradually fell into place, thanks to this new teacher and his object lesson in Love. Like all plain teaching, it only showed her what was common sense, what she had deduced already on the verge of sleep and on the brink of waking. Standing behind her now, he went on unfastening her dress like a squirrel tackling a pine-cone.

'Your wife asked me if I weren't eager to be pleasured by a lover. I couldn't answer her then. This is what she meant.'

He was greatly encouraged by the tenor of her voice – slow, sleepy and sliding down swollen sinuses. He ruched up the back of her dress and tucked the folds into her belt. 'And what answer would you give her, now you understand the question . . . Lean forward, Vérité . . .'

He was delayed by the need to unfasten his own clothing, and she moved away, like a ewe wandering off forgetfully from in front of the ram to nibble grass. She freed her skirts and let them fall back into place. 'Of course. I have appetites. I have curiosity, too. I was raised to be curious. I don't like to rest ignorant of anything,' she said.

'I'll unlock the secrets of Love to you, dearest, never fear it.'

'But I took a vow.'

'Well? So? My heart's faint with sorrow that I can never call you wife,' said Estienne briskly, 'but is that any reason for you to go untended? Unloved? Unserved by a chevalier in thrall to your beauty's needs?' There was something utilitarian about the way Estienne lapsed into perfunctory poeticism.

'My vow was never to allow a man into my bed,' she said.

'So? Is there a bed here? Do this pair here have need of a bed? Love's as soft as swansdown, sweetheart. You'll think you've been couching on . . .'

'Nor into my body,' she said. 'Those were the words my father used.'

Estienne was barely put to the trouble of a detour from the directness of his path. He made great play of grasping a sudden insight. 'Ah! I see it clear now! So that's what kindled the great Victoire's fire, eh? Lusted after his daughter so much he wouldn't suffer another man to have her. In time he'd've had you himself. I've heard tell of the like.'

She drew in a sharp, unsteady breath. 'Like Lot and his daughters,' she suggested.

'Who? Oh yes, exactly! I've heard tell of the like. I'd just not realized that my own beloved was so abused by those with charge over her. Thought he was just careful of your inheritance – wouldn't suffer the Sablois to be got from under you. La! Much simpler reasoning, by Christ! Devil's reasoning! . . . You realize, of course, it would be wrong to keep a vow forced out of you by a man like that? Tantamount to giving him his way. I see I must teach you what your father meant to keep from you – or keep to himself!'

Vérité fastened the last hook of her dress and began to replait her hair where it had become dishevelled. 'I'm greatly obliged to you, monsieur, for the kindness of your offer,' she said crisply. 'I shall consider it and let you have my decision.' It was as though she were talking to an argentier who had offered her the opportunity to buy a new boot scraper. '*Monsieur de Dénezé!* Pray come hither and show us the piece you made as an apprentice to your craft.'

De Dénezé came sheepishly into the cave from the spot to which guilty anxiety had drawn him to spy on them. 'That. That piece. There,' he mumbled. 'I was very young. My chisel work . . .'

'Your chisel-work showed much promise even then, my friend.

Unfortunately I was somewhat mistaken in what I would find here. I was hoping to find a good worker in bronze. For an equestrian statue.'

'Ah! A bronze,' said de Dénezé stupidly.

'Of Lot on horseback,' she said.

'Lot was never on . . .'

'No. I know it.' She put on gloves, and with one more comprehensive glance around the Cave of Initiation, she left it ahead of them and was mounted before either man could offer her assistance.

'It's very late, coz!' called Estienne, breathless at hurrying after her. 'Mustn't risk your safety to dark roads. Better pass the night at our house. Yolande will be there by now and we . . .'

'I have no fear of the roads over the Sablois, Estienne,' she said, wide-eyed with surprise. 'What? Do you think my father's spirit will be lying in ambush for me? Pray don't fret on that account. Inexperience has left me grievously lacking in some respects – I realize that. But I beg to suggest that nigh twenty years of life can't have left me entirely simple. For the most part I am green-ignorant about the nature of my fellow men, I admit it. I've met so few, you see. I realize it makes me gullible. I suppose there's only one person in the world I'd claim to know through and through. *And that's my father*, Monsieur de Puy. Victoire de Gloriole I did know – rather better than I know my Saviour. And certainly better than I find I know you.' And she put her horse to a canter and then to a gallop, leaving them uncertain of their way on the shadowy maze of paths through the Vendôme forests which border the Sablois.

'Women are always sharp after a lying-down,' said Estienne, salvaging his dignity as best he could. De Dénezé looked him over dubiously and wondered what else to disbelieve.

And so the moat held.

TWENTY-FOUR

Stepping Stones

The relief was so great, the fear so sharp in looking back, that Vérité took to her bed complaining of shivering and headaches and locked her door even against the Little Sisters. Still, she recovered quickly. She had met with Temptation, and if those were all the blandishments it had to offer, her vow would be easy to keep. For after years of dim, vague imaginings, when she had come face-to-face with Love, it was no more than Estienne de Puy fumbling his way to a mistaken conclusion.

She had thought she was ignorant. But she had known everything all along, by instinct. When he had tried to tell her a falsehood about her father, she had been able to say: 'No, that's not true. How do I know? Because Victoire taught me to judge Good from Bad.' When Estienne had tried to tell her that fornication was the same thing as joy, she had been able to say, 'No, that's not joy. That's sin. How do I know? Because Barnabas taught me to judge holy from profane.' Ellen de Gloriole, that creature of myth, had known intuitively the secret of herbs and medicinal flowers. Vérité knew something far more useful: that fornication was sin and that she could overcome the temptation to it.

She congratulated herself. The priests had always made Temptation sound such a difficult and deadly foe. And yet she, vulnerable and stupid as she was, had won out against it. She *had* been tempted. She had been curious. Was Estienne not an admirably handsome young man? Was he not a masterly lover? His own wife had said as much. And yet he had not been able to seduce her into lasciviousness, even in that pagan setting amid all those inducements to sin.

In short, Vérité, in escaping the sin of lechery, fell prey to the sin of pride. But the angels stayed around her bed. Even when she dreamed of that cave, of that coupling. Even though Estienne de Puy – poor, slow-witted, unsubtle Estienne – sent her a string of paintings for the wall of her bedchamber. She knew she was impervious to their influence and that the angels would stay around her bed even when the pictures were in place.

So she hung them and studied them ardently, morning and night. They were dire paintings – copies of copies done by artists in a descending chain of talent. The de Puys did not have money to waste on excellence. *The Rape of the Sabines, A Bacchanalia, Leda and the Swan, Europa and the Bull* . . . Lovers historical, lovers classical, lovers in flagrante, lovers in extremis, lovers no matter who, no matter where, so long as they were both graphic and ecstatic. The recommendation was plain. The education was comprehensive. Even the youngest children learn from pictures what they cannot be taught in words. But Vérité was impervious. She had no need of a lover. She was missing nothing. Her father must have imbued her with great strength of character and a degree of his own heroism.

When Estienne de Puy called at Gloriole next, the Little Sisters told him that the Chatelaine was ill. She rather thought she must be, for it would have been cowardly to hide from the man. 'Next time I shall give him audience,' she said when they came to sit round her bed and sew and nurse her with tender, anxious sympathy. 'Next time I must not be so uncivil as to give him a wasted ride.'

De Puy, as he rode away, was distracted, desolate, amazed. Failure had been a stranger to him in all his dealings with women. On his arrival home, his father hit him with the barrel of a flintlock, then kicked him down a flight of stairs in easy stages, pausing at each landing to tell him precisely which creeping, crawling creatures of creation he resembled. He scrupulously avoided kicking Estienne in the face, however, so as to allow him no excuse for failure another time. Estienne's own sense of humiliation smarted far worse than anything Geoffroi could do to him. Lying at the foot of the stairs, he began to compose in his head a letter:

'Adored and cherished cousin – so far above me in estate, further still in merit, and higher in nature than the angels themselves . . .' He tried to get up, but fell over again, clutching his ribs.

Just then his brother came in from the paddock. He looked Estienne over while clapping a pair of gauntlets over his own shabby clothes to drive the dust and dung out of them. 'What trampled him?' he asked, without much concern.

'He's dying of a broken heart,' said his father. 'Get over to Gloriole with the news of it. He's at death's door. Deliver it in person to the woman of the house.'

261

'What, now? Buggered if I will. I've been breaking horses since first light. I'd not mount up again today for the Queen of Sheba. You go. You know what you're talking about.'

Geoffroi, who had hurt his foot in the kicking, launched out with the flintlock. 'Get you to Gloriole, rat's-head, or you'll feel the pangs of heartbreak yourself and a few more besides.'

'I thought a letter . . .' said Estienne, trying to use the banister to get to his feet. 'Cyr could take it.' He was ignored.

'Tell her *what*?' snarled Cyr.

'That your brother's suffered a fall from his horse and it's only her encouragement'll save him rendering up the Holy Ghost. Keeps speaking her name. Keeps asking for her. And make her believe it, if you want to come home and find houseroom!'

Cyr de Puy shrugged and stepped out into the yard. On some days he held Life a detestable thing: a flyblown midden. He preferred to keep to the perimeter and out of the heat at the middle. If he could, he would have avoided people altogether, and his family like the Plague.

'So you're Estienne's whore,' he said, sitting down and putting his dung-covered boots on the embroidered stool. It was not a promising beginning.

'*No!*'

'Lover. Should I have said "lover"?'

'It would not have made you more accurate. You mistake, sir. Who told you such a thing?'

'I don't know. Common knowledge. I thought . . . Anyway. He's fallen off his horse. Death's neighbour. It's thought you'd want to know. Seems he's asking after you. No one else will do. Will you take a carriage?'

Cyr de Puy was a professional soldier – an artilleryman. He had contracted smallpox in the Ardennes and his cheeks were scarred by it. He also wore his hair helmet-shaved up the nape so that the blue veins of his head showed through, and close-cropped over the rest of his skull. An exploding cannon had showered him with burning wadding, and he kept on his gloves to hide the mess he had made of his hands in putting out the flames.

'I didn't know Estienne had an older brother,' Vérité said as she digested the news and the notion of herself as Estienne's whore.

'He has three years over me,' said the visitor peevishly, but was clearly accustomed to the mistake.

'I'm very sorry. For your brother. How did it happen?'

Cyr was irritable in the extreme. 'I don't know! What d'you mean, how did it happen? He fell off his horse. Doesn't he seem the manner of man to fall off his horse?'

'Yes. But not the manner of man to call on me with his dying breath.'

Cyr took his boots off the stool and scraped some of the dirt on the andiron and into the grate. 'Never short of breath, that one.'

'And you don't seem overly concerned, monsieur.'

'Oh me. I'm a military man, aren't I? See it all the time. What d'you expect? Wet breeches? I came as fast as I could.'

'I'm indebted to you.' But she still did not stir from her great audience chair pulled up to the grate, opposite his.

He said impartially, 'You look better than at the funeral. I'd envy Estienne – except you say I've no reason to.'

'Envy a man knocking at Death's door? No, sure.'

He scowled. 'Do you always accept presents from lovers you mean to disappoint? I seem to recall the exchequer was too bare to buy me a new horse lately, thanks to my brother's ardour.'

'Should I not have taken them? Should I have sent them back? Forgive me. I'm green in these matters. Estienne will tell you . . . if he has breath enough, I mean.' She sent at once for the pictures from her bedchamber. She felt brittle and vicious in the face of his contempt, or she would not have chosen to part with them, her proofs of invulnerability.

He got up and paced about the room, looking at everything in it, touching patinas and embossments, measuring the length of the broadsword on the wall with the span of his hand. 'Did he really use this? The Veryvictorious Victoire?' She objected to the scepticism in his voice and did not answer. 'Would that I could carve my way to such a fortune,' and he looked up at the ceiling as if it offended him beyond stomaching. 'But then he didn't use his sword, did he? Silk and whispers. That's what Gloriole's built on, isn't that right? You did very well from the son-and-heir's disgrace.'

'Do you remember Fils?'

'Of course not. Do you? I recall I was raised to rejoice in him being racked to death as a traitor. I recall thinking it wasn't a very cousinly sentiment.' Out of the corner of his eye he saw her cross herself. 'You didn't know? She didn't know! Green's the colour, as you say.'

'You're a mortally offensive man, Monsieur de Puy,' she said.

'I am? No, sure. It's the world that's offensive. I just do it justice.'

The paintings arrived. They restored Vérité's confidence. 'Not so green after all,' she imagined him thinking. She said, 'Tell me, what do you think of them, cousin?'

Even the disconsolate droop of his moustache could not mask his contempt. 'Cheap stuff. Worthy of my brother. I wonder you didn't burn them sooner than hang them alongside the rest. Your father – now there was a man with taste – or a respect for quality, at any rate.'

'Oh yes! I see your good opinion writ large on your face, monsieur. My house *delights* you so,' Vérité said with vitriolic sarcasm.

He was genuinely taken aback. 'Of course it delights me! Aren't I eaten up with envy? Why wouldn't I be? Envy's the lot of the second son. I've coveted this place since I can first remember. Accident of birth. I was born with the appetite of a first son and the opportunities of a second. No bite at the carcase till the first one's fed. No use of a thing till it's once used. That's why I joined the army, isn't it? Armour's made to fit the man. No chance of being put into Estienne's plate. Also it gives me the chance to kill men richer than I am, without hanging.'

She should have stayed in bed. She should have feigned sickness. To think she had fought shy of an interview with Estienne and had agreed to entertain this evil-humoured melancholic! This black devil's man was far more menacing. And whatever she said only made matters worse. 'I see you are a Leveller, sir.'

'Crap. I'm no one's equal. I'd out-climb 'em all if ever . . . Well? Do you mean to save my brother from desperation or not?'

'No, I don't believe so,' she said coldly, standing up to imply dismissal.

It was terrible. What demon had hold of her by the braids? The Gospels taught her to 'give and ask no question'. Saint Paul bound her to visit the sick and sorrowful. And yet all she could do was vie with this spiteful, peevish wretch to prove she was more heartless than he. What if Estienne was truly hurt to the edge of death? She had no right to ignore the message just because the messenger was repellent.

'Then you've more wit than I credited you with, Chatelaine. I'd rattle at the latch myself if I thought you really have bolted and barred against Estienne.'

'I don't rightly understand that.'

'It was an obscenity, lady. Do you suppose Estienne and his paintings hold the only licence to be obscene?' He bowed peremptorily and made to leave.

'You've forgotten the paintings.'

'D'you expect me to ride home lumbered like a pack ass? Estienne can collect his own trash.' The look that passed between them acknowledged that he had just betrayed his brother for a liar and a charlatan, and the message for a ruse. It did not seem to cause him much guilt.

'In that case you may burn them for me before you leave.'

How foolish! To prolong the villain's presence in the room purely to be revenged on Estienne! She was amazed at her own folly. Cyr de Puy returned to the pile of pictures and laid them lock and stock in the grate. Smoke was deflected out of the chimney and into the room. 'No! One at a time, or you'll smother us all!' He would think she was forcing on him the role of a common menial – 'Stoke the fire, slave!' All well and good. She would not look him in his dismal face and be made to feel apologetic. She would fix her eyes on the grate and prove her icy indifferencc to the world of men, whether the one drawn by Estienne's trite flattery or by this barrack-room cynic.

He watched, too, as Solomon and Sheba writhed on couches of fire, their heat of passion reanimated in the melt and stench of oil, in the curling of canvas, in the fat red flames. Bathsheba's bath bubbled and blistered like a rusty cauldron. The swan between Leda's thighs moulted – white feathers into black ash. The rutting bull roasted over Europa.

When Vérité could finally tear her eyes away from the incineration of naked Lucretia and her rapist, Cyr de Puy had gone.

Adored and cherished cousin – so far above me in estate, still further in merit, and higher in virtue than the angels themselves, my brother tells me that he found you too ill to trouble with my own minor mishap. I pray God to spare no healing benison for me until my adored Vérité is restored to health and happiness. Perhaps I was brought low by sympathetic anguish for your person, seeing how conjunct is my soul with yours . . .

'Was she truly sick?' said Geoffroi de Puy. 'Or did she smell a ploy?' His second son shrugged his indifference. He was not about to admit to the conversation that had taken place. Cyr was able to lie with great conviction. His father said, 'Well then. Let's leave her to stew in her chastity for a season. I'd serve a year in Hell to know if she's put a name to that *affrairementum* yet.'

'If she has, who's it going to be but me?' said Estienne, tilting a new turban this way and that on his head to find the best effect in the mirror. 'She doesn't know another soul. If she's not done it yet, I'll write it in myself inside the month, tup me if I don't.'

'Oh there's quicker and surer ways than you to get the Sablois,' growled Geoffroi. 'If I knew that *affrairementum* was blank, cousin Vérité would suffer a lethal accident before Wednesday week. Us being nearest by blood. Maybe I'll take the risk. Better than rest reliant on a pizzle like you.'

'The nuns would take it all,' said Cyr through a mouthful of food.

The other men stared at him along the table at which he sat eating his dinner with the asperity of a heron catching fish.

'What d'you say?'

'I say if she dies without signing the *affrairementum*, the estate goes to the Little Sitters-Pretty. And holy orders exist in perpetuity, so that's an end to your hopes of Gloriole. I found out as much in ten minutes. Nothing to be gained by snuffing out her candle. Damp your fires, do I? Sorry.'

Geoffroi spat a plumstone into his heir's dinner. 'See? Two months of sniffing up her skirts and you couldn't find out what he finds out without getting off his horse! Nuns? Nuns? I'd like to shoot'm like rooks. And you! Why didn't you tell us straight off? Keeping it to yourself. Cocksure bloody waster!'

Again Cyr shrugged and, picking his boots and coat off the table, shambled outside to the peace of the yard.

He was glad they had no excuse to murder the Chatelaine of Gloriole: they would be sure to bungle it. How he hated incompetents. Sometimes he hated them worse than the rich. Even well away from the house he could hear his father – endlessly optimistic, endlessly changing tack – moving round to his next angle of attack: a burglar trying every window till he found one left open. In the long run, she stood not the ghost of a chance, that green, lonely, silly, frustrated virgin over by the Sablois river.

*. . . and knowing your fondness for the green places and know-
ing the restorative merits of God's fresh air, I crave that you
will allow my wife and I to commend a ride through the Sablois
where, for so many years, I watched you at peaceful recreation
with your noble father and kept secret my soul's yearning for your
sweet company. Yolande begs you, with all the earnestness of a
neglected friend, for one short day spent hunting in the Arcadia
of the Sablois.*

'What, will the man never relent!' cried Vérité, crushing the letter
in her fist.

'You said you would entertain him and not be uncivil,' said
one of the Little Sisters charitably, and Vérité was chastened and
nodded and smoothed the letter out again on her knee.

But she did not go hunting alone with Estienne and Yolande. She
went moated around with dogs and *valets de chien*, all the ladies of
the neighbourhood she could muster and a phantasmagoria of birds.
Even the Little Sisters accompanied the hunt, riding in a wagon with
a barrel of hare's meat, rebaiting cords with which to summon home
the hawks.

On every arched wrist sat a little peregrine – ornamental as a
cockade and vicious as a ferret. The motion of the horses set the birds
fluttering, and the heady novelty of so many women set at liberty
set the ladies twittering. Yolande was outshone. Estienne was outnumbered. The fat partridges flew out of the bushes as numberless
as an Egyptian plague and were clutched down out of the sky in a
rain of coloured feathers. Here and there, a lady declined to pit her
bird against the rest, because the creature on her gauntlet was stuffed
– merely stitched on by its gilded feet – but the owner's enjoyment
was hardly the less for all that. The trees embroidered the hem of
the sky with bare intricate blackwork – turk's-heads of light which
had threaded its way through the twigs.

Vérité's black mourning swagged among the white horse-hounds
and dappled pointers. Her black hennin, overspread with its white
butterfly veil, gave her an appearance more nun-like than any of
her Little Sisters. If she had wanted to whet a lover to desperation,
she could not have done more. Her hawk took a partridge out of
the very claws of Estienne's bird which was sent reeling into the
topmost branches of a tree where it moped for a long time.

Estienne de Puy was hugely depressed. He had discussed with his
father the staging of some piece of theatre in the forest. Something

dangerous. Something to make Vérité feel the need of a male defender. A bear perhaps? And there again perhaps not, since he would have to prove his indispensability by actually *doing* something. Bandits, then? Yes, bandits recruited from a cast of discreet and well-rehearsed serfs who would shrivel obligingly before the flames of his wrath.

But the plan had to be abandoned when he learned what a vast expedition was planned. All these women would intimidate the staunchest bandits, if not ride them down. Now, in the event, he could not even get near enough for long enough to convey the message he was sure Vérité wanted to hear: that her modesty had vanquished all his hopes of pleasing her physically, and his determination was to live only for the approval of her eye. It seemed that whenever he approached her, she either unhooded the ferocious brute on her wrist or was swinging the line to summon it back again.

He gave thought to a piece of arson that would happily destroy all wills and *affrairementums* that stood in the way of his family's advancement, but had to admit that he was not the practical one among the de Puys and could not imagine how to begin. To restore his wilting spirits, he flirted with a demoiselle – and succeeded in catching the eye of the Chatelaine for the first time that afternoon. His head ached with grinning. The curl in his hair drooped as the evening dew came down. He began to feel a quite uncommon degree of desire for this Amazonian queen with her army of women. So he comforted himself that that was her intent. She clearly wanted to prick him on in his suit, or why else would he feel so pricked?

How elegant the mares crossing the causeway, their hocks as delicate as the balusters of the bridge! How sweet the smell of attar and essential oils on the evening air! Even the fish in the moat rose up to scent it and left expanding circular targets for the moon to aim at with its slender hunting bow. And there waiting to greet them, kneeling upon the berm like an expectant child permitted to stay up late, crouched the Master-at-Arms. It startled Vérité to see him.

The horse-hounds ran ahead and licked his face, appreciative of the fact that the top of his head had been quite blown away by flintlock fire. But in their excitement they overbalanced him so that he fell into the moat face-first, and the weight of his mail vest sank him. It took grapples to fetch him out.

The other guards had had no time to put on armour of any kind: they floated like stepping stones – two, three, four, five – across the moat, almost as if the scene were stage-managed for the maximum visual effect.

Scorchers, the household said. An opportunist robbery. Thank God, they said, that Vérité had been out of the house, for the marauders had made much of what they had in mind for the Chatelaine and her nuns had they found them at home.

Estienne de Puy was quick to say that it proved the vulnerability of a woman on her own. Said that it proved her need of a champion. Said that it proved the word was out: the Chatelaine de Gloriole was an easy prey to the wicked. Consequently, she looked at him and wondered if he could be responsible for the attack.

So next day she sent instead for Cyr de Puy and said, 'I am in need of a master-at-arms.'

'So I hear. But I can be vassal in my own house, Chatelaine. What terms are you offering?'

'A good wage. Congenial quarters . . .'

'I'll ask about. There's plenty men can be had for a wage. I'm not one of them. Good day to you, madam.'

'What terms *would* interest you?'

'A house for my wife.'

'I had no idea you were married. She may have the best of the hunting lodges. What else?'

'To manage the estate. To lend advice on its improvement.'

'*Its improvement?*'

'Well? So? There's a world of ways I'd bring it on. It's no great achievement to have made this neighbourhood envious, you know? They were born covetous. But I'd make you the envy of the Loire if you gave me a free hand . . . Still, if all you had in mind was to get you a tin man to prop against the door and have his brains blown out like the last . . . my thanks, but I'd get more advancement in the King's Army.'

'I might value your advice, sir, if you could temper your manners.'

'Ah! I'm a disappointed man,' said de Puy. 'Show me a path out of disappointment and I'll temper my manners quick enough. I might even put off my next planned enterprise.'

Vérité was hypnotized by the sheer incandescent discontent of the man. 'And what was that, pray?'

'Faith, to hang myself, lady. What else?'

'God in Heaven! What did Life ever do to you that you hate it so much?'

'Gave me appetites above my expectations, madam. Shall I have the post? Estate manager. Master-at-Arms.'

Though she longed dearly to change her mind, there seemed

no way of withdrawing. It would have meant bringing down everlasting night on this poor, unlovely madman. Charity alone demanded that she should try to pacify this unhappy creature. 'You may have the posts. On condition that your brother doesn't use it as an excuse to come calling. I find I'm not as eager of his company as I was formerly.'

'Madam, there was never love lost between us. If I wash my hands of my family, I'll be the richer and so will you.'

So it was agreed that Cyr de Puy should move his wife and his few possessions into one of the hunting lodges in the Sablois forest and establish himself in a room at the chateau. Vérité did not know whether to feel relief or pity for the wife – a chirpy robin of a woman – that the man chose to spend both day and night at Gloriole taking up the reins of his new employment. He certainly proved most industrious, conscientious and competent.

She requested, after a time, that he dine with her, and deterred her Little Sisters from joining them – the better to discuss his plans for the estate. She hoped too (she confided to her companions) to pluck from Cyr the black feathers that grew so sharp out of his soul. She recognized in him (she said) the misery of loneliness, and would not rest till it was eased by Christian counsel and a little kindness.

At night she lay awake especially to give thought to his plans and the plight of his soul. How could he be better clothed in her livery – being so long in the waist and thighs and looking so cadaverous in maroon? Even her dreams were troubled by the problem of Cyr de Puy.

Of course, he frightened her with the sheer energy of his discontent and his barbaric manners. Even his appearance frightened her in a way that his soft-upholstered, limp-wristed brother never had. She dreamed several times – a ridiculous dream – that he came to her room to unburden himself of a tormentuous, agonizing secret: that he loved her! and that it was for her that he had left home and inheritance and made himself vassal to the Chatelaine of Gloriole. The fright of seeing him there, on her threshold, would jar her awake.

But such foolish, outlandish fears were entirely unjustified, of course. Of course he did not presume to come. Of course when she woke, no naked, wolfish man stood at the door of her chamber.

In fact it was she, finally, who had to make the long, bitter-cold walk over splintery, creaking floorboards to the chamber above the armoury.

She expected the room somehow to be furnished in black or battle-clad with weapons and mail. But he had obeyed her instructions to make his quarters comfortable and in keeping with his status.

She expected to have to wake him, but he was awake already – as if he had known she was coming.

She expected to have to speak, to explain herself. But there was no need. Cyr de Puy perceived his duty to his Chatelaine, even in the few moments that she hovered in his doorway with her fingers on the rings of the door-curtain to silence them. He flapped down the covers of his bed, and his body said that he had been expecting her all along.

When later she asked if he loved her, he replied, 'Naturally. As you wish.' And since words could not encompass how much she wished for him to love her, what better reply could she have hoped for? Far greater, though, was her need of someone to love.

For all Estienne had unwittingly primed his brother's gun with erotic suggestion and sexual curiosity, he had laid too great a store by Vérité's vanity. To a woman raised in her formative years on self-denial and humility, flattery and adoration were far easier to resist than the chance to love: to pour herself selflessly into another's welfare. It was what her childhood vocation had prepared her for.

So the moat was breached by Cyr de Puy – with nothing more than the help of a few old army friends masquerading as Scorchers, with two, three, four dead guards floating like stepping stones across the river, and with the expenditure of a little lead.

PART III

When King Charles VIII set his mind to marrying Duchess Anne of Britanny, he besieged Nantes and Rennes. He paid her troops to desert her. He harried and laid waste her country. And although Anne was already affianced elsewhere and Charles had himself gone through a form of marriage, he saw no impediment to his plans. The season had passed for honouring vows. Charles had put away such childish things and become a king — a master of expediency.

Anne was persuaded of the excellence of Charles's suit, and all at once it was a love-match made in Heaven. Not that he thought love could be purchased for nothing. Two silver-gilt flagons and two large, enamelled red bonbonnières added weight to his declarations. Seven hundred and seven marcs, four oncas and seven gros of weight, to be precise.

The bride beggared her exchequer with the price of a dress, but it failed to hide her short leg and false heel, just as her heart-shaped face failed to hide a granite personality. At the service, the King teetered forward, overburdened by his length of Valois nose, picking at his hands, knotting his fingers. His mouth hung open in perpetuity, and he was so slow to speak his vows that he seemed to be waiting for his wits to rejoin him. An awe-inspiring sight. Even the guests turned their backs and chatted by the fire, so moved were they by the proceedings.

And yet there was a kind of love. Beyond Charles's passion for Britanny and Anne's passion to be Queen of France, there was a kind of love. It was a match of kindred spirits, and it flourished, pulling round it a caddis cocoon of beauty at the chateau of Amboise by the Loire.

TWENTY-FIVE

Material Evidence

Further upstream than Amboise, in a tributary of the Loire, another caddis pair gathered around it the material evidence of happiness. Not that they much resembled Charles and Anne, for there was a physical vigour about Cyr de Puy that drew respect, and a rare beauty in his woman. She shared her beauty with him, in the shape of gorgeous presents, clothes, horses, and happiness.

Happiness. Envious moralists will want to say that it was lacquer over base tin, a grand disguise for an inward emptiness. But that is nonsense. Wealth is only hollow to those who perceive other, intangible riches slipping out of their moneyed fingers. Here were two people primed to measure their worth as growing children are measured against the jamb of a door. Vérité yearned to own beautiful things. She had owned nothing until she was loved; she remembered love's arrival, hands laden with beautiful presents. It had been no sham love – goods in place of affection. It had been real. And the only sibling with whom she had had to share her father's love was the Chateau of Gloriole. Why should she not love material things, then? Why should she not love Gloriole? Was it not, in some way, her step-brother? Why should she not prove her love by buying it things – beautifying it, as the devout beautify the relics of saints? And why should she not lavish money on Cyr de Puy, since she loved him twice as much and since it rescued him from the sin of despair? In short, it made him happy, and that is the duty of a lover.

Cyr de Puy, bred in a household utterly devoid of love, the unfavoured second son, raised on constant reminders of his own worthlessness, could not remember a time when the family had not looked down the road to Gloriole with a seething, calculating envy, as the devout look to the City of Light as their ultimate goal. Now, all of a sudden, he was tenant of Gloriole, darling of its Chatelaine, and wealth rained down on his head like the golden apples of Paris. He was a wonder in the eyes of his father, a usurping king in the eyes of his brother. They fawned on him like Court sycophants. When, as Vérité's champion, he wore a black journade over his gilded armour and a tourney-helmet moulded into the gilt snarl of a chicheface, the sheer opulence was proof to them – material proof – of his merit.

It was no hardship to do the Chatelaine the little service she wanted in exchange. And his days were left free to satisfy a much greater lust: the yearning to acquire beautiful things – to make his mark on Gloriole-sur-Sablois.

He built up the silk trade and it thrived so well that however much he and his mistress exerted themselves to spend the income, the silkworms exerted themselves harder. And the estates that had rendered up schist and tufa were just as ready to offer flint. He licensed first flint-knapping, then the manufacture of flintlocks for the wars in Britanny and with the English. Sometimes he even went to fight.

It was a dire blow to Vérité when he mustered a levy of Sablois men and rode off to join the King's troops. He left only his proxy in her bed: Loneliness as bulky and tangible as ever he had been. It claimed her in the middle of the night; it rose with her in the morning, kept her company during the day. Then it was night again. Disproportionately often, it was night. And that was when she began to think of her sin.

They would be discreet. No one need ever know. But that did not mean God could be kept in ignorance. She knew that if she confessed herself to her new chaplain, he would make nothing of it. The man was a toady (one of Cyr's rare lapses in judgment, or so she thought). He had a way of snickering over the childlike paucity of her sins, as though he knew places to go where one could find a far better breed of iniquity. There was no purging to be had there.

For a long while, her Little Sisters also rested in ignorance. She wanted to confide in them, as she had confided all her happinesses, small and large. But for the first time in her life it was impossible. How could they rejoice in the knowledge? What could it do, other than upset them?

Then one day, just after Cyr's departure, Petite-Agnès came flying to the chapel in a state of abject terror, and the flapping of her sleeves as she prostrated herself on the altar steps extinguished several of the candles Vérité had just lit for Cyr's safe return. 'Sanctuary! Oh sanctuary, madam! Don't let them lock me in the armoire! Tell them it's true! I'll do penance, but not in the armoire, please! I can't abide small places! I'm mortally afraid of small places!' Other nuns came into the chapel, more sedate but as implacable and hard-mouthed as black Inquisitors closing on a prisoner. 'I'll do penance here! I'll fast here!' Petite-Agnès shouted out, but it did not stave them off. 'Oh tell them, lady! Tell them I wasn't lying!'

Vérité stepped between Agnès and her persecutors. It was inauspicious that her prayers for Cyr should be interrupted, that the candles had gone out. She tried to complete inside her head the invocation of Saint Cyr so as not to give the saint offence. 'What's the matter here? Tell me.'

The accusers tightened their lips. It frightened her to see them look so altered – grown-up – parentally angry.

'They say I told an untruth!' wailed Petite-Agnès, dissolving into hiccuped tears. Losing faith in the safety of holy sanctuary, she slid down the steps and clung to Vérité's dress instead. 'But I didn't! I only said what I saw. I didn't make it up. Why would I make it up? How would I?' The girl's nose was running on to the tan velvet of Vérité's dress; Agnès noticed, tried to wipe it clean and made matters worse. 'I only said I saw the Master-at-Arms kissing madam in madam's bedchamber before he left. Ursula said she was glad he was gone because he frightened her with his fierce face, and I said there was no call since he didn't fright madam, plain as plain if she could kiss him. Oh, I don't know what I said wrong, but I'll do penance! By my soul, I will! But don't let them lock me in the armoire, Chatelaine! Please, Chatelaine!'

The oldest nun, *mère ancille* Catherine, directed her eyes somewhere below Vérité's and seemed unwilling to pursue the matter in front of the Chatelaine: almost as if it were none of her concern. Catherine had entered the order as a widow. She did not share Petite-Agnès' ignorance, even though she secretly shared Ursula's fear of de Puy. At last she whispered, 'The child said more, madam. Of what he did. She has a licentious turn of mind that one. Your reputation's not safe with her.'

It seemed to Vérité that Mère Catherine saw through her as through glass. She blushed scarlet and, unnoticed, the taper she was holding curled back on itself like a ramshorn. Mère Catherine stepped forward and knocked the dangerous wax to the ground with one hand, while with the other she set three fingers to Vérité's lips and forbade her to so much as answer the charge. She took a grip on Agnès – firm to the point of cruelty – and the others laid hold of her too and dragged her out of the chapel.

Vérité returned to lighting candles. But now they burned so vigorously that they scorched her cheeks. She knelt to say her prayers, but the prayers turned to vinegar in her mouth. She trailed after the unaccustomed noise of anger and fright, followed it up the staircase, turned away from it towards her own room. Had she begun already to spoil Eden seeing that her blackbirds had become as strident as starlings?

After the Little Sisters had withdrawn to their roost beyond the plank drawbridge, the hysterical thumping of a fist on the inside of the armoire door continued unabated. The pitch of Petite-Agnès' voice was too high to carry as far as the Chatelaine's room.

She was amazed that they could be so cruel, to inflict such a penance on one of their own little sisters, knowing her fears, knowing her to be innocent. She wondered that she could be so wicked herself as to allow it, knowing the girl to be innocent. So sin was born, then, like a baby. Once the head was out, the rest came tumbling after with ease. One vow broken and already she was perjuring herself by keeping silent. Now here she sat, lying by her silence, inflicting pain on her little friend, sowing dissent among her dependants.

And what of God, watching her through the lattice? The more mired she got, the less she could hope for her prayers to be acceptable. And that made her sin a hazard to Cyr's life.

Her skirts hampered her as though she was wading through water as she ran to the cupboard on the landing. It shook and trembled – a Pandora's chest full of sin and ill fortune pounding to be set free. She unfastened the latch, and Petite-Agnès spilled out at her feet, sobbing and shrieking and inconsolable. The pulley squealed and the drawbridge lowered a little until a row of heads was visible mustered in the doorway of the loft room. Vérité went to the tripwire and the skirts of her dress brushed the bells and set them ringing.

'What Petite-Agnès told you is true. I did kiss Cyr de Puy. I'm very fond of the man.'

All but Mère Catherine melted away – back into the darkness of the loft. This was a subject they knew nothing of. Men.

'You must send him away, then. Or your vow's broken,' said the older woman decisively.

'I only vowed not to marry.' It was not true, but Catherine was not to know it and it was something of which Vérité had convinced herself long since: her father had simply meant her not to marry and place Gloriole in the hands of an outsider. Even so, it was an unnatural vow, a cruel vow.

'So what will come of it, Chatelaine? I'm sure he says he's fond of you too. Yes?'

'He is. He loves me with a great tenderness. He is a very gallant gentleman.'

'He wants possession, that one. He won't rest short of owning.'

'Ah what kind of nonsense is that? He's married, you know that! It's impossible I should break my vow! I wouldn't have him in the house otherwise, naturally.'

The head on the far side of the drawbridge bobbed about like a puppet in the window of a booth. 'He'll soon set her aside, poor woman. Divorce, they call it. He'll lay that sin to your charge before long, as I'm a Christian he will. Like the King. Divorce he'll call it, but I'd call it worse . . .'

'No! I'd never allow that!' protested Vérité. 'I never would! We're friends! Friends-in-love. Cyr doesn't look to own Gloriole! Of course he doesn't! I only employ him, you know that. He knows my vow. Of course he won't divorce his wife! Pshah! He knows I'd turn him off if he did anything so wicked! You're talking nonsense. I don't know what's beset you. He's not the breed of man to care about rank and title. Look. Didn't he demean himself even to be Master-at-Arms and in service to me? His birth's really too high to fit him for the post. I'm hard put to recompense him.'

With sobbing and with desolate hand-signals Petite-Agnès made suit to be readmitted to the State of Grace beyond the gulf in the landing. Catherine let down the drawbridge, and the girl scurried across as though the open cupboard behind her might close its gaping jaws on her once more. She did not so much as glance up at Vérité, but ran bent double, black and white, like a badger going to earth. Vérité too ran forward on to the bridge. 'Look! See here!' She seized the crucifix at Catherine's breast. 'See here! I swear I'll never break my vow and marry Cyr! I'll never give him cause to set his wife by! I swear it!'

Mère Catherine looked down at the crucifix and seemed confused to the point of bewilderment. 'What, then? What's to come of it? Anything else would be mortal sin. Anything else would break the Seventh Commandment.' She eased the cross out of the Chatelaine's fingers, and Vérité backed away from a territory that was not hers to enter.

'It was an unkind vow to force on me! It was an unnatural vow! My father had no right . . .'

'That's not for me to judge,' said Mère Catherine, pulling on the rope once more. But in her eyes was an undented devotion to the memory of the dead Comte. A gulf opened up between the two women that it would take more than planks to bridge.

And afterwards the Little Sisters of Pity discussed her in the privacy of their loft. She was their daily icon. They had as many dealings with her as with the Virgin Mary. They would reserve judgment. It was not their place to judge. What, in any event, could they do? They depended for their livelihood and shelter on this their benefactor, and if they wished to go on living in her loft, eating her food, praying in their new chapel, what could they do but go on loving her? Hers would have to be a very great sin indeed before they chose beggary and homelessness in preference to the Chateau of Gloriole. This present sin could not be so very serious. After all, they had known Vérité too well, for too long. They cradled her too tight in their prayers.

Besides, as time wore on, they did not see the change in her that sin would have wrought. They saw no transformation into a Jezebel, no painted cheeks, no immodest clothes, no lewd talk, no falling off in religious devotion. In fact, the Chatelaine astounded the neighbourhood with a sudden outburst of religious patronage, as though her goodness had grown too great for the confines of the chateau and overspilled in a flood of generosity. She endowed the lazar house at Troo with a new dormitory. She sent two candles weighing forty pounds apiece to every church in the comté. She gave thirty livres to the Brotherhood of the Minimes at Tours to mention her house and household in their Masses, and had a bell cast for the Church of Saint-Cyr in Ormes. She visited sick soldiers at the Hospital Sainte-Jeanne, and granted pensions to their families. It was rumoured that a local wife had once maimed her demobbed husband with an axe in the night 'because he'd fetch more home that way than ever he had with a sword and musket'.

The stables at Gloriole were constantly infested with vagrants in Cyr's absence. He said – when he returned from campaign and hurled them into the moat – that Vérité was never to endanger her health again by opening her gates to such diseased scum. (Although somehow he phrased it more tenderly.)

Consequently, when she began to feel unwell, and when her monthly flow dried up shortly after his return, she dared not tell him. What if he were right and she had contracted something fearful from tending the sick? For his sake, she kept to her own room and would not so much as kiss him.

He could not understand how he had offended. At first he was curious, then peevish, then blackly morose. The man she found seated on her bed in the middle of the night was the same malcontent who had burned her pictures in the grate. 'Has someone poisoned you against me, lady?' he demanded to know. 'Have those little saints in the attic won you back to a frost?'

'No, Cyr! No! Don't be so foolish!'

'Is it your season, then?'

'Y-e-e-s. Yes, that's it! It's my season.' But she was not yet so accomplished a liar as to sound plausible, and it only made matters worse.

'So. I've crossed you, have I? By turning out all your good causes?'

'No, Cyr. Not at all. It's not that.'

'But I've surely lost ground while I've been gone, haven't I? I'd better go home to my wife if I want a wifely welcome.' And he left her, failing to hide his bad temper or to tread quietly in the long corridor.

Vérité resolved to go after him. But when she got up, it was as if her illness took a hand in restraining her, for she was suddenly gripped by violent cramping pains. She called out to him, but either he did not hear or he did not choose to hear. In all her life she had not been ill. Now demons were warring in her belly. She thought, 'and all for want of Confession and a broken vow'. She wanted to summon her Little Sisters: they had virtue in plenty to protect them and could perhaps spare enough to throw over her like the tails of their scapulas. She rang the handbell: it put her at one with the leper ringing his bell, shouting 'unclean!' and dying in loneliness for the sin of being ill.

When the haemorrhaging began, all she could think to do was to cling to the wooden feet of the madonna in her room, as the woman clung to Jesus' robe to sap Him of goodness. She thought of the contract of *affrairementum* and was glad that Gloriole would be bequeathed to God when she died. Part-payment for her sins.

Having no notion that she was pregnant, the miscarriage struck terror in the Chatelaine. At first it was an immeasurable relief when Mère Catherine explained it to her. But as the nun leaned over the fire, burning bloody rags with a ruthless eagerness, she was tight-lipped and knowing, siding with God in His decision to abort the fruits of adultery. She had been thinking, she said: Vérité was right: the vow extracted from her by her father was wrong and unnatural. The Chatelaine should opt for the lesser of two sins and accept marriage with a man of rank rather than adultery with a man so far beneath her. This miscarriage proved it. Catherine suggested a quick marriage – before rumours spread, before it was known she was deflowered.

It was a foolish, ill-timed piece of advice. Just then, it seemed to Vérité that the finest thing in all the world would be to be reconciled to Cyr de Puy and to have his child.

When he came back and heard her news, he was contrite to the point of speechlessness, desolate to the point of tears, word-perfect in solicitude. He swore it the greatest loss he had ever suffered, and when she looked into his eyes, there was no doubting the truth of it.

'Another child will come,' he said, when it was the thing she most wanted to hear. 'Another child will come.'

'You know I can never marry you, Cyr. It's sworn and double-sworn.'

'I never pressed you, did I?' he replied. 'Enough to plant my seed in your fields, lady. More than enough.'

She stroked his hands where they lay, unpresuming, unambitious on the counterpane. When she stroked his face with her fingertips the pitted surface was as beautiful to her as chased plate, his razored hair as soft as the silk pile of Moorish carpet. He had trained her up, after all: made her an aficionado of Beauty. She *would* marry him, vow or no vow. 'They say you'll divorce your wife to be free to marry me,' she said.

'Who says so?'

'Oh people. Slanderers.'

'I hope you opened them to the truth, then. I'm content with things as they are, lady. I'd never lay such a sin to your store or mine. I hope you know it, too.'

'Yes, love. I know it.' And after one single wicked pang of regret she was glad to be allied to so very good a man, one so unambitious of sin.

So Vérité de Gloriole remained the mistress of a lover who refused to be elevated to the status of her husband or to divorce his wife. A plain thing, he said, and ill equipped to raise him to a passion, but content (happily) to rest barren as a result. Vérité called on her often, with little presents and comforts, and was touched and relieved to see such a wealth of ignorant welcome in the pleasant, provincial face. Marie did not seem so very plain to Vérité. But then she supposed there must be truth in what she had heard somewhere – where was it? – that each heart carries within it the blueprint of the one and only face and form it is destined to desire.

Poor woman, to be barren. Poor woman, to lack the wherewithal to remake the image of Cyr de Puy. Still, Marie had no Gloriole to bestow upon a child, nor half such a strength of passion, nor half such a debt of gratitude to repay.

When Vérité fell pregnant again, she clamoured at the very gates of Heaven to accept her thanks. She set about converting the Chapel Saint-Cloud into a rising star on the hilltop, with triangular side chapels radiating from the nave all radiant with coloured light when their various angles of stained-glass trapped sunshine or moonlight. As for the castle chapel, she commissioned the merchant Vache to fetch her Carrara marble, pellucid, baby-white and veined with yellow. Out of it she had niches made in square fluted columns where a platoon of brightly painted saints might stand on gilt plinths to bless her at her prayers. The Oratory of Pity fanning out from the base of the East turret was peopled with angels clad in cloth-of-gold and crowned with circlets of silver. She sent to the choir school at Psalette and begged for choristers to aid her in the praise and glorifying of the Saviour. And when they came – children in the perfection of boyhood – they put her angels and her wooden saints to shame with their fluting voices and warm skin. Their treble psalms overshot the hulking ugliness of everything man-made in parabolas of sweetness. And Vérité's obsessive pleasure in her unborn child vanquished all other ambitions. 'If all's well, I'll go on pilgrimage to René d'Angers' shrine,' she whispered in the ear of her most favoured guardian angel, as Cyr feathered his flight over her and she clasped his magic superstitiously close.

Even her Little Sisters prayed now for the child, filled with a vicarious hunger, driven by their own suppressed longings. Petite-Agnès had seen Cyr de Puy weep in the privacy of his own room over the loss of the first child, and the community decided they had misjudged the man. They made reparation to him in their prayers for slighting him in their hearts.

And all the while the house grew greater, as if to house a multitude of children, as if in anticipation of tribes of Glorioles. An upper storey was added to the wings of the chateau. Linenfold panelling – like a petrifaction of billowing Sablois silk – lined the new upper corridors. And busts of noble men turned their backs on every cross-mullioned and transomed window, white-eyed, unblinking and never tempted to look over their shoulders at the changing views outside.

Parklands were considered a more fitting surround to a lady's house than the rude chaos of natural forest. And so the perimeter of the woods was pushed further back, burned in swathes of linenfold smoke, far beyond the river. Swatches of unvarying green grass rolled out on every side – a copse preserved here, a spinney there, a row of planes to block the view of unscenic Croix-Rouge. Circlets of rose bushes lay about the park, haphazard as quoits shied wide of the columnar trees. As Nebuchadnezzar made a gift of the Hanging Gardens of Babylon to Amytis, so Cyr in his assiduous stewardship made gift to Vérité of two hundred apples-of-Paradise entwined with currant bushes, a hundred musk roses, white asphodels by the dozen, and a pair of Judas trees.

Giant amphoras of cardinal-red marble blossomed like megalithic tulips; and Greek urns and fat, blithe cupids. A hornbeam maze was planted, too, though in its infancy it was impossible for Vérité to appreciate the cleverness of its convolutions. Cyr designed it.

All about the great-hall, the red leather wall covering was flayed downwards and a frieze begun in bas-relief, to depict the hunting of the unicorn. But de Puy had great plans for a still greater hall: a phantasm of a room brilliant with windows and mirrors and gilding and a coffered ceiling painted with a hundred different vignettes. Vérité urged him to speak of it often, for it implied his presence in the chateau for decades to come. His plans were so grand that he might stay a lifetime and never see them fulfilled. Her grand plan was only for a lifetime of Cyr. Her passion for him grew like the child in her womb, requiring a more and more expansive gown. Small surprise, then, if Gloriole were to spread out its walls to infinity.

Then the King went into Italy.

Despite the Queen's tears and the cost to the treasury, he formed designs on Naples and marched into Italy. It was said that the campaign might start in Italy but that it would end in Constantinople – a crusade to replant the Cross where the heathen crescent had supplanted it. Seeing it in that light, the devout Queen Anne could hardly raise serious objection. In the meantime, though, Charles was content to fix his sights on the Kingdom of Naples, flattered that his

Angevin blood entitled him to it. Ten thousand men crossed the Alps from Grenoble and among them rode Cyr de Puy. Despite the Chatelaine's tears, he crossed into the Italian sunshine and left her darkling.

TWENTY-SIX

The Good Christian

'What must I do to please God above all things?' she asked her chaplain. Her lonely vulnerability brought anxieties clustering round her like sharp pieces of metal round a lodestone.

His answer was categorical – as though he had lacked only the conversational opening. 'Rid the Jews, madam.'

'The what?'

'The Jews, madam. Are you aware how these Spanish Christ-killers are breeding hereabout? It's a shame and a degradation on your house. Every cottage that comes empty in Rocheblanche, there's a Levite new come from Spain with his moneybags to buy it. The place is a den of thieves and heathens these days.'

Vérité was taken aback. She knew, of course, that the expulsions from Spain had sent thousands of Jews drifting through France, and that many had lodged on her estate, like thistledown lodging in a hedgerow. But she had quite failed to notice any ill will arising from it.

'I didn't know,' she said. 'Has anyone preached to them? Do they give offence?'

'In the nose of Heaven? Rank as sardines drying, I do assure you,' said the chaplain. 'It's your Christian duty to purge the Sablois of them root and stock. That's to say, if you do nothing, it could be misconstrued, madam. Your estates could gain the reputation of a safe haven for blasphemers and villains. It's been on my lips to say it a thousand times.' This seemed true, for the man's lips were chapped and flaking and he licked them to excess.

'And you think the matter of the Jews might prejudice the success of my prayers?'

'Nothing more certain. How could the Lord Jesus look kindly on those who shelter His persecutors?'

Such harsh words. The crucifix on the wall suddenly cut her at the eye like a double incision. But Vérité hesitated. Barnabas had never raised his voice against the Jews, though she knew her father hated usury. 'If only my Master-at-Arms were here,' she said, 'I could trust the matter to his hands.'

'The excellent chevalier de Puy would undertake it with a good heart and Christian valour. He's spoken of it often to me in the past.'

'Valour? You mean they'll take up arms?'

'Ah,' said the chaplain inscrutably. 'Let me levy an army of God-fearing men. Surprise overcomes all difficulties.'

But Vérité had lost that independence of thought that Barnabas had made such efforts to instil. She wrote to Cyr for his advice, and in the meantime she asked the opinion of the nearest person to hand. Joachim Vache called that afternoon to recommend to her the cargo of a newly docked barge. 'Do you think, Monsieur Vache, that I ought to burn out the Jews?'

He stared at her. Of course, she thought when he failed to answer. He will wait for some hint as to what answer I want. The man's sycophancy was a trial to her. But this time the silence lasted so long that it seemed Vache must have no opinion whatsoever on the matter of the Jews.

'Competition is always a healthy thing in trade,' he said at last, coughing to clear his throat.

She was disappointed: commercial arguments never stand up against theological ones. 'I see. The Jews don't trouble you, so you have no objection to them.'

Vache laughed short and loud – an unprecedented thing never to be repeated. 'Ah. Ahem. Indeed no. The Jews don't trouble me. Not at all. Not at all. Ahem.'

'But they killed Christ.'

'No, sure. No one in the Sablois?' he said, and his cheeks made a last convulsive effort to free themselves of rigor. 'So very long ago.'

'Don't they kill Him anew every sabbath with their vile rituals?' Strange. She had rather wanted arguments with which to counter the chaplain, but found herself using the chaplain's arguments herself.

'My lady has decided already, it seems,' said Vache pulling the rim of his turban ridiculously low around his eyebrows and over his ears. He wore the same expression as when he was calculating in his head a lengthy account less discounts plus interest and allowing for shipping tax. 'May I beg to part from your ladyship's exquisite company somewhat hasty-like this morning? They're greatly put out at the jetty by this vessel gone aground.'

She could see it from the window. The alteration to the river's flow caused by the Gloriole moat had, over the years, raised a mudbar below the bridge. Even for those who knew it was there, it made the approach to the jetty awkward. Now one of the big guild-monopoly barges had rested its keel on the bar, settled, stuck fast. The upper river was effectively closed to all but the smallest vessels.

'Can she be got off?' asked Vérité, anxious to change the subject.

'No. Her back's broken. Better burn her and be done.' For a moment the merchant stood beside his customer looking out of the window. His head came only to her shoulder. She knew he had plans for a new jetty further downstream – a warehouse, a wagon depot. Vache's world, like Gloriole chateau, was an expanding empire, though he seldom had the opportunity for such a panoramic view of it. 'Not burn, maybe,' he said. But she mistook him – thought he meant the barge – and he did not correct her, such was his haste to be gone.

No sooner was he out of the room than he pulled off his turban and snatched the skullcap from his head. The clip grazed his scalp. After praising God for his Chatelaine's ignorance, he rode directly home, setting his household a-flutter like a dog in a farmyard.

The Vache family fortune was based on usury, and usury on the pettiest scale of money-lending to the poorest of the poor. But no sooner had it lifted the family above the status of their neighbours, and brought them a house, a ship and a plot of land, than Joachim Vache eschewed the title 'money-lender' for that of merchant – argentier – and lent in the name of credit to those who thought the mention of 'price' and 'cost' and 'cash' somehow indelicate. It was the age of the merchant. Not since the Phoenicians had the owning of a ship promised such wealth to those who survived the storm, the rocks, the disease, the vicissitudes of the market. And the pogroms.

His house was far, far removed from Rocheblanche's rue des Juifs – a ten-room gentilhommerie of chevron-patterned brickwork under fifty-three thousand and four hundred tiles: he had shipped the consignment himself. The doorposts were so ornately carved that the mezuzahs barely drew attention to themselves. He plucked them down one by one as he went through the house summoning his family together. It was a big family: as many as the branches on the menorah candelabrum, as his wife delighted in observing.

'I have a thing to say and when it's said, it's done,' Vache announced. A favourite dictum of his. The commandments he delivered from on high were carved in stone, unalterable. To explain or justify himself would have weakened his status as King-among-subjects. Besides, the pace at which he lived forbade him to waste time on explanations. If he made his children tremble, all well and good. It would fit the girls for marriage and the boys to run families of their own with as sure a hand one day. Dutifully the children assembled in ascending order of height, resting their fingers on their lips.

'Ahem! Today we are become a Christian family!' He unwrapped two holy pictures – goods surplus to some customer's consignment – and laid them on the table, inviting defiance. The line of children bent as the youngest edged forward to stare at the pagan baubles. The older ones simply widened their dark eyes and stared at the wall. 'We'll go tomorrow and be baptized by the Abbot in Croix-Rouge. It is arranged.' At home Vache spoke plainly, without the frills and ornaments of speech afforded to his clients. He circumcised sentences with a clean thrust.

'What, an' eat pig?' said his youngest daughter. He pulled the kerchief from his sleeve and pushed it into her mouth as he did when she dribbled food at table.

'I can flog you all to a willingness, and my arm won't tire.'

Face by face, the children turned towards their mother. They none of them believed what their father said, but they had to rely on their mother to deflect this latest tyranny. Madame Vache was a thick-set woman who, in her husband's efforts to make her like the gentry-folk, had been encouraged to eat herself fat. She revelled in her layers of flesh as she revelled in the other wrappings and trappings of wealth. She dressed for evening in the middle of the day and her hair was overarched by a gold-wire birdcage which she took off only at night. She had made herself obedient to her husband's bullying since the day she married him. Now she said, 'Your father has taken leave of his senses. Samuel – take those filthy pictures out of my house.'

'What I've said is as it shall be,' said Vache with oracular grandeur, crossing his arms over his belly.

They argued past nightfall. At least Leah Vache argued, beginning with the comforting certitude that her husband was drunk, deranged, momentarily under the influence of demons, incapable of persisting in his blasphemy. She warned him gently that God would strike him dead. She screamed at him that his children would spit on his grave and the dogs dig him up to piss on him. She prayed out loud, shaking her hands in front of her face and cursing the tongue in her mouth that she should ask for reasons and be left so unanswered. The children listened, round-eyed, passing the holy pictures from hand to hand like uncomprehended pornography.

Towards midnight, the shouting quietened to a low drone of voices. Perhaps Vache gave his reasons. Probably not. But towards midnight he was heard to say, 'Consent or die. Which is it?'

Leah Vache called on God to strike him dead then and there. Then and there, Joachim Vache called on the seven-branched menorah to stove in the gold-wire birdcage and the more fragile skull beneath it. Then he summoned the children one by one and showed them their mother, still convulsing a little on the floor, though in silence. He asked each if they chose to turn Gentile and be dipped by the Abbot, and while they deliberated he held the brass candelabrum over their skulls.

Next day they made a touching sight – a family of eight all sure and certain in the hope of salvation, being baptized in the shallows of the Sablois (because the good Abbot doubted the power of his font to wash away so very *much* Jewishness).

Vérité could not recall the precise moment at which she had granted the chaplain permission to purge the Jews. Somehow the thing took on a momentum of its own, and an opportunity presented itself so pat that the chaplain said it must be Heaven-sent. The Assembly of Merchants had decided the fate of the grounded barge. It must be shifted without further ado.

All of a sudden one morning the guard were gone from the chateau, told by the castle chaplain that the orders came from their Chatelaine. Word went ahead of them, and a great many of the houses on the rue des Juifs were abandoned by the time the raid began, their doors swinging open, their tables left strewn with uneaten bread. But since the campaign had been mounted with military care, a pincer movement from either end of the street contained the fugitives within a closing cordon of soldiers. There was no resistance at all, owing to the heroism of the Gloriole chaplain who risked contamination and actually passed among the enemy spreading word of a forced removal to Brittany. Naturally the Christ-killers reviled him for the loss of their belongings, but began grudgingly to go aboard the stranded barge, thinking they were bound for new, Breton homes. They learned better before embarkation was complete.

The river was high: there were some worries that the barge would refloat after all and drift downstream. But the weight of those loaded aboard soon bedded it securely into the bar. When the evacuation ceased to proceed voluntarily, a breeches-buoy was rigged and those put into it were invited either to jump down into the hulk as they passed overhead or be dropped, on a slack rope, into the river to drown. Most opted for the wreck, hoping that the intention was to set it adrift and entrust their lives to the river. Eventually however it proved necessary to mount crossbowmen on the old jetty and bank to shoot any who jumped into the water.

The sheeplike bewilderment of man, woman and child worked in favour of their shepherds. They bleated, for the most part, in Spanish. Perhaps among themselves their complaints sounded more persuasive than they did to a French guard. Within three hours the hulk was filled from end to end with families. Only then did a universal silence settle over the refugees. The chaplain smiled at this well-orchestrated diminuendo. It remained only for the Chatelaine to be sent for and to take credit for this splendid deed of holy purification. He went to fetch her from the chateau.

'The vermin are culled out, lady,' said the chaplain, rapping his heels into the ribs of his horse at every pace to keep up with her. 'It remains for you to give the signal.'

'What signal? What particular neighbours am I blighting? Where are we sending them?'

'To Hell, naturally,' he replied, and his horse shook its withers irritably: excitement had marred the man's co-ordination. Though she did not understand, she did not query it. All would become plain, she was sure.

The crowd was excitable too. Its noise greeted them with fully half a mile to go. It was a triumphant ride, the way lined with religious women, debtors and small traders whose salvations would be sealed by the expulsion of the Jews. They held Vérité de Gloriole responsible for their good fortune. Some still held furze bushes – great skeletal globes of kindling which they gave their children to bowl along like hoops.

Enthusiastically they had all helped to gather this kindling, and there was far too much to line the hulk and to fill the raft moored by the jetty. The tinder raft. Still more bushes floated on the river

– a fleet of furze globes blown off the raft or thrown overboard by cramped refugees making room for themselves on the stranded barge. Officials of the Merchants' Committee lined the jetty, dressed in ceremonial finery, to witness the destruction of a hazard to shipping. The clergy were there too, to witness the destruction of a hazard to social purity, the dredging of a treacherous spiritual mudbar. Some seemed less at ease than others at the prospect. Because of the great weight of spectators, the jetty had bowed to the very level of the swollen river and the men of rank shuffled their feet about dismally in a shine of water. Someone laid down a sheet of gabardine so that the Chatelaine should not wet her shoes. A pleasant bonfire had been lit near by.

Vache and his sons were there, too, the father pointing out the demerits of the jetty to anyone and everyone, recommending the virtues of the new one he was building downstream. He exhorted his boys from time to time, in a shrill excitable voice, to be grateful for some favour he had done them, but they only stared out across the river with big, unblinking eyes, as still and inexpressive as the rotten posts fencing in the wet landing stage. A ballad singer was improvising a song to commemorate this notable day in the history of the Sablois.

Vérité could make no sense of the scene. She supposed it must all have sprung from her command. Why then could she not understand what was happening? She realized, with a pang of shame, that she had allowed everyday decisions and the overseeing of detail to slip out of her hands. She had become a woman dependant. Her father would not have approved. In a feeble attempt at least to appear abreast of the proceedings, she did not ask, 'What's happening here?' But her eyes darted about nervously, taking in the dignitaries crowding the jetty, the hordes of onlookers, the raft stacked pyramid-high with spidery bushes. A crocodile of choirboys – her own choirboys but under the instruction of the chaplain – filed down to the river bank and sang an anthem in the direction of the stranded barge. Her eyes were drawn there last, but were held longest by a woman on the vessel kneeling up against the bulwark, holding a baby at full stretch about her head. The baby was sound asleep.

'You will observe how the raft is on a rope and can be drawn across the river from the opposite bank,' said the chaplain, taking hold of her elbow in his excitement, and steering her to her position in the centre of the gabardine sheet. There were dark circles under

292

his eyes from the sleepless hours he had spent choreographing the day's splendour. His hand was hot through her sleeve. 'If my lady would consent to light the tinder aboard the raft, you'll observe how it can be drawn alongside the barge without Christian hand having to touch the . . .'

'You mean to *burn* them?'

The momentum of the chaplain's sentence, suddenly dammed up behind his lips, turned him a little blue in the face.

'Naturally. Of course. In accordance with tradition. Always fire to destroy the . . .'

'Don't be ridiculous.' She took the torch out of his hand and plunged it into the river.

Thinking she had missed her aim, a soldier immediately ran forward and threw a helpful bucket of coals on to the raft which burst into a rage of flame so high and so bright that it seemed to snatch all the oxygen out of the air and engulf the jetty in light. The choirboys, obedient to rehearsal, burst into song. The crowd raised a cheer. The cargo of the stranded barge began to scream and wail, as though the river were already a lake of fire in Hell. On the opposite bank, a team of men began to pull on the rope, and the raft with its burden of flame drew out on to the water shedding burning balls of furze that hissed themselves to extinction.

'I forbid it!' said Vérité. 'On pain of death.'

The soldier with the empty bucket panicked and began to run, shouting the change of plans to soldier and civilian alike, gesticulating wildly to his comrades on the far bank. But they only took it for encouragement to pull harder and faster. The raft yawed through its own bright corona of reflected fire.

A man and woman threw themselves overboard from the hulk and found the water, unexpectedly, only waist-deep. As they drew themselves to their feet on the mudbar, the woman's skirt spreading out on the water, crossbow bolts struck them, six apiece, and they fell flat and spun downstream in the wake of the festive, burning bushes.

Vérité put both hands into her chaplain's face and pushed him off his insecure footing. '*In my name? This? In my name? I never meant this! Not burning!*'

The man's fastidious ceremonial degenerated into a shambles, with people running this way and that in sodden boots, their words confused with the dogged strains of the choir's anthem, the cheers of the crowd, the screams from the barge. Close by the minstrel sang, in utter self-absorption,

> Now give unto the lady fame,
> Whate'er so be thy station;
> For she hath lit a candleflame
> To light them to damnation . . .

The team pulling on the rope hesitated. The raft drifted downstream. A bush toppled from the pile and burned through the rope, leaving the raft to be taken by the current. Those with boats moored downstream began to curse the danger of this unpredictable bale of fire spinning towards their craft. Three more youths jumped from the stranded boat and swam aimlessly against the current, not daring to carry their lives ashore amid the bloodlusty spectators. They tired in the current and were swept back into the lee of the hulk and lost from sight. The violence of panic aboard the wreck shook it like ague, and it began to twist and wallow and shed fragments of its bulk, though the mudbar still held it fast by the stern. Like a prisoner in the stirrup, it writhed.

'Send out a barge to take them off!' said Vérité to a dozen intractable faces, before a schism of dissenting clergymen sprinted away to redeem their innocence. 'Oh God! Oh God! Oh God!' she heard her conscience praying in the vacuum of her soul. But she did not know how to finish the plea. She had snatched her sacrificial gift away from under God's very nose. She had defied her chaplain – withheld his burnt offering from the altar of the Lord. 'But women and babies!' she said aloud, without any hope of the Godhead hearing her above the chaotic dissolution of the day's fun.

She exiled the Jews downriver to Brittany, but no news came back of the welcome or fate they met with there. The townspeople consoled themselves by pillaging the rue des Juifs with a sudden Christian fervour. A couple of long-established, non-Spanish Jewish families, who had thought themselves immune from the pogrom, had the roofs burned over their heads, and their donkeys hung up in the vines with their throats cut.

The Vache children, observing this, embraced their new faith with a shudder of mixed revulsion and relief. They thanked their father (if not their Heavenly Father) for their lives. They went on offering up thanks. It was required of them. Weekly. Vache himself thanked God with a scrupulous attention to detail. He dispatched his sons on pilgrimages, his servants on penances, he endowed the abbey in Croix-Rouge and acquired an assortment of religious decorations – crucifixes and crucifixions – from a supplier in Brittany he could hold to a good price. He gave a son to the choir school at Psalette and a daughter to the order of the Little Sisters of Pity.

The girl did not demur. Her world was simple, haunted by nightmares of her mother's ghost. Once installed at the mother-house of the order, the nightmares stopped. The oppressive shadow of her father lurked only outside the convent walls. She felt safer in her novitiate white. It was not even a struggle to renounce her own name when the nuns randomly retitled her 'Cecille'. The Abbot with the fierce hands, holding her backwards under the cold of the Sablois until the water came in at her nose and the silt made her retch, had told her that the name Rachel was a Jewish abomination. She cast it aside willingly enough. She did not struggle with Fate as she had struggled for air under the Abbot's fists. This time she allowed events to flow round her, over her, through her, without recourse to thought. She did as she was told.

Vérité, of course, had not done as she was told. The stiff-necked and self-willed Chatelaine of Gloriole had spared God's enemies, and though she tried to excuse it on grounds of compassion and a humanitarian upbringing, her chaplain left her in no doubt that the Lord would look down and see only squeamishness and obstinacy. There would be a price to pay.

When word came from Cyr, proving him safe and well after the battles which secured Naples, she breathed a profound sigh of relief that his dear life had not been confiscated to pay the fine. Perhaps, like Cyr, the Almighty had been absent during the matter of the Jews. Of course! Had her prayers not invoked God to keep her Cyr company on campaign? The Lord God was in Italy, and the Alps had temporarily obstructed His view.

I have seen such things! [wrote Cyr de Puy from Rome] *Domes and towers and spires fit to house the gods! What pillars! What statues! The artists here paint truer than life – I swear they recall Heaven from before they were born, for they carry such scenes in their heads as I would cleave open my brain to possess. Such palaces! Such scale! The sun draws up plants no home-bred Frenchman would credit, and I believe it infects the bricks, for they climb up with a sappy ambition that makes all things French* seem small and mean. May the Devil reward me if I don't lap up a taste of this place and carry it home to Gloriole.

All the saints have passed this way and left their parts and pieces to show for it. The countryside fair runs with miracles. If I could I would send you home some of this Italian sunshine to make the child flourish in you. In place, I send water from the Holy Fountain of Santa Jiminia which I saw keep a man from certain death . . . Such bridges, lady! Such arches and steps! Such materials and makings! Such gold-smithing! They build conduits here to piss in finer than we French build to christen our children. God quit me if I don't do a thing or two for Gloriole in this Italian style! I am sending a youth to you – one Giulio Gigliamo. I've seen his work and have sent letters commissioning him to come to you, and I pray you employ him wheresoever and howsoever his skills warrant, for they warrant much, believe me, despite his years. I can't vouch for his table manners, having not laid eyes on him, but the boy has more genius than any seven French compagnons asleep in the one bed. Let no one steal him out of your service. Such men are the prizes of the age.

As for the matter of the Jews whereon you wrote, I say kill them all if there's profit or luck to be had by it. I measure the chaplain a sound man, and his advice most likely to be sound.

Until I may pay my respects on your person with better than pen and ink, I pledge myself your servant lasting to ever-lasting.

CYR DE PUY, MASTER-AT-ARMS

She read and reread only the last. Appalled that she had put Cyr's child at risk by her disobedience, she gathered round her, like a greedy magpie, all the gifts he had given her to preserve the unborn. Once she had called him a superstitious soldier, but now she shielded her baby from every slight of misfortune with a piece of black wax wrapped in cloth-of-gold, with six serpents' tongues in a snakeskin bag, with a rosary of chalcedony and jasper. She counted the first seven stars to rise on seven successive nights and she placed carved wooden babies as votive offerings at the feet of the Virgin. And of course, she drank the holy water from the fountain of Santa Jiminia, seeing in her mind's eye the confection of pink marble glistening in the sunlight.

She did not see (as Cyr had not) the troop of dysenteric deserters from the army routed by King Charles's glorious conquest of Naples; how they had pitched their last hopes up against the cool marble, and clung sobbing to the little pink saint while her benison washed down their filth and fever into the gnat-blown pond at her feet. They had believed implicitly in her powers, as Cyr had believed in them when he scooped up a phial of water from the base of the fountain and dispatched it to his mistress to preserve the heir within her.

The Neapolitan deserters died. But Vérité was better tended and better placed to survive a bout of dysentery. Even the child seemed like a live thing, so urgent to escape the disgusting mire of her body that he fought his way free of it two months early. But it was only an illusion of life. They assured her the child was dead.

After a short while she said, with a flash of inspiration lit by fever, 'Of course! His father's a lion! You fools! Leave me be. I must be private in my den.'

No amount of argument would dissuade her. She set her jaw. She hauled her hank of hair out of the sweaty trough of her backbone. The shift stuck to her, front and back, in dark ruts, like sleigh tracks through snow, and her hands were icy-cold. But she turned the women out of her chamber and locked the door, commanding them to pray to Saint Mark whose beast is the lion.

Little Mother Catherine set a stool outside the door and entreated her endlessly to open it. '. . . Sweet lady! What's this talk of lions? How can we pray? How can we? What must we pray? Sweet lady! Open and tell us what to pray!'

But from beyond the door came only a sound like purring or a soft growl. For Vérité was a lioness.

Her reading had taught her how the lion's cub is born dead and only lives after three days' assiduous love from its mother.

At the end of the third day, the Little Mother, rattling once more at the door, found it open under her hands and, beyond it, the Chatelaine lying on her bed with the baby still in the angle of her arm. Catherine put her sleeve over nose and mouth and carried the bundle away. Vérité did not demur. 'I'm not a fit mate for my lion,' was all she said. 'I couldn't be a lioness for him.'

The chaplain, who came to daub her with the healing oils, was smug with self-congratulation. She could read in his face the conviction that God had rewarded her justly for her sentimental so-called compassion for the Jews, just as she could read his disgust at the room's smell. He larded her with the holy oils as though he were basting her for Satan's oven. He even expressed the opinion publicly that she had been poisoned by the Jews. She did not contradict him. She did not know the source of the illness that had lined her face and emptied her dresses of their curves. She simply knew that it was God's means of killing the child within her, the child she had vowed not to bear. Her vow had ensured it. Her disobedience had guaranteed it. She could see it now. Though she turned her face into the pillow and wept, it was not with outrage, for she understood the justice of what had happened. Her only emotions were impotent repentance and infinite regret that Cyr should have been so ill-served by her.

She in part came to believe that the house of Gloriole lived in reflection – a mirror image of Life's intended pattern – just as its chateau reversed its image in the waters of the moat. For life was lived backwards within its walls, the young dying before the old, in absolute contradiction of the Natural Order.

TWENTY-SEVEN

Italian Sunshine

Young Giulio Gigliamo arrived like a sunburst between banks of cloud. Arrayed in slashes of yellow and green, like an ogen melon cut open, he wore his hair in long glossy curls whose confused tendrils hung to one another with a desperate passion and were bound into bouquets with lengths of yellow ribbon. He pushed back his sleeves with quick, alternating hands to reveal forearms freckled with ochre and cobalt and red lead, and his face was as brown as a gypsy's. The white creases radiating from the eyes asterisked his changes of expression and made him appear always to be talking in exclamation marks. In the beginning, he had not a word of French.

Here was Cyr's artistic discovery, a youth to be employed for the sake of his promise – in the hope that he might become a name of note – and because of the Italian sunshine running in his veins. The heat of it gave rise to a great volatility. It seemed to Vérité that he might run, like a bright spider, vertically up the wall and begin to scribble intricate patterns in silver thread extruded from his own abdomen.

Vérité was anxious only to hear about Cyr – the state of the King's army, whether Gigliamo brought news, a letter, a message. But questioning him was like trying to catch a cricket under a cap. And besides, the Neapolitan knew nothing but his paintbox. He had not even met the good Captain who had commissioned him. She managed to discern (using what little common language they could pool) that Gigliamo was still seeking a patron and was as ready to go anywhere and undertake any work in order to prove himself. Even so, it was the first time he had ever left Italy.

He moved so fast, he darted so martin-like along the corridors and terraces, and talked aloud to himself so incessantly that the nuns fled him, crossing themselves. They wanted to ask him about the Pope, about the Vatican City, about Savonarola and the new crusade, but dared not so much as channel questions through the Chatelaine. They begged her to keep her distance from the 'odd foreign gentleman'. He was a mystery to them, noisy and ardent about everything, responding to the beauties of the chateau like a yellow canary mobbed by starlings: he practically covered his head with his arms, so great was the assault of loveliness on his senses.

It was hard to know where to employ him, having seen nothing of his work, and Vérité asked him to show her sketches. He immediately produced from his baggage a succession of portraits of a lovely girl with large, moist eyes. '*Mia moglie*,' he said and closed his lids so tightly that beads of saltwater were expressed along the long, curling lashes. Vérité rather wished that Cyr would confine himself to sending her inanimate presents.

It took six thousand mules for King Charles to transport out of Italy the assortment of animate and inanimate treasures he had gathered on his Italian campaign: architects and icons, books and barbers, weapons and linnets, musk grains and monumental masonry, golden coin and even more golden hen chicks. Hatched out on the journey, the baby chickens tumbled intermittently out of the saddle pack holding the intriguing novelty of an incubator, and blew away like the heads off so many dandelions. Cyr de Puy watched them, torn between disgust at being placed in charge of a mule train and covetousness of all this extraordinary treasure trove.

The campaign had soured beyond all expectation, with the disparate little kingdoms of Italy suddenly uniting to hound out the French. Now, out of ten thousand 'new crusaders', a thousand were dead of camp-sickness and the rest were straggling back to France over the Apennines, with no more booty than a pretty memory or two of Naples. Cyr had acquitted himself well enough, but no particular flash of merit had caught the King's eye. Now he found himself shepherding livestock and chattels along a mountainside – incubators and chickens, monkeys and a wagonful of vine stocks. And none of them his. Such spoils as he had taken had gone to pay his expenses. All he would have to show for Italy was a stomach full of appetites.

King Charles barely knew what treasure he had scooped together into this absurd, trundling souk of ill-gotten gains. He had not made a considered selection but had, as it were, swept the entire tabletop into his lap, then parcelled up the table too. There was no inventory of his treasure. The man who knew how could filch himself a fortune, and the takings would never be missed. As it was, Cyr de Puy had to content himself squirrelling away ideas and novelties. He too would incubate chickens at Gloriole; they would simply have to be French chickens laying French eggs. The Italian sunshine that had dazzled him with so many wonders could not be carried home: it trickled through his fingers like sand. Instead, a sterile, dirty wind blew from the direction of France, full of moribund dust and swearing.

Swearing? He emerged from thought to find himself looking down on a curve of river that might well have been a reach of the Sablois looping round a Touraine village. It was in fact the village of Fornova, cradled in an arm of the River Taro. And alongside it, like a field of sunflowers gazing up at the sun, an army of thirty-five thousand Italians stood arrayed in battle formation, to cut off the French on their ignominious retreat. The standards of Gonzago, Marquis of Mantua headed those of a dozen other petty states and cities. The dust and smells following in the wake of the French Army seemed to catch it up and envelope it in eddying filth and noise.

Cyr was separated by a mile from the heavy artillery, and knew that the men of his own muster would have been deployed and officered by the time he reached them. His responsibility was for a half-dozen of the wagons which straggled single-file as far as the eye could see. A vexation as big as the sea overwhelmed de Puy. To have such plans for the future and to be cut off from them by a last-minute ambush, an eleventh-hour massacre! He rummaged through the events of the previous week to find what he had done that had brought this bad luck down on his head.

Outnumbered four-to-one, on unfamiliar ground, by Italians whose morale was high and whose guts were sound, the French scattered in panic leaving the wagons strewn about the mountainside. The King was the ultimate treasure to be defended. Cyr contemplated riding downhill to join the swirling mass of riders converging on the royal banner. And yet there were things in those wagons . . .

In the heat of vexation, outrageous heresies were forged in Cyr's head. There was the King – sickly, puny, dithering, as well equipped to scintillate as a lump of coal in a sack – and here were treasures of art and science too many for him to house, leave alone appreciate. What if that little liveried horse *were* to stumble and fall, and its royal rider miscarry? Would it be so terrible a sight? Cyr could imagine worse. He could imagine pitched battle stampeding in among the treasure-wagons, overturning and spilling them, buckling and ripping and trampling their contents. He could picture the battle-followers picking over the wreckage – plucking the jewelled eye out of an icon, getting drunk on a rare vintage, using an Uccello to mend a broken shutter, a triptych as a firescreen, using a chased Toledo blade to skewer a supper of crimson flycatcher over the campfire. The mortal pillaging the immortal. Better to save such treasures than dive into the Sablois to rescue a baby: the things preserved would live longer and be of greater value to future generations. 'You! Turn off the track! Drive in among the trees! You behind! Follow him! Get as high as you can!'

The whole hillside had been born out of geological catastrophe and the boulders strewing it – giant shards and balls of rock – concealed caves and crevasses. They could serve to conceal wagons, too. When the thing was achieved, Cyr rode higher still in search of a vantage point from which to assess the dire prospects of the French.

So Cyr's initial reason for diverting his few wagons was to save them from destruction, come what might. He accompanied them up the wooded mountainside track not to save his own skin in battle. After all, de Puy was no coward. But it did occur to him, when one hundred feet of wooded precipice separated him from the mêlée below, that his life was also well worth saving. Formerly he had been nothing but a captain-gunner, almost as dispensable in his own estimation as he was in the reckoning of senior ranks. Now he was a man of influence and means; a connoisseur. Formerly his life had held nothing that particularly warranted saving. Now it was loaded down to the axles with advantages and promise. There was Gloriole; there was the baby on its way (for he knew no better then); there was . . .

What he took at first to be an exotic bird escaped from one of the wagons fluttered above a nearby rock. But then he saw that the gaudy peacock plumes were attached to a gilded ferrule on top of a silver helmet. A moment later the owner emerged, seconded by two other knights also on horseback, wielding axe and sword. When they saw de Puy, entirely alone, they lifted their bevors to assess his clothes and ask themselves whether he was worth a ransom. Cyr looked behind him, but his wagoners were way back among the trees and he had no help to call on. 'I am Cyr de Puy of the Chateau Gloriole-sur-Sablois in Touraine,' he called as the two knights trotted towards him holding their reins elegantly high in gloved fingers beneath arched wrists. They swung their weapons with a gloating nonchalance.

Cyr took a flintlock from beneath each flap of his saddle and shot both men through metal, leather and wadding. They fell up against one another, their helmets clashed, and the bevors interlocked with a quaint Mediterranean intimacy. The third man was so startled that he hesitated while de Puy began to reload. Then making a fleeting estimate of the time it would take to cover the ground between them, he drove in his spurs.

The horse was confused at the sudden need for speed on steep, broken ground. It wasted time in sidling and plunging; it stumbled over a thornbush, and ground the bit between foamy teeth. It wasted time, but wasted only seconds. Only as long as a volley of arrows took to dispatch fifty men in the valley below and for their souls to spiral up on the backs of dislodged rooks. Only as long as it took for the crash of a cannon to echo to and fro across the river. Only as long as it takes a dying man to review his life and regret its mistakes. Before Cyr could reload, the Italian was close enough to smell cordite from the first two shots. Then he found himself looking down the small black mouth of a flintlock and had to rein in two sword-lengths from de Puy.

His face was a picture of horror. 'A gun? Do you mean to show no account of yourself as a soldier?' Cyr shook his head. 'Gun against sword? Have you no sense of honour?'

'Have you no common sense? Why should I kill you at a yard when I can kill you at two?'

The Italian crossed himself, took off his helmet and held it under one arm. 'But you will not kill me, monsieur. I am a man of considerable means.'

'And stand to be of considerably more before the day's out.'

They both looked down on the fragmented mosaic of battle below, the noise and the intermingling colours. 'We do have you greatly at a disadvantage,' the other admitted. 'But my person would guarantee you safe passage should the day favour us rather than the excellent King Charles.'

'And you think, do you, that I'd be allowed to leave with so valuable a commodity as yourself?'

'My word of honour on it, monsieur.'

'And is that a parole worth having?'

'Sir! I am Il Duce di Malatesti! I would have said it was for the Italian chevalier to doubt the word of the no-sword French bandit!'

De Puy looked down at the gun, holding it in his open palm. 'I set up a manufactory of flintlocks on my estates. It would be a kind of disloyalty, don't you think, if I favoured a sword above good Sablois flint?' ('My estates', had he said? He only said it as a kindness to the Duke, of course – to imply that he was in the hands of a nobleman.) 'Besides, we must travel with the times, signor.'

They retired to the natural shelter of a rocky trench which the sun warmed and the wind overshot, and there they sat, like two old Romans at the bath-house, while below on the river-plain the fate of King Charles's expeditionary force was decided.

In fact they discovered mutual interests enough for the afternoon to speed by. It seemed that whenever one or other raised his head to reconnoitre the situation, a thousand more lives had gone in a twinkling.

'He collects cheeses, you know,' said Cyr at one point.

'Cheeses? *Formaggio?* Who?'

'Charles. The King. He built a house for them at Blois. A whole household of cheeses.'

'To be a connoisseur of cheeses, it shows a kind of . . . discrimination, no?'

'One might say he has "good taste", you mean?'

'I think you are a man who would not collect cheeses yourself. And do you not like the things he has collected in these wagons? Have I wasted my breath sending men to seize them? Are they full of cheeses?'

'No, no. I almost wish they were. It irks me, you know. To see such things herded all together into one or two palaces. It's like cramming eggs into a pot: the end won't be as wholesome as the start. Let's say I'd prefer to see the eggs still spread about the farmyard.'

'You feel so great a concern for us robbed Italian chickens?'

'I was thinking more of the hungry man who might have chanced upon a couple of eggs. His pleasure would have been greater. A couple of perfect eggs. They could make a hungry man very happy.'

'So you have the taste for things perfect, do you, signor?' Cyr shrugged. 'You have a hunger for the contents of these wagons? A bigger hunger than the King's?'

'I could wish he would confine himself to collecting cheeses.'

'Then you are a man after my own heart, Monsieur de Gloriole. I own I entered this adventure in the cause of Beauty rather than

304

for love of King and State. The Neapolitans are not my greatest friends, you understand, but they have works of art worth . . . preserving.'

Overhead the wind grew opaque with the burden of souls it was asked to carry away from the river-plain below, and dusk came down early, augmented by smoke. With the dusk came the wagons Malatesti's men had succeeded in capturing. They climbed, pitching and rolling, up the mountainside, their drivers rattling at the cheeks with horror. 'Do you see? Do you see what's happening? It's the Devil minding his own!' Cyr had no need to kneel up in the trench to know what fluke of luck, what strategic stroke of genius, what divine intervention had done to Gonzago's army. The shocked terror of these fugitives told him everything. They were so anxious to escape with their lives that they were indifferent to the reeling tons of treasure piled up behind them. Gonzago's army had lost the day. Cyr could smell the characteristic smell of death. There was a pontoon across the River Taro made up of Italian dead, the water turned purple, the gaudy banners hung in tatters on the trees. Though God or the Devil knew why, the Italians had been routed.

All that the Duke said was, 'Damn.'

'There are caves hereabouts where a wagon would be safe, no matter what,' Cyr volunteered. 'So deep out of sight it might slip the mind altogether. I stored three or four there myself earlier in the day.'

One by one the Duke's raiding party were deserting their stolen wagons and setting off to run towards the peak of the hill, as if they would leap up into the safety of the sky. Malatesti stared at de Puy. 'A man might collect them later, at his leisure, you mean.'

'A free man might,' said Cyr, uncocking his gun. 'And dispatch them to his friend abroad under a different canvas. In a month or so. A gift from one man of taste to another.'

'A gift from a man of his word to a kindred spirit.'

'Just so. What very excellent French you speak, mio Duce.'

'The things would be recognized. The friend would be marked down for a traitor.'

'There's no inventory.'

'*No inventory?*'

'Half. A half for me and a half for you – if you'll not unload the dross on me.'

'Why? Is there dross?'

'A certain amount of cheese, you might say.'

So they climbed out of their safe haven and saw the wagons stowed, both men heaving and straining like labourers to back them out of sight into the dark crevices of the mountainside before cutting loose the horses from their traces. When they returned to their bunker, Malatesti found that he had thoughtlessly left his sword lying there. He picked it up and sheathed it and they shook hands on the bargain. There was a thrill for Cyr in that handshake that jarred the blood in his veins and set the doors of his heart slamming. To conspire with ⅂ duke is tantamount to being his equal. To steal from a king is tantamount to being his better.

Malatesti wiped the sweat from his top lip. The tide of battle was driving more and more Frenchmen uphill in pursuit of Italians to kill. His escape must be made quickly. 'If I leave this place with my skin . . .' he had begun to say when Cyr's own wagoners came suddenly into sight. They were chasing on foot a lone Italian pikeman and caught up with him by the brink of the rocky trench and cut him down. The man's last futile prayers tumbled down on to Cyr's head like soil on to a coffin. Conquest had made the pursuers brave, and when they saw their commander sitting there, out of the battle's traffic, a look of foolish contempt came over them. They had sat out most of the battle themselves, but for a captain to have done the same . . . Then they saw the Italian.

'Prisoner, sir?' They leapt down into the trench and seized Malatesti one by each arm. The Duke stiffened from head to foot, rigid with dignity.

'That's right. Where have you put your wagons?' asked Cyr, priming his empty second flintlock.

'Still in the caves, sir, where you said, sir. Safe enough. We'll fetch 'em down, shall we? It's a miracle, they're saying. God delivered 'em up. Sheep to the slaughter. The river's full of 'em. Ran, they did. Ran clear in and drowned themselves.'

'Like the Red Sea closing on the Egyptians,' said Cyr, cocking first one gun then the other. 'Now stand back from the Italian.'

'What, not good for a ransom, sir?' said one, pressing himself against the side of the trench to leave a clear target.

'And he looks worth plenty,' said the other stepping away; he even drew Malatesti's own cloak between them so as not to be splattered with his blood.

'A man of his word, did I say?' The Italian shook his head in disillusionment and despair. Cyr de Puy took aim with both

306

flintlocks and fired them simultaneously. The flapping wind plucked the smoke out of the trench like nesting material for the growing banks of cloud.

Distastefully, Il Duce di Malatesti extricated his cloak from the grip of the dead Frenchman beside him. His shanks were shaking. He was aware of having been teased with his own death and it enraged him more than he was willing to show.

'Observe. Didn't I say I was a man of my word?' said de Puy. 'I trust you are too.'

'I'll send your booty to you in three months' time. I wish you joy of it. But if you love your life, don't let that King of yours find out.'

They emerged from their rocky hiding place, and paused to view the triumphant French victory of Fornova. Strange, but having stood apart from the desperate clashes, the frantic charging and discharging of cannon, the small heroic one-to-one struggles conducted in the heart of the bloody maelstrom, it all looked a little futile and hugger-mugger – a trifle passé in an age of more civilized behaviour.

When Cyr saw a treasure cart cheerfully burning, the robes inside indistinguishable from the canvas tarpaulin – both ash – he could almost have wept at the world's loss.

'Chatelaine! Chatelaine! Please come! Please come and do something!' The Little Sisters clamoured round her, tugging and cajoling her towards their private chapel. And yet she was no sooner there than they were pulling on her clothes to stop her going any closer to the altar rail.

Giulio Gigliamo lay sprawled up the steps like a landslip. His brushes were bunched in one hand; his hair lay about as shiny and black as spilled ink, and he was beating his forehead on the marble. The candles banked in front of the Madonna communally trembled at the sound of his sobbing.

'What seems to be the matter?' said Vérité, and had to raise her voice above the din.

Three weeks earlier, finding that he was skilled in goldwork, she had put him to work gilding the carved heraldic device over the causeway gate. Unfortunately, a kind of pervasive dampness was in the stone which the mason called 'the tufa cancer' and which Gigliamo attributed to the damp river air. No amount of effort would persuade the leaves of hammered gold to cling to the muzzle of the carved chicheface or to the letters, RIEN MEILLEUR, below. After a week there was nothing to show for Gigliamo's talent.

So she had asked him instead to paint a triptych for the nuns' chapel, and he had been overjoyed, declaring he would make it a celebration of the female kind. He gave one panel to Martha and Mary, another to Mary Magdalene and the centre to Mary at the foot of the Cross. The triptych stood in a south-facing room at the top of the chateau, though Gigliamo resorted often to the Chapel Saint-Cloud and the chateau chapel for inspiration. But it seemed the Madonna in the nuns' chapel bore a striking resemblance to his wife and because of it he chose to worship there, getting under the nuns' feet and thoroughly irritating them with his everlasting Aves. Whereas they would whisper, like scholars in a library, Gigliamo would sing like a milkmaid in a field. Charitably they told themselves that David had danced before the altar of the Lord, but they firmly believed in their hearts that King David, had he ever come to France and found it absolutely necessary to dance, would have had the decency to do it in Tours Cathedral and not in the private chapel of the Little Sisters of Pity. Now Gigliamo was sprawled sobbing across their altar steps and the time had come to fetch the Chatelaine for help, even though they were loath for her to go near the deranged foreigner.

'What seems to be the matter, signor?' she asked. But all that he would do was lift his forehead off the marble steps and wail, 'O care mio! O care mio!'

Vérité scolded herself. She must be decisive. She must not keep looking for the return of Cyr to put everything to rights. She must, if nothing else, show this eccentric gentleman a little Christian charity instead of wishing he would go away and weep in Italy. She crept close, like a sapper checking an unexploded charge, and put one hand on his shoulder. 'Signor Gigliamo, pray don't upset yourself.'

He rolled over, seized her hand and pressed it to his forehead. She tried to snatch it away. She even tried to free it using her other hand, but he only seized that too and pressed it to his chest. The nuns lifted their hems and fled.

'Mio cuore, madonna! Come può uomo lavorare senza cuore – senza gioia – senz'essere ispirato?'

She ventured a guess. 'Your muse has deserted you?'

But no, on the contrary, Guilio had deserted his muse. He had left her in Italy while she was big with child, and his first

308

son would be born with his father a thousand miles away. Guilio Gigliamo, it seemed, was in love with his wife, and all the chateaux in France could not compensate for the loss of her company. '*Mi manca tanto!*' he cried and plunged his head at her chest and nestled it there between her breasts.

Vérité was entranced. If he had been trying to curry favour, he could have found no more sure way. 'I do understand how you feel,' she said, absent-mindedly stroking his hair.

'You also? You also? You have maybe the great love also?'

'No, of course not. Certainly not. No.'

He took no notice. 'But of course: a woman *si bella – si simpatica!*' And he loosed a fusillade of Italian remorse at the plaster Madonna, begging forgiveness for his unfeeling ambition in leaving his wife for the blandishments of France.

'You must go home,' she said. It was out of her mouth before she could retract it. 'I'll give you the cost of the journey. You're not to worry about the triptych. You can be home in time to see the child born.' She had to repeat it several times before he either understood or believed her. He protested that his name would be ruined, that a man must follow his calling, but his eyes begged her to repeat the offer, to let him go home to Naples. She felt like Pharaoh setting free the Israelites.

And almost as soon as he had gone to pack up his frugal few belongings, she wanted to harden her heart like Pharaoh and tell him to stay. What would Cyr say when he got home and found his protégé had come and gone with nothing to show for it? She practised the explanation, but in her words it sounded sentimental nonsense: 'He was lonely for his wife. He could not bear for them to be apart for another moment.' After all, Cyr had had to follow his trade just as far as Gigliamo, and his letters were not tear-stained. He had not deserted his post to be restored to the arms of his pregnant lover. Perhaps if he had she would not have lost . . . but then that was a wicked and futile train of thought. Perhaps if she afforded happiness to one man and wife, a similar happiness would be afforded her. Yes, that was the way to look at it. That was the way she squared it with her conscience. That was her superstitious remedy. If Gigliamo was restored to his wife, perhaps Cyr would be restored to her. He surely could not object to such motives when she told him.

She even paid Gigliamo for the half-painted triptych, since he could plainly not afford to waste two months of his youth in earning nothing. But she hid the panels out of sight. Worse to own half such a promising painting than to have no painting at all. Fleetingly, it crossed Vérité's mind to wonder why she should be inventing excuses to offer Cyr. Was he someone to be afraid of? Certainly not. Were the house and authority not hers to do with as she liked? Naturally. But she hid the painting even so.

Gigliamo swore he was so indebted to her that he would run to fetch her the golden apples of the Hesperides if she only asked. She replied that she would not think of putting him to the trouble of such a long trip, given his tendency to homesickness. The closer he came to leaving, the greater his gratitude grew, until she doubted he would be able to squeeze out through the door for the expanse of it. If ever there was anything he could do . . . If ever there was a way he could repay her . . . If there was ever . . .

She prised him off his knees and towards his horses with all the difficulty of shifting a snail along a wall. 'I promise I shall call on you, signor, if I ever have the need. But as you see, I am greatly blessed. I can easily spare you your happiness out of the great store of my own.' And on impulse she bent over and confided in his ear, 'There *is* someone I miss, as you miss your wife.'

'*E im più, tu gli manchi!*'

She felt herself blush with a foolish, adolescent pleasure. 'And he misses me, yes.'

Gigliamo burst into renewed tears of joy and was still sobbing as he passed out beneath the carved, ungilded keystone of the gateway. As he diminished to a distant figure in a landscape, Vérité found she was regretting the loss of him not for the sake of his painting but for his own sake. She almost wished the Red Sea of the moat would close across the causeway and prevent the little Italian from leaving. They could have gone on talking about Love, and how it feels to be parted, and he could have told her again how Cyr was missing her. What were his artistic talents compared with the ability to do her such a service?

No matter. The magic worked. The kindness of sending home Gigliamo (or so it seemed) brought the King out of Italy and with him Cyr de Puy, sharing in the triumphant Victory of Fornova. He came with the evening flare of river sunlight in his eyes and carrying a white leather cradle embossed with lions for his child.

At the news of the child's loss, the sun went out in his eyes and he excused himself with a wintery formality and disappeared into the forest. She imagined him there, making a secret of his grief, rolling like a hedgehog through the leaves, spines outwards and soft parts curled away, until the pain could no longer touch any vulnerable place.

In fact, when he returned, his forest-dwelling, homely wife had mended his torn battle-clothes, polished his helmet and fed him the square meals he lacked. There was even a shine restored to his eyes, but not French daylight so much as Italian sunshine. He told Vérité, as they lay in bed, of the consignments of treasure on their way from Italy.

She was aghast. 'Cyr! You mean you stole from the King?'

'Only what was stolen already from others.'

'But you joined with the enemy to steal the King's wagons?'

'There's one-third of them lost. The few Malatesti and I diverted, they're hardly worth the counting. They'll never be missed among so much missing. Charles didn't come away empty-handed, I promise you.'

'But it's treason! It's treasonable! To steal from your own King! If anyone found out! You'd hang in a chain! God knows what they'd do to you if it were found out! Send to this man! Write to him! Tell him you'll have none of the booty. Let him keep it all! We've got enough!'

He was brazen, though. 'And succour the enemy? No. What difference does it make whether the things are at Amboise or Paris or Gloriole? They're out of Italian hands and into French, aren't they? Jesu! If I could've got Rome on to a sled I'd've brought it home tower-and-chimney. There's nothing to match these Italian architects. One day I'll . . .'

'But to steal, Cyr! To break the Eighth Commandment! To steal!'

He turned his eyes on her full of that glittering foreign light and as injured as innocence. 'Don't you understand anything, you foolish woman? I did it for you.'

She was silenced.

'Rather than come home empty-handed. Rather than use your own wage to buy you love-gifts. To bring you something by the strength of my own right arm. Don't you understand? *They're presents for you, my love*. I risked it all for you.'

She opened her mouth to protest she had never wanted it, but no words came out.

'For you and for the child.'

That last sentence chained her to the Fornova treasure as sure as a dead sailor chained to an anchor to keep him down. The guilt was hers, not his. She could see how a simple, rough soldier would reason like that. She was sorry to have carped at his love-gift.

Even so, when he asked, 'Where's my Italian? Did the boy come? What did you put him to?' she simply said, 'No. He didn't come. Perhaps your message went astray. Perhaps he couldn't come. Perhaps the war . . .' It was a lie, but only a small lie. What was a little lie alongside theft? There is a hierarchy in sin. Break one rule and all the lesser ones below it in rank seem insignificant afterwards.

Even when the goods began to come – delivered up by the serpent river like Man's first temptation – they brought her less joy than Cyr's previous presents. Pretty and novel as they were – the onyx bowls, the black marble pillars, the chamois bags and wrought silverwork – they seemed to Vérité all a little sullied. Market-soiled trinkets. She might have liked the incubator and its fluffy yellow chicks, except that the contents of the one which arrived had hatched and suffocated weeks before, and all that tumbled out of the crate was an intolerable smell.

Cyr, of course, delighted in each wagonload of assorted plunder, and she was happy for him – would not have detracted from his pleasure for the world. After all, for a materialist to lose his delight in material things is like a priest doubting the existence of God. *His* only regret was for the wagons he had failed to divert – the ones burned at Fornova or kept by Malatesti or run off by other opportunists or preserved for the King's treasure-houses. 'If only I could have laid hands on the goldwork,' he said. 'If only I could have brought you an Uccello.'

She tried to tell him, the real treasure to come out of Italy was you, but the notion bounced off him like rain off a rook's back.

'All the same, I would have liked the parrots,' he said.

'Then ask Vache to buy parrots, Cyr. Order as many as you please.'

Cyr was so very sure that his stolen booty would pass unrecognized. It caused him not the least concern that some member of Court would recognize a chair or a lamp and go running to the King. Vérité, on the other hand, felt that merely by looking at her, her neighbours would know she had in her possession this or that book, such-or-such a tapestry. So it was some time before she felt at ease at Court, and she rarely accepted its invitations.

Nevertheless, in '98, on the eve of Palm Sunday, she found

herself at Amboise for the Easter celebrations. Already it was like a little outpost of Italy, the men in broad stripes and piratical caps, sporting long hair whether or not they were blessed with enough to warrant it. The women all wore high waists and low necklines. The chateau and the gardens were becoming so Italianate that it was said the echoes reverberated with a Roman accent.

Crowds did not suit her – the bright, frenetic babble of the high-bred in hot pursuit of the trivial irked her; it made her feel old beyond her years. Most of all she was conscious of their eyes, all the time watching, watching, like windhovers over a field, one eye forever fixed on the King for the cue to laugh, to gasp, to applaud. She would not have come there for Easter but that Cyr wanted a description of the new tennis courts so that he might build similar ones at Gloriole.

There was a strange atmosphere at Amboise that day. The King went from sport to meal to promenade to entertainment like a child lacking the concentration to persist at any one game. The Queen Duchess was at his shoulder, sharp and argumentative, and behind her dawdled the men and women of Court eternally awaiting the signal to break off and indulge in whatever the King next chose to enjoy.

'He looks very unwell, don't you think?' Vérité had the temerity to observe to the woman alongside her.

'Not at all! Not a whit! He's quite forsworn his old ways, you know, since he was ill in January. Quite forsworn them. Ah well. Sigh and sorrow . . . but he *was* quite incorrigible, you know.' She said it delightedly, wishing to imply that she had been on sleeping terms with the King before his virtuous New Year resolution. Vérité turned aside, but was immediately accosted by a woman of more discreet years.

'I dare swear it's the worry,' she said, bunching her kirtle with one hand so that Vérité might see it was embroidered inside and out. 'Have you heard the rumour?'

'No. Thank you,' said Vérité, who had no wish to hear.

'A letter's come from *that man* commanding – I mean *commanding* the King to go back into Italy.'

The younger woman blundered back into the conversation. 'It'll be all the gentlemen gone again for sure. And the grape-pickers and the horses. So tedious.'

'What man? Go back? Why?' said Vérité.

'To put the Church to rights, of course,' came the answer,

uninformed, simplistic, untouched by the significance of what she was saying. Again Vérité slowed her pace and dropped back to escape the conversation. Unwarned, the person behind collided with her and she turned to apologize. Her breath caught in her throat at the sight of a demon juggling with green goblins. She had never seen a black face before, and to meet the royal parrot-breeder carrying his birds on forearm and shoulder and glove was so bizarre as to be nightmarish. With the collision, the parrots reeled on their big, horny feet and spread green wings and ducked black heads to regain their balance. Their great nostrils, big as snail-shells, protruded from bony beaks over-full of anthropoidal tongues, and their eyes were shuttered with white film. This was the novelty of the hour, and for its sake a man had been transported across oceans and shipped upriver and clothed and housed and paid and stared at, in order that he might breed more birds to decorate the gardens of Amboise.

She shut her ears against the chatter, but Vérité could not fail to learn the current rumour in full. Savonarola had summoned Charles to be his armed right hand and by brute force to reform the Church at Rome. If he turned down the privilege or made as poor a show-ing as the last time, the hand of God would rest heavy on him. So said Savonarola. Looking with fresh eyes, Vérité could see already how something had bent Charles's shoulders and had turned him a sallow, unwholesome yellow. Damn him.

He strolled along between his confessor and the Bishop of Angers, talking inconsequentially or simply trying to think despite the loud opinions of his talkative wife. All the weighty discussion had already taken place in private rooms, between those three men. The decision was probably already made. His second Italian campaign was prob-ably already in hand. Curse him.

He would take his army and hurl it up against the immovable rock of Rome, but the damage done would be to heads and limbs and eyes and trunks, not Establishments. He would take Cyr and ten thousand others and leave them strewn about, like a child's broken toys, a thousand miles from home. She hated him for it already, before it was accomplished. As she promenaded through the King's walks, among the King's friends, to the sound of the King's musicians, she hated the King with a covert, conspiratorial loathing.

A flurry of laughter, a new corner of the palace she had never seen before, a clatter of Italianate boots on stone flagstones, and the entourage hurried indoors to watch the tennis in progress on the courts. The King bent and ducked beneath an archway and cracked his head against the architrave. It quite stunned him for a moment.

'Oh my lord King!'

'Your Majesty!'

'Are you all right, my dear?'

'Shall a surgeon be sent for?' The usual, foolishly exaggerated reaction to a little mishap.

Vérité wished him a worse fortune than that. She wished him worse than a grazed scalp. Sooner than have him go to war again in Italy, she wished him all the ill in the world. War is not a game of tennis, except for kings and generals who can sit at a distance and safely watch the balls fly to and fro.

The train of courtiers and guests sidled in between the benches which overlooked the real-tennis, and Vérité found herself sitting immediately behind the King. She had never come so close to him in her life before. She could see each strand of his velvet, clear as blades of grass. She could see the dewdrop shadow cast by his pendulous nose, the shine of saliva on his big lower lip, the blood sitting in ruby beads on the graze, the shaling of the fingernails each time he put his hand up to the injury.

'Tenez!' cried a player on the court and served the ball.

No one on that bench in front of her had their thoughts on the tennis. Several times Vérité heard on the Queen's lips the name of Savonarola. She pronounced it oddly; it was a point of principle with her that she, better than anyone, knew how to pronounce a name. Charles was talking economics with the Bishop of Angers. Anne was talking theology. No one mentioned that they were talking war.

No matter, thought Vérité. He was ill. His womanizing had seen to that. He was not robust enough to go campaigning again: his Valois antecedents had seen to that. His commanders would oppose it. *Her prayers would prevent it.*

In front of her, Charles gave a small gasp of pain. 'Something in my head . . .' he said in a puzzled whisper so insignificant that perhaps only she heard it. Then he keeled backwards into her lap: the King of France in her lap.

His eyes were in the top of their sockets, the whites flickering between eyelids all but closed, his hands twitching like gaffed fish, the spasms in his legs thumping the court wall. For a moment the game of tennis went on in ignorance, then, after the players stopped, the ball went on merrily bouncing down the sloping buttress of the end wall. Bounce, bounce, bounce. It held the eye, that ball.

'*Look to the King! The King!*'

One side of his face was drawn up into the mockery of a grin. His hair was oily with scent; her fingers smelt of it for hours after. His boot went on thumping the wooden wall. She tried to lift him back into the sitting position and he weighed so little that she could have done it but for the arching of his back and the thrashing convulsions. The Court closed in around her, climbed on the benches, vied to get closest, trod on her dress, left their footprints on its cloth. The Queen's hands plucked at her husband's nose – '*Charles!*' – almost as if she were cross with him.

Four strong men lifted him and, possibly thinking to carry him somewhere more sober than the stalls of a tennis court, ran with him until they panicked. Panic grew to a consensus that he should be laid down till the fit was past. They were in a dank, low passageway. Like any discreet corner of a castle, it smelled of piss. Everyone recalled that afterwards. Having put him down, no one had the courage to lift him again, and a physician could not be found. Perhaps they could all recognize the situation and ran to change their Valois reds and yellows for the colour of Louis d'Orléans. Perhaps they thought that if there were no eyes to see it, the impossible could not happen. But whatever the reason, just for a while, no one but Charles and one nervous, chanting prelate remained in that reeky passageway. Then the crowds regrouped, soft-soled and moist-eyed, mouthing prayers and whispering their consternation, making mental note of the scene for their absent friends and the chroniclers of history.

Not Vérité. She remained crouched in one corner of the tennis court's gallery, waiting for confirmation that the King was dead. It took a great many hours to come, but she never doubted it. She had wished him dead and he had died.

There was only one other person in the room. But for the bilious parrots sidling up and down his arms, the parrot-breeder would have remained invisible, sitting in a shadowy alcove, whispering to his birds. Only the white flash of his teeth as he chuck-chucked his soundless encouragement, and the green flicker of their clipped wings, drew attention to him. His lids were too much closed to tell if he was looking at her, and neither person called out a comment on the King's accident. It was too terrible a thing for words. She told herself she must speak with the man – after the earthquake finished and the stars had ceased to fall – and ask him where she might come by parrots for Gloriole. Cyr had wanted parrots since Italy. Cyr must have his parrots.

For Cyr had merely stolen a little surplus treasure from the King, whereas Vérité had wished his breath away. She took mental note of the paume-court and its net-hazards and jutting end walls: Cyr would have an identical room at Gloriole. He could have what he liked. She could not understand how she had ever dared to pass judgment on him for such a little crime towards the King: she who had wished her monarch dead at the age of twenty-eight.

Twenty-eight and he was dead. Between sunrise and sunset he had met Death in a stinking passageway and was nothing but a piece of litter to be cleared away. Between fastening her hair in the morning and unfastening her hair at night, Queen Anne had become a widow. So Cyr must have tennis court and pleasure garden and his grand gallery with the Italianate roof. While the breath of Life had the grace to stay in his nostrils, Vérité intended to make each minute a coffer filled with treasure. If Death could creep in so subtly and steal Life away in a few sordid minutes, provision must be made urgently. She was already far older than the King – the former King, the dead King, the trash in the passageway. She must act fast to guarantee Cyr's happiness in the event of her death. She must fill up the void beyond the wall, so that when Death breached the wall, a compensation sufficiently vast would tumble at Cyr's feet. Material things could never compensate *her* for the loss of Cyr, but then material goods had lost their magic for her of late. Not so for Cyr.

So on her way home she called on her man-at-law. And she made Cyr de Puy heir to Gloriole-sur-Sablois, in case he ever had to bear this unbearable separation, this everlasting exile, this intolerable parting: bereavement.

They were such very pretty parrots that she brought home – not pond-green but fire-red, not zoological oddities but pleasing chevrons of scarlet, flitting, despite their clipped wings, from crate to beam to corn-box. They could walk miraculously up walls and their toes pointing to front and rear seemed as ready to walk into the past as the future. They were birds of the present moment, noisy and cheerful. Some billed amorously in the angle of the joists while others chattered in magical foreign tongues.

'Do you think it's true they can learn human speech?' said

Vérité, watching the gratification on Cyr's face as he opened the last crate.

'No. Too much tongue, sure. All swollen, like a man with typhus. A man with typhus can't speak.'

'But you like them.'

'Excellent, excellent. And neat. Quick. They're as good as anything I saw in Italy. The greys from the West are too slow. You were right to get these.'

'But where will you keep them, sweetheart? Must I build mews specially? Won't they fall to a civil war with the hawks and falcons if they're mewed up together?'

'Won't mew them at all,' said Cyr opening the double stable doors. 'If they're too tame they'll come close at the sight of a man – defeat the object.'

'What object?' she asked, but he had followed the toddling explorations of a few eager parrots out into the yard. The birds clambered up the stonework, finding footholds where the stone looked as smooth as glass. They were even more red against the white tufa – brilliant plumes of incandescence, like the glowing ash from a bonfire rising up and up. Their comical grinning beaks and their implausible strolling up vertical walls made Vérité laugh out loud. She clasped Cyr's elbow: it was not his way to say thank you for presents – not in so many words – but if she stood close enough she could often sense his pleasure – feel it in the squeeze of her hand between sleeve and waistcoat. This time, however, he was so delighted that he pulled away. 'I must show the men!'

Like a child showing a new toy to his playmates, she thought fondly. Maybe only a childless woman is so susceptible to the charm of childishness in her lover. Perhaps only a childless woman treats him to presents and tries to make him laugh.

How would he react, how would he look, what would he find to say when she broke the news of her most splendid gift of all? (She had been saving it up so as not to diminish his joy in the parrots.) She would tell him next time they lay in bed together. Or at the coronation of Louis d'Orléans. Or, if she could no longer bear to hold the secret hot in her hand, next time they found themselves alone by the river, where the waters of the Sablois pumped like the vascular artery through the heart of the estate. Their estate. His estate.

Cyr went into the house and returned with a crossbow and three or four men from the wardroom. The guards shielded their eyes against the light as they pinpointed where the parrots had perched along the sills and pediments, and exclaimed at their extraordinary colour, their bizarre faces. Cyr loaded his bow and took aim at a bird perched on the ridge-cresting of the mews.

'What are you doing? Don't! Don't kill them!' She spoiled his aim and he was annoyed.

'What d'you mean, "Don't kill them"?'

'Well what do you want to shoot them for?'

He was baffled. 'Why ever not? Buy targets and not practise on them?' The guards were embarrassed and edged away.

'Targets?'

'Why buy parrots otherwise? It's why the King has them. It's why they're breeding them up and down the Loire. Why else for God's sake? For songbirds?' He should not have shown such disrespect in front of the guards.

'People say they talk,' she said, though it sounded childish.

'They could recite Rabelais but I'd not waste houseroom on them if it weren't for target practice.'

'But they're so pretty, Captain de Puy. I like them so.'

'Ah yes. I forgot. You're the one who banned stoning wrens on Stephen's Day.' The guards laughed; he encouraged them to laugh so that her foolishness should not get a foothold. After so long, he could judge when a whim might grow into obstinacy. He could see even now that she was not ready to give way, so he resorted to temper. 'What? D'you grudge the money, then? D'you not want your present out of the box if it's to get broken? Just as you like, lady. You paid.'

'No! . . . Very well.' She was not prepared to quarrel in front of the other men. 'No. No matter. I misunderstood, that's all. My apologies, Captain de Puy. I thought they were kept for decoration only. Do as you like. They're yours to do with as you like.' And he gave a curt grunt, acknowledging her mistake as understandable in a woman.

The parrots made a challenging target, costly of ammunition. But Vérité had not yet left the yard before the first successful hit was scored. The bolt tore wings from body like a seedcase from a sycamore twig. The scarlet feathers came slowly down to settle on the new 'Italian pavement' of black and white flagstones – a fleck of blood on a chessboard.

When she had seen it, she went indoors and wrote a letter to her man-at-law. She instructed him as follows: that on no account

319

must the contents of her new *affrairementum* become public. If the lawyer wished to keep her patronage, he must also keep her secret. No one but he and she must know that Cyr de Puy was named heir.

Not even the heir himself.

TWENTY-EIGHT

Rachel and Bilhah

A new century. It approached as slowly and as implacably as a glacier and yet would arrive within a single second. For Vérité it lay like an impenetrable wilderness of briars, toiling and coiling across her path. It would snag her skin and leave lines there. It would snag her hair and bleed it of its colour. It would overgrow her bed and drain it of what last fertility survived there. With the old century, her youth would peter out. With the new one, middle age would start like a narrowing corridor – unlit, sloping and slipping down to a blind end. Unless she took a stand against it.

With the latest recruitment of girls to the convent in the loft, the departure of older Sisters was dramatic that year. The last faces to have peopled her childhood decamped to the mother-house at Rocheblanche. Those who came to replace them would never touch her as close. The human heart gives more readily to first acquaintances than to later ones. Later friendships are looser, shallower unions. These new nuns did not remember her father, were not associated with that sweet, naive regime irretrievably lost.

The cartful of newcomers – all under the age of sixteen – gaped around them like fledgling birds cramped into a windblown nest, as they bowled over the causeway and in among the branching miracles of the chateau towards the meal laid ready in the refectory. Vérité came to welcome them, her keys bright in the folds of her skirts, her hands clasped at her waist, her lips reddened a little in retaliation at their youth, and her authority over them written in ornate ciphers of rich embroidery on her hood. Timid and excitable, they gazed at her, willing her to be the benign benefactor of which they had heard tell, willing her to speak simply to them in a French they could understand.

What do they know? she thought, and the twenty years' difference in their ages penned them round like the fence that kept her mastiffs safe inside their kennels.

'Please remember,' she told them, as she told each new intake of Little Sisters, 'that I am your friend and will remember you in my prayers in the hope that you will remember me in yours. If there are any among you uncertain of your vocation, you must not think that the promises of your parents have bound you past remedy. There's no sin or disgrace in a change of heart, and I won't let ruin fall on any of you who'd rather serve God in the Outer World.' She always said it (though she was never believed). After all, no one's life should be blighted by a vow. They wondered at her charity.

Within a week, an incident occurred, so unseemly that the Convent of the Little Sisters of Pity shook with fright at it. A novitiate with the given name of Cecille stole a small silver gilt cream jug in the shape of a cow.

It had somehow become one of the secular duties of the nuns to clean the small, portable valuables of the house. It was inevitable that Cecille would be found out. Her fellow Sisters could not fathom her reasoning. The jug bulged awkwardly through the breast of her habit when she was first questioned. The fact that the jug was fashioned in the shape of a golden calf added a horribly sinister biblical dimension. The girl was locked into the wardrobe on the landing – she did not complain – and a deputation of sisters confessed the crime to Vérité, only daring to speak to her through the drawn curtain of her retraite. They begged the Chatelaine to pronounce a secular judgment, rather than refer the matter to the ecclesiastical courts so that the whole order was defamed. Cecille was, after all, only a novitiate at the time of the theft.

'Send her to me,' said Vérité.

As she awaited the girl, her head was full of other thefts – thefts on a much grander scale, and another thief she had found easy to forgive. She got up out of the Italian chair sent there by Il Duce di Malatesti. By the time Cecille arrived, dishevelled and pulled about by the violence of her sisters' fear, she was like a piece broken off the Chatelaine's conscience – an offshore island of a continental guilt.

Her face was not pretty, with such pronounced cheekbones as might have been swollen by blows and such deep-set eyes as might have been quarried by shelling. She moved with one shoulder and one hip slightly to the fore – like the small carrion birds who dart in to tear at a carcase for as long as the bigger, fiercer birds allow it. Confronted with the Chatelaine she went down on her knees with a weary resignation.

If she says she stole the thing to help some needy relation,

I shall acquit her, thought Vérité. One must be charitable.

'Why did you steal the jug, girl?'

'It was so beautiful,' said Little Cecille.

'But what did you hope to do with it? Sure, you couldn't hope for it to go unmissed? Did you not think you'd be found out?'

'It was so beautiful,' said Little Cecille again with a helpless shrug. She had so little expectation of being understood that she could see no point in searching for words.

But Vérité understood her all too well. She knew every contour and landmark of Cecille's crime. 'It wasn't seemly for a child of your calling. Don't you want to live the holy life?'

'I suppose.'

'I mean, don't you want in your heart of hearts to be a Little Sister?'

'Yes ma'am.'

'Say I sent you home to your family and wrote that you weren't well suited to the calling?'

'Pa'd kill me,' replied the girl matter-of-factly. After a moment's thought she repeated, 'Pa'd kill me.'

'Ah!' said Vérité with the wisdom of insight. 'That's very dreadful. No one should be put to Orders unless it's of their own choosing. So what's to be done? Do you not want to be a Little Sister?'

Again Cecille shrugged. 'Wouldn't mind,' she said.

She did not lack intellect, but she lacked any sense of self-determination. Her life was the possession of others; she watched it go past like a boat out on the river bound for the rocks. No amount of shouting would save it, and so she kept silent.

When, instead of having her flogged or imprisoned, the Chatelaine made her a maiden-of-the-bedchamber, Cecille's jaw momentarily dropped in amazement. But then she accepted that Fate must have intended to save her for some later calamity, and she crouched like a frog at the poolside, hoping that if she kept sufficiently still she might just escape an early death.

The nuns were a little appalled at Vérité's bizarre judgment. They reminded themselves often of the parable of the vineyard hireling, where the least deserving was paid the same as the hardest workers. But when Cecille passed them on the landing and the train of her cotton brocade lapped over their black wool, it stirred them to new sins of resentment, as though her covetousness were a contagion that would have been better isolated and treated with harsh medicines. She infected them with wicked thoughts, just as other aspects of Vérité's life troubled them to the edge of discontent.

To mark the turn of the century, there were meant to be bonfires and beacons, and candlelit barges full of music accentuating the river's course through the denser darkness of parkland. In the event, a cold tedious rain soused the bonfires so that each hilltop belched a volcanic geyser of smoke, and guests turning their faces skywards to watch the beacon baskets hoisted up on chains met with arrowy, pricking rain. They bent their forearms across their brows like wailers at a funeral, and still the drops ran down their cheeks. The music from the barges was subdued by the hiss of the rain and the awnings drawn over the musicians – so much so that as the boats circled the chateau, Cyr sent word that the awnings must be dropped. The music-makers must suffer the rain to rain on them if they wanted to taste the sixteenth century.

He had begun the evening well enough, and had no guests attended the party he would no doubt have ended it just as cheerfully. But already two virtual strangers had jovially suggested to him that the festivities would serve as a wake for the dead baby. Tradition, it was true, did mark down a baby's entrance into Heaven as cause for celebration, but personally he could find no grounds for rejoicing. Vérité was spared the crass remarks – mothers rarely observed the tradition – but everyone felt free to say it to Cyr, implying knowingly that the Chatelaine's child had been his.

He could say nothing in reply. It would have been disloyal and improper for him to acknowledge that a child had ever even been conceived. He was obliged to wear a look of ignorant bewilderment, to ask 'What child are you speaking of?', and excuse himself on the grounds of some pressing household task for which his rank fitted him. So he vented his spleen on the musicians, who stood like dismal water clocks, drip-dripping over their instruments, feet splayed against the rolling of the barges and their boot-cuffs filling up with rain. The dripping was unsyncopated.

Even so, the chateau was ablaze like a fireship riding downtide, bearing down on the next century. Each time a door opened, the house refilled its lungs, took breath, for every fireplace was lit and sucking greedily on the warm, overcrowded air. The passage of guests through the house was marked, like the high-water line, by a detritus of food scraps and discarded drinking cups.

'Gluttons and bibbers,' said Cyr misanthropically. 'You should have gone to Amboise, Vérité, and had the King pay for the night's follies.'

'And been apart from you at New Year? Not for the world. I have a present for you.'

'A present? What?'

'Ah no. You must wait till midnight.' It gratified her to see the childish flash of excitement in her lover's face. No one else would have seen it, but she who had made a career out of pleasing him had the measure of his face. 'Something momentous for a momentous night,' she said. Though sometimes it seemed she had to jump higher and higher to clear the obstacles to Cyr's happiness, still she could usually find a way to appease him, to please him, to dispel his blackest moods. No matter that this one New Year present would cost her more than she could truly afford. He was a good man; he had given her his all; he must have whatever it was in her power to give. This auspicious night would bless the giving.

Cyr looked round the stateroom as if he might spot his present hidden under drapery or lipping from behind a curtain. But all he saw out of the ordinary was the small, ashy figure of Little Sister Cecille (he still thought of her as a nun), her big pomegranate breasts and broad hips squeezed into a brown dress of Vérité's, so that she looked like a bollard worn into grooves by ships' rope. Her eyes were staring at him. When he countered the stare, bright, cherry spots sprang up to her cheeks and she looked intently at the floor. But after his search moved on round the room, he could feel her eyes batten on him again. At last he caught sight of someone far more interesting. 'Isn't that your man-at-law, lady? Why's he here?'

'For the same reason all the world's here,' she said, jealous of his attention drifting. 'Don't be too civil in drinking healths this evening, my love. I need you sure and sober at midnight. For your present.' She went to take the cup out of his hand, but he turned away as though he had not seen her reach for it. He went and put an arm around the man-at-law.

She hoped he would not drink. She liked him to seem perfect in the eyes of her guests, and when he drank he had a tendency to lapse into barrack-room obscenity and to jab with his finger and pluck at people's clothing for emphasis. And she did so like him to shine in company. That suit of midnight blue sat well on him, and for all he would not wear his hair in the Italian way, how much more of a gentleman he looked these days than his brother. There was Estienne now, dandling his fingers in the palm of a lady (not his wife), telling false fortunes. He had run to fat since his father died, and rumour had it that he was selling off his farm in penny pieces to subsidize his gambling. When he saw her watching him, he kissed his fingers to her with a strangely indecent intimacy – as if he still intended the room to misconstrue him.

'Are you quite well, Cecille?' Vérité asked. The girl said something but her throat clung on to the words. 'Are you afraid? There's nothing to be afraid of. I told you.'

'No. Not feared, ma'am. Not really.' She was panting shallowly. She scratched at her groin through the dress. 'If he's agreeable. If it won't pain much. And you say it won't pain much.'

'Pish! You make it sound a hardship. How could Nature recommend itself if it weren't . . . tolerable. Do you think all the poets lie, on purpose to fool you?'

'I never read a poet,' said Cecille.

The Chatelaine felt for the reassurance of her keys, but they were missing, of course, from the festive finery of her gown. 'He's a good man. You've got no call to fret.'

'My ma said different. She fretted plenty sometimes when . . .'

'Are you content or not? Say not and I'll look elsewhere.'

'Content! Content,' said the girl, like a child who sees sweets about to go back into the jar. 'Can I see the year die first, though? Can I?' She should have said, 'see the New Year born'.

'No. Go now. I want you ready by midnight.'

Cecille dropped a small, inept curtsey and overbalanced against Vérité: her hands on the woman's forearm were hot and damp.

Across the room, Cyr said to the man-at-law, 'And have you accomplished any business for my lady today?'

The lawyer was round-shouldered and wore a velvet turban with dagged flaps that hung down on to either cheek: it gave him the look of a beagle. He lifted his nose at the scent of a fee. 'Business? Faith no! Has she some business she wants seeing to? I'll attend on her now!' He crammed a meat bone into his mouth to suck it clean the quicker.

'No. Pray don't trouble yourself . . . You mean you've not drawn up . . . anything recently, at her request?' The lawyer looked troubled and grated his teeth against the bone. He choked a little as Cyr clapped his shoulders between unpleasantly hard hands. 'Well, no matter! Don't hurry away, for all that! Eh? There'll maybe be an announcement at midnight. Maybe be business for you in the morning. Eh?'

'Oh! Excellent! Excellent!' The man-at-law was flustered, covered with embarrassment. Cyr could see him, beyond the shutters of his

326

eyes, guessing, speculating: a marriage? a deed of consort? another child? It pricked de Puy to an even greater agitation and he turned abruptly away and took two cups of wine off the table and drank them both down.

In the centre of the room, in a wrought-iron stand, a huge candle burned, with a red ribbon tied around it at the exact band of wax designated midnight. Unfortunately, each time the door opened, the draught from the fire sucked the candle flame down to drown in its own wax, and a page-boy would have to relight it from the grate, easing and squeezing his way between the guests with a lighted spill. The new century was thus being postponed further and further into the night with each gust of air. Cyr de Puy drank off a cup of wine with every accidental extinction. The Chatelaine too seemed agitated; she liked her ceremonial to pass off faultlessly. Little by little, the red ribbon was over-trickled by cataracts of white wax as the old century melted away. The flame tugged backwards unwillingly. It blew out again.

Like a badly primed gun, Cyr de Puy leapt on to the table and clapped his hands with a big, hollow, startling noise. 'Honoured guests! Most worthy and excellent gentlemen – ladies.' Plainly he was drunk. Stewards drew the bowls and dishes away from around his feet. Vérité hid her hands in her pockets and made fists of them. 'Before the old year is out, the Chatelaine Vérité of Gloriole has a word to speak! An announcement to make!' He reached down to help her up on to the table. The trestle rocked unsteadily and a houseboy dived beneath it to drive the chocks deeper home.

Vérité blushed and struggled to salvage a smile from among a chaos of emotions. 'I fear my Master-at-Arms is impatient . . .' she began, but stopped short, unwilling to criticize Cyr in front of these . . . gluttons and bibbers. 'Dear friends. Most excellent and honoured Tourainois. Your presence here tonight does the place and person of Gloriole more honour than can be repaid!' And the guests cheered themselves, applauded themselves, thanked themselves for coming. 'I did so want the pleasure of your company, so that the old century should not pass without honour nor the new come in without due ceremony.' She looked around her for Cyr. His face was flushed with wine and the expectation of something more, but she could think of nothing else to say. 'Let the bells of Saint-Cloud toll till the old year's dead, and then let the cannon salute the fifteen-hundredth year since the birth of Our Saviour!'

Mustered like little white sheep into a small, frightened flock, the choirboys from Psalette hurriedly assembled overhead in the gallery to sing the anthem they had rehearsed for midnight. Their music drew the eyes of the guests away from the Chatelaine and allowed her to climb down quickly and draw her Master-at-Arms away towards the stairs. He protested loudly, '*Is that all? Nothing else?*'

'What did you expect me to say?'

Cyr was only narrowly in possession of himself. 'A present, you said. I thought . . .' He tripped against the newel post and in retaliation kicked out with such violence that he crazed the lacquered panel and left the mark of his boot on it.

'You thought I'd break some news! A baby! You thought I was pregnant! Oh Cyr, I'm so sorry.'

He admitted grudgingly, almost unconvincingly, 'Something of the kind. A present, you said. Something momentous.'

She laughed, if a little shrilly, and led the way upstairs. She was conscious, even as she spoke, that coquetry was grotesquely silly in a woman of her age. She was also intensely angry with him for being drunk. 'So impatient? So eager for your present? If you knew what it was, you wouldn't have me stand on a table and declare it to all the world! You would not! Ha ha! That would startle the neighbours for sure!'

'A toss for the neighbours,' he muttered, but if she heard him she pretended she had not.

She led the way to the door of her room and entered its antechamber and sat down abruptly on a little spindle-back chair. 'I wish you were sober.'

'A toss for sober. I'd best go and check the cannon for your "salute".' But she took a firm hold of him around the thigh.

'Listen, Cyr. Listen. You know the story of Rachel and Bilhah?'

'Who?'

'How Rachel couldn't give Jacob any children? So she gave him Bilhah . . . gave him her handmaiden . . . You must remember it!' She threw her arms round both his legs, like a sailor reefing a sail, and began to kiss whatever part of him she could draw within reach. She wanted to digress from her story, but had at long last won his attention. He pulled away from her. 'I want a baby, Cyr! I want an heir for Gloriole! Oh, I want a baby, Cyr! I want your baby! It must be yours! Oh God, give me the means! I love you so fierce. It hurts like a pain.' She placed his hand where it hurt her. 'So bad. So fierce some days I think it must be the Devil's doing.'

His hand rested on her belly, unambitious of exploration. She was obliged to say, 'Lie with me! Now! While the year's turning! One last time!'

He snatched his hand away, furious. 'What d'you mean, "one last time"? Is that the present? *One last time?* Is that what you've been saving for me? Make shift without?'

'No! No! That's not the present! I told you! Rachel and Bilhah! I've found you a Bilhah!'

'Who?' He had not been listening. She had to explain all over again. Then he shook himself, gave a panting laugh: '*Who?!*'

'No matter who. Little Cecille. No matter who! It doesn't matter who. Just so you get a child on her! A daughter. A son. A baby for us! An heir for us.'

He gave a snort of disbelieving laughter. 'Cecille? The thieving nun?' He was, after all, completely taken aback by her surprise present. He made two circuits of the room before he could wholly grasp the notion. 'And if she whelps . . . if I make a child on her . . . you'll adopt it heir? Make over Gloriole? The child in place of the nuns? What does she say? The girl?'

'Say? What should she say? I've promised her she can live fine as fine – everything she wants till the child's weaned, so long as she keeps silent. I'll claim it for my own, you see. Live close and secret while it grows . . . What's the difference? Her womb or mine?' Her nonchalance was quite hysterical. 'It's all agreed. She'll be my proxy. She'll bear our child. Then she'll take her vows – somewhere else, I mean. It's all agreed. If you consent, I mean. It all depends on your willingness, of course it does.'

He scowled. Her voice was keeping him from mastery of all the implications. But the more he scowled, the more she talked, trying to make things plain to him:

'I couldn't share, you see. I couldn't bear to share you. Not like Rachel. And maybe afterwards I couldn't compare so very well. Now I'm grown so old. It's not the same with men. Time's not so villainous to men. This way you'll never sicken of me. I'll never see you sicken of me for growing old. And my sin won't light on the child. You see? If I keep my vow – from today onward. Look at me – forty almost! I'll be no great loss to your bed, will I?' She laughed as she said it. She said it in order to be contradicted. Her intent was steadfast. Her mind was made up. In the new century she would keep her vow – forswear her sin . . . But he must contradict her, even so. The sky would shatter like glass if he did not contradict her. Then, as he returned from another circuit of the room, she realized that he had not been listening, but had taken in only the bare essentials of the plan. It was understandable. She had been fashioning it for weeks, had sewn closed every loophole like Penelope at the loom weaving her own undoing. To Cyr it was a novelty. It made him grin.

'I told my damned father I'd earn my way with my sword,' he said, unfastening his belt and letting it drop to the floor. 'Where is she? Where've you put her?'

Vérité stood up and intercepted his eagerness in her arms. 'You and I though first, sure! Before midnight! One last time, before the century's done!'

A distant noise of cheering grew like a woman's contraction: from an inkling to a great roaring, all-encompassing pain that shook the house with its violence. The red ribbon had charred, caught, flared, burned, dropped away leaving the great candle bare and white, its flame secure from draughts now, inside a tessellated battlement of wax. The new century had come in.

'Too late by all accounts,' Cyr said, freeing himself of her arms. 'Besides, you flatter my stamina. You wouldn't have me disappoint Little Sister Cecille, would you? Let me get about my duties. We'd better discuss my wages if you're going to lay extra work of this kind on me! She's not any manner of a beauty, that one. Favoured like a Jewess, I always thought.' He was happy. She had disinterred his happiness from where it had lain buried along with the last dead baby. Vérité congratulated herself. To see him happy was almost reward enough for what she had sacrificed. Almost.

'I loved you to the peril of my soul, Cyr,' she said, rubbing her face against his, endeavouring to take lasting possession of his sweetness by breathing in the breaths he let go, clinging on to him as though he were the precipice at the century's end. But she could not cling on for long.

'And I you,' he said perfunctorily. 'That's why I must go and hunt out my present. Show me the way.'

But it was he who went ahead, throwing open each door in turn until the slam of wood against brick was met by a timid shriek. Cecille knelt up on a testered bed, her arms around the corner pole and the curtain pulled round her shoulders against the cold. She stared at them both, as white-faced as her shift, and her feet edged one of the pillows on to the floor with a thud.

Vérité dug in, like a plough-anchor, and pulled Cyr back into the previous chamber. 'You don't have to do this! You can refuse!'

He relented almost at once, and put his arms around her and rocked her against his body. His face was over her shoulder: she could not see his expression when he said, 'Yes, but think of it, Vérité! A child! A child, without hazard of your dying! And without God's blight to smother it. Think of it. Think. Just like Rachel and . . . who was it?'

'Bilhah.'

'Yes. Her.'

From the bed Cecille gazed out into the chamber, staring at their kisses, staring at the Master-at-Arms rocking the Chatelaine to a passivity. Vérité could not reach the doorhandle to shut her out of their embrace. At last it was she who pulled away.

'Where are you going?' said Cyr. He pulled his tunic over his head. The scars on his arm were as livid as passion. 'Don't you want to stay and see it well done?'

It was a man's joke, a soldier's joke. His soldier's laughter pursued her down the corridor as she ran – fled, to be out of hearing of the shutting door and the turning key.

She went up on to the roof where the cannon had been primed (by Cyr) to fire in salvo a salute to the new century. The first explosion sounded just as she emerged through the hatch. It shook loose the nailhead stars and brought the night sky down on her, a suffocating, flapping blackness. The round, recoiling butt of the cannon came towards her, smoking at the touchhole, smoking at the mouth, hasty with news that it had smashed the old year to atomies, speeding to tell her that a new age had won the field. The gunners came to fetch it back to the gunport, dragging at its collar with rag mittens, like dog-handlers dragging a wayward hound back to its kennel. The second gun went off. There was scant space behind it and it touched the sloping, gabled roof, breaking slates with a sound lost amid its own. Vérité put her hands over her ears, but each successive salvo still broke over her like surf, its undertow throwing her off balance. She reeled on the roof's edge. The gunners grinned, and toasted her in ale, while the two bright guns thrust themselves backwards and were thrust forward again through the gaping parapet. Six – seven . . . ten – eleven . . . She could hear the fragments of noise falling through the house in shards – cheers and shouts and barks and drums and bells and singing and music. The guns went to and fro, to and fro beside her, pitching invisible balls into her sleeping comté, setting the harts and herons flying in terror, ejaculating fire. Twelve – thirteen . . . To and fro the little ornamental guns pumped, though their loudness had deafened her at last. Fourteen – fifteen . . .

On the last recoil, the carriage on the nearest gun cracked – simply, like a toy breaking. The smoking barrel slithered slowly off its moorings. The gunners sprang away from it, as though some monstrous juggernaut were careering across the roof. But it seemed so small, that domestic cannon. It moved so slowly and had such a small distance to fall that Vérité did not even step away. The carriage twisted and split into planks and splinters. The barrel was shed like the cuttle off a fish and rolled towards her across the roof, crushing shards of fallen tiles. It stopped alongside her feet, and the hems of her dress charred with a strangely disagreeable smell.

The artillerymen gibbered with fright. They burned themselves on the wrecked gun in an effort to expiate the dreadful risk they had caused to their Chatelaine. They ran for buckets to douse the gun. They fractured its barrel in doing so. They sobbed their innocence; they confessed their guilt. From the top of the hill, the Saint-Cloud bell went on tolling, tolling the death knell of the fifteenth century: no one had sent word for the ringer to stop.

Vérité frowned a little, examining the damage to her dress in the square column of light that rose through the roof hatch and spent itself like a fountain over their heads. The gunners' panic '– coulda been crushed . . . coulda been unlimbed . . . !' – was a mystery to her. The cannon lay spent and cooling on the roof, small and harmless.

'One salvo too many, I suppose,' she said peaceably, to acquit the men of blame. 'One century too many, that's all.'

TWENTY-NINE

Patience Rewarded

Absurd to think that one night, however momentous on the calendar, is big enough to fence off one era from the next. Babies are not got in one night just because they are wanted or because there are guns firing overhead. It took three months of assiduous effort for Cyr de Puy to get Cecille with child. Hollow-eyed and preoccupied, she haunted the house, tinkling like a frosty tree with the jewellery and religious ornaments she borrowed from Vérité's closet. The chalcedony and jasper rosary hung at her waist and she slept with a salt cellar, a candlestick and a silver-bound book of days under her pillow so as not to be parted from their prettiness. The weight of her dresses grazed the landing floor, so thick were they in gilt wire.

Her pet monkey ate supper with them, while she crammed herself to a nausea with every edible morsel that came to table, and drank herself tipsy. Then she would suddenly interrupt the conversation with an effort to describe how, the previous night, she had pleased the Master 'better than any Italian *[hiccup]* he had ever known'. Seeing her failure to impress, she would lapse into contemplative silence or anxious tears while Cyr squirmed in his chair and Vérité tried hesitantly to pick up the threads of conversation. Once, late at night, the Chatelaine overheard the recompense Cecille received at the hands of her lover for one such outburst: the slaps and the swearing carried all the way to the first chamber and set the Little Sisters of Pity fluttering in their pigeon loft. The sound horrified Vérité. It thrilled and mollified her. For though she had granted Cecille equal status with herself and the right to possess and enjoy all the delights of Gloriole, Vérité had underestimated the Kraken jealousy that would be roused up from the seabed of her soul. She longed for signs that Cyr undertook his work with distaste or unwillingness. His love was still hers: he frequently said so, wiping the supper from his beard and departing for Cecille's chamber. He would rather be in Vérité's bed: that was what the shouting and the slaps meant. Surely.

Then Cecille was pregnant and could not be hit. Nor thwarted, nor gainsaid, nor even hated, for to have let fly one sharp fleck of malice might have punctured the swelling prospect of a child. Vérité closed up the castle gates – isolated Gloriole against outside infection and the spread of rumour, and imprisoned herself alongside her proxy for the long, intolerable wait.

Naturally, there were rumours in plenty, nevertheless. What tradesmen and callers could not discover by entering the chateau, they invented. There was sickness there. There was madness. It was a vow to live contemplative. It was the wish for discretion on the part of some visiting lover who came by secret tunnel and left by darkness. They badgered the household, but the household claimed to know nothing; only that the Chatelaine wore maternity gowns once more and took Mass every day and was inseparable from her fat, spoiled favourite to the exclusion of all others. Every day Vérité and Cecille would spend together, locked in one of the single-storey, self-contained wings of Gloriole which bowed out from the main building like the outrigger of a punt.

She felt cast adrift. She wanted to look up and see land in the shape of Cyr. But he kept scrupulously apart; spent his nights now in the forest lodge with his wife; held good to Vérité's plan; respected her renewed vow. He allowed her no backsliding into the wonderful sins of the previous century.

'I want to go out in the air,' said Cecille after a month's confinement between the linenfold walls.

'There's pestilence abroad,' said Vérité, one hand resting across her own diaphragm as she sat reading. 'The air's dirty. You must stay safe indoors.'

'Why doesn't Cyr come now? At night, I mean. He don't come. Tell him to come. I don't see a mortal soul from day's end to dawning.'

'My Master-at-Arms must be about his work . . . As for you, his work there's done. You can't expect him to labour when he's reached his goal . . . Besides . . . men don't lie with a woman when she's with child. Didn't you know that?' She was not certain why she said it. As a kindness? Because she knew herself the disappointment of waiting for the sound of footsteps which never came? Because Cecille must be kept placid for the sake of the child? Whatever the reason, Cecille did not believe her.

She told herself that she loved Cecille, for the sake of the child within her. She told herself that she must love Cecille as dearly as herself, because somehow then the baby would be more truly hers. In fact, she was so intent on sharing the pregnancy that she felt the sickness herself, eased her own clothes, replicated the symptoms, as a mirror is obliged to replicate reality. It is mine, she thought, as the gown creased and uncreased of its own accord over the younger woman's belly, over the quickened child. It's my heir.

'I itch, and my back pains me,' said Cecille. 'Would to God it were out of me.'

'Amen,' said Vérité, pressing the heels of her hands into her own back. And she sewed a shift of soothing silk for Cecille to wear, because she told herself that she loved the girl as dear as dear.

When Cecille was brought to labour, there was no midwife present to hear how she called on her dead mother and cursed God. Only Vérité and one trusted Sister of Pity were in attendance, and they did not recognize Hebrew when they heard it. Still, Cecille was a sturdy, beamy girl, and though she swore she had changed her mind and would not bear a child – no, not for anyone – she found that matters had been taken out of her hands, as usual. Though she fought the inevitable with a ferocity that tore the bedsheets, rended the pillows and bloodied the mattress, still she was delivered of a boy who reached out one hand into the world ahead of his skull, to grasp the moment in a purple fist.

And all the time she assisted, wiping Cecille's face and suffering her hair and clothes to be torn by the girl's anger, Vérité felt her cervix gripe and her innards rend, like Cerberus whose puppies re-entered their dam to chew out her womb. She bit her lip. She prayed her prayers for Cecille's well-being. But when she caught the slithering, newborn baby in her apron, such a reserve of energy went out of her that it was all she could do to bear the weight. She consigned it readily to the nun and went through to her own room and lay down in a cold sweat. 'Yes, Lord, if need be. My strength before his,' she prayed. 'His good before mine.'

The indisposition passed. Next day she was able to take sole charge of the baby (except for feeding) and to receive the formal congratulations of the household. The Sisters of Pity obediently acknowledged God's gift of an heir to Gloriole, even though they were a little bewildered to see the sin of bastardy glossed over so easily.

Some had long since deduced the truth, as well.

They kept their distance now, like small black daws on the rim of a battlefield, watching and waiting. It was not as Vérité remembered in her childhood. But then she was no longer a child and it would have been immature to look for the old companionship.

She sent for her man-at-law and her Master-at-Arms, to bear witness to the birth, and addressed them from her bed. The child lay swaddled and cross-belted in her arms (as though, by a wave of its fist, it might give away its secret). 'Gentlemen. In the light of the birth of my dear son, Rémy, I wish to draw up a new will. This same Rémy is my heir and the heir to the lands and possessions of Gloriole-sur-Sablois, and after him his issue. Will you see it properly recorded, please?'

The lawyer nodded his head vigorously, taking unnecessary notes of the proceedings with a crossed nib that scratched.

'Naturally there must be a guardian to act on his part should my son inherit before coming of age.'

The man-at-law interrupted with the required politeness: 'Ah, but your ladyship will live to see the little fellow bearded and married and with sons of his own!' From over by the window, Cyr de Puy shot him a look of acute impatience.

'I pray God permits it,' said Vérité with equal politeness. 'But one must provide for the will of God to be otherwise, and I name Cyr de Puy, my most trusted steward and Master-at-Arms, to hold in charge the interests and welfare of my heir in the event of my death. Are you agreeable, Captain de Puy?'

'As if he were my own dear son, madam,' said Cyr, bowing courteously, unflamboyantly. The scars on his face coloured with emotion.

'Very good. Very good,' said the lawyer. 'But you'll wish it kept secret, I suppose? As before? You may trust my discretion perfectly.'

'Before?' said de Puy.

'No,' said Vérité. 'As my father acknowledged me, so I acknowledge my son and my choice of guardian. Publicly. You may tell whom you choose, sir. Now, Cyr will show you to pen and paper and you can come again as soon as you please for my signature.'

She was teasing Cyr. She was making sport of his wish to be alone with her and his child. She was savouring the moment she had looked forward to so long that she was almost afraid to taste it. Cyr must go with the lawyer. Time enough for them to be together, alone, with the baby.

When they had gone, she slipped out of bed and carried the listless child through to Cecille for feeding. There was a sweet smell in the room of surplus milk and praline. Cecille sat eating shelled hazelnuts from a bowl, with a tirelessly rhythmic lift-chew-swallow. It was as if she wished to maintain the warm cloak of fat that had come with pregnancy and saddled her shoulders and back. She resented the baby's hungry nuzzling, and winced at the ferocity of its greed.

'How are you, my heart?' said Vérité, starting to shell more nuts and replenish the bowl. 'I've done as you asked and found a wet-nurse, so your part is almost ended. I've not been idle on your behalf.' Cecille crammed her mouth with nuts and did not reply.

Meanwhile, Cyr de Puy guided the lawyer towards a retraite where he could draw up the necessary documents and conclude his business without ever leaving the chateau. Pen, parchment and ink were all set waiting, and de Puy lifted the chair in behind the man and kept hold on it till the work was done. As the crossed nib scratched in the name of guardian, he said casually, 'From what you said, do I take it there was a testament before this one? Made in secret?'

The man in the chair laughed at the unlikelihood of Cyr's ignorance, and let fall the secret he had kept successfully for three years. '. . . a very great reward, monsieur Captain, though I've no doubt your merits warranted it . . .' Before he had finished explaining about the previous will, he had to lay down his pen: the chair was jerking so much in Cyr's grip that he was afraid of blotting his completed work.

'You mean to say she made me her heir in '98? Disinherited the nuns?'

'Well, provision was made, of course – as it is here, indeed! The nuns have security of tenure and livelihood, naturally.' Cyr did not hear him. He was laughing too loud.

The man-at-law joined in, relieved that Cyr took the news so well. He might, after all, have felt demoted, dispossessed by the infant heir. 'But you knew! Sure, you must have known!' he exclaimed, and sprinkled sand over the document's drying ink.

'I've arranged for you to enter the Convent of the Immaculate Conception at Nantes,' said Vérité. 'I've assured the Prioress there that you need not duplicate your novitiate: you can take the veil immediately – as soon as you arrive.'

'Nantes?'

'Of course, you shan't travel till you're quite well and strong again, and I'll send you in my very best barge – you'll ride smoother than by coach. But you must dress warm, mind.'

'I don't want to go to Nantes.' The girl squirmed down beneath the bedclothes, like a lugworm burying itself in sand. She left the baby on the pillow.

'Nonsense. I hear it's a lovely place. Looks clear to the ocean. Treasures sent by the Pope. Come now.' She pulled the covers back with a sure hand. 'Don't tell me you thought to rejoin the Little Sisters? No! A new beginning. You'll be happy at Nantes. It seems to me you'll be fit to go quite soon.'

'But I don't *want* it.'

'Of course you do.' Vérité drew the bedding fully back, briskly, like the bait-digger laying bare the lugworm. Cecille curled up within her shift; pulled her knees up to her chest. Her back was chevroned with rolls of fat.

'And live in one room? And sleep on a plank? And wear a shroud? *And cut off all my hair?*'

'If God called you to it. How else? No more foolishness, now. It's as we agreed.' Unaccountably, the sheet between Vérité's hands ripped. She stared down at the tear wondering how she had come to make it.

Cecille stared at it too, her eyes white-rimmed with hysteria. 'You said I needn't!'

Vérité laughed without humour. 'I hardly think so.'

'*No one should be put to it*, you said. No one, except of their own choosing!'

Vérité could feel her face growing rigid. It had been cast once in warm wax for a plaster bust, and she could feel that same cooling stiffness rigidify her top lip and jaw and cheek muscles. She was plumbing, for the first time, the depths of her loathing for Cecille – that fat, fertile leech she had wilfully laid to her breast. 'And by your own choosing you entered into our bargain. To live in all material comfort till the child was born and then to continue on your road as before. Have I failed in my side of the contract? Have I?' She argued from a position of strength, knowing she meant to

338

give nothing more to Cecille if she lived a hundred years.

The girl had no more words at her beck than a grizzling, thwarted child. 'But now I've had it, and I know! They won't let me keep things! Not anything!' Her nose drizzled down on to her pouting top lip. 'It's not just! It's not fair! I want things now I've had them! I want them! I want all the things!'

Standing at the foot of the bed, Vérité began stripping the linen and folding it vigorously into untidy parcels. 'You're like the man who sold his soul to the Devil, then complained when the debt came due. Get up. I'm weary of listening to you . . . Or am I to send you home to your father?'

'Pa?'

'With the news that you don't choose to keep to your vocation.'

'Pa?'

'And tell him about your thieving?'

'Tell Pa?'

'And your sleeping with my Master-at-Arms, when all the while your poor father thought you were living a life of prayerfulness with the Little Sisters?'

'He'd kill me dead!'

'You said as much, now I recall. Dress. I'll send a barber to you to cut your hair. It'll show humility of purpose when you get to Nantes.' Vérité had no notion who the girl's father was, but her memory was sound enough for the essentials. And as she left, the baby clasped in hands as binding as swaddling bands, she locked the door on Cecille's screams:

'*God never called me! He never! I'm a* . . .'

At the landing stage, Vérité gave orders for the voyager's trunk to be opened and emptied on to the frosty spikes of grass. Inside were a jewelled chain, a silver-gilt pomander, a pair of embroidered sleeves from Vérité's damask-silk gown, a lacquered casket, a phial of perfume and a ground-glass stopper from a wine-server. But Cecille said nothing. She was utterly silent once more, watching her fate flow down on her with the inexorability of the Sablois river. Earlier, at the sight of the razor, she had blurted out to the barber that she was a Jewess and ineligible for the veil. But the barber, who was simple, had only laughed and lathered, laughed and cut, laughed and dragged the blade over her skull with a noise of rasping. Now she prayed that the man would keep silent, forget what she had said, forget to recount the joke. For how was it better to be burned or hanged for a thieving, counterfeiting Jew than sent downriver to a dismal future?

Besides, it was not true. This very river, bent on bearing her away down to the sea, had washed the Jew out of her and left her without a reliable God to call on.

She wondered if the Chatelaine would have her hanged in any case, to ensure her everlasting silence. There was no need. The power of speech had fallen from Cecille along with her hair and her beautiful gowns. At the sight of the pretty things on the grass, Cecille only shrugged. She could offer no explanation. She did not know herself why she had taken them.

'I fear they'll not let you keep such things at the convent, my dear,' said Vérité tenderly, loudly, and ordered the trunk to be closed up again, leaving the baubles on the grass. 'Now God keep you and bless you for the service you've given me, Sister Cecille. Safe voyage.'

Vérité stood on the jetty and waved the boat farewell. Then she hurried back to her coach and to the warmth of the chateau and to her baby and to her restored joy in Cyr de Puy's unshared company.

Within a few days the news was cried round the estates – both heir and guardian named publicly. 'Do you think I should send word to the Queen?' Vérité thought aloud when she and her lover were alone together by the crib. 'Would she take it amiss, with another stillbirth so fresh in her mind? And ours a son, and her only a daughter living? I'm loath to triumph – you understand what I mean? Not just out of charity. I mean, it may bring bad luck!' But her expression did not anticipate bad luck. She held Cyr's face between her hands as if it were the bread and wine of her salvation. 'We must have a party, though! How I long to see faces again, after so long shut up.' She could not get mastery of his eyes. He would keep looking over her shoulder at the crib where their baby lay asleep. She was touched to the point of tears: that a man so fierce and virile should lay such store by a little child. She drew him by the elbow to the side of the cot. 'Our son, Cyr. Jesu, I can scarce hold the joy of it! You've given me everything, Cyr! Everything! Whatever shall I do to repay you?'

He put his hands to front and back of her skirt and she wilted against him with all the dependency of columbine on the briar. 'No, Cyr! God will see! God will punish us! God won't let our baby thrive!' But she said it with her eyes shut, feeling the waxen mask of her face soften again into its pliable tenderness. He took away his hands.

'But you asked what you could do for me,' he said, breathing fast and shallow and speaking so close that the words clung like damp rose petals to a bride's hair.

'It's true. And what would I deny you?' She caught sight of herself in the white and gilded mirror, and just for a moment the incongruity of her greying hair made her feel too old, too fortunate, too uncertain. So she closed her eyes again. The baby stared up at them and whimpered. Her contentment was absolute. 'So what shall I do for you, my Cyr? What?'

He took hold of her plait and wound it once around her throat. 'Die, madam,' he said. 'Die and be damned.'

THIRTY

Penance

The rope of hair bit deep as hemp into her throat and closed her windpipe for so long that a red roaring fire engulfed her vision and charred all the room to blackness. Her flailing hands tasted the texture of Cyr's shirt, doublet, belt, points, hose. His glossy leather boot struck her in the ribs, but there was no wind left in her to dislodge in a cry. She could hear the baby crying for her instead.

'Twenty years!' he said, kicking and stamping at her as if she were a campfire finished with. 'Twenty endless, stinking years you've made me jig for this! Your ape! Your dancing bear! Your bedwarmer! Blood, but you lift my gorge! Have you any inkling of the pleasure I'd've had in cutting your throat while you slept?' He went to jump on her with both feet, but parted them and came down astride her, squatting down, pinning her to the floor with hands and hips. 'Twenty years of toiling to breed on a spayed bitch of a bastard whore! Twenty years of fawning and fumbling and bowing to a piece of trash fit for the muster-yard. I've had better nights on an Italian bawd with lice! Twenty years watching my wife grow old and tired in a dog-box in your woods! Twenty years of telling her, "Be patient . . . Soon . . . Nothing's got by haste." I'll tell you, there were times I wished I'd left you to Estienne. But I've spent my life to win this place for myself, and every minute you stay in it's a cut in my winnings!'

'You won't kill me!' she whispered, already as rigid under him as a corpse. He pushed his face down and spat into hers.

'Why? Why would I deny myself the pleasure? Now you've signed the deed. Now my son's got Gloriole for me. Now you've served your term.'

She screwed up her eyes to shut out the sight of him. 'For love. For love's sake! We love each other! Cyr! This is madness!

Cyr! Please! Let me go. Let me see you tended to! You're mad! You don't know what you're saying!'

'Let you go as far as the midden and be buried there and never missed! "Disappeared", I'll tell them. "Gone swimming and drowned and aren't we all heartsore and forlorn." '

He deliberately set her free. She was clumsy in getting to her feet – encumbered by skirts and hobbled by terror. He stamped on her hems and brought her down twice more on to her hands and knees. The hems ripped away in great swaddling hoops that tangled her feet as she broke for the doorway, but she managed to bolt through one adjoining chamber and through the next – into the armoury. Her mouth gaped, silent as a fish straining under water. Her voice had been crushed in her larynx by the noose of hair, and though she screamed for help, the armoury and guardhouse were empty of guards: the Master-at-Arms had instigated manoeuvres in the forest.

She cried out for her nuns to come. But even as she called she could hear the anthem of thanksgiving she had commanded, spiralling up from their chapel. They were as far removed as Heaven. When she looked back, Cyr had taken down a boar-sword from her father's collection of weaponry.

'A fitting bore for a sow,' he jeered, weighing the sword in both hands. She threw open the door of the tocsin tower and started up the spiral of stairs. She would sound the alarm bell and alert every living soul.

By halfway up, her legs were worthless cords of string – fleshless – boneless – the bones melted in their own hot marrow. She was crawling on hands and knees, and the tip of the flame-shaped, scalloped sword-blade was resting on the base of her spine. He let her climb all the way to the top, then stepped over her and flipped the end of the bellrope high out of her reach over the cast-iron crossbeams of the belfry. He prodded her with the sword: her shift and underclothing bled whiteness through the broken weave of her dress.

'Now, Chatelaine. Mistress. Beloved. Am I to grant you the ultimate consummation?' The grey metal came to rest among her keys, and severed the leather cord from which they hung. 'Or will you jump over?'

She looked down through the pierced stone parapet and the dizzy height struck her like a blow. An icy wind snatched away all the breath she had left, and the tower seemed to sway like a reed in the northerly blast. She could see the river – stretch upon reach of the river – wriggling like the Serpent through Eden, like the cord binding Gloriole to its savage mother the forest.

Cyr barracked her: 'Pray, give me my orders, mistress. Yours to command, lady. Servant. Serf. Yours to enjoy by *droit de seigneur*. A lackey. So give me your orders. Shall it be impaling slow and easy or a fall sweet and clean into your own moat? Obedient to your every word, ma'am. The model of obedience, that's me. Pray test the metal of my devotion.' But the swordpoint came on through her dress and shift, impelled by its own weight as his wrists tired.

'You won't kill me!' she said, spitting the windy hair out of her mouth.

'And spend twenty years in the relish of it, by this hand. Or are you still trusting to that great *Love* of ours?'

'Self-love! I trust to self-love!' she said, snatching seconds out of the rattling air. The bell above them quietly hummed its note with the sheer incessant hammer of the wind. 'And fear of things to come! Swear by your hand? Well, by my soul I swear! By my soul, I'll haunt you!' She shouted it, contending with the wind. 'May my soul never rest nor find its way to Heaven till my spirit's brought you to madness. You think I clung tight to you while I was living? Just see how I trail after you in spirit! Visit you by sunlight and dark. Haunt you to a madness! You're halfway mad already, God knows! Best believe me, Cyr! If I was mistaken in all things about you, that's one back door into your nature I do know!'

His scarred cheeks twitched like dunes infested with sandhoppers. She held the thought in place with her eyes and drove it home with oaths and vows. 'God hear me! High up here! Never take my soul into glory till the man who murders me is damned and burning. Damned to madness living and burning dead!' Cyr seemed suddenly to feel the cold, for he closed his shirt collar across his throat. 'Let me live, Cyr. Let me live and I'll spend my time praying for your good. You can have Gloriole! Take it. I know it's God's judgment on me! I know it! But before God, don't kill me if you have a jot of self-love!'

Like a stage-devil through a trapdoor, her tormentor suddenly disappeared. He dropped backwards on to the stairs and could be heard running down them with a salt-soft shuffle of shoe-leather on the gritty steps.

For what seemed like an hour, Vérité lay under the humming bell, clinging to the delicate masonry, watching the wheeling terns flash their ice-white undersides to and fro in blizzard flocks over the surface of the distant river. She grew so cold that she lost all feeling in her hands and feet, and after creeping into the shelter of the staircase had to slide down, sitting, from step to step. As she reached the anteroom to the armoury once more, Cyr de Puy stepped from behind the door jamb, stepped close in at her back and held her arms by her side while he said quietly, 'I've rethought the situation. You'll have the lodge in the forest. My wife'll take your place here – as my Chatelaine. Keep silent. Hold your peace, and the child inherits. Raise a clamour and I'll name its mother and say how you murdered her.'

'*Murdered?*'

'Well?'

'Cecille's not dead.'

'No? You didn't really mean to let Cecille spill her history in the confessional, did you? And make you a laughing stock? My men were posted to cut her off downstream. "On orders from the Chatelaine", naturally.'

'Oh Jesu, not murdered,' she whispered. 'Jesus have mercy on me! Murdered?'

'It was plain enough you wanted her dead.' After so long an acquaintance, Cyr too knew the back door to Vérité's thinking. When she examined her conscience she found quite enough venom there to have poisoned Cecille.

'I mayn't keep the baby?'

'Keep him? Hinder your *own child* from inheriting Gloriole? Now there's an unnatural mother.' He had regained all his confidence and was enjoying the novel pleasure of absolute power. 'I've given you your life, haven't I? And you've got the comfort of knowing Our Boy will own the Sablois. It would be greedy to want more, sure! What more could you want?'

Vengeance. The word stirred in her like Original Sin. She wanted to spit it in his face – shout it above the placid monotony of the nuns' anthem. But all she said was, 'You'll never be Comte de Gloriole. Guardian, that's all. You'll never have the title.'

'Do you really think I care? So long as I own the place? So long as it's mine to make and milk? Even got a son to pass it on to, haven't I? Don't fret on my account. I'm content just to carry the keys of Gloriole. How's a title going to make that sweeter than it already is?' He slung one arm round her as he might a drinking partner, and drew her downstairs – along white and gold passageways, through a linenfold maze of panelling and tapestries, over an acre of mosaic floors, under the unmoved gaze of a hundred haughty portraits. He hurried her down flights of stairs flowery with lacquer garlands and summer landscapes, past the doorways to endless empty rooms. 'We'll give out that you swore to live solitary if God would only grant you the joy of a son. Yes, that's what. Your bargains with the Almighty are famous hereabouts. It's time you kept one of them, don't you think, Chatelaine?' He was warming to the several possibilities that arose from sparing her life, even though he had spared it out of purest superstitious fear.

'Shan't I pack a chest?' she asked. '. . . clear my things out of your wife's way?'

'Nay, that's not biblical. One shirt to your back. Isn't that all you need for the track to salvation?' The arm round her neck speeded her along – would not allow her to snatch up in passing so much as a cloak before they were out-of-doors, buffeted by the wind and the smells of the stable.

'How shall I live?' she asked, with a new kind of panic. 'Will you give me my bread?'

He made a show of questioning his conscience, then said, 'No. I don't believe so, lady. I'm granting you shelter, aren't I? Earn your keep, why don't you? There's always a thing or two a woman can sell, if she's a need.'

He led her horse by its headstall, out across the berm and on to the causeway. The water lapped in quick, nervous waves against the piles. He forced the pace to a jog-trot and she clutched at the pommel of the saddle with barely a chance to turn her head and look back at the chateau. Behind them Gloriole receded, receded, until its bulk shrank to the scope of a single glance. Across the parklands he accelerated to a canter, and then the forest rides swallowed them up as the Labyrinth swallowed Theseus. A twig snagged a single thread of Vérité's gown and unravelled it, as though by its help she might one day find her way back to the mouth of the Labyrinth and so to the daylight of Gloriole. But the thread soon broke, and she knew in her heart of hearts that labyrinthine darkness was all that remained to her of her father's inheritance.

'Shall I not see my women ever again, Cyr? My Little Sisters? May they visit me?'

'Not unless they care to forfeit their place by it . . . Still, I see your argument. You think you'll lack for company. Tell you what

I'll do. I'll tell the guardhouse where there's a woman in need of company and earnings. That should furnish you with trade enough to live by and the means to pay your rent and feu. Am I fair or am I just?'

'Cyr . . .' But his agitated elation was so bright-eyed and twitching that anything she said would only incite him to more and more imaginative cruelties, so she broke off.

She wondered at the vastness of his grievance against her, the volcanic eruption of so much molten spleen. It was as if she had sewed her beloved a shirt of fire and forced him wear it for twenty years.

His wife ran out of the hunting lodge at the sound of hooves. At the unexpected sight of Vérité, she cowered against the wall and even dropped a kind of curtsey, for fear the plan had gone awry. Vérité saw her run an appraising eye over Cyr and take the measure of his frenzied excitement. She knows him as well as I, Vérité thought with a pang of jealous astonishment. Still less was she prepared to see the way he leaned down out of the saddle and put his fingers to the round, timid face and trapped her paw in his and spilled his triumph at her feet, rich with endearments.

'You didn't kill her, then?' The wife greeted his news bright-faced with relief.

'You didn't wish it, so I brought her here instead. You shall fill her place and she'll fill yours.'

Vérité wanted to blurt out, 'Ah, so you lie to her too! Have you told her about your Italian bawds? About Cecille with her throat cut in the river?' But a bottomless weariness had sealed up her mouth, and she could only watch the intertwining of those fingers, the uncharacteristic tenderness in Cyr's face. She got down from the horse without being told to do so.

'I've packed nothing! What'll I bring?' asked the wife.

'Nothing. Leave it. Trash, all of it. There's things more fit at the chateau. Everything's at the chateau.'

And so this wife, who had waited twenty years in patient obedience to her husband's ambition, mounted Vérité's horse with an apologetic shrug of one shoulder and a sideways bend of the head towards the woman who had commandeered her husband for a lover.

'Madam, your husband's a thief and a villain,' said Vérité. But the woman's universe was governed by her husband's law, and she only shrugged again and bobbed away through the trees towards

347

the next phase of her existence, unquestioning. She had as much volition as a cork bobbing on a stream.

'Look at her. Her soul's owned by him,' Vérité thought aloud. 'They'll go down to Hell together like two witches tied back to back. That's what my father meant to save me from. The tyranny of marriage.'

Then she looked around her at the vast oppressive dark of the forest. The day was failing. Cold sprang out of the ground like the armed soldiers that sprang up to harry the Argonauts. Hedgehogs rustled loud as wolves; wolves prowled as quiet as ghosts; ghosts stripped naked of their flesh howled at the prospect of everlasting cold. This was what her father had brought her to, rather than see her nestle in the warm possession of a man.

She wandered through the lodge. It was in sound repair and well furnished. Cyr had seen to that. There were clothes in the presses, a fire in the grate, a loaf and cheese under earthenware, herbs hanging to dry from the rafters. There were spiders and woodlice, too; birds in the loft and rats under the plank floor. The lodge was an ark floating in its sea of green to which every manner of beetle, slug and cockroach had resorted, to ride out Chaos.

Here was the bed to which Cyr had come to escape for a few hours his subjection to his Chatelaine. He had come here for solace from the hard labour of pretending to love her. Vérité sat up all night rather than lie on it. There was a madonna, too, and more crucifixes than there were tie-bolts to secure the roofbeams.

She knelt down and begged forgiveness from the soul of Cecille; from Mary Magdalene for her lasciviousness; from Saint Frideswide for valuing a child before chastity; from Saint Pancras who abhors the oath-breaker; from her father for the loss of Gloriole. From Cyr de Puy for the peril to which she had put his dear, dear soul.

In the middle of the night, horsemen came riding by lamplight. By lamplight they fumbled their way to the door. When Vérité ran to bolt it, she could hear their drink-sodden oaths as they rattled at the latch, and then as they circled the lodge. She snatched up a blanket from the bed and crouched under it, as though its wool weave would make her invisible. But the cheerful redness of the dying fire showed her outline to the faces pressed against the one tiny window, faces flattened against the glass, faces masked by their own breath.

'Open for trade, woman! Open! Let us in out of the cold!' They tapped the glass with their money. They swore on their mothers' eyes that they were free of the Italian disease. They did not recognize her, for all they pressed their skin white against the pane, and their eyeballs glisted red in the firelight. They had simply been told of somewhere new – a change from the brothel in Rocheblanche. Besides, they were not expecting to see their Chatelaine, and men see only what they are expecting.

When she still did not open the door to them, their tempers kindled in the firelight. 'Shall we burn the place down? Shall we kick in the door?' The glass tinkled softly to the floor. 'Shall we mark your face for you? Open for trade, you legless cow! Fetching us out on a night like this!'

But finally they contented themselves with soiling her threshold before spurring their horses back towards Gloriole and the warmth of the guardroom.

Vérité stayed shivering by the grate, on hands and knees, for an hour after they left. She had tried to return to praying, but it was as though the disturbance had frightened away all the saints, like so many swallows off a wire.

She would not stay in this place.

Poor Jeanne of France. Stunted and hunchbacked, swarthy, lame and ape-like, she disgusted even her father. Louis d'Orléans only took her at the King's command. Her or the priesthood: that was how the proposition ran. And Louis sixteen and she twelve. After the wedding, he left her at the church door to go hunting. Poor Jeanne.

Poor Jeanne. The moment King Charles VIII was dead and Louis made King of France, he petitioned the Pope for a divorce and found he could have it for a modest twenty thousand crowns and a dukedom. Cesare Borgia, the Pope's son, filled the dukedom, and it was he who delivered the annulment. After all, an ecclesiastical court had quickly proved the marriage non-existent.

Had her poor husband not been terrorized into the match? Was she not so ugly as to repel any man? Was she not so deformed as to prevent all consummation? Had her so-called husband not made his loathing plain from the outset? Case proven. Poor Queen Jeanne.

Poor Queen. She swore it was not so. She trusted her whole case to the conviction that her dear Louis would not perjure himself in a church court. And then he swore he had never slept with her. No one thought any the worse of him, even if they suspected him of perjury. Everyone knew it was vital he should be free to marry

349

the dead King's widow and so keep Brittany bound to France. The truth was irrelevant alongside such considerations of State.

Poor truth.

So Jeanne withdrew – un-married, unmourned – to the Duchy of Berri and founded the Convent of the Annonciade at Bourges where she devoted herself to the sick and the poor. She endowed churches and colleges and hospitals; she composed a rosary of ten Aves in honour of the Blessed Virgin, and she did penance for her great weight of sin. Poor sinner.

When Vérité de Gloriole knocked at the door of the Annonciade, she already held the perfect attitude of mind to fit her for its rule. For she too was racked with guilt. Only a lifetime of self-denial would compensate for the grief she had caused to her Saviour and to others.

Had she not placed a greater value on the physical than the spiritual; on treasures of this world rather than the next? Had she not used her temporal power to force a man to gratify her gross lusts? Had she not broken an oath sworn on the Bible? Had she not ridden rough-shod over an innocent life? Had she not prostituted a sweet novitiate girl powerless to defend her virtue, and brought about that girl's murder? And had all the events of her life not brought her full circle to confront this one truth: that she had been promised to God from the outset, as a Daughter of Joy, and had flouted a life of penitence in vainglorious pursuit of worldly things? Now that disobedience was behind her. All she craved was the means to make amends for her wickedness.

So she put on the grey gown of penance, the white cloak of purity and the red scapula of Christ's blood. And in place of the keys of Gloriole hanging in the folds of her skirt, all that swung there was a rosary and breviary. She confined herself to a freezing kennel of a cell, watching the lichen weave its fronded green brocade across the damp bricks. She mortified her flesh with hessian, and she fasted.

But whenever hunger griped at her in chapel, she found her thoughts wandering to those few weeks she had spent in the forest lodge. She had found that the soft life of privilege had rendered her so helpless that she could not so much as rekindle a dead fire, cook a piece of dried meat, earn herself a living once the furniture was sold. If Victoire had not taught me how to fish, she found herself thinking, I should have starved to death. And then the savour of those fishes came back to her – how good they had tasted, how redolent with happy memories . . . The liturgy of the Mass flowed round her like a draught; she realized she had not been listening. So she begged the saintly Jeanne to teach her how to empty her mind of things past.

The oracular, wizened little *mère ancille* told her news of a terrible defeat the French had suffered at Gonsalvo on the banks of the Gavigliano in the holy Italian Wars. She herself was still engaged in praying for the soul of the late Pope Alexander, she said. Vérité might busy herself praying for the souls of the French soldiers who had been all but exterminated. It would occupy her mind and make real to her the brevity and fatuity of life.

The remedy worked. She prayed, and the praying reminded her that life is nothing but a vale of tears. But as she industriously prayed for each man in turn, turning over each anonymous soldier-corpse in her imagination to lie chest-up in the Italian sunshine, each one seemed to have the same face. Cyr's face. And then she would commend his soul to Heaven with a fervour that was neither unselfish nor holy.

And then at night she dreamt of Gloriole: sweet dreams of her childhood – of a magician who could conjure doves from his codpiece and a juggler who could hold fire to his breast and not burn. She dreamt of particular dresses, of specific days dazzling with the golden dapple of lit water alongside white stone; of white ceilings and gilded mouldings. She dreamt that her father was standing at the door of her cell, shaking the bars with gauntleted fists and begging her to come away.

So she begged the saintly Jeanne to teach her how to empty herself of sinful Beauty and the indulgence of sleep. Sharing the confidence as other women confide a trick of cosmetics or a titbit of gossip, Jeanne pressed her little body against Vérité in a sisterly embrace, allowing her to discover by touch her treasured secret of sanctity. Vérité was deeply grateful. She too acquired a length of heavy chain and, shackling one ankle, wound it around leg and belly, ribs and shoulders in a tight diagonal spiral. Though it did not impede her work much during the day, it served to make nights a sleepless torment of exquisite pain. The white island of Gloriole no longer had the opportunity to rise out of the sea of night.

Very occasionally, during a momentary lapse into sleep, her father would still rattle at the bars of her cell, calling her, calling her to come away and to be Chatelaine of Gloriole But the gates were chained shut against him and he could not kidnap her soul this time out of the realms of grace.

351

THIRTY-ONE

The Free-Thinker

Perhaps it was Vérité's prayers or perhaps it was the Devil whom Cyr de Puy had to thank for his life. But he was not among the dead at Gonsalvo. His days of campaigning were over. In his estimation, his responsibilities as Guardian of Gloriole could not spare him for the King's service. He sent a muster of Sablois men; he sold Sablois flintlocks to the Royal Army, but he paid scutage and stayed home with his wife and son and enjoyed the fruits of success.

Within weeks, the reign of the Chatelaine was forgotten. For a time the name of Vérité de Gloriole was handled in every market-place and great-hall in the Touraine. A very virtuous lady to be sure. A deeply devout and Christian lady to exchange Gloriole for a life of holy devotion. And yet some said she should not have left her babe alone, nor entrusted her chateau to a hired man, *whatever* she had promised God in the rashness of childbirth. Some said she should have stayed to see the boy weaned; some said her sacrifice would guarantee an era of unprecedented prosperity; some looked forward to the child of such prayerfulness holding sway over the Sablois. In fact, with so much handling, Vérité's name wore thin, threadbare; all texture and character were lost. Vérité de Gloriole (who had, after all, closed her doors on the outside world a long year beforehand, at the start of her confinement) was hard to recall as a person. She was simply an insubstantial genealogical fact, a one-time portrait among countless others, a pallid plaster bust on a plinth.

Cyr de Puy quickly removed all trace of his mistress: every bust and portrait, every purchase she had made without first asking his advice. There was not much: she had come to trust implicitly in his good taste and in his plans for the chateau.

As soon as they heard of the Chatelaine's departure, Estienne and Yolande de Puy hurried round to call on their brother, striving and struggling to make sense of the rumours. Naturally they did not believe the official version of events, but were not much troubled to guess at what had really happened. Sufficient that Cyr de Puy had, by fair means or foul, taken hold of the keys of Gloriole and had a legal paper to prove it.

They were received by Cyr in the great-hall, he and his mouselike wife, Marie, perched on new chairs-of-audience whose backs rose almost to the ceiling in lattices of gilded oak.

'So! You've won Gloriole for us at last, little brother!' exclaimed Estienne, throwing one thigh across the corner of the table with a homely familiarity.

His wife settled herself amid a rick of satin skirts which she patted with enthusiastic little hands. It was she who had persuaded Estienne to come. Her grey hair was attenuated into a horse's tail of borrowed red. '*Dear* Cyr,' she said, as if overtaken by a surplus of fond affection. 'Shall you change the name? Shall you retitle the estates? Oh, how happy you must have made our ancestors in Heaven – to think how the de Puys have risen!'

Cyr counterfeited surprise. 'How? How have they risen? *Dear* Yolande, I don't doubt that if they're dancing in Heaven it's with rage – at seeing the runt of the litter thrive. No, I shan't change the name. Gloriole's what I wanted from the first. Gloriole's what I set my mind to. Gloriole's what I boarded and took. Why would I retitle it with one less auspicious?'

'Well, so, what's a name, ha ha!' Estienne wiped his sweating palms down his plump thighs. 'You'll surely combine the estates? Conjoin the families? While you've got the legal muscle to do it?'

Cyr drew his heels up on to the rim of the chair-seat and clasped his knees. 'Ah! I didn't realize. You're here to sell me your land, farmer de Puy. Well, you'd better recommend the idea to me. I don't see it myself. Why should I buy it? Where's the commercial sense in it? Why tie a wood barge behind a galleon? You'll own it's not the best land in the Sablois, that mire of a croft. Now if you had knapping flint on it . . . or quarrying stone . . .'

'Blood, man, what are you at?' Estienne abandoned any show of comprehension. 'Here you are – you've got your feet under the table at last in a home that should've been the de Puys' by right fifty years back . . . I don't know how you did it, but you've done your duty by the family. Now how are we going to take a firm grip on the place? That child's not got your name, you know? You've got controlling hand now, but when it comes of age it could wipe you off its backside like so much shit . . . your pardon, madam . . . Yolande and I have children, you know? There are other de Puys to be considered. The future! Consolidate, man! Consolidate our advantage!'

Cyr, too, abandoned politeness and got up out of the chair. His wife keeled visibly away from the unpleasantness to come. '*Our* advantage? Whose advantage is that? Yours and your fat wife's? Your mongrel bastards 'got hither and yon? Listen here, you pig-truffler! Here's news for you. The Prodigal Son's made good on his travels. He's got no call to come home grizzling. I got Gloriole for myself! I climbed up to get it and to get out from under the boots of Father and Grandfather and their little blue-eyed boudoir puppy. "Older brother!" "First son!" First pukeling! If I'd been drowning you'd've pissed on me, the pack of you. Devil tup you and your brats. If I do nothing else with this *advantage* of mine, I'll fix it fast on paper that no de Puy farmers ever stick their pitchforks into Gloriole. I took it for myself, and I'll keep you off it even if you breed faster than rats in a drain! Better learn to farm, Estienne. I hear you're nigh beggared for want of agricultural wit. I'll have your land yet for a pan of acorns, and scratch out "De Puy" and write "Gloriole" on it.'

He was by this time holding Estienne by his protuberant ears and banging his head backwards against the wall, having hounded him into an alcove. Yolande stood behind Cyr, slapping at his shoulders and swearing shrilly, calling on God's angels to damn him. He turned and put the flat of his hand into her face and pushed her on to her bottom amid a welter of taffeta and silk. She floundered for a while, then turned her abuse on her husband for not helping her up. They left the room as shaky on their legs and as raucously incoherent as two drunkards turned out of an inn, and quarrelled all the way home. The theme was not new. They had been quarrelling at regular intervals for twenty years about Estienne's failure to seduce the Chatelaine while he had the chance.

In the great-hall, the baby Rémy began to cry and Marie, gazing down at it in horrified bewilderment, plucked the cover a little higher, in the hope of lessening the noise. Cyr de Puy went back to the table where he was drawing up architectural plans.

But Cyr de Puy was not base lead, dull to the powerful magnetic pull of heredity. The large, sluggish, pallid baby who had given him control over Gloriole in turn controlled Cyr's thoughts and actions.

It spurred him on to work with the manic intensity of a soldier-ant to swell the gross white chrysalid at the centre of his nest. His son. His posterity. His lasting hold on the material world. Having no title did not trouble him. But his son must have one. His Rémy must want for nothing, must suffer no obstruction to his prospects, must look out of his eyes at nothing squalid or second-rate. Cyr was, in that respect, a true Gloriole by birth; the motto *Rien Meilleur* was etched with acid on his soul.

The Best was not to be had in France. The Best, it was clearly understood, came from across the Alps. The Court decked itself out in more and more Italian plumes, and deeper and deeper grooves were worn through the Alpine passes by the fetching and summoning of Italian genius.

Jerome de Fiesole came to carve statues, Andrea del Sarto to paint pictures and Pacello to lay out gardens *à l'Italienne*. Il Baccatore came to turn the royal chateau at Blois into a little piece of Italy. And of course Il Diavolo came to build his staircases and towers and chimneys, like a vast force of lava driving its way upwards through the cores of a dozen paltry mountains so as to render them blazing volcanoes. People had called him 'Diavolo' ever since his excommunication, although it was said he suggested the name himself, delighting in his reputation as a blasphemer and dissident. Il Diavolo was a free-thinker – that's to say a heretic. The things he said had left the whores crossing themselves on the banks of his native Arno and sent the old women running, for fear they be clipped by the ensuing thunderbolt. If it were not for his talent, he would have been burned, or sunk in gaol years before.

He was a big man, built like a miller, with rolls of fat over his scapulas which pushed his shoulders forward into a belligerent hunch. His hair was a bright, incendiary red, bound up into a plume above his head – a burning bush of a head which never stopped talking. The big face, shield-round, boasted an ugly boss of a nose and a hooked underjaw like a salmon in breeding fettle. As he told Cyr, recommending the idea, he had had all his teeth removed in his twenties to thwart the barber-surgeons. His hands were never clean of ink, and since he sketched only in red, gave him the appearance of having come fresh from a job of murder. He had a reputation for profligacy and dissolution. And yet his patrons picked up the bills in his wake like grooms following after a carriage with bucket and trowel. For to secure the services of Il Diavolo was to be the envy of the world, even if it did feel like stabling the Minotaur.

355

'I'll build you a Tower of Babel!' he said, biting the heads one by one off a score of spring onions from the gardens of Gloriole. 'This trash here can go and I'll raise you up a piece of something worthwhile. You cattle French, with your long barns! I'll add you on a storey. One chamber – not carved up into loose-boxes like the rest of the place. The kind of room you'd ask for if you had the wit. And give you a roofline worthy of a second look. You French – you think a few mansard tiles and a ridge-crest and you've built a palace.' He jabbed at the side of Cyr's head with a stubby finger and left a red stain on the temple, like a bullet-hole. 'A Babel of a staircase, that's what!'

'Just as long as it doesn't suffer the same fate as Babel,' said Cyr, trying manfully to appear casual.

Diavolo shook his head. 'If I'd been hired to build Babel, there'd be a brick or two up God's left nostril, I can tell you.' Knowing that his reputation travelled ahead of him, gross and exaggerated, he felt the need to fulfil his patrons' expectations, growing a little larger than life with every new commission.

Cyr was still astounded even to find the celebrated architect sitting in his great-hall talking in terms of undertaking any task at all, leave alone a new storey. Marie, buried beneath a sprawl of boy, tried unsuccessfully to catch Cyr's eye and query the cost of such a project. They were speaking Italian, which she did not understand, but she flinched from the tenor of Il Diavolo's voice. She wished she had hung drapes over all her sacred objects. She also wished she knew what such a prestigious heathen would charge for his services.

'Show me! Show!' said Il Diavolo, dragging himself to his feet. 'Show me what I must contend with.'

They progressed through the house. The indolent Rémy, once roused, was fascinated by this crude foreigner. When Il Diavolo entered the nuns' chapel without genuflecting, Rémy did so too. When Il Diavolo broke wind in the nave, Rémy strained to do so too. And when Il Diavolo heaved his rump up on to the high altar and sat flapping his heels against the altar cloth, Rémy demanded to be lifted up there too, though Marie sincerely pleaded with him not to do so dreadful a thing. The child's eyes glittered with defiant daring. His father too was enthralled to find there were such people in the world. The revulsion amounted almost to admiration.

'I can base it here,' said Il Diavolo of his projected staircase. 'You've a surplus of chapels already.'

Cyr explained about the nuns and the Order of the Little Sisters of Pity. The Italian was intrigued and insisted on seeing the convent in the loft, filling the chapel with a long, loud, spontaneous laugh which the child imitated.

'What does he say? What does he want? Why are we going up here?' whispered Marie, plucking urgently at her husband's sleeve as they all squeezed up the narrow spiral stairs leading directly from chapel to loft. None but the boy had ever dared to infringe the nuns' privacy by using this flight, for it issued directly into the Sisters' inner sanctum, setting them a-flutter like doves in a cote. They snatched up their sewing, their books, their music; they darted their heads through the neckholes of scapulas and smoothed out their creases; they wriggled their feet into discarded shoes and fell silent, since they had been in the middle of discussing 'the foreign gentleman'. They knew nothing of his reputation – only that he was an Italian and therefore an artist and therefore a man of sensibilities. They remembered such a man once weeping on the altar steps. All the same, they found it a little shocking to be visited via the chapel steps and to have men setting foot where no laity had trodden since the staircase was completed.

'I'm sorry, Sisters, I'm sorry,' said Marie puffing and panting after the climb. 'Signor Diavolo wished for a complete tour of the chateau . . . He's an architect, you know. He's going to build the most wonderful staircase . . . and a hall up above, and . . . oh, grand things!' But she could hardly make herself heard above the persistent, bellowing laughter of Il Diavolo and the shrill hinnying of the boy. 'Rémy! Please! There'll be tears before night. What've I told you? Stop that at once.'

The nuns smiled indulgently at the boy. Not that he was the easiest of children to cherish – he liked unkind tricks and anal jokes – but it kept their eyes from the more alarming sight of Il Diavolo.

The visitation swept through the dormitory loft, and the Little Mother hurried to open the door and let down the drawbridge on the outer landing. Its block and pulley seemed to afford the foreign gentleman even more mirth. The Guardian of Gloriole also wore a fixed, rather uneasy grin as he ushered his guest deferentially away.

'The signor is going to do wonderful things!' exclaimed the Guardian's wife, and ran across the drawbridge for fear it would give way under her. Contraptions frightened Marie.

'We'd better discuss the cost of this transformation, signor,' said

357

Cyr de Puy over dinner. But his heart was already set on hiring the man. Il Diavolo stirred the adrenalin in him, struck him with a kind of childish awe. Here was a man in thrall to no one – not even to God Almighty who nevertheless let him prosper. Cyr had no intention of following him beyond the bounds of damnation, but it was titillating to hear him lampooning the saints, pulling the wings off angels. And to employ him! That was to walk the Sablois with a dancing demon on a leash and be the envy and admiration of the Touraine.

'You have stone in plenty, don't you? And the labour? It's for you to say how much you spend painting the ceilings once they're up.' (Il Diavolo had made plain his opinion of artists, both Italian and French. They were titivators, decorators, a frippery.)

'But yourself. Your services. To design and oversee the building. They say you Italians know how to put a price on your worth these days. The King at Blois . . .'

'Bed and board.'

'I beg your pardon?'

'Bed and board merely,' said Il Diavolo with a glittering smile and exaggerated languor, pinching the dough of his bread into dirty pellets. 'My industry and genius haven't left me a poor man, Captain. These days I work where I choose – where my muse beckons, so to say.'

'Of course. Naturally. I'm honoured that Gloriole attracts you – invites your interest, I . . .'

'I have my tariffs, of course. I wonder you've not heard tell. These days I find a price fitting to the project. Something with the power to gratify me long after money would be spent.'

Somewhere deep down Il Diavolo knew he had degenerated into a fairground performer. He knew how to grip an audience. He knew that Cyr de Puy had determined to employ him – not because of his architectural genius but because of who he was, what he was; because of his reputation. And a reputation is a thing that needs maintenance if it is to hold its commercial value. Knowing such things had made the Italian sour. The price he would have asked, above all others, would have been the return of innocence, but the patron did not exist who could pay him such a fee. He arched his top lip in a supercilious sneer. 'My last venture, for instance. For the Duc d'Oise. I had the use of his wife for the duration . . .'

Cyr's carving knife grated on some bone in the joint and slipped out of his hand.

'. . . With his daughter a bonus for early completion.'

Marie blushed and squirmed under the Italian's flagrant staring, for all she did not understand what was being said.

'But in this case . . .' said Il Diavolo deliberately, looking Marie up and down, up and down. 'In this case, I think not.'

The great staircase was to comprise an octagonal tower half embedded in the outer wall. Its landings would provide balconies on every turn, on which to pause and look out across the courtyard. Its steps were so shallow, so broad, that they barely ridged the smooth, winding ascent, past the exposed rafters of the old roof, up to the vast new shell of Cyr's long-awaited gallery-room. New chimneys, too, were to rise through the house, impaling it to the sky. And over the gallery, an elongated, oval dome – a new Heaven over a new Earth. One sight of the plans shackled Cyr de Puy to Il Diavolo with admiration, and no amount of fretful doubts expressed by his wife could deflect him now from employing the architect. He accorded the man absolute power over the welfare of the chateau, and pillars were fractured like shins, and windows were shattered like ice and a silver-grey treasure of roof tiles was carried away in preparation.

No advance warning was given of the demolition of the nuns' chapel. No sooner had matins finished and the Little Sisters filed up their private staircase to the loft, than the altar window burst inwards in a rainbow shower of glass. Grapples dislodged the carved roof beams, and cold hammers beat their way from apse to sanctuary. The nuns tumbled back down towards the noise, but found the door at the base of the staircase locked against them and only a billow of stone dust under it to indicate what was happening. They ran the long, circuitous route up, along, down and round to the courtyard, and found stone-saws already flaying the chapel of its walls. They plucked at the workmen – Il Diavolo's handpicked demolition crew – but they might as well have been birds pecking at the backs of grimy cattle.

'For shame! For pity! What are you, Visigoths? Stop this at once! Stop this instant! In the name of God! Stop it, you pagan gentlemen!' But the migrant workers only shouldered them aside.

The nuns ran this way and that, bound together by fright into one scudding cloud of billowing black, searching for the Guardian. His wife would have been a better protector, but they knew she had left for Paris only the day before at her husband's suggestion.

So it was to Cyr that they ran, clamouring round his retraite with blessings and questions, questions and blessings.

'Regrets,' was all he said. 'The new design demands it. You were years without a chapel . . . there are two others . . . not such a privation, surely.' And then he moved off backwards, shaken by small, flinching spasms of anger at their ingratitude.

They returned to perch at the perimeter of the courtyard, darting in under the picks and mallets from time to time to retrieve precious items from the rubble: stations-of-the-Cross carved in white marble; a painted crucifixion; a plaster madonna. With this salvage they retreated to their loft and sat about like so many pietàs, weeping over the pieces of broken sacredness in their laps.

'We should rejoice,' said Little Mother John, reminding them of the special dictates of their order. 'We should rejoice that something beautiful is coming out of the Italian gentleman's visit.'

'Yes, but our chapel, Mother!'

'What can't be altered must be borne. La! I dare vouch there'll be a new chapel for us in the plans. In a bigger building? It's a certainty!' Her eyes settled to her lap and she stroked the wooden Christ propped across her knees, as though she were soothing a child. She was ashamed of the tears in her eyes: they would discourage the younger girls.

'If the Chatelaine were here . . .' But nobody knew how that sentence ought to end. There were nuns there to whom Vérité was simply a historical fact, an oft-recounted story: they had come too recently from the mother-house to recall the actual woman. Of course they remembered her in their prayers, as they remembered her father who had founded this their loft-convent. But the days were rare now when the Little Sisters' conversation turned to the subject of Vérité. Even those who recollected her did not quite know how to think of her. They felt they ought to understand how the Chatelaine's vocation had called her away to the contemplative life, and yet they could not fully understand how she could leave her newborn son – or, for that matter, leave her Little Sisters without a word. The Guardian, thank God, had observed the traditions of the house and kept them fed (though they feared it was only at the insistence of his wife).

'Do you suppose the Chatelaine knows this is happening, Mother?' asked Sister Edmund. 'Do you suppose she gave her consent?'

'Perhaps, perhaps. She may think our lives are too full of luxury and lovely things. I hear tell the Annonciade is a very different matter from our little convent.' But her hand travelled unconsciously to her pocket where lay the only terse, unilluminating letter yet to come out of the Annonciade in reply to her own:

> *My sins have hunted me to the door of the Convent of the*
> *Annonciade where I shall suffer them to chew on me in this*
> *world sooner than carry them into the next. I pray God spares*
> *you all to pray for my loved ones and enemies in equal part. Have*
> *a care of Cyr de Puy.*
>
>

She who was formerly
VÉRITÉ DE GLORIOLE

A strange phrase that: 'have a care'. An unnecessary injunction and one Mother John found slightly unseemly – an injunction to cherish a carnal lover. If only (Mother John mused) the Chatelaine had not stumbled into the realm of great sins. Then such great penances would never have been necessary. Life at Gloriole could have gone on in the sweetness of simplicity all the days of her . . .

The noise of demolition, the frightful scream of bowsaws through stone, drove involuntary sobs from some of the nuns and novitiates, and the sobs undermined the resolve of the rest until there was a general desolate rocking to and fro, a cradling of salvage and a wholesale, unconfessed, inexplicable terror pervading the room like stone dust.

'I believe we would be better served singing our devotions,' said Little Mother John briskly, and after a couple of false starts everyone was gathered into the reassuring fold of musical harmony.

They did not venture out again. No doubt when the Guardian was less busy he would see fit to explain where their new chapel would stand or whether he wished them to move to some new niche of the chateau. At twilight the noise died away. In accordance with routine, Little Mother John went to haul up the drawbridge and lock the convent door.

In some unaccountable way, the pulley had become unthreaded, and the rope, instead of hanging through its ferrules beside the door, was dangling over the balustrade of the landing. It was too dark to puzzle out the mysteries of block and tackle tonight, and she left the rope neatly coiled on the plank bridge, a task for the morning.

But when she came to lock the door, she found the key gone too. Little Rémy, no doubt. So very fond of practical jokes and petty vandalism and pilfering. The child should not go so completely unpunished, she found herself thinking; every wilful sin should carry its penance.

Just then there was a movement on the stairs – the slow thud of a heavy man and then the quicker, lighter steps of the Guardian speaking that pretty language of the Pope which he had picked up with such facility on campaign. They were coming, perhaps, to apologize for the disturbance or the unmannerly behaviour of the workmen.

'. . . e adesso, mio pagamento . . .' said Il Diavolo.

'You don't need me,' said Cyr de Puy with a snicker of nervous laughter.

'I'm a big fox,' said Il Diavolo in French, 'but among so many chickens? Join me! Join me, why don't you?' The gesture was expansive, Italian, magnanimous (but then Il Diavolo had assessed his host and did not expect to be taken up on the offer). Again Cyr laughed an anxious laugh strangled with nervous excitement. He continued in Italian, 'You take smaller care of your soul than I do, Diavolo.'

'Ah! But there is no soul, my excellent good friend. How often must I tell you? There are no souls. Only bodies! And the hungers of the body to be fed. No God! No "souls"! No "everlasting fires". Only these fires here. Only the fires of appetite to be quenched.' He had been drinking, and leaned heavily on Cyr as he embraced him.

'It'd best be over and done with before my wife gets back,' muttered Cyr, extricating himself.

'Oh, tonight! Tonight! Well . . . two maybe.' He grinned a grin devoid of teeth. 'But they must stay! Once they're gone, I go too! That's my wage. I must have my wage!'

Cyr nodded wearily. He had been over the ground many, many times since Il Diavolo named his price. 'You have the key, don't you?' he said by way of an answer.

Il Diavolo held up the key with a triumphant flourish. He showed it to Little Mother John who was still standing on the unsecured drawbridge.

At the sight of it, she moved backwards, fumbling for the handle of the door without looking behind her. Her eyes were on Cyr de Puy. Her pallor was the whitest glimmer on the unlit landing. 'No! By all that's holy! No, Monsieur Guardian! As God's your judge! Only a devil . . .'

He shrugged, avoiding her eyes and, as she scrambled through the door and closed it behind her, took the key unwillingly from the Italian.

'Lock it behind me,' said Il Diavolo. 'And stay close. I may need your French to make myself understood. To explain what's needed, you know? . . .'

No time for barricades. The fox went into the chicken coop quick and sure, with the farmer's consent. The squawking and the flurry of feathers and the beating of wings against the cave and the wet-mouthed noise of feeding went on till morning.

While the farmer stood by and listened.

THIRTY-TWO

Regression

Estienne de Puy did not recognize the creature in front of him as Vérité de Gloriole. As a great convex mirror gradually distorts, the silica trickling down under the burden of gravity, so the curves of her body had disappeared, her shoulders bowed, the flesh and lines of her face dropped downwards. Strange weltish lumps bulged through her clothes, and her hands were claw-like and purple with raised veins. Her mouth, whose shape had been determined originally by the exercise of smiling, had collapsed, the musculature dismantled like scaffolding.

The deterioration of her eyesight was almost visible in the lack-lustre of her eyes and the flaky red soreness of the lids and the dark, moat-deep sockets. She was listless, and fidgeted continuously, with the unpleasant bristling noise of a hedgehog and a slight clanking sound. He thought that his trip to Bourges, to the Convent of the Annonciade, had been wasted. 'Madam, you're dying,' he said in the first unguarded moment of their interview.

'No indeed, monsieur, I don't believe God will grant me that reward just yet.' Even her voice was as thin as a wire flexed to breaking point; corroded by lack of use. It disgusted and discouraged Estienne.

'I've come to tell you what your so-called Guardian's about.'

'Please don't trouble, sir. As you clearly know, I have retired from the world. I can't lend you anything more than an impartial ear. I pray daily for Captain de Puy and for my dear heir to that temporal . . . pleasantness.' Her voice was as tedious in intonation as the shuttle of a loom travelling to and fro to weave dyeless ecru.

'So it's right enough with you, is it? Everything he does? No more interest? Even though he's put that fat cow of a wife in your place?' She started to leave, pulling herself to her feet like an old woman struggling out of a low chair. He shouted in her face, 'Too worldly a crown for you, was it? Gloriole? God called

364

too loud, did He? Well maybe you could ask Him what He meant for the rest of us – next time you're on your knees, eh? Once I tell you what Cyr's done?'

She held up one obscenely tremulous claw. 'I'll tell you first what he's done. He has released me to a life of prayer and praise and penitence. I rejoice with Saint Elizabeth of Hungary who found greater riches outside her castle walls.' She hobbled towards the door and fumbled with her enfeebled grip to open it.

'Saint Elizabeth? So he did turn you out, then! I knew it! I told Yolande! "She never gave up that place of her own free will," I told her. Saint Elizabeth, eh? Pillaged of title and estates.'

'I am content,' she replied, using both hands on the handle.

Estienne slapped his head. What was the use of enlisting the help of this gutted sprat? She would not serve to catch anything half as big and vicious as a Sablois pike. But he bellowed after her, 'And d'you think your nuns are content too, eh? Your Little Sisters?'

She turned back. 'My nuns?'

Estienne hunched petulantly in his chair, almost tempted to withhold the news now that she wanted it. 'Your precious Guardian – the one you asked God's blessings on night and day – your precious Guardian has hired himself an architect and got in builders. Made *improvements.*'

'So. He finds no room for the Little Sisters. The loss is his. They can return to their mother-house. He won't find it so easy to evict God from his . . .'

'He's not evicted them. They're still there. But the improvements. Don't you want to hear? The change to the drawbridge, for instance? It lifts now from the other end.' Estienne took out his dagger and scraped an illustration in the table top. It made a repulsive grating sound. The woman's eyes seemed to have difficulty in focusing on the diagram. She did not want to be troubled with it.

'He's made them prisoners, you mean?' she said, plainly disinclined to believe him.

'*I mean he's made them callets* – put them at the disposal of his architect. Il Diavolo, he calls himself – some heathen from Italy. They say it took three nights to break every maidenhead. He instructs them now in the Italian ways.' He did not know whether to say it again: her face was such a blank of incomprehension. 'There's two have jumped from the loft window. They say there's one he throttled for trying to beat out his brains with a statue of Saint Denys. There's some'll starve to death, for sure, hoping the saints'll send someone to their rescue. I know better, though, don't I? I'll tell them, shall I? I've applied to their sainted Chatelaine, but she was too busy praying for their gaoler – for their pander. I'll leave you to contemplate it – how their nights are for them, shall I? In the Devil's lair?'

He made a half-hearted show of leaving, fully expecting her to call him back. But he was unprepared for the weird, unearthly, piercing cry that came when his back was turned – like a seagull driven inland by a storm far out at sea. When he turned round, he had to doubt whether the noise had come from her at all, for she seemed as before, perching on the edge of her stool, her hands clasped round either bony wrist. He sat down again and waited for her to speak, but he had a considerable wait in store.

'Do you know,' she said at last, rocking forward and back, 'Jeanne of France – our Superior? – she died in the winter.'

'God rest her soul,' said Estienne perfunctorily.

'The King her husband wouldn't suffer her so much as a funeral in her rightful name and title. For fear it might be read as remorse. For casting her off. For perjuring himself. For his adultery.'

Estienne held his peace. He had the impression that Vérité was engaged in some attempt to turn anger back into charitable sorrow. If she was, then the struggle was in vain. She said slowly and deliberately, 'I think there's no humanity left in the world. I think it died in the drought and the famine. I think men are bent on quenching all the brightness of women so they can do their sinning in the dark.'

'Maybe the King's sickness is a judgment, then,' said Estienne, not quite knowing what else to say. But the illness was news to her.

'The King's sick?'

'At death's edge, didn't you know? Oh, he rallied when he got to Blois from Paris, but he sank again after Easter. You didn't know?'

'So,' she said. 'So. The King's sick,' and sank into a contemplation of the fact for so long that Estienne despaired again of the interview. 'So Justice can still strut, can it?' she said at last. He pounced on his opportunity.

'You must come back, then, and take Gloriole away from Cyr! Put him out! Cancel his guardianship! You can't start a thing then hide from the upshot! Some of the blame's yours, lady, after all. You made him Caesar and it puffed him up to a tyrant. But you can undo him! You can be *God's instrument* in bringing him down!'

The silence settled again, muffling, stifling. Estienne loosened his collar.

'Cyr de Puy's your own brother, monsieur, and you want my help to undo him?'

'Ah. Well. Naturally. Yes. However much the family stands to gain *materially*, our honour cries out against such a godless villain. He's slurred our good name with his crimes.'

'I see,' said Vérité. 'You mean you've just deduced that your prospects of profiting from Gloriole are worse now than they were when I was there. You're a fool, Estienne. I could've told you as much ten years ago.' His mouth fell open and he nodded despite himself. 'Very well. Very well, then, Estienne.' The voice was changed: tempered somehow. 'Gloriole is yours on my death. I'll disinherit the child. Since he's not mine.'

'Not . . .'

'You didn't know? No? So you see I can still surprise you with a tasty piece of scandal, even in here. I'll need a coach here tomorrow: I'm too thin to ride a horse. And petition an ecclesiastic court to sit in Rocheblanche. Have it summon Cyr to answer charges . . . What's the matter? Aren't I well enough placed? I'll look the world's fool. I'll be disgraced. I'll maybe even hang for murder, but I think I cut a plausible enough figure these days, don't you? Suitably penitential?' Cynically she indicated her habit and the weary body inside it. 'For once God will take the whip hand in this world rather than the next. I'll be His scourge . . . think of it, Monsieur de Puy. It'll be a novel thing for you, won't it? To further your interests by way of Law and the Church?'

Estienne beat the tips of his fingers on the table between them as though he were playing a drum. He had heard very little of what she said after the first sentence. 'Have Gloriole?' he said incredulously. 'Inherit Gloriole?' And he grinned a grin of childlike delight, beaming up at her with genuine, affectionate adoration: God's scourge of his detested brother's back.

The noise of the whips cut from the air a breathy sigh, like a gasp of religious awe, and the congregation took up the sound. The front ranks rose from their knees, and those behind, rather than be denied a view, got up, stood on tiptoe, craned this way and that, fingering their necks, flinching their cheeks, whimpering their prayers and here and there breaking out into cries of ecstasy. It was as close a noise to cheering as most churches ever hear.

Standing round the naked man spreadeagled on the altar steps, four monks leaned fastidiously backwards to avoid the cords of the whip, leaving only one effeminately pointed sandal pinning a wrist or ankle to the floor. They wore their hoods drawn forwards and their heads turned aside, and all but one maintained the correct rhythm in his chanting despite the confusing counterpoint of the whip's lash.

Cyr de Puy, though it ran counter to his nature, gave vent to a crescendo of cries and groans which excited the congregation to a still greater pitch. The clergy of the Sablois covered their faces and wept, their copious tears illuminated by such banks of candles that they vied with beads of sweat. Soon the whole nave resounded to a cacophony of grief.

Blood, too, sprang like tears, and Marie de Puy swooned quite away rather than see the flesh jump, the muscles knot, the old burn scars blaze, the feet cramp.

The flogging ended. The sandals lifted. The same four monks held up a prudish blanket to enable Cyr de Puy to get to his feet without offending the matrons of the town. A prelate brought him a platter of water and a sponge to wash his face, as his valet enveloped him in a penitential robe of black wool lined with silk, whose cowled back left the wounds uncovered to the base of his spine. Then the Guardian of Sablois bowed to the altar, accepted the Bishop's benediction and slapped bare-footed away across the memorials of the dead in the aisle. The crowds pressing round the church door fell back to a respectful distance.

Marie hastily recovered and bustled after him. She flinched mouse-like from the great combers of sound that broke over the sunlit forecourt. 'God save the King!' 'God save the King!' A church officer moved her aside so that the marks of flagellation should be seen by as many as possible.

For his part, Cyr was aware of his wife's pattering feet behind him. He experienced, not for the first time, a kind of irritation. It seemed to him that she had changed somewhat since he installed her at the chateau. Changed, and not for the better, from the adored and ethereal figure he had been free so rarely to visit in her forest exile. He blamed Vérité of course that by the time he had obtained a fitting setting for his lifelong love, Marie had become a little – what? – commonplace, unremarkable, silly.

The good citizens of Ormes craned to see his back. Their wives vied to glimpse his nakedness. He pulled the robe close and turned in to the Bishop's residence. Someone shouted, '*God bless you, Gloriole!*' The pain abruptly diminished.

'A fine gesture! A noble sacrifice!' exclaimed the Bishop, dancing about and hampering the surgeon who was applying a flax dressing to Cyr's stripes. 'The Lord God must surely incline His ear to such an eloquent plea!'

'I did no more than follow the example of my betters,' said Cyr. 'I hear the churches of Blois and Amboise are running with the blood of men more worthy than I. But I pray you're right and that we win God's clemency for the King.'

'May he recover and thrive to hear how his subjects love him!' said the Bishop gushingly.

'May he recover and thrive,' said Cyr, conscious of having said it forty times since morning and forty-times-forty since the King's illness became known. It had become the fashionable greeting: 'May the King live.' 'May God restore him.' In Blois and Amboise, priests and noblemen had been trooping to church floggings by the dozen, offering up their pain in exchange for an improvement in the King's health. In the Sablois, only Cyr de Puy had thought to follow suit. The novelty had made him quite a celebrity among the clergy and petty gentry and general peasantry. In fact his prestige had soared.

'I'm so very sorry that you should be troubled with this *other matter,*' said the Bishop because he felt he could not avoid all mention of the forthcoming court case. Then he left Cyr to recover and rest on the couch, in the company of his tearful, over-excited wife.

'Oh Cyr! Oh my dear Cyr! What a wonderful thing!' Marie sobbed, drying her eyes on his shirt as though it were Saint Veronica's veil. 'What a wonderful, terrible thing!'

He turned his face in towards the couch's faded upholstery and groaned. 'If I could get hold of that whip-man I'd cut off his hands. Two livres I slipped the bastard to pull his strokes.'

The journey home of Vérité and Estienne was also touched by the King's illness. The uncertain political situation brought about by Louis' possible death had led to some wild precautions. Anne of Brittany had loaded her silver plate and furniture into three ships to effect a speedy departure should her husband's successor choose not to honour the clause in her marriage contract entitling her to it. Several thousand guards had been posted along the banks of the Loire. The countryside was suspicious of travellers.

So there was no time for Vérité to rest before she detached herself from Estienne – 'Your envy wouldn't help my cause' – and paid her respects to the ecclesiastical court. It had convened at her request in the guild hall of Rocheblanche.

'Give your name and state what matter brings you here,' said the summoner.

Like a little duck landing on the white glare of water she was startled by a sudden confusion of sharp images. There sat three bishops on a dais. She knew none of them, though four years before they would have been of her social circle, her intimates, her servants almost. There sat Cyr de Puy in a comfortable chair beside the dais, his legs stretched out and crossed at the ankle, his wife demurely intent on sniffing a pomander. Vérité had expected the court president to explain the business of the day: she had apprised him by letter. It took her time to collect her thoughts.

'I am Vérité de Gloriole, Chatelaine of the house and estates of Gloriole-sur-Sablois, and I come here to make a declaration before God and the Law. I wish it known that the child called Rémy and named my heir is not mine but born of the union of Cyr de Puy and a woman of my household. Wishing the name of Gloriole to live on in my father's house, I adopted the child and put my name to him – I admit my sin in doing it. And I made the man de Puy guardian over the child and over the interests of my estates, thinking he was a fit man. I freely own that, in my vanity and wrong-mindedness, I wished the child to be thought mine, but I say again that he is not, and I dissolve the contract of inheritance and the guardianship of Cyr de Puy, along with his employment. I'd rather have the Sablois lost to the name of Gloriole than have the like of de Puy parade under Gloriole colours. I would like to resume my charge and office as Chatelaine, but I bow my head to such judgment as the Church sees fit.'

She expected the court to convulse into an uproar. Out of the corner of her eye she assessed her audience – row upon row of men, young and old, shabby or cheaply fashionable, silently, gauchely shifting their weight from one thigh to the other, their eyes darting between her and the dais. The news that should have burst like a shell and scattered them lay undetonated between their tapping feet. They seemed to have known it all along. Or had the world grown so naughty that her public confession lacked all power to shock? Beyond the windows, the people of Rocheblanche and the surrounding country were gathering at Estienne's instigation, to witness the ousting of Cyr de Puy.

'A moment, madam,' said one of the presiding churchmen. 'If I might clarify a thing . . . You say it was your *vanity* to be thought the mother of the child.'

'Yes, sir.'

'Surely not. You are unmarried, are you not? Most ladies would think it a shame to bring forth a child outside the fold of marriage.'

Yes, she could see how he might be confused. He did not know all the circumstances. He was a man, after all, and a childless celibate. She explained as simply and concisely as she could. 'Sometimes, for a woman, the shame is worse to be barren . . .'

'Worse than to be an adulteress?'

'Ah, but I took a vow . . .'

'More than one, I seem to think!' He applied unnecessarily to the papers in his lap. 'At the Convent of the Madeleine, and later at the Convent of the Annonciade. And yet you tell us you are come back to the Sablois to be Chatelaine. What became of your holy vows?'

'I made a vow to my father . . .' she persisted.

'Whereas the others were only to your Father in Heaven. Well. So. Continue.'

She was loath to let him simplify so complex a thing. 'You don't understand. Those who know me – know the circumstances – people in my household . . .'

'Ah yes. Your *household*,' he said returning to the papers on his knee but allowing himself to be interrupted by the bishop on his left.

'Do you come here to alter a will or to defame Captain de Puy?'

She turned her eyes on Cyr and was filled with gratitude to the saints for a sense of quiet power they replenished in her breast. They recommended that she heap coals of fire on her enemy's head. 'Only to undo what was done in folly and vanity, my lord Bishop. Captain de Puy's actions are a matter for his own conscience. They're between himself and God.'

'And yet your statement casts a great many blots over the gentleman's name. Is he not to have the right to speak in his defence? Do you wish to speak on this matter, Captain?'

'I do,' said Cyr without rising to his feet. Arrogant and churlish not to get up, thought Vérité. He would antagonize every man there. She was glad he stayed lolling in his seat. But why a tapestried arm-chair for him and no offer of a seat for her? He said, 'Though it ruin me, still I must speak, for the sake of the child, who's grown dearer to me than I could have believed.' He then recounted his version of history in such a voice as mesmerized her with the depth of its sincerity.

'Nigh twenty-five years ago, in good faith and fealty, I took the station of steward and Master-at-Arms at the chateau of Gloriole. Within a three-month she – I mean that woman there – had corrupted me to her lust. I don't tender any excuses – unless it's the threats she used to win my compliance. Against my wife here. My dear wife.' He paused as if to reflect on this Achilles' heel of his. 'Yes. She knew my weakness, for sure . . . My wife here will vouch to you the hard terms that confined her to a poor den of a place in the forest – just as I was confined to the chateau . . . But so. No excuses. I complied.' He hung his head, then seemed to remember one more extenuation. 'I confess that pity lent me the means to gratify the lady. I pitied her loneliness, I admit that. It's always seemed to me that the rich are planted round by great plantations of loneliness . . .' He allowed the thought to crystallize, then smashed it with a fist banged down on the arm of his chair. 'Still. It was put to me that I should labour like Jacob for only seven years to win back the company of my wife and a sound conscience.' Marie covered his hand with her own and he turned and made confession of his innermost heart as if to her and not to the court at all. 'The child Rémy was born to the Chatelaine. I believe I am the father. There was a witness . . . the girl called Cecille.'

'*Ay, and where's she?*' shrieked Vérité, bearing down on him like the Angel of Death in her billowing white cloak and blood-red scapula. Her face was so white that it was impossible to say where flesh ended and wimple began. 'Murdered at your command! The milk still in her breasts and turning the river white!'

'Fie, fie, madam,' he replied very softly. 'You'll surely confine your charges to ones less fantastical. I pray the court's patience in hearing the testimony of Cecille of Nantes.'

Cecille entered the hall with a rustle of habit and hood. Her black skirts were white at the knee from praying on the chalkstone floor of her Breton convent, but wholly unmuddied by the long journey – as though angels had wafted her, intacta, to Rocheblanche. She went to the dais and kissed the ring of each bishop in turn.

For four years Vérité had believed her dead; had carried her on her conscience like the rotting joint hung round the neck of a corrupt butcher. For one uncomprehending moment Vérité believed that Cyr must have conjured up the Dead. She could not speak a word.

Cecille began her testimony on a cue not from the bishops but from Cyr. She plunged directly into it, chanting it with all the spontaneity of her catechism: 'I served as waiting woman to the Chatelaine of Gloriole during the time that she was big with child, and I waited on her when she was delivered of the boy called Rémy. All that time we lived secret, she and me, in one part of the place. She thought it a shame to be seen the way she was: said if the child were born marked or maimed ('cos of the way it was begot) I should say it were mine. It was born fair enough, so I was let go. I was sent down to Nantes, when I wouldn't go to work in the loft, and it's been pleasanter to live poor, I can tell you, than ever it was among all those velvets and satins. As to the father, I couldn't say. There were so many.'

Vérité, turning and turned about like a grey rat in a field of flails, ran to the court's lectern and pulled down the Bible whose pages lay open to irradiate justice. It was too heavy for her emaciated arms. She half dropped, half threw it against Cecille who was obliged to save it from falling to the floor and crouched with it caught in the lap of her habit. Vérité pressed the plain face down into its gully of pages and screamed, 'Swear! Swear by Saint Pancras who sends madness on oath-breakers! Swear on your soul that the child's not yours!'

Cecille looked up at her out of that round, bovine face, its small nose hooked like a beckoning finger, and said with all the gentleness of good nature and with her hands spread on the Bible, 'The child is yours. I swear it. Before all these good people.'

Vérité snatched away the Bible. The creaking and cracking of its precious spine held the attention of every spectator, as though a thing of finest glass were being tossed from hand to hand. She lugged it towards Cyr yelling, 'He told me he'd killed her. He told me he'd kill me! He drove me out of my own possession! He won't deny it! I know him. He's more superstitious than a drowning sailor! He won't perjure away his soul!' Cyr's hands found hers under the great burden of the Bible, and for a second they shared the weight between them. She watched his face for her moment of triumph.

Sure enough, he cast about him for assistance. His face asked to be spared. It was desolate, anguished, piteous. She gloried in it. She and her saints had him outnumbered. Then he turned his eyes on her.

'I see you will put me to it,' he said. 'You have read me rightly, Chatelaine. I'll not swear away my soul – though I wonder to hear you call that superstition. I'd rather call it honest fear of God.' He took the Bible into his lap. Still he was sitting down. Still the indolent villain would not rise to his feet even to confront the Truth. He only raised his voice so that everyone present should hear his confession: 'I admit that I did oust this lady from her rightful place. I own I did it by trickery and threats. She unwittingly put in my hands the means to wrest the house and lands of Gloriole out of her grip, and I no sooner had the power than I drove her out. What manner of man does that? Fealty aside, what manner of man parts a newborn child from its mother?'

'Wait . . . That's not . . .' Just for a moment, just for the second in which weariness, hysteria and obsession met in Vérité, she lost sight of certainty.

Had the child been hers? She remembered wearing the gowns. She remembered the pains. She remembered three days in a room with something silent in her arms. She remembered . . .

'I'll tell you, sirs, what manner of man would do it,' Cyr went on. 'A man sick of self-disgust. A man who couldn't any longer stop his nose against the stench of corruption. A man made foolish by affection for a child, whether his own or not.'

' "Yours or not?" '

The president of the court pounced, as though on an error tricked from a heretic. 'You say then that the child was fathered by this gentleman?' She had no patience to answer him, but dismissed his stupidity with an exasperated wave of the hand. She could not detach her eyes or attention from the horror of Cyr de Puy's mouth chewing her Past into a different, grotesque shape.

'So, out of the love I bore the child and the respect I bore its grandsire, I drove this scarlet out of her bawdy-house, hoping to save the name of . . .'

'Hoping to own Gloriole!' she broke in, ranging up and down in front of the dais. 'Thinking to spend its wealth on his vanities! Meaning to deliver my Little Sisters to a rape! Ask my Little Sisters! Send for the nuns of Pity! Send for them, won't you? He has them prisoners at Gloriole! Send and see!'

But in place of outrage, a ripple of laughter was all that moved the court. She saw the comedy climb from shoulder to shoulder like a monkey – a smirk here, a giggle there, a bobbing Adam's apple. The presiding bishop helped her to understand. 'Your whores, madam, are all removed to the convent of La Madeleine where, with God's help, they may repent of their sin and the slur they have made on their calling. Their order is broken up. Let the next witness be called.'

And then the men rose, one by one – this courtful of strangers, this impartial audience she had thought to horrify with her revelations. And one by one they testified – some in a garbled monotone, some with the grandeur of oratory, some afflicted with nervous smiles so that they dragged at their beards as they spoke.

'I testify that on or about Martinmas in the year 1498 I did lie with the Chatelaine of Gloriole within the bounds of the castle, according to her commands and wishes . . .'

'I testify that in the year 1499 I did often lie with and enter in upon the Chatelaine of Gloriole in place of paying feu . . .'

'I testify and confess that on many occasions with the drink on me I did use and pleasure women of the Gloriole brothel, and on one time, around Whitsuntide, did likewise with the Chatelaine.'

They trooped up to bear witness to abominations beyond her imagining – to Roman excesses, to pagan luxuries, to biblical Babylons of sin.

'I testify that on every night between April and June of 1501 I did attend the Chatelaine of Gloriole in her bedchamber, though I couldn't always . . . well, you know . . . do as I was bid.'

Comedians. Penitents and whiners. Braggarts and whisperers. And their wives.

'I testify that my husband (who's dead now an' it please your honours to pity me) was sick of the clap in the first of the century's new years, and when I put it home to him where he should take such a thing he said he had it from the stews of Gloriole – from the women who dressed like nuns.'

They all pulled together, sharing the same community of purpose with which she had seen them haul up a heifer by its heels and cut its throat for an ox-roast. None looked at Vérité as they gave their evidence. Many let their eyes trail over the Guardian, reminding him of the bribe now due, the money he had promised. And yet with every new, implausible testimony, the bishops settled deeper into titillated outrage. With smug opprobrium they wrapped their hands across their bellies, and their eyes burned bright with the coals of damnation they saw in store for Vérité.

'*Look at me!*' she howled, reduced to the distracted pacing of a caged wolf. '*For Jesu's sake! Look at me! What do you see? What kind*

375

of Jezebel?' When she stretched out her fleshless wrists and twiggy hands in self-defence, she had the look of one of the espaliered trees crucified against the sunny walls of Gloriole. Faces staring in at the window – faces not party to the trial – crossed themselves and whitened their cheeks against the glass, straining to listen.

Cyr de Puy got to his feet at last. An officer of the court hurried to help him – lent him the support of an arm. He stooped under the burden of his injuries and his voice implied a pain bravely borne. 'One may gild over rotten wood, Chatelaine, but time will lay it bare again.'

That was when the chains – the other chains which had bound Vérité long before she ever entered the Annonciade – burst and fell away. Her heat of hatred for Cyr de Puy unforged them. The absence of God at the witness bench – His resolute refusal to appear – freed her too, after a lifetime lived in terror of His wrath.

Suddenly, standing surrounded by Cyr's jeering and fleering hirelings, she was that child again, barracked in the courtyard of La Madeleine, shaven-headed and wrapped in sackcloth against her will, against her nature. Her nature called to her from beyond the bars, from the wolf-grey forests of the Sablois, from the snow-besieged caves. The tamed animal was reverting to the wild. Though she stood still to hear the deliberations of the court, her soul was, in truth, pelting down the tiled passageway of the Madeleine, climbing the iron-barred gate, tumbling into the grip of a dark anarchy. Escaping. Regressing. Reverting to the wild.

'Captain de Puy,' said the presiding bishop. 'You are like Michael whom God set at the gates of Eden with a blazing sword. You did well to drive out this Eve before she could bring about still more harm. I confirm you in guardianship of the child. More. I am glad to say that I'm not alone in noting your merits. As you've no doubt heard, the gracious Father of the People, King Louis, has – praise God – been restored to health by the prayers and intercessions of his subjects. Hearing how you, Captain, took upon yourself the pain of holy affliction for his sake, and being informed of the proceedings in hand, His Majesty has seen fit to vest in you the title Seigneur Chatelain de Gloriole, to bequeath as you see fit.'

'God bless and save the King,' said Cyr de Puy with a complacency that showed he had known the news since morning.

'Is the King living then?' said Vérité, not knowing she had said it aloud. 'So God goes on sleeping. Till Judgment Day.' She looked at her lover and smiled. ' "The pain of holy affliction", Cyr? My,

my. I dare swear you have a little more of that in store one day.'
The words were full of Hell.

'Woman,' said the bishop. 'You have made your father's house a brothel, and the house of your soul a sty. I might have you whipped at the cart's tail for your depravity, if it weren't that the King in thanksgiving for his miraculous recovery has issued a general pardon.'

'God save the King,' said Vérité with a wry insolence.

'I free you therefore to a life of shame and penitence, and recommend that no man solace nor shelter you against hunger or the elements if he values the health of his soul. Nor shall the comfort of Holy Communion be yours within the realm of France.'

Vérité de Gloriole inclined her head a little, in the most mild and gracious acknowledgment, and looked him in the eye. Though he had been readily convinced by Cyr de Puy's version of events, and all too glad to see a female bastard ousted from such a powerful social position, it was borne in on him for one short moment, by that one steady glare, that the *sang de noblesse* flowed in those purple, distended veins.

By the time Vérité left the court, its evidence and conclusions had spread to the crowd outside. They too had escaped bondage after a fashion. An hour before they had belonged body-and-soul to her, by right of fiefdom. Although the ownership had passed intact to Cyr de Puy, they revelled in an illusory sense of freedom. After all, they were free to spit on their Chatelaine, imagine it! Free to cock their fingers, fists and forearms; free to shout into her face and into the nape of her neck, 'Whore!' 'Strumpet!' 'Bawd!'

She looked for her transport, and for Estienne de Puy. But the wagon by which she had come lay on its side now, wheels spinning, upholstery pulled out like viscera, and Estienne was nothing but a curled head of hair far off in the crowd, hauling his horse against the flow of traffic, failing to look back.

Soon the jeerers packed her round too close for her to go forward or turn back into the guild hall: a sparrow mobbed by starlings. She cursed the self-denial now that had wasted her in spirit and physique. She knew now that it had been a kind of treachery against Life, a betrayal of her body. But then she had come to perceive the whole universe in terms of treachery and betrayal.

With a rumbling of metal-rim wheel over the stony strewings in the street, a long black wagon rattled into the mêlée with murderous disregard for those in its way. The driver was wearing a hood, its cord pursing the black wool shut over all but eyes and nose. It seemed to Vérité that Death himself had come reaping. She held her ground with a kind of heady elation. The wagon's cover, stretched over its hoops of iron, panted like bellows, funnelling the wind, and within the bellows naked white figures swayed and teetered, clutching their hands to their breasts, reeling and rigored with cold. The driver put down a hand and summoned her into the cart. 'Get up, Chatelaine. Get up.' And she clambered up past the snaking whip, past the brake paddle and in to the flapping funnel of black waterproof.

A consignment of small plaster statues – nymphs and fauns, dryads and cupids – jostled each other with a hollow ringing sound as Joachim Vache drove his wagon on through the chanting, blustering, whistling, hissing, babbling rabble of a crowd. He felt the indignity sharply. Vache employed men to transport his merchandise about the countryside, and it was beneath his dignity to find himself driving one of his own delivery wagons.

THIRTY-THREE

Buffoons

'Are you the only man in the Sablois with any Christian charity?' she asked when Vache took off his hood.

'It's necessary for a man in my line of work to be a judge of character, that's all,' he replied. 'He must know the nature of his clients. I was a frequent enough caller at the chateau, wasn't I? Besides . . .' He nursed some weighty resentment between cupped hands, in among the tangle of reins. 'Besides, doesn't a man know when his own daughter's lying?'

'Daughter? Your daughter? Which was she?'

'The nun, lady. The nun they called Cecille. The mother of the child. "Mother", ha! No more than a man's duty to take sides against a daughter like that – thwart her in whatever she intends.'

'Monsieur argentier! I had no idea! I lived right close to her . . . I never knew she was . . .'

'Ingrate. Parasite,' he snarled at the swaying rumps of the horses. 'Clothed. Provided for. Put in safe-keeping. The safest. Her life to thank me for. And what does she do?'

Here is a man, thought Vérité, who honours the social order, who cannot bear to see the social pyramid torn down. His daughter has offended against his image of the ordered, feudal world.

'I'll tell you what she does. Sleeps with a Gentile. Eh? Does what? Sleeps with a Gentile! Ei, what kind of a daughter is that, tell me? What kind of a daughter? Sleeps with a Gentile.' And he spat on the rump of the nearest horse.

Vérité struggled unsuccessfully to piece together the picture. 'Cecille is a . . . Jewess, monsieur?' she asked as daintily as possible, given that it constituted such a term of abuse.

He wagged his head from side to side, nauseous with disgust. 'Oh no! Oh no! Better provided for than that! Was there any advantage I didn't give her? When you'd a mind to kill the Jews, didn't I save her hide? Didn't I Christianize her? The whole family? Safe in the

379

fold? Didn't I make her as Christian a girl as ever put on black? And how does she thank me? Sleeps with a Gentile, the slut.'

Vérité drew back into the shelter of the cart and left the merchant to be pelted by both rain and gall. Not for her to query his logic. Not for her to speak in defence of Cecille of all people. She would shield behind his righteous indignation and hope that his curse – whether Christian or Jewish – might prove potent. It was not till he was helping her down from the wagon that she ventured to say, 'I owe you my apologies, monsieur. I've treated your people to barbarities when there were enemies nearer home who merited it more.'

He shrugged. 'My people? You stopped short of a burning, didn't you? And besides, they're not *my* people. I'm a Christian now, thank God. Thank God. There's a new pogrom coming, you know? That Bretonne, she's vowed one in thanksgiving for the King's recovery. She's so grateful, she says. A race could die of so much gratitude . . . But that's nothing to do with us Christian folk.' And with a gesture so Jewish that she wondered she could ever have mistaken Joachim for a Christian, he ushered her into a house bulging with holy artefacts. A synagogue of saints, an ark of the covenant stashed with icons and crucifixes, a shabbat of Christian lip-service: the Christian house defiled by a daughter who had slept with a Gentile.

And there she stayed, discreetly immured, until the flesh came back to her bones, her cropped hair grew down grey and the process of metamorphosis was complete. A handsome woman emerged from it, but one not readily associated with the dark, agile, ingenuous girl who had ruled over Gloriole.

She kept house for Vache, widower as he was, and all the recompense he asked of her for the shelter of his roof was that she should eat at a separate table, with different utensils, and abstain from conversation on Saturdays. All that hung now in the front folds of her skirt was the crude innovation of a tinderbox to light the fires. She lit the fires, but the house would never be warm. It gratified her a little that the box contained shards of Sablois flint.

Cyr de Puy made efforts to discover what had become of her. He guessed that she had fled France if only to find Holy Communion, but he could get no proof of it. He asked, for instance, his argentier Joachim Vache to make enquiries as he went about his trade. But the old merchant could discover nothing. In place of news, he brought to Gloriole samples of South American hardwood, and melon plants, news of the garden being planted out at Villandry, and an Arab pony for the boy.

The boy wore the pony's soft mouth into leather, then flogged the beast for its unresponsiveness.

Returning home from Gloriole, Vache brought Vérité news of the refurbishments, above all of the dome. He described how the new roof bellied up into a great oval – an astigmatic eyeball of a bulge staring up into the firmament, cataract white, awaiting only the artist's alchemy to make it the envy of all Touraine. Even an artist (Vache told her) had been supplied by the Fates which prospered Cyr de Gloriole.

My dear Malatesti,

If ever the spirit of ingratitude has made me dull in remembrance of you, your latest kindness would upbraid me. I ask you the whereabouts of a man, and you furnish not directions merely but the man himself from under the wing of your patronage! Nor does the fellow promise to empty my exchequer, for all his fame has grown so. For he swears his talent is not for purchase and flies where it will. And he is filled so with admiration of my architect's work that he says he would paint my ceiling were it the final week of his life!

I have lighted for my subject on the story of Aeneas' descent into the Underworld and shall furnish my Anchises with the face of the King. You see how I am become a diplomat in my advancing years . . .

Cyr de Gloriole broke off from his letter to silence the anxious twittering of his wife.

'If he wants it he must have it, woman! I've told you before, how else can he learn to have aspirations?'

Marie de Gloriole heard this often. 'Whatever Rémy wants, Rémy must have.' Sharing no blood link with the boy herself, she had an unbiased view of the damage it was doing, but would not have dreamt of questioning Cyr's philosophy of child-rearing. Everything Rémy wanted, Rémy must have. So when, at the age of nine, Rémy expressed the wish to be married, his father's proviso was only that the nuptials should wait until the ceiling of the Great Chamber was finished.

Since his elevation to the true aristocracy, Cyr had indeed grown quite agile in matters diplomatic and political. He knew full well how to set about finding a wife for his son. Queen Anne had few pastimes beside her devotions, but one was match-making among her ladies-in-waiting. She accumulated young women around her, squirrelling them in from every good family in Europe, as her previous husband, Charles VIII, had once collected cheeses. And if there was one thing she liked better than the company of this seemly, virginal retinue it was to arrange marriages for her virgins. A romantic foible, she pursued it wherever she went. The Pope even gifted her a portable altar so that she could solemnize marriages in an emergency, at a moment's notice – like the pyx carried into battle so that men need not die unshriven. Emergencies did not present themselves quite as often perhaps as she would have liked. So when the Comte de Gloriole wrote entreating her to find his son a fit wife, perfect in Christian virtues, and to solemnize the marriage herself, she proved marvellously obliging. What though the boy was . . . immature? What though his marriage could hardly constitute an emergency? What though the father lacked blue blood in his veins? Rumour whispered that he agreed with her about the infallibility of the Pope and that was more than the King himself did. So despite the fact that she could scarcely spare the time from catechizing the King in his duties, Anne of Britanny agreed to honour Gloriole-sur-Sablois with her presence and with a protégée of the royal Court.

'But will it be finished?' he called up, and his voice scrambled ape-like through the trellis of wooden scaffolding, up into the invisible dome.

'It will be perfect! My finest work!' came back the answer, sliding down shrouds and dust-sheets made rigid with multi-coloured splashes of paint.

Cyr shifted his feet uneasily, plucking them out of the mire of paint coating the floor. 'I don't fear for its perfection, maestro, simply its readiness.'

'It will be perfect!' came the reply, and Cyr gnawed on his lip. His eye scanned the scaffolding, planning a route by which he might climb up to the topmost platform. It would not be impossible, despite the fact that his artist hauled up each of five ladders as he ascended in the morning. It would not be impossible to reach the top. To view the dome. It was tantalizing past all tolerance.

He could judge where the figure of Aeneas must be standing

within the oval, because he would be holding the golden bough of mistletoe which was the light source for the entire ceiling. It drove back illusory shadows to the very cornice, the rays splaying out through a leafy dapple to where the words of Homer were picked out in gold above the end chimney-pieces:

> Roman, remember that this is to be thy skill . . .
> to wage war until the haughty are brought low.

But the central encounter between Aeneas and Anchises was still obscured by the scaffolding. It was tantalizing past all patience.

Anticipation of seeing the finished whole filled the Comte Cyr with an excitement almost too sensuous to contain. The choice of subject had been his – a soldier's choice, but a politician's too, as he had explained to Malatesti. Aeneas descended into the Underworld to hear the ineffable wisdom of his dead father. He himself would be represented in the heroic figure of Aeneas and the all-wise Anchises would have King Louis' face. It was a *coup de diplome*. Anchises' vision of the triumphant future in store furnished the excuse for various scenes of military triumph from the history of France. The concept had seemed grand inside his head, incubated out of the ovals and parallelograms scribbled incessantly on sheet after sheet of paper. But the realization surpassed all his best hopes. The painted ceiling was as insubstantial as a thunder cloud, its flat plain conjured into three dimensions, its angular edges invisible, its figures borne on pallets of light and dressed in the tissue of rainbows. The painting was tangible music. Nothing in all Touraine had ever been touched by such genius.

Cyr set his foot into the cross-struts and tried whether his weight would pull loose any of the planks.

'*Sir!* Do I make a demanding on your hospitality? Do I offend the rules of your house? Respect please my wishes only. Let the whole be finish before the part is seen. Every day I beg you this!'

The reproach rattled down along with an empty bowl of paint that spun a noisy circle of scarlet on the filthy floor. Cyr backed away from the scaffolding. He was nervous to the point of panic at the possibility of giving offence and perhaps endangering the miracle of completion. Even with the pressing deadline of the wedding, the man must not be chivvied. He must be cajoled and humoured. He was irreplaceable. Cyr might comb France for a year and not find a talent comparable. This foolish little Italian with nothing much to say for himself but Aves and Caves, had to be handled like Venetian glass. He was of the aristocracy of genius, his time past purchase, his status only a little lower than the angels. He was fashion's ultimate prize. To have acquired his services at all was a miracle not to be questioned or queried.

But to see the figure of Aeneas! To see the Golden Bough held aloft blazing its false daylight at the heart of the painting!

'When? When can I see it?' he called.

'When is marriage?'

'A ten-days. And the room's to be made fit. When?'

'Will be ready,' came the reply. 'I give my promise. I never break promise.'

There was nothing to be gained from hounding the fellow. Peeling his boot soles off the puddling paint, Cyr gave the room one last, longing look and left it, closing the doors reverentially behind him.

But with each passing day, his wife fretted more and more balefully. She had too little time to prepare, she said. She was dogged by ill fortune. Disaster and shame were bearing down on her and nothing would avert them. There was a conspiracy to make her look foolish. For example, the parrots had colonized the gutters over the berm and used passers-by below for retaliatory target-practice. Cyr sent crossbowmen to dispatch them, but the parrots' aim was truer than the archers' and the men returned brushing their hair and shoulders and missing several dozen arrows. The only *papegault* to die fell into a downpipe and decomposed slowly and pungently. The rest dispersed about the inner courtyard and sat like malevolent red goblins on the stanchions and pediments, tapping at their reflections in the stained glass.

Then there was the horoscope that Marie had an astrologer cast for the day of the marriage: the fool rolled it too soon and wet ink smudged some of the happy conjunctions of stars. As for Rémy, the child bridegroom rattled and kicked at the locked door of the Great Chamber, insisting that his day would be marred 'by stupid foreigners who couldn't work faster than spiders'.

The merchant Vache kept them waiting until the very last moment for a buffoon, but then redeemed himself by delivering two – a married couple, and both grotesque to a degree. Their humour, he said, was in their discord, for they maintained a pitched battle of quite ferocious violence, barging each other downstairs and hurling food at mealtimes. For all they were the fashionable necessity of any grand home, the Comtesse Marie found them faintly distasteful. The boy relished them well enough. He asked if he might have a whip to train them (but then he had always had difficulty distinguishing between household and livestock). The buffoons went by the names of Balon and Batonne, and their deformities held so much in common – the hare lip, the elongated earlobes, the glaucous eye, the bubble nose – that Cyr suspected they were brother and sister as well as man and wife. He kept the thought to himself: Marie had reached an age where her habitual anxiousness was easily enflamed into panic. If she thought there was a biblical sin at large in the house, she would never let him rest till he put it out of doors. In fact, once an idea had taken root in her, she snagged him with the thorns of it every time he brushed past her. He would have liked to be less irritated by it, but found that all his reserves of patience had been eaten up.

'Finished or not, the carpet must go down this afternoon!' he bellowed through the locked door of the Great Chamber the day before the wedding. The door opened unexpectedly, and he found himself face to face with his artist who said, in soft, unhurried tones, 'Scaffold is downing. Floor is washing. Soon. Bring carpets and hangings. Leave all here.' Cyr went to push past him into the room to see the finished spectacle, but the Italian pulled the door to behind him. 'Signor,' he said in a sibilant, soothing whisper. 'Is room for your boy's wedding, yes?'

'That was the hope.'

'I am sentimental man, you know.'

Cyr tossed his head like a checked horse. 'You want the boy to see it first, is that it? I'll go and find him.'

'No. No. The boy – he love dwarf and dog and shooting small animal. The eye for Beauty it grows late in Man. Not till he is full-grown man. To him is nothing. Is picture on ceiling is all.' The grinding of Cyr's teeth was plainly audible. 'No. Il Duce di Malatesti he send me to you because you are lover of Beauty. Because you have the Eye. Because you have the passion for Beauty, yes? You want beautiful things and I give. But is like wedding. This is how I wish it to be always when the eye see my work. The bridegroom he makes down the bed covers. He sees his bride. Uncovering for the first time. Is moment of great consuming, yes? Never again is like this first time of making down the covers. I wish for you to share this with your boy tomorrow. He the bride seeing. You the ceiling. Finish. Perfect. My best work ever.'

'But the floor! The shrouds! The furniture's still to be set out, man!' protested Cyr thumping the door jamb with his foot. Even so, he was relenting, succumbing already to the idea.

'My boys do all. Hanging tapestry. Putting chairs . . . But not floor. You give me them please for washing floor.' He pointed at the two little buffoons yapping and yelping on the stairs.

'You. Fetch water and brushes. Scrub the floor in there and help to lay the carpets.'

Balon's face relaxed while he assimilated the command, and he assumed a look akin almost to intelligence which irked Cyr somehow more than the usual vacuity. Suddenly the look was gone, and the dwarf had seized Batonne by the scruff of the neck and was shouting in her ear, 'Bucket! Bucket, you pig's head!' They tumbled away down the stairs, as round as twin wheels of fortune bowling downhill.

'I go now to make myself good for wedding. Clothes fit for Queen. I go. I come back.' And locking the door behind him, the little Italian ducked beneath the Comte's arm and leapt down the stairs three at a time, overtaking the jesters and throwing them the key to the Great Chamber. Cyr would not put himself to the indignity of pursuing it. So long as the room was ready he could wait a few hours more to see the finished masterpiece. It was true what the maestro had said. There is titillation in unseen Beauty that can only be gratified the once and that gratification never repeated.

The artist took with him, on his expedition for wedding clothes, his entire retinue of boys and servants and his bouncing Amazonian mistress with the dark eyebrows. He had presumably some depot in the locality that housed his large wardrobe of gaudy suits – somewhere he resorted to slough off his paint-smeared gambeson and put on a plumage of brash reds and yellows. A vain, strutting little cockerel of a man, thought Cyr, who if it were not for his talent would never have gained access to Gloriole: he clashed with the decor. Cyr would certainly not have invited him to a wedding or a royal visit. He wished there was some way of dispatching the man now that his job was accomplished.

Balon and Batonne returned to the Great Chamber with bucket and brushes, and locked the doors while they worked – 'so that none might tread on their washed places while they were still wet'. The sound of their quarrelling echoed loud in the vast, empty room now that the scaffolding was down and before the hangings and carpets were restored.

The cavalcade of Italians straggled out across the causeway, against the flow of incoming deliveries, and across the park towards Rocheblanche. Once out of sight they were forgotten. The chateau was in too much uproar to wonder what became of them.

'Is done, madonna. My work is done. I must go back to Italy and quick.' Giulio Gigliamo perched forward on the merchant's couch. He was wearing parti-coloured hose and a huge brim of yellow felt. With no crown to his hat, he gave the impression of an angel who had ascended too quickly in his carolling and buckled his halo. The boisterous black curls tumbled quite as liberally over his shoulders as they had years before, though traces of paint streaked them exotically and his eyes were bloodshot from too much close work.

Around their feet sat his entourage, and curled up between his knees the buxom mistress smiled vacantly up at Vérité. Though she had spent five months at Gloriole in the company of Gigliamo, she had acquired not one word of French. Now and then he stroked her like a dog and at one point justified her place in the universe with a single declaration: 'Her armpits smell of Arcady!'

Vérité, disconcerted at first, had long since realized the constitution of the man. 'Your wife will be right glad to see you again, Giulio.'

He clasped his hands prayerfully to his throat. 'And I she, madonna! Ah, my lovely lady! My most dear treasure! I weep that you do not see her! I weep also nightly that *I* do not see her! One time always I take her everywhere. Always I must send her home so,' and he swept his hand in an enormous curve over his own sparrow's waistline. 'Seven commissions, seven babies! Seven! Good God, He rains on me the little fruits! But if you see my wife . . . what's to be done? I ask you, what's to be done? I am slave to Beauty or why am I artist?'

'Your world view doesn't change, I see, signor.' She would have liked to soften the look in her eye: she had no intention of reproaching him. And yet it seemed that in these days there was something of the Medusa in her eye; she had only to glance at the lively little Italian to still his exuberance and turn his face stony white.

'Ah, the angels are men!' he said. 'Every day I see this more and more! The angels all are men! They have no care for the sad ladies. You have not one baby! Not one little one!' His eyes filled with tears.

'Like the fig tree in the Bible, my friend. But it's as well,

isn't it? It's for the best, wouldn't you say? And I have friends.'
She reached forward and touched his sleeve, and the tears overspilled his lashes and splashed her wrist. Gigliamo's tears were a
wonderful phenomenon. She could no more understand them than
those miraculous carved madonnas whose wooden eyes were said to
stream with pity. She herself must be more wooden and less flesh
than they, for she had not wept since the trial. She could lay out
the facts of her story impassively, like a game of patience, and was
merely puzzled to see them provoke such sorrow in Gigliamo who
beat the cushions with his fists and tore holes in a kerchief with his
teeth.

'You come with me. You come back in Italy with me. I tell
Malatesti to give you house. He do everything I tell.' He pushed his
tongue wryly into his cheek and smiled. 'I am "prince of genius". *Il
Principe del Arte.*'

'Well. Perhaps. Perhaps I will,' she murmured unconvincingly.
'Perhaps I'll follow on in a day or two. When I hear word from
my informants. Monsieur Vache did well to find them, don't you
think? As I say, I'm fortunate in my friends.'

Gigliamo shook his head. 'A true friend would have lended you
sword or poison. Poison. That is way to kill rats. And what do I
do? How I serve my madonna?'

'Enough. Enough, Giulio,' she said soothingly. 'No less than
I asked and better than I hoped for. You did what was needed.'

'I think you love him still that you are so gentle!' protested the
Italian, sorting agitatedly through the thrums of his mistress's hair.
The thought seemed to strike Vérité as amusing.

'I? Gentle with Cyr? Let me tell you something, *mio amigo*.
When I was young, my father taught me the way to catch a
cock pheasant – the peasant way, you know? Do you know it?'

Gigliamo blew his nose in apology.

'You tilt an upturned basket on a stick, and up to the basket you
lay a trail of grain. And inside the basket you hang a mirror. The
cock pheasant has two vices, you see. He's greedy and he's vain. He
eats the grain right up to the basket; then he sees himself in the mirror
and in he goes. Into the basket. To admire his reflection. When he
goes to kiss the reflection . . . Are you partial to pheasant, signor?
Roasted on a skewer?'

It was so early that it was still dark when, on the day of the
wedding, Cyr de Gloriole began slapping with his leather scabbard

against the box-bed where Balon and Batonne slept. 'Where's the key? What've you done with the key? The steward says you have it still.' Twin gargoyles bleared at him over the covers.

'Key, master?'

'Key, master. To the Great Chamber, master. Do I have to thrash it out of you?'

'What's o'clock, master?' said Balon, his speech slurred with sleep.

'One minute before your undoing if you don't give me that key.'

There was much fumbling in pockets and purses. Batonne suggested, 'He's lost it! The oaf's lost it!' But Balon threw her a glance which said he did not hold life so cheap, and the key was found.

So Cyr let himself in to the Great Chamber. In the draught from the door, the hangings lifted and moved like ghosts, but the walls of the room soared too high for any candle's light to scale as far as the painted ceiling. He even stood on the table and held the candlestick high above his head. But a window left open to disperse the smell of drying paint blew out the flame. So he sat down where he was and waited for dawn to sift through the vast palisade of fanlights. He did not know what unease had brought him there: he could barely differentiate between misgiving and anticipation.

By the time Batonne and Balon had dressed and crept upstairs in his wake, there was enough light to see the Count sitting there cross-legged on the table, letting the sun's first rays fetch the sights of the room to him like servants fetching individual garments. The dwarfs stood to either side of the doorway, still and silent, round and lugged like urns, watching.

Span by yard, the room's true dimensions emerged from the darkness, the silver-white carpets visible first like porpoises glistening under the prow of a night ship. Then the chimney breast welled out of the end wall, embroiled in stucco girdle-cords and overrun with ermines in honour of Queen Anne. What though he detested the woman? She had brought forth nothing but daughters and dead sons: the country would be rid of her as soon as the King died. She had served her purpose by putting an end to the unprepossessing House of Valois. She would serve to furnish Rémy with a thoroughbred breeding mare, then the ermines could easily be exterminated from the chimney breast.

A trick of the increasing light lent shape even to things not visible. He fancied that just wide of his field of vision someone stood waiting in attendance on him: a monk or a prelate of some kind. Momentarily, it was so vivid an impression that Cyr actually spoke his chaplain's name aloud. But no one answered.

Only the exquisite painted figures of Gigliamo's imagination – the Dead of the Underworld – drifted airily round the cornices in a vortex of cloud that swept the eye round and upwards towards the artist's source of light. There, directly over his head, Aeneas stood – a stocky, grizzled, unidentifiable figure, his back turned on the room. But lit by his upraised bough of blazing gold, and filling the oval dome was not the figure of Anchises at all. It was the great dog Cerberus, guardian of the Underworld. Nor was it the monstrous bitch commonly depicted but a simple, mild distortion of a female form, her belly ripped open and her entrails (in accordance with legend) dragged out to feed her own puppies in perpetuity. There were two grotesque whelps party to the torment. One had the round-chopped, curl-nosed face of the child Rémy. The other, far larger beast, its cringing back curved for the aesthetic purpose of framing the dome, wore the pockmarked muzzle of Cyr de Gloriole, full-face, snarling down into the room with a bloody mouth. A scrolled banner arching the head of Cerberus – or rather the Chatelaine Vérité – read

Veritas filia temporis – Truth is the daughter of time.

For a long time the Comte only sat and stared. Then with a mechanical, methodical logic he scanned the remainder of the ceiling. He found his likeness in several other places – last-minute alterations by Gigliamo, he supposed. He found himself in the vignetted depiction of the Battle of Fornova, standing at the shoulder of the Duke Malatesti, his pockets and the folds of his clothing stashed with treasure. He found himself at the massacre of Gonsalvo, picking over the bodies of French dead. He found himself among the Moorish opponents of French crusaders – one white among the black, crucifying a nun with hammer and nails. And he found himself among the pantheon of gods (who presided over history from one corner of the ceiling) committing abominations with the boy-god of Love.

Cyr began to laugh. He laughed until he was sobbing with laughter, his hands drawn back inside the sleeves of his jacket, and the cuffs thudding on the table as he rocked forward and back.

THIRTY-FOUR

Reconciliation

When Queen Anne arrived later that morning and was introduced to the bridegroom, she took his fat face between her hands and crooned, as if over a cradle, 'Ah! lovely, lovely child! If only my first hadn't died or my last had lived I should have a little boy like you. Now, isn't that sad?' It did not seem to worry her in the least that she had come to prompt this jolly infant through the rites of marriage.

She also admired Balon and Batonne, and when Cyr said modestly that they had only one brain between the two she rejoined, 'That's as it should be. My husband's fools think they have wit enough to be offensive, and that's one wit too many, don't you think? Fools should be simple.'

The Great Chamber was locked. All day long the arriving guests trooped upwards, like the dead in hope of Heaven, only to find their way barred by military men and the doors bolted. 'The room was not finished in time,' said Cyr. 'The place is all lath and plaster.'

'But you've had Gigliamo here for months, sure!' they said. 'Can't we see what he's done?'

'He won't stand for it,' replied Cyr. 'And besides, the man's a drunkard and a dissolute. He hardly progresses. I rue me that I commissioned him. Can't recommend him, on my life I can't.'

His wife at his elbow was hysterical with uncomprehending anxiety. She plucked and whimpered, giving away his secret without even knowing it: '*Why* can't the room be opened, Cyr? Why ever?' The guests speculated that Cyr de Gloriole's well-famed love of Beauty had driven him to one of two follies: either he had been so eager to impress that he had boasted of gaining Gigliamo's services without ever doing so; or else he had turned miser so completely that he could not bear to share his prized ceiling – not even with the Queen of France.

Young Rémy did not confine his outrage to a whisper. He

demanded loudly and incessantly that the doors be opened, until his father took him by his flax-limp hair and thrust his face into a mantel-shelf and left him with a swelling cheekbone and blacked eye. The boy, unused to being gainsaid in the smallest matter, grizzled and swore, while his bride grew, by the minute, more and more aghast.

She was a girl of immense, classical beauty. It was impossible to say so, seeing that every compliment payable must be paid to the Queen. But there were a great many admiring eyes cast in the direction of Margaret of Drumlochie. Parting with Margaret from out of her retinue did not cost the Queen a huge grief, however. To have parted with the Boleyn girl, say, would have hurt more. But this particular Scots lass had come only newly to Court, and her French was still of the Highland, unintelligible kind. After a few days' impatient efforts to understand her, the virtuous Court circle had rather swept Margaret aside and left her to a solitary small world of her own. Much the same thing happened at the wedding. After half-hearted attempts to communicate with the bride, even Rémy left her and clung close to the Queen, often brushing up against her and allowing himself to be caressed and crooned over. Perhaps he thought the pollen of royalty might drop from the nodding head of the twice-crowned Queen into the stamens of his hair. He was besotted with the notion of royalty.

So Margaret of Drumlochie drifted to the corner of the room, like a twig caught in the back-eddy of a river, and watched. The proceedings of her marriage rolled past her like the wagons of a pageant. She was only relieved to find it was not the Comte himself for whom she was destined, as the unprepossessing man seemed overfull to slopping, with a claret-red rage.

The Queen's portable altar was unwrapped from its swaddling and placed at one end of the old great-hall. It was a room marred in its splendour, for extra pillars had been built to support the floor of the far grander room above. The symmetry of its twin-barrelled vault and the splendour of its unicorn frieze held no novelty for the guests, who had seen them often before. Like the Magi, they travelled always in pursuit of some newborn magnificence.

Queen Anne heard them talk about the room overhead. She heard the boy Rémy whine his disappointment. And so after the service, when Batonne and Balon took her each by a hand and begged her discordantly 'to see the pretty room above' she was easily persuaded up the old straight-flighted staircase to the locked double doors.

Seeing her venture where they wished to go, the wedding guests pressed after her in a noisy throng. Their curiosity was about to be satisfied: Cyr de Puy would never dare refuse a direct request from the Queen to see the painted gallery.

The guards fell back, lacking the confidence to stand in the Queen's way. It was left to Cyr to leap up the stairs and to cut her off.

'Your Majesty! I regret – the room – it's not complete yet.'

'Still. I may see how the work progresses,' she informed him as a statement of fact.

'But the tinctures are wet. The plaster . . . Your gown would be spoiled . . .'

'Oh, but Amboise was all stone dust and dirt during the improvements,' she responded with a gush of sentimental nostalgia. 'I know the disruption so very well. No one better. What hardships my dear Charles and I endured in the name of Beauty! Oh yes. *Do* open, my good Comte.'

'I fear the key's not to be . . .'

But Balon produced the key with the triumphant flourish of a conjuror. There was no understanding how he had come by it, but now it lay in the Queen's palm. She passed it to Cyr. 'Do show me this ceiling I've heard such talk of.'

Her detractors called her a mule – *La Duchesse Âne* – and it was true that at the merest touch of a headstall, the merest suggestion of tugging, she would settle herself back on her hocks and haul with all the obstinacy of a pack animal. To contradict her was to guarantee defeat. It said a lot for the miracles of Almighty God that He had kept her from teeming with heirs. 'Do pray open for me, Monsieur Comte.' The crowd on the stairs pressed upwards. There was a danger the Queen would be jostled. Cyr fumbled with the lock.

Beams of sunlight solid as cabers hurled through the high windows of the Great Chamber, and the crowd fell back, dazzled. It allowed Cyr time to slam the doors in their faces, so that he found himself all alone in the room with the Queen; the two dwarfs dangled from her hands like dolls. The beauty and horror of the white and silver room enveloped Cyr like a gill-net tangling up a salmon's movements and breath.

'Please, madonna! Please!' urged Gigliamo, already mounted, already left behind by his party.

'Madam. It is time to go,' said Vache and produced a purse of coins which he tried discreetly to give her.

'Oh dear. Do I trespass upon your hospitality, friend?' she asked looking blankly at the purse without taking it. 'I'd've dearly liked to stay and hear your little spies report home.' She saw him flinch at the thought of her staying. 'But of course there must be no trace of a connection made between you and me. I've presumed enough on your kindness. I'm everlastingly indebted to you, sir.' And she accepted the merchant's help in mounting the horse he had given her.

'It's your safety I'm thinking of, madam,' he said. 'The de Puy man won't rest in his resentment.' But in his thoughts he was already back inside the house, busily barring the door against any involvement, barricading it with plaster saints and icons against Gentile intruders. When she looked back from the gateway of the elegant bourgeois house, Vache had already gone indoors to forget her.

'You'd think a man would savour having his grandchild heir to the Sablois,' she remarked to Gigliamo. 'Rémy is his grandchild, after all.'

'These Jews are clean,' replied the Italian. 'Always after they shit, they wash hands.' Giulio did not try to conceal his anxiety to be gone, the terror he felt for his own life. It shamed him and she was sorry to be the cause of his shame. In his own estimation, all he had done was scribble an obscenity on a wall, then turn tail and scurry away before the schoolmaster came along to read it. It was a poltroon's revenge. She would have done him more honour by asking him to slit the Comte's throat while he slept. (Not that he would have done it, but to have been asked would have been an honour.) But this graffiti, this scrawl on a man's ceiling . . .

'It's a brave thing you did for me, Giulio,' she said to his hunched, jogging back. 'Your life was in danger every day you were under his roof.'

'Is nothing. Such a very *small* revenge.'

'If you think that,' she said, 'you haven't understood the man.' But he did not hear her. In his imagination, Gigliamo was still there, under the oval dome of Gloriole chateau, picturing how easily his work of five months would be eradicated. An absurd revenge.

He was too absorbed for a time to notice that she had reined in her horse. When he looked back, the direction of her gaze drew his attention to the topmost chimneys and the dome of Gloriole projecting above the treetops to their right. He thought she was indulging in sentimental recollection. 'Is no time to be sad. Be sad in Italy,' he said.

But she answered, 'This is where I'll leave you, Giulio. Greet your wife from me. And a kiss for all your little fruits of Heaven.'

His horse wheeled round on the spot, sensing his keenness to be gone and to catch up with the rest. 'No time to waste, madonna! You come in Italy with me! You greet wife yourself. Plenty room in my house. If you like, I have Malatesti build you a house all your own. Come now! Hurry!' He refused to see her shake her head. He urged his horse on into a canter, a gallop, persuading himself that she would follow. But when he caught up to the others and looked back, she was nothing more than an interference to the light between the trees, a darkness weaving its way down into the denser woodland towards the stripped parkland of Gloriole. He watched for her to emerge into the open, to wind a path between the rose-circles towards the Sablois bridge. And when she did not, he told himself that she had some other place of resort, some other friend in the forest; that she was not so reckless as to be heading for the chateau at all.

The Queen turned her little heart-shaped face towards the ceiling. Cyr could see there the bulge of her plucked natural brows swelled like twin welts beneath the pencilled imitations. Her cupid-bow mouth was red with carmine. Her small blue eyes swept the ceiling with all the care of a silversmith sweeping his bench at the end of the day.

'Charming. Charming,' she said. 'Quite charming. Who was the artist, did you say?'

'Gigliamo, the Neapolitan,' said Cyr without breathing.

'Ah yes. Some of these Italians are most useful. Most.'

Gratified with having won her own way, the Queen Anne returned her short-sighted gaze to Cyr de Gloriole and blessed him with a winsome smile. 'You should have held the wedding here, Monsieur Comte. The room is not so very *déshabillée*.'

'I defer to Your Majesty's better judgment,' he replied, while over his head the impotent demons and hounds of the painting writhed, powerless to harm him, out of range of the Queen's short-sightedness. He could have howled with laughter.

The fires were not lit at either end of the gallery. The Queen shivered delicately. 'I must leave you now, Monsieur Comte. My heart is quite set on paying homage to the dear Virgin of de Puy. It's not far from here, I understand. I dare say you've been there yourself.'

'Oh, many, many times,' said Cyr. The woman's entire ignorance of his background and history – her utter indifference – pleased him more than the most extravagant flattery. He protested strenuously that she should stay overnight, but sent quickly for her coach.

The guests on the landing, though they pressed forward eagerly to glimpse the room, were all turned back, diverted in a babbling torrent down the stairs, unsatisfied. In among them, buoyant as fishing floats, bobbed the two dwarfs Balon and Batonne, squabbling and scrapping until those around them were hawking with laughter, eyes streaming, cheeks red, kicking at the panels of the staircase with delighted mirth at the sight of such strident, ugly, violent, cruel deformity.

Vérité spent one night at the hunting lodge in the Sablois forest before riding on to the chateau. Even then she allowed time for the last wedding guests to disperse, for her business was only with the man and not with his neighbours.

As she crossed the causeway, it was as though all the perspective lines of her life met now in Gloriole. The vanishing point. The point beyond which neither the eye can see nor the imagination extend. Nothing remained but to return home. She paused to watch Rémy walk his bride through the formal gardens, regaling her with his small repertoire of jokes, his paucity of experiences. She heard him say often, 'My father this' or 'My grandfather that', as though he derived a vicarious heroism from the valour of his forebears. The Scots girl watched him with rapt attention like the lovely miller's daughter confronted in her prison cell with a Rumpelstiltskin. Vérité appreciated that no option remained to the girl but to make the best of the marriage: a royal dowry of thirty thousand gold livres had sealed the bargain. But why, in the name of Heaven, did she bend and scurry to keep a sight of his face while he spoke? It was not a sweet face. It was not a lovesome face.

Rémy looked up, but he did not recognize the woman on horseback at the rim of the gardens.

This was the boy she had wanted so much; so much as to pass him off as her own. This was the boy to whose good she had sacrificed happiness, reputation and future. Suddenly it was beyond comprehension that heredity should count for so much.

There were people dearer to her than this under every roofbeam in the land: Gigliamo or the saintly Jeanne, Mère Catherine or Little Agnès; her father's dog or her first caged linnet. There were peasants asleep now under oak trees, vagrants she had never met that she found easier to love than this bumptious boy with his sagging rump and bitten fingernails. And yet she had been prepared to pay with her fortune and her immortal soul to ensure his prosperity: to have 'A Son'. What foolishness, to place such weight on the Future, to the detriment of the Present. It was like filling a ship so full of treasure that it founders. Heredity. It was as futile a principle as denying this world in favour of the next; denying happiness in the hope of Heaven.

'And how fairs the ambitious Cyr de Puy?' she asked when she met him on the uppermost staircase of the chateau.

'Gloriole. I'm Cyr de Gloriole these days.' He did not waste time wondering where she had come from, but immediately turned back up the stairs so that they might talk uninterrupted in the Painted Chamber. He asked casually, 'Do you know where I might find Signor Gigliamo? I owe him his fee. His recompense, at least.'

'The good signor is long gone,' she said. 'And if he didn't present his account, I should take it he wanted nothing but the reward of a job well done.' She looked up at the ceiling – a wonder only described to her in words until now, only sketched in dull pencil. 'And it was a job well done, wasn't it, de Puy?'

They stood at a considerable distance from one another. But in spite of the carpeted floor and clad walls, the acoustics of the room still conveyed their voices with perfect clarity.

'What inducement could *you* find, I wonder, to make the man undertake it?' He ran a spiteful, derogatory eye over her middle age.

'Sure, none of those you used to pay Il Diavolo. Simply a past kindness . . . But I mustn't use a foreign language. I forget: you never learned the vocabulary of kindness. The word has no meaning for you.'

Although there was a sort of apoplectic tension in de Puy which made the whole globe of his cranium swell and throb, setting the short hair bristling and a tic flickering by his eye, he persisted in smiling, smiling, smiling. 'Why've you come here, nun? If you want my loft for your cell, I fear it's occupied by my dwarfs these days. Since your Little Sisters turned whores, I mean.'

397

But she would not rage for him, either. 'Oh now, Cyr. I wonder you need to glory in Il Diavolo's sins. I'd've thought you had enough of your own. And I came to see this ceiling of yours, of course. This long-awaited, glorious room of yours. The one you've always been planning. This dream you've harboured under your doublet since you could first dress yourself.'

He smiled more broadly if anything, and moved closer to her, circling her with his wolf's tread, patronizing her with his wolf's-head grin. 'Look your fill and welcome. Though I never found you a connoisseur of art before. Dirty pictures and gilded toys were more to your taste, I recollect.'

But her soul presented too narrow a target for him to wound. It hopped out of his reach like a red parrot with a slashing beak. 'It's a beautiful room, Cyr. It's every scruple as lovely as you ever dreamed, I can see that. Jesu, how often I had to listen to that dream! Of your Painted Gallery. And here it is. And here it stays. And you can never, never, never let it be seen, can you? And you'll never, never, never bring yourself to destroy it, will you? It'll hang here like Damocles' sword – an everlasting danger overhead. An original Gigliamo masterpiece. Gigliamo's masterpiece of masterpieces. The best he ever painted.'

He closed on her from behind, his hands round her throat. She went rigid with courage, like a swan rising to stretch itself. But he was only teasing her. He lifted her grey hair and whispered in her ear, 'And do you suppose I mind? Don't you know me at all, lady? Didn't I tell you once: I never coveted the title to Gloriole – just to own it? Just to have the place for mine? Don't you think it's enough just to *own* this room? What makes you think I need the stares and compliments of my esteemed neighbours? Ignorant philistines. D'you think I need their flattery? I've a mirror and an argentier for that. Admiration I can buy. It's as easy had as a comté. I'd've been harder put to buy Giulio Gigliamo, but I presume I have you to thank for his services. I could hardly believe my luck that Malatesti should send me Gigliamo. But then I didn't know you had the ear of the artist himself to persuade him to come. I'm everlastingly grateful, my dear. His masterpiece of masterpieces. His best work ever. Of course, you thought the Queen would see it and carry my head home to the King in her portmanteau, didn't you? But I'm sorry to say the Good Duchess Anne has eyes as feeble as her intellect. As you see. My head stays where it is – to wear the coronet of Gloriole.' He dropped each syllable in at her ear like hot

398

lead, then kissed her throat, flicking his tongue against the skin like the Serpent seducing Eve.

As she broke away from him, the end doors opened and Rémy, breathless from hauling his fatness up all those outer stairs, and dragging his wife by the hand, found that his persistence was at last rewarded: he had found the Painted Chamber unlocked.

At first he could not understand the situation. The room was finished. His glance, as indolent as the Queen's had been short-sighted, could find no offence in the ceiling. 'Which is me?' was all he wanted to know. 'Where's *my* likeness? Where am I?' It had to be pointed out to him, though the young Scots girl looked with more perception and gave little gasps of breathless horror and finally covered up her eyes. Rémy had to have the painted insults explained to him.

Vérité felt a pang of guilt then, at having Giulio include the boy's likeness. After all, Rémy had been an innocent party to her undoing. She was on the very point of an apology when the boy's legs began to twitch. His eye fixed on the depiction of his own face, and his knees began to lift. He drew his fists up against his chest, then all the surplus flesh on his body shook as he began to stamp out his tantrum. Faster and faster the fat little in-turned knees lifted until he was running on the spot, eyes shut, ears, lips and eyelids red and straining. His hands snatched for vengeance and his teeth chattered while he coughed and hawked and spluttered out subhuman shrieks of rage that used up all his breath. His wife stared at him in silent amazement. So too did Vérité.

'Why? Why? Why? Why? Why?' squealed the child like a pig with its windpipe open.

'This woman bribed the Italian to do it,' said Cyr, seemingly unmoved to either revulsion or pity by his son's tantrum.

As if a restraining tether had been cut, Rémy hurled himself up against Vérité, kicking and punching and butting without opening his eyes to see where the blows fell. The sheer aggression overtoppled him and he fell on his hands and knees on the floor and resorted to pounding at her feet inaccurately with his fist. Vérité stepped out of his reach. The vibration unsettled a pile of logs from beside the fireplace and they tumbled across the carpet.

'Get rid of it! Get rid of it! Paint it over!' he howled, incorporating his father in the blame with flying slaps to Cyr's shins and thighs. Cyr too stepped back.

'No.'

That one unprecedented word. It pulled Rémy up as sharp as a curb bit, bending the corners of his mouth into a grimace. He began to argue, but the same unfamiliar word came again. 'No. The painting stays. It's of the best. And the best you never part with.' Vérité laughed out loud and clapped her hands.

The boy gazed up open-mouthed from his hands and knees. His bottom still twitched with inchoate rage. Before he could gain momentum again, Cyr said, 'What's to be done with the woman, say you?'

It was a wedge of honeycomb thrust at a crying baby. It stopped up Rémy's mouth. It riveted his attention. He savoured it, knowing better than to rush his choice, looking Vérité over with eyes bloodshot by the sheer exertion of his tantrum.

As if to fill in an awkward silence at a dinner table, Vérité remarked to the Scottish girl, 'I am Vérité de Gloriole, Chatelaine of Gloriole-sur-Sablois.' The girl, catching sight of a face turned in her direction, a mouth speaking, was flustered and began to apologize. It was only then that Vérité realized what no one else had troubled to notice – that the girl was three-parts deaf. Again she laughed. How it would vex Cyr to find he had bought imperfect goods! But then perhaps deafness, blindness and dumb stupidity were the perfect prerequisites for a chatelaine of Gloriole. She herself had displayed all three.

'*Lock her in the room and let her starve to death!*' said Rémy.

She had handled enough fierce dogs in her time not to incite him with sudden movement or panic. She simply said, gently and quietly, 'Rémy. Listen to me. I am your mother. In a court of justice, with his hand on a Bible, your father swore to it.' Rémy sniggered and snickered and looked to Cyr for contradiction.

'She's no one. Nothing. Did you ever see her before?' said Cyr.

'You're no one. You're nothing. Look at you.'

'How else do you think you come heir to Gloriole, Rémy?' said Vérité peaceably.

'His father is Comte, isn't he?' replied Cyr. 'How else?'

She was impressed. 'Have you managed to keep him that much in ignorance, my dear? In this day and age? I thought only my father could work such a feat. In the old days. When the world was altogether more simple. How long do you think to sustain it? Everyone discovers the truth one day. Even me. Rémy, listen . . .'

'You overlook a possibility,' Cyr interrupted. They addressed each other over the child's head, with the mutuality of a long-married couple. Indeed, Cyr was aware of feeling more at ease in conversation with his former lover than ever he did with his wife: less needed to be explained. 'Perhaps my son has learned his worldly wisdom already. Perhaps he knows only to understand what's useful to understand.'

'And can you still find it in your heart to *like* him, this mongrel?'

Rémy's fury was rekindled by the careless insult. He began to rant, 'Lock her in the room and let her starve! *Lock her up and leave her! Lock it and leave her!*' He grabbed both wife and father by the sleeve and dragged them towards the door. Vérité went to follow, but her dress had snagged under some of the fallen logs and she had to turn and disentangle the cloth. When she turned back for the stairs, the double doors were already shut, the key turned.

She scorned to rattle at the handle. Cyr would return after the child had been spanked and put to bed. Cyr would not humour such an irredeemable brat. She sat down, her hands clasped in her lap.

The sun moved from lancet to lancet, like the eye of a circling giant peering in. While she waited patiently for Cyr to return, Vérité lay supine on the long table and studied the ceiling: the ceiling Cyr would never bring himself to destroy, the ceiling that would ensure his filthy architect's work was never admired, that Cyr's sublime room remained locked for ever. A sweet and an apt revenge.

The sun declined below the window sills and the ceiling melted into shadow, then into obscurity, then into darkness. When Cyr returned, she thought, he might threaten her with death, but his superstitious timidity would save her as it had saved her before. Not that she could envisage where life would take her from here. Nor had she any great desire to escape death. It had followed at her heels for many years, like a devoted dog. She could almost sense it now, in the room with her, dark and fur-shouldered and just outside her range of vision. To be summoned with a word. The warmth engendered by the departed sunlight sank down through the building and left the Painted Chamber cold and dark. Cyr did not return.

There was dirty water in a wooden bucket by the door, left from the scrubbing of the floor. It would not be thirst, then, which took days, but hunger which took weeks. Especially for a woman who had disciplined her body to the rigours of regular fasting.

She rattled at the doorhandle and hit the glossy, lacquered panel of the door with one fist. 'Cyr de Puy! Let me out!' Her sharp, bassless voice rose into the dome and was deflected in myriad directions. It humiliated her. She had been wrong to panic. A man who could conceive such a room – a zenith of civilized influences – could surely not be capable of such a barbaric act. A man who could not bring himself to destroy or even maim a painting would hardly be ready to destroy flesh and blood. Besides, Vache's intelligencers, Balon and Batonne, would come if no one else did, and open the door after the household had gone to bed. She resolved not to shout out again.

Somehow, on the path between Gloriole and the Vache house, Batonne and Balon missed meeting with either Vérité or the Italian entourage. Otherwise they need not have travelled so far to deliver dutifully their account of the wedding day. As it was, Vache would barely open the door to them. He shooed them off his steps, said that their association was at an end. The woman was gone, safe, into Italy with the artist rabble. Now was the time to keep silent, to deny involvement, to plead ignorance. No, he did not want to hear the Comte's reaction to seeing the ceiling, nor the Queen's neither. He had found the couple employment, hadn't he? He had furnished Cyr de Gloriole with dwarfs? There was no extra money to be had any longer for their spying and gossip.

Balon and Batonne recognized the nature of the man's fright: they had felt it themselves as they led the Queen upstairs, insisting she see the Painted Gallery. They were also relieved that the Chatelaine had gone. Now they need not recount how small the impact had been of her intricate revenge. Cyr de Puy had not been exposed as a traitor and a villain. The whole elaborate exercise had surely put him to no greater trouble than the hire of decorators. Still, Vérité was gone now, to Italy, and could imagine whatever happy conclusion she wished.

So Balon and Batonne took a leisurely return route to the chateau by way of the tavern in Rocheblanche. All the while they remained outside the purlieus of Gloriole they were safe to express their affection for one another, and hold hands, and talk in soft, low voices. So they did not hurry home, and did not reach the boundaries of Gloriole until sunset the following day. At least they took it for sunset, as they crested the same rise where Vérité and Gigliamo had parted company.

When no help came, and Vérité realized that Cyr meant his son to have his way, she forgot to keep silent. She called on Margaret of Drumlochie, but Margaret could not hear. She called on Marie de Gloriole, but Marie refused to hear. And she called on Rémy, who heard well enough and delighted in every syllable of fear.

The screaming lasted a matter of hours, cannonading through the chateau in salvoes of rage and terror. But its source was high up in the house, isolated. And it was nothing in comparison with the sounds heard in the days of Il Diavolo. The men drowsing in the guardroom found they could readily ignore it. The household staff in their noisy subterranean kitchens and cellars never even heard it.

She hurled the fire-irons through the tall lancet windows. She smashed the verminous plaster ermines which swarmed up the chimney breasts. She threw the bucket of water at the portrait of Cyr de Puy hanging on the wall. And all that the complacent castle did was deliver up to her its daily smells of cooking, of lit fires, of clattering livestock out-of-doors. Even the parrots busy colonizing the roof-ridges outside raised only a curious interest in the jagged broken windows and the sight of a woman immured in the great white chamber.

No, perhaps after all the inanimate chateau did do more. For it seemed to deliver up memories, like a timid well-wisher posting morsels of food under the locked doors. First Vérité remembered Little Agnès locked in the landing cupboard to repent. Then she remembered how her father had dropped over her head a golden sarcenet that clung to her face and seemed to stifle her with the weight and dazzle of its beauty. She remembered locking her door against those that wanted to take her stillborn cub from its lioness. And she remembered the lion.

She remembered the deceitful nine-month confinement to those corridors and chambers full of Cecille's whining. She remembered the claustrophobia of Estienne de Puy's chivalry and the tendril twinings of his insinuating flattery. She remembered the sculptors' cave and the embrace more objectionable than that length of chain in which she had wound her penitent body. And she remembered Estienne's brother.

She remembered Cyr's helmet-shaven head purple with angry veins, his boots muddy with dung, measuring in hand-spans the broadsword on the wall, glaring up in jealous admiration at the starry, coffered ceilings; burning the lewd pictures Estienne had sent her. She remembered how the smoke had belched out into the room, choking and black, smutting the walls as if with traces of the artists' grubby preoccupations.

Vérité dragged a heavy oak chair across to beneath the new, flattering portrait entitled *Cyr de Gloriole*. Precariously balanced on the curved slats of the seat and at full stretch, she was able just to reach the base of the frame and to dislodge the heavy square from its hanger. It crashed down, rolling obligingly from corner to corner towards the hearth. She paused to listen for footsteps on the stairs outside. Cyr would soon come if his room was at risk. But no one heard the portrait fall, and she was almost relieved, half elated.

All that now hung within the front folds of her skirt, where the keys of Gloriole had once hung, was Vache's tinderbox, her badge of office in the august station of housekeeper. So she gathered the spillage of logs into the grate and, armed with the flints of Sablois, struck a spark. As the fire took, she lifted the heavy portrait and walked it on its corners into the chimney breast to lean against the logs and deflect the smutty smoke out into the room. Like an exhalation of Hell, it began to breathe its dirt up into the painted dome, smudging and obliterating the work of Giulio Gigliamo. A sweet, still more apt revenge, surely, to give the child his longed-for toy and then to deprive him of it!

Another kind of destruction suggested itself to Vérité. She began to daub, with ash-blackened hands, along the white wall,

    Cecille is a Jew. Your heir is born of a . . .

The day before it would not have seemed like an insult. But reflection on things past had convinced her of the anti-semitism that smouldered in Cyr. He would burn at the thought. He would burn with misery.

Her enthusiasm for the work of ruining the room gathered momentum. She dragged the rugs of silvery silk pile up to the fire, like the trains of a bridal gown. The sight of the fire trickling in viscous red down the maze of Moorish patterning had a beauty all its own. Perhaps it kindled, in this woman reverted to the wild, pre-memories of a smoke-filled, fire-lit, dome-roofed cave full of screaming: a place where she had previously come to life. The pall of smoke belching out of the hearth filled her head to a drunkenness. It seemed to her that she saw a figure made indistinct by the tears in her stinging eyes: a dark-clothed figure or a fur-maned beast watching her with golden eyes, waiting beyond the pain.

The tinderbox hanging from her belt ignited first, swinging

once too often into the fireplace. It lit her dress with a strewing of straw-fire flame that she thought to brush away impatiently with one hand. Then flame enveloped her in a single cloaking embrace and incorporated her in the swirl of fire and smoke spiralling upwards into the painted dome with a grandeur which surpassed Gigliamo's mere painted imitation.

Watching the scene from a distance, Balon and Batonne saw the white dome of Gloriole fracture like an egg and release, amid yolky streaks of orange fire, a black phoenix of smoke. The greater the shape grew in the sky, the more it seemed to diminish the fragile nest from which it had hatched – the Chateau Gloriole perched precariously on its branching bough of the Loire.

PART IV

The stone called tufa grows a purer, more glistening white with age. Unlike men or the sons of men. In those years, all the branching Loire blossomed with exquisite, white castles, their defences purely decorative, their purposes pleasurable rather than military, their chatelains courtiers rather than soldiers. Courtiers, merchants, financiers, politicians: it mattered less than it had before who called himself a nobleman. After all, who can judge the nature of a man's blood when he is never called on to spill it? And when a king needs money, there is surely a kind of nobility in the man who supplies it. A kind of heroism? A kind of knightliness quite as glorious as outfacing Death on the battlefield.

No? Well, then, a usefulness that cannot be overlooked.

As for the chateau of Gloriole-sur-Sablois, it stood on its river bend like a beautiful woman leaning on the elbow of an admirer, cloaked in gardens of millefleur and a dress of snowy magnificence, chaplets of rose bushes strewn at her feet and the streaming clouds combed through by her cresting. Her injuries healed. Those who had seen her injured forgot. Her youth was indestructible. Unlike men or the sons of men.

THIRTY-FIVE

Thibault

The stone that Cyr was made of only grew blacker with the passage of time. He repaired the damage, but with a kind of half-hearted joylessness – like the sick man who buys himself an outfit of clothes he knows he will never wear. He was right to suspect that he would never reconstruct his Painted Chamber. No dream can be faithfully reconstructed after waking. Not only was the ceiling a thing irreplaceable, but the repairs alone were the work of years.

And after the first novelty, domestic security palled too quickly for Cyr to stay at Gloriole and see the work through. He found the place oppressive, as if Il Diavolo's extra storey bore down on the rest of the house, increasing the air pressure, making the dark more dense at night. It gave him bad dreams. He would not speak of the dreams to his wife, but she imagined – to judge by the way that he woke with his arms over his face or beating at his clothing – that they had to do with fire and falling masonry.

So, to be out from under that great weight of brick, he offered his services to the everlasting, the interminable Queen Anne in the wars with the English. The English. They were an endemic disease, but Cyr felt no strong antagonism towards them. He would have fought Spaniards with as good a heart. This time it happened that the Bretons were pitted against the English and the theatre of war was the sea. De Puy had never fought aboard ship, but it occurred to him that the skies must be broader there than anywhere, and the dreams less likely to pursue him across water than across land. Water to counter fire; wooden walls in place of masonry. The science of superstition is both precise and logical.

'That's nice, my dear,' said his wife. 'The fresh air. It will mend your constitution.' He thought he saw relief in her eyes when they parted, and could not quite remember a time when separation had meant anything different for either of them.

He boarded *La Cordelière* in Brest. It was captained by Hervé Portzmoguet, a Breton whose contempt for the English was only matched by his contempt for life. But Cyr had thought correctly. At sea the skies are bigger than anywhere, and never more than a plank or two between him and the clouds. Even the heavy, immovable earth of the Sablois was replaced by liquid motion, and tufa walls by billows of white canvas.

Cyr did not realize his mistake until the hour in which *La Cordelière* joined battle with the English flagship, *The Regent*. They were outgunned, and yet the wind brought them down on *The Regent* with a confident bluster. Timber as heavy as roofbeams began to fall on to the confined decks of the ship. The English ship grappled them with iron claws. Portzmoguet, the Queen's encouragement in his pocket and glory in his heart, kindled his ship, and *The Regent* clasped to her wooden breast five hundred tons of fire.

The sea circled them round – the ultimate unbreachable moat. There was nowhere to escape from the fire. It swarmed up to the mastheads of both ships, usurping the sails in flapping sheets of orange and red. It did not differentiate between Breton, Frenchman or Englishman, between soldier or sailor, between good man or bad, between those who prayed or those who cursed. It simply took possession of one small patch in the vast realm of sea before itself ceding the ash and cannon to the numberless ranks of waves.

Several thousand men, including Cyr de Gloriole, burned to death aboard *La Cordelière* and *The Regent*. Queen Anne was deeply proud. Rémy commissioned a painting of the incident for her, but she too was dead before it was completed. He was desolate, bereft. He had once met the Queen, after all, and been made much of by her. His distress over her death quite prevented him from mourning his father or comforting his mother who was left adrift in an empty world.

He was not an acquisitive man, Rémy. He had not the imagination to think how Gloriole could be improved. It was as if, having asked as a child for every material thing he could think of, he had wearied his intellect and jaded his palate. It takes a certain amount of energy to be ambitious, and energy was not a commodity Vache could supply. From his mother's timidity he learned how to be timid; from his deaf wife he learned how to talk without listening. Only his father's blood guaranteed a streak of ruthlessness sufficiently strong to hold the estates together. But the days of the Loire arms boom were over, and neither the Sablois flint or flintlocks found as easy a market as before. In the year of the Field of the Cloth of Gold, all the Sablois wine-harvest was requisitioned to swell the river of French hospitality which gushed out to meet the English. His steward told him of such things, had Rémy been listening. To Rémy, life was a book he had bought with every intention of reading one day. When he died, he had barely grasped the gist of the plot and had certainly not foreseen how it would turn out in the end.

To be charitable, it should be said that he felt no need to contribute more than he did, having furnished the world with Thibault, his son. For just as he had derived vicarious glory from his predecessors, so he took vicarious credit for the merits and achievements of Thibault who was everything Rémy was not.

Thibault was a son in whom even Cyr could have rejoiced. He reached back over the head of his father to derive all his characteristics from an earlier, more heroic generation. His mother's looks he did inherit, however, transcribed into the masculine by an unsubtly harsh geometry. Thibault's face was a stained-glass window, leaded with demi-circle, diamond and rhombus shadows, fused with perfect precision out of excelling materials. It was a face implying a commission by angels undertaken by Genius. The long columnar nose and scrolled Doric pediment of the nostrils lent a central strength and nobility to the structure. His straight mouth kept the equilibrium of a spirit level. Thibault's face was a stained-glass window. Women worshipped before it. But as with all stained-glass, it was animated by the prevailing light, and if Rémy had taught his son only one thing, it was the source of all light.

Everything desirable emanated from the Royal Court – from the King. As the flower turns towards the sun, so Thibault turned towards the King. His earliest memory was of the Field of the Cloth of Gold, its phantasm of palaces and banqueting halls and chapels of such ethereal beauty that their seemingly solid walls rippled in the breeze, their interiors ran molten with dripping gold. Many years later it was revealed to him that what he had seen was the stage-scenery of wood, canvas and scaffold. Even the English King's beard was an artifice of golden wire. To a small child, there is little difference between reality and imitation. The six thousand English smiles had seemed real, too, and proved just as artificial. The gorgeous panorama of dazzling grandeur scorched itself deep and irrevocably on Thibault's brain, like a man who has gazed at the sun and damaged his retina. It coloured his outlook and vision.

Up and down the Loire Valley women cast longing looks towards

Gloriole. Every rumour of Thibault's marriage plans was greeted like the news of a death, every counter-rumour greeted like an Easter morning. When word came that he, as well as the King, had been taken prisoner at Pavia in Spain, a great many young ladies of the Court flew their hearts at half mast. A gale of weeping blighted all the vines.

His mother Margaret made copious efforts to brighten his lot as a prisoner. As to a child promised a pony to tide him through an illness, she wrote:

> I have secured you a wife of excellent house and exquisite features, smiled upon by the Court itself, if you will do yourself the honour of agreeing the match.

He knew the Tolon-Peque girl somewhat, and being quite unable to think of a more suitable wife, wrote that he 'would contemplate such a match as soon as liberty shall be restored to me by those who hold me dear'. There was a grievance implicit in the words, for he could not understand why his ransom had not already been paid. The matter of a bride seemed slightly academic while he was obliged to spend his days paying courtesies to the wives and daughters of his Spanish 'host'. It was not as if the sum set was as high as the King's, after all, or required a realm to muster it. But there again he did not have sons, as the King did, to deliver up in temporary lieu of ransom. His was a civilized imprisonment – not unduly uncomfortable. He had the company of a cousin, Sebastian de Puy. He was nevertheless very glad to hear the wails of anguish from all the little senoritas on the day his ransom arrived.

To greet him, Gloriole cloaked itself in flags and brazed its walls with clarion trumpeting. He arrived on a dapple-grey horse won from his host in a game of cards. His cousin rode a respectful distance behind, on an undersize, dung-coloured nag.

Rose Tolon-Peque thought Thibault the most beautiful sight she had ever seen, this suzerain of a snow-white chateau, mounted on a snow-white horse. She had been staying as the guest of the Lady Margaret ever since the match was agreed in principle, and had three months' acquaintance with its battlements and walks. She believed she had found the solution to the hornbeam maze and the many hiding places where one could guarantee to be found. When she envisaged his formal proposal to her, it was at the heart of the maze, where a small Grecian circle of fluted stone pillars held up a cupola of orange tiles. A kiss perhaps. A boat ride to follow.

Margaret had warned her not to idealize marriage, but then what did she know who had only been married to Rémy?

The servants and certain key members of the communities of Rocheblanche and Croix-Rouge formed an avenue of honour and shouted 'Noel! Noel!' as spontaneously as if they had never been primed. Thibault's fur-lined dressing gown was brought him by his *valet de chambre*, and a fond embrace by his mother, along with the news that his grandmother was dead from sheer joy at his release.

'Then would to God I had been held for ever,' he observed, and there was a small burst of appreciative applause.

Margaret too wore her indoor fur, for it was a windy day and the draughts were as enthusiastic as the peasants, shouting in at every open door and window. But the woman sitting at table between the Bishop of Sablois and the chaplain of Gloriole scorned to cover up her finery. She wore a bodice of cobalt blue laced with red, and cuffs of bright scarlet to complement her perse gown. White underlinen peeped out at armholes and corsage, and a small oval hood augmented the charm of the ringlets in front of her ears. The nagging unease abated in Thibault. Here was an acquisition indeed on the part of his mother. His stomach churned with excitement, confused also by a sudden splash of Sablois claret.

'Son, let me present to you the Lady Rose Tolon-Peque who, I vouch you, shed more tears at your misfortune than a . . . than a . . .' said Margaret, her eyes unfocusing as she searched for an apposite simile '. . . than an orange!' she said nervously snatching one up and toying with it till her nails holed its skin in several places and her hands were full of juice.

Rose coughed shyly. 'Were it not that I've seen your dear family's grief, I'd make bold to say that I wept more than any.'

'Oh, say it! Say it!' Margaret urged generously. 'You were much sadder than we!'

'And had I held a better picture of the Lady Rose in my mind, my chains would have chafed twice as sore,' said Thibault. He rested his feet up on a faldstool and allowed the fur gown to drop back, displaying the shape of his legs and his green and gold trunk hose.

'You mean you forgot me entirely while you were gone?' she asked in genuine panic. She stared at his legs, knowing that she should not.

'I mean that the girl I remembered was only the bud of a flower which has clearly blossomed since then.' (The clerics smiled approvingly, indulgently.)

'The sorrow was heartfelt throughout the parishes, Comte,' said the Bishop. 'No sooner invested Comte than the enemy have you fasting in want and pain. It's no wonder your good family felt so cast down. Can a house stand without its centrepost?'

Dropping his bread and bending to pick it up, Thibault was able to see that Rose wore black hose and small white pattens. He was amazed at his mother's good judgment and determined to take *la bella Rosa* walking in the garden as soon as the meal was over. The maze was his usual resort. Many a woman had offered him up their most well-kept secret in the little Grecian bower at the centre. The sooner the meal was over, the sooner the walk could begin. On reflection, the sooner the meal *began*, the sooner it would be over.

He could also see the feet of the household buffoons, Balon and Batonne. They had crept into the room to bring a message to the Lady Margaret. Since they had been taking their orders from her for so many years now, and since she relied so heavily on lip-reading, they no longer troubled to use their vocal cords but merely mouthed their messages. Returning after a long absence, Thibault found it faintly ghoulish. Now that he had come to his majority he would not permit it. They ought to report to him.

Margaret de Gloriole looked a little flustered at their news and adjusted the hood of her dress so that her silent-mouthed reply should not be seen. Then noticing that Thibault was looking at her, she smiled warily and said, 'Some problem with a stove in the kitchen.'

'You have plans for the Sablois, no doubt, my lord,' said the Bishop. 'After all, you've had all too much time to put your mind in frame.'

'*Exacto!* But first a marriage, I think!' and he feasted his almond-sweet, dark-lidded eyes on Rose so that she gave a small involuntary cry of pleasure and the whole table laughed. They were relieved that the Comte's happiness was so simply secured. The bread on the table was nearly all gone. No food emanated from the kitchen. 'And then, I think, an invitation to the King! I feel I'm equipped to create the kind of place where a man who has been deprived of sweet liberty for many a month can once more relish the sweetest elements of freedom.' There was more appreciative laughter.

'Oh, but it's already so *beautiful!*' insisted Rose, clasping her folded hands to her breast.

He looked around him at the decor, glorious but unchanged

since he first opened his eyes on the world, except that with each passing year it grew a little more shabby. 'It's adequate,' he said. 'No more.'

They were there again, those two elderly dwarfs, flapping their hands, distorting their faces hugely round their petty anxieties, drawing attention to themselves. Even the household dwarfs had grown old and shabby, he thought to himself. Margaret shooed them away, trying to make the gesture look as though she were flicking breadcrumbs off her clothes. As they left, they made wet footmarks on the carpet runner. The guests looked expectantly at Margaret. The chaplain's stomach rumbled hopefully.

'Was it very dreadful for you, my lord Thibault?' said Rose. 'Was it a great trial? Manacles and so forth? Rats?'

The description did not entirely tie in with his experiences in Spain, and it was some time before Thibault could make sense of the question. But recollection roused up a sudden unanswered question in his head and he replied, to the table in general, in a tone of puzzled reproach, 'It was unconscionably *long*, I must say. I began to think I was quite forgotten.'

There was an awkward silence. The chaplain's stomach sounded as if it had been kept waiting every whit as long as Thibault had for his ransom.

'It was a very great deal of ah . . .' said Margaret anxiously. Life with Rémy had not given her the momentum to reach the end of a sentence.

He made a joke of his affront. '*Como?* Could you not decide whether I merited the outlay, Mother? I know! You ladies thought to found some Amazon state here on the Sablois! Saw no need of a comte on the comté.'

'Oh Thibault! I mean, my lord! I mean, it wasn't that your mother didn't *ache* from day to day to send the ransom!' protested Rose. 'But what with the ransom for the King's sons, and the rot in the vines . . .' The Bishop looked as if he wanted to speak in support of the ladies' efforts, but confined himself to a nod which could easily be overlooked.

'Rot? Someone has been teasing you, my dear lady,' said Thibault indulgently. 'The vines rot every year. The *noble grise* is all a part of the ripening . . .'

'Not the noble rot,' said Margaret, misjudging her volume so as to sound unfortunately terse. 'Just the rot. The rotting kind of rot.'

'Vintners are in despair the whole length of the Sablois!' the chaplain confirmed helpfully.

Thibault's eyebrows rose like twin ospreys feathering their flight over dark pools. 'I fail to see . . .'

The dwarfs returned, this time soaked and gibbering, their hair plastered to the knobbly malformations of their scalps. Feeling that he was perhaps the butt of some bizarre running joke, Thibault interrupted their mime, shouting, '*Where the devil is dinner?*'

Balon hopped from foot to foot, evidently in favour of Thibault being told, but Margaret was in such a consumption of anxiety, for fear she should be blamed, that she waved the dwarfs away, determined not to be told of any problem. While she did not know of them, they did not exist. It was Margaret's overall strategy in life. She had learned it from her mother-in-law. 'A small leak in the kitchen,' she said to the table at large. 'Perhaps a walk is in order – to assist our appetites.' She was incapable of hearing the sleet rattling against the windows. The gentlemen at table looked to Thibault to defend them from a bracing walk in the sleet on empty stomachs. How would he assert himself, this debonair courtier who had gone away a boy and come home to be Chatelain of Gloriole?

He had meant to begin his reign by laying out a pleasure park for the King, and he found himself expected to deal with a leak in the kitchen. He was as keen as his mother not to acknowledge it.

'So a feu was levied, I take it? I have my peasants to thank for my liberty, do I?'

'Oh no!' cried Rose, as though she had been keeping the best news till last. 'I thought it would be most dreadful to begin your time so unpopular! Your mother said we would have to wait till next apple harvest – or even till the winter flint-gathering. But that was more than I could bear! I said: "There is another way!" ' She was proud of herself, tripping over the words in her haste to take credit for his release. He saw Margaret draw away a little from her, wanting her to keep silent till later. A warm gratification settled itself in Thibault's bowels.

His betrothed was not of the timid, dithering breed of his mother and grandmother. While they had hesitated, Rose had acted – a guest in a strange house and without so much as the guarantee of a lover's proposal to spur her on. She would have that proposal, though. She was a woman worthy of Gloriole. She had undoubtedly gifted over a portion of her dowry for his release.

He got up, walked round the table and rested his hands on the back of her chair. He saw the frisson of physical excitement set her trembling and her hands clasp the side of her chair-seat. 'Is this true, Mother?' he said. 'Is it my future bride I have to thank for my freedom?' But Margaret was preoccupied with watching the door – did not see his lips move – did not know what he had said. He leaned on his vocal cords: '*Is it true, Mother? That Rose was my redeemer?*'

'What? Oh. It was her idea, yes,' said Margaret wincing. She had not been shouted at in all the time he had been gone. 'She was most insistent.'

'A few acres of trees, that's all. A few acres of trees are easier spared than the dear Comte Thibault, I said.' The back of her neck was red with delight.

Suddenly the doors burst open and Batonne stood with her headclothes in her arms like a pile of sodden washing. She shrieked, '*For Jesu's sake! The cook's near drowned trying to stem it! Won't anybody come?*'

In his anger, Thibault failed to disentangle himself from Rose Tolon-Peque, and dragged or trailed her after him down the staircase to the reception floor, then on down into the excavated cellars and kitchens. 'You did *what*?' he repeated on every bend of the stairs. 'You said *what*? *You had them sell off Sablois?*'

'Just a few acres! Trees are easier spared than the dear . . .' She could not refrain from repeating it. She had rehearsed saying it for so long.

'*But they didn't believe you?* Say they didn't believe you!'

'Just a few acres of trees . . .'

'*You sold part of the Sablois, between you? Jesu! Sold Gloriole land? And kept back your dowry? Land sooner than your dowry?*'

She giggled hysterically. 'Oh, but such a large sum! My dowry . . . you could have had that, of course! But such a little portion! Such a tiny . . .' He hated her now for the insult of a paltry dowry. He hated his mother for finding him an unmoneyed, stupid wife.

As they descended the stairs they collided with servants fleeing the basement kitchen as though a beast were in pursuit of them. A dreadful, unidentifiable grating and grunting spiralled up the old steps hollowed out of rock and rock-hard earth, as though they were about to enter the Labyrinth.

The bottom-most steps were already awash. Oil-lamps hanging from the ceiling swung wildly in the turbulence of air where formerly draughts had never stirred. Now and then another lamp extinguished itself. A tilth of mortar and sand and Sablois silt made the floor soft as a garden bed underfoot, and over the tilth ran three feet of water, cold, black and seething.

The diverted river, eddying in the lee of a flying buttress, had chafed and chafed at the massive old schist footings until the mortar was gone and the holes filled by nibbling water and swirling grit. Finally, in the river's unfailing grip, boulder had rolled against boulder, and water spilled through into the basements of Gloriole: first a mould and then a smell and then a trickling and then a puddle at the cook's feet. Then with a plop like the bung from a vat, a piece of frost-fractured rock fell inwards and smashed on the kitchen floor. A spurt of water, such as Moses struck, gushed into the room. The spurt grew to a torrent of slime and cold.

Now, just as Thibault caught his first sight of the cavernous, vaulted room, two more boulders in its end wall shouldered against one another like drunken trolls before slumping forwards and crushing a pine table to matchwood. The river came to greet him, an uninvited guest belligerent at not having been asked in before. A fathom of water broke against his chest. Thibault kept his feet, but his breath was snatched away by the cold and he was jostled by a wooden bench and tripped over a cast-iron spit battened into the floor. His trunk hose filled with water, ballooning out preposterously. He shook off his fur robe rather than have it saturate and drag him under.

The cook, wearing only the flimsy shirt in which he normally sweated, gibbered on a plate-chest. With the box submerged under the rising flood, he appeared to be sinking, like Saint Peter, into the Sea of Galilee, for want of faith. 'The river's on us! The river's coming!' he continued to shriek as he had been doing since the first breach appeared. It was the end of his world. His territory was inundated. He still had hold of a sack of grain with which he had tried to dam the hole.

The dog that had been turning the spit-wheel swam up and down, barking after fragments of meat. Thibault waded up against what remained of the disintegrating joint: it felt like a drowned thing. Utensils and trestles and loaves and vegetables were washing from wall to wall in a Charybdian whirlpool, until the huge, implacable body of water moving by outside began to pluck out the spoils of its invasion. A wooden spoon spun with a slow inevitability towards the gaping hole in the wall. Thibault made a grab at it, and when it slipped out of his fingers he reached and slapped and lunged after it as if it were the Great Seal of the Kingdom and the safety of the realm depended on it. It evaded him, even so. The river swallowed it through the lamprey bite it had made in his castle wall.

The water found its own level. His head was still higher than the flood. But the kitchen had become the possession of the river – annexed by enemy encroachment. Rose Tolon-Peque sat on the staircase shivering, her arms and décolletage blue with cold, her fear for his safety giving way gradually to a different kind of alarm as he waded towards her waving a salvaged hazel whisk. '*You sold part of the estate, you stupid . . . You women, between you? You sold land? Who to? Who to?*' She did not know. Otter-black he came up out of the water still raging on the same theme – almost as if the flood in the kitchen were part and parcel of the same disaster. He stormed from staircase to staircase, finding the fuel-wood awash, the wine tuns broken loose. And as Rose trailed at his heels sobbing with cold and regret, all he said was, 'Sold the Sablois? Sold acres? Sold land?'

The land deal proved to have been with Joachim Vache. Thibault sent word immediately that he would buy back the few orchards concerned, though it was not clear what he would use for the transaction. It took some time for the true state of his domestic economy to be brought home to him – to realize that there was no loose cash at his disposal. It would not have mattered if there had been. Word came back that Monsieur Vache was unable to conduct business that day: extreme old age had demanded its toll and Death had closed all accounts.

The old man called his grandson Joshua to his bedside on the day before he died and was a long time in taking his leave. He bequeathed to his heir – inasmuch as a commoner can be said to have an heir – all outstanding debts and credits, all his tied warehouses, his ships, his several houses, his bed and bedding and those few orchards on Sablois land. He also bequeathed (it was guessed) a secret. The speculations grew from the look on the face of Joshua Vache as he emerged from his grandfather's bedchamber. It was a look such as the high-priest Zachariah probably wore, emerging from the Holy of Holies after the angels had dumbfounded him.

THIRTY-SIX

The Dragon of Saumur

Not until the land was sold did Thibault realize how deep-seated was his sense of heritage. It was as though Rose had cut off his arm to pay for physic to one of his fingers. She and his mother had cut a patch out of his trailing knightly cloak – not so very large a patch but enough to mar the whole.

He had every intention of buying back the ground at the earliest possible moment. But in the meantime it was necessary to put to rights the accidental dwindling of household funds. The end of the armaments boom, the rot in the vines, the indolent land management of his father were minor factors alongside the King's ransom. Getting back the two sons he had given as surety was costing the nation more money than the average war, and all to be found from the nation's heartfelt love – that is to say from levies on such estates as Gloriole-sur-Sablois.

Empty coffers did not accord with Thibault's plans for Gloriole as a resort of King and Court.

Then there were the repairs needed to the castle. (Who would have thought that a little water could do so very much damage and take so very much work to oust?) Far from repurchasing from Vache's grandson, Thibault in fact found it necessary to borrow a little more, using the mill and surrounding land as collateral. But then the redemptions could be made all at once. As Joshua put it – better one combined loan than two little ones: the transaction was cheaper to handle.

It irked the Comte that his destroyed supplies of firewood should be replenished with trees cut down on his own land and sold to him by his *petit argentier*. But it was purely an interim arrangement. Thibault had plans in mind to solve his economic shortfall once and for all.

He would marry money.

Having found her lacking in so crucial a sense of historical responsibility, he would no more have married Rose Tolon-Peque than harbour the King's enemy. It would have been a kind of treason against the *noblesse d'épée*, against the *noble sang*. Why the girl's father could not understand that was incomprehensible to Thibault.

'But the sale was in your own interests, surely? You gained by it, didn't you? God knows, no one else did!' complained the old man, absently turning his hat inside out with an angry fist.

'Lose a portion of my birthright and the birthright of my heirs? You clearly have no sense of continuity, monsieur.'

'But it wasn't even Rose who undertook the sale! Your own mother . . .'

'She was incited to it, sir, not being blessed with the strongest of intellects. And if I had made your daughter Chatelaine of Gloriole, would we not have seen a field sold here and a vineyard sold there each time she favoured a new dress?'

'Oh come, sir! That's mortally offensive!' The father's fingers stripped the herls off the feather decorating his hat. 'Her thoughts were all for your safety and welfare.'

'You mean she was impatient to be married – as I am impatient for the trees to grow that can replace the ones . . .'

'God strike me, but you're a jackanape!' The spine of the feather threaded itself between Tolon-Peque's fingers. 'I said I'd speak for her to you. I said I'd level out any misunderstanding. The girl's silly in affection for you! But I find no misunderstanding here! Only a haughty, puffed-up peacock of a villain looking for a way to set aside a sound marriage duly sworn!'

'Marriage sworn? Come now. No such word was ever spoken. I've made my marriage arrangements in quite another quarter, I do assure you. I admit the loss is all mine: your daughter's a matchless flower in the wreath of womanhood and so forth. The sacrifice was a hardship.'

It is quite possible that Thibault believed this when he said it, for there had been nothing in his short life to teach him better. He truly thought that his pang of pleasure at seeing Rose Tolon-Peque, and the warm anticipation of marrying her, were the stuff and substance of Love.

'Young man, you have a great deal to learn about hardship,' said Tolon-Peque, cramming his mangled hat on to his head. 'My daughter came to rest in your house in expectation of a marriage. She leaves it unmarried, and that's a blot on her honour.'

'Oh hardly! Not while I was languishing in a Spanish . . .'

'A blot. Seen from many miles off. I shall be suing you for the cost of her time misspent.' And he stamped out, holding his cloak clasped tight round him as if to contain the blast if his temper exploded.

Thibault was almost happy at the mention of a lawsuit, for it confirmed him in his opinion that the Tolon-Peques were small-minded and mercenary. Having concluded as much, it seemed all the more fortunate that he had escaped marriage to them. Besides, how can a man be morally at fault who, for the sake of feudal responsibilities, undertakes such a personal sacrifice as marriage to Berenice de Saumur?

He could not remember who had first recommended the family to him; the notion had come from the King himself, who declared himself most eager for Catholic and Protestant to co-exist amicably. Saumur was well known for its eiguenot persuasion, and its vast private wealth, both noble and bourgeois. Thibault left it in the hands of his agents to discover just which house could furnish him with the largest dowry. He was prepared to bend his neck beneath any yoke, he said, for the sake of Gloriole and the King. But nothing quite prepared him for Berenice.

Word has travelled far of your daughter's qualities [he wrote] *and I have none to match them. Only by the grace of God will my entreaties win your consent to hear my suit . . .*

He expected to hear only from the father. He was astonished when the lady herself replied.

Reputedly the grace of God has been kinder to you than to me already, but if you do crave to marry, I can think of few other ventures as agreeable in which to invest my dowry. Only one impediment remains, sir. Will you change your religion?

'Lord save us. What manner of woman is this?' he asked rhetorically as he read this. 'She wants me to turn eiguenot. What next?' He said it too loudly, with a derisive laugh, for the benefit of his chaplain-confessor. To his surprise, his chaplain did not throw up womanish hands of horror.

'One may be a thing on one's wedding day, sir, but who's to say what one becomes the following morning?' He was a sly old man who had exerted himself for most of his life in moulding a comfortable theology around the indolent, zealless Rémy.

'You mean, turn Protestant to get her, then reconvert after?'

The chaplain was pleased with himself. He saw a way of tricking Protestant wealth out of the stronghold of Saumur and into Catholic coffers. So simple. So foolproof. Anything else would have been the sinful waste of an opportunity. So even her religion did not detract from Berenice of Saumur. Only Berenice herself did that.

It was really quite titillating – the thought of marrying an eiguenot. It smacked of dabbling in the occult or with alchemy, of supping with the Devil off a long spoon. When he suggested it to his mother, teasing her with the idea, she went and fell on her knees in the Chapel Saint-Cloud to beseech a change of heart. It made him all the more keen.

But it was Joshua Vache who decided him finally. The merchant's business, both before and since his father's death, had taken him often to Saumur and he knew the household well. 'Of course it would put you in the King's shoes, somewhat,' he said. 'He with Queen Claude, you with the Lady Berenice. With the deepest respect in all the world, sir, she is not the city's loveliest asset. Though she is its richest.'

'You are impertinent, man.'

'Yes sir. I die a little at your rebuke,' said Vache prosaically.

But to put himself in the King's shoes! To take an ugly wife in the reign of a King with the plainest of wives imaginable. Astonishing how an idea can gain momentum from such a small push.

He and his cousin Sebastian were three-parts wine-sodden when they composed the letter to Berenice concerning Thibault's conversion. Sebastian de Puy had also been held hostage with Thibault after Pavia. His rank being so much more humble and his lands so dependent on Gloriole, he had, in some unplanned, accidental way, crept under the Comte's wing and been freed on payment of the one hostage-price. The frustrations and boredom of captivity had led to a closeness, a camaraderie between them. That is to say, when Thibault wished to get drunk, he chose Sebastian to drink with. When Sebastian wanted to get drunk, he deferred the pleasure until it next suited Thibault to override the social difference between them. For the de Puys were nothing more than mud-grubbers since losing all their vines to the grey-rot.

Honoured Lady,
For some time now, I have harboured secret sympathies for the New Faith but have hovered, uncertain . . .

'Timorous. Make it timorous,' suggested Thibault, reading over the other's shoulder. 'It makes me sound more like a rodent. Women like rodents – small furry rodents. Say "timorous".'

. . . but I have hovered, timorous, on the brink for fear of bringing grief to my mother . . .

'Oh good! Marvellous good! A mother's as good as a neck-verse for winning a pardon. Put the Old One in, too. Grandmothers are even better than mothers.'

. . . grief to my mother and grandmother, and confusion to my peasants.

'So? Strike it out. D'you want her to think I go in fear of my peasants?'

'I thought peasants counted for rodents,' said Sebastian. 'On a par with small furred things.'

'Very good. I'll concede you the peasants. "Confusion to the peasants".'

Perchance you are the spur sent by God to drive me to a full commitment – to coax me away from the Roman fold . . .

She replied:

Sir,
 Do not burden me with the task of swaying your allegiance towards the Truth. The Truth will answer for itself, and I am a poor exemplar of so fine a thing as the Christian life. Still less must you let my dowry sway you. However, should you choose to marry me in the face of the Low Church Community of Saumur, I shall consider myself allied to you in the eyes of God – howsoever the Pope may view the situation.

He felt, when he read it, like an adolescent put in his place by an adult. He blamed this uncomfortable feeling not on himself for being adolescent, but on Berenice for being older. Much older. Five whole years older. 'Shall I mind her *great age*?' he said to Sebastian as he packed for the journey. Sebastian knew he was not intended to answer. But there was a tacit understanding that he would be accompanying the Comte to Saumur, to lend moral support.

So it was to Sebastian that Thibault observed, the first time he saw Berenice, 'Good God. I heard that Saumur had a dragon, but I hadn't thought to marry it!' After a month in his mother's company, he had quite forgotten how to modulate his voice. The remark coincided with a general lull in conversation. Now the whole room fell silent.

'But lo. Here comes Saint Sylvester to conquer the dragon, does he?' she answered from the far end of her father's gallery.

The press of wedding guests shimmered, like silver-fish, into hiding places and would not be winkled out again. The parents were left caught between bride and groom like civilians trapped by crossfire. 'You'll find no lack in her conversation, my lord, I do assure you,' whispered the father bristling hot with a mixture of outrage and embarrassment.

There was nothing to be gained from back-tracking. 'I talk to my horse,' said Thibault, 'but it was not my object in buying him.'

'Here the transaction is the other way about, however,' said Berenice. 'And were your horse to have bought you, he would not have done so for your manners, I dare swear.' She had dropped her voice to a deep, dragony purr that lifted the pile of the carpet on its way down the room.

Her nose was drawn out and flattened at the tip, the line of her jaw corrugated and indistinct. Sunken black eyes looked out from under hooded lids, and there were woolly tufts of hair on the tips of her ears. Moles disfigured her top lip. Thibault knew how Francis d'Angoulême had felt when he stepped up to betrothal with the Princess Claude. He wondered if the Crown of France had been worth such a depressing moment. And in that same moment, he was warmed by imagining himself in the King's shoes.

'Will you to church, madam . . . mademoiselle? It is a custom in my part of the world to mount marriage as though it were the gallows. The bride is at fault who takes offence.'

The guests burst into grateful sobs of laughter and nodded to one another, suddenly and gratefully remembering this novel 'custom'.

'And in Saumur there is a similarly foolish custom that bride and bridegroom be civil to one another,' said Berenice, curtseying to him graciously so that he was better able to see the congenital droop of her collarbones. 'Quaint, I know. But let us humour the local traditions.'

Unaccountably he found himself without words, and felt for his pocket as if he might find some there. The belt was unfamiliar: it was some time before he could find his pocket, leave alone the wedding present he had there. If there was one thing for which

Thibault was renowned among ladies, it was his panache. Could it be that this frowsy witch of a woman could wilt his panache by the sheer contagion of her ugliness? He fixed his eyes on the bodice of her gown which was exquisite, encrusted with gems and bullion-knotted embroidery. It calmed his misgivings.

The gift was a printed copy of *Le Viandier* rebound in white leather embossed and tasselled in gold. Vache had recommended it. He said it would please. She turned it over in her hand as Sablois flint-knappers turned a flint. She ran her fingertips over the pages. 'It's beautiful,' she said without one note of qualification. 'It's perfect.' He fixed his eyes on her belt which was inlaid with coral. A thousand facile remarks trooped up at his back, but he dismissed them, or stood them down at least for some later skirmish. She saw them go.

Saumur Chateau was not susceptible to the insinuating river which passed it by at a reverential distance. Only to the wind. From end to end of the huge, hilltop bastion, draughts chased the wedding guests into their carriages or away into their separate chambers, and left Thibault alone with his bride. The bedroom's draperies moved incessantly in the breeze. It was as though the room was rife with eavesdroppers, voyeurs. 'I'll wish you sound sleep, madam,' he said, scratching at a food stain on the skirt of his doublet. 'I've a damnable rheum on me.'

She was unfastening her hair. The strands were so brittle and wiry that even unpinned it stayed in place, only drooping. The parting was wide and bare, like a path cut through meadowlands by the habitual passage of sheep. 'Did you ever read Chaucer's story of the Round Table knight?' she asked.

'God spare me! I may have turned Protestant, but I've not stooped to reading argot English. Is that where your dissenting took you? *Chaucer?*'

'A knight once fell short of his chivalric vows and was condemned to death,' she persisted. 'His life would be spared only if in space of one year he could find out the secret of what women most desire. For eleven months he searched the world, and in the despair of the twelfth month he met an old crone who said she would give him the secret if only he'd marry her. Take one, take both. What else could he do?' She paused to be sure he was listening.

He said impatiently, 'It's a worn story. He married her. She was a fairy – could transform herself at will. Come now, madam. If we are being analogous here, let us not exaggerate. You're neither a crone nor a fairy. I simply choose to spend the night . . .'

'The fairy gave him the choice. Would she be beautiful at night in bed or during the day when his friends were standing by to see?'

'And his answer was to let her have her own way.'

'Since that's the secret of what women chiefly desire. Bravo.'

'Do I take it I'm intended to ask your choice in the matter? Whether I stay or go? We are grown past the Age of Fairies, madam.'

'And dragons too, monsieur. And chivalric knights, it would seem. Even so. If you were to ask me, I'd say, do as you please.'

'What?'

'But first get a child on me. After that I'll not make demands on you, nor dampen your reputation as darling of the Court.'

He was shocked. Not that he had ever intended to let marriage stand in the way of amatory adventures. Men with wives twice as lovely as Berenice considered the marriage bed a mere heraldic shield on which to combine initials. But it did rather empty his sails that she should grant him permission. It meant he could not slight her with her ugliness. Besides, it was unflattering and he was a man accustomed to the flattery of women. Two at least at the wedding feast had signalled their availability should the bride prove too dreadful a prospect.

'Tell me, ma . . . Berenice. Was your opinion asked on the subject of this match?' he asked, absent-mindedly poking at the fire with a log-roller. 'At least – were you hot against it?'

'Sweet Luke, no! Quite the contrary. My father was, but not me. I *honed* him to a willingness, you might say.' Without him noticing, she had slipped into bed and taken with her his fur house-gown to wear round her shoulders. 'Once, when I was younger, I passed through the Sablois on the way to Lyon. I saw your chateau. I've never forgotten. The sun on the river. The sun on the stone. The thought of living there. Why wouldn't it draw me?'

'Ah. Then this is a land transaction for you,' he said. 'Then we're both satisfied. I'm pleased to gratify your childhood wishes.' But there was a kind of frosty resentment in his voice; it surprised even him. So vain, he thought, that I should covet the lusts of this old beldam.

'As to you . . .' She said it casually, off-handedly.

'As to me?' He bridled. He wished he had left earlier.

427

'You're as I expected.'

'I'm *what*?'

'You're as I expected anyone to be who belongs with Gloriole-sur-Sablois. Well. Why say it? You know what you are.'

'Oh pray. Do say.'

'I say you know your advantages. You've been told them by women better able to judge than I.' For the first time he noticed that although she seemed calm and self-possessed, her hands were in fact trembling where they held the edge of the bedding. The red cover pulled into taut folds, radiant flames diverging from the Saumur dragon. 'You're in keeping with your chateau, sir. Naturally, I'm as moved by the sight of you as by the sight of Gloriole. It goes without saying.' She admitted it with a restrained dignity, just as a devout married woman might admit wistfully to a proscribed and unfulfillable longing. 'Do you suppose I'm blind to physical beauty? I who can be impassioned by a great heap of stones beside a river? Do you suppose I'm immune just because I'm not blessed with beauty myself?'

The fire crackled and they both started. A cinder was thrown out on to the floor at Thibault's feet. He extinguished it with his boot. 'D'you suppose I have any interest in the matter?' he said and left the room, wishing he had done so ten minutes before. He resolved to leave Saumur the next day. Not only was it inhospitably cold, but it was home to a strange atmosphere as well. It was as though he were all the time trying to play real-tennis in a court built off-square. He would stand a better chance of winning on his own ground.

He even failed to find where either one of the pretty and obliging young women were keeping themselves. The chateau was a maze of draughty corridors, and his own warmth was left behind with Berenice. The fur cape, that is. The fur cape.

THIRTY-SEVEN

Masque

It was some days after their return to Gloriole that Thibault steeled himself to consummate the marriage. She was perfectly right, of course. The sooner heirs were achieved, the sooner the marriage could take on its day-to-day formality, and a comfortable estrangement grow up between them. He even told Berenice that he, too, had no objection to her taking lovers in due course, though in truth he only said it because her looks made it implausible and her virtue made it unthinkable. Besides, she seemed too perpetually *busy* for intrigues. From long before he rose until after he retired to bed that first fortnight, Berenice was writing letters, interviewing the staff and tradesmen, familiarizing herself with the accounts and routines of the Sablois and acquainting herself with the estate. His mother paddled forlornly about, like a duck ahead of a farmyard broom, and was shocked to find her opinions being asked when twenty years of marriage had drained her of any she ever had. And such strange opinions in return! On the infallibility of the Pope. On the Immaculate Conception. On the Imperial Elections. On the succession to the English throne. On the Plantin typeface. On the merits of the Dutch. On Thibault's conversion. Conversion indeed! Margaret could not for one moment pretend she understood what Berenice was talking about, for all the woman took great pains to speak clearly and distinctly. Instead, she invariably diverted the conversation on to the subject of the forthcoming masque and the visit of the King. Thibault had invited King Francis to join in the marriage celebrations.

He had left himself far too short a time to make preparation. There was no opportunity to consult with Vache and repurchase that land. There was no time free to counter the lawsuit of the disappointed Rose Tolon-Peque. (With more time he could have settled with less money.) There was no time to have a new masque composed and he had to make do with one used at the wedding of the Duc de Bourgogne from which the King had been absent. There was no time to instil grace in the lumpen daughters of Rocheblanche and Croix-Rouge, who were to represent the stars and planets. He entrusted the task to Berenice and threw his energies into designing a gantry for the roof on which sun and moon could rise.

It was a blustery, cold spring and his hands and cheeks were forever cold from overseeing the joinery in the stable-yard and then its installation along the front of the roof. And every so often, as he worked, his stomach would flinch at the thought of the King on his premises; at the honour, the opportunity to please.

It was not mercenary. He told himself that his exchequer had already been replenished with Saumur gold: he had no need to win royal donats. It was simply something he had promised himself as he kicked his heels in Spanish captivity: to entertain the King under his roof and to do it better than anyone expected.

Consequently, the nervous energy he consumed each day left him weary and preoccupied. By bedtime on Tuesday the twelfth it took all his concentration to put out of mind the bedding of Berenice. He had listed it among his tasks for the day and, having struck off all the others by ten o'clock, repaired to her room with a fatigued resignation, filling his head with other things. What to do if it rained on the King's masque?

He had given her a chamber at the other end of the central building. When he entered it he found her sitting at her desk in her shift and a mantle, writing letters. He noticed that the middle finger of her hand was, as usual, stained with ink. She looked up with alarm. Only then did he remember that he had not actually *mentioned* to her that she was among his tasks for Tuesday the twelfth. 'I'm thinking to fasten sky hooks into the masonry to canopy the courtyard with blue silk,' he said.

She rallied at once. 'However many widths would it take?'

'A hundred and twenty, by my estimation.'

'Best rake it, though, or the view of the roof will be baulked for those at the back.'

'Very good. I'll rake it,' he conceded, blowing out a lamp or two.

'About the room beyond the drawbridge,' she said.

'The fools' room? What about it?'

'May I have it?'

'What for?'

'For my own purposes.'

'As you please. It's no size.'

'No, and the bridge has worm. But it suits. And you'd not mind noise coming from that quarter? Not undue noise, I mean?'

'Noise? Music, you mean? You're not going to master *another* instrument? Whatever for?' He fed logs to the fire and began to shed pieces of clothing on to each piece of furniture, like a deer preparing for spring, brushing strips of velvet haphazardly from its antlers on to every bush and tree. She put down her pen, wiped her hands and got into bed, extinguishing the candle beyond the pillows. He did not appear to notice. 'I'll oust the fools. They've been carping for a change for months. They can have somewhere nearer the kitchen. How are the Stars and Planets progressing?' Between them, they began to dismantle the stacks of pillows against which she would have reclined to sleep.

'Oh, they're in the ascendant I'd say. You may judge for yourself tomorrow. They'll rehearse in costume.'

Thibault put out the last lamp and only the red firelight was left, lapping no higher than the foot of the bed. She drew shut the bed curtains to exclude even that, and no further remarks were made concerning the King's masque.

Towards the end of the second watch he woke Berenice by getting out of bed and blundering about the room.

'What are you looking for?'

'The means to light a candle, woman. Where's your spills?' She did not answer, and soon he was sufficiently awake to slough off the foolishness that sometimes grips a man in the middle of the night. He had dreamt – or half-dreamt – that he was party to that Chaucerian story of the Round Table knight: the antique crone transforming herself in the wedding night into a fairy. Thibault returned to the bed, knowing that if he lit a lamp it would still be the dragon of Saumur watching him from the other pillow. And yet there was no denying the pleasure . . . the unexpected enjoyment . . . the quite unprecedented . . .

He felt obliged to pass encouraging comment on what had passed between them. In his considerable experience, it was a folly women expected, particularly virgins with romantic illusions to preserve. But just when he was trying to couch some understated compliment, she undermined him. Once again she undermined him. She observed wryly and peaceably, 'The dark's a great leveller, isn't it? I've heard it said we're all one between the sheets, when the light's out. Indeed – I've been counting on it.'

The cost of the masque was staggering. The wild beasts alone, which Thibault pitted against one another in a birchtree pen as an opening *divertissement*, sank their fangs deep into Berenice's dowry. Fourteen wolves buried a bear under a quicksand of fur, and pulled it down. A lion fought a bull, both unwilling. The lion, whose lionesses had always slaughtered his meat for him, was astonished to find his ribcage shaken to pieces on the horns. Overhead, the canopy of silk cracked and billowed, noisy with gusting wind. It stirred the colony of parrots to a restless, uneasy swooping and trapped them – silly, nervous creatures – on the underside. The King's retinue gazed up at them and applauded, as if the birds were choreographed participants in the prelude to the main event.

Then the King, gorgeous in cloth-of-silver, his shoulders massively exaggerated by his padded tunic, left the remnants of a sumptuous dinner behind him in the hall and picked up his broad-toed bulbous shoes over the wet grass. It was intended he should open the masque by sweeping across the stage to take up his seat in the midst of the scene: a more rigid canopy had been erected to shelter him from the possibility of rain. But he was engrossed in a philosophical discussion with Berenice on the subject of unicorns when the music began. It was only by sheer tact and diplomacy that she swerved his attention towards the entertainment. Then, with grandiose gestures and stylish charm, he invited bride and groom to be seated on either side of him. The Stars and Planets came tripping in from all quarters of the stony Universe.

High on the roof, riding on an arch of cogwheels more intricate than the Mind of God, a white metal moon rose above the parapet and reaped the reflected glimmer of a thousand torches in its crescent scythe. It was pursued into the sky by a copper sun spinning to its zenith so that its raggedly serrated edges cut the air with a whirring savagery: Apollo hankering after Diana. The wind, shaking the wooden structure, added to the frustrations of Apollo. Down on the stage Planets and Stars yearned towards the King in their elliptical orbits of dance, and he smiled patiently on them, having long since accepted that it was his lot to sit through interminable masques. As the chorus sang of the virtues of Apollo, Francis turned to Berenice and said, 'Jean Thénaud saw them on his travels through the Holy Land, you know? I've read his accounts. The thing's well authenticated. I've seen a horn! – I forget where. Part of someone's treasure somewhere. This long. Like a sugar twist.'

'You amaze me, Your Majesty. I'd always thought them lost at the time of the Flood.'

Thibault watched them both, his mind too distracted to join in the conversation, his eyes bright with anxiety and gratification. His hands moved on the arms of his chair, subliminally conducting the music, beckoning forward the gauzy, white-limbed girls glimmering in careful constellations beneath his windows. The King, like some giant-whorled snail, had crossed his threshold and left a glittering silver trail there for all to see. In all the days of his father no such thing had ever happened. For Rémy had never summoned the energy to attempt it. He had contented himself with going to Court, with standing at the back of the jostling crowds, with gaping rapt over others' shoulders to see the King's face. Now, when Thibault looked around him, everything satisfied. Everything excelled. Everything was fit. Everything was beautiful.

His wife's voice – 'You should breed them, then, to draw your carriage, Your Majesty' – put the lie to his thought. She was the dragon in the Garden of the Hesperides. And yet even the King was saddled with an ugly wife. Francis would not hold against him this one lapse in the aesthetics of his decor.

A chilly solar wind blustered the Planets through several seasons of the year. Hermes, descending from Heaven on a rope and harness, miming his message of benediction, was grazed against the window pediments and had to keep himself from spinning with one hand against the brickwork. A cornucopia was brought in by a buxom Vesta and laid at the King's feet. He picked it up and examined its construction. He put it to his lips as if about to blow a hunting horn. His courtiers roared with laughter and disconcerted the singer whose false soprano wavered for a moment. Overhead in the cloudy purple of the night sky, the artificial sun reached its zenith and vibrated in the wind with a noise like a bowsaw flexing.

'God's neck, it's cold,' said the King and got up. Strolling down through a meteor shower of child dancers, he cleared a space for himself in the front row of seats with a wave of the hand. He beckoned bride and groom to join him there: he had not finished his discussion of unicorns with Berenice. 'And what do you think, Comte? Shall we have unicorns in the royal menagerie before long? And will they be hunted and taken as your splendid frieze suggests, or with net and pit?'

The wind, veering of a sudden to the north, shouldered against the mechanical wooden arch on the roof parapet. The sturdy young

433

man steadily winding the handle which turned the copper sun on its spindle found the windlass snatched out of his hands, and the sun began to spin at the mercy of the wind. The thick wooden axletree bolting it to the gantry broke with the slightest of sounds and Thibault, looking up, saw the sun grate once or twice against the parapet and then come hurtling down. The dancers joined hands, in Arcadian innocence, for a circle dance.

The giant metal teeth of the disc tore through the canopy where the King had been sitting a moment before, then rolled like a shining coin across the plank staging, severing partner from partner, Planet from Star, music from action. Some of the audience, unsure of what they were seeing, drew their swords. Others turned tail and fled. The sun, losing momentum, began to roll on its rim with a louder and louder cymbal-crescendo, until it clashed flat.

The King's eyes travelled from stage to roof and then settled on the ruin of the chair and canopy where minutes before he had been sitting. It was not an assassination attempt. Not by his host at least. Surely, Thibault himself would have been killed where he sat.

A woman lay on the stage clutching her leg; another had been all but decapitated by the serrated disc. The cornucopia was shattered into a thousand pieces.

'You should embark on it, my lord King,' said Berenice's voice close by his shoulder.

She avoided looking at her husband: the mosaic of his face had been shaken out of its excellent pattern. He stared at the stage as if his grave had been gouged out by the great wheel of fallen metal.

'Embark on?' Even the King's voice was reedy, wedged somewhere between rage and devout thanksgiving.

'On a hunt for the unicorn, Your Majesty,' said Berenice, as though nothing more serious had happened than a garland slipping over Vesta's eyes.

The King stared at her, digesting the meaning of the words and the extraordinary aplomb of the woman. Not an assassination attempt, he decided. Merely an unfortunate accident. 'I may do that, madam. Or there again I may ask some loyal subject to undertake it for me.' And offering her the crook of his arm, he drew both her and her husband away from the distasteful noise of the woman on the stage screaming.

THIRTY-EIGHT

The Unicorn

When Sebastian de Puy called next at Gloriole, he found some peculiar work of fumigation in hand. Peasants in sacking hoods, with sacking bags slung from neck-yokes, were sprinkling lime into the angle of every wall, across every threshold, across the base of every staircase. And a sulphurous smoke rose from a row of braziers that had filled the chateau with noxious fumes. He hesitated to go any further, until Thibault summoned him from an upstairs window. 'Have you got the plague in with you or what?'

Thibault was not forthcoming with an explanation. He shrugged off the smell – 'an infection merely' – and behaved as though nothing worth mentioning were disturbing the routine of his household. 'Come up, man. Come up. You're late.' Sebastian climbed the stairs to the great-hall. The fire, which twenty years before had taken out the roof of a third storey, had destroyed, too, the coffered ceiling of the room below. But it had made such a clean excision that the Unicorn Frieze was left intact. Now half a dozen men sat about in the great-hall looking at the painting as if it were newly finished or contained the clue to some hidden treasure. 'Are you game for the Holy Land?' Thibault asked Sebastian.

'To hunt unicorn? Certainly! Have you made up a party? Can you afford to leave the Sablois?'

'Why not? I have a dragon to leave on guard, haven't I?' There was a deal of laughter: the joke was by now a well established one. But Thibault drew Sebastian aside to confide in him, 'She's whelping, you know.'

'With child, my lord? Congratulations!'

'The surgeon hears two heartbeats.'

'Twins, you mean?'

Thibault broke away with a show of indifference. 'Who knows? Who knows what prodigy might come out of a dragon, eh, de Puy? Twins, yes, I suppose. Well, man? And how do you say

435

we set about this hunt? How do we net a unicorn for the King?'

'As the books say, I imagine,' Sebastian said cautiously. Thibault would follow his own method, in any case.

They studied the frieze as though it were Holy Writ – as though the moving finger of God had daubed it there and not some allegorical home decorator. 'The virgin must go with us,' said Thibault. 'There's no certainty of finding one in Palestine. We could be sold a nag. Fontenac, see if you can't recruit a nun from the Madeleine or some such.'

'Must it be taken alive?' said another. 'We could put down poisoned bait otherwise.' But it was generally agreed that the animal was not quite zoological enough to tackle like a fox or a stoat. There was an unspoken acceptance, too, that actually killing a unicorn might bring bad luck to them and to King Francis.

In a corner of the room, Joshua Vache had been busy making out a more practical list of requirements and submitted it for approval:

Three nets in silk and gut & 1 chain x 20 spans
One halter; leather and hemp
2 pr. hobbles: Egyptian hemp
1 saw (antler)
Victuals to the provisioning of 12 men
Provener   ”   ”   ” 15 horse
1 chair (travelling)
Camp cots x 12 + tents to suffice
Rock salt
Horse blanket . . .

The travelling chair was intended for the virgin. The huntsmen demanded comfortable, upholstered seats. The list of provisions grew to a prodigious length. Vache received each addition with a deferential bow and a smile of acknowledgement. He was a man willing to exert a quite ridiculous effort to please: contemptible, but of great use. Thibault's credit was bottomless. It seemed that Vache's greater profit was to be useful to the aristocracy. He never submitted a bill. Of course the man was wealthy to the point where profit could no longer give him much satisfaction. But there was no doubting the joy he took in dancing attendance on Thibault.

Thibault liked to think of the hunt as his idea. At least he liked to think so until two months later when he was sitting out yet another vigil in a charmless landscape of semi-desert. The virgin, a robust but fidgety girl of ten, had an aversion to cedar trees: they blocked her sinuses and made her cough, and the white of her dress attracted large flying insects. Fontenac had used his initiative and recruited a pretty child of devout parents and irreproachable youth, and promised her the company of her mother plus twenty livres if she could 'sit still in a chair in God's good fresh air and keep her hair combed'.

It was delectable hair of écu-shining gold, though that too attracted the insects as well as the attention of Palestinian locals. They gathered in noisy crowds to watch the bizarre behaviour of the French pilgrims. This was not the leafy idyll of the Gloriole frieze, of glades carpeted with flowers enshrining a pale maiden with a single lily.

The locals were endlessly forthcoming with news of unicorns. They spoke (as they jingled the French silver in their palms) of seeing such a beast 'only last week'. Thibault disbelieved every word, but went on asking.

Thibault saw strange animals, too: beasts quite wonderful enough to put the unicorn's existence past doubt. He saw camels and ostriches, locusts and scorpions. When he sailed south along the coast he saw dolphins and porpoises and shark. His mind was a bestiary of wonders. But the unicorn taunted him from behind every thicket, from beyond every mountain. It was there and it would not show itself. He began to wonder if it were not, like the Holy Grail, a thing invisible to all but the purest knight.

It would not profit him to be gone from the Court circle for longer than a few months. He would return a forgotten man. And if he returned without a unicorn for the King's menagerie, he would be nothing short of a ruined man. Thus, after two months' fruitless hunting, he began to blame the idea of the hunt on his wife and curse her for ever diverting the King with talk of unicorns.

They erected their corrals; they sat their bait on her camp-stool; they strung their nets; they followed unfamiliar hoofprints over miles of baked and barren land. But no unicorn was drawn to lay its head in the maiden's lap.

Thibault offered a large reward for a live specimen. He was brought horses with welts on their heads, mules with one ear cut off, cattle and goats with malformed horns. Members of his expedition sailed for home. The date of his wife's deliverance came and passed, and yet he had no way of knowing what children she

437

had borne, whether they had lived, whether Berenice had lived. He longed to be back in France. And yet his search took him further and further south into lands for which he had no maps and with which he wanted no acquaintance.

At last, when his enquiries had taken him once more down to the docks and in among the sailors' stories of sea-monsters and siren mermaids, his dog-eared sketch brought a different reaction. The man who glanced at it said casually, not waiting for money to change hands, that just such a beast was newly landed and that two or three had passed through the port in recent months bound for Italian menageries. Thibault was so taken aback that he let the fellow stroll off holding the drawing.

They found the ship still in dock. The cargo had gone. Thibault gouged a picture of the unicorn on the green mildew on a capstan. Yes, said the gestured reply; not a day since, it was here. The beast had been watered and put aboard a dhow to be transported along the coast, reshipped from Darmietta. Yes, a horn on the centre of its brow, yes. They pulled at their noses with cupped hands, as though in some ritual desert salute. A horn on the forehead, yes, and one on the end of its nose. It unnerved the Frenchman, the mention of that second horn.

The virgin's mother began brushing her child's hair into a crackling cloud of gold. By nightfall they would at least lay eyes on a unicorn if not harness it for the King's possession. The men pursued it along the coast on horseback, the women following on more slowly in a wagon.

The dhow was soon visible, keeping the coast within sight of its starboard bow. Whatever it took – money, diplomacy, brute force – Thibault was determined to secure the unicorn for King Francis and, at a coup, ensure that the light of the royal countenance shone for ever on Gloriole. He wondered just how the beast had been taken: a net probably . . .

But a net would not have sufficed for the beast disembarked from the dhow. The usual crowd of locals gathered to beg from the foreigners. When the dhow put in at their jetty and put ashore its crated cargo, they greeted the sight of the unicorn with a noisy, hysterical babble. But the Frenchmen simply stood and stared, their cold northern blood turning colder in their veins.

It was vast and slab-like; a pig on the scale of an elephant. Neckless, its head was merely a portion of its body; a third of its length beginning with a fold of flesh behind the jawbone. Its tiny eye would have passed for a gill or a tear in the hide but for the marbly swivel of a dull black ball. The legs were trunks shrouded in hanging skin. The three-toed feet had made trefoil impressions on the wood of the crate, and its bottom jaw moved to and fro incessantly. It was gross. It was grotesque. The horns on its face were excrescences a yard long that seemed to weigh down its thick, beaky lips to the very ground.

'God in Heaven, it looks like my wife,' said Thibault and the laughter caught in the beast's ears like flies and made them swivel – round, hair-tufted ears twirling where the brainbox should have been.

Here stood the symbol of purity, mired in its own pats. Here stood the mythic zenith of hunting's art: the ultimate capture, the most elusive essence of beauty. Had travellers' tales truly flattered this monster into the milk-white equine grace of tapestry and painting? He could not say, 'This isn't a unicorn!' for he could give no other name to it, and there was the horn – the double horn in fact – kept where no other beast keeps its horn.

'What do we do?' said Fontenac, holding his nose delicately between two fingers.

'Shall you buy it?' asked Sebastian de Puy.

Thibault's chronicler, a monk from Rouen, was drawing the beast in charcoals, muttering under his breath prayers of thanksgiving to God interspersed with prayers to repel the Devil, uncertain of whose handiwork he was witnessing.

'Is the girl come yet? We'll wait for the girl,' said Thibault. And while they waited, every breed and variety of beggar converged on the gentlemen thrusting stumps and babies and cupped palms under their noses.

When the girl arrived and saw the unicorn, she screamed and swooned and prayed to be spared going near it. The men would not have insisted, but her mother, embarrassed at the trouble and money expended by 'the lovely gentlemen', insisted. 'Pay no heed to the child. She's perfectly willing. A game girl, she is.' Pinches and slaps persuaded the girl to sit one last time in her camp-chair and to have her hair brushed into an electric storm around her shoulders. Large dark ovals of sweat darkened the sides of her dress and her face was purple with the heat, but she took her place a dozen yards from the crate. Thibault gave orders that the end should be levered off and the beast freed – to lay its head in her lap or not, depending on whether or not it was a true unicorn. It was an arbitrary way to decide the matter, but the monk was of the opinion that God would oversee the proceedings.

Was Thibault mad? Had he drunk seawater? Had they brought this catch down six cataracts of the Nile to let it loose for a pack of madmen? How did he propose to recapture the beast once it was loose? The transporters tossed their heads till their turbans unwound, and flung up their hands for the arbitration of Allah. A dozen rope halters had to be made and a dozen hands touched with the alchemical magic of gold before it was agreed the cage should be opened.

And then, at every application of the claw-hammers, at every tinkling of a nail to the ground, the girl got up out of her chair and began to run. The spectators caught her each time and brought her back.

Then all at once the child became oddly acquiescent – unsteady, then drooping, then limp. The mother, anticipating trouble all along, had administered a sleeping draught, and the girl had succumbed to an open-eyed unconsciousness in which her beauty deserted her. Her mouth hung open and her head lolled moronically. She slumped in her chair and snored loudly. The mother's eagerness to please was somehow repellent to the men. They found it unnatural. But then it was a day for the Unnatural. And in any case, the child was more content than formerly. She did not stir at all when the end fell out of the cage with a crash as the unicorn lent its weight to the work of the claw-hammers.

Its journey had brought it down six cataracts of the Nile and placed it on an open sea. It was unsteady on its feet, hungry, thirsty, terrified. It lumbered forward out of its crate and its small arc of defective vision showed it bright colours and a glaring sun. The little eyes were set so far back in the head that it did not see the furniture in its path.

'It's drawn to her! Look!'

'It has the smell of her!'

The ears swivelled at the noise. The crowd evaporated away. The transporters rattled a wooden bucket of water under the promontory of a head; the creature ducked its nose to drink, but only knocked over the bucket and spilled it. Then it gave the illusion of a purposeful lunge towards the girl. In fact it blundered into the chair, catching the beak of its lower jaw in the armrest. The unexpected collision alarmed the animal still more, and it turned on the spot, hind-quarters overturning the flimsy leather and wood chair and buckling it. Unnerved by the noise, the animal turned right round, and the arc of its horn caught the seat again. Virgin and unicorn became entangled in a dance of panic.

Suddenly there were scarves waving and men shouting. The Arab boys with the halters dashed in, but could find nothing small enough for their nooses except the horns, an ear and the tail. The beast shook them off like cuckoo-spit. Their din and gaudiness excited it into slumping from foot to foot, turning and turning, sawing to and fro with its great bluff of a head. It grunted and wheezed and gargled, and the breath from its nostrils raised gouts of sand off the wooden jetty.

It was the monk who drew a gun from the depth of his sleeve and discharged it into the hairless, sagging hide. The report froze the turmoil into a tableau of chaos.

'Damn you,' said Thibault to the monk, and willed the oafish monster to survive the gaping hole in its shoulder.

His will prevailed, surely, for the unicorn, after lurching drunkenly about, crossing and uncrossing its unwieldy feet, turned towards the monk and ducked its head to charge. Again the hind legs buffeted the camp-stool and sent it skidding across the jetty, the girl still roped and limp inside it.

The monk was on the waterfront, the beast on the pier. Brainless and raging, the rhinoceros struck a straight course towards its persecutors. It cut the corner between jetty and waterfront, and ran directly out on to empty air, somersaulting into a fathom of water. Only its feet, instantly inert, poked out of the water like four rope-scored bollards.

'You fool,' said Thibault in disgust.

'It put its head in her lap,' said Fontenac, more hopeful than certain.

'We should salvage the horns,' said Compiègne.

The sailors wept and wailed in transports of mourning, tearing at their clothes. Small Arab boys leapt into the water, turning head-over-heels in imitation of the unicorn. The virgin's mother could not unfasten the ropes around the chair: she was going from person to person asking to borrow a knife, but was unable to make herself understood. Sebastian suggested it would be necessary to pay the value of the beast to its captors if they were to escape Egypt with their lives.

That was the least of Thibault's regrets. Days later he was

still spitting venom at the loss of his prize, still asking Sebastian for corroboration: 'Did it go to her lap? It did, didn't it?'

He arrived home unannounced, anxious to take Berenice by surprise, rob her of her unwelcome facility with words. And then, after all, it irritated him that no one should be waiting to greet him, that he should have to rummage through the rooms of his chateau to track down his own wife.

A strange, incessant but muffled din drew him upwards through the house. Perhaps it was the clanking of a log winch over some remote hearth. Or his armed men at pike practice in the yard. But no, the noise was inside the house. As he turned along the passageway towards the room that had once housed his dwarfs – the room beyond the drawbridge, he grew more and more alarmed by the steady clanking, as of farm machinery, and said aloud as he opened the door, 'And what sorcery is the witch about now?'

He was greeted by the sight of a monster with more arms than the Kraken, flailing and thrashing its afternoon shadows over the figure of his wife perched on a stool beside it. 'I should've known I'd find the dragon *in flagrante* with a prodigy.'

She looked up defensively. 'You said I might have the room for my own purposes.'

He wanted so badly to make sense of the machine that his eyes would pass on nothing but garbled images to his brain. Then he saw the little sheets of paper lying face up to the assault of the metal plate – pure white disfigured by inky intricacies of print. Each time the plate lifted, the ink stuck for a little while before the paper peeled itself away and dropped back with a pale flutter. A pile of finished pamphlets lay by the door: *A Life of Martin Luther*. He pocketed one without knowing why. So big a machine in so small a room was intimidating. He was glad when she got up from her work and moved quickly out on to the landing. The metal giant was closed up in its room, as the ugliness of his two dwarfs had formerly been.

'Change your clothes, my lord. I'll have food and drink brought to the stove. Has anyone gone for washing water? I'll go myself.'

It was a room built *à l'allemande*, with a big German oven filling one corner. The day was warm and the heat given off was oppressive, but then Thibault was missing Mediterranean warmth. He had his wife sit down in the armchair beside the oven and brought the horn to her there, staggering under its weight.

'There you are, lady. The horn of the unicorn. The horn of Love in the lover's lap.' He laid the great sawn-off tusk across her thighs. It amused him: plainness clutching the grotesque; that pastiche of so many tapestries and friezes. 'Well? What d'you think? Does it disappoint the romantic in you? Still, it is the unicorn's. I hewed it off myself.'

'It's very . . . interesting, sir. I've truly never seen the like. Look how it's made up. Compacted hair. Not bone at all. Will you ream out its centre before you give it?'

'What?'

'So the King may drink from it. To be safe from poisoning.'

Only the lengthening of his long top lip and the straightening of his mouth indicated the least unease. She had seen through him to his misgivings, but it was unthinkable he should admit to having any. He recounted the hunt, and when he had done so, all she said was, 'I pray the King will overcome his preconceptions. Was the little girl killed?'

'Trampled only. She'll live. Though the unicorn may have seen to it she stays a virgin.'

He saw her lean forwards a little, try to ease the weight of the tusk further down her thighs and fail. All of a sudden he jumped forward and pulled the thing off her, letting it fall to the ground. 'Well?' he said. 'I'm to guess, am I? So taken up with your mechanical toys, are you? Am I to rot in ignorance? Must I guess or what?'

'Not at all,' she said. 'Twin boys. I bore twin boys.'

'But.'

'But?'

'But?'

'But nothing. They're thriving, praise God. In fact they're right pretty babies if you'll take my word for it. And if you won't, they're in the corner there. See for yourself.'

So there was no need for Thibault that night or on any future night to creep into the den of his Saumur dragon. He went there, even so, wagging her pamphlet as though it were the incriminating letter of some secret lover. 'Aren't there enough zealots in the world without you adding to them?'

'But you've no objection to me using the room,' she said by way of reply.

'What? No, why should I? I take it the estates have gone to ruin and rack, though, while you played with your new toy.'

She offered to show him the accounts, but he waved the offer aside. For he was busy wondering why he had just decided to stay the night. Perhaps the sight of his baby sons had rendered him magnanimous. Perhaps the presence within his walls of the aphrodisiac horn gave rise to exceptional impulses. And there again perhaps the chateau and its dragon were still exerting their pestilential magic.

Once again it almost frightened him when the swaddling bands of darkness bound him to his witch. Something, something in the room kept reminding him hour by waking hour of the story of the Round Table knight and his fairy-crone of a wife. He could not get it out of his mind.

In the morning he woke to find, laid across the end of the bed, a long white horn. It was milk-white mottled with cream, a yard long and twisted like stranded sugar into a spiral point – as unnatural a natural shape as the trumpet of a lily or the harp of a lyre-bird. It was hollow, too, like the cornucopia. And beautiful.

He pushed the covers back and crept to within reach of the lovely knurled rapier of bone. 'Where did you find it? Where? When? Where?' But he found he was alone in the room. She had already gone to her prayers.

He picked up the horn – it weighed next to nothing and was sensuous to touch. He fumbled his feet into his shoes and carried the horn downstairs, cradled in his arms like a child. His long bare legs startled the house serfs sweeping the floors, as he hurried out-of-doors. The sunlight had already warmed the stone where he knelt down on the brink of the moat. Taking a sure, two-handed grip on the wider, open end of the horn, he dipped it into the water of the moat.

The horn of the unicorn can, it is said, free water of all impurities and leave it cleaner than the rivers that watered Eden. Never again would the vines of the Sablois rot, the apples blemish with rust, the cattle throw dead calves, the sheep bloat and die. The Sablois river, heart's blood of his estate, would run pure as meltwater. This magic phallus would swell his rolling hills and make them big-bellied with life. Everything whose roots reached down for Sablois water, everything that drank at the river's edge would thrive. He looked about him for a vessel of some kind so that he could taste the result.

'What are you doing?' she asked. She made her devotions in the gardens or, as this morning, beside the moat.

'Purifying the Sablois, of course. Look at the colour of it! Look at the shape! Where did you lay hands on it? How?'

'I'd seen one in a book,' she said mildly. 'In your library. It was there for anyone to see who looked. But I only set it by you in case you think the King won't appreciate the other. Will you give him both?'

'What? Of course not! I'll give him this! I'll give him this!' When he held it at both ends between his two hands, it was as if he had just wrung the spiral into its white spike. 'How did you come by it? How was it taken?'

'I believe it beached itself.'

'It what?'

'On the western shore of Scotland. It's from a whale. A narwhal, they call it. I consulted with the man Vache. He was of the opinion one could be got, and he was right.'

'Not a unicorn?'

'Not unless you're of the school that thinks Noah's Flood overtook the unicorn and transmogrified it. By all accounts, the narwhals don't bear a close family resemblance.'

'Why, then?' he wanted to know.

She was bewildered. 'To save the King a disappointment, naturally . . . Oh, are you offended? That I didn't trust to your efforts? Please don't take it amiss. You know I've always thought there was no such animal. So I took precautions in case you found I was right.'

He stood up, the horn hanging from his fingertips, unvalued. 'With what in mind? To deceive the King? To fool the King with a – what? – a *swordfish*?'

'To satisfy the King's expectations, of course. But since you have the real thing, it doesn't matter, does it?' She took the horn out of his hand and went as if to throw it, like a javelin, into the moat. He snatched it back, and the silence that followed made it plain which horn he would present to King Francis.

'If I could've brought the carcase of the other . . .' he began to say, but could suddenly remember the stench of that monstrous decaying beast hauled out on to an Egyptian beach by chains to rot in the sun. The sight of the twisted, milky horn had undone any conviction he had of having captured a unicorn. And he had not the smallest doubt which Francis would choose to believe came from the mythic *monoceros*. 'It's anathema to me,' he told her haughtily. 'To deceive the King. Confidence tricks. It's a kind of treason.' She bowed her head penitently. 'This once. This one time.

Since the money's spent . . . And I dare swear Vache charged dear enough.'

'He's not submitted an account yet,' she said meekly.

He looked down at the steaming puddle on the berm's hot stone where the drops from the narwhal's horn dripped down and turned to vapour. It might be true, after all, that the Scottish whale was some hybrid descendant of the unicorn which had waited too long to enter the Ark and been left to swim.

When he arrived at Amboise, the chateau was in uproar. He found most of the Court cast out into the courtyard in a state of extreme agitation, sheltering from a light drizzle under the colonnades. Every now and then some would attempt to shelter on the open staircase whose balconies would give them ascendancy over the rest. But a soldier of the royal bodyguard would turn them back on to the cobbles.

Was the King ill? Had there been an assault on his person? Rumours were rife. Madame d'Etampes had fallen from favour? Or a duel! That was the favoured story, for ever since the splendid if unfulfilled challenge between Charles V and Francis, duels had become quite the fashion; a pierced spleen, a severed artery quite the most piquant source of gossip.

At the sight of Thibault de Gloriole, sunburned from his journey and dressed in velour the colour of lionskin, many of the Band of Ladies threw up their cuffs of Picardy lace and exclaimed that Adonis was returned from the hunt. He did not smile for them. He rarely smiled for them. But then smiles were a debased, overminted currency at Court and the ladies only thought him more broodingly passionate because he did not smile.

'What's in the wallet, my lord Comte? What have you brought for us? Is it a present from the Holy Land, Gloriole? Who's the fortunate one? Who is it for, dear Thibault?' The longer he was kept waiting, the more the gift under his jacket diminished in significance: a beachcomber's curio, a fishbone. He refused to unwrap it.

He had thought to stride directly into the King's levée and to make account of himself to the King alone. As it was, he was obliged to jostle and wait with the rest, while more and more women descended on him like starlings on a lawn. A half-year before, he had envisaged leading a milk-white equine miracle into the yard and letting the clatter of its golden hooves draw Francis to his window overhead. A cry of astonishment; a message to 'fetch up Monsieur le Comte this instant' . . .

Thibault considered turning about-face and leaving – calling again another day. But the women had him surrounded. He could no more sink out of sight than Odysseus could manage to drown. In any event, it was necessary to know what disturbance to the State had taken place overnight. He was as gripped by curiosity as the rest.

Another foray set off towards the open staircase and Thibault joined it. But a young guard, recently employed and unfamiliar with Thibault's features, was suspicious of the Mediterranean sunburn and pounced into the mêlée of courtiers to snatch him by the collar.

'What's in the packet?' He stood only shoulder-high to the Comte and had no advantage other than surprise. 'A sword! A blade! Sergeant!' Already excitable, and having been berated once already that day for incompetence, the Guard fell on Thibault as blind as sharks. Several young women, silly with fright, tried to repossess him, and there was an undignified tugging. His ruff came away in the struggle and was trodden on. More and more troopers arrived in a hysteria of zeal and dragged their prisoner to the top of the stairs. He was aware of a sobbing lady bending to retrieve his ruff as though it were Veronica's veil dropped on the route to Golgotha.

It was not the way he would have chosen to achieve an audience with the King, but even so Thibault found himself in the uppermost gallery of the building and not far from the man himself. He was the cause of such a stir that the King left off a tirade of cursing to see what the matter was.

'We took him with a hidden weapon!' gasped the ardent young soldier.

'A weapon concealed on his person!' The fact that Thibault was also carrying a sword on his hip only confused them.

The horn was unwrapped. The Guard did not know what they had found. They lost momentum. 'Gloriole, it's you,' said the King, failing really to notice Thibault's predicament. All he saw was an ear receptive to his grievances. 'D'you know what, Gloriole? The gall of the devils! Hell's open and no mistake! Gall? I'll give 'em wormwood! Where were the Guard, that's what I want to know! How did he do it, that's what gnaws on me! In the middle of the night! A bucket? A pastebrush? Heretics roaming the place unhindered? Look at it! Blasphemies! Just look at it, will you?'

They moved towards the King's bedchamber. A page with a wet cloth and a palette knife was scratching at a placard pasted to one panel of the door. Only a few words of the original, lengthy tract were still legible.

> . . . this pompous, preening Papal Mass . . . the Pope and his vermin of cardinals . . . other mumblers of the Mass . . .

'An insult to Christ! Where were the archers?' Francis was still saying. 'Can you wonder the heathens are knocking on the gates of Vienna if blasphemous little paper-hangers can roam free round a royal chateau! Where were the Guard? Look out, you! Look where you've damaged the paint!' Francis' hand made a hollow crack against the page's skull. Flakes of paint lay on the threshold like devout Catholic tears. Suddenly the King asked, 'What was that about just now, Gloriole? That business on the stairs. People thrashing you.'

'Oh. That. A misunderstanding. I simply brought a present for Your Majesty.'

'Present?' He ground the paint flakes violently into dust.

'You recall I've been travelling. The Holy Land, Africa. In pursuit of the unicorn.'

Momentarily Francis' attention was stayed. 'You found one? You brought one home?'

'I regret . . . A horn only,' said Thibault choosing his words carefully.

Francis was disappointed. He did not trouble to conceal it. 'A horn, eh? Good, good. Useful. Just as well. Today broadsides pasted on the door, tomorrow poisoners. Riots and insurgence. That's what things like this say to me,' and he tapped at the scratched door with his knuckles. 'Is it true a man can't be poisoned drinking from a unicorn's horn?'

'I haven't tested it, Your Majesty.'

'Useful that. If it's true. You must tell me about it all. The hunt, I mean. Another time. Currently you must excuse me. I have heretics to burn.'

Thibault was almost grateful that his tribute had been so obscured by the events of the day. He had not been called upon specifically to lie, and his honour could therefore be said to be intact. Besides, the unicorn's horn was planted in the royal treasure-house. Its magic might still touch the King's imagination at some time in the future. A cup fashioned from it might even save him from an assassin's poison . . . Because now that it was out of his sight, Thibault began to fancy there must have been magic to it after all. Perhaps Berenice had lied – disguising magic with a pretence of banality, since magic was so out of keeping with her banal, *scientific* religion . . . The possibility would always be there.

A week later Sebastian, calling at Gloriole to pick up the old routine of sports, diversions and drinking, encountered the chaplain leaving the chateau. He was savage with resentment, muttering vituperations under his breath and cinching his saddle with a violence that made his horse gasp.

'He's still not reconverted, then?' de Puy ventured to guess. 'I've told you before. He's teasing you, sir. You shouldn't take it so to heart.'

The chaplain blew out through plump wet lips – a snort of disapproval. 'A man shouldn't toy with his immortal soul. It's no joking matter.' Not for him at any rate. While the Comte persisted in pretending to adhere to Protestantism, the chaplain was without a living, without succour. He was inclined to think the joke had worn too thin for mirth after all this while. He had begun to worry whether Thibault would remember to recompense him fully for the months and months of this charade. 'And if you're so well acquainted with the workings of his lordship's mind,' he said sourly to de Puy, 'pray tell me the significance of this *sulphur* everywhere. The place smells of a plague pit!' Sebastian could not explain the sulphur. Clearly the fumigation had not yet worked to drive out whatever pestilence Thibault feared.

Only after several bottles of wine did the Comte let slip to Sebastian an incoherent and embittered hint as to what was going on in his mind. 'The first Comte, you know . . .' he slurred, trying unsuccessfully to create a prismatic rainbow with the side of his wineglass and a shaft of sunlight '. . . bewitched by some Englishwoman. Against all likelihood, they say. Some kind of aberration. These things . . . they cling to the brick, you know, de Puy . . . Cling. Like bedbugs. Never rid them. Steeps the air. Infects it. Smell! Can't you smell it?' Thibault raised his head from where it rested on one sleeve on the table top, and snuffed the air like a hound. 'Can't you smell it?'

'Smell what, my lord?'

But Thibault could not bring himself, even in his cups, to put into words so great a fear. Too terrible a thought, should sulphur not suffice to purge it: that the walls of Gloriole could still, after a century, be riddled with the woodworm of Love. And its larvae already be at work in him. But what other explanation could there be for the irrational and ludicrous way that his thoughts ran on his wife and his footsteps turned towards her door every night?

THIRTY-NINE

The Salamander

She knew. He never acknowledged it publicly, but she knew even so. Publicly? He never acknowledged it in private, but she sensed it all the same – that unfair advantage she held over him. The witch. It was so powerful, so implausible that it was tantamount to magic. Ten years later Thibault was still resentful, still blaming an infectious spoor in the walls of Gloriole. It had colonized every turret and stair, as the red parrots bought for target practice had colonized the roof, and bred. Ten years later Thibault still resented Berenice de Saumur for undermining the rational ethos by which he had thought to live.

It was not quite so irrational that he should love his sons, Thomas and Kempis. He did make a point of treating them with qualified affection for the first few years owing to the unreliability of children, their propensity for suddenly dying. But once again that bacteria in the tufa stones infected him, undermined him, made him worry about them when they were ill, take them into bed when there was ice on the windows, ask after them when they were absent, mention them too frequently in conversation with his friends.

Berenice's religion was just as insidious as she was. It was clever. It was cunning. It appealed to his intellect and to his xenophobic hatred of Italy. His intellect told him that the only truly sensible course was to wear the same religion as the King, but after ten years he had never quite taken the step of reconverting. Francis' hatred of the Protestants was never as hot before or after the day he found their placard pasted to his bedroom door. The punishments he had executed then were not so very great; no more than forty or fifty printers, booksellers, schoolteachers, disembowelled, quartered and burned. He had his radical sister's restraining hand to keep him from any real religious intolerance. But he had banned freedom of the press. Francis, who had been so very urgent to educate and edify his nobility, who had granted printers privileges and pensions, had overseen the rise of

451

that civilized phenomenon, the scholar-publisher-printer: that same Francis had also seen the risk of too much enlightenment and had cut short the freedom of the press.

So Thibault could not understand why he, a loyal subject, allowed Berenice to keep her printing machine in the East-turret loft, why he indulged her in her hobby of writing and printing her little pamphlets. He had told her to be rid of it, but when she declined he did not, much to his surprise, take a cold-hammer to the machine and reduce it to pig-iron. It shocked him to know that he harboured an illegal device in his house, against the express wishes of his King. But somehow she held him too much in thrall, too mesmerized for him to exert his authority and ban her harmless little pastime.

Of course he considered himself a Catholic beneath it all, but somehow he held to the Protestant disguise he had put on for the purpose of his marriage. It was ridiculous, he knew that. Even Berenice considered him a Catholic still, and kept to herself her coterie of eiguenot friends, declining to make him an arc in her circle. But he read all her pamphlets even so. At first he did it furtively, like a jealous husband suspicious of finding love letters among his wife's underclothes. Then it was with the excuse of proof-reading her copy for errors. He looked for foolishnesses to gibe at, for nonsenses to snigger over. But in time it came to seem blasphemous to make sport of such as Calvin and Melanchthon, the Ninety-Five Theses or the *Inspicientes*. He stopped being amused by the spiteful wit of Murner and he did nothing to stop Berenice 'opening his sons' minds' to the arguments involved. Of course he saw how she swayed the boys towards her way of thinking, but he did not mount a counter-argument. Let the priests in the pulpits defend the Church of Rome as they were paid to do. It was not a man's job. Let women, children and clerics concern themselves with the imitation of Christ. Gloriole's salvation would grow out of imitating the King.

All the while that Thibault was growing from boy into man, another chateau had been growing on the Loire: a chateau so vast in concept that it dwarfed Gloriole and Amboise both together, dwarfed all but Chinon. The wall that bounded its estates was twenty miles long; its parklands covered thirteen thousand acres. Chambord was to be the royal chateau among chateaux – to intimidate rivals, impress visiting monarchs and invite admiration and envy from the builders of the world. Futile to compete – irreverent, too – but vital to flatter a work of such grandeur by making it the acme of fashion, the pattern for all imitation.

So Thibault tore down the painted panels of the boxed staircase, tore down walls, opened up the storeys of Gloriole into cavernous voids, then drove a staircase up through the old stairwell, up through the great-hall, up through the very roof itself, and capped it with a lantern dome in the likeness of Chambord. It was a double helix of stairs, the one intertwined with the other, within a well of pierced and painted stone. The structure of the building was not suited to it. Ceilings sagged, load-bearing walls bellied, the overall sum of rooms was reduced. But at noon a shaft of sunlight rived the chateau from roof to foundations, with rods of light diffusing through the huge open cavities of each landing. The King came to see it.

He said, 'Tell me if you find an answer to the draught.'

It was perfectly true that the shaft had the qualities of a flue and drew in air at the ground floor to funnel it, in an eddy of cold, up into the blowy sky itself. As it rose, it drew in all vestiges of heat, a Charybdis swallowing warmth into its ever-spinning vortex. Still, the double staircase was greatly to be admired for its modernity – as the panelled, straight-flight stairs had been before it.

'I styled it in on your own work at Chambord, of course,' said Thibault to the King. 'It was Leonardo who designed that, was it not?'

To his surprise, Francis said, 'No. No. I dare say there'd be no draughts if Leonardo had designed it. Oh, he drew a few sketches, but then he died. Besides, his design was for four staircases, not two. The builders simplified. Of course. You know how they are. Small-minded. Couldn't cope with a genius that big. Ah, how I miss that man's mind! He would've solved the draught.'

They paused before Thibault's copy of the King's own picture at Amboise. It depicted the death of da Vinci in the arms of the King. Thibault had placed it at the head of the stairs in the misguided belief that they took their genesis from Leonardo.

'Came across the Alps on a mule, you know,' said the King, dewy-eyed. 'The *Giaconda* and the *Virgin of the Rocks* in his saddlebag. I gave him Cloux manor-house for the twilight of his . . . He was my dearest friend, you know.' Francis bowed his head in sentimental humility. Thibault had heard it a dozen times before, but he listened with the delight of a child hearing a familiar fairy story. (Berenice said, laughing unrestrainedly, that it was a 'great nonsense' and that Francis had been nowhere near Cloux when Leonardo died. But Thibault's childhood impressions were not so easily defaced.)

'There was the canal too, of course,' Francis was saying.

453

'Canal, my liege?'

'Canal, yes. Of course. Simple enough idea, God knows. Between Tours and Lyon. To drain the Sologne. If only he'd come over to me earlier. If only he had. Hey-la! What he and I could have achieved!'

There was a pause which Thibault sensed he was intended to fill. 'Drain the Sologne?'

'Consider the profit to the man who did it! Eh, Comte? And to work with da Vinci's plans! A little piece of immortality that would be for a man in itself, don't you agree?' Thibault did not answer. His expression was a little vacant. But he agreed; no doubt about it. The idea had stuck to his brain like flies to a sugar paper. It was Francis' intention that it should. 'I'd undertake it myself, but these wars in Italy . . . They sap the exchequer. I've had to stop work altogether at Chambord, you know? Besides . . . the place is an ice-house at this time of year. Damn stairs.' And he went to change into his green felt.

With him he had brought his huntsman, a lieutenant, twelve riders, six valets-of-bloodhound, six grooms, fifty archers and an army of halberdiers to erect tents in the Sablois forests. Thirty six-horse wagons stood waiting to carry the floors, roofs and hangings of the tents. Though the exchequer did not extend to canals, it still furnished the essentials of kingship.

The Sologne was a wilderness of soft marsh and heath. Its dark low buildings of wood and cob crouched beside small, shallow lakes and flyblown meres. Road-builders, in bypassing its spongy heatherlands, had left the peasants there as autonomous rulers over a kingdom of snipe, gnats and toads. As fast as they felled the trees, the trees remaining closed ranks. As fast as they cut heather for their beds, their cattle, their roofs, a fresh tide of green rolled in to fill the gap. The trees waded knee-deep in bracken. Their roots reached through shifting swamp in a futile search for firm ground. The only outsiders to brave its inhospitality were pilgrims to the church in Saint-Viâtre; jaundiced sinners in search of a cure. For Saint-Viâtre held out the cure for malaria to those who believed. As Berenice said, 'Why else would anyone want to go there?'

Thibault did more than just go there. He emptied the estates of men. The vines grew untended, the Sablois apples fell to the worm, as he poured manpower into the Sologne. And when all the men at his command were deployed, he shipped in more – tens by scores by hundreds of others – vagrants, itinerants, wolf's-heads and cripples.

He envisaged a canal of crystal clarity flowing as straight as a ruled line through the dark bewilderment of the Sologne, bleeding it of its impurities, purging it of its foul humours. In fact the first time he visited the starting site, the broom was blossoming and fountains of flowery yellow gushed upwards like cheers all around him. Sunlight flickered on lakes too numberless to have been named, and mistletoe hung in dark green clusters from every tree. Shrike, widgeon and pheasants leapt up to salute him, and boar shook the undergrowth like pardoned prisoners clamouring along their bars. There was wildlife enough to feed an army of labourers. He deployed huntsmen to forage. He employed cooks to roast the catch. Then he went to Chambord to take possession of Leonardo's great plans for the Canal du Sologne.

Berenice did not demur at the inroads made on her dowry. The money was no longer hers, after all. Thibault was free to do with it as he chose. She and the children even accompanied him to Chambord. The palace sat like a resplendent potentate enthroned on the green cushions of the Sologne. Berenice stood with her husband among the Alhambra of chimneys and turrets and he pointed out to her where his canal would run – from one green horizon to another and far, far beyond. Only from up here was the scale of his task brought home to him. Imagining it already accomplished, the magnitude of it filled him with happy amazement. His fingers plucked nervously at the moss already growing in abundance along the newly finished parapet. 'D'you see, Thomas? D'you see, Kempis? A man-made river, all the way from Tours to Lyon.'

'And will it carry ships, Mother?'

'Like the Sablois, Mother?'

Why ask her rather than him? And why could she not answer them? Her silence infuriated him. He tried to startle his sons with the grandeur of his expectations: the profits that would accrue, the credit it would afford him with the King: the pollen of fame that would stick to his fingers in handling da Vinci's plans. 'And pray what *do* you think, lady?' he asked at last in exasperation.

She looked around her at the cupolas, chimneys and minarets. 'This place reminds me of the Temptation of Christ,' she said. '*And then the Devil set Him on a pinnacle of the Temple* . . . I fear Francis is akin to your canal, husband. He passes through his empire draining it as he goes. I hope you realize – he'll never reach out a hand to curb extravagance. It's his favourite vice.'

'Silence, woman! How dare you!' Thibault fumbled with his

rage, and finding his head empty of words and his hands full of moss, seized his wife by the cords of her cape and pushed the green velvety fungus into her mouth. 'Never let me hear you speak ill again of the King!' Terrified, the children took to their heels and fled. 'And in front of my sons!' he reproached her. 'How dare you say such things in front of my sons?'

She looked back at him implacably, her lips smeared with green and little fragments of moss held in the pleats of her ruff. She swallowed with difficulty once or twice, but even after her mouth was empty she said nothing.

The concierge who delivered the da Vinci plans into Thibault's hands was surprised that the man should find them so sketchy. 'He was a right antique gentleman,' she said. 'I were at Amboise then – just up the road from Cloux. Used to see him every day. Paralysed he was, in the hands. And his eyes weren't good for much. He just did little jobs for the King. Costumes for parties, that sort of thing.' She turned and scuffed away, her voice and echoing footsteps hardly impinging on the vast silence of the empty chateau: empty rooms stacked one upon the other by the dozen, by the score, by the hundred.

The da Vinci plan for the canal consisted of a straight line ruled from Tours to Rouen across a monotint map of northern France.

After one glance Thibault swiftly rolled it up again and replaced the ribbon. 'Surveyors,' he said cheerfully, and ruffled Kempis' hair. 'It occurs to me that I must have more surveyors. I'll send to Paris.' He avoided looking at his wife. He arranged for her to travel home independently while he took Thomas and Kempis to cut the first sod at Saint-Viâtre.

Summer was barely over on the Sablois when work came to a halt on the Canal du Sologne. The Overseer sent word to Thibault to come and see the problems which prevented further progress. When he arrived it was raining. He took it for a day's inclemency at first, but found that the Sologne had been enjoying torrential rain for seven weeks.

'Shall you disband the teams till spring, my lord? We'll get no forwarder till the other side of winter.'

'Do what?' The scene was a quiet one, the gentle tints of autumn blurred by silver drizzle, the soothing tambourine tap of raindrops falling on tens and twenties of taut white tents. The shape of them was pleasing against the ovals and curves of treetops and poolside.

'Disband them? And have what to show for two months of food and maintenance? Disband them? What've they *done*?'

The Overseer turned and indicated, among all the pools and puddles, one particular isthmus of water. 'The ditch keeps filling with rain, sir, and the way's too mired up for supplies to come in from Viâtre.'

Thibault was pacing out the length of the waterlogged ditch. 'And is this what you have for me? In two months? A furlong of pondwater? Jesu! You idle pack of bastards! I'll have you before the assizes! How much have you siphoned off while you all kept holiday at my expense? Blood and nails! Did you think to get by with a furlong? You must take me for half-witted!'

The Overseer protested his industry. 'Idle? I've had 'em working dawn till dusk for six days in and out, God witness! These are ploughing men, sir! They're used to flint and loam, not swamp! Even the army sappers've never worked in the like of this!'

But Thibault would have none of it. 'Since Adam was in Eden, men have dug holes in the ground. Get 'em out of their tents! Get 'em out and digging, or must I?'

They did come out. They shovelled up random spadefuls of earth here, there and anywhere, just so as to keep from drawing the eye and wrath of the raging Comte de Gloriole. The burden of their shovels could be heard falling wetly, like a hundred cow pats, in among the steaming trees.

But it was like poking hibernating badgers with a stick. They could not be kept from inactivity for long. Soon the water filling the cut gully froze, and the water puddling the ground with tarns froze too, and the soft ground froze hard as metal. Raw, saw-toothed winds ripped through the trees, and a tedious black sky sat so low over the Sologne as to rest on the bracken roofs of the cob houses. When Thibault visited his enterprise in December it was bound hand and foot in manacles of ice and black frost. It could not move forward one fraction of an inch.

His workforce dwindled away: filched their tools in lieu of payment and walked off the Sologne into the anonymity of distant comtés. He mustered one afresh: boys and demobs, flint-gatherers, women and pensioners. Only the local people resisted the temptation of Sablois gold and hung back under the eaves of their grim little houses, watching and shaking their heads. Where they stood in his way, he fired their hamlets in the name of the King. They came back at night and stole his timber shorings to build new homes.

Then in the spring the weather improved. Purple heather grew so thick on either bank of the new trenching that the earth looked bruised. Huntsmen riding out from Chambord and Tours expressed amazement as their horses leapt the ditching. They heaped praise and encouragement on de Gloriole. The fawning, adoring Vache begged the Comte to proceed with all speed, and insisted on loaning more funds at a derisory rate of interest.

And all the while, the Overseer's letters mewled, begging Thibault 'to come at once and see', 'to reconsider his last instructions', 'to hunger less after the impossible'. The face and name of the Overseer had changed a dozen times, but the letters might all have come from one man. And when Thibault stood on the roof of Chambord chateau and looked out beyond its velvety green parks to the sunny Sologne, there was still nothing to show for two hundred thousand écus. It was as though the Sologne, having swallowed them, had closed its mouth and set its lips against him in smug derision.

At last he determined that if he could not force men to work by power of will, he must do it by brute force. The letters which went ahead of him said that he was taking personal charge of the project.

The sun was brassy when he left the Sablois. The Sologne, however, was in thrall to celestial palaces of creamy nimbus cloud. The tarns were vats of sunlight curded with weed; there were clumps of blackness too which proved to be whole nations of engendering flies. The sweet air, like wine spoiled by lees, filled a rider's mouth with gnats.

And though the heat was really too oppressive even for the exertion of riding, when Thibault reached his Canal du Sologne, the navvies labouring in the bottom of it were clothed as if for winter, their sleeves and breeches bound in tight with twine at wrist and ankle, their hoods pinched close round their faces to keep off the mosquitoes. Their sweat burst in black patches through their garments, as blood oozes out of a man hit by grapeshot. It was as if they had sweated pint upon gallon into the trench and mired their own digging, for they staggered splay-legged through knee-deep mud, slipping and falling and scrabbling to their feet again, their fingers elongated with gules of slime, their breeches bulging, then emptying brown water through the open weave. When they paused for breath, they would spreadeagle themselves against the brown mud walls, barely distinguishable from the amputated tree roots groping the soil beside them.

He came across a wagon sunk axle-deep in an emerald-green bog. He came across expensive stirrup-pumps half interred in the ground. And everywhere he came across sweaty peasants gibbering under trees and in among bushes, imbecilic death's-heads shivering under blankets on the ground, curled up on their knees, their foreheads to the ground, like Moorish worshippers. And dying. He took the noise in his ears for indignation, but it was only the whine of mosquitoes.

The Overseer, clearly as ravaged by malaria as any of his crew, greeted Thibault as though he might be just one more hallucination. With a blanket clutched round his shoulders and his knees pressed together so as to balance on the insteps of his feet, he gave a wild sweep of the stick he had been leaning on, condemning the countryside at large. 'It's the water table. Dig and it comes up to meet you. Like digging a beach. Fills up soon as it's dug. See for yourself. Collapses in on you. Can't get a clean lip. It's all the time slurrying down. Sometimes five men go at one time. Slurry swallows 'em. And they walk off, too. How am I meant to keep 'em from walking off? Look in the tents! They're dead or they're gone.'

'Damn them to Hell,' said Thibault.

'Oh, they'd go there and thank you. Anywhere, so the ground's firm.'

Thibault walked from tent to tent, snatching back the flaps. It was not true that the occupants were dead, though many believed themselves to be in Hell already, rolled up in blankets, clutching illness to them like a lover. Mosquitoes whined their tittle-tattle in his ear.

Something dropped out of a tree on to Thibault's shoulder and in trying to brush it clear he only succeeded in frightening it into the shelter of his collar, the warmth of his neck. It scurried down inside his clothes. He was in a consumption to be rid of it – those cold, scaly feet scrabbling against his back, round his ribs, quivering on the brow of his belly. He dragged his shirt out of his trousers and shook himself like a dog. 'Get it off me! Get it out of me!' But the group of men gathered round a fire, tempering broken tools, only stared at him hollow-eyed, unaware who he was. A lizard the length of his palm dropped on to the ground. Without thinking, Thibault kicked it into the base of the fire.

'Won't be rid of it that way,' said the man on the far side. He clapped down a hand and snatched the same lizard out of the ashes. It had run clean through the fire. 'Salamander, that is. Likes fire, it does. Eats fire. Millions in this piss-hole.'

But it was like a sign from Heaven to Thibault. A salamander! The heraldic symbol of the King himself. His heart lifted. His head swam with the significance of the omen. He was filled with renewed fervour for the task. He would snatch glory from this desperate, filthy slough! That was what the omen signified. He reached out to take back the priceless creature from the man's hand. But the smith too had grown disgusted at the feel against his flesh of the tiny claws. To him it was one more creeping thing in a wilderness of insects, lizards, leeches, toads and lice. 'This whole stinking place is crawling . . .' And he threw it over Thibault's head and into the flooded canal where it panicked for a moment before drowning in plain sight.

Just then yet another wedge of bank about the size of a table slumped into the water with a swirl of brown. Without reverence for the genius of da Vinci or the wishes of the King or the efforts of the Comte de Gloriole, the Canal du Sologne was returning to its primordial constituents of mud, slime, ooze, bog and swamp. The mosquitoes seemed to have penetrated Thibault's eardrum and to be excavating his brain.

His wife did not triumph in his defeat. She merely equipped a fever hospital in Viâtre to nurse the survivors. She even ministered to Thibault's injuries – his wounded pride, and the loss of face he felt in the eyes of his sons.

But how was Francis to be told? Thibault was torn between the horror of admitting to his failure and the terror that Francis would hear the news from someone else.

At last his hand was forced. The Steward of the Royal Hunt called to inform him that the King's Hunt would be riding through the outskirts of the Sablois next day and that a banquet should be furnished for its huntsmen. Thibault steeled himself for his fall from Grace. For Lucifer the fall from Heaven could not have seemed so far or so terrible.

'But what exactly is it you're afraid of losing?' Berenice asked. 'The friendship of the King? If it's a stuff that relies on tributes and successes, it's not worth having, surely?'

He dismissed her stupidity with an impatient hand. 'The greatest man in France? The greatest king among all the Kings of France? Greatness doesn't tolerate failure.'

She continued with her reading, then permitted herself to say, 'I hope you're not mistaking stature for greatness. I agree Francis is a very *tall* man. He takes an uncommonly large size in boots. But that doesn't make him a Titan. Half the government disaffected from him . . .'

'Hold your noise, woman. "Disaffected"? There's a fine euphemism for treachery.'

She was still at pains not to cross him. 'Perhaps I meant disaffected from his mistresses. After all, it only calls for *over-generosity* on his part to give away the country's revenue to his whore . . .'

'Enough! The King only bestows his favours where they're merited.' His tone of voice was intended to forbid all contradiction.

'Oh Thibault,' she said, startling him with the rare use of his name. 'Don't try too hard, my dear. Do please remember how you despise and disparage poor Vache for trying to please and serve you. You wouldn't like Francis to feel like that towards you.'

He was open-mouthed at her impudence. When she raised the subject of the royal mistresses he had expected a prim lecture – the usual cluck-clucking of dry old women and pious frumps. He had not expected to be called a toady. There was no gibe bad enough to repay the insult. '*I* have a mistress *too*, you know,' he said.

But if he expected horror and tears, he was disappointed. She looked at him with the vestige of a puzzled frown and said, 'Yes, I know, dear. Forgive me, but I can't quite see the relevance of that to the argument. Indeed, I'd've thought she might object to you lavishing such affection on someone other than her . . . Anyway, all I started out to counsel was ease of mind over this business of the canal. It wouldn't have made you a friend of the King if he didn't care for you already, and if he does, then a canal undug won't unmake you in his affections. You spent deep enough, God knows. You meant well.'

She was right, as it happened. The King had so completely forgotten the Sologne project that he needed reminding of it. 'No matter,' he said blithely. 'Would've ruined the hunting, I dare say.' And he graciously granted Thibault the right to carve the Royal Salamander over the outer gates of Gloriole. 'I'll give you something else, too, Gloriole! In recompense for your effort!'

Thibault's heart was rocked by cheers. He had expected reproaches, at best forgiveness. Reward for failure was beyond his imagining. 'I'll tell you as useful a trick as you ever heard!' said

Francis, leaning out of the saddle to confide his secret in Thibault's ear. 'The dogs in your villages – they cut down your game birds one in three. Don't tell me they don't.'

'I suppose . . .'

'Cut one leg off 'em, that's what! *Swicht!* You'll find your sport picks up past measure. A leg off every dog in the comté! I've tried it! I've proved it! You do it and see! One leg! Woop-là! Do it!'

'I'm honoured by your advice, my lord King,' said Thibault. And standing in the shadow cast by that gigantic form, warmed by the beneficence of those slanting, vital eyes, holding the stirrup of that straddling Colossus, it was perfectly true.

Thibault often dreamed he was back on the Sologne. He would be hewing away at the end wall of a trench when all the solidity would go out of the spade he was holding, then out of the boards under his feet, the soil in front of him. Everything would begin to swallow him down like a wet gullet, sucking him down until the quagmire reached his neck, his lip, his nose. He called for help, but all that came were mosquitoes who clustered in clouds round his head, whining with a shriller and shriller excitement. He would wake swatting at his ears and cheeks. But it proved not to be the noise of the mosquitoes whining in his ears. Only his blood racing.

FORTY

The Duel

Madame Dideron, Thibault's mistress, was not a source of unalloyed joy to him. She did not have the generosity of spirit to match the voluptuous proportions of her gorgeous body. Although she was blonde and of Pisseleu stock (like the King's own current mistress), this promising formula had not proved as auspicious as it might. She was forever asking for things, in the songbird flutiness of her high voice. But what she gave in return had no Arthurian magic to it. In bed her unimaginative compliance was like racing a sloth up a tree: he knew dejectedly that he could win every time.

Every so often he tested her shortcomings against other lovely satellites of the Court, and she did not compare badly. But in the context of that other, that unnatural passion of his – the one which stayed in his blood like malaria and flared up just when he thought he had shaken it off – Madame Dideron simply could not compete. Perversions are like that: they sap the appeal out of ordinary wholesome pastimes. He tried not to admit it to himself, but his wife had ruined him for the simple, Christian pleasures of a mistress.

He did not very often trouble to visit Madame. She did not take issue over it. She was besotted with his face, hypnotized by the sight, touch and sound of him. But it was prestige enough to be associated with the beautiful, the excelling Comte de Gloriole. She was the envy of her friends. How could a man of such personal attractions fail to rise at a Court which lived in pursuance of Beauty? She maintained that he would be given a ministry at Court before he was thirty and have chateaux like Montmorency, money like Louise de Savoie, and farms in Italy. He liked to hear her say it, but not because he coveted the wealth.

It was an age of money. Along the Loire, commoners were building chateaux – even buying titles. A contradiction in terms, that. For in Thibault's mind the virtue of a title rested in that which could not be bought – natal nobleness, a genetic quality of blood, a God-created accident of birth. He perceived, in his imagination, the glory of the Godhead descending in a diminishing brightness over the wings of His angels, the head of the King, his kin and noblemen, their subjects and chattels, their kine and cattle. That key place in the pyramidical structure of Grace was the priceless bequest he held in trust for his sons. Material assets were simply proof of God's approval.

He was in half a mind to do with Madame Dideron as the King was reputed to have done with Diane de Poitiers, and bequeath her early to one of his sons. But Thomas, on consideration, would probably neglect her as much as Thibault, being a studious, frail, underfleshed boy with eyesight too poor to appreciate Madame's assets. He had one of those childlike, cherubic faces which would not age at all, before suddenly shrivelling into that of an old man. His genius was for pure mathematics, a subject whose name alone would forbid it to some young men but which suited Thomas down to the ultimate decimal point. His looks came from his mother's side and, as such, Thibault would have liked to despise them. But gentle, effete little Thomas was a target too small to invite contempt: it slipped to either side of him like the river round an eyot. Even his brother, who at twelve was a master at the tilt, never directed the point of his wit against Thomas.

As for Kempis (who had his father's looks and the promise of acquiring every knightly accomplishment) – well, he simply deserved better than Madame Dideron.

No pair of twins could have been less alike. Their father took it for granted that he loved better the handsome, accomplished Kempis, every time he saw them seated side by side at table. Thomas would never amount to much. He was a clerk, a book-keeper, an accountant. There would be a place for him in the life of the Gloriole estate; he would have a certain functional usefulness. But Kempis would sit in feud over Gloriole-sur-Sablois or teach his brother to keep up a semblance of order while he went into Italy on the latest royal campaign. From time to time, Thibault threatened – whenever Thomas showed more soup stains than usual on his doublet, or a black eye from walking into a door – to take him on campaign to Italy and make a man of him. And the boy's eyes would flicker with alarm and he would bite his lip more agitatedly. But there was something squirrel-like and vulnerable about him which protected him from Thibault's most forceful ambitions. He was, like a used nose-rag, not quite respectable enough to be brought out in fashionable company. And yet he seemed to accumulate friends, just as much as his velvety, upward-growing hair collected pollen, blades of grass, strands of thread, brick-dust. He could not be socially noxious; it must simply be that he travelled by different and circuitous routes towards the same end.

Thibault was thinking this as he jabbed his heels into his horse to catch up with Thomas. He had just caught sight of the boy across the cattle market in Rocheblanche. A cast horseshoe had unexpectedly diverted him to the smithy there. He was surprised to see the boy: Thomas had not said he was going to market. He called out to him, but the incessant, tragic bleat of sheep and nagging of chickens swallowed up his shout. Besides, Thomas was immersed in a book, reading as he rode, his head sunk down between his collarbones, his back hunched. Thibault fixed his eyes on that nape of glossy, dense, velour hair and shook his reins impatiently.

Both horses were awash to the knees in a flock of noisy sheep; he could neither raise a trot nor attract the boy's attention. A sheet of paper fluttered down behind Thomas's pony. Thibault felt a pang of fond despair for the woolly-brained youngster surrounded by his woolly peers. The pony's reins were dangling loose; it seemed to be wandering at random, taking its direction from the flock. Another page floated to the ground, then another. The book must be disintegrating between his two hands, and still the boy was too engrossed to notice. Thibault dismounted and groped for the first fallen page, like a wader in white woollen surf, till he picked it up from among the sheep's hooves. He valued his library too much to let a book be so irreparably damaged. Only when he noticed how the second sheet resembled the first did he look more closely and see that they were not pages at all. They were handbills. In the meantime Thomas had dropped four and five more.

Encumbered by his horse, Thibault scurried after them to snatch them up.

. . . who burned to death the saintly Berquin . . .
. . . who smiled on the massacre of 800 holy folk at Vaudois . . .

Thibault let go of his horse and ran in pursuit of another five, six, seven sheets that Thomas had let fall. The shepherd boy, seeing his efforts, ran and fetched two more. 'Good boy, good boy. A sou for every one you find.'

465

. . . who is lackey to the butchers of the Sorbonne . . .
. . . who is blind to the sins of his clergy while they fill his coffers . . .

Thomas, like a baby with its eyes shut, thinking it cannot be seen, rode doggedly on, head down, not looking back, believing his actions as furtive as night.

. . . who is ruled by petticoats and enslaved by letchery . . .
. . . who makes France a beggar to win vainglory in Italy . . .

Though the shepherd boy was determined that every sou should come to him, Thibault enlisted more and more tradesmen, herdsmen, wives and drunkards to gather up the handbills. Thomas's propaganda fell like snow, and no sooner touched the ground than it melted away. Triumphantly the treasure-hunters ringed Thibault round, their arms aloft, their hands full of bunched and crumpled paper. He had to back-track to his horse to fetch money. The payment of rewards was complicated by a lack of change. He watched the crowd for those who showed signs of reading the handbills while they waited for their money. Then he would snatch the papers out of their hands and count them flamboyantly, aloud.

. . . who is a puppet for the Pope . . .
. . . who is very wicked . . .
. . . who gave his sons into captivity that he might be free . . .

Thibault's son meanwhile grew more and more distant, showering his treacherous litter in a sparse trail towards the southern horizon. At last an enterprising youth, impatient of competing for the litter, caught up with the pony and snatched the entire remaining ream out of Thomas's hands so that the boy looked up, startled and alarmed. He turned round in the saddle, caught sight of his father, and with a mouth as round as an O, jabbed his heels in and took off at a trot. Then Thibault's view of him was obscured by the enthusiastic crowd, all vowing they had no change for his silver pieces. There was a great shortage of change in Rocheblanche that day.

By the time Thibault arrived home at Gloriole, he was riddled with spleen and his doublet was stuffed to bursting with crumpled papers. 'Where is he? I'll take the hide off him! This is your doing, woman! Did you know he was using your press? Did you allow it? Blood and water, woman! Can't you keep a tighter lead on your own pups?'

466

Berenice said, 'I don't know what's grieved you, my dear, but there's business afoot in the stove. You have a visitor.'

'Oh, damn visitors. Visitors can hang themselves. Where's Thomas? I'll beat him inside out and right side out again, sly little beggar. He'll have us all hanged!' And he flung down a ball of handbills on the table.

She extricated one. 'He's accurate at least. A rather wild spelling of lechery, but then it's not a word he has much to do with. You should thank God you have a son who can tackle "Berquin" better than "lechery". I think your visitor is urgent to see you.'

'I should thank God that my horse threw a shoe this morning and put me in the path of your son undoing us ... What d'you mean, he's *accurate*?'

'In his portrait of the King. Out of the mouths of babes and sucklings ...'

'... comes what was put there by their mothers! You mean you endorse these – these – *blasphemies*?'

'The King would be hard put to deny them,' she said, with her usual soft-spoken placidity, smoothing out each bill with a kind of tenderness before feeding it to the fire. 'Your visitor goes by the name of Dideron and she seems greatly alarmed for your mutual safety. I really think you shouldn't let the excellent lady suffer another moment's unshared anxiety. I put her in the stove-hall: her dress didn't seem adequate to the weather.' She always denied him an outlet for his spleen: he always had to carry away from an argument as much as he had brought.

Despite his amazement at finding his mistress had called on him and had received a civil welcome, he was still preoccupied with rage against Thomas. The first thing he said as he slammed the stove-hall door behind him was, 'D'you know what that son of mine's done? The boy's a half-wit! A numbskull! Wait till I take a hold on him. I'll thrash him to the Vatican and back.' He went on divesting himself of waste paper, throwing it into the stove. Madame Dideron picked up one sheet which fell out again and browsed over it.

'It's a strange age he's at,' she said routinely. 'Boys can be a sore trial.' Then she recalled her tragedy. 'Oh dear! Oh God help us! Thibault, listen! My husband means to kill you!' And she plucked his arms round her like an otter stole and burst into tears against his chest.

'He what?'

'A duel. He means to send you a challenge to a duel!'

467

It certainly slowed Thibault's momentum, for all it was a ridiculous notion. 'I thought he never left the Vendée? A duel? For God's sake. What offence does he think I've done him?'

She looked at him a little reproachfully, but was too busy explaining how the impossible had come about. 'It was the King, Thibault. It was quite, quite dreadful. He invites Jacques to Court – even has him to table. You know how he loves to pace up and down – the King, I mean – up and down, round and round the table, telling jokes, touching the ladies. You know how he does, while a meal's on the table. Well, round and round he goes, up and down, and when he's behind Jacques' chair – God help us – doesn't he put his fingers up to his forehead like this! There's Jacques sitting across from me. Looks up – looks in the mirror over my head – sees the King! You should have seen the colour he went. Lord ha' mercy! Black! Not purple, black! There's people laughing, of course – looking at me and laughing. Oh dear heart, it was terrible!' (And yet Thibault gained the strong impression that the shine in her eyes was from the excitement of reliving that *terrible* moment.) 'Up leaps Jacques – well, struggles to his feet all wheezes and grunts. Turns round. His chair overbalances – right on the King's toes – Lord that must've hurt! "And who, pray, have I to thank for such a pair of horns?" says Jacques. You know how he speaks – that boar-grunting of his. You know it. Well, His Majesty does a great capering dance – oh, I mean everyone there felt just too awful for him! – So *like* Jacques to embarrass his host. He couldn't wait till after and take issue in a private place – oh no! "Who have I to thank for such a pair of horns?" ' She mimicked unkindly, and still Thibault could not help thinking how she cherished that sentence and would cherish it till Death sealed up her mouth. ' "Not me!" says His Majesty. So light-hearted, bless him! And he *would not* give your name – gentleman and saint that he is. Jacques had to drag it out of him by prayer and supplication, never doubt me! He went down on hands and knees, that old lobster. He played on the King's pity before Francis would give you up to him.'

'The King named me?'

'Jacques had too much wine in him, of course, or he'd not have made such a spectacle . . .'

'The King *named* me?'

'Wine always makes Jacques wet at the eye and sentimental. Hey-ho.' She lost her place just thinking about it, then rallied and cantered on to the matter of the duel. 'He swears he'll send you a challenge – instantly – now – today! I believe somebody put him up to it for the sake of the sport, and now his mind's set fast and no budging. But you won't fight him – you shan't! He might hurt your poor dear face.'

Preoccupied, he snatched his face out of the clasp of her two damp, scented hands. 'He must still be drunk to think of it. He's my worse for thirty years. I'd spit him like a woodcock.'

'Ah, but he might scar you.'

'Don't do that. I'm trying to think.'

'Tibby!'

'What did the King mean by it? Name me? Why would he do that to me?'

'Oh, the King wouldn't have done it for the world! He was quite abject with me after. Quite!' (The best yet. The day had confirmed her happy: the King had dandled in her palm and apologized abjectly.)

'Not see a mirror? Once, madam, once it might happen by accident. But I've heard the story before, and such accidents don't happen twice. So why?'

Madame was at a loss. Accidents she could understand. Guile was too complicated. Thibault could sympathize with her stupidity: he could grasp that there was mischief afoot but not map its complexities. He was strongly inclined to call his wife and ask her. Instinct recommended Berenice, as it recommends a ship's mast to a migrant bird lost over the ocean. Meanwhile, Madame was still forbidding him to put his pretty features at risk from her husband's swordpoint. 'What will you *do*? What *will* you *do*?' she wailed balefully, plunging her prayerful hands inside his doublet and finding yet another handbill. She pulled it out and looked it over idly, but she had time only to see:

Unite and rise up against the tyrannies of a viceful King!
. . . who burned to death . . .

before Thibault snatched it away.

'My boy's folly. His mother's doing. She shouldn't have let him play with her toys.'

'Your wife has a printing press? Fancy. How very . . . *masculine*. But Tibby, what will you *do*?' The owls in the tocsin tower could not have hooted so loud or melancholy.

'Fight him, I suppose,' he said dubiously. 'If he really is fool enough to send a challenge.'

469

'And I'll be your second!' An incipient swoon was forestalled by a burst of romantic energy. 'Yes, yes! Don't thwart me! I'll dress as a boy and play your second! A black cloak – a tall black hat – oh yes! I shall be on hand to give you courage!'

The thought might have seemed more dreadful but for Thibault's conviction that no fight would ever take place. 'Don't fret, my dear. It'll never happen. I'm sure your excellent husband cherishes life as dear as I do. Go home now . . .'

'Home?!'

'Back to Court, I mean. And be so good as not to flout the proprieties quite so completely another time.' She blinked at him, still reminiscent of the owls. 'By calling at my chateau, I mean. God speed.'

The challenge did come, nevertheless. Berenice said: 'Have a care. Refuse it. Don't play into the King's hands. As I see it, he has it in mind to confiscate Gloriole and use your killing Dideron for the excuse.'

'Jesu, woman! What a kennel you have for a mind! How do you conceive such plots? I see now who schooled Thomas in his warped opinions!'

'No matter,' she said. 'It's of no account. Believe it or don't. Just as long as you don't fight. It's your place to name weapons. Name unicorn horns.'

'Are you being facetious? At a time like this?'

It was not even as though he had told her about the duel. He resented bitterly that she should have guessed everything without him confiding one word in her. 'I'm not joking, Thibault,' she said. 'Honour's served. The fight's impossible. Name feathers. Name oak trees. Name what you will so long as throats can't be cut.'

He dismissed the cowardly suggestion with a snort of disgust . . . but carried it away from table with him furtively. He named broadswords, thinking that Monsieur Dideron's great age would forbid him hauling a two-hander through the woods to the rendezvous on the tufa cliffs above Gloriole.

But Dideron had swum too deep to turn back and reach shore with his honour still in his teeth. He accepted broadswords and arrived at the place with his eyebrows spangled with dew. Little wedges of grey shadow held his face rigid, though he had still managed to cut himself shaving.

Madame too was there, but masked and clinging to the crook

of Thibault's arm with a debilitating excitement. She had already been prettily sick in a bush. Thibault kept disengaging her grip but it kept coming back with the stranglehold of convolvulus. Her big bosom strained the resources of her especially tailored doublet, and there was jewellery on her hands. Dideron was either too much of a gentleman to comment on her presence, or too preoccupied with dying to see clearly. The joints in his wrists cracked loudly as he shifted the weight of his borrowed sword. As his second he had brought his son, who showed signs of embarrassment at his father's stupidity. Thibault wondered what manner of man would bring his son to see him dismembered. He wondered, if Kempis were to have come, whether he would have criticized Thibault's technique; whether Thomas would have read a book throughout.

The view was intoxicating, the sun rising under a furrowed brow of cloud, and the river shimmering into life. Yellow euphorbias and purple iris flew rival banners on either bank, and a surf of nettles broke up against the cliff with a spray of rose-bay willow herb. 'Let us be agreed. The loser shall be transported secret from this place,' said Dideron through dry larynx, 'and given burial – sudden but holy – and the cause not be made known.'

'Agreed,' said Thibault. He pushed the tip of his own sword to and fro through the leaf-mould and across a moving line of ants. The ants never faltered. Some died, but the overall column never faltered. 'Who put you up to this, Dideron? Was it the King?'

But Dideron only shook himself like a dog, as though Thibault's impropriety of words could be shaken off like water. It was not *comme il faut* to speak. It was *comme il faut* only to kill or to die.

The old man had been practising in the intervening week. He could parry in all four quarters. But Thibault made no serious attempt to strike home. The insult was heavier for Dideron to bear than the sword. He swung a frenzy of slashes, cleaving up divots of earth wherever the sword-tip dropped back to the ground. But Thibault simply stepped out of its way. The sight of the stained steel blades and the bestial grunts torn from both men by the sheer effort of lifting them sobered Madame. She withdrew to clutch at a tree, as though ensuring a third lover to see her safe home. The son ran away to a safe distance. The single dull note of steel hitting steel resounded through the forest like a funeral knell played on a cracked bell by a drunken sexton.

Lactic acid filled Thibault's fists, wrists, forearms, until he was wearing gauntlets of pain, and each time he parried a blow, the jolt that travelled down the hilt jarred his knuckles against one another like a game of fives. He began to retaliate rather than give ground and find himself among the trees, hindered by branches overhead. He noticed that Dideron shut his eyes in the very instant of his sword landing. It would be easy to take him then with a double lunge, a forward feint then on into the gizzard or throat. And then? The eyelashes that closed with each blow were grey; Thibault noticed that, too.

He cursed Berenice for her insinuating propaganda. The King plot to confiscate Gloriole? What had Thibault ever done but his damnedest to fulfil his fealty? Where in the whole kingdom was there a truer subject? What had he ever done to invite persecution? He could hear his wife's sinuous voice soothing him with heresies.

'You mistake private enterprise for public justice,' she had said. 'He took Chenonceau from Bohier and gave it to Diane de Poitiers. He takes Gloriole from you for Anne de Heilly. Just deserts don't come into it.' Such cynicism. It was not becoming in a woman. He blamed her religion. A few dissenters burned, a few authorities butchered, and she was prepared to accuse Francis of any vice in the world. He held it a kind of madness to maintain political views quite so strongly. Still, just in case she was right, he held off from the double feint that would slit Dideron's carotid artery, topple his head off its neck, and just maybe give the King an excuse to confiscate Gloriole.

The old man attempted a ballestra and his feet skidded on the leaf-mould as he came down, and he staggered, impelled from side to side by the momentum of his sword. Thibault barged him shoulder-to-shoulder and sent him sprawling. He pitied the man the humiliation of being spared. In Dideron's place he would sooner have felt the blade.

He was a rapier man himself. That's to say he practised with the rapier for sport. The unaccustomed use of such very different muscles suddenly made them cramp and one hand open of its own accord. He kept hold of the sword but it fell out of the air, unstoppable, and he had to drag it after him as he retreated from Dideron's renewed onslaught. The old man grew mad-eyed at the possibility of living after all.

The rhythm of broadswords is a slow one, inexorable but patient. Dideron wanted to hurry it, tried to speed up the ponderous parabola of the arcing blade, took it high above his head as he pursued Thibault to the lip of the cliff, pulled the hilt down into his face with two impatient fists, and made to rive Thibault down the backbone while his face was still turned away and his weapon still down.

But instead of wheeling forwards, the weight of the blade continued its backward arc, falling, falling, falling down behind Dideron, pulling his elbows up until they were above his head. He could have dropped the sword, but he clung to it, swerving to regain his balance, his back arching, his arms twisting in their sockets. One foot only went over the cliff edge at first and it seemed he would recover himself. But like a drowning man clutching for safety at an iron girder, he obstinately clung to the broadsword which found no impediment in falling a hundred feet towards the river below.

He lodged only a few feet from the cliff's base, on a white ledge of tufa garlanded with eglantine. Looking down, they could see him quite clearly; foreshortening seemed to put him almost within reach. The eyes were open at first; they perused the sky, examined the oxlips in minutest detail, then picked out his wife, her lover and his son high above. He opened his mouth to call something but either thought better of it or found his throat blocked by shards of his backbone, and closed his lips again. Then he closed his eyes. The eglantine ceased to quiver except at the interference of the wind.

Madame Dideron was utterly silent at first. She stood looking down at the river, letting its current carry her gaze downstream towards the chateau. Gloriole was not visible, but the Sablois' undertow was quite strong enough to carry the imagination down reach and bend and sandbar to the ox-bow moat encircling its white chateau. The wind blew her cloak above her head. How big-bottomed a woman could look in man's puff-breeches. Her hat blew away and her hair came unfastened. When the cloak emptied of wind, she pulled it round her, feeling the cold.

'My profoundest condolences, madam,' said Thibault, at which she sighed sentimentally and replied, with characteristic inaccuracy, 'Ah well! That's life, I suppose.'

'You killed him,' said Dideron's son, the thought only newly come to him.

'He fell,' said Thibault.

'You really killed him.'

'I meant him to live,' said Thibault.

'He fell off his horse,' said Madame incisively. 'His horse stumbled and he was thrown over. You heard what he said: "The cause not

473

to be made known". There'll be no wounds on his body: it's plain he didn't die duelling.'

'You're no better,' said the boy. 'You killed him too.' His skin was pale with shock. She tweaked his nose spitefully.

'Hold it in, Dickie. The Comte means to make you a very rich boy indeed.'

'Your mother has just suffered a great blow. Your thoughts should be for her,' said Thibault.

'You see? The Comte's a man of sensibilities. While you're a bumpkin and a shame to your mother.'

The boy looked up and down his mother's ridiculous disguise. 'I want five thousand now.'

Thibault bridled, flaring his nostrils, but without engaging the boy's eye. 'Five thousand *what*?'

'Ecus.'

'Oh ten thousand, by all means!' exclaimed his mother, leaning heavily once more on Thibault's arm and leading him away from the cliff edge.

'Your son bears a striking resemblance to you, madam,' he observed. 'I'd not noticed it till now.'

'He *is* a fine-looking boy, thank you,' she simpered. 'Ah, sweet Thibault! What a very dear thing you've done for us! We three, I mean.'

'I trust your boy won't make it cost so very dear. I'm loath to hang for a scuffle.'

'Oh, you mustn't worry about Dickie, sweetheart! He likes to be peevish. But he'll like it better being son to the Comte de Gloriole. He won't risk that for a moment.'

He had too recently finished wondering where ten thousand écus could be come by to welcome new surprises. 'Are you saying you want me to adopt him? Poor fatherless boy and so forth?'

She smiled again, poutingly, blushingly, and hung as a lead weight on his arm. 'That will follow naturally, won't it? When you become his mother's husband.'

Thibault looked over his shoulder. Something as cold and sharp as a broadsword had struck him low in the back, and he fully expected to see the ghost of Dideron smiling at him out of the greenwood. 'Are you not overlooking one slight impediment?' The rectitude of his backbone grew upwards into his speech which emerged with a terse, clipped formality. Madame did not let it deter her. Words slipped out of her like spangles of grease from a dish of melting butter. 'No very great impediment, surely. My Saint Martin! Fearless on the banks of the Loire! Slaying the dragon! That is what you call her, isn't it? The Saumur Dragon?'

'I'm sorry you misconstrued the analogy,' he said as if each word cost him a livre to speak it. 'I draw the line at laying sword to a woman – even my zoological phenomenon of a wife.'

'Oh, my silly boy! I didn't mean *kill* her! Not actually *kill* her, ha ha! Not do it yourself, ha ha!'

It was rumoured Françoise de Foix, cast-off mistress of the King, had been stabbed to death by six masked men let into her chamber by her husband's key. Was that what she had in mind?

'Her life's under my protection,' he said icily.

'Ah yes! But if she were a traitor, it would be your bounden duty to cast her out – deliver her up to justice, wouldn't it?' She said it coquettishly, as if she were spurring him on to some jolly practical joke. 'I thought you had it in mind a three-weeks since. Does she really have a printing press?'

He perceived it, all at once, like a man in a beach cove noticing the incoming tide. 'A what? Oh. Well. It's nothing. A toy. No. She doesn't. Not any more.'

'And she's poisoning your son's mind against the King, plainly.'

'Thomas? Pah! He's a baby. A noddle-head. His politics will be changed all about by next week. You know what boys are when they're rubbing flanks with manhood. God knows you've got one of your own!' He tried to laugh dismissively, but the muscles of his face were too rigid.

'Anyone would think you didn't crave to marry me.' She said it so sibilant-soft that he could feel the dampness through his shirt, like syrup trickling.

'You know my heart has been at your disposal for many years,' he said peremptorily. 'But don't you think a slur of treachery against my wife might swallow up me and mine as well?'

'Not for a minute! No! Never! I know just the judge would welcome a single conviction and not be greedy for more . . .'

'Besides, as I say, there's no crime to find her out in.' She did not believe him, but was not in a position to argue. 'I regret, madam, our love must stay as it is – and who could wish it any other way, seeing what pleasure it's brought to us both? Leave us not mix pleasure with marriage or the one will canker the other for sure, like butterflies in a lettuce patch.'

She smiled, a tinkling waterfall of a smile, and sighed so deep

475

that her doublet burst a hook and eye. She clasped her hands in front of her belt as though about to recite an appropriate verse of poetry, then gave a girlish shrug and turned away. 'Just as you see fit,' she said, and there was a hint of barely restrained tears.

Thibault descended to the river bank and succeeded in dislodging the body with a tree-branch. The broadsword, which had continued on its way, like Excalibur, into the water, had left no incriminating mark on Dideron. It was possible to put him across a horse and dispatch him home, the victim of a lamentable riding accident. Madame Dideron was persuaded to accompany him and make her son word-perfect in his version of events, though Thibault was obliged to repeat the promise of ten thousand écus before parting tenderly from his silent, thoughtful lover.

He replaced his broadsword over the hearth where it had hung undisturbed for as long as he could remember. He was breathless from riding home at the gallop: there were fragments of leaves still caught in his clothing. Berenice stood pale and silent by the fireplace in a blue silk skirt that made her look like a bulrush in a pond. 'Wouldn't it be better to cart the press away? Break it up? Hide the pieces?' she asked, pressing her knuckles to her mouth.

'No time. No time. They could be here by nightfall.'

She followed him meekly up the staircase, carrying the other end of a rolled tapestry torn down from the gallery-tower. She fetched him a chair to stand on. She fetched him nails and a mallet. 'I could only find horseshoe nails in the stable,' she said. 'Will they serve?' Her hands were shaking so much that she had spilled half before she reached the house.

They pushed and dragged the armoire to the door of the East-turret room: the dwarfs Balon and Batonne helped them, balancing the chair on top of the armoire and hanging precipitously out over the banister to secure the topmost corners of the tapestry with horseshoe nails. 'Oh do be careful! Do be quick!' Berenice pleaded. She twisted a strand of hair alongside her face – round and round two fingers. 'How soon, Thibault? How soon do you think they'll come?'

'There's time. You may rely on a certain vegetable slowness in the woman.'

But there was a fine sweat on his face, condensation on the stained-glass of his features, and as he pushed the armoire back into place, the blood vessels swelled purple and knotty in his temples and his eyes bulged in their sockets.

'What makes you think she'll do it at all? Why should she do it? Without encouragement?'

'Count on slowness, woman. But don't count on the Madame denying herself anything she's once set her heart on. She has no experience of it. She'll inform against you. I saw it in her face.'

He pointed out a bulge in the arras where the handle of the door behind it pushed out the cloth. Balon and Batonne each drew up a bottom corner of the hanging, and Thibault smashed off the handle with the back of an axe. He did the same to the block and tackle through which ran the rope of the wooden drawbridge, and threw all but the rope over the banister. The woman and the dwarfs retreated down the corridor and Thibault, tying the rope round his waist, threw them the other end to make fast while he hacked away the drawbridge.

When he lifted the axe, all the same muscles in his wrists and hands cramped and ached as when he swung the broadsword. As he sank the axehead into the planking of the drawbridge, the jolt jarred his knuckles. But the sheer necessity of isolating that room, that machine, that pocket of disobedience inside his loyal house, gave him the strength to smash his way through the very floor he stood on. It left him unbalanced on two joists, while the planks fell away into the room below, twirling like oakseeds. The joists were thicker – dense, chestnut beams that flexed under the soles of his boots but would not shear away from the wall. One at last fell, with the slowness of a broken mast, and he was left straddling the other. He got back to his feet, but could not hold his balance to swing the axe. So he had to sit astride, the room beneath gaping for him. He could feel his palms sweat, the axe slip with each blow, the beam jerk under his crotch.

'Get downstairs and clean up the dross!' he bellowed at the dwarfs, and he had no sooner said it than their round, potato faces were goggling up at him from the room below. 'No, no! You! Crone! You go to the roof and keep watch for riders!' He had to pause for breath. 'Why am I doing this, woman? Why?' he asked Berenice. 'Shielding an illegal practice? Sheltering a lawbreaker? Harbouring an enemy of the King?'

'Because the King's your real enemy. Because he's manoeuvring to take Gloriole from you,' said her voice from the landing behind him.

'You really are subversive, aren't you, woman?'

'I think my own thoughts. I wouldn't inflict them on others.'

'And here am I, helping you. Colluding with you. Keeping your little secrets.'

She paused before speaking, though not out of uncertainty. 'Love's a powerful slave-driver, isn't it?'

'*Ha!*' He laughed loudly, aggressively, and found the strength to take four more swings of the axe, sending chestnut shards flying in all directions. 'So you fool yourself I love you, do you!'

'No, Thibault. I don't fool myself.'

He laughed again, and would have gone on laughing, but for a cock crowing incessantly in the yard outside. He could hear it gibing at him; he swore he could hear it. It renewed his indignant energy, and he slammed the axe once more into the angle of beam and wall, severing enough timber for the joist to sag downwards under his weight.

It snapped off clean at the other end and pitched from between his thighs into the room below. Balon skipped aside, his arms over his head. The axe wedged in a bench near by. Thibault meanwhile twisted and writhed in mid-air, suspended by the rope. But the armoire round which it was made fast began to shift slowly, slowly along the landing. Berenice threw herself in front of it on hands and knees, but it pushed her along too, closer and closer to the gaping hole in the floor.

Then Thibault righted himself, took hold of the rope, made a half-turn in it for his foot. His hands appeared over the edge of the smashed floor, snatching at the splintered wood as he pulled himself back up on to the landing, snagging his clothes and swearing foully. He cursed her ancestry of dragons, her ageing ugliness, her politics and her God.

There proved to be time enough. There was time to make good the woodwork, clear the wreckage, make the landing appear that it had never led anywhere but to a banistered cul-de-sac. No trace remained of the door to the East-turret room. No access remained to the printing press which crouched behind that door like a monstrous spider.

The searchers came – a platoon of guards from Tours acting on the advice of an anonymous informer who said there was an unlicensed printing press in the house. They searched, but they found nothing. (Thomas's books and possessions were smouldering in the stove for fear they concealed yet more juvenile calumnies against the Crown.) They looked but they found nothing. They even asked after access to the East turret and satisfied themselves that there was none.

'My fools asked it of me,' Thibault said to the sergeant-at-arms. 'They had it for an apartment once, but they came to me with talk of ghosts.'

The sergeant looked the dwarfs over dubiously.

'Women,' said Balon.

'Screaming,' said Batonne.

And Berenice added, in a strangely distant, detached voice, 'I never heard women. A baby sometimes. Crying.'

They came and they searched, but they found nothing. The printing press sat immured in its little room like one of King Francis' prisoners whom, for his fancy, he liked to wall up for life, away from the light of day, powerless to stand or sit.

If Francis did have plans to lay hold on Gloriole – if that was the story behind the duel – so small a setback would not have thwarted him. He would have found a way to take it. But a rather greater setback thwarted his plans that year. Death came and, for its fancy, immured him in a coffin, away from the light of day, powerless to stand or sit.

So the quarrel was never settled between Thibault and his wife. She went on believing that the King had connived to dispossess them. But she refrained from ever saying so again. Berenice was indebted to her husband: she had no wish to hurt him. And to have undermined the faith of a man so dedicated to the notion of Holy Kingship would have been like disproving Heaven to a dying man. So Thibault went on believing in the honour and perfection of Francis.

Or what if he did not? God's divinity now shone round the head of a new monarch – Henry II, his son.

FORTY-ONE

A Closed Circle

'She paints her face,' said Thomas with a prim hostility. 'And her family are all murderers and libertines.'

'I hardly think the one sin ranks with the other,' said his mother who warded off pomposity in her sons whenever she was able.

'Have you seen her ride a horse, though!' said Kempis with a roué's swerve of the eye.

'You can scarcely tell your grandchildren that you were privileged once to glimpse the Queen's bloomers though, can you? It lacks the romance of Ronsard.'

'Oh I don't know! I could write you a sonnet on the joys of *la planchette* and no hardship.'

Though they were grown men, the brothers had a tendency still to squabble like adolescents, for the joy of arguing. There was no aggression in it.

'I think, don't you, that Catherine de Medici has contributed rather more to the life of France than bloomers and the planchette saddle?' said their father. (There was nothing Berenice could do to preserve him from pomposity.) 'And I fail to see how the use of certain unguents and colours healthful to the skin has any bearing on whether I build an observatory or not for the Queen Mother.' He could see Thomas muster the courage to retort, and glared at him.

Thomas closed his eyes and clenched his fists. It was a mannerism left over from childhood when he had dared his way through many a beating for his idealistic radicalism. 'You called her a tradesman's daughter yourself when Henry first married her.'

'It's a sign of maturity to temper your views,' said Berenice, and Thibault thanked her stiffly and said that he could conduct a conversation without her help.

The room was draped in black. Every mirror, every picture, every tapestry was obscured by swags of funereal black for the death of the King. It seemed to Thibault only yesterday that the drapes had hung there in mourning for Francis. Now Francis' son was dead too, and in such a way as to shake at the tree of heredity and set Thibault's leaves trembling.

He wondered at his son's resilience – to be joking, arguing, eating as usual after so narrow an escape! From time to time, his glance rested on Kempis and took stock of eye, ear, hand and hair. Then Kempis would catch the look and laugh it off all over again. 'It wasn't Montgomery's fault,' he kept saying. 'It could've happened to anyone! No one will hold it against Montgomery.'

'No more than they held Pontius Pilate culpable,' said his mother. 'I rather suspect they'll peel his body from his soul to find out if he intended it, and when they find he didn't they'll discover – ah shame! – they can't piece the two together.'

'And you next in the lists,' said Thibault for the fiftieth time, pinching the table linen into tuck-pleats. He recalled in his mind's eye Amboise's claustrophobic combat yard, every pavilion, every caparison, every squared foot-cloth and tasselled oriflamme, every favour, every thicket of lances planted in the ground. And the helmets – shining golden skulls visored with lions' marks and leopard snarls; horseheads maned with flowing hair; the chicheface of Gloriole waiting in the lists. Only one combat still to go: Gabriel Montgomery against the King. Montgomery, Captain of the King's Scottish Guards, would lose to Henry: the King's arts in tourney were very fair and Montgomery was not a complete fool in the realms of diplomacy. Then Kempis would have ridden out to contend with the winner. Thibault's son crossing lances with the King of France! Thibault had even reached out, in a momentary aberration, and squeezed his wife's hand for the good she had done him in bearing such a son.

Then the waver of a lance, the wrong evasive snatch of the head, and women were screaming, men were shouting, and the little Florentine Queen, in her buttoned sleeves and Spanish bodice, was staring ahead as if the lance had entered in at her own eye, pierced her own brain. It took Henry eleven days to die. And it might so easily have been Kempis de Gloriole who accidentally killed him and not Gabriel Montgomery.

'Kings *are* mortal, you know,' said Berenice, interrupting these absorbing, circular thoughts.

'What am I supposed to learn by that, woman?'

'And Henry's son looks more mortal than most.' She said it like a warning – that Thibault's latest toy would not stand up to rough play.

'Are you going to judge a man in his twelfth year?'

'He'll be a puppet to the Guises,' said Thomas, 'and then the real apocalypse will come.'

Thibault threw down his fork and the pickle impaled on it. 'Where do you *get* these ideas? How d'you sleep with such a bedful of melancholy? Must you perpetually be so dismal?'

'I thought you wanted us to mourn,' Thomas retaliated, stammering nervously, wiping his palms.

'The dead, not the living!'

They lapsed into silence. The whole meal had progressed like April – little flurries of foul weather interspersed with peace. Dinners were not always so fraught. Generally Kempis and his father would laugh and joke: usually about Kempis' 'secret lover', the one too high of birth for him to aspire to. In fact Kempis did the laughing, for Thibault's face was not built for laughter, being too rigid a construction of symmetrical lines. But inwardly Thibault rejoiced in his son's over-ambition, resolving regularly, once a day, to match Gloriole's fortunes to those of the unknown mistress. He even admired the man's ability to keep a secret so well, and it entertained him to look over the ladies at Court and guess in which trunk Kempis had left his forester's blaze.

Thomas wore his heart too much on his sleeve to manage a romantic intrigue. Still, there was something to be said for that, after all. Thibault never had actually ruffled the hair of his lesser son – that was how he thought of him – his lesser son, as in Ursa Minor and Ursa Major. No, Thibault never had. But inwardly, at some depth he would never dream of letting Thomas fathom, he would like to have ruffled the chap's hair.

'A wonderful science, this astronomy. Now it's being brought to a perfection. Nostradamus predicted the King's death. And Ruggieri. There's a lot to be said for astrology.'

'Father, you're incorrigible,' said Kempis, making room for the unwanted food Thomas invariably passed on to his plate.

'And Luc Gauriac sent a letter warning him to avoid combat in enclosed spaces. Something to that effect. Blindness or death, he said. Blindness or death, and it turned out to be both. Absolutely astounding.'

'The Medici woman will see you coming. She's not simple, whatever else she is,' said Kempis laughing agreeably.

But Thomas became suddenly agitated, scratching his head and picking up his plate to reposition it a dozen times. 'Please, Father. Don't get involved with Ruggieri. Not even to please the Medici woman. He's a convict and a devil-worshipper. He conjures. He'll hurt your soul. Don't have him in this house.' Thibault was rather touched that his lesser son should give any thought to his father's soul. But he paid no attention to his opinion.

Kempis patted his brother on the sleeve. 'Never fear, Thomas. Father's not as interested in the science *per se* as in ingratiating us with *la bella Katerina di Medici*. He thinks she's a friend to any man with an observatory and an interest like hers in all things celestial.'

Thibault sat back from the table sulkily and turned his face away towards the window, effectively declaring the meal ended. 'What kind of a word's that? "Ingratiating",' he said. 'Astrology's the science of the moment. What? D'you want to shut your eyes against enlightenment? D'you want to go on living in the fifteenth century? We have to progress.'

'Why can't he just stand on the roof?' Berenice interrupted banally.

'Who? What are you talking about, woman? Why can't who stand on the roof?'

'Your astronomer . . . when you have one. Why can't he just stand on the roof to look at the stars? Or on a hill? Why do you need to build him a *particular piece* of roof? It seems to me these astronomers are very greedy of space since the only tools they have are their eyes and they carry those in their heads. They should be able to make do with a chimney pot and here you are talking of building half a wing.'

'Ah, Ruggieri does have his *magic mirror*,' said Kempis who found the whole thing entertainingly absurd.

'Ruggieri's no joking matter,' hissed his brother hotly.

Thibault, though he was at a loss to know exactly why astronomers needed towers or, as yet, what exactly marked them out for observatories, heaped contempt on his wife's foolishness. 'What's a chateau these days without an observatory? What Chaumont can do . . .'

'What Chaumont could do was build an observatory facing the wrong quadrant of the sky,' said Kempis, startling everyone that he knew anything at all about it. 'If we're going to build, then for God's sake let's build one facing the right way.'

Thibault was overjoyed. The light of enterprise animated his face like a tree moving behind stained-glass. His son was interested after all! Kempis might seem giddy and frivolous, with his sports and fashionable clothes and romances and jokes, but at heart he had the Gloriole sense of what was necessary, what was fit. Thibault had convinced himself of that long since.

'Is there money enough to pay for it?' asked Berenice. All three men looked at her, astonished at such a bourgeois consideration.

'There is *always* money enough to gratify a queen,' said Thibault sententiously.

But she was not reproved. She only smiled at him, shook her head maternally and said, ' "Gratify." What kind of a word's that? I preferred "ingratiate", myself.'

She was perfectly right, of course. There was no limitless source of money for such a fashionable frippery as an observatory. But Joshua Vache, unctuous as the cup of oil anointing the psalmist's head, undertook to furnish not only the materials 'cheaper than for any Loire pig-sty', but labourers and architects too, 'consolidating many debts to one' that need not be paid till the job was done.

'You'll say that no person worth knowing would grant me the honour of his acquaintance, sir,' said Vache, fixing his eyes on the floor as though he were talking to the Burning Bush. (Thibault half expected him to take off his chamois shoes as he entered on Gloriole's hallowed ground.) 'But I know of an astrologer most proven in the science and with such an eagerness to pursue it that the only burden falling to you would be in granting the privilege or licence to pursue it under your roof, or rather . . .'

The sentence threatened to engulf Thibault in an avalanche of words: he could already feel himself losing his footing. 'He'd cost nothing, you mean?'

'Precisely, my lord.'

'Don't be absurd, Vache. Nothing worth buying costs nothing.' Vache bowed abjectly. He was a tiny man, rendered square by a robe such as a mandarin might wear. His hands were always muffled up in his sleeves. His face was round and ingenuous. Having raised his eyes as far as the Comte's bottom lip, he let them slip back to their rightful station in life, sweeping the floor. 'Naturally. Naturally, my lord. We should offer this person a wage commensurate with their talent, though having the honour to serve your lordship, and being permitted to reside here in this most exquisite of residences must surely be incentive enough for . . .'

'Besides. Do I want an astronomer here? On the premises? Every day of the year? Ruggieri may come and go often, if he finds the place to his liking. Personally I don't crave predictions for myself day and night.'

Vache stood like a rabbit at the entrance to its burrow, stock still, his nose flickering as it always did at the scent of something inadvisable or in bad taste. 'Not have a resident astrologer, sir?'

'What of it? The observatory's the thing, surely?'

'It's simply that . . . Well, they do say . . . It is thought . . . well, since the death of the poor King – God grant him rest – that the Queen his widow – that's to say the Queen Regent is . . . well, anxious for portents – eager, as you might say, for news from the starry intelligencers. And that calls for constant vigilance, as I understand the science – though you'll tell me I never could aspire to such cleverness. It is an exceedingly tedious process, as I hear. But as you see fit, of course. Naturally. As you see . . .'

'Send him, then. Send your astronomer. But only till he can teach me the science. Then I'll do the job myself.'

'I'm honoured by your trust. I'm overwhelmed at your tolerance of my presumptuous interference, my lord.'

'But not till the work's finished. I don't want to be feeding and clothing the man while he kicks his heels.'

'As you wish, sir,' said Vache '. . . though I'm sure the roof would suffice for look-out in the meantime. Or a hill. As I understand it.'

The work proceeded without setback, but slowly, slowly. He was in competition for labourers with Catherine de Medici herself who, having ousted her dead husband's mistress from the love-nest at Chenonceau, was adapting it to her own tastes. To inconvenience her would have defeated the entire object. So Thibault waited for the craftsmen to finish there, and to find their way up the Sablois river to Gloriole.

The observatory was a conversion of the twin-coned dovecote on the corner of the stableyard. Observing the style which Catherine favoured at Chenonceau, he had the outside walls embellished with caryatids – giant stucco women standing on the lower cone and bearing the upper one on upstretched, Amazonian arms.

'What, are they sheltering from the rain?' asked Berenice.

'Father! Come quick and tell this painter to strike out his work!' called Thomas. 'He's painting cabbalistic signs!'

The interior of the dovecote was transformed far more than by the caryatids on the outside. Its honeycomb walls had been lined with white ash and painted – white at the base, rising through pale blue and turquoise to darkest navy and black. Planets in glazed ceramic bulged in spiral brightness out of the matt wall. A spherical astrolobe and below it a cast-iron clepsydra were suspended in the centre of the room, the timepiece letting Time dribble inexorably away, drop by glistening drop. A score of windows and a score more skylights lit the platform within the roof-void, whose only furniture was a desk with ten great flat drawers for maps. Between the planets on the wall were constellations of stars in gold paint, the music of the spheres written on staves of silver, and a miscellany of zodiacal signs, like Heaven's krill drifting in shoals on every side.

'I like it well enough,' Thibault told Thomas conclusively.

The total cost of transforming dovecote to observatory was absurdly low. He supposed the bourgeois Vache was better able to strike bargains, cut costs, hold suppliers to their quotes. There were certainly enough of them building on the Loire these days: so many storekeepers (as he said to Vache) as laid end-to-end would make a veritable street-market.

'And their blood no richer than mine,' said Vache nodding his big head on its little body. He had round, pouchy cheeks, long earlobes, and protuberant front teeth, and put Thibault in mind of the timid coney rabbits that colonized the Sablois forest. He had never liked the animals. Their huge, undetectable burrows could too readily subside and break the leg of a good hunter and pitch its rider on his face.

The building of the observatory was an entirely selfless enterprise inasmuch as Thibault thought he had no interest in discovering his own future. Like Kempis and Thomas in their different ways, he tended towards the opinion (whatever he said) that all astrologers were conjurors and knaves. Not that he believed astronomy a nonsense. It was perfectly sound and proven. The Pope himself had an astronomer. But like a plough too overgrown with nettles to warrant unearthing, the science was too beset by charlatans. Thibault was not prepared to risk the insult of some rogue's attempt to gull him. That was Thibault's reasoning.

Berenice said that he was afraid of what he might find out.

Never for a moment did Thibault expect Vache's protégé to be respectable. The royal astronomer Ruggieri had served time in the galleys and was as unsalubrious an individual as one could chance to

486

meet at twilight, creeping about the terraces of Blois. But nothing prepared Thibault for the astronomer Vache sent him two days later. Not Italian. Not agedly wise. Not bunched up in expensive clothes to prove past successes. By God, not even male!

She arrived on foot, presenting herself at dusk to Thibault as he sat chewing a tobacco quid on the shadowy berm. 'My name is Urania,' she said

She had long auburn hair which she wore uncovered and unfastened except by a browband with a star in the centre of her forehead. Her dress was the contoured blue of the night sky, overlaid with cloud-grey swags of sarcenet silk. Her eyes were those of a nocturnal animal, huge and glistening, and her face wore the melancholy of Mnemosene who was doomed to know everything there is to know and found it too much to bear. In her hands she carried a pair of brass compasses, a rule and a rolled map, and a quiver of pens hung above one hip, feathery like the goddess Diana's moonlit arrows. 'You wish to learn star-science,' she said. 'Shall you begin tonight?'

Her timing was so well judged, the surprise factor so great, the narcotic effects of the tobacco so dampening on his temper that he did not send her packing then and there. He could do that tomorrow. He would let the sunlight dismantle the illusion of her. He would laugh off Vache's impertinence tomorrow. After all, there was novelty in it. How many other women astrologers would Catherine de Medici have met? How many male charlatans had as sound a sense of the theatrical? If only she could have some rudimentary knowledge of the science . . .

He got up and led her to the observatory. Here as everywhere, the parrots had found their way in and were perching along the high cornice mouldings of zodiacal beasts. The compass star inlaid in black marble in the floor was already soiled with droppings. He thought the girl would be daunted by the potence ladder which was the only access to the platform in the roof. But she simply parted her dress at the centre front to reveal bloomers after the style of the Queen Regent's hunting clothes. Then she set off up the ladder. It proved to be Thibault who had lost his taste for heights, as he followed slowly on behind her, palms sweating, feet wet within his boots and knuckles white on the rungs in front of his face. By the time he reached the observation platform, Urania had sat down cross-legged, for lack of a chair, unrolled her star-map and pinned it flat with rule and compasses and a lamp. Thibault was rather glad to sit on the plank floor, away from the edge of the platform.

She said nothing about herself, her credentials, her record of phenomenal predictions all-proved-true-within-a-twelvemonth, her clientèle of devoted admirers whose lives she had saved with timely celestial advice. She entered straight into a lesson on the geography of the night sky in the month of June – its constellations, its prime stars, its planets and nebulae. 'You are familiar with the Dog Star here – the Plough, Orion and Cassiopeia. These will be our landmarks in finding out the rest. I've sketched here, along the sides, such landmarks as can be seen from the chateau by daylight – the bend in the river here; the spire of Croix-Rouge . . . Ah, but the elm-clump's gone now, hasn't it?' And she deleted the pencil sketch in the margin.

'You knew you were coming here, then?' he said, nodding with a sardonic scepticism. 'You've known for two years or more.'

She looked him squarely in the face with those large, desolate eyes. 'Oh yes. I've known I was coming here for a great long while. Since before this tower was built. Since I was a child.' He snorted his disbelief and indicated she should return to the subject of the map. 'Now I shall point out the major constellations. Here's the Great Bear. Here the Little. Here the Swan and here the Flying Horse. Here's Cepheus. Here, just rising, are the twins, of course. Your sons' natal star . . . is here. And of course, over all the Dragon.'

'The what?'

'Draco. The Dragon. Your own star is among it –'

'No,' he said categorically. 'Where? "Among"? Where?'

'Here, sir. From close by Hercules up to the border of Cepheus, curved round the back of Ursa Minor. The Dragon. And here's your natal star.'

'No.' He said it as a statement of fact, as if by saying it he could remove his nativity to some other precinct of the moving sky. It struck horror into him that his life should represent one scale on the back of so giant a beast. 'I've heard tell there's a unicorn. Show me the unicorn. Is it true? Is there such a thing?'

'Monoceros? Oh yes, sir. Down between Hydra and the Little Dog. But it's of the Middle Heavens, sir. You'll never see it. Not from here.'

'But from somewhere else. If you travelled south far enough.' It was Thomas's voice. He had seen the lamplight riming the roof of the observatory and had come in behind them. From below he began to climb the ladder saying, 'If a man could board the Great

Ship Argos and sail in it through the sky . . . think of it . . . he'd pass by Noah's Dove and the Whale.'

Beside Thibault the woman breathed a deep sigh. So she too craved to sail in the constellation of Argos with its poop and keel and mast of stars, did she? Thibault at once deduced that she was a parochial oracle. She had probably never set foot outside the Touraine. He felt at liberty to mock her because of it.

'And when's my death, then? Such foreknowledge of coming here: you must've divined that much out curiosity? Eh? Where's it to be and by what means?'

'When? On the last day of your life, of course.'

'Huh. I knew it. Quibblery. And where's yours? Show me. No, wait! Let me guess. I've heard this one times past number. The stars say that your death'll fall the day before mine, isn't that the game you people play? The ultimate assurance of a long and sheltered life.'

She looked at him with a childlike bewilderment. 'My life is of no importance. The stars have nothing to say on a subject so insignificant. Why should they?'

Just then, Thomas completed his climb, and his head emerged over the edge of the platform. 'Have you considered the possibility, Father, that she might be honest?'

Thibault shook himself like a dog and got up. 'You? Defend a fortune-teller? A star-monger? Wonders surely never cease. And what exactly will you *do*, madam? I mean *do* with yourself, while you eat my bread and waste my means?'

'If I'm left free to it, sir? Build a quadrant, sir. After the thinking of Tycho Brahe. Inset it yonder, in that wall, to help track particular stars. And watch, sir, of course. For portents and things out of the ordinary. I observe, sir. I don't interpret. Others may do that.' As she looked out across the dark Sablois, several separate shifts of moonlight converged on her through the new windows of the old dovecote despite an overcast sky. 'Tomorrow the weather will be better – clearer. I shall point out these same constellations to you in the firmament.'

'Ah! Our first prediction! And so soon, too!' gibed Thibault. 'D'you hear that, Thomas? "The weather will be clearer tomorrow!" You see she'll be useful come harvest-time, Thomas. She divines the weather!'

Once again she cast that look on him which questioned why a grown man should talk such foolishness. 'The wind direction suggests a change,' she said, 'and your workers were netting the citrus trees against a frost as I came by.'

Abruptly Thibault turned on his son instead, as though his unkindness had all been by way of a test, like putting a new mare through her paces with whip and goad. 'Well. What d'you think of her, then? Will she do? Will she satisfy Catherine?'

'Excellent well,' said Thomas immediately. It numbered among the few times in his life that he had ever spoken an untruth.

In truth he rather thought Urania too honest to satisfy the violently superstitious tastes of the Queen Regent. But he gave his answer quick as the flash of a shooting star. 'Excellent well, Father. I think you should employ her.'

Thibault wanted to show his new acquisition to Kempis, whose opinion he valued a great deal more than Thomas's. But Kempis was clearly out putting the starlight to better use than for astrology, scallywagging in Tours or drinking the tavern dry at Carrefour. Thibault comforted himself that he would ride to Blois without delay, the very next day, and allow it to be known at Court that he was in possession of an observatory and an astrologer of considerable rarity value.

But when he reached Blois it was as empty and abandoned as a plague-ship. The Court had been at Amboise for a matter of weeks. It put Thibault in mind of his worst nightmare as a child, whereby the Last Trump sounded while he was out playing and he returned to find everyone gone to Heaven without him. He was in half a mind to turn about and go home. Afterwards, he attributed his perseverance to an angel whispering in his ear. He turned for Amboise instead.

As he approached the town, he gained the impression that some martial party game was in progress for the entertainment of the boy-King. Soldiers would keep leaping out at him from every bush, doorway and gatehouse, demanding to know who he was. When he told them, they seemed uncertain as to what it signified: friend or foe. They insisted on disarming him. He accumulated a triumphant foot-troop of Scots Guards, one leading his horse by the head, and entered the castle by the Hurault Tower. Its shallow spiral pavement swept him up between tapestries still hung out to welcome the King, but for some reason it was more the gargoyle lamp-holders which caught Thibault's attention: shouting, grinning, grimacing contortionists carved in stone; monkeys and goblins, all screeching a warning at him in a language he did not understand.

Someone suspected a danger to the King. Every brick in the place said so. Blois was too open to defend, whereas Amboise was impenetrable. Someone suspected rebellion and Thibault (absurd to think it!) was not above suspicion.

And yet the atmosphere within the isolated inner sanctum of the Royal Apartments was all gaiety. A quite inordinate air of fun surrounded the young King Francis, a great tossing of headdresses, a great flouncing of taffeta skirts, an aviary of high-pitched laughter, a through-draught of bagpipe music. The chimneys sang too, from the unaccustomed draw of so many grand fires.

As uniformly big as if they belonged to some separate race of Titans, members of the de Guise family stood about the King, protecting him from all influence but their own. They tended to adopt a position in any room which dominated its sight lines and exits. They kept watch, balanced on their stilt-long legs, for any easing in the merciless jollity.

Naturally, Thibault paid his compliments to the King. Perhaps it was in contrast to the Guises, but young Francis II seemed, in defiance of Nature, to be growing smaller with age rather than bigger. In his hand he carried a steaming bowl of water clouded by the acrid stench of naphtha. 'Don't speak to Us, whoever you are,' he greeted Thibault. 'We've got a foul disease.'

'Then God have mercy on France, Your Majesty.'

'A toss for that. God have mercy on Us first.' He snuffed up the vapours from the bowl. They made him retch, and he spat a rheumy gobbet on the floor at Thibault's feet. 'It was just the sinuses before, but it's got into Our ears now, beggar it. And to top it all, they want to kill Us.'

Just then he was picked up, like a crab from a rock, by a wave of red silk, and his wife insisted he 'come and hear the sweet poets rhyming extempore'. Mary Stuart was two years older than the King, but with her hand through his, she looked like an old man's young comfort. She was dancing the flesh off his bones. Perhaps that was what he saw as a threat on his life.

Suddenly the Queen Mother was at Thibault's back, rustling in black serge silk, rattling with jet beads and gold chains. Her lace sleeves were a magpie collection of buttons and gold braid, and her coif and collar were crêpe. 'Can my lord your son be correct, madam?' asked Thibault. Even on one knee he was almost as tall as the Queen Regent. She looked him over, her powdered features a little yellow at the edges – like a parchment drawn from a very secret place. Then she looked sidelong across the room to summon a Guise. 'Monsieur le Comte does not become any the less . . . debonair with age,' she observed in the meantime. 'A man should age if he is to be gallant to his lady friends.'

'But madam! I was only following your example, and that badly,' replied Thibault. He went to get up, but found that the Guise was now at his side, standing on his short-cloak.

'I don't recollect that you were invited to His Majesty's fête, monsieur.'

'I own I knew nothing of it.' He turned back towards Catherine. 'In fact I went first to Blois to present a piece of news to Your Majesty . . .'

'You and your business may wait downstairs, Monsieur le Comte,' said the Guise. 'One of my men will escort you.'

A cast of pity or sorrow clouded Catherine's eye, and she reached out a hand and squeezed Thibault's shoulder. 'I have great hopes of reconciliation if this thing blows by.' Then she drew her skirts away from him, as from a puddle in a stable-yard, and allowed herself to be drawn away towards the flautists.

Thibault got up, his hand on his shoulder where she had touched him. He wanted to hurry after the Medici. He wanted to smash that smug palisade the Guises had made of themselves around the King. Not welcome? Wait downstairs? Insinuating bigots, Berenice called the de Guise clan. And he never liked to be in agreement with his wife.

A ring-dance was forming itself without any apparent instigation. He determined to join it and to strip-the-willow as far as the Queen Regent and re-present his compliments with more insistence. He had, after all, the burden of an observatory and an astrologer to lay at her disposal, and they weighed heavy till he could make of them his *grand geste*.

Easier said than done. The ladies still greeted the sight of him with a drop of the jaw, the snatch of a hand to the breast, a dilating of the pupils in their lovely eyes. But then some afterthought would make them join hands hurriedly and shut the circle against him while continuing to gaze over their shoulders. He was shut out, humiliated like a fat child excluded from a game of paume. And he could see de Guise's men coming to escort him downstairs. A hand on his collar and by God he would bloody a nose or two!

Gracelessly he shouldered his way into the circle between satin and velvet and took hold firmly of a hand on either side. To their mutual astonishment, he found he had inadvertently partnered his former mistress. Madame Dideron looked at him with round, painted eyes. Her breath smelled of cinnamon.

No parting had ever taken place between them – no recriminations, no unpleasant impropriety of anger, and yet they had not spoken for fifteen years. She had grown old. He had not. The fullness of her cheek had trickled grain by grain down towards the sides of her mouth; the top of her breasts was marked by a crease; the skin over her knuckles was tissuey; the distinction between lip and face had been made with an Italian crayon. He saw those lips flicker with nervous delight and knew that she found him unchanged in his appeal. But she said, 'Go away. We want no eiguenots here.'

He laughed out loud. 'Me? An eiguenot? Fah! My dear madame, I thought you knew me better than that!'

So. The time had come to reconvert, he thought. The days of religious tolerance were well and truly over.

The stewards hesitated, unwilling to risk an unpleasantness in the same room as the King.

'Nothing will come of it, you know,' she piped. 'Nothing at all! It's known. The when. The who. It's all known! Traitors are always betrayed, you know. The Prince of Condé's summoned here to make account of himself! The Guard will be waiting for the rest.'

The circle began to move to left and right, and all at once it felt to Thibault like the wheel on which condemned men are broken. He had to break free of it. He laughed again, louder than before, but said in a voice whose indignance would be heard further off, 'If "all's known", you know that I'm entirely ignorant of what you're talking about, madam. I see you are a great way behind the times, too. Did you not know I returned to the joys of Holy Mass years ago? My dalliance with all things Erasmic was an *affaire d'un jour* – the merest affectation of fashion, I do assure you. The merest means to a marital end.'

One twirl of the dance and Madame Dideron found her partner gone, her hands in those of a woman, and there was a momentary jostle and giggling confusion as the circle readjusted to the loss of one dancer.

Thibault was surprised they let him leave. He was surprised the guards (since he was suspect) did not detain him for fear he might take his intelligence straight to fellow conspirators. But they were so confident, so sure of themselves, circled round by the pink walls of Amboise that they felt safe simply to close the circle against him, exclude him from the dance, make it plain that the plot was known, and that he and all Protestants had been found guilty by association. He was no longer welcome at the King's Court.

It was the most desolate loneliness Thibault had ever felt.

But he had no time to indulge his misery. The misunderstanding could be sorted out, given time; a state of grace could be recovered. But nothing could be recovered – everything would be lost if Thomas, his fool of a Protestant delinquent, crusading, harebrained son had joined Condé's conspiracy. The more he thought about it, the more likely it seemed – that Thomas was about to destroy Gloriole with a futile political gesture, to damn his soul with the sin of High Treason. As he rode, nothing seemed more probable, nothing more certain than that his half-witted son was about to squander everything Thibault held most dear – including his own, half-witted life.

FORTY-TWO

Treachery

It was March and wet. The rain was driving in under the lantern-dome at the head of the great staircase and streaming down the central pillar, the balustrades, the steps. His boots slipped on the wet stairs as he ran up them calling for Berenice. She emerged from the library saying that a log had just spat wood-ash in her eye – look, here, in her eye. She had a kerchief clutched in her hand and the eye was running. He grabbed her by both wrists.

'Where's Thomas?'

'Thomas? Why?'

'*Where is he?* He's not come home, has he? I saw him saddling this morning. He's not come back. Tell me.'

He did not hear her the first time. She had to say it twice. 'He's here, yes. He's here with me.'

'Are you sure?'

'What do you mean, "Am I sure?" He's here with me, in the library. He's been reading to me.' She was furtive. She was honest. She was deceiving him. She was telling the truth. With so much at stake he lost the ability to read her face.

'There's a rising. Your pack have finally turned rabid. A plot to kill the King! Rebellion, by Christ! The Prince of Condé's party.' Thomas came to the door of the library and Thibault let go of his wife to grab his son, like a bear snatching a silver salmon out of the air. 'Still here, are you? Too slow by half! And it's all up now! You're expected, you and your rabble! They're lying in wait for you. Anarchist! Traitor!' He clipped at Thomas repeatedly, making his round, furry head bang against the door jamb. His eyeglasses fell to the ground and broke.

'Father, I don't . . . Father, I haven't . . .' No sentence finished before his temple cracked again against the timber. Thibault bellowed for the officer-of-the-watch to raise the drawbridge and to keep it raised till he was ordered to lower it. Then he drove both

son and wife like sheep ahead of him into the library and locked
the door and threw the key on to the back of a lit hearth.

This room would be his ark against the Flood to come. Here he
would batten up himself and his animals while God destroyed the
wicked. Dragging chairs out from the long table, he thrust Berenice
and Thomas into them, then sat down himself at the table's end. 'And
here's where we stay, till the harm's done and the guilty taken!'

'Father, I don't know what you're talking about,' said Thomas
repeatedly. But Berenice did not leap to his defence – did not protest
his innocence. She simply sat with her mannish hands spread flat on
the table and her eyes shut. Thibault had only to look at her to know
that she also believed her son was capable of treason.

'This is your doing, woman! This is where your religion took
him.'

'Perhaps,' she said.

All evening they sat, and when his protestations of innocence
had no effect, Thomas fell as silent as his parents. At midnight he
got up and went to rake at the fire with a poker, searching for the
key.

'What d'you think you're doing?' demanded Thibault.

Thomas sighed. 'Histrionics are all very well, Father, but now
none of us can get to bed till the fire's dead. You surely don't mean
us to sit here all night with nothing to say for ourselves.'

'All night and all day and all week if need be, till your plot's
foiled and your friends taken.'

Thomas gave a snort of disbelief and rattled the door. He paced
up and down the room, his resentment gaining momentum like a
garden swing. 'D'you mean to say there's a rising going on out
there – everything turning about – and we're sitting on our hands
here like nuns in a cloister?'

His father replied with a slow pedantry, pressing the tip of
one finger down with each word as though he were reading off
the table top. 'All that's happening out there is a piece of folly by a
few hot-heads and half-brains. There's a trap ready and waiting for
them. They've only got to walk into it.'

Berenice said suddenly, 'They'll not persist, though, if it's known.
If the plot's uncovered. They'll not attempt it.'

'I hope and trust they will,' said Thibault ponderously. 'An
opportunity for the country to be curded of its scum.'

'Oh yes? And leave us with the de Guises leading the King about
by the nose? They're the real scum of France!' Thomas clenched his

thumbs and shut his eyes and began the familiar argument. But it seemed his mind was elsewhere and the peroration dwindled away to silence. He made a show of reading a book, but without his eyeglasses he could see nothing. And the more he thought, the less his eyes rested on the page. An hour later he said, 'Kempis will laugh this out of countenance. Shut up here. Waiting for the End of the World. Kempis will laugh the door off its hinges when he gets back.'

'Kempis is under the covers with his lady of birth and high degree,' snarled Thibault. 'He told me so. Then on to Périgord for a boar-cull. Would to God you'd spent your youth on a little dissolution rather than plotting treachery.'

'For Jesu's sake! How many times? I tell you I've plotted nothing!'

'All well and good. Then you've no prior appointments I'm keeping you from . . . I know your nature, Thomas, and it's not in your nature to pass up a fool's adventure like this. These stirrers can churn you from milk to butter with one turn of the handle.'

The fire was out. There was only one oil-lamp filled in the room and it too began to gutter and fail. In the last of the light Thibault saw his son reproach him with such a look of grief and bewilderment that his worst fears died with the flame. 'Maybe you knew, maybe you didn't,' he said almost tenderly to the darkness. 'But that's why we'll all three stay here till the danger's passed.' He could not see how his son responded. His growing certainty that he had misjudged Thomas, and the lightness of heart it lent him, was encouraged a little while later by the sound of his lesser son snoring gently. A conspirator, surely, on the very day of a coup, would not have such a conscience as to let him sleep.

Thibault could hear his wife's breathing too. She was as wakeful as he. He whispered, 'Damn it, woman, he must surely grasp that it's for his own good!' There was no reply. 'I only want to keep his head off the block! He'll see that in time, when he hears what becomes of the rest.' He waited for her to speak. It was dark. The magic of her grew like the scent of a night-perfumed flower. He got up and groped his way round the table to where she sat, and felt for her hair or a piece of her clothing. He had been rather foolish. There had been nothing to fear, nothing to make him gallop home and leave his horse sweating in its stall. He had brought his children up sound, after all. He should have known that even Thomas was not such a reckless, impulsive half-wit as to be snared by rascals with no respect for God's Anointed. He found a corner of her hood and put it to his cheek like a child its blanket. 'Damn it, Berenice, doesn't he realize it's only done out of love?'

Still she did not reply. He felt his way along her hood to her shoulder and up her throat to her face. He was amazed to find her whole head bobbing rhythmically and to feel the sharpness of her teeth against his hand: she was crying silently, open-mouthed, desolate. He held her head against his stomach, but she left her arms dangling down, limp as a doll.

'I'm sorry,' he said. 'I shouldn't have doubted him. But his *reputation*, woman! His *reputation*! He needs an alibi or he'll be suspect for sure, seeing who he makes friends of and goes about with. This serves for an alibi.' But nothing he said could persuade her to speak: he concluded that she was weeping for poor France, torn in half by fools.

In the morning, Balon and Batonne brought breakfast and a pan of water and left them outside the door. On the mantelpiece of the library a clepsydra dribbled its grains of crushed enamel, burying the minutes one by one with perfect precision.

Forty miles away a band of boys and young men burst out of the woods behind Amboise and emptied an odd assortment of pistols and muzzle-loaders towards a fortress as big as a city. Yes, they had known the plot was betrayed. Yes, they had been thwarted by the Court's removal from Blois to Amboise. But like children running downhill they had been powerless to stop themselves. Only after their shots were fired and the unharmed giant turned his head to scowl did the Lilliputian rebels about-face and flee, hurling their weapons into the bushes, weeping into their sleeves, wondering if they would ever dare go home.

Thibault de Gloriole stood at the window of his library where all morning he had been burning Protestant books. The time had passed for choosing one's religion. From now on it would be a question of birth, and those born noble were born to be Catholic. He would reconvert as soon as he could do it privately and unnoticed. His spirits were entirely restored, though he felt a little sheepish at having doubted his son's integrity. Now he wondered how he was going to open the door without seeming to have overstated his case in the first place.

Thomas was saying his prayers, his elbows on the seat of a chair, his hands gripping the spindles in the chairback. His mother bent and kissed him above the ear, then she too knelt down. 'Won't you join us, Thibault?'

'I can wait till Holy Mass,' he said pointedly.

'But wouldn't you say there's a rather urgent need to pray for the King's safety today?' she asked with that firm, maternal assertiveness which always made him feel like a child and wrong. He gave way and knelt down. And no sooner did he rest his face in his hands than his lack of sleep from the night before took hold. He prayed for the King's safety. He prayed that the rebels should not hold off their attack so that they might all be captured and expunged from the face of France. Then he sat back on his heels. He prayed that his wife should see where dissenting politics had led, and cling to him while the ship of Protestantism broke up and sank. Then he rested his forehead on his hands. And he leaned a little towards her, as he did at night when the feel of her back gave the security he needed to fall asleep. He leaned and he leaned, without opening his eyes, until the chair in front of him almost capsized and he had to unclasp his hand to keep from falling. Berenice was no longer beside him. She was at the door, her hands and dress black with ash from fumbling in the grate, the dirty key in the lock.

'What the devil . . . ?'

'I heard a horse on the causeway. It must be Kempis returned,' she said. Her cheeks were hot and red, but then the fire had been smouldering while she scrabbled in it for the key.

'Why didn't you say so?'

He got up wearily, unlocked the door and crossed the cavernous landing. But as he descended the slippery stairs, he could feel the unusual phenomenon of his wife's hand clasping the half-belt of his doublet. Thomas crept down the steps behind them, like a timid, velvety fieldmouse still nervous of the scythe. Berenice even showed signs of helping the guard to lower the drawbridge which was stiff through lack of use. Thibault had to tell her to come away. He resolved to have the gate overhauled. If the country was to descend into madness and rebellion, he must make shift to keep out marauding bands of eiguenots. He resolved, too, to tell Kempis how foolish it was to bring a horse home at the gallop. It was bad practice to leave them all lathered up in the stall, in peril of catching cold.

No sooner had Kempis dismounted than Berenice went and embraced him. It was raining still – fine, long drops like threads of the mystical net used for taking unicorns. Perhaps it was that net of rain that held Thibault in one spot, disorientated, unable to make sense of the scene being acted out before him.

Kempis was wild-eyed, unintelligible. He kept putting his hands into his hair so that like Struwwelpeter it stood out around his head in wet spikes. 'Oh Christ, Mama. Oh Jesus, Jesus, Jesus. It was a farce! A fiasco!'

'I know.'

'It was known ahead of time!'

'I know.'

'I mean everything! Everyone! The waste! Such a paltry show! Such a . . . *nothing!*'

'Hush now.'

'They'll come for me! They're behind me now!'

'Shshsh.'

'They were waiting for our coming! Like culling pigs!'

'Peace, son. It's not for you to speak now. Your speaking's done.'

She had him lie down on his face in the wet stable-yard and she placed herself between father and son.

'Listen, Thibault. Your son's life rests with you now. They'll be coming for him soon. He'll be safer well hidden here till the reprisals are done – safer than trying to get him to Germany or the Low Countries now. I tried to argue with him. I tried to dissuade him, but his conscience was set on it.'

'*On killing the King?*' It was Thomas who said it, incredulous to the point of laughter. Thibault could not have managed so many words.

'Killing? Of course not. They only meant to abduct Francis and Mary out of the sway of the Guises. We were betrayed by one of our own, of course. Judas among the disciples.'

' "We".' He should have known. He should have known that his wife was one of them, one of their kind – only used his house as a base for her filthy politics. Used his house. Used his son. 'So you *were* party to it.'

'We. We eiguenots, I meant. We Protestants. I told you. I tried to stop him. D'you think factions are anything to me beside the life of our son? I tried to stop him. He just wouldn't be told. But look, Thibault! You differ in opinions. Well? So? You differ in hands – you left-handed, he right-handed. Would you let strangers kill him for the fault of being right-handed?'

Thibault realized that she had had all night to think out her defence of the man's life. She was scripted, whereas he must ad lib, improvise, find words where there were none. He seemed to be trapped in a treadmill of the same thoughts turning, turning. 'Yes, but a traitor to the King . . .'

'What's he, then?'

Thibault knew what the King was. A foul-tempered, adenoidal, ailing, impotent runt, weaned by his mother and herded by the Guises while his foreign wife jigged him into an early grave. He knew what his son was, too – his greater son, as he had always thought of him. Kempis was a man of conviction; discreet, responsible and self-contained; handsome and full of promise. You only had to look at him. Flesh of his flesh. A soldier in a plausible campaign that had gone awry, as campaigns commonly will. Bone of his bone. Heir of his earthly powers. Thibault shut his eyes.

'Tell him to hide on the island in the centre of the lake,' he said, 'till after the house's been searched . . . If houses are to be searched.'

She bent and kissed his hands before hurrying Kempis to his feet. There was mud on his cheek and ear, and the fur of his lapels was matted flat like two crushed animals. He also attempted to kiss Thibault's hand: 'Thank you, Father! Thank you!' but Thibault snatched his hand away. The risk of contagion was too great. Mother and son ran towards the gardens and the dinted grey of the ornamental lake.

Behind him, Thomas let fall an involuntary groan. Had he taken any account of his lesser son, Thibault would have seen earlier the agony of disappointment on Thomas's face. Bad enough to have been excluded by the Prince of Condé from his futile conspiracy. But for Kempis to have been chosen and then to keep his own brother in ignorance . . .

At last Thibault saw him standing there in the rain. 'I see it now,' he said. 'Who'd trust you with a secret? Your brother can keep things close, but you – look at you. It's all written on your sleeve. It always was.'

Consequently, they took their misery in opposite directions out of the stable-yard.

Only some of the riders were captured on the day. It did not greatly matter. The informer, Pierre de Quenelles, could supply most of the names needed. The rest were furnished by those taken prisoner and put immediately to the torture.

From where he waited for the Guard to come – in the armoury above the causeway – Thibault could see the lake, the island in it, the functionless Greek portico, the derelict pleasure-barge swamped by rain, the bronze of something biblical stranded halfway between island and shore. He could see how the herons, frightened off by the disturbance of a rowing boat, had returned now to eat his fish. He could see the rowing boat adrift where Berenice had failed to secure it properly on returning from the island. The hull banged up against the sluice-gates as if it were yearning for the river beyond.

Berenice was glad he had chosen to wait in the great-hall. Before she left him alone there, he had seen her look up at the tapestry of the Prodigal Son, drawing his attention to it without a word more spoken on behalf of Kempis. But all her assertiveness, assuredness, independence were laid aside. She had subordinated them to her gratitude. She would obey him in all things, because he had taken pity on her.

It was she who showed the Guard into the great-hall, anxious no doubt to see that Thibault was believed when he witnessed how Kempis was on business in the south of France – had been gone a three-week, would not be back for another three. The riders were mired from days of riding to and fro, from chateau to farmhouse to inn, rounding up conspirators. The mud caked their clothes a reddish brown, like dried blood. They said, 'We have a warrant for the taking of one Kempis de Gloriole, for an attempt on the life of his most Royal Majesty the King Francis. All those loyal and true are charged to assist in the capture of the King's enemies.'

'There's some mistake,' said Berenice, small and meek and frightened, unconvincing in her efforts to convince. 'Kempis is out of the Touraine these three weeks. Isn't that so, husband? Isn't that . . .'

He knew what the King was. A surly, sickly, snot-nosed runt who would not reach Kempis' shoulder if they stood side by side.

But they did not stand side by side. That was the crux of it.

'You may find my son on the island in the heart of that lake yonder. Don't hurry yourselves. He'll stay for you till you come. He has a horror of water and can't swim, you see. Since he was a child. A horror of water.'

He knew what the King was: a puny, malformed, contemptible, snuffling pat of fifteen years. And God's anointed spokesman on Earth, his body formed of the chrism of royalty, his blood the distillation of heredity century by slow century. Perhaps not he, perhaps not his son or his grandson would be a Saint Louis or a

Henry Plantagenet. But once in every few hundred years, as God willed it, an embodiment of kingship would emerge from among this anointed tribe whose life was the very purpose of history, the very explanation of Man's estate.

Thibault knew what Kempis was: a man who could make no further contribution to Gloriole-sur-Sablois. Except as a sacrifice to the sacred will of the Crown.

FORTY-THREE

The Tumult of Amboise

Every day the list of known conspirators grew longer. The Prince of Condé expressed amazement that his name should have been mentioned, for he knew none of these people nor had the least desire to make their acquaintance. It was generally acknowledged that he would have been mad to stand by his friends.

To those who loved the King (said de Guise) his happy escape was cause for celebration and festivity – for expressing publicly one's private joy, for reaffirming one's undiminished loyalty. So those who were not at Court already flocked there to demonstrate their devotion and to sanction the just punishment of those who had transgressed. Neither Berenice nor Thomas would attend. They said the Cardinal could make of it what he chose. But Thibault argued that to stay away would be to risk drawing down Kempis' fate on all their heads. Many agreed with him. So the King's Lodging was uncomfortably crowded that day, the men pressed round by the women's satin dresses as though they were already in their coffins.

What process of Law was in progress at Amboise and where in the castle it was taking place nobody could say, but most certainly penalties were being awarded more quickly and efficiently than Adam conferring names on the animals of Creation. They were as imaginative, too.

Guests slipped to and fro, apologizing, passing back-to-back, not stopping to talk, even to their closest friends, for fear of being thought to share doubts worth whispering, for fear of being thought factious. It was a masked ball, for although there were no masks worn, there were smiles instead which distorted familiar faces into grotesque grinning grimaces, and there were glazed eyes which looked without seeing. Thibault did not smile. It would have been out of character. It would have aroused suspicion. He was nevertheless obliged to talk, to move incessantly around the room, like a horse on a lunge rein, and made to leap the obstacles placed in his way to trip him.

'Your wife not here, de Gloriole?'

'No. No. I find her presence hampers me in society, you know. She hasn't the features one would wish on one's friends, nor the broad-mindedness one would wish on one's *petits amours*, if you understand me.'

'A Saumur eiguenot, isn't she?'

'She is as I tolerate her to be, my lord Cardinal, and if the day comes when she's not . . .'

'Ah, what then?'

'Then, since marriage is indissoluble I must clearly change her. She is, after all, as much my property as I am the King's.'

'Ah! The King. He's not well, you know. What would we do if we were to lose him?'

'God would provide, I dare trust.'

'I see the death of a king holds no horrors for you, Monsieur le Comte?'

'Should I begrudge Heaven one of its saints?'

'And do you think your son will go to Heaven, Monsieur le Comte?'

'Thomas? I pray God for it daily.'

'Why no. I was rather thinking of the other . . . what is his name?'

'I fear you're mistaken, my lord Cardinal. I have only one son.'

'Oh but sure, I'd take an oath on having seen the Gloriole name among the list of those condemned.'

'If someone chooses to wear my name, there's no more I can do to prevent it than if they took a coach out of my stable without my permission.'

'Still. You must be glad that noble necks escape the noose.'

'Nobility, sir, is in deeds as well as blood, don't you think?'

Thibault did not for one moment believe that he was being informed of clemency for Kempis. To say that noblemen cannot be hung is not to say that noblemen cannot be put to death. There were a dozen headless trunks already lying in the courtyard to prove it. He was surprised not to have seen Kempis among them. If he had, perhaps the demon fantasy would have left him alone by now. Instead he was plagued by imagined possibilities: a royal pardon . . . the intervention of Kempis' elevated mistress – which was she among all these? – winning the King's sentimental forgiveness. A ram caught in a thicket. He remembered now what bronze that was that spewed up a fountain between island and shore of his ornamental lake. Abraham and Isaac. Well, Thibault had been perfect in obedience to his feudal god, hadn't he, and delivered up his son? Perhaps, after all, when his god saw such perfect obedience he would find a way . . . The fantasies continued to dance in his brain. Would to God the thing were over and the demon exorcized once and for all.

'Watch! Watch!' exclaimed the King startlingly close to Thibault's shoulder. 'The Cardinal de Guise has an entertainment for you, my friends.' He still reeked of naphtha – his hair, his eyebrows, his breath. His ears were packed with plugs of wool and he carried a hot, metal pomander of camphorated oil. His face was full of pain. The infection of his sinuses had spoiled his sense of balance; he reeled up against Thibault; the smell of medication made de Gloriole's eyes smart. 'Watch!' said the fifteen-year-old clasping Thibault's sleeve. 'Just watch!' The room went on smiling, everyone smiling.

The men outside the windows smiled too, after a fashion.

Three hundred iron hooks were sunk in the face of the chateau where it looked towards the river – three hundred hooks intended for the flags and tapestries decking Amboise on feast days. Some took the weight. Some did not.

Two ladies had been standing by the doors to the balcony, discussing a particular shade of cloth. One pointed to a panel in the other's dress and said, '. . . closer to that. A shade darker than that and in silk rather than . . .' She was startled by a sudden eclipse of the light and looking up had to leap aside or receive a blow in the face from a pair of boots. The kicking was wild and uncoordinated, however, and only set the rest of the body spinning and swinging and banging up against the open window. A moment later there were two, barging and shouldering each other, drunken and unmannerly, dancing an appalling drunken jig in empty air, grunting and sucking for breath. The third broke his neck cleanly. The seventh plunged directly to his death on the castle footings with a coil of rope and a billhook and a shower of mortar for benediction.

The guests fell back from the window but were ushered forward again for a better view. Why, they had only to stand on the balcony to reach out and touch, push, tease the hanging men. What entertainment the good Cardinal had furnished for the afternoon! Mary Stuart, the King's Scottish wife, turned white, then green, and begged permission of her mother-in-law to leave the room. A great many napkins were laid to mouths, a great many smiles

506

slipped away. But the young men at the windows went on grinning and dancing, jigging and pulling tongues, banging their feet against the windows, plummeting off the roof – seemingly out of the sky, like three hundred Lucifers falling.

A column of polite Scots Guard apologized to guests for discommoding them as they led through the room a string of youths – all bloodied and bruised, some wounded, some fresh from the torture. They wore their nooses already round their necks, but were kept waiting while the other end was secured round the balcony rail. There was not room for them and the soldiers and the dead to jostle on the balcony, so for a time they had to share the States Chamber with the courtiers. No word was spoken; their hands were tied behind their backs; they had no resort to gestures. And yet afterwards it seemed to many who remembered it that a conversation had taken place.

The prisoners searched the faces of the guests for pity. The guests searched their faces in return – for relations, acquaintances, perhaps, or favourite enemies. Thibault looked in each face for his son, but Kempis was not there. After they were gone – bundled clumsily out on to the overcrowded balcony and thrown over to dance in front of other windows, outside other, lower rooms, he eased his way through the press and out into the afternoon air. He needed the air.

Looking both ways along the chateau's façade, he could see it decorated from end to end with a bunting of corpses. The sun was too bright: the distances too great. If one was Kempis, he could not tell which.

He had to know. Seized with a quite irrational panic, he had to know which balcony, which rope, which member of the Guard, what clothes his son was wearing, what kind of death he had made. Whether anything was said. He returned indoors and crossed through one room to the next and the next and the one beyond. He began to walk faster and faster, along corridors of endless, indistinguishable magnificence, past guests clothed in indistinguishable splendour, and faces indistinguishably inert with horror. They washed about like stirring kelp in the inlets of a rocky shore, unable to get away, unable to stop still. A smell was beginning to pervade the galleries and landings – a smell that should have been confined to the dungeons.

Thibault saw more than most that day. Whereas the rest could turn away their eyes, he must leap to each window in turn, often convinced that a pair of bound hands were those of . . . waiting for the wind off the river to swing the body about and . . . always proved wrong by the blackening face that turned out of the wind. His search took him down through the chateau to small, unplanned intricacies of the building – little courtyards and stairwells and rose gardens and washing yards and chicken runs. And everywhere men were being butchered, as if there were a Mardi Gras haste for meat. A boy bound to the leg of a water tower was being hacked to pieces by three men with small firewood axes. He called out to Thibault to help him live. An older man spreadeagled across the cover of a well was being disembowelled. He called out to Thibault to help him die. On a bonfire the quarters of several men were failing to burn. The trees on the terraces cast a red dapple on the ground. The stones underfoot were slippery with blood. They cried out to Thibault for washing, but he had no time to spare them. The whole sky, the whole body of Amboise air was charged with screaming. It was so penetrating that even as he looked, the mortar was shaken out from between the bricks of the chateau and blood was oozing out through the gaps. It limed the roof tiles where the birds were sitting; it stained the heads of statues. The river below crawled by, almost too viscous to move. Culprits of no social rank, unworthy of torture and with no information to give, were being thrown down from the battlements into the river. It would never do. Someone would have to put a stop to it, or what of the fishing, the river sluices, the castellar moats? The laundry. Red. The bathers. Red. He did not have time to consider all the ramifications. He had to find Kempis and know that he was dead.

Looking down from the walls, he could see that the surfeit of Justice had overspilled into the town and that the city walls and street arches and iron gates and trees and lamp-holders and balconies were festooned with bodies. He was unaware that the minutes of his search had given way to hours, the hours to half a day. He found himself back in the States Chamber of the King's Lodging. He would be methodical. He would be systematic. A list must exist, along with instructions for disposal.

'And did you find your son, Comte?' enquired the Cardinal de Guise. Alongside him, the King barely came as high as to his scarlet, cowled shoulder.

'How could I find what's lost?' replied Thibault. 'I was simply looking for the Queen Mother to tell her of certain improvements in hand at my chateau which may be of interest to her. An observatory.'

'What's that? A bribe? The current rate is more costly than an observatory, my dear Comte. Today I've been offered . . .'

'My hand beneath your foot, Lord Cardinal, but I fear you misheard me. I said that I had an item of news for the Lady Catherine. If the word "clemency" had inadvertently entered my mouth, I feel sure I should have tasted it and spat it out. As far as I know or care, Kempis-known-as-Gloriole is already among the chickens whose necks you've wrung this afternoon.'

'Oh, but he isn't, my dear Gloriole. I happen to know he's still to be executed. Won't you speak a word with him beforehand? I'm sure it would raise his spirits marvellously. He must be seriously downcast. Don't you agree, Your Majesty?'

The King was rubbing his cheekbones, puggling his ears and blowing down his nose to try to ease the pressure in his head. His small eyes with their prominent blood vessels moved only dilatorily between Cardinal and Comte.

'By no means, my lord,' said Thibault. 'By your leave, it would turn my stomach to see him again and think that I gave life and breath to a godless jackanape.'

'Oh for shame, for shame, sir. And you of the Sword–Noble. I would've thought it would gratify you to see His Majesty's justice carried through.'

King Francis grasped the game that was in hand, and lent his weight to de Guise, as he had been well schooled to do. 'Oh do. Do by all means, Gloriole,' he said rattling one finger in his ear and wincing with pain.

So Thibault was obliged to follow the Cardinal out of the States Chamber. Two pillars supported its exquisite vaulted ceiling, stuccoed from base to top with the ermines of Anne of Britanny. The whole room – the whole palace swarmed with ermine. They played the strangest tricks on the eye, seeming all the time to move, to swarm upwards into the roof cavities, like maggots crawling up out of a carcase. Thibault realized that he had not eaten all day. Perhaps that was why his head swam, why the ermine swarmed. Everywhere piles of food were heaped on tables untouched while the guests moved incessantly to and fro between, unable to leave, unable to remove their seal of approval. They shimmered like silver salmon on the spawning beds, their stomachs occluded, incapable of eating amid limitless food. Now and then, without having expressed anything amiss, a man or woman would faint discreetly, the smile still on their ashen lips, and those they were talking to would turn aside and reanimate the conversation with someone new. Only those of very great power dared pass free comment on the tableaux of butchery in every window.

'No good will come of this,' said the Duchess de Guise to Catherine de Medici. 'Blood calls to blood.'

Blood calls to blood. Was that what she said? It explained the throbbing in his ears and the clogging of the sluices in his heart where the blood swashed while he walked. He followed the Cardinal down endless passageways diminishing in size as though towards infinity. Finally, where an adit no wider than a man's shoulders led to a courtyard full of flowerpots, they came to a herb-drying house being used for a cell. In place of the stench of blood and burning, there was a sudden smell of basil and thyme, lemon mint and bay.

The windowless hut let in light only through the cracks in the plank door, and the gap underneath it where it made a white rectangle like a lover's covert letter slipped under the door. Each prisoner sat with a folded sack and bound hands in his lap.

'Father!'

It had to be borne. It had to be gone through. He would have preferred not to have to justify his decision to Kempis, but it had to be borne. He felt irritable: how much more did he have to do to prove his loyalty to King and Court? Now look. The Cardinal was untying his son's hands.

Fortunately Kempis gave every appearance of having forgotten that his father had betrayed him: he made no reference to it. At first he mistook the untying of his hands for the signal that he was free, and praised God and his father in equal parts. Then the Cardinal disabused him. After that, all he did was to plead for Thibault to buy his freedom. 'Give them anything, Father! Give the King anything! For Christ's sake, give them a ransom! Exile! I'll go into exile! Only let them bail me, Father! What's happening out there? What's happened? The rumours in here . . . they grow and grow. I'm condemned to die, Father! Don't you understand? I'm condemned! Are there pardons being given? Is the King giving out pardons? They're saying he is. They're saying he's not. They're saying he's already hanged some.'

'Hanged some. Gutted some. Burned some,' said Thibault inexpressively. 'What d'you expect? Traitors, the whole pack of you.' The men sitting cross-legged on the floor, knee to knee, shoulder to shoulder, looked up at him blankly, silently. Some began to sway forwards and back. Kempis did not appear to have heard him.

'Father, give them Gloriole! Make a present of it to the King! *Give them anything!*'

'Give away Gloriole,' said Thibault smiling. 'What an extraordinary notion. You're plainly mad. That's plainly how you came here. Madness. And vice.'

'Father?'

'Can we leave now, my Lord Cardinal? I find I have nothing to say to this young man.'

'Father!'

'Ah, but the King finds it so hard to credit. This dichotomy of views in a single household,' said the Cardinal sinuously.

'That's because the King is young,' said Thibault. 'When he reaches our time of life, my lord, he'll realize how powerless a father is to curb an unnatural son.'

'Not powerless to punish, however. After the event.'

'Indeed so,' said Thibault. 'What then? Does the King invest in me the might of his justice? I'm indeed honoured.'

'He does, he does. And what punishment will you mete out to your son for the crime of conspiring against the Crown – for planning violence upon the person of the King?'

Thibault regarded his son. Astounding that a man could so resemble his father outwardly while inside he was of a different species. 'Sell Gloriole?' he recollected, as if the meaning of what Kempis had said had only just reached him. 'Huh! You claim yourself equal to a peasant and yet you think yourself worth more than the sum of all your ancestors and forebears. No, sir, a House may shed a man. A man doesn't merit the shedding of a House. What a waste. What a profligacy. All those meals eaten. All those clothes worn through. I should have drowned you in a bucket the day you were born.' Then turning to the Cardinal again he said, 'The man's a Leveller. So. Let him share whatever fate was allotted to his peers here.'

Like a battering ram the light suddenly broke into the room through unsuspected double doors in the far wall. Like slashing the blindfold off a horse, the calm of the darkened hut was suddenly destroyed and the prisoners began to thrash out with bound hands, and struggle to their knees, and shout, and name themselves, and protest their innocence, their reasons for living, the reasons why the world could not spare them. Kempis, by contrast, became abruptly calm. He had seen his false hopes broken, whereas his companions were only now raising theirs.

'I'll pray for your soul, Papa, but God curse you, body and brain. You've placed the King so high in your sky that he's thrown the rest of us into eclipse. What manner of man loves his King more than his own flesh and . . .'

Two guards took hold of him, tumbled him off his feet and threw him into the wagon outside like a rag effigy for burning. The sacks allocated once in such an orderly way, one to a man, were gathered up again and thrown in on top of the prisoners, hugger-mugger. Then the cart trundled away at walking pace towards a side gate, for the hut proved to be on the very perimeter of the chateau.

'I shall direct the King's attention to your loyalty,' said de Guise surlily. He had been so convinced of Thibault's Protestant sympathies that he was simply disappointed to find his suspicions unfounded. He had never liked de Gloriole on the same unconscious grounds as most men: jealousy of his looks, of his fascination to women. Now he found he was still more disgusted to find him just like the rest, abject in obedience. (Since the Cardinal had aspirations to rule the country from behind the throne, he naturally felt contempt for such men.) 'We shall be watching you from above. The King and I.'

So Thibault followed the cart, not quite knowing why, or what more was expected of him when it came to a halt. Ridiculous to think of the King watching from the balcony – any more than God was watching out of Heaven. He followed the cart out on to the broad, beautiful bridge, even so; out over the Loire.

The setting sun was colouring the water. It made the castle behind them flesh-pink, too, as though it had overexerted itself in the cause of Justice. Or perhaps it was not the sun at all, but the blood seeping into the tufa, suffusing it with rosy blushes. The windows caught the sun, making them too pricking bright to look at, and Thibault turned his eyes back to the river.

One by one, the prisoners' hands were untied and they were invited to put on, for a shroud, one of the sacks. Then the cord that had tied their hands was used to knot shut the sack, before two guards heaved it over the parapet of the bridge and into the river far below. So very labour-intensive, thought Thibault. So very extravagant of man-hours. So many guards needed to dispose of so relatively few, while keeping the rest in order.

They were flour sacks for the most part, and sturdily made,

but some tore. A hand or an elbow or a foot poked through. And of course the hessian did not muffle the sound so very well. He wondered whether any were from the Sablois flour-mills.

A crowd gathered – not a crowd exactly, but four or five dimly aware that the day would live in the history of the town and that history would value eye-witnesses. They held off at a distance – expressionless, deadpan, deferring opinion till they were safe home behind locked doors. One mistook Thibault for an officer-of-the-court overseeing the execution. He asked deferentially, 'Why this way for these?' Thibault could not answer him.

They could not expect a nobleman – a comte – to hump sacks like a miller. They could not expect a man dressed for a ball to dirty his clothes with flour dust and husks. They could not expect him to labour like a stockman in an abattoir. The sinking sun was overtaken by cloud, and left nothing but a single beam of light pointing downriver like the beam from the eye of God.

The soldiers were faster at tying reef knots than in disposing of the bulging, wriggling sacks. A backlog had built up of bagged prisoners propped against the parapet. Thibault went forward and lifted one. A hand grasped him through the sacking, but could not keep hold. A leg kicked. There was a cry as the backbone swung against the bridge balustrade. Thibault hadn't the art: could not get the awkward load high enough to rest on the parapet, but just kept banging it against the wall. A soldier came to his aid. Then the rope got tangled in the archer's brace on his wrist, and slid off the collar of the sack. As it dropped away from them into the river below, Thibault glimpsed a tuft of hair on the crown of a head, inside the opening bag.

'Just leave it to us, sir,' said the archer patronizingly. Thibault moved away to the end of the bridge and watched the river purge the sins of Amboise chateau, carrying its burden of corpses through the reddening reflection of evening. It was the first plague of Egypt. The river had turned to blood.

The water pushed fast between the arches of the bridge, but where the flow slackened further downstream many of the sacks resurfaced and bobbed away between the sandbars, the pilings, the reedbeds, the eyots, as far as the eye could keep trace of them. And there was no bend in the river as far as the eye could see. Who was to say where those sacks might end, what perverse current might snatch them into what culvert, what Loire tributary, what ox-bow backwater, what castle moat?

FORTY-FOUR

On the Stairs

For a man so completely successful in subordinating heart and mind to expediency, it should have been easy. Easy to disregard another person's feelings. And yet somehow, all the way home, Thibault could not help but speculate on his wife's reaction. And the nearer home he came, the more convinced he became that Berenice would show stamina and persistence in her grief as she did in everything else. Fortunately, something happened as he neared the chateau which distracted a mind already determined not to think on the subject.

As the causeway came into sight, he found his horse moving against a tide of peasants, townspeople, students, beggars, monks and nuns, all carrying pieces of his property. Portraits, tapestries, carpets, salvers, plate and pottery. In these days of vandalism, pillage and casual slaughter, he at once assumed a raid. But was it Catholics punishing the Protestant leanings of his House, or Protestants wreaking revenge for the slaughter at Amboise? He drew his sword and rode into a group of the marauders, scattering them with the sheer weight of horseflesh. Where had his guard been? What danger or disaster had overtaken Gloriole while he was busy ensuring its safety? What would he find on the other side of the causeway? He picked up a scrivener by his linen crossbelt, and the man's inkbottle came up under his armpit and spilled down him like a chest wound. He dropped the books he was carrying. One was *Le Viandier*, bound in white leather.

'What's to keep me from killing you?' The scrivener seemed astonished, quite taken aback – a perfect day marred by the unfairness of a bully. '*Whose doing is this?*'

'What, lordship? What?'

'Who started this loot, this sacking?'

His feet dangled. He kept looking down to the ground below them. The horse turned its head and nipped at him. He tried to keep the ink from staining Thibault's clothes as well. 'She gave it! She gave it us!'

'Who? Gave you what?'

'Everything, master! Everything! She gave it all to us – summoned us hither – gave it! Past luck of dreaming, it was sir! Before God, sir! By this hand!'

The hand he swore by was inky red and looked like an assassin's. Thibault let him drop. When he picked himself up, he went and squatted over the fallen books, staking ownership but unwilling to touch them before he had wiped his hands clean on the grass.

All the way across the causeway Thibault snatched items back out of the arms of his chattels and neighbours; their groans and protests closed behind him like the Red Sea. He could see members of his guard standing about on the berm, watching the pillage, pointing to certain loot with recognition, shaking their heads, discussing it. As soon as he was within earshot, he began to bawl at them to put a stop to the robbery – to help him – to take back the goods. The half-tester of a bed came swaying across the bridge towards him, like a player on stilts. The soldiers seemed confused. They hesitated. They looked up towards the armoury window where the figure of Berenice de Saumur stood like a black wraith.

He did not need to ask for an explanation. She volunteered one. 'You gave away what I valued most. So I've given away all it was in my power to give.'

His arms were encumbered with salvage: a serving dish, a harness, a little chair, a dress of hers. He let them all drop. 'Then you'd best make shift to recover them, woman. Nothing's yours to give.'

'Mayn't a wife give charity out of her husband's goods? Anyway, how will you punish me for it? Drown me in a sack like a kitten?' It seemed that no matter how fast a man rode, his news could travel faster.

He thought to step closer, to justify himself and express regret. But for every pace he stepped closer, she drew away from him, without ever seeming to move her feet. Like Eurydice away from Orpheus, into Hell, without a scream. He should have realized that perpetual winter had set in at Gloriole. He had lost her good opinion for ever.

But he did not realize it. Instead he thought, she'll come about when the wind changes. He thought, it's for me to set the period of mourning. When I decide it's done, she can be told to put off black and to let the memory lapse. Such decisions were his; she must abide by them. Besides, he was seethingly angry to look out along the causeway and see the contents of his house borne away like blades of grass on the backs of a colony of ants. He could not stay to argue with her; he must recoup as much property as could be found. Then there would be time enough to make her acknowledge the necessity of what he had done. If need be he would thrash her till she saw the right of it.

So it was some time before he discovered that Berenice had afforded him the last interview she intended to grant. She confined herself to her rooms, stripped bare as they were of everything portable, and when he pestered her there, she removed to the servants' turrets, sewing rooms, pantries and wardrooms, annexing new land every time he made her cede the old. He discovered, too, that she had sent Thomas away – to travel as the fancy took him till the religious bloodlust had eased in the countryside.

He wrote to her family at Saumur, demanding reparation for the goods she had given away, but received not so much as abuse by way of reply.

And whenever husband and wife passed, it was always on the stairs. That double helix of stone was so illusory in its properties that he would think he glimpsed her ahead of him and hurry after her, only to find her always on the other spiral and out of reach. He could change, at the next landing, on to the other staircase, but somehow she would always elude him and be seen descending a flight or two below. He could have put a stop to this foolishness, but he had other things more pressing to attend to. Besides, her grief embarrassed him, worn as it was with such tenacity, such unseemly obsession. It never once *slipped her mind*, it seemed, and allowed her to hum a song (as she had done all the time before) or to investigate the intriguing sound of strangers arriving, or venture inside the observatory to see the quadrant finished. He put off and put off beating her, but she showed no appreciation of the fact by casting him a morning greeting across the stairwell. They were as North and South on the weather-vane – fixed always to travel at a permanent distance from one another, no matter how hard the wind blew. He put off and he put off forcing his way into her bedroom and taking what was his by right. But it could not be put off for ever. Did he not need solace himself, after all? Had he not lost a son as much as she?

But how was he to draw her eyes? A foolish time to realize it, but only now did he acknowledge knowing that his wife had loved him all along. Her eyes had always been on him. He had often taken that for criticism or maternal watchfulness, but now that she kept her eyes turned away he could feel what radiant warmth there had been in coming face to face each day with his dragon of Saumur. Now she would no sooner look him in the eye than the like poles of two magnets tolerate each other's company. And he did not know how to set about recovering what was lost. It could not be lost for ever. Did he not need solace himself, after all? Had he not lost . . . Would to God that he could have put her foolish obsession into a sack and dropped it into the Loire.

'What's this meat?' he demanded of the kitchen woman when she brought him a stew of broth.

'Mutton, sir.'

'Well, it's rank, woman. Smell it.'

The woman sniffed the broth tentatively. 'It's the rosemary is all, sir.' And she pointed out the rosemary leaves floating like waterboatmen on the surface.

He pushed it away. 'I tell you it's rank. When I say a thing's rank, have the goodness to take it from under my nose!'

But the beef was no better. Despite the bay leaves crowning it like a victor's wreath, it smelled of blood and decay. And when Lent brought nothing but fish to the table, it too turned his stomach. Tarragon could do nothing to mask it. He sent Vache to Blois to examine the ice-houses the Queen Mother was introducing to all her houses, and had him commission the excavation of three beside Gloriole's kitchen garden. But when he went to see how the work was progressing, he heaped abuse on the workmen for digging up some forgotten cesspit. Little wonder the food tasted of corruption and filth when the herb garden – once so redolent with basil and thyme and lemon-mint and bay – stank like a ploughed graveyard. He could not even stomach standing near by. With his handkerchief held over his nose and mouth, he circled the house in search of a more pleasant thing: his latest acquisition. Forty flamingoes, pink as baby's flesh, stood about in the shallows of the ornamental lake. He had ordered the removal of the bronze of Abraham and . . . from the water. The fashion was not so much for art as for nature these days, not so much for the familiar as the exotic. So there stood his birds, blushing with embarrassment at the surfeit of their own beauty, slitting the still surface of the lake with cleaver bills so that the rims of their beaks and their absurdly long tongues were stained red. It was not sunset, and yet their tongues were stained red. A strange phenomenon. Their feathers were darker, too, since their arrival. A trick of the light perhaps, though it looked more as if the water droplets scattered down their backs during feeding had darkened the herls.

He hoped there were shrimp enough to content them. He did not want them wandering off. He had clipped the wings of the peafowl he bought, but they had still decamped into the cornfields, presumably walking there to be free of Gloriole. He must ensure that his flamingoes had no incentive to go. Someone, it seemed, had thought of this ahead of him, but with a crass lack of subtlety. A sack of offal had been thrown in, to encourage the shrimps: there, in among the feet of his flamingoes, so that their scything, pendulum beaks slashed through its hessian, loosing the contents. His men were all fools and incompetents. The birds would choke themselves! He found himself running the perimeter path of the lake, waving his arms, shooing them into the air – a peach and pink spring cloud of twiggy blossom. The startled flamingoes chattered and gabbled and shrilly protested, and their comical, splashing feet churned up the water, destroying their own reflections. The sack of offal was submerged by their panic, and Thibault was not about to wade in up to his waist to grope about for it underwater. So he returned to the house, dispatching every person he passed, from gardener to fool, to the lake to recover the sack.

They found no sack. They said there was no sack. But Thibault, knowing better, told them that the undercurrent must have taken it out through the sluices into the river. He demanded of his water-man whether such gross methods of feeding were really necessary in an ornamental lake. But the water-man looked as blank as one of his carp and claimed that offal was 'nothing to do with him, master'.

'The King is dead.'

He threw it to her across the stairwell as a suitor might throw a nosegay of flowers. She was climbing, he descending, but each of course on a different staircase. For the first time she stopped and regarded him, through the pierced stonework of the stairwell wall, her black eyes blacker than her dress.

'So? What's one more after twelve hundred? Who have we now, then? Another child to pull the legs off every crawling thing?'

He was quick to reassure her. 'We're in good hands till Henry comes of age. Catherine de Medici will keep us in safe hands till

Henry comes of age. You know she's urgent for peace with . . . you Protestants.'

Now that at last she favoured him with her eyes, he could not be free of them. He felt himself turning to stone in her Medusa stare. 'We Protestants? I protest, you need not number me among any body of Protestants, Thibault.' She waited for his pleasure to show itself, like waiting for a louse to creep out from under a stone before treading on it. 'What good is protesting? When did it ever persuade a cruel man to hold off his hand? Or God to lift a finger.'

Thibault shivered violently in the draught. A door far below was banging in the wind, and the tackle on a flagpole on the roof could be clearly heard rattling above. He had not realized that anything she said could be as bitter as her silence. 'Berenice,' he began assertively, 'you've grown unsound. You must submit to physic. Melancholy can poison the best constitution, you know.' He hitched one thigh on to the stone sill and leaned out across the stairwell. In doing so, he noticed how household litter was collecting in the base of the shaft, fifty feet below: fruit skins, candle stubs, strewings, something black like a nun's hood, something white like a baby's swaddling, something bulky wrapped in hessian. The hair of his head lifted in the howling updraught of air. 'I'm concerned for you, lady,' he said, and it seemed as if the echo would travel all over the house, whispering distortions out of every fireplace and stove: '*I am concerned for you, lady. I love you.*'

She too leaned across the stairwell, one hand darting out, the fingers stiff, the nails intended to claw troughs in his cheek. But the scale of the staircase was vast. Her hand came nowhere near him, nowhere near. 'You? You're concerned for no one but your precious kings and queens. No beggar in the street ever grovelled as low as you in your lust to climb into royalty's placket!'

Now she was ugly. Now that there was no love in her face, he could see how it had been possible to love a plain woman. The face had been all gentleness and humour, wit and vigour. Now all that had dropped away. Now she was ugly. She went to continue on her way, climbing her lonely spiral, but Thibault, having determined to end this nonsense between them once and for all, was not prepared to let her have the last word. He too ran upstairs, glimpsing her on every turn looking misleadingly close. He thought of leaping the stairwell, then thought better of it.

'I shall come and find you out tonight, woman!' he shouted. 'I've paid grief its due! Now I need some recreation. You hear?

I'll come to you tonight!' Near the base of the shaft, faces began to poke out and look skywards, trying to make sense of the shouting. 'I'll purge melancholy myself, you hear, woman? I know a cure for it most infallible!' Berenice continued upwards. Like lovers in Dante's Inferno, it felt as if they were to be blown round in a vortex of wind from everlasting to everlasting.

But the furthest she could go was the roof, and Thibault would reach it at the same moment. His tone changed. 'The third time was too many, Berenice! Once, yes. Twice, yes. Twice I deceived the King for your sake. But you can only ask so much!'

She stopped abruptly. 'What does that mean?'

He did not quite know what he had said. He had to catch his breath before he could also catch hold of thoughts that running had jarred loose in his head. He rested his head and hands against the pierced stone screen marring his view of her. 'Well?' he said. 'Well? I lied to Francis about the unicorn, didn't I? I conspired with you to hide the printing press, didn't I? D'you know what it costs a man like me to lie to his king? To deceive his king? To be a traitor to the truth?' He was unaccustomed to running. He was fearful that the noise of the blood pumping through his ears and the breath in his throat would prevent him hearing what she had to say in return. But she waited until he had recovered himself, waited till she could see his face clearly among the scrolls and lacework of carved tufa. Her own face was whiter than ever. But the vicious animosity had slipped away. It was the face he had always known was there beside him in bed, whether or not the lights were lit.

'Yes. I do know,' she said with an air of enlightenment. 'So the third time was once too often.' She nodded in his stead, readjusting her perspective on events long past. 'I see now. I overtaxed your sense of honour. I overtaxed . . .'

'Yes!' he exclaimed triumphantly, having at last made her understand. 'I *just couldn't* break faith a third time. I could not.'

'Couldn't break faith. No. I see that now.' Her voice was dreamy, distracted. He went to say something else, but she put her finger to her lips to stop him, as if she could not assimilate any more revelations for the moment. She turned and went on climbing, but slowly, wearily now. 'I see now,' she said repeatedly. 'I see now. I'm as much to blame.'

Thibault emerged on to the roof, but since the other spiral of the staircase gave on to a different, slightly higher terrace, it was some time before he caught sight of Berenice between the chimneys, lanterns and cupolas of the roof. A forest of pinnacles decorated in mosaic inlay broke the wind into a hundred swirling eddies. The rope beneath the bell of the tocsin tower snaked like Lucifer in the Garden. All about them lay Gloriole and the lands of Sablois. The patterns of the gardens were levelled to a tame, two-dimensional millefleur tapestry, the yellow of spring bursting like flock stuffing through every seam and tear. The river beat like a vein in Thibault's temple.

He suddenly realized, with a terrible certainty, that he had said something amiss and would never have the chance to retract it. He began to run again, grazing the palm of his hands as he swung round angular columns of stone. Suddenly she stood in front of him on the lip of the roof, thirty paces away.

'In Cathay,' she said, 'I've read that dragons fly.' And having said it, she walked off the edge of the roof as if she had contracted with God for the angels to catch her.

The angels' backs were turned. She plummeted down the face of the building. Its several pediments, water spouts and sills pawed at her opportunistically. Rejecting all its advances, she plunged on to the black and white paving stones of the inner courtyard, not far from the spot where Thibault's coppery sun had first fallen during the King's Masque.

It was deemed wise that Thibault's first Communion after re-entry into the Catholic Church should be accomplished on the same day as his wife's trial. Not that it was taken at a public Mass, but in the privacy of his own chapel. His chaplain, however, considered it would divert him. Only a churchman could suppose his rituals and ceremonies sufficient to distract a man from his wife's trial. Thibault took Mass, then rode to Rocheblanche and was there in time for the conclusion.

Had Thibault not already elected to re-enter the Church he would not have had to make Confession. If he had not had to make Confession, he might have described his wife's death rather differently. But as it was, the chaplain was eager that justice should be seen to be done. Suicide was an endemic evil to be suppressed with all the zeal right-thinking society could muster.

So the body of Berenice de Gloriole was brought to trial: propped up in a high-backed chair and covered over with a sheet. It was excommunicated by Church and condemned by State for the crime of desperation. It was sentenced to be hanged, then cut down and drawn through the town on a hurdle as an exemplary warning to others.

There was a poor showing for the hanging, the memory being so recent of the presents she had given away. They said they'd known then that she was mad . . . but they did not go to see her body hanged, even so. And when the hurdle passed them in the street, pulled by a donkey and horse yoked together, the citizens stepped out of its path into doorways, and crossed themselves, and chose to believe that she had been murdered by Thibault for giving away his furniture. The possibility of suicide could simply not be held in the mind; it scorched with an inextinguishable fire and made the head spin with the smell of sulphur.

When the hurdle reached its destination in the flyblown tumulus of the town's litter, it was intended that the maimed local dogs should eat its cargo. But though they balanced on their three legs to sniff at it, they spurned to touch the corpse, perhaps because some were Gloriole souillards given away by Berenice out of the Gloriole kennels.

She was gone by morning. Some said that her relatives from Saumur had come and fetched her away, but it was not true. Suicide is a non-denominational sin – one that united Catholic and Huguenot in repugnance and righteous outrage. Her relations chose to forget she had ever been born.

Only Thibault was condemned to love her from everlasting to everlasting.

FORTY-FIVE

The Storm

Several dozen men were studying at the 'academie' of the Chicheface Inn in Rocheblanche: dealing the cards to play triquetrac, oie and chouette, with a noisy game of nine-pins going on in an alcove of the same room. Only the week before there had been yet another edict from the pulpit banning gaming and skittles. So when there was a hammering at the door it was of course taken for a raid.

Cards and dice were swept into hats and sleeves and boots; those with good cards cursing and those with large debts crossing themselves in gratitude. The skittles were rammed into a wine-rack, and someone cut through the rope by which the skittle-ball hung from the beam. Two or three other tell-tale tufts of rope still decorated the beam from earlier raids. By that time, the hammering had been replaced by the thump of a boot which bowed in the planks at the base of the door.

'*Since when did inns lock their doors?*' the Comte de Gloriole demanded to know when the tapster finally opened to him.

'Midnight, sir. I always make fast at midnight,' said the man losing his hands behind the bib of his apron as though they too should be hidden out of sight. Strictly speaking there should have been no one there but legitimate, transient travellers, but since the room rose *en masse* at the sight of their liege, it was plain that the men were all local.

The Comte was muffled up in a black, waterproofed cloak, and his hair was damp and wild. He was out of breath with riding. 'Maidens!' he said, searching the room for co-operation. 'I need maidens! Don't just stand there! Find some!'

The men looked at one another. No one made a move.

'Maidens, by Christ! There's a tornado coming'll cleave the place in half if it's not put off! There are the boats out here. D'you want 'em sunk? Make 'em fast. Get the canvas off the wagons if you don't want 'em ripped up. Get the animals indoors.

I want men up at the chateau to stand guard over the animals. If the palings go there'll be dogs loose in with the horses and God knows what else. I want sandbags on the berm: the wind'll drive the waters up. *Maidens*, damn your eyes! Can't you understand plain French? Daughters! Haven't you got any daughters in the whole cockless pack of you?'

Understanding dawned slow as morning before men began pulling on their caps, snatching up their hoods and heading for the door. A man who had slipped an illicit dice into his boot cursed and limped hoppingly after the rest, and their noise grew, like a pack of hounds, from a babble to a common baying note. 'Women to the bells! Women to the bells!' Shutters banged open. Fuddled sleepers rolling out of bed on to their knees thought that rowdies were beating up the town, and rummaged for swords in their presses.

'I need men to load the cannon. You! You!' bellowed Thibault, snatching at the flying cloak cords of the turn-key. 'D'you have men in the lock-up? Let 'em out! I need men to charge the cannon up aloft!'

The throng in the streets grew every minute, running to and fro, spreading out to wake different alleyways and streets, then reconvening for mutual encouragement. 'Load your guns! Load your guns! Where's your gunsmith? Break down his doors! We must have guns to fire!'

When he was certain that he had shaken the town out of its inertia, Thibault rode back to Gloriole as fast as he had come, flogging his horse till it sweated blood and the veins stood out from its cheeks. His chaplain stood on the causeway clutching a blunderbuss which he kept snatching away from the persistent grabs of the armourer. 'I may carry it! I may carry it! It's the law now!' shrieked the priest shrilly, and in defending his rights was almost ridden down by Thibault returning at the gallop.

Already, a girl from the kitchen had been mounted, like the Witch of Endor, on the very top of the tocsin tower and told to ring and to shout without ceasing till the danger was past. In her shift she weighed barely enough to swing the alarm bell, and the exertion left her no voice at all to bellow at the gale. 'Away! Away! Foul weather away! Be gone, storm! Be gone another way!' Her sister joined her there, a blanket draped around her neck, and they screamed themselves hoarse into the deafened hollow of the swinging bell above them. They could see the tiny white shapes of other women running barefoot up the hill towards the

Chapel Saint-Cloud to add its bell to the din. The church bell in Rocheblanche made a third.

No purpose would be served in sending to the vines or orchards. The shoots and blossom would have to fend for themselves in the grip of the tornado. No means existed either to save the red deer from the falling timber of the Sablois, or the crops from being churned back into the ground by the harrowing rain.

Thibault gave orders for the doors throughout the house to be axed off their hinges, because the wind, funnelling through the house, would slam them, slam them, slam them. The compression of air, he said, would shatter the windows. But he was obliged to carry through the salvation of his house single-handedly, as though he were towing every other slave behind him on a rope. For when he gave commands, they stood dumbly about, mouths agape, asking stupid questions, wasting the precious moments before that Charybdis monster of wind and rain came swirling out of the Sologne and drove its path of destruction through the Sablois. 'How d'you know it's coming, master? How d'you know?'

'Are those girls dead up there?' he demanded, shaking both fists up at the tocsin tower. 'Why can't I hear them? What are they doing?' In the end, the paltry chinking of the bell and their reedy childish voices led him to such despair that he mounted the steps himself and pulled on the rope till his ribs gapped and his belly ached and the two little kitchen girls cowered down beside the wall with their hands over their ears.

> Away! Away, foul weather! Away!
> Be gone, storm! Be gone another way!

But the storm would not take fright. The fright in Thibault's own bowels told him that the storm would not be deflected from its determined course. History had wound it, like a dark clock-spring, and this was its due time to strike.

It came like an invader, razing the surrounding woodlands. Landslips overpowered and crushed vines to a bloody smear in the chalky mud. The tornado levelled the parklands like ten thousand running feet. It piled up the water in the river into a tidal bore whose crest was white with fish and spray. It spun the waterwheel of the mill off its axle and rolled it over the race to smash against the apple barges and turn the river cider-sour. It pushed a fold of water into the moat to circle the chateau. It swamped basement doors, bit curved morsels out of the base of buttresses and smashed the rowing boats keel-down on to the causeway. The wind lifted out of the troughing waves a treasure of orange carp which it showered like Danaë's gold along the berm.

Birds ripped from their roosts or out of the air came pitching through the windows like thrown stones or were broken against the leading in bloody gouts. The roof was alive with them, unfeathered, hopping, blowing about, dying. Lengths of fencing snaked and cracked like flags and, like flags, grew ragged and frayed. When the fences fell, they freed the boar to ravish all the shrieking, Sabine sows. Bears danced to the tabor rattle of thunder. The hawks, chained by their legs, were spilled into the jaws of dogs escaped into the mews, and monkeys swarmed over the face of the building gibbering with cold. The scarlet parrots huddled together, clotting like blood.

Breaking over the chateau, the wind drove the smoke back down the chimneys of two-score hearths and pushed choking fumes and soot back down the flues. Archangels of sheet-lightning flew on six-fold wings through the smoke-filled rooms. The carpets undulated like sea waves and the tapestries bellied out, reanimating their static heroes just as, outside, the rain was gouging up the burial grounds, reanimating the dead, washing clean the white faces of muddy skulls. And the bedding was torn from Thibault's bed and strewn about like graveclothes.

Up on the roof, the bronze cannon of Gloriole fired never-ending salvoes into the belly of the storm, but the cannonfire of its thunder was louder, its chainshot more destructive, as it tore off cupolas, minarets and chimneys, bell-lanterns, flagstaffs, water-spouts and ridge-cresting. The weather-vane tried to fly away but was brought down at once by a crossfire of hail. And over Thibault's head, as he heaved on the tocsin bell and bellowed out the wonted formula, the storm hovered, raptor of all raptors, sinking its talons into the very fabric of his castle, slashing at him with jagged beaks of lightning.

> Away! Away, foul weather! Away!
> Be gone, storm! Be gone another way!

Cataracts of rain converged on the lantern-dome of the stairwell and poured in interlacing cascades down the double helix of the grand stairs filling the basements, swilling rats from their subterranean nests to swarm in a black plague across the ground floors and chatter along the mantelpieces. Stained-glass smashed from the rose window above the courtyard lay on the black and white flagstones like the red mosaic of a supine woman, while in the gardens the storm-fiend went to earth down the rose walk and into the walled garden where it plucked down the espaliers clinging by their finger-tips to the miserable shelter of the walls.

When it was over, the swollen river drew back to within its banks, taking with it the detritus of the storm: shrubs and punts and gates and piers and drowned cattle and wagons and rabbits. And tree branches and barns and the spires of churches. And the contents, surely, of some grainstore, for hessian sacks by the dozen, by the tens of dozens floated and spun and wedged and went aground down all the length of the Sablois. From where he clung to the bellrope, his hands burned by its fraying strands, he could count them all, all of those sacks.

The little girls had crept away. There was only one other person in sight and that was his chaplain, squatting against the causeway parapet, asleep with his blunderbuss between his knees. Thibault surveyed his estates, his eyes coming to rest finally on the rose walk and the rose petals lying in bloody pools at the feet of their slaughtered stock. He could see them. He did see them.

Even though there was no such storm that summer on the Sablois or anywhere throughout Touraine. Only in the mind of Thibault de Gloriole.

FORTY-SIX

The Silent Stars Are Strong

When the concordat was signed between Catherine de Medici and the Prince of Condé, Thomas de Gloriole felt safe to come home to the Sablois. Catholic and Protestant would live together in peace from now on. It must be so. It had been set down on paper, with royal signatures below.

Even by the time he reached home, the Basilique Saint-Martin in Tours had been burned down by Huguenot mobs. They broke into the Annonciade, too, and burned the relics of poor little Jeanne of France, so uncomfortable in life, for fear she might give comfort to others in death. Murders and riots were commonplace, but at Gloriole the illusion of peace was perfectly preserved. It was as if no outside world existed, no unpleasantness. No mention of religion was ever made. Though nominally Catholic, it was a no-man's-land from which all debate and rancour had been excluded. But then so too had God.

The rumours Thomas heard en route of his mother's death proved all too true. The rumours that his father was mad thankfully proved groundless. Indeed, despite everything that had happened there was no marked change in Thibault's character, except perhaps for an increase of energy – a certain urgency, a certain magnification in his ambition. For instance, when Thomas arrived, it was night and yet the whole chateau blazed with light. He thought there must be a party in progress but there was not. There was scaffolding everywhere and, lashed to the scaffolding, a thousand reckless torches. Moving across the ground were the giant, distorted, flickering shadows of bricklayers, tilers, carpenters working by torchlight. Thibault was extending the chateau and nothing must hinder the work – not darkness, nor rain, nor feast-days nor fast, nor lack of funds nor lack of industry on the part of his workers.

'*Rien meilleur.* Nothing but the best,' he told his son, shaking him by the elbow. 'I dreamed it. A castle floating on the river.

Piles sunk clear into the riverbed; storeys riding over the top. Make Chenonceau look like a jetty. I dreamt it.'

'Like Venice, Father.'

'Like Venice, son.'

No comment was passed, no acknowledgment let slip of the fact that Thomas had been absent for two years. He drew no attention to it. He allowed himself to be received back into the household like blood seeping through from one side of cloth to the other. His father did not ask him, 'Where've you been? What've you seen?' and he did not volunteer the information. But in the gloom of evening, by the base of the observatory, he did mention it to Urania.

'I went to Poland. And Copenhagen. To see if any of it were true. Any of it. Copernicus. Any of it.'

'The heresy? You could've stayed closer to home and I'd've eased your mind. What did you find?' Like a hedgehog creeping through the evening dewfall, she was a rustle among the shrubs, a half-seen movement among the arbutus.

'Oh, it's disproved. Discredited. Of course.'

'Of course. If the Earth were moving round the sun, the distance between the stars would look as if it were altering – by reason of parallax. Did you have to go so far to find out that?'

'I had to go so far,' he said. 'What I did when I got there was immaterial. Still.'

'Still. You're returned now,' and she stepped towards him.

'What purpose was there in staying away? The structure of the universe wasn't all I re-proved on my travels. It's true what the Scriptures say. There's no escaping a foul conscience. Even in the uttermost parts of the . . . even in Poland.'

'*Conscience?* Why should you have a bad conscience? Why?'

'I'm alive, as you say,' he shrugged. 'That's crime enough these days, to my mind.' His dejection was like a cold draught that buffeted her away and she moved back into the shadows and diminished to a glimmer of pale skin among the snowberries.

He did not trouble to resent the fact that, on his return, no status devolved on him, for all he was heir to Gloriole. The place of deputy had been taken up by Sebastian de Puy with whom Thibault shared his tobacco, spirits, loose women and confidences. De Puy could no more have swayed the Comte's thinking than he could have conjured demons, but his listening ear was companionable and his silence shrewd. Thibault was freed from the nuisance of dealing with Vache and other tradesmen, by delegating to de Puy the undignified process of haggling, wording contracts, setting prices. Sebastian was even empowered to sign in the Gloriole name as Thibault's chamberlain. Thomas was not. To his father, Thomas continued to be 'the lesser son', and to the people of the Sablois a gentle, slightly simple-minded creature not to be entrusted with their hopes or fears. To suppose Thomas simple was not entirely fair; he could speak five languages and had read the entire contents of Gloriole's library – every account of exploration since Nicholas of Cusa. But alongside his father, seemingly built of iron, glass and stone, little Thomas with his plush hair and heart-shaped face, his unbelted doublet like a flag wrapped round its post, and his eyes forever lowered like a penitential maid, left a nebulous, soft impression on the mind. The peasants and townspeople did not seek his help even when they were sorely in need of it, for it did not seem as if Thomas could help himself, let alone a whole community of souls.

That sore need did arise when Thibault, standing on the roof one day to survey the work in progress, sighted the village of Croix-Rouge. This was hardly unusual; it had stood there for as long as the castle and with more continuity of occupancy. But today, like a hole in the retina, like a lash in the eye, it irked him, that unplanned straggle of wattle cottages, the church with its twin Norman towers ugly as Balon and Batonne, the barn with its broken-backed roof. What he could not see, he could imagine: the kennel running yellow down the main street, the three-legged dogs yelping and shivering on incontinent flanks, the wagons waiting for repair like ships that had foundered up against the cooper's house. There were similar scenes in Rocheblanche, but that was out of sight, hidden from Gloriole by a tactful fold of terrain. Only Croix-Rouge had the bad taste to show itself – like a beggar at a wedding – alongside the pure white splendour of the growing chateau. Its impertinence could not be tolerated. It must be banished. It must be erased, purged, forgotten.

At ten in the morning he commissioned his steward to inform the town that it was to be destroyed at four. Like Jonah sent to condemn Nineveh, the steward did not want to go. The soldiers in the wardroom were already busy making the incendiaries. Some of them, whose families lived in Croix-Rouge, begged him to ride like the very devil and give time for the household goods to be got away. But he dithered and fretted, said he must have protection if he was to deliver such a message. He did not say as much to the Comte, of course, but to the Comte's son.

'I'll go myself,' said Thomas, and seeing the urgency of the situation, moved uncharacteristically fast.

He apologized to the people of Croix-Rouge. He told them the town would be resituated – better built and with planning and foresight instead of the confluence of accidents that had given rise to it over the centuries. He said there would be compensation. He promised far more than it was within his ambit to give. He said that the chateau was sympathetic to their plight. And when they pelted him with litter out of the streets, he told them not to waste precious time. He expressed regret and sorrow, and they looked at him with eyes which said, 'How unlike his father he is. No stomach for his cruelties. Better to be eaten by a lion than mumbled to death by a bushy squirrel.'

The wreckage of carts around the cooper's yard disappeared; for the evacuation, everything and anything with one wheel or more must suffice. The litter disappeared out of the streets, for it was all someone's possession and the prospect of homelessness lent it all some possible future use. By the time the sappers arrived, Croix-Rouge had the clinical cleanliness of a fever hospital scrubbed out after the Plague has killed all its inmates. The householders loitered about at a distance, watching, feeling obliged to watch, lending moral support to the inanimate buildings like tender parents standing by at their baby's circumcision.

As the fires leapt like ginger cats from roof to roof, and a few mean explosions toppled the sturdier buildings, women one by one turned their faces in against their husbands' chests and children cried at the loud noises. The ugliness of Croix-Rouge, which had offended against good taste for a thousand years, ceased to give offence. Already the ivy was growing which would mask and soften the ugly rubble. Later the villagers returned to pick up firewood for their campfires. Someone set about salvaging the church bell which, if he could find a cart strong enough, would make him richer than he had actually begun the day. The wilder boyos, their blood set racing by such wanton violence, turned their faces towards Rocheblanche to beat up the town and raise hell. There was nothing to hold them back. A deputation arrived at the chateau next day from Rocheblanche to complain at the behaviour of these Visigoths and Vandals and to plead the protection of manorial law. No deputation came from

Croix-Rouge, of course, to protest at the behaviour of Thibault de Gloriole.

Thomas did not return directly to the chateau from Croix-Rouge. He went instead to the hunting lodge in the Sablois forest. He was in the habit of meeting Urania there. Any peasants who saw it no doubt supposed more than there was to suppose. For Thomas was a man crippled by despair, a fact which Urania was only gradually discovering.

No one, of course, had done her the disservice of christening her 'Urania'. But Thomas, though he knew it, never used her proper Christian name for fear he let it slip one day within hearing of Thibault, and undermined her. Today he went further than to avoid speaking her name. He avoided her eyes, too, and all manner of conversation. He simply sat on the rotting timbers of the half-dismantled bed and, with his hands clenched between his knees, stared into the fireplace. Every piece of kindling was a home, every stick of wood was a roofbeam, every tile of peat a wall collapsing in the dissolution of Croix-Rouge. She went and sat down beside him, but he did not acknowledge the hand she laid on his shoulder.

'Don't I always tell you? It can all be set right in time. Everything he does, you can undo. Else we can board our Mare Navis and sail away among the stars. Where would we go?' Her voice was sweet and animated, though untheatrical and higher-pitched than when she made her weekly astral reports to Thibault.

He narrowed his eyes, a habit born of short-sightedness and migraines. Once they had dreamed for hours at a time. Now he could no longer bear for her to try to rake alight a tired old game. 'There's no escaping it. I'm penned up here till my dying day. Now there's nothing I can do. Then there'll be too much. Too much to do. Too much to look after. Look at today. This one day. I'll have to make amends to the Sabloises for today – and a host of days like it. I'll be lucky if I have years enough even to put right what he's done. But that's what's laid to my charge. Nothing's served by pretending. There's no breaking away. Fate's immutable.' He added sardonically, 'You should know that. Look in the stars and see.'

'But you won't let me!'

He was the only man she had ever met who had not, within an hour's space, asked to know what fate lay in store for him. Catholic or Protestant, devout or profane, lay or cleric, they all asked her that same question, and all went away disappointed. Grinning or anxious, serious or supposedly in jest, no one failed to ask her, 'When will I die? What will become of me? What do the stars tell you about me?' The fact that Thomas thought astrology a blasphemy and a sin and held good to his beliefs made him remarkable indeed. It may even have been the reason she first loved him.

'And I'm supposed to believe you haven't done it anyway? Cast my horoscope? Let me guess. I was born and I'll die. I can even tell you what falls between. I'm Gloriole. I'm the future Gloriole. When Kempis died it was decided then and there. Every last minute I draw breath. It's my sentence. For not being the man my brother was.'

She did not argue. He was right: she had cast his horoscope. Even before she set foot inside Gloriole, she had cast his horoscope. But being a twin, his nativity was compounded with that of his brother. The stars spoke strongly of death and loss, but which was Kempis's fate and which Thomas's? The Geminian twins rolled in each other's arms for eternity, one dead, one living, while the other constellations growled and roared through the bars of cloud.

'I keep telling you!' she said jumping up. 'I know, I know, I *know* everything will turn out for the best. You must trust me. Why can't you trust me?'

'I'm sorry,' he said obdurately. 'It's as well we never . . . gave expression to our love.'

She gave a cry of exasperation and walked quickly up and down the room, hair blazing like a beacon fire declaring a state of war. 'Ah, that! I wondered when it warranted mention! Your mother didn't seem to think it such a paltry thing – a thing so readily put by!'

He watched her move about. Poisoned as his system was by the disease of melancholy, she was nothing more to him just then than proof that he would cause sorrow all his life long and be powerless to ease it. He said, 'I wouldn't lay any store by my mother's strivings in the cause of Love. We were part of her revenge, that's all. She was avenging herself on Father. Not very sound grounds for a marriage, is it? I've had time to think about it and it doesn't seem very sound grounds for . . .'

'Is that what we did, then? Is that the top and bottom of it? Instruments of Berenice's revenge? I'm sorry. I'd not realized we had no motives of our own.' The fury of her skirts was agitating the fire, the strewings on the floor, the moths gaping in at the window. Her hair separated into rivulets of glowing lava that would have burned his hands to touch. But Thomas remained unmoved. His depression, his despair, his sheer guilt at surviving when others had died weighed him down like the leads that carry a dead sailor to the bottom. He saw no purpose in opposing God. And his vision of God had changed over the years, from a wayside companion to some great freezing river of darkness, washing the stars towards their appointed reefs.

What an unkindness had been there. For Berenice to bring them, jump, to minister and vows, and bless a love they had kept secret from everyone but her. They had married on the day of Kempis' death, before Thibault even reached home. 'A ray of light on a dark, dark day,' Berenice had said, with a face as bitter as sin. But the dead Kempis had been there as bride and groom kissed. The cold hand of tragedy had dampened every potential joy. Urania said Berenice had simply meant to salvage a little happiness, after the Tumult of Amboise. Urania maintained adamantly that one day they would have everything they had ever dreamed of. But at present even she struggled to find any joy in being secretly married to Thomas de Gloriole.

There were other arguments in favour of despair – arguments Thomas was not prepared to expand on. Tell Thibault of the clandestine marriage, and Urania was more likely to suffer a sudden, unaccountable death than to become Chatelaine of Gloriole. There had been too few witnesses to the marriage: a man of influence would soon see it undone, dissolved, annulled. It was no more real than it had been when Thomas, wide awake, had stood at his chamber window night after night and yearned towards the tall tower of the observatory with a thrilling desperation. If Thibault were to die . . . if Thomas were to become Comte of Gloriole . . . what fantasy could he not command to come true? But Thibault would not die. And besides, the prospect of inheriting Gloriole was as loathsome a prospect to Thomas as the prospect of living without the companionship of Urania. Whichever way he looked, Thomas saw no salvation. His life was a string cat's-cradle between his father's hands in which a single string had slipped and left a hopeless, insoluble tangle from which he would never escape.

One day soon, Thibault would find a wife for him whose blood was compatible with the glory of Gloriole-sur-Sablois, and Thomas would be forced to choose. He must choose between relinquishing an unconsummated love-match made for mischief's sake by his distracted mother, or defying his father who was constitutionally incapable of brooking defiance. Then Thomas's world would come tumbling down. He did not know which was worse: to be crushed under the debris or to live waiting for the fall.

Even so, when the general subject of marriage arose, Thomas was able to swear with his hand on his heart, as his brother had always done, that his affections were already given to 'one above him'.

'Are you trying to make sport . . . ?' demanded his father, blushing with the strength of emotion still roused by mention of Kempis.

'Not at all, Father,' said Thomas meekly, and glanced at the ceiling. 'I swear to you, on Christ's body. My affections are given to one whose station in life puts her high above me.'

'Then you'd best change your affections, man,' snarled Thibault. But so far he had not pressed the issue, perhaps out of some superstitious reverence for his lost, greater son.

FORTY-SEVEN

Kingdom of Stone

Lodged in the crop of an African parrot, a sharp-hooked seed travelled, unmoved by cartwheels stumbling over jungle tree-roots, by the pitching of waves, by the grating of keels, by the blast of a colder sun, to fulfil its destiny. Finally it fell, in a weary whorl, into a garden bed at Gloriole-sur-Sablois. Other guts, other seeds, other germinations, and within fifty years fleshy green-black leaves wrestled with the hornbeam hedges, and the rose trees were strangled where they stood, by the tendrils of nameless exotic flora. Fleshy flowers with velvet mouths devoured the paltry French insect life. Worms in the earth were severed by the speedy plunge of razoring roots. And perfumes ranging from that of brignole plums to newly opened graves vied in the big nostrils of the parrot's descendants. The bats staggered on their nightly promenades, intoxicated by foreign scents. The Temperate was overrun by the Tropical, the primordial, the outlandish. At first the invasion was tolerated for the sake of its novelty. By the time Thibault extended Gloriole out across the river, the tropical weeds had embraced his garden in a grip no gardener could break. The builders paved over acres more grass, quarried the banks of the Sablois till its tufa cliffs were worn away like the teeth of an ancient horse. But for every stride in architecture, Nature took two.

Shortly there were no gardeners to fight the unequal fight. Thibault turned them off for leaving sacks of leaf-litter piled up against the house at the end of a day's weeding. Any that might have replaced them were already at work on the building. Men and women, however skilled, unskilled, willing or apt were fetched in from Rocheblanche and the whole rural estate daily to dig foundations, to saw rock, carry tiles, solder lead. Night and day, summer and winter, they laboured, as wistful as any Israelite in Egypt for the lost days gone by. Their land went untended, their homes unmended, their businesses unplied, their boats unsailed, their vines ungrafted or picked. The agricultural year passed by unobserved, obscured by high white walls of tufa. The river was powerless to fetch down season by successive season, for it was dammed to a puny trickle upstream to allow for the pilings to be sunk. A temporary canal was built to divert the water.

From downstream came protests at the repercussions – the loss of depth, the silting, the boats aground, the shallows exaggerated. Thibault had applied a tourniquet to the river and it would turn gangrenous if he did not loosen it soon. He was interfering with Nature. Thibault said he would loose the river soon, very soon, as soon as the piles were sunk. But his critics still shook their heads and said that the massive, ever-growing island of Gloriole-sur-Sablois was a clot in the arterial river and normality would never be restored.

Who could ever say now where the keep of the ancient castle had stood, where the bailey motte, where the curtain wall? The chateau grew like a town in the grips of a trade boom. And yet it was an unpopulated town full of empty streets, paved with slabs of marble that never saw a footprint, afforested with belltowers so far from human ears that their bells were never heard.

It was the wonder of the Sablois. Thibault was congratulated on it at Court by everyone – even by the Queen Regent herself. But she congratulated him merely on the strength of rumour, for still she had never ventured as far as the Sablois to see this tribute of beauty to her and her son.

It did not surprise the Comte. He was aware of something, something indefinable which, however high or huge he built, marred the place, marred it somehow.

'You're so ugly you make my gorge rise,' he told Balon one morning when unexpectedly confronted by the tiny, frail old man tending melons in the walled garden.

'Ah, but where would Beauty be without its opposite, master?' said Balon, thinking he was called upon to argue for the sport of it. 'Good tailors would be out of fashion, and flatterers would find nothing remarkable to remark . . .'

'Look at you. How could anyone eat that after you've handled it? Take your crone of a shadow and get off the Sablois. You turn it rank.' Balon was open-mouthed, speechless, waiting for the stroke of wit to justify the abuse. But Thibault had no new witticism to rehearse, no clever verbal rapier thrust to run home before laughing off the offence. 'If I ever see your pig's-head again, I'll stick it on a spike with an apple in its mouth and your sow's beside it.' And he snatched the melon out of Balon's hands and impaled it on a bean pole which bowed and sagged and nodded and bled melon juice into the ground.

The two little household buffoons were nearly seventy years old, and belonged nowhere in the world but Gloriole. 'We'd thought to die here and be buried down yonder where the dogs are remembered,' Balon told Thomas. Behind him, Batonne clutched a blanket-bundle of clothes to her chest and sobbed into it. 'I know we shoulda died sooner, master, but it weren't God's will, and it didn't happen, though we look for it daily, sir – on our lives we do!'

'Gently, Balon, gently.'

'And I'd not trouble you, sir, but we're chattels, sir, fixtures and fittings.'

'And never paid, sir, except in bed and board!' whispered Batonne into the weave of her bundle. 'So how *can* we travel – even off the Sablois? How *can* we?'

'Now, now, Batonne, don't upset yourself.'

'We've no money, and our clothes aren't big enough for any who might've bought them!'

'Please. Don't distress yourselves. Please. I'll find a place for you. The hunting lodge . . .'

'Oh no, sir! We wouldn't dare, sir! What if the Master went hunting and found us?'

'What then? He'd be ashamed to have dealt with you so unchristianly. This is only a passing humour of his. I'm glad of the chance to give him pause to think again.'

But Balon and Batonne believed Thomas no more than he believed himself, and he agreed to find them somewhere outside the Sablois: a hearth, a roof, a plot of land. He felt the loss of them already, while they were still standing in front of him. They were part of his childhood; toys well dog-eared before he was even given them; soft, circular shapes in a lifetime too full of square stone slabs and angular scaffolding. 'I shall send for you,' he said, giving Balon his purse. 'When I . . . When there's no curb on my power to treat you as you deserve.' But he knew they would not live so long; knew that his father was only at the beginning of his hereditary tyranny.

'Please. There's no call to do that, sir,' said Balon hurriedly, ecstatically. 'A hearth, a roof, a plot of land. Who'd be an owned man who had so much?' It was a reckless thing to say. Some lordly

538

men don't like the servile classes to talk in terms of freedom from ownership. Some would have withdrawn their offer of help. But Thomas was not one of them. Balon had seen them come and seen them go, and could judge such men.

Still, even he was surprised by the bitter vehemence with which Thomas said, 'I'll tell you who. A hearth, a roof, a plot of land, and still owned body and soul? I'll tell you who. An heir to a comté, that's who.'

'Yes, sir. I'm sorry sir,' said Batonne, her happy face still wet with tears. 'You'll call it an impertinence from the likes of me to talk of pity. But I've always pitied men who was owned by wood and stone and ancestors. Wish I could see how the future lies for you, sir. You know we come into this place as spies. It's terrible to leave it so ignorant of what'll befall.'

Thomas did not pursue her little confession. If she wanted to confess, then it must be to a priest. He had no space left on his shoulders for carrying another person's guilt. He watched them go. A hearth, a roof, a plot of land – no matter where – and they were hand-in-hand and happy to the point of capering.

In truth Thibault was grateful to Balon for being in his garden that morning. It revealed to him at last the secret of his discontent. He knew now what it was that was marring the beauty of Gloriole, no matter how fine or how high he built. It was the people.

Vicious, imperfect, unlovely, intrusive, foul-smelling humanity wriggled in every corner and cleft of his estates like maggots wriggling in a carcase. He purged them. In as far as he was able, he routed them. Any house-servants who could come and go and fulfil their duties without being seen were tolerated to stay. As for the rest, any goitre, any scurf, any shaving rash or arthritic swelling, and pages, guards and footmen found themselves tilling fields – an inoffensive speck erased by dust behind a distant plough. The first grey hair, crow's-foot, rotten tooth, and a maidservant, seamstress, desmoiselle of Gloriole's *petit-Court* found she had out-stayed her welcome.

The town of Rocheblanche, instead of centring its existence on the chateau, found itself both unwilling and unfit to send its daughters and sons into service there. An uncomprehending resentment filled up the growing gulf between castle and town.

So there were no gardeners to replace those turned off; no one to hold back the infiltration of tropical greenery into the arbours, into the bowers, into the orangery, herb garden and ice-houses. But when Thibault looked out on this peculiar chaos, it pleased him. Its ferocious, luxuriant beauty was unlike any other chateau-garden in the Loire Valley. A hundred thousand umbelliferous, gaudy flowers panted open-mouthed through petal lips beaded with drooling nectar. And because every emperor-despot needs subjects, he peopled his empire with stone statues: perfect, flawless, inert, reliable dryads and fauns and cherubs, and glittering bronze heroes, their horses high-stepping over the toils of South American flora. This was his kingdom, these his subjects, biddable in perpetuity, faultless in obedience and everlasting in their beauty. Unlike man or the sons of men.

Fortunately, Thibault himself grew more magnificent with age – different, but more notable, more commanding, more certain. Women at Court who had once giggled and said that 'de Gloriole must have trysted with the Devil to get such a face', no longer said it, for it seemed far too plausible.

'Get me crocodiles,' he told Vache. 'Crocodiles and elephants and gibbon.' And the little merchant bowed so low it seemed he would lift Thibault's foot and place it on his neck, such was the pleasure he took in subservience.

'I shall do my very utmost, sir.'

'By the way, Vache. Tell your Company of River Traders that there's carelessness halving their profits if they would but open their eyes to it. Cargo falling overboard in the canal. Sheer carelessness. Every day I see it, in the canal and down on the river. Sacks – bales of cargo – floating down. Tell 'em. Sheer carelessness. Dozens of sacks. Every day.'

And then a new star rose in the firmament. To be precise, it did not rise but burst into being, combusting Space within the constellation of Cassiopeia. Everyone said it was the Star of Bethlehem returning. Some said it meant the End of the World.

He summoned Urania at once. When the babbling excitement greeted him at Blois – *'Have you seen it? The new star? An omen! A portent!'* – he was able to say, 'I've heard about it. My astronomer is observing it.'

But his astronomer had not yet told him what it meant. She would measure its passage, she said. She would observe and record. But though he had taken hold of her by her solar corona of flaming hair and shaken her, and locked her in her observatory without food, she would not attribute a meaning to the star. He also knew that when she did, he would probably not believe her.

The End of the World? 'Too soon! Too soon!' he had shouted through the window of his chamber at a blood-red moon. 'I've not finished yet!' He could not bear the waste of effort involved if the world were indeed to end before Gloriole was finished, perfected, and had raised him to the King's special favour.

The Queen Mother was desperate for an interpretation. Fiery swords, shooting stars, eclipses had ravaged the night sky over recent years, but the return of the Star of Bethlehem! Twinkling there for all to see, night after night in the jewelled finery of Cassiopeia – it was the portent of the millenium, the seal at the base of some codicil God had written on Creation as an afterthought. A dozen times Thibault had told her of his observatory, of his astronomer and his astronomer's quadrant, and a dozen times the words had washed over her, indistinguishable from the flattery of a dozen similar tributes. Now she took him by the sleeve and said, 'Can your woman divine a meaning? The rest are at a loss. They don't *know*. They don't *know*. I can tell. Can your woman fathom it? Can she?'

'With time,' said Thibault, his face as unrevealing as the oracular Sphinx. 'She's methodical. She has a device – a quadrant. She's taking measurements. Very soon she'll have the exact meaning.'

'I must come and see her, then! I must come to Gloriole! I shall make Royal Entry there . . .' She recovered herself with an effort. 'If you will be so good as to extend me an invitation, my dear Comte.'

And Thibault bowed lower than the knot of jet beads that hung sparkling in the lap of Catherine de Medici. 'The honour would render my household happy while the stars continue to shine,' he said.

'It'll bankrupt us,' said the syndic with a gesture of helplessness that spilled his ale. He had no compunction about saying it in front of the Comte's son. It was not as if the town had any say in the matter.

Thomas was acting as his father's factor – he had taken upon himself the role of intermediary between lord and subjects, always hoping to absorb the impact of the blows which fell on them. Consequently, like the sole between the foot and the ground, Thomas grew more worn and thin and shineless day by day.

'A chance to enjoy yourselves, surely! A carnival. A farce. Some sports.'

'There's a famine coming. T'aint commonly a cause to hang out banners.'

Thomas raised his hands in a gesture of encouragement, but let them fall back on to his knees. He rocked a little, forwards and back. 'I'm sorry, man. Is it really come to that?'

'Famine, sir. Famine to the point of babes dead in the womb, old folk left, villages quit. Wandering and begging and dying on the way to somewhere better. Famine. It'll be worse here, for lack of proper attention given to the fields. That's how things are set. And we must lift up our aprons must we, and caper in the town square, and empty the coffers buying masks and ribbons? Christy's laid a burden or two on us before, but this'll break our backs, sir.' It was a thinly veiled civility which made the syndic blame his Saviour rather than his liege-lord.

Thomas did not need to persuade the town's representative of his duty. Resignation was already hanging in the man's face, deepening the lines. But weariness and worry about the devastating harvest had emptied his head of ideas. He could not recollect the last time the town had celebrated anything or how it was done. So Thomas read out to him his father's notions of a fitting Royal Entry. He couched them as suggestions, but the syndic, his face twitching with pain at each new expense, took them for orders which indeed they were.

When it was done, the two men emerged from the back room of the inn and took up their places at the big table in front of the village assembly. Thomas said a prayer against the coming famine and a provisional date was set for sowing. Then it was formally announced, what rumour had already voiced throughout Rocheblanche – that Queen Catherine, mother of the King, would give them cause to rejoice and make merry when she made Royal Entry to their town a week hence.

No one was very much to blame. If anything, Tradition was at fault for inventing so many different ways of welcoming a queen. At some time long past, the gracious passage of some sainted king through a town full of well-wishers had caused paroxysms of genuine delight, left ploughs abandoned in mid-furrow, lined the roads with cheering children and been recorded in village annals as a day of unbridled joy. Now the thing had been formalized, the need for jollity set down in statutes, the spontaneity ordered up ahead of time. When Catherine passed through Rocheblanche, the little children lined the high street and shouted, '*Largesse! Largesse!*', but they didn't receive any. Her only gift was a peal of bells for the church there, and those, as yet uncast, would be paid for by the local federation of merchants. Sponsorship was crucial to a successful Entry, and sponsorship was not voluntary.

But when Catherine looked around her on that brief, magnanimous ride from one town gate to the other, she could have been forgiven for thinking her visit had brought happiness and recreation to the people of Rocheblanche. On four separate stages, mountebanks were performing: a farce, a morality, a sottie, a concert of songs. The winner from the wrestling was being led in triumph by an escort of oboists who broke off at the sight of the Queen, their reeds silent in their round, open mouths. Every tapestry that had ever hung in church or home or hall was flapping like washing at the windows, and the side-alleys and passages echoed to the noise of skittles falling. Trestle tables stood out in the street ready for communal supper, and from the town square where a band was playing, a carnival spilled out – young men masked as demons or animals or saints. She paused only to accept from the hands of the town dignitaries a miserable hundred golden livres in a white skin purse, in token of the people's love.

In truth, there was no supper worth a mention to be eaten off the trestles. Also, the young men had been drinking on empty stomachs and would profit from Tradition by breaking into houses, pawing the girls and punching the old women. As soon as the Entry was accomplished, the owners of the tables would hurry them indoors again to prevent damage. But Catherine rode away imagining a bucolic scene of Arcadian merry-making closing behind her – which was all that really mattered.

A masker in the guise of a she-goat stepped into the street behind the royal procession and dropped his breeches as a political comment. He was wrestled out of sight by bodyguards and found face-down in the watercress beds next morning. But as far as the Queen was concerned, the carnival music behind her played to a faster and faster beat as her coach drew away towards Gloriole, and every now and then during the evening the wind brought it as far as the chateau – unless that was simply a trick of the imagination.

Thus Catherine de Medici arrived – like all of the Magi compressed into one grey satin gown – to view Gloriole's observatory and quadrant, and to learn the meaning of the new star. It was, in point of fact, a fast day. It had taken a dispensation from the Bishop of Sablois to hold carnival. Permission was only granted on the grounds that every communicant member of the parish would afterwards do penance and pay a fine to the episcopal court. (It all added to their grounds for rejoicing.) Thibault was not required, however, to offend against Church Law, for his chefs confined themselves to the Lenten fare of fish. The oceans had been depopulated to feed lady and retinue, but canon law was served to the last hair-fine fishbone. He laid before her pike, salmon, codfish, Sablois lampreys, oysters, turbot, swordfish, sturgeon, allozes, and gurnards with mustard and cress. Tours champagne and a Gloriole red washed away the salt-sea thirst before apple tart, a flammèche and fruit ices completed the meal.

After it, she drifted through the various levels of the chateau like a frilled anemone, assimilating her impressions of it imperceptibly and without comment. Such charm, such gracious nonchalance! The subject of the star had never once been raised. She looked at every single item of his curio collection – and there was no curio collection to match it in any of the Loire chateaux: astrolabes, animal horns and skins and tails, maps mounted on wooden rollers, seashells and fish-skins from the Southern Seas. There were portolans, ancient medallions and antique arrow-shafts, a fossil and several etchings of South American native scenes. 'You have a hunger to travel, my lord Comte,' she said, trailing her finger across the spines of a hundred travel-books.

'My son, madam. My son Thomas likes to travel – within the confines of his imagination, of course.'

'Naturally. What place is better than home when it has such treasures?' And still the subject of the star was not mentioned, though no one there doubted its significance for the Royal House of France. That God should have sent His sign to another nation or to someone of a lesser rank was past imagining.

On every day of the previous week, Thibault had summoned Urania to his retraite and demanded to know what she would say to the Queen Mother when asked about the star.

'I'm still observing it,' she would say. 'It's too early to reach any conclusion. If I might walk for a while in the garden – I find it hard to think under lock and key.'

But he was afraid that, finding nothing to say, she would run away, so he returned her to her towering prison and zodiacal warders. Next time he sent for her she said, 'I told you. I don't divine.

544

I observe.' But the answer was unacceptable and he returned her to the observatory and locked the doors on her. Next time she said, 'If I might have some food . . . Hunger is not conducive for watching stars: they muzz. They blur.' But he only gave her a whistle and told her to blow it when she was ready to do as she was employed to do and interpret the meaning of the new star. Perhaps he thought that if he treated her like Joseph in Egypt she would prove as true an interpreter of dreams – an interpreter to make his dreams come true.

When the whistle sounded, the noise went through him like an arrow fired from a high tower. He barely dared to give her audience. He barely dared to say, 'Well? And have you something to tell the Queen Mother of France when she asks you the meaning of the star?'

'I've received a letter,' said Urania. 'Your son just brought it to me. I'm ready now to interpret the new star.' And her eyes were bright in a way that hunger alone could not account for. He had expected her to make it up – half expected her to invent some plausible and flattering story. It was all he wanted, after all – to bring delight to the Queen Mother – and know that it was not the End of the World. 'It changes everything,' she started to say. 'It changes the whole nature of . . .'

'Very well. You may go.'

'But don't you want to hear . . . ?'

'Will knowing alter the unalterable?'

'But that's exactly the . . .'

'I can wait to share enlightenment with the Queen Catherine, thank you, lady. Go now. I'm busy.'

It was as though he had read the words of John the Divine: 'Write the things which thou hast seen and the things which are, and the things which shall be hereafter . . .' and slammed shut the book so as not to witness the Revelation. He had thought she would invent, but had only to look at her to see that she had read a phenomenal truth, pricked out in code on the vault of the sky. He had been so sure she would invent an answer. He almost wished she had.

They were both as overwrought as each other, host and royal visitor. The star was not mentioned, but their pleasant stroll around the vast expanse of new rooms, terraces, arcades and gardens was going to end – both of them knew it – at the twin cones of the observatory tower. Catherine paused on a little rustic bridge in virtual darkness to throw meat to a ton-weight crocodile, tethered by a noisy chain, within a deep damp pit. The collar was lifting the scales of its neck, showing raw meat. 'I heard you had a dragon,' she said, only half recollecting such as she had ever heard tell about the Comte de Gloriole. The crocodile lashed to and fro. Its violence and menace excited Thibault. He was in the habit of coming to feed it himself. (The animal-keepers could not be trusted – not since the time he had seen its teeth tangled with river litter and the poor beast gagging on an old, rotting piece of sacking.)

At last, nowhere remained for Catherine to visit but the observatory. She took from her pocket a small book and presented it formally to Thibault: 'The current almanac of forthcoming events as discerned by my astronomer, Signor Ruggieri. I trust you will find it useful. Perhaps we might view this most interesting quadrant of yours, Comte. At very least I can then inform Ruggieri of its nature.' She stood on the black marble compass like the blade of a sundial, and the torches on the wall cast her shadow to every cardinal point.

'And this is my astronomer. As remarkable in her profession for her honesty as for her sex.'

Urania was wearing a man's coat embroidered with astrological symbols. It was Thibault's way of apologizing for her being a woman. She bowed rather than curtseying, as she had been instructed to do.

'And this is your quadrant,' said Catherine.

'Yes, ma'am. Built on the guiding principles of Tycho Brahe, to register the movement of the stars relative to the Earth.'

'And this *new* star . . . It is a *new* star, I take it?'

'Oh yes, ma'am. Quite new. Never before seen. Born out of nothing.'

There was a pause, a silence, in which Catherine wiped a little non-existent dinner from around her mouth and admired two or three of the ceramic planets decorating the wall. Urania looked to Thibault for her instructions. Was she intended to go on? Thibault was staring up at the roof, his hands behind his back.

'And this *new* star. In your opinion. Does it have any significance for my . . . for us mortals? My own man has his own opinions, of course, but you, with the benefit of this . . . this . . . implement . . .'

'Oh yes! Yes! Yes!' Urania crossed to her quadrant, a curlicue of brass inset into the ash of the wall, with crude dated crayon marks spoiling the beauty of its design. She was invigorated by the knowledge inside her. Thibault saw his guest shiver with alarm at the confident certainty of the woman. 'Never anything more so, ma'am! In all the history of the world! Never anything more so. I've replicated Tycho's work – measuring the distance between the new star and Polaris. Aristotle is quite undone. Quite.'

'*Aristotle?*'

Racked with anticipation of news of the death of kings or the second coming of Jesus Christ, Catherine was not prepared for Aristotle to be undone. Her black eyes bulged a little in their sockets and her top lip swelled.

'I observe, you understand,' said Urania. 'I don't divine.'

'*Divine, blast you!*' exclaimed Thibault, and everyone started and quivered and was silent till the echoes of the shout had finished ricocheting around the drum-shaped building.

'I was going to say,' said Urania, 'that the observed facts leave no room for doubt. Aristotle said that Space is immutable; that the stars are unchanging. But this new star – and it is a star, I do assure you, not a comet or any such – well, it proves that the pattern of the universe can alter – that it wasn't fixed at the time of Creation from age to age everlasting. Fate is not *accomplis*, so to speak. The future's not indelible.'

Her voice died away in the vacuum of Space amid the planets and constellations.

'Is that all?' growled Thibault menacingly. 'No war and pestilence? No flaming chariots dipping down? No *dates*?'

Catherine laid her hand on his cuff, chewing her own saliva as though it were too hard to swallow. Her shrewd brain was shuffling the implications of things said – and not just by Urania.

It suddenly occurred to Thibault – why had he not thought of it before? – that Catherine had not waited all this while to see what Gloriole's astronomer would say on the subject. She had consulted Cosimo Ruggieri and a dozen others, comparing their predictions, searching for contradictions, wanting second, third and fourth opinions about some adverse diagnosis for the future that she did not want to be true.

'You don't predict, you say?'

'Prediction's an inaccurate science, ma'am. I leave that to others . . . And now I see why it's inaccurate! The Heavens are changing! The Heavens are all the time changing! It's not as Aristotle said at all!'

A smile broke over Catherine's face so sudden that it displaced powder from her cheek in a little puff of interstellar stardust. 'Yes indeed! It *would* be inaccurate in that event! I see that. And you're quite sure?'

'There's no doubt about it, ma'am. I've only replicated what Tycho's already proved.'

'Good,' she said. 'Very good. Very, very good,' and as she drew Thibault away, back towards the house, the implications of what Urania had told her were clearly growing better and better with every lively step. Something her other astronomers had told her had overshadowed the future in a fearful, harrowing way. Now that same Future might alter. Its terrors might be diverted. The mere possibility was all she needed to be restored to optimistic happiness. And Gloriole's astronomer had granted her that happiness.

Urania turned her face up towards the dome and watched Thomas climb down from the platform on its roof. 'Someone has cast the lady a black horoscope, wouldn't you say?'

'And now she hopes it's avoidable – whatever it is that Ruggieri's seen in his magic mirror.'

'And it is.'

He paused on the ladder and looked at her from above – a face only amid a pool of burning hair. 'It was a fine, politic answer,' he said.

But she shook her head. 'I told you before that I was going to tell her the truth. I told her the truth. The stars aren't immutable. The Future's changing all the time.'

'God. God. God,' he said, chafing his cheek against the ladder's rung. 'If only it were. Not fixed. Not decided.' He shook himself, as if to keep optimism from settling on him overheavy.

'Perhaps there's no such thing as Fate at all,' she said.

He mistrusted her bright delight. She was forever reaching it towards him like Eve's apple, like delicious Temptation. Once again he managed to push it away. 'And if it weren't. There'd still be Responsibility.'

She was disgusted with him, pushed her wrists under her heavy hair and lifted it up in a luxurious feline stretch. 'Well, you may do as you please, Thomas. I shall live in hope. There are things going to happen soon you know nothing of.'

'I thought you didn't divine,' said Thomas, so full of inexplicable desire that his ribcage seemed to buckle inside him.

She shot him a glance which admitted she had said too much,

and let her hair drop down again. But she was still so full of vague, happy expectations that she shone white in the oppressive grey darkness. He wanted to leap down on her like the swan on to Leda and seize the moment from under the dangerous, teetering Future. But in the very last second, as he let go of the ladder, he snatched hold again, for he had just caught sight of his father's figure in the doorway.

'What are you doing here?' asked Thibault.

He was a helpless, hopeless liar. It took Urania to say, 'Lord Thomas expressed the desire to see this new star for himself. From the roof.'

'Ah. Just my own thought,' he said, and Thomas at once jumped down from the ladder, like a young buck giving way to the old bull stag. 'The Queen Mother has retired to bed.'

'And was she satisfied with your observatory?' Thomas did not really need to ask. There was a badly suppressed glory in his father's face which he had felt himself a moment before towards the woman he loved. Thibault could plainly foresee the imminent consummation of all his hopes and ambitions. He had won himself a place in the heart of Catherine – given her what she wanted and been rewarded with the promise of great rewards.

He said as he climbed, 'The gracious Lady was pleased to say that she places the greatest confidence in me and would like to see me close to her son's shoulder. She begs me to attend on His Majesty at a party shortly to be held at Plessis-les-Tours. To receive the award of a post "befitting my potential to serve", as she was kind enough to phrase it.' Thibault rose amid the lesser stars and planets of his plaster constellations like a star soaring into its ascendancy. 'She mentioned the post of Royal Falconer, but it rests with King Henry to say exactly which . . .' No fear of heights any longer. The higher the better. Urania followed him up the ladder and snuffed out the lamps which would spoil their view of the stars. She led him out on to the balcony which circled the tower and pointed out to him the constellation of Cassiopeia and its bright new component.

It was a clear, frosty sky. Every star that eye had ever seen was visible that night. It was pelting stars. Cataracts and cascades of stars rolled over him, washing the breath out of his nostrils. A solar wind stood his hair on end. The swirl and eddy of Heaven's glittering river washed from prehistory away to the end of Time, and the menagerie in God's moat roared with dragons, beasts and giants. Thibault gripped the rail in front of him, the torrential stars making him dizzy. Maned nebulae reared up over him. The twelve houses of the zodiacal heaven raised towers of infinite height and endurance; and trine and quintile planets danced in a ring which seemed to close its hands and turn its back on base and grubby Earth.

There was Thibault, so close to his zenith that he half expected to knock his head against God's shin, and yet even up here, at the summit of his Tower of Babel, aphelion God was nowhere to be seen – just this swirl of stardust lifted by His robes and settling now, settling.

'Damn Him,' said Thibault under his breath.

'I beg your pardon, my lord?' said Urania. He had forgotten that she was standing alongside him on the balcony.

He encompassed the view with an inarticulate sweep of the arm. His teeth were clenched in frustration. 'Damn Him, I said. Damn Him. He has *out-decorated* me.'

FORTY-EIGHT

King's Favourite

'It was that new star decided us,' said the syndic, having begged leave to speak with Thomas on behalf of the community of Rocheblanche. He did not wish to give offence. He did not want to make difficulties. 'We asked the priest what it meant, see, and he said it was the Second Coming like as not and to watch and pray and do penance. So we watched and prayed, and then what? No Second Coming. Then this chap, this scholar from the seminary at Saumur, he comes by and says it's nothing of the kind. It's the coming of the new religion. And we took a plebiscite, sir – man, woman and child, sir – and it came out in favour of the new religion. And the priest went home and took up arms and began shouting and shooting, and that made up minds as weren't made up already, so now we reckon we're Huguenots. Well, we may as well starve in the one religion as the other, so we thought to give this new one a try, and I must say it suits us right well so far, though our bellies are just as empty and the town's just as beggared by that Entry. And that was partly what decided us, too. That and the hurricane that never came. And the wolf cull.'

'The wolf cull.'

'Twixt Christmas and Epiphany.'

'Ah yes. That wolf cull.'

'I mean, wolves is one thing, but werewolves are a danger to a man's soul and everlasting life. The wives won't wear another hunt for werewolves. It had them jangled to hell this year, and I was scared, I don't mind saying it. Men was scared past what just duty can put them to.'

'Are you talking rebellion, syndic?'

'No. No. No. 'Course not, sir. For now, we're talking religion is all. But 'twas religion the Comte your father gived as grounds for the hunt, and me for one'll follow any religion that don't tell me to hunt werewolves in the midwinter freezing cold.'

'I hope you don't suppose the God of Luther will turn away famine better than Holy Rome,' said Thomas, but the man only looked at him with a gauche bewilderment and said, 'Now the chateau won't help us, we reckon we've got to help ourselves, that's all.' Thomas wanted to embrace him, to apologize to him, empty gold into his pockets and make amends; run indoors and empty the bread jars and meat cellars into Rocheblanche. But he was no one in the syndic's eyes: the Comte's factor, the instrument of Catholic neglect, simply the correct person to inform of a change in circumstances.

'You'll find there's some wildness been loosed by this new seminarian,' said the syndic, 'but I'd beg you not to lay it at our general door. It's only the wild boys, and they'd be factious no matter what. It's nothing to what's been done to Huguenot folk these past years.'

The wild boys' revenge on Papistry took the form of vandalizing the Chapel Saint-Cloud; the sarcophagus was smashed with a pick and an attempt made to open up the grave underneath. The marble had defeated them, but the fire they lit had taken out the roof and left Victoire de Gloriole's last resting place open to the rain and God's decorations of the night sky.

Thomas did not know how to tell his father that his estate had converted, or that they had desecrated the family tomb. He feared that the repercussion would be too dreadful, that he would be unable to stand by and see Thibault exact justice. He would be forced to take up the cause of the people. He was almost amused at the possibility that the Wars of Religion might, in the end, cost him his life. After all, it would not be religion which forced him to take sides.

It appalled Thomas that he should so much lack denominational conviction. Once upon a time he had seen it all so clearly – the two paths – one austere and scholarly, the other ornately tawdry and blood-soaked; the Protestants trooping up to Heaven, the Papists sliding down to Hell. And yet the Wars, the atrocities, the wider and wider gulf, the failed treaties, the murdered nuns, the burned dissenters, they had all closed on him like the confluence of two great rivers and all he could make out now was a tumbling, dirty confusion of souls spilling towards a shoreless sea of wrong. He wanted to leap between and hold the two sides apart, like pit-dogs set to tear out each other's throat. Sometimes, when Urania spoke of 'everything turning out for the best', he even imagined he could.

Then he would catch sight of himself – gentle and timid, with his slight body and plush-haired head full of arcane knowledge, and he knew that the dogs would chew him to pieces and never even notice that he had got in their way.

So what to tell his father the Comte? It could not be kept from him: his chaplain would soon tell him if Thomas did not. The priests and bishops would come flocking to the chateau in outrage, demanding protection and reprisals. Plebiscite indeed! There were words abroad in the Sablois that were as outlandish and doomed as the poor dead crocodile in its pit or the tapirs waddling through the hornbeam maze.

He dared himself to break the news. He mustered his courage; he said his prayers and took an oath on the shattered tomb of Victoire de Gloriole – to lay down his life sooner than see Rocheblanche persecuted for its faith. The marble was cold as ice under his clenched hands. The birds roosting in the holed roof pecked ash down on to his head. On the plain below him, the vast empty chateau clothed the entire river bend in inert white tufa. The quarries were emptied of it. The cliffs were gone. Green Nature had ossified into white beauty. It was Thomas's inheritance. And the sight of it turned his flesh to stone, walled up his heart, stifled his blood's flow as surely as Gloriole blocked the river's natural course. In that moment he made a rather dreadful discovery: that he in fact *wanted* to lay down his life in this cause – any cause – and make good his escape before the unimaginable horror of inheriting Gloriole. 'I haven't even the courage of my mother,' he told himself. He unfolded his hands, brushed the ash off his shoulders and the stone dust off his knees, and descended to the chateau.

'Father. The people have turned Huguenot,' he said.

Thibault was being fitted for a suit of clothes: a doublet and long trunk-hose quartered in the Queen Mother's favourite black and white. He held a black velvet beret with a white ostrich feather trembling in the draught. 'Which people? Who?'

'Your people. Our people. The Sabloises. They are turned Free Church by common consent.' The tailor was so astounded that he ingested a pin he was holding between his lips.

'Nonsense!' said Thibault brightly. 'They're as I am. What I am, so are they, let 'em think what they like.'

And for that, Thomas had lost a night's sleep and screwed his courage to the sticking point and outdared Death. 'Is that all you've got to say?'

'No,' said Thibault as he recalled something that had been at the back of his mind for days. 'Are you bedding the astronomer?'

'What?'

'Urania. The astronomer. Are you laying her down? No? Oh. Just a something passed through my head when I saw you with her the other day. No matter. Might have served to keep her from straying, and I prize her now for the good she's done us. Think on it, if you can spare the time and the taste for it.'

Thomas had never seen his father so elated, so leaven-light with anticipation, so magnificently handsome. The new Gloriole did not outscale him. Its pavements and black-and-white chequered marble were mere imitations of his garment; the sunburst architraves over its windows were mere copies of his starched lace ruff.

When the suit was finished, the day come, and his horse saddled, the footcloth too was squared in black and white and trailed past the mare's hocks to her oiled hooves. His retinue were also all in new clothes – black for the men and white for the women, and among them were Thomas, the Master-at-Arms, Sebastian de Puy and Urania. With such a fine equipage, de Gloriole's horse was transported inside a wagon and only at the gates of Plessis-les-Tours was it unloaded and mounted and the ostrich plume attached to its bridle.

'Choose a wife tonight, Thomas!' Thibault was still filled to overspilling with cheerfulness. 'I'll conclude the details before we leave. Is your mistress here? She must be, sure! Fetch her to me. You'll have her, or I'm a Spaniard. The night's our making. Above you? I'll put her under you before the month's out!' and he reached down and tousled Thomas's hair in a kind of premature blessing of his marriage.

'My mistress is here. She . . .' said Thomas, clenching his thumbs inside his palms.

But a sudden disturbance ahead of them on the driveway stopped him in mid-sentence. A dozen young women in trunk-hose and with their hair blowing loose came leaping out from behind the flaps of a cloth pavilion pegged beside the drive. They were naked to the waist and their little breasts bobbed cheerily as they cantered towards the latest arrivals. Thomas took several steps backwards. Thibault struggled to control his horse without moving hand or heel. A dryad put one foot through his stirrup and jumped up at him, and he was obliged to put an arm around her or let her fall backwards on to her head. He therefore entered into Plessis balancing

554

the woman on one thigh and resentful less of her impertinence than of her *pinkness* marring his chequered equipage.

A pail-mail course had been laid out in the gardens, and wooden balls encased in red velvet and brass were flying like meteorites along the alleyways, occasionally becoming confused with less violent games of billard and cochonnet. Concealed behind high hedging, the festivities could be heard before any of the guests could be seen. But the very first person Thibault passed was a familiar enough visitor to Gloriole, though not one he expected to find moving in such exalted circles. 'What are you doing here, Vache? Have you a hand in the catering?'

'No, indeed, Comte. I'm here for the conversation merely. A word with you, for instance, would be greatly appreciated.'

'Later! Later!' said Thibault and urged his horse on past Vache to where a female groom, also in breeches and little else, held his horse's head. She giggled and said he would 'spoil the fun' with his mirthlessness. He was rather taken aback, for mirth, if it had ever touched him, was quite thriving this evening.

'Is the King entered yet?' he asked her. But she could not answer before a fanfare of trumpets announced Henry's emergence from the house. As Thibault hurried to join the general salutation, he had shouldered aside several indignant doublets and hose before he realized what the groom meant.

The ball was in travesty.

The monkey was presumably female, for it perched on the King's forearm in beret, puff-pants and waistcoat, sharpening its teeth against a metal pomander with a vile scraping noise. As for King Henry, he wore a brocade dress in pink and silver, deep-plunging to show his chest hair and navel. Pearl drops hung from his ears and his mouth was painted with carmine. He had powdered his hair with sparkling silica of some kind, and a little crown with a top knot of false hair was fastened on with grips. His beard was grizzled with face powder. 'By Jezebel!' he exclaimed, falsetto. 'What jollity!' and gave a shrill giggle before lifting his skirts to negotiate the steps in treacherous silver pattens. The monkey clung on as best it could, bearing its teeth and gibbering with fear in the glare of torches and lamps. The nymphs and dryads ran forward and sprinkled the King with rose petals. Someone was attempting to sing a hymn to Flora. It was not a woman, but a gross, sweating castrato perched at a window overhead. Henry paused to kiss the back of one hand and blow the kiss in the singer's direction – a *coup de théâtre* that brought uproarious laughter and applause from the assembled guests.

Then the party adjourned to the pail mail alleys where a great arguing ensued in the mustering of teams for *grand coups*. Henry, noticing Thibault near by, threw off the tedious jabbering monkey and, hitching the plunge of his dress back across his nipples, called out, 'You'll make up my team, won't you, Gloriole!' Thibault hurried forward with an elegant bow. 'I wish you'd carry these for me,' said Henry lispingly, and passed two of the velvet-covered balls into Thibault's hand. 'Yes indeed, I *wish* you would.'

The whole entourage shambled confusedly along the wood-kerbed lanes, disputing each other's shots, cheating and digressing to dance with each other or the nymphs that sprang monotonously from behind every hedge. But at one point the King did say to Thibault, 'I recall you now, of course I do. When my mother mentioned you first, I couldn't put a face to the name, but I have you now. I have you. That's to say I'd greatly like . . . But you're not in travesty, Gloriole! Everyone should be in travesty! What? Would you defy my ruling?' It was said laughingly and Thibault responded with a laugh. The idea of putting on a dress and jewellery and painting his face was as repellent to him as going naked. He had that quality of sober dignity which those with a sense of humour can never aspire to. 'My mother invited you, didn't she? Trust Catherine to censor our fun. She sent along these little wood nymphs: missionaries to convert the unconverted, you know. Still. She commended you to me, so you see she does have taste in some things. By God, Gloriole, but what's been keeping you? Should've been at Court long since! I mean properly at Court. So cut off. So remote up there on the Sablois. Too remote by far.' A page passed him his mallet and held the ball still on a tussock of grass with one finger while Henry took his swing. The ball flew in a perfect line over the others, and as he swept along the alleyway to take another stroke, the skirts of the silver and pink dress brushed his opponents' balls into the gullies at either side. 'Put on travesty, though!' he called without looking back over his shoulder. 'You absolutely must put on travesty or I shan't speak another word to you!'

Thibault returned to the stables and retrieved his saddlecloth which, by strategic knotting and pleating, he succeeded in making look like a toga rather than a gown. He was aware that such entertainments were fashionable – popular with the effete youngsters that babbled about the chateau circuit, but . . . He cautioned himself against the intolerance of middle age. The visual effect was most spectacular, after all – so many Amazonian women towering over their mates, and the little hermaphrodite attendants flitting to and fro.

At Gloriole he had taken to distilling spirits – a new and intriguing art which he applied to fortifying Sablois wine. The taste so pleased him – had pleased him ever since the Saumur Dragon left him in peace to indulge the practice nightly – that he never went anywhere any more without a flagon of the liquor on his saddle. He took a drink of it now.

In several of the trellis bowers of the garden, pairs of lovers were already struggling like fish in a net. There would be Saturnalian exploits by morning. The spirits gave him the inclination to join them, to warm the little groom-girl who had greeted him on arrival. But then he would have to puzzle out afresh how to put on his chequered toga. He postponed the pleasure. Besides, it gave him the adrenal edge he needed to press his suit to the King and secure the post of Royal Falconer or Keeper of the Royal Purse or whatsoever title Fate held in store for him. He caught sight of Sebastian. 'De Puy! Find us out a pair of dryads for later! I feel a need to touch wood for luck!' and he hugged his friend to him with sheer surfeit of goodwill. 'The best or nothing, mind. *Rien meilleur!* It all comes together, Seb. Tonight it all comes together!'

An incredibly sweet smell of herbs drew him towards the main building of the chateau. Its dour, forbidding exterior was well disguised with bunting and hangings, flags and silk drapery. The light was kind. He was aware of it being kind to him, too, that all signs of age were wiped away by merciful torchlight and that he looked like a man of thirty with the demeanour of a fifty-year-old. He drew the attention of every eye. He began to carry himself like a king. For to be the King's favourite is surely to be a limb and member of the King himself. The smell drew him, strangely enough, to the carcase of a spitted, roasting ox. He stood and looked at it for some time, trying to make sense of the heady perfumes congesting in his head: lemon-mint and thyme, bay and rosemary.

Something touched his forehead and he put his hand up to brush it away. It was not an insect but a flowerhead – a wreath of flowers, in fact. A burst of laughter made him look round and he found the King standing at arm's length from him, holding the chaplet over his head as a man signifies his choice of partner for a braule. 'I believe I shall dance with you all night long,' said Henry sibilantly, and clasped hold of his hand.

'Sir, I don't dance,' said Thibault. He could see the look of animosity on a dozen rosebud lips among the King's transvestite entourage. His mignons. His favourites.

'Then I shall teach you!' The grass was wet. The pink and silver was dark at the hem. The King kicked off his pattens, and large hairy feet protruded now and then from under the brocade. It brought him down to a height lower than Thibault's chin. 'I'll say this for Mother. She's never wrong in her judgment of a man. And she says you're wondrous loyal – intelligent, and have a chateau would put this place to shame and tears.'

'I hope, my lord King . . .'

'Henrietta! Tonight you shall call me Henrietta. Tomorrow you may call me as you find me,' and Henry reached out and removed a flower petal that had fallen and lodged on Thibault's saddlecloth. The toga fell away and was left on the grass. Thibault was restored to male status. He found he wished for the warmth of the chequered cloth again. He was cold in the small of his back. Very cold. 'Yes, I'm quite decided. You shall be my Grand Falconer. You've quite earned it over the years . . . And if you've not, you soon shall!'

The orchestra had a ribald, squawking brassiness in the open air that made it sound like a peasant band. It struck up a *volta* – a dance that had been the vogue, *le dernier cri d'une vogue* ever since Catherine introduced it to the French chateaux-balls. Some of the men had even gone to the trouble of wearing the special chastity belts their wives commonly wore to dance it: it was the source of quite convulsive laughter. The King had not, it seemed.

The dance was an exercise doomed to failure; the doubleted women might be able to seize their transvestite partners by the crotch, but they hadn't the power to heave them into the air with the wild abandon called for. Still, it served the King's notion of entertainment and there were those among the King's mignons who had practised in private and could carry it off to perfection, man dancing with man.

'Come now, Thibault,' said the King, and the use of the first name struck home every whit as deep as Thibault had ever dreamt it would. 'Are you honest? Have you truly never danced *la volta*? Well! Even so. You've only to watch to see how it's done! Simply put your hands here . . . and here . . . and you have me. Now all you have to do is up me – or do I mean raise me up? The rest will *come* quite naturally.'

A crack of artillery. A flash of bursting crystal. Thibault thought it was inside his head, but it was not. The dance circle smashed like a dropped plate, and its dancers ran pell-mell towards the rear lawns for a better view of the fireworks.

Italian fireworks. Not the paltry French squibs that Thibault had seen at previous balls, but great pavilions of golden fire, geysers of blood-red sparks; vainglorious wonders that faded to nothing; exclamations of brilliance; hoots and whoops of exultation. He was a made man. He was a King's favourite. He repeated the words over and over to himself. They tasted like wormwood and gall in his mouth.

Minarets of silver came tumbling down like Babel's Tower. Mirage palaces dissolved into nothingness over his head. The stars were falling out of their spheres to the music of a squawking band. Someone was flaying the night sky till even after the scorching was done the heavens stayed lacerated with after-light. The noise climbed in at the ear and ransacked the brain. Somewhere a dog was howling. A storm of fire broke over Plessis-les-Tours, a retribution of brimstone fell on it, but people went on smiling and laughing and gaping and gasping with polite, well-modulated wonder. Had they seen such things before that they could take them so calmly – the night turned to day by phosphorus, the House of the Gods brought down by shellfire? By the time it was over, nothing was left remarkable beneath the visiting moon. The torchlight was tarnished and dull, the moat was slubbered, the nearby river nothing but a bent, shineless streak robbed of its fishy reflections of gold, crimson and green.

'Might I ask a moment of your time?' said Joshua Vache, who had moved to stand by Thibault's shoulder as he gazed up at the sky.

'Not now, Vache. Not now.'

'Oh, but I think it's a matter that merits your interest,' Vache insisted. 'Indeed, I don't think it can really be put off a minute longer.'

There was something different about him. Thibault could not immediately place what it was. Then he realized that the merchant's hat was on his head, rather than in his hands. 'I must congratulate you, Comte. I see you are become a King's favourite tonight. I might have advised you on the cost, if you'd asked me earlier. You might have saved yourself a very considerable outlay. Extensions, animal hunts – when all that was called for was a little bending.'

Thibault thought he must have misheard the man; but then

559

he barely trusted the evidence of his senses – his dazzled eyes, his scent-stifled nasal passages, his hands still caked with the touch of a pink and silver crotch.

'But you must congratulate me, also,' said Vache. 'And I must own a debt of gratitude that I find myself welcome here tonight, in this august company.'

'Why? Whose sodomite are you?' hissed Thibault venomously, making as if to brush past the little man and go. He had to escape the cacophony of the fireworks, the explosions still going on in his head. He needed to find the stable once more and take a drink of liquor. His life's lodestone was crumbling into dust. He must get away to the peace and isolation of Gloriole where the people in the garden were all danceless stone and the ground under his feet was his own.

Vache rocked his big head from side to side, and his mouth worked like a ruminant chewing the cud. 'Well, I suppose you could say that I was yours; forever bending and bending.' Even now the habit of years made him stand with a stoop, bringing his head still further into the foreground so that it appeared even bigger. It seemed to fill Thibault's vision – those dog-jowl cheeks, those dreadful teeth, the silken sheeny velvet, that forest density of fur. 'No, don't apologize, my lord Comte. It was worthwhile. It was always such a joy to serve a man of your birth and calibre. It accustomed me to the ways of gracious living – how it could feel to live in a place like Gloriole – how I should deport myself when I in turn became noble.'

'Noble? You? *Noble?*' Again he went to push past. He knew what was going to be said. It offended his politics and if he did not hear it, he need not be irritated. He needed that drink.

'Yes indeed! Tonight I'm become your brother in nobility. Councillor in the Parlement of Rouen. *Noblesse de robe*, naturally. No swordsman myself, ha-ha!'

'So you've bought yourself a title. Bravo. I shall have to look about for a new *tradesman*.'

'I do wonder that you scoff. And you so much in admiration of the great King Francis. He sees no objection to a man spending money to better himself.'

'How much?' asked Thibault bridling with contempt. 'What is the current rate for a tin coronet?'

'The councillorship? Oh, twenty thousand. But my income, you know, in any event my income exceeds ten thousand livres per annum.'

'And that makes you equal to nobility? Jesus! The money-changers have bought the Temple! D'you really suppose money . . .'

'Oh precisely. I agree. Money's insignificant. Money ceased to hold an interest for me long since, beyond its capacity to bring me where I wished to be.'

'And just where do you plan to make your *seat*, my lord Shop-keeper?' He did not want to be here. He did not want to be having this conversation. He wanted to withdraw to somewhere unpolluted by squalid thoughts, common lusts, noise and the untoward. To his horror, tears were pricking at his eyes. He did not want to put his hands up to his face, either. Not until he had washed off that secretion of pink and silver, of red velvet and brass.

'My seat?' said Vache. 'Oh, I thought Gloriole would suit my retirement. Such an amiable place. And so very much beyond your means, I fear. Now that I come to present my bill.'

FORTY-NINE

Debts

He had brought it all with him – every piece of paper, every letter of commission, every sub-contractor's account.

'Of course, most was incurred in the Sologne,' he said referring to his figures. 'The unicorn was relatively speaking inexpensive. These last extensions – ah, it's appalling how the costs of basic materials have soared. It amazes me. But then there's little precedent for work on the scale that we've undertaken, you and I. And all loans secured against land, as you wished.'

'Against land? Never! You always said . . .'

Vache laughed good-humouredly. 'Ah business, business! So many words. I forget. And my brain's not so young as it was formerly. I forget so much. Show me the paper. Where it's set down, what I said, and that's a different matter. That's always been my policy. Set it down on paper and there you have it: an *aide memoire* to last till Doomsday . . . But I do recollect quite clear how you told me your astronomer must be well paid. And as her agent . . .' He unearthed one sheet from the dozen he was holding; several others seesawed to the ground. He had, in his capacity as Thibault's agent, engaged Urania at a salary of one thousand livres per year, taking ninety per cent for his commission.

'Well and what does it come to? What figure have you invented, you usuring leech?'

'And then there was the compensation to the Merchant River Guild while the river's stopped up. I settled it myself – not liking to trouble you when your thoughts were so occupied with creativity. I do so admire an artist – men of taste and discernment like yourself, with a sense of continuity and a thirst for the very best in every respect. You'll agree I've always supplied you the very best of everything you've requested – *rien meilleur* – entertainers, horseflesh, furnishings . . . How is the crocodile faring? And the tapirs? Of course I haven't your taste for curios. Very fashionable,

I know. But I'm a home-loving man myself. French through and through. Fish-skins hold a limited interest for me – except on the side of my plate, as you can see – I regret!' He patted his flat stomach which, if he was truly a glutton, concealed the vice as thoroughly as his fawning and cringeing had concealed his lifelong, patient, inexorable intentions.

'The figure, for Christ's sake! What do I owe you?'

'Owe? Oh. It's all here. Everything's detailed. In total it comes to – you may have an accountant verify the exact sum – but in round numbers my calculations, allowing for interest accruing on the loan at a percentage of fifteen – very moderate – you won't find a lower anywhere . . .'

'*How much?*'

'Say three hundred thousand livres. Secured against thirty thousand acres of the Sablois.'

'Oho! I see you leave me enough for my grave, dog-face! Only thirty thousand? You're too modest in your ambitions! You've left me a place to lie down and pull the earth over my head!'

Vache scratched his hair. 'Have I? You recollect, of course, that your family purchased your freedom from captivity in Spain with a sale of land. I bought two thousand then – the remaining thousand to finance your repairs to the chateau and the lawsuit with that annoying Tolon-Peque girl. To be of assistance to you, if you recall? But naturally, I can afford you the use of your family vault. I'd be an unnatural and a godless man else.'

'Sebastian! De Puy! Come here! Quick!' He beckoned urgently to his friend whom he saw coming with a strumpet on each arm and three goblets of wine clasped awkwardly between his hands. Thibault shooed the girls away and put his arm round Sebastian, not just for moral support but to hold his head still and his eyes engaged on Vache. 'This lamprey thinks he has his head sunk in me up to the gills. He's bored and bored his way into my substance, he says. He's only trying to lay claim to Gloriole for settlement of debts!'

Sebastian struggled to disentangle a strand of his hair from around a button of Thibault's doublet. 'Is he though? And what does he say they've mounted to, these debts?'

'Three hundred thousand's the magic number. As good as any, don't you think? A handsome enough figure in its own right.'

Sebastian whistled appreciatively. 'I never knew money could be spent so deep.'

'By fraudsters and embezzlers, why not?' said Thibault, snapping his fingers in Vache's face. 'But you'll bear witness, won't you? That he did it all out of love and philanthropy? Begged me for the *honour* of doing me good? Revelled in the glory that rubbed off against his name?' The contempt he had felt for Vache at the time redoubled. Did he honestly believe he could filch an entire comté? 'I'm afraid, Monsieur Shopkeeper, you'll find cause in a court of law to wish you'd stopped short of forgery.' And he ground his heel into the fallen papers on the grass. 'Look, Sebastian. Find me a paper with my signature forged upon it, before the villain tries to withdraw and destroy the evidence. They boil forgers in vats of oil, Monsieur Lamprey. Were you aware of that when you took this perverse and wreckless little adventure into your worm-eaten head?' De Puy thrust two of the spilled goblets of wine into their hands to be free to stoop and pick up the crumpled, muddied sheets. 'Well? Do you find my name signed in pledge of any land to secure a loan?'

'No. No. Nowhere.'

'Oh come now, Vache. Try to gull me with unsigned papers? Has this full moon turned you dog-mad? What kind of a . . .'

'Only mine,' said Sebastian.

'He's forged your signature?'

'Well, let me . . . No. No. My name's only where I set it down on your behalf, acting as your signatory.' He knocked his own cup up against theirs with a tinny clash. 'But before you sully the night with business, let me ask you – on a more cheerful note – to drink a toast. Just one toast. Well, more than one if the fancy takes you, but so . . . To me. To Sebastian de Puy. This being a night of great moment and magnitude. Yes.'

'De Puy, you're drunk.'

'I mean my betrothal.'

'Your what?'

'Don't I, Joshua? My betrothal, to the good Councillor's excellent daughter. But you're not drinking, dear old friend Thibault. Dear old companion-in-captivity. Dear old wine-butt confidant!' There were tears glittering in Sebastian's eyes, but they were tears of hysteria and not remorse.

'You've plotted with Vache to strip off my land?' said Thibault. His voice was high and breathless with disbelief. His eyes searched de Puy's face for a landmark, some means of reorientating himself within an unknown place. 'You've schemed with this worm here, taken his scurvy daughter for a bribe? You've betrayed the Sablois into his hands? For why? Does he own your soul?'

Sebastian waved his hand airily, intoxicated on the store of words he had kept hidden for so very long. 'I'm sorry, cousin. Nothing personal, you understand. Call it a family tradition. Goes back generations. Generations of contempt. Humiliation. Grubby farmsteading. My father . . . grandfather . . . his before him. The pattern's held good these hundred and fifty years. Always ambitious for a taste of inheritance. Never climbing higher than beggary. I was raised on covetousness, in truth. At my mother's breast, I was fed on it. Always one remove from inheriting – next-in-line – always kept down by your sheer bloody refusal to die out. "Pull him down." "Restore the family fortunes." That's our family motto. Seemingly it goes back to the English wars, though more surely it goes back to your turd of a grandfather. He did gain a grip but then he promptly shed his name. Nothing personal though, Thibault. No great personal wrong to avenge, nothing so grand. Though I've a great curiosity to know how it feels to be treated like a man instead of a hearth-hound. So there it is. The de Puys back in the family title-seat. No loss of continuity. It should be a comfort to you that – knowing there's a piece of family at Gloriole even after you're not. *Santé!*'

He was just like Vache. A whole life given over to the cause of vengeance, and for ills Thibault was not even aware of having done him. Thibault turned his face away from de Puy and looked at the merchant. 'You'd better give him a plot of land for dowry, Monsieur Lamprey. Even Judas Iscariot must have his Field of Blood . . . Ah, but you'd not've read the New Testament to know it, would you, *Jewboy.*'

Calmly now. It was no great matter. Already Thibault was making adjustments within his head. The two must be mad to stray so far from the house lights, into so shadowy a part of the garden, and to stand so close to the moat. One does not hold a lamprey off by the tail. One cuts it off close at the throat. It was plain as the inconstant moonlight. The men must both die. He would hold that head, that square, jowled head with its ugly teeth and its dagged turban – he would hold it under the water of the moat, push his fingers through its eyes, reach so far into its skull that he could close his fist around that calculating, insinuating leech of a brain.

Vache pulled at his nose thoughtfully with two fingers and plucked at his top lip. 'I take it you use that for a term of abuse, my lord Comte? "Jewboy"? Now that does surprise me, I have to admit. Given that I take Communion as often as the next Christian man. And given your bloodstock.'

And as for de Puy . . . He would erase his farm from the maps of Sablois as if it had never been, and wrap him in hessian for a gravecloth . . . Thibault's mind sailed back, on streams of liquored sentimentality, through all the times when Sebastian had sat at his drinking elbow and they had laughed the creeping world to scorn.

Vache was still talking, still talking, saying, '. . . confided the truth of it to me on his deathbed. How my aunt gave birth by proxy for the Chatelaine Vérité – the one they call just "The Chatelaine". Or "The Madwoman". Or "The Bastard". Not in our household, mind. Oh, the name's held in great respect there, I might tell you. I believe my grandfather had a great tenderness towards her, you know? Towards your grandmother. Or that's to say the one credited with bearing your father. She'd've liked to disown the boy – she tried with all her might – but her lover prevented her. Blackened her. Lied before a court of law. That's your grandfather, Cyr de Gloriole. Cyr de Puy before he sloughed off the name like the beetle he was. Isn't that right, son-in-law? So you see, all this acrimony, all this talk of Jewishness – all so very inappropriate between us. After all, I am kin to you, and not so very far removed. And we've both left our Jewishness behind us, haven't we? No wonder I've always held you in my heart with such affection.'

Thibault stooped down and grasped a handful of water and splashed his own face. Perhaps he thought it would wake him out of the nightmare. Perhaps he thought it would wash the flesh off his bones, the blood out of his veins, the contamination out of his soul. He knew it was true. He denied it as damned lies, but all the time his lips were moving he could feel the Jewishness inside him, growing like a cancer, poisoning his noble blood, strangling the letters of his name, smudging his title. He could almost feel himself falling as the Truth nudged him out of his hereditary place in Heaven among the white-robed aristocracy of saints crowned in familial coronets of light. Vache was relishing his hour of triumph, but he had no concept, none whatsoever, of the depth of torment he had achieved for Thibault.

Yes, he had used the word 'Jew' as a term of abuse. The name of any other animal in Creation would have served as well to throw at Vache. Thibault was an anti-semite in an age of anti-semites, without time to spend on reasoning out why. But if, in that moment, he could have found the particular recess of his body in which the offending foulness lay, he would have taken a knife and cut it out. He wished even now to cut off his hands that they might never make a gesture deriving from Cecille Vache. He wished to castrate his son that the mutant stock of Gloriole should not survive to pollute the pure stock of Aristocracy. He was a Jew who had aspired to a nobility which nothing but birth could bestow. He wanted to crucify the Barabbas in himself.

All he said was, 'Lies. I wouldn't expect other from you. Lies. Fraud and lies. I'll see you in the law courts to keep my land, and I'll see you in Hell after, Monsieur Bourgeois. By these eyes, I will! As for my chateau . . .'

'As for the chateau, we have you blockaded,' said de Puy with an air of puzzlement, as if he did not see how Thibault could have overlooked it. 'You can't come or go without crossing over the Councillor's land. And if he chooses to toll the road, who's to say how high he mightn't set the toll? If this were chess we're playing, this would be the time to "castle", eh? But since it isn't . . .' He drank down the wine left in his cup, his sniggers making bubbles that burst against his cheeks.

'As for my chateau,' said Thibault deliberately, pulling de Puy so close up against him that the goblet pressed deep into the man's diaphragm and left him powerless to speak, 'since you say I'm a Jew, it won't startle you to learn that I'll never again let hogs and swine set foot inside, nor never countenance the sight of them unless it's with their throat cut!'

He tore himself away from them like a sheep from a toil of brambles. He could have sworn he was bleeding. The land, after all, had been flayed off his chateau. How could it live without its flesh? The house too would die. It was true what Sebastian had said. He was blockaded and all means of income were in the hands of his enemies. A year from now his situation would be such that Vache could buy the chateau from him for a handful of sous, a mess of potage.

He must find his son. He could not tell why, but he needed to see a face which would give the lie to this waking nightmare, one face which would not unmask before his very eyes into a grinning grotesque. He ran through the gardens, looking for Thomas with the desperation of a parent for a lost toddler – pushing, barging, his breath sobbing in his throat, the name held between his teeth. 'Thomas. Thomas. Thomas.'

And Vache came after him. Wherever he looked, wherever he turned the bend of a pail-mail alley, Vache was approaching him – a finger raised, a hola! in his throat, hobbling along as fast as he could go on an arthritic hip, trying to add some codicil to the horror he had just scrawled across Thibault's life.

Thibault ran from him. He was the black dog that had pursued him in childhood nightmares, the brown mud of the Sologne welling up to engulf him. He ran like a man demented, searching for his son, searching for Thomas so that he could go home in company. Just go home. To the library, to the stove, to the bed whose curtains closed him round like a little hero's pavilion, to the small domestic corners of his chateau.

He must have run in circles, for Vache was quite equal to him. 'A moment, Comte! A word!' All the old mannerisms of humility were in evidence again, the stooping forwards, the raised eyebrows, the simpering mouth, the petty-petitioning voice. He folded one hand into the other as Thibault allowed him at last to catch up. One hand inside the other, as communicants hold the holy wafer for later, secret consumption. 'You were too quick for me! I was afraid you'd go home without me catching you. Do let me crave a word out of the hearing of Monsieur de Puy. I would've said it before, but he was upon us before I could say my fill.'

'I do assure you, eel, you have said *my* fill and plenty besides.'

'Oh, but of course, of course, of course I don't mean to take your chateau from you! It was never my intention! The Sablois is a comté! What's a comté without a comte? Pray calm yourself, my lord. No, indeed. I don't wonder you were put out by my unpolished opening.'

So. It was a jest. It had all along been a practical joke, probably orchestrated by de Puy. Thibault laughed. Not funny now, but in a little while, when his heart was restored like a statue to its pediment, he would appreciate the humour of it. He admitted to himself, he had never enjoyed the warmest sense of humour. He tried to laugh again. Yes, it was easier that time.

'There's a ready solution to our difficulties,' said Vache. 'It would please me so much more than lawsuits and destraints and so forth. Blockades indeed! What are we doing talking of blockades and tolls? We friends? We *men with children.*'

He stopped there. But it was only like a fiddler stopping in the middle of a well-known phrase. The brain continued it on irresistibly to the last note. Thibault clasped his hands together and raised a cheer of congratulation. He slapped his knees and tweaked Vache by both cheeks, then took the dagged cap out of his hands and placed it back on Joshua's head. 'My dear sir! Well, well, well! I have you! You are the soul of clarity! Would to God I had understood you earlier! Yes, yes, yes! I have you! Indeed I do! *You mean our children to marry!*' A smile twitched Vache's face. 'My Thomas and you . . . your . . .'

'Germaine.'

'So! You do think like me after all! *Noblesse de robe* is no noblesse at all! Not by the side of the *noblesse d'épée* – the *noble sang*, the blood noble! You mean us to join our bloodlines and be related in true and earnest! Father and father-in-law. Joint parents, as it were. Husband and wife!'

Oh, Vache wanted it. One look at his face confirmed that. As Caligula wished to be a god, as Icarus wished to fly as high as the sun, as Midas wanted gold, Vache wanted his daughter to be Chatelaine of Gloriole, his grandson to be born to the title and lineage, Comte de Gloriole-sur-Sablois. He flinched from Thibault's noisy cheering and dancing, and his mouth hung a little ajar, unsure whether the smile on it was premature. But he wanted it, just as much as Thibault had ever wanted to win the King's favour or make Gloriole the finest chateau in the Valley of the Loire. He wanted it.

'And you and your daughter would come to Gloriole, and the children reign together in nuptial vigour, and we two old men could dawdle out our lives in the shade of the orangery, drinking claret on the terrace, and – who knows? – shuffle our slippers to Court sometimes to lend the King the benefit of our sage advice. Tell me . . . do you have more than one daughter, or shall we be disappointing poor Monsieur de Puy yet again?'

'I regret. I did rather mislead Monsieur de Puy in my eagerness to enlist his invaluable help. To have his co-operation when it was needed. I do have another daughter. But not for the likes of him, I think. Still, I'm sure some other small compensation can be found for him.' Still Vache's small eyes moved nervously between half-closed lids. This exuberant, capering, roaring man seemed taller than ever, physically awesome: he set Vache's sharp-tuned nerves jangling.

Just then, a monkey came leaping along the alleyway of hedges, one paw down, trailing diaper bands and a leather leash. It leapt up at Thibault, shrieking, teeth bared. He thought it was a demon come to carry his soul away to Hell.

But the King came in pursuit of it, trailing a retinue of giggling youths, all frocked and powdered. 'Ah, you see how Our baby takes after Us!' cried the King, striking a declamatory posture. 'Does it not show Our excellent taste in men?' The party was too far advanced for jealous rancour. The youths all laughed unreservedly and clustered round Thibault to recover the monkey from where it clung to his hair and ruff, turning round and round and round till it had manacled itself in the leash. They lifted it down, though its long fingers clung on tight and had to be prised open. 'Tsk, tsk, friend Thibault,' the King reprimanded him, slapping him on the wrist. 'You may have her *after*.' He made a stage-grand show of looking furtively over each shoulder, then whispered behind his hand in Thibault's ear, 'I have a little bitch puppy dog is better by far. You shall prove if I'm a liar.'

And for this Thibault had built and planned and laboured, engaged his every intellectual power, obsequiously ingratiated himself with the Queen. For this he had buried a year of his life in the swamps of the Sologne. For this he had hunted unicorn under an African sky. For this he had hunted werewolves under a winter moon. For this he had seen his wife leap to her death. For this he had killed his son. He knew in that moment how God felt on Good Friday when He saw on what He had wasted Creation.

The King turned to Vache. 'What? Not gone yet, Councillor? Pray don't let Our little soirée keep you too late from your bed. We want the Comte here. By Lucy, We do!'

After Henry had gone, Vache was genuinely agitated. 'I've kept you from the King. I mustn't detain you. But if we could just settle . . .'

'Naturally! When I tell him the nature of our contract, the King will understand perfectly well why our business couldn't wait another day.'

'Then there is a contract?' exclaimed Vache.

'But of course, man! What? Undone and remade in a single night? There's cause enough to celebrate, sure! . . . One small amendment, though. I would make one small amendment to your eminent plan – or should I say your plan for eminence?'

Immediately, Vache was all guards up, bristling with suspicion, too close to his goal to dare believe in it.

'Might I suggest that *I*, and not my son, should marry your

570

excellent daughter? No delay, then, for you in seeing a Vache made Comtesse de Gloriole. No risk of your dying with your ambitions unsatisfied . . . Come now! Don't gawp at me, man! Am I not a widower? Am I not eligible to marry howsoever I please? Tonight, why not? Tomorrow, anyway.'

'Your honour . . .' Vache was overcome. He put three fingers into his mouth as though he were licking honey off them, then was confused to find them there when he came to speak. 'Could we? Could you? Oh my soul! Oh, my good body and soul!' He could not help commending his daughter's intelligence, youth, sweetness of nature – hawking her to him like the salesman who reflexly continues his patter after too easy a sale. Thibault held up a silencing hand.

'Bring her on. You saw the Dragon of Saumur? Your girl can hardly compete with such ugliness and sourness of nature.'

'Oh indeed! She's a good girl! An excellent! Well, you know her qualities already!'

'Oh, I've met her, have I? God strike me, but I can't call to mind that particular privilege.'

'Oh yes, oh yes. And she's done you good service, though you'd never have credited her genius if I'd told you she was mine, ha-ha. Far more talented than her father. Far more, ha-ha!'

' "Germaine", you say? I can't recall . . .'

'Oh but you know her by her professional name, of course. You know her by the name of Urania.'

He did find Thomas at long last. He was with the astrologer woman, which Vache thought was marvellously fortuitous since they could be informed both together of the evening's remarkable outcome.

'No, no,' said Thibault, trying to restrain the merchant's outburst of joy. 'Don't speak of it straight off. I must take steps to *commend* myself to your daughter.'

But Vache was close to the lodestone of his ambition, powerless to change course. 'Germaine! Germaine! It's concluded! It's decided! Tonight I've secured you a happiness you'll bless me for on your deathbed! You shall be Chatelaine of Gloriole, as I've always promised! Come and give your father a kiss. I've matched you to the finest husband in the Touraine!'

She drew herself up so tall that her white neck was swan-curved, and the hollows of her throat deepened. She turned on Thomas a smile so incandescent that his cheeks flushed as at the opening of a stove door. 'At last!' she said very softly. 'Finally.' And she hurried to kiss her father and thank him. She could not quite bring herself to look Thibault in the eye, but as she crossed the ground in front of him and her glance skirted his feet she said, 'Did I not say I'd known it all my life? That I'd come to Gloriole, monsieur?' In her delight she moved like a peacock, her hems lifting and falling over the grass. She returned to Thomas and took hold of one hand between both hers. 'Haven't I always counselled you not to lose heart, my love?' she whispered.

The flush did not fade from Thomas's cheek. 'Vache is your father? But your surname – you told me your . . . You're Vache's daughter?' She laughed with pride at her well-kept secret.

'Ah, but our plan is a little amended,' said Vache hurriedly, perceiving a complication he had known nothing of. He spoke heavily, pointedly, for his daughter's benefit – a signal that she should not jeopardize their good luck. 'The Comte here has expressed the desire to marry you himself, and of course I wouldn't stand in the way of such a chance for you to rise up, Germaine.'

'The Comte?' she said, as if in need of translation. 'But it was always going to be . . .'

'*You*, Father?'

'In settlement of outstanding debts. Councillor Vache has spent a world of time in arranging this marriage. A world of time. It's been an evening of revelations, I have to tell you, son. But there it is. My hand given on it. My word as a Christian nobleman. I crave the joy of marrying Mademoiselle Urani . . . Germaine, is it not? Providing she can cast a favourable horoscope and light on the best and most auspicious day.'

'What?' said Urania.

'Top grade!' exclaimed Vache. 'She shall! She shall!' He pawed at the air, trying to catch hold of his daughter's hand to draw her to his side, but she was a world away, lost among her disappointments. 'Tomorrow she shall cast a horoscope to settle the date, and on that day – well! – I shall light a victory bonfire with these!' He tapped his breast. So many papers lined it that it sounded hollow, empty. It was Vache's way of asserting one last time that his was the ultimate power, that the feudal pyramid had been overturned and that he was at its peak now, master of Gloriole.

'Oh, she shall do it tonight, by all that's sacred!' said Thibault peaceably, softly, incontrovertibly. 'The days are gone for patience, surely? And the finest astrologer in the world can hardly work by daylight. If we go now, she may yet have time to sight an omen speaking yea or nay for the match. Come, lady. Let us become acquainted on a more agreeable footing than previously. I dare swear I've not always treated you to the attention your beauty deserved. But you must own, I've been at a disadvantage all these years. I mean to say: you were aware of what lay in store for my future. By the rules of your profession, you should surely have told me!'

She could not raise even the most wan of smiles. 'Begging your indulgence, sir. I didn't read that knowledge in the stars, and I was not employed as your fortune-teller but as your astronomer.' She turned towards Thomas to see when he would speak up, when he would bear witness to the impossibility of such a marriage. But he seemed too stunned to speak. His face had taken on the inexpressiveness of stone and glass and lead.

'But what of the King?' asked Vache anxiously. 'The King wants you!'

'The King?' said Thibault. 'What's he?' Then, to dispel the look of horror on Vache's face, 'What's he, I mean, in comparison with securing my house and future happiness? Shall we go, lady?'

The fact that Thomas would say nothing did not mean that Urania could not. As they rode towards Gloriole in the darkest watch, Urania said to Thibault, 'My father always said he intended me to marry your son, Thomas.'

'Then I'm glad the evening held some surprises for you, also. Now you shall be raised to the rank of Comtesse immediately and not be put to the tedium of awaiting my death.'

'Oh that'd be no great hardship,' she assured him hurriedly. 'I hope that I'm not so very vainglorious as to chase after worldly titles.'

'I am the more fortunate, then.' Thibault sealed the subject so closed that they had ridden another mile before Urania dared reopen it.

'I fear I was so much of that impression that I gave your good son certain . . . encouragements to care for me. And I allowed my heart to attach itself to him.'

He turned and looked at her, an equestrian bronze turning its head to address a passer-by. 'You mean you're not a virgin? Pray don't be afraid that I'll hold it against you. The times are such that I'd have been more surprised if you were. What's a momentary disappoint-ment in these times of . . . readjustment?'

'I meant no such thing! Of course I'm . . .' Breathlessly she gabbled it out, her own particular revelation in a night of revelations, her long-awaited coup: 'I mean, sir, that we're married already. Your late wife witnessed it – gave us her blessing.' The face did not react. 'So. If we could return to my father's first solution, you won't be troubled with the burden of an unhappy woman for a wife and your dear son will be well reconciled to the . . .'

'Oh, but I was burdened with an ugly and strident woman in my first marriage. Alongside that, it seems to me no trouble in the world to be burdened with an unhappy one. Pray don't fret on that account. And still a virgin? Strange marriage! Worse and worse for Thomas. Better and better for me. If it's the matter of vows that worries you, I can reassure you there, too. I had it proved to me this evening that I'm a Jew. So I think all contracts between God and my house are quite annulled, don't you? That surely holds good for Thomas as well?'

'But we love each other!'

'Ah. That.' Thibault stood up in his stirrups to look for some directional bearing in the increasing light. He said most earnestly, 'It's the brickwork, you know. I couldn't get it out of the brickwork. But you mustn't concern yourself, my dear. I do believe the spoor are entering a dormant period.'

This bizarre, incomprehensible remark so unnerved Urania that she shut her open mouth with a slight snap and allowed her horse to fall back into the wake of the Comte, following the flickering pattern of the chequered horsecloth creasing and uncreasing.

Only a very few stars were still visible against the pallor of morning by the time they crossed the causeway (now levied with cliffs of new buildings) over the drained and lightless moat. The statues hailed them, arms raised in a perpetually servile salute, called out silent salutations of '*Noël! Noël! Largesse! Largesse!*' The caryatid women beckoned them, only the tips of their buxom breasts stand-ing out beyond their recessed niches to be stained milk-white by moonlight.

They dismounted by the door of the observatory and he had her go ahead of him up the potence steps. While she unrolled a current map of the summer sky and laid out her rules and charcoals, he patiently prepared for a long wait by laying down his cloak for a seat on the draughty plank floor of the loft.

574

She was nervous, agitated. The tools looked like strangers to her. She made a show of scanning the sky and checking her maps, of looking for portents and phenomena. But her nerves and concentration were jarred by the sudden alteration in other people's plans for her lifetime and by his impressive, oppressive presence.

'Might I be of assistance?' he asked after watching her every movement for ten minutes. 'I know full well what you'll tell me at the end, so might I not save you the energy of invention?'

'My lord?'

'You'll tell me that the stars are not propitious. That they speak an urgent need for you to marry with my son. That such a union would be blessed with a veritable constellation of little ones. That nothing good would come . . .'

'Sir, I . . .'

'The stars are entirely right, of course.'

'Sir?' Though her back was turned to him, she sensed him get up.

'Do you have a sister?'

'Yes sir. Two. Why?'

'Excellent. In that case, I offer you a choice. Between love and vainglory. I'm touched, you see, by your brave declaration of love for my son. But as your long acquaintance with this house must've taught you, I'm cursed by a peevish nature. I take disloyalty hard. Would you say that was true?'

'I –'

'Yes. So. Imagine my feelings, now I find my son and heir's married behind my back – deceitfully – with his mother's connivance. I'll own I do rather choke on that. My argentier make a mock of me, yes. My best friend gull me – not the first time in the history of the world. My astronomer keep me darkling – well and what's new? But my own son? Ah now. That's something different. No matter. I must practise Acceptance. I must acknowledge the mystical power of Love, I suppose,' he said banally. 'I must consider how to embrace this new development. So what say we divide gain and loss evenly between us, Thomas and I? I disinherit him of Gloriole but give him back his bride. That's to say, I marry your sister.'

'My *sister*?'

'A fair compromise, eh? Or you can marry me. Consider! How long can I last on this earth? And with my death you can pass to Thomas as a part of his inheritance . . . Not as his wife, of course. Oh no. We must join Gloriole to the noble house of Vache, mustn't

575

we? Your father insists. So *Thomas* must marry your sister. What d'you say? Comtesse of Gloriole, or a blissful but impoverished bride with the man of your heart's choosing. Which is it to be?' He allowed her time to think.

'You're making sport of me!' she protested, but he assured her that he was perfectly serious. She must choose. Gloriole or true love. 'I'm very fond of my sister,' she said at last.

'What does that mean?'

At first even she did not seem to know what it meant. Her nervous, scribbling hand was gradually, unconsciously obliterating the constellation of Gemini on her map within a charcoal whorl.

'She'd be in such very good hands with Thomas, don't you think? He is so very gentle. And you . . .'

'Can I believe my luck? A willing bride after all? I'm sorry: you were about to say: "and me"?'

She dropped her head forward almost penitentially, turning it so as to look at him out of the corner of half-closed eyes. 'It's well approved – you are the most handsome man in the whole Touraine.'

So she wanted it, too. She wanted Gloriole. As her father and his father before him. There was, after all, no disease more hereditary in the whole world than the desire to own the Chateau of Gloriole-sur-Sablois.

Thibault laughed: at least there is no other name for the animal roar that emerged from behind the rigidly impassive face. She was frightened to look round at the face that made it. She turned her back again and stared at the map.

'Praise God. She loved me all along!'

'Well, I always . . .'

She sensed rather than heard the ringing rasp of his sword being drawn. Her hands closed over the sides of the desk and, unaccountably, she could not unfasten them.

'But whatever would the stars say?' he asked with exaggerated awe. 'Do tell me what the stars would say to it.'

'The stars, my lord, are silent. They have no voice.' She said it without breathing or turning her head.

'Oh, but that's absurd!' His arm came over her shoulder and he picked up her metal rule. Then one by one, as he ran from window to window, he smashed the panes to let in the noise of the stars. 'Don't you hear them? Such shouts of protest! Such Cassandra wails of warning! So piercing! So deafeningly loud! What, and you can't hear them? Out there – set in their ordered spheres by the hand of God, never to digress or falter or fail? Listen to them! Well and how could they countenance such an abomination? Such an aberration?'

'As bigamy, sir?' she whispered.

'*As marriage between lord and serf. As betrayal of a sacred trust into the hands of a tinker. As pollution of the* noble sang. *As nobility bending its knee to a bourgeois!*'

'Sir, there's good precedent . . .'

'For sin? Ay, plenty of precedent for sin. There's damnation for it, too. How credulous can a man be?' Once civilized pretence was done with, nothing civilized remained in Thibault. 'Does your creeping maggot of a father really think he can extort his way to nobility? Doesn't he know he'll never rise higher than the noose draws him?'

'You seemed content, my lord . . .' The feet of the desk actually lifted off the ground, so rigid were her arms and back, and so tight her grip.

'Yes, well, "seeming" is the sport in fashion, mademoiselle, as you must confess yourself. As your father has taught me. Don't think me rash. I gave it deep consideration as we rode. I'm not an impulsive man.'

'What will you do to me?'

'I'm not a reckless man, as I say. I have a royal friend who'll teach your father the sum of his true worth.'

'You won't kill me! Pray God you won't . . .'

'The King himself will settle my debts. Then plant Monsieur Vache in the outermost colony of Hell to boil in a vat of forger's gold for ay-and-everlasting.'

'Yes, yes. As you like. Pay or don't pay. Good, good! I'm happy the King'll pay. I'm happy he's such a good friend. I'm glad of it. Settle your debts or don't! Your quarrel's with my father, not me! I never liked this way of doing things. I always said he should be more open!' She went on talking, even as the tip of his sword cut one by one through the laces of her dress, then through every strand of her hair. The fallen curls, the broken laces made cabbalistic signs on the plank floor.

Yes, he would go back to the King. He would abase himself to whatsoever degree ensured the redemption and survival of Gloriole-sur-Sablois. The proud, the noble, the intact Comte Thibault could not have done it. But the bastard son of a Jewish slut could do it –

577

could do what was called for. Now that he understood how two strains of man had occupied the one body, he could make better sense of things in his past. He was full of enlightenment. He understood, for instance, the perversion of love he had felt for the Saumur woman, the affection he had felt for his poltroon of a son, the hardship – yes, now he could confront it – the difficulty he had had in killing the traitor Kempis. He was two men in one: the common, vulgar weakling, Jewish Thibault and the true Comte de Gloriole, the nobleman, the demi-god, the upright and uncompromised chevalier outsoaring the dirt, the squalor, the sinful and the foul. No matter. He would subjugate one to the other. The Jew could be made to serve the aristocrat.

'Unrobe, woman.'

'Oh God. Oh pray God you won't kill me for being obedient to my father? I had no choice!'

'I gave you the choice and you damned yourself. Blood shows, sure enough. You're a piece of your father. Unrobe.'

'I was a true astrologer, wasn't I? I knew my science. There was no fraud in my reading of the stars?' The swordtip pierced the stiff buckram of her bodice with a loud popping. She dropped her shoulders forward and allowed the open dress to fall away. 'But I was a prisoner to my father's plotting, sir! He used me!'

'Then I'll use you, too. I mean to use you as common women were meant to be used. And afterwards, you can carry a message to your father. Tell him, let him send his account and I'll settle it. I'll send money enough to bury him and interest enough for him to choke on. Just as you are now, you can carry the message. Then let him sell you on to whosoever he can, once you've walked to Plessis in the *noblesse de robe* God gave you!'

Her scream was the loudest noise the observatory had ever contained. It spiralled down the ash-lined cylinder of the building, then spiralled up again to the rafters, intermingling voice with echo, echo with voice. It unsettled the scarlet parrots roosting in the uppermost beams, and the roof-void so amplified the noise that it seemed angels or demons must be carrying the old dovecote away.

He should have left her her hair; it would have given him something to hold on to. As it was, she was a dirty white comet whirling him round – ice-slippery and insubstantial. She pulled out of his hands and ran, her eyes closed in panic, round the precipitous edge of the platform. When she slipped, and one foot plunged over the rim, he did nothing to help her pull herself back on to the splintery planks, but when she had done so, he was waiting for her, scraping his swordtip across the only pane of glass still intact. The noise made the parrots buffet their combs against the conical roof in a frenzy of alarm.

She pulled away from him again, grabbing at the rope from which the cast-iron timepiece swung, darting behind the great sphere of the astrolabe which hung from a chain centrally over the platform. As he feinted to right and left, taunting her with the ease of his conquest, the futility of resisting – 'Am I not the most handsome man in the Touraine, after all?' – the astrolabe spun between her hands, first east then west. The seemly and proper rules of the universe were out of joint in that claustrophobic little loft. With one last desperate shriek of terror, she pushed the iron globe at him – a puny, futile push that far from injuring him only swung the thing within reach of his hands. He caught it at the apogee of its swing.

'Fate, you see, is not immutable,' he sneered at her. 'A man needn't submit to events. Isn't that what your studies taught us? A man may choose whether to be the cat's-paw of a tinker or the favourite of a king. Whether to marry a greedy whore or drive her out of his castle with her maidenhead between her hands.' And to prove his strength he pushed the astrolabe, on its chain, in a wide, circling orbit of the platform; one that cut her off from the staircase, one that made her duck down with her arms over her head. Round went the sphere, the air humming through its iron cage, the chain grating in its hasp with an ugly kind of music. As it completed its orbit, Thibault put up his hands and stopped it dead.

The next moment, his face was all changed – masked – visored in a scarlet tourney-helmet of sheeny feathers, chevroned with white and red, and braided with blood.

Throughout the white empire of Gloriole, the parrots had multiplied and expanded their territory with an imperialist aggression. Now, in niches of blue-black tile, in pediments of Carrara marble, in lamp-holders and tie-beam joints, in cellars and attics, stables and high halls, on stairwells and in the cast-iron contrivances of the observatory, they had withdrawn to an annual quietness to breed and raise their young. The particular parrot brood that had made its home in the astrolabe prized their domestic peace. When they found themselves shaken and spun about and deafened by laughter and screaming, they naturally retaliated. Without respect for his rank, without sensitivity to his feelings, without admiration for his personal beauty, they mobbed the Comte de Gloriole and ripped up his exquisite face.

FIFTY

Rien Meilleur

The Gloriole contingent of party-goers did not know what to do once the Comte left Plessis. They were unwilling to travel home in dribs and drabs, since the countryside was infested just then with gypsy marauders. So they gathered around the empty wagon on which Thibault had brought his horse and, by mutual accord, set off together for Gloriole. Thomas felt an instinctive need to contain the news of Vache's foreclosure and forthcoming marriage – to keep it within the household – though of course, with Vache still on the loose, the whole French Court would probably know about it by morning.

Once a convoy was formed, there was no unwillingness to come away. The extraordinary revelations had dampened down any fire lit in them by drink or fireworks or licence. The bushes tossed with love-making, the trees had put on a blossom of discarded clothes, and those revellers too drunk or unfortunate to have found a partner were baying like werewolves at the setting moon. It was a thing repellent to see with sober eyes, and the last outcrop of fireworks bursting over the house too much like brimstone falling on Gomorrah. The Gloriole party set their eyes on their horses' ears and did not look back, for fear they would turn to salt like Lot's wife.

Sebastian de Puy felt as if he had already turned to salt. The reward that had made him Vache's cat's-paw, that had made him encourage Thibault in all his extravagancies, spurring him on to folly after folly, had melted away in an instant. He had been promised an alliance with Vache's family and a seat therefore in the great-hall of Gloriole. Now it seemed he had served Vache's purposes only to be relegated once more to farmer and tenant. He was too disappointed to be angry, yet too apprehensive of what would become of him if Thibault was suffered to remain liege-lord of the Sablois.

He rode beside Thomas de Gloriole, but they did not talk. He was not sure whether Thomas knew the full extent of his involvement. It did not appear so. Grief and shock were written large on the man's face, but not resentment or revenge. Sebastian had long since guessed that Thomas was in love with Urania . . . Perhaps there was something to be made of that. Surely he could sow the seed of usurpation in a man robbed of his lover by his own father? And once he had an ally, Sebastian would be one step closer to defeating his enemies . . .

He began to muster his strength and patience once again, to steel himself for the long climb towards possession of Gloriole-sur-Sablois. If not his generation, then the next. There is always a chance when the blood tie is so short and tight. And when the blood tie is so tight, it manacles a man to a lifelong labour of striving, planning, contriving.

'Vache is taking a risk in marrying his daughter to a man so full of years,' he began casually. 'I mean, God forbid, but what if he were to die, the Comte? Before he's had a chance to get children on the astronomer? Where'd be that noble link Vache is so zealous to win? Gloriole would be yours and Vache would be no more than a guest in your . . .'

Thomas pulled up his horse and Sebastian had to turn his in a wide circle to come back alongside. But Thomas's amazement was not at anything de Puy had said. It was at the sight of a naked woman running through the woods towards them like a damned spirit chased beyond night by Hellequin's hounds. She held her hands to her head as though her sawn-off hair were truly on fire and not just the colour of flame. The closer she came, the less spirit-like she looked, for though the goddess Diana might run in nothing but sandals through a hunter's landscape, she would not slap out at the twiggy boughs or shriek her way through waist-deep nettles or curse the tripwire ivy that made her stagger and collide with tree-trunks. 'I want my father! I want my father! I want my father!' she screamed into the faces of those who rushed forward to cover and console her.

Thomas reached her first. He wrapped her inside his cloak and the cold of her body struck through his shirt and hose.

'He's mad! He's stark mad! He never meant to marry me! He thinks he can do anything! He thinks he's above everything! He thinks the rules don't stand for him! High and mighty Gloriole! Does he think a title'll shield him from hellfire? I hope my father leaves him in rags . . .' She recovered herself as she recovered her breath. 'But it's all right. It's all right. The King won't have him now! The King won't pay his debts for him now! Oh Thomas, Thomas! Why couldn't he leave well alone? We had it planned so everything would be perfect. It was all going to be perfect. Perfect. Perfect.'

Thomas rocked her against his body. He said very gently, 'And this was how you knew never to give up hope. This was the "something coming" that would set our fortunes all to rights. You knew from the very start. I wish you'd trusted me with your real name. And your father's plan.'

'Oh and it *will* make everything right, Thomas! If the devil bastard dies! If the birds've done for him! It'll be as it was meant all along: Gloriole and Vache. Just as Papa intended it!'

'Birds? Hush now. Peace now. Explain about the birds, little Germaine.' His voice was soft like a lullaby and he continued to rock her, but just when it seemed she was pacified, the memory of what she had seen sent her hands flying to her face and she actually scratched it with her nails in her triumphant recollection.

'The parrots! They tore off his face! God sent them to save me. He must have! They pulled out his eyes! I ran. I'd be dead now, otherwise! For all I know they're feeding on his brains right now!' and she spat on the ground with a gesture worthy of her great-grandfather. 'May he rise without his face! May he rise without his face! May he rise without his face on Judgment Day, as a witness to what he tried to do to me!' Her voice broke under the burden of feeling.

'Monsieur de Puy,' said Thomas. 'Would you be so good as to see Mademoiselle Vache tended to. She's been sorely abused. The wagon will serve for a litter. Pray be so good as to lead the party to your own house. I must . . . assess the situation at the chateau. I'll send for you all when it seems fit to come. I trust you'll use the eyes of a gentleman not to see what a woman would not choose to show.'

He stepped out of his cloak, leaving Germaine its only occupant, and Sebastian saved the lady from swooning unsupported. As Thomas rode on alone towards Gloriole, she called out after him, 'All's well now, Tom! Everything will be all right now!'

The cook greeted Thomas at the door of the observatory, her hands and forearms full of dishes and balanced trays of unidentifiable things. 'Something fearful's happened, sir! Thank God you're come! He won't let anyone near. He looked down on me from up there and – O Jesu! – that face! He's up there still. He won't let me near with a salve or nothing! Oh Christ-a-mercy, sir, that fine, handsome face!'

'Let me alone with him, Juliette . . . Oh, and Juliette – send musicians to play. Over there. Not too near. Something sweet and soothing.'

The cook nodded sadly. It was what the doctors did: put music to a madman. She nodded as if to say, 'It's been coming a long time.' 'There was a young woman seen running off mother-naked, sir. We think in the house she must've took a knife to'm for taking what wasn't offered.'

'That was Urania, Juliette. Did no one think to help her? Stop her? She could've met her death in the woods.'

'Help her, after she crossed the Comte?' said the woman aghast. Her loyalties had been sealed at birth: to feed whom her liege liked and shun whom her liege disliked.

'And it was the birds racked him, not the woman.'

'Filthy foreign things. Here. Take these up to him if he'll let you. This is hart's-horn; the pills are sulphur; here's the English drops . . .'

'You keep them, Juliette. I'll fetch him down to his bed.'

She was pacified. She could stop worrying about what should be done. Someone of rank had lifted off her the onus of Thought, and she could creep back into the security of Obedience.

Thibault was still sitting on the plank floor of the platform, one leg curled under him, the other knee raised and his shirt bundled together into a wad between knee and forehead. His sword lay on the floor beside him, and as he heard footsteps in the rungs of the ladder he slapped its tip along the planks. 'Leave me alone. Keep down, will you! I gave orders for no one . . .'

'Father, it's Thomas. There's matters too pressing for me to leave you in peace. I'm coming up. You must do as you like.'

No sword met him as his head rose above the platform edge. Thibault's hands were encasing his head, as though the skull might fall in pieces if he let go. But his face was hidden in the white shirt – the red shirt, rather. Thomas crawled on hands and knees to the cloak lying on the floor, and laid it round his father's shoulders which were cold as tufa to the touch. 'Let me see, Father. Let me see your misfortune.'

A stained-glass window smashed by fire sometimes hangs together, but the panes are crazed and the lead melts and sags and the sense of the picture is lost. Angels might as well be demons, saints heathens, a Saint John lamb a burnt offering made by some Old Testament Jew. The perfect tapestry of Thibault's face had been ragged about into a tinker's bundle of coloured ribbons and laces, the inexpressive mask torn in two. One eye was gone and the cheek below it laid open to the teeth. His left ear was dagged like one of Vache's turbans, and the oak-straight tree of the nose was blazed with notches, as if marked for felling. Blood exaggerated every wound. Above, in the rafters, the colony of parrots shuffled uneasily, blushing with remorse.

Inside Thibault's head, in a continuing storm of scarlet lightning, pain swooped to and fro tearing pieces off his brain with raptor claws and beak. Every time he tried to construct the smallest, frailest structure of thought, the wings would come beating back and demolish it and leave him lost on a flat plain of red desolation. He knew that he should destroy this son of his, but could not for the moment remember why. He wanted to cry for the loss of his face, but his tears were dammed up behind a ductless socket, like the Sablois river pent up behind its dam.

'Well? And do I make a promising mignon for His Majesty?'

'You're spared that, thank God,' said Thomas.

Thibault turned his head, finding that he could hear through only one ear. 'It's a kind of relief,' he said, straightening out his legs and toying with the shirt in his lap. 'It would've come hard for me. I know you think I'm an unnatural man, but there are things that are past . . . There are trespasses on a man's body that can't be . . . Ah!' He gave a cry of pain that came from the arrival in his head of a great black memory that settled on the boughs of his brain and began to tear off its food. A Promethean pain. 'You've done it, haven't you? You've achieved it with your "secret marriage". You've given that lamprey the coronet he's worked for all these years. I suppose this is your happy ending, your grand coup of good fortune,' and he spread his hand like a claw in front of his face as if he would complete its destruction.

'No, Father. No. I don't account myself married to Germaine. The thing was done in deceit and for a motive. Under a false sur-name. That could be put to rights. I admit I loved her. But finally – when hearts are laid open, as they say – I suppose I'm too much Gloriole. Too much Gloriole to help along a plot to seize on it, to take it by force. You could say, the Lady Gloriole in her distress makes a greater call on my honour than the Mademoiselle Vache.'

Thibault stared at his son out of his blindness, convincing himself that he saw him better now than he ever had with two eyes. The hand that had patted for his sword felt forwards across the floor to take his son's hand. 'You mean it? You won't marry her? You won't give him the title? You won't give him my chateau?'

Thomas covered the hand with his own. He spoke as if to a child about a treasured toy. 'No, Papa. I won't give Vache your chateau. He'll take it anyway. But I won't be a party to giving it.'

They sat on in silence while voyeur daylight peered in and the sun made a round, gaping, foolish mouth of amazement.

Thibault suddenly lurched up on to his knees, pulled himself to his feet and lumbered towards the balcony. His son jumped up to support him, restrain him, whatever. 'Oh marry her! Marry her! We're Vache already, aren't we? Her grandfather's stock! His aunt's progeny! Marry her, why not? What d'you think you're preserving? The purity of the *noble sang*? This is the *noble sang*. See it? Smell it! You can smell the Jew in it!' He pressed his bloody palm against Thomas's face so that a perfect handprint was left there. In his shame, Thibault bellowed out his lineage over and over again. Was Thomas stupid not to be bent double by the revelation? By the loss of his noble illusions? By his sudden relegation to the ranks of commonalty?

'Noah had three sons, Father,' said Thomas in his library-soft voice. 'I can't say which I'm descended from. Nor Vache. Knowing that, I've never been able to see this fine difference you've always drawn between noble and commoner. Myself, I suspect it's a fallacy put about by kings and princes, for the ease of living basely in the midst of civilized folk.'

They went outside on to the balcony. A solitary oboist wearing only his shirt had begun to play a plaintive, doleful, repetitive ditty, like the first bird of a dawn chorus: music for a madman. But it did not seem to impinge on Thibault. His fists gripped the rail of the balcony and it turned and scraped in its ferrules as he heaved on it like a prison bar. 'It gives you no pain, does it? For this place to pass into the hands of a bourgeois? For money. A commodity on the market-place. The ground doesn't writhe under your feet. The earth doesn't crack open and voices shout up from below to forbid it. Pah! You must be dead already not to *feel* the wrong of it. I've watered the ground with our blood to make it grow. I've stocked the river with our stock to make it teem.' He broke off. His brain was bleeding words through his mouth. He could not staunch the involuntary flow.

'And what does it teem withal?' asked Thomas gently. 'How many sacks today?'

Then Thibault knew that his mask had been torn irrecoverably, for his son could read the very thoughts off the surface of his brain, the nightmares engraved on his skull. 'How should I know? I'm blinded. I can't see with just the one eye. You count them. How many?' He held Thomas by the nape of the neck and directed his face towards the river. He would not look himself, not until Thomas failed to speak. Then he searched and searched, the pupil of his remaining eye shut down against the bright morning light so that there was virtually nothing visible except the brightness of the river. He could see no sacks floating downstream. 'But there were thousands before! Coming down on every rain.'

More musicians began to arrive in the courtyard below. Their panic to begin playing, to begin in unison, to choose an apt piece, to settle on a suitable tempo, had just the opposite effect from the one intended. Thomas regretted sending for them. 'Music for a madman,' said Thibault bitterly.

Thomas put his arms around his father. 'Because you were mad formerly. Now it seems to me you're sound again.'

Thibault tried to push him away, like a child rejecting its mother and in as little hope of succeeding. 'Of course I'm sound. The parrots bled me, didn't they? A proven cure . . . Ach! I don't understand you, man. You're a different breed. A man who'd let the Sablois fall into the hands of a tradesman!'

'Oh God! Into the hands of the Devil and willing!' cried Thomas so loudly that the quarrelling musicians broke off and looked up at the summit of the observatory. 'Don't you know anything about me at all? Don't you know anything? This place is a prison to me. Big cells – oh, huge dungeons! – but d'you think I'm not penned in by it just the same? It walls me in. It buries me alive. It lays nine thousand halters on me – one for every man, woman and child on the Sablois with their needs and their wants and their wishes and their fears . . . All I ever wanted was to travel. Study. Have you any notion of the size of the world? What places? What people? What things undreamed of? I'd like to walk it from end to end. And here I am pinned down to the one spot like a fox in a gin. Christ! I know why a fox'll chew off one leg. So would I, too. So would I.'

Thibault's protest was self-pitying and shrill. 'But I built it for *you*!'

'No, Papa. You built it for the glory of it. To say, "I built this." "I left this mark on the world." For the glory. But the only men I ever knew who found glory – real glory – they were the ones busy looking for something else.'

Hearing the aims and goals of his life written off one by one, Thibault retaliated with the only indisputable truth that clung to his brain, '*It is the best. Rien meilleur.* It demanded to be built.' Their faces were so close that Thomas could see a broken blood vessel in the Comte's torn lid pumping out blood in great welling drops, like tears. He cradled the head against his shoulder and stroked the hair streaked with red and grey, and he said, almost to himself, '*Rien meilleur. Rien meilleur.* Oh yes. Now there's a motto I hold as heartfelt as you, Papa. *Rien meilleur.* "Nothing would be better." Nothing. For myself, I'd like to destroy it brick by stone for the things it's brought us to.'

A kind of rigor shook Thibault. He raised up his head, and written on his face was a manic rapture that no amount of tearing could make illegible. '*Oh so would I too, son! So would I!*'

Thomas went from room to room, and every time he met with a member of staff he told them to pack their possessions and leave. 'Councillor Vache has purchased the chateau. He will certainly re-employ you, but in the meantime, until he takes up occupancy, my father has no wish nor means to keep you.'

They trooped out across the causeway, between its towering cliffs of wrought tufa, burdened down with goods.

'My father is, as you know, a man of pique, and foul-tempered to a degree. Consequently, he wishes Monsieur Vache to win as little pleasure as possible from the purchase of his house. Nothing I say can dissuade him. So would you take, before you go, any piece of furniture or plate or trinket as may serve you usefully in the future and remind you of the era when the Comte of Gloriole owned the Chateau of Gloriole.' There were few members of staff remaining and some still on their way back from Plessis. 'Do take things on behalf of those not here,' said Thomas. 'They'll come home to find the gates shut against them, so you would do them a kindness to clear their quarters thoroughly.'

Thibault's chaplain cautioned against peevishness. Then, being a pragmatist, took a collection of books from the library, blessed the Comte and his son, and left speedily. During his period of office, he had done everything he could to keep in favour – seen Thibault's hallucinations, believed in his storms, moulded God to fit the image of Thibault de Gloriole. Now, in all probability, Joshua Vache would need a chaplain. He searched his conscience and discovered it was his duty to alert Vache to the pillage going on at Gloriole. It would take only half a day to reach his house beyond Rocheblanche.

The staff trooped past the jacaranda trees, the empty crocodile pit, the implacable statues and out beneath the salamander crest surmounting the portcullis. Rain, weather and the Sablois cancer had eroded the lizard so that the face of the Chicheface concealed beneath was starting to show through again. The only traffic moving in the opposite direction was a train of quarry carts arriving from Rocheblanche full of saltpetre.

So Vache too would be continuing the madness of Gloriole, would he? That was what the household concluded, scattering nervously away from the caravan of wagons. But what rib would he manage to find in the body of the earth to quarry for yet more tufa, to build yet more wings, towers, peristyles and terraces? Enough was enough, they said. But then the household at Gloriole-sur-Sablois, year by year, had been saying as much for a hundred years. Enough is enough.

Thomas found his father pouring a keg of gunpowder into the grain hopper of the new pigeon loft and into various other bowls and boxes of grain. 'The parrots eat the grain then fly into every nook and cranny ready to explode – *Bang!*' Thibault explained with the enthusiasm of an inventor.

Thomas put the lid back on the keg and sat on it, till his father's fertile imagination and excitable energy diverted him to some other ingenious project. His head was parcelled up in silk bandages like a man newly risen from the grave on Judgment Day. The half of his face left showing was uninjured, so that it was possible to imagine that he retained his looks beneath the disguise of wadding and Sablois silk. And he trailed a cloud of maniacal euphoria. 'It's a kind of freedom,' he said repeatedly. He was celebrating his escape from the tyranny of obedience, from the slavery of feudal devotion.

It was as though the Spanish captivity he had shared with King Francis I was only just ending and his soul was at liberty to roam as far from the royal side as legs would carry him. No more manacles of admiration, no more chains of fealty, no more tributes to be paid. He was as free as the unrequited lover who learns that there are other women, other beds. His blinded vision was crystal clear. He perched in his chateau like an owl of infinite wisdom sitting in a great oak tree.

Meanwhile his son, with quick, unobtrusive quietness, scampered the height and breadth of that tree, squirrelling away his provisions in every hollow and knot. He knew the building – not as a grandiose flowering of Renaissance ambition, but in precise architectural detail. Undazzled by the glories and prospects of the place, he saw it purely in terms of uprights, load-bearers, conductive hollows, stressed surfaces, weakened footings, unstable cantilevers. His acquaintance with the 'Lady Gloriole' was that of whoremaster; knowing her physically better than his father who had loved her with a blind and spiritual love.

Having dressed the house for her enforced wedding, suddenly there was nothing more to do than to wander through the rooms together, to acknowledge the pallid salutations of the eyeless busts, the fireplaces attired in gilded stucco, the mirrored lamps refracting their light across bare, stripped walls. They freed the dogs from the kennels, the hawks from the mews, the horses from the stables. In many of the new galleries nothing but spiders had ever set foot, and their webs were the only drapery. In the great-hall, however, the unicorn on the frieze still paused short of laying its head in the maiden's lap, as it had paused for so many years. Over the fireplace, to their surprise, they found no one had taken down the old broadsword for spoil. It hung where it had done as long as Thomas could remember, as long as Thibault could recall. 'Shall you take it?' he asked his son.

'Take it? I could barely lift it. No. You take it. It's for a man of your build.'

'Not at all,' said Thibault. 'Men aren't built any more of the stature to use it. I wasn't. I couldn't.'

They walked up the stairs together, using only one of its twin spirals, and stood on the roof overlooking the gardens and lake. 'Where will you go?'

'To the Americas,' said Thomas. 'Or maybe only to England. I have Huguenot friends there. Or maybe only to Belgium. Or to Paris.'

'Oh, say Rocheblanche! Are your ambitions so shrunk? I thought you meant to explore new worlds!'

'New worlds start closer to home than Paris, Papa. New worlds start beyond the moat.'

'And you'll go alone?'

'Till I find a woman prepared to go with me. And you?'

'Ah. A woman. Yes.' He brought his face close up to a little chimney stack to examine how its pointing had been eaten away by weather and by roosting birds. Suddenly he gave it a kick with one foot, and the stack collapsed, and bricks skidded this way and that. He picked up a handful of cheesy rinds of mortar and crushed them between powerful hands. 'I can't see the spoor. Can you see anything? This damned eye. Can you see a spoor in there? It's green, I think. Or yellow. Used to be bad, I remember. Right through the house.'

Thomas took the mortar his father held out to him and put some into the wallet at his belt. 'I know the stuff you're talking of. It's endemic. Didn't you know? Hardly a house in the land free of it. Not just Gloriole. You'd be lucky to find a place safe from infection.'

'Ah,' said Thibault, enlightened and impressed. 'All that reading. You youngsters know so much more than we ever did.' He added with a sudden stroke of inspiration, 'You could always sleep in a tent to avoid it, I suppose!'

Thomas shrugged. 'Oh, I'm not so very afraid of catching the infection, you know? I've a sound constitution – and a great liking for the physic.' It was the kind of joke Kempis might have made. It was the kind of ribald gesture Kempis might have used. It earned the kind of smile Kempis had earned from his father – one man to another. 'And you, Father, where will you go?'

Thibault's hands came up to his face, as though like the Beast in the fairy tale he ought to confine himself to an empty manor-house remote from the light of day. 'There's the hunting lodge. That will serve for tonight. After that, who knows? New worlds, as you say. Beyond the moat . . . Quick! It's time! They may come from de Puy's place any moment – jump – and thwart us. Is the dam set?'

'Best I know how. I closed the sluices on the canal this morning. We'll make a start here, then go up to the dam.'

But Thibault had taken fright at his own suggestion. He was all the time looking now for riders on the north road. Hampered as he was, he could convince himself he saw them – a clotted string of horsemen and women, with Vache and his daughter and de Puy among them. 'You go. I'll see to this and come after. Quick! Quick! Or they'll prevent us for sure!'

No one but Thibault de Gloriole could have overridden Thomas's better judgment. But then Thibault de Gloriole had all life long been a force greater, less resistible, than the voice of reason. Thomas mounted his horse.

'Vache will rebuild, you know,' he said.

'A gentilhommerie. A folly. A monument to trade. Not this. Not Gloriole!' and he spread his arms like a swan on brood over her straggling island nest. 'Be quick! I'm on fire till it's done!'

'I love you, Father. Despite yourself.'

The blood rising as a blush into Thibault's features renewed the pain in his wounds. 'Of course. Of course,' he blustered. 'It's in the stone. And I gave you your own way. It's as Chaucer said in that damned fairy tale. What all women desire: to have their own way. Go on, woman! What are you waiting for?'

Thomas shook his head in amusement, and left the chateau ahead of his father. As he crossed the great trans-moat extension, he could hear Thibault calling after him, '*The parrots will carry it into every part! You wait and see!*'

He rode up to the dam where the great bulk of the Sablois river was pent back to leave dry a vast reclamation area on which to build. The temporary canals diverting the flow round Gloriole were sealed up, and the water flowing down from the high lands was already brimming up to the lip of the dam and spilling over it, thanks to the closing of the sluices.

Thomas surprised himself. Not for the first time that day, he found that he could turn his hand to a task never before attempted. While the book existed that he could study, there was no skill, no accomplishment he could not master. This realization came to him as a picture inside his head – a pathway of stepping stones across a fearful moat, and each stepping stone a book equipping him to make good his escape. There was no great artistry to demolition, he told himself . . . though he also told himself that he would wait for his father to join him and have Thibault check the petards along the foot of the dam.

Then he looked north and saw a party of horsemen on the furthermost horizon. Vache and the turncoat chaplain and a hired escort of armed men. 'Come on, Father. Where are you? Come quick now!' he said under his breath.

Fireworks. The picture was still bright in Thibault's memory of those Italian fireworks pluming over Plessis – that fiery panoply of immaterial sparks, that illusion of Armageddon. While the parrots had clung about his head, while their beaks had chiselled out their alterations to his face, he had been treated to a second display of bright, searing light and to deafening noise. Now it was his turn to mount a display for the King of France, for the Court, for the whole French noblesse – of épée and robe alike. He lit the cord round his waist and carried the glowing end from room to room, lighting the fuses which coiled like exotic snakes throughout his cold, white vivarium of a house. There was an order to it, an intelligent sequence to be followed if he was not to cut off his own means of escape. It demanded concentration and forbade deep thought. He simply said to the portraits on the wall, to the gargoyles on the water-spouts, to the parrots sidling along the cornices, 'It's a kind of a freedom, you know. A kind of unburdening.'

He outstayed his safety margins. He dared God to hoist him with his own petards: 'If I'm defying the Divine Will, destroy me!' And God did not allow a single device to explode, a single incendiary to ignite ahead of time. At last, with the grandeur of a knight riding out to the joust, Thibault walked his mare with slow swaggering braggadocio, out across the causeway, between towering barricados of stone and glass, towards the Sablois forest. In his stirrup stood a banner from the armoury: a beast rampant on a white field. And the morning and the evening were the Last Day.

Fireworks. Italian fireworks. Even from as far away as the northern horizon, where Councillor Vache came trotting alongside the Gloriole chaplain, the lights in the sky compared well with the finest Italy could offer. The whole flat backdrop of the sky flickered like a wall catching the indirect light from a hearth. Plumes and jets of yellow brilliance were overlaced with filigree red, and new cloudbanks of sunset splendour enshrined a new sunset of purple, orange and gold.

'Devil roast him! Satan gripe him! *My chateau!*' cried Vache, rending the embroidered lapels from his robe. He tumbled off his horse to scramble to the top of a steep knoll for a better view, and when he gained a better view, he grabbed up clods of earth and broke them against his own forehead. 'My chateau! My chateau! My chateau! Stop him, won't you, God? Somebody stop him!'

Fireworks. Even from the mud-caked yard of de Puy's farmstead, set around with rusty ploughshares and scythe blades and harrows and fleecing knives, the contingent from Gloriole on their way home from Plessis believed at first that they were seeing a rival display of fireworks. All day long, Sebastian had been paying his utmost attentions to Germaine Vache, consoling her for her treatment at the hands of Thibault, avowing his undying friendship, his love undented by her father's broken word. If he had read the situation aright, that righteous little Thomas de Gloriole was disillusioned in his lover. So there might be hope yet of marrying into Gloriole . . .

Now all at once he was pushing her aside, swearing at her for blocking his view. 'My house!' he breathed softly, in awe of the borealis in the southern sky. 'My chateau! The mad old boar has fired my chateau!'

From the head of the dam – an unhandsome heap of slag and dredged silt and boulders and mud – Thomas de Puy saw his father ride out of Gloriole under the banner of the Chicheface. 'At last,' he said aloud and irritably, and fired a flaming crossbolt into the nearest keg of saltpetre. Its explosion detonated the rest in a salvo of destruction.

The dam could not hold its shape. Its loosened aggregate sank down like a sea-wave into a flatness, and the water behind it rushed to take back possession of its chateau.

With those petards Thomas unlocked the balance of his life and set it free. As prisoners are set free on the Entry to a town of a monarch, Thomas was freed by the river's re-entry into its rightful territory. All he carried away from Gloriole, into the outer world that so empassioned him, was a piece of mortar infested with the notorious spoor of Gloriole: Love. Virulent, contagious, pandemic, it was to infect his every future action, his every resting place.

Only the Sablois could ever truly be said to have owned Gloriole. For the coiling river had made that first circle of defensible land, laid bare the tufa for the quarrymen, watered the timber used for its roofbeams, slaked the thirst of its builders and occupants. Now, as if resentful of being kept from its property, the Sablois river returned to claim its own.

Already the centuries of passion that had seen the river embrace the base of the chateau walls had kissed into the buttress footings, eroding the rock, permeating the porous schist. Now as it returned, it took huge, ravenous bites, fracturing walls, swilling away whole tons of soft foundation rock till the refilled moat churned red-brown. The new pilings, sunk into the wholly inappropriate silt of the moat, were washed away like the struts of a wooden pier, and whole arcades of tufa and glass crumbled with a silent grace into the noise of rushing water. So Thibault saw his dream fulfilled – a chateau floating on the river – water on every side and water below. Then, like the house in the parable built on sand, it began to slide away, the solid made fluid, the vast made small by the relative power of the river; the massive made lightweight; the permanent made the stuff of a few remaining moments.

In the centre of this, like a galleon burning at sea, the Chateau of Gloriole exploded into an animation of fire. The serene chastity of its white stillness was overwhelmed by a passion of fire. While explosions made its chimneys, minarets and belltowers dance to their tumbling deaths, a central pillar of fire took up its stand on the great staircase: twin helixes of fire that thrust out boughs of scarlet across every open landing, simultaneously reached out tubas of flame into the cellars, the stable blocks, the mews.

It was a sight that demanded veneration. Thibault paused by the rim of the forest. This was of his making: this palace of towering radiance, this architecture of conflagration, this animate masterpiece of fire. The heat was terrible. He dropped his cloak off his shoulders. His face began to sweat beneath the bandages and he pulled them off too. The river, refilling its natural course, momentarily rose higher than its banks in a white, seething foam, then settled back, swamping and recoiling from the banks as each section of tower and wall slumped down into the moat.

A man who could build such a chateau could immortalize his name. He could defeat Time's determination to bury a man and his memory under muddy tons of history. Even vainglorious kings were trapped there, like flies in amber: kings were defeated by Time. So the man who could defeat Time, what might he not do? What pure maiden of goodness might he not rescue from the dark towers of past mistakes and sins?

So when Thibault thought he saw figures among the fires of his roofs, on the steps of his great staircase, in the coffered furnace of the old great-hall, he knew with a sure, unalarmed certainty that he could ride to their rescue and bring them out under the singed banner of the Chicheface. The stocky figure, fur-shouldered like a bear, the woman with a flash of silver in the lap of her black dress, the boy leading young white dogs down through the rose walks, the swaddled baby thrust for safety out of an arrow slit; the boy hiding on the island in the midst of a lake of fire; the woman teetering on the brink of the roof above the black-and-white paved courtyard . . . Amazingly remiss that the presence of these people should have been overlooked. But no great sin once he had brought them out. There would be glory in it. And a kind of unburdening. He rode his horse back across the causeway.

Who would have thought that insubstantial fire, its flames as flittering and crimson as birds in an aviary, could fly up against cold baulks of stone without dropping down dead and broken at the foot? Who would have thought that stone, so ungiving and unforgiving, could be so moved by tongues of licking fire: licking, licking, making the weather-vanes moult their feathery gilding, the vaulting ambition of ceilings shatter and empty their coffers to beggary, the stairs and the turrets incandesce with ecstasy until their blood-black domes tossed plumes of fire into the night sky? Both the fire-filled air and its reflection in the river trembled uncontrollably in a passionate consummation.